I, ELIZABETH

ALSO BY ROSALIND MILES

FICTION

Return to Eden
Bitter Legacy
Prodigal Sins
Act of Passion

NONFICTION

The Fiction of Sex
The Problem of *Measure for Measure*
Danger! Men at Work
Modest Proposals
Women and Power
Ben Jonson: His Life and Work
Ben Jonson: His Craft and Art
The Female Form
The Women's History of the World
The Rites of Man
The Children We Deserve

I, Elizabeth

A Novel
by Rosalind Miles

DOUBLEDAY

New York London Toronto Sydney Auckland

PUBLISHED BY DOUBLEDAY
a division of Bantam Doubleday Dell Publishing Group, Inc.
1540 Broadway, New York, New York 10036

DOUBLEDAY and the portrayal of an anchor with a dolphin
are trademarks of Doubleday, a division of
Bantam Doubleday Dell Publishing Group Inc.

This novel is a work of historical fiction. Names, characters, places and incidents relating to nonhistorical figures either are the product of the author's imagination or are used fictitiously. Any resemblance of such nonhistorical incidents, places or figures to actual events, locales or persons, living or dead, is entirely coincidental.

Book design by Paul Randall Mize

ISBN 0-385-47160-2
Copyright © 1994 by Rosalind Miles
All Rights Reserved
Printed in the United States of America

FOREWORD

Like all who approach Elizabeth I, I owe an enormous debt of gratitude to those who have written on her before, all her biographers, chroniclers, admirers and critics whose work I have drawn on in the preparation of this book. My thanks are due to so many that a list of acknowledgements would be endless: suffice it to say that the years I have spent working on *I, Elizabeth* have shown me that the richness of our history is equalled only by the genius of our historians.

But this is a work of fiction, and my chief aim has been to give a sense of the extraordinary creature who was England's most famous Queen. To that end I have taken the simplest routes through the maze of Elizabethan history, protocol and nomenclature, and also tried to present events and people as they would have appeared to Elizabeth, not perhaps as we are accustomed to seeing them with the benefit of hindsight. While I was writing this book, individuals ranging from a Cabinet minister to a taxi driver told me that she was their favourite character in history. Reading the various biographies has also taught me that there are as many Elizabeths as there are people to write her story. I have tried to fill out a portrait of the woman who, like so many others, I have admired and wondered about since childhood. If any readers feel at the end of this that they know Elizabeth better than they did before, I shall be well satisfied.

To those who have supported this book with love and faith, my dearest thanks.

ROSALIND MILES

PLANTAGENET

EDWARD III m. Philippa of Hainaut
d. 1377   d. 1369

House of Lancaster   ## House of York

Edward "The Black Prince" d. 1376

Lionel Duke of Clarence d. 1368

John of Gaunt Duke of Lancaster d. 1399 — m. ① Blanche d. 1369 — m. ② Constance of Castile d. 1394 — m. ③ Katherine Swynford d. 1403

Edmund, Duke of York d. 1402

Richard Earl of Cambridge ex. 1415 — m Anne Mortimer d. 1411

HENRY IV (Henry Bolingbroke) d. 1413 — m. Mary de Bohun d. 1394

John Beaufort d. 1410

Richard, Duke of York killed at Wakefield 1460

① HENRY V m. Katherine of Valois m. ② Owen Tudor
d. 1422   d. 1437   ex. 1461

John Beaufort Duke of Somerset d. 1444

EDWARD IV m. Elizabeth Woodville
d. 1483   d. 1492

Margaret of Anjou d. 1482 — m. HENRY VI murdered in the Tower 1471

Jasper Duke of Bedford d. 1495

Edmund Earl of Richmond d. 1456 — m. Margaret Beaufort Countess of Richmond and Derby d. 1509

EDWARD V murdered in the Tower 1483

Richard Duke of York murdered in the Tower 1483

Edward Prince of Wales killed at Tewkesbury 1471

TUDOR

HENRY VII m. Elizabeth of York
1457–1509   d. 1503

Arthur "The Rosebush of England" 1486–1502 m. Katherine of Aragon

Margaret 1489–1451 m. ① JAMES IV of Scotland killed at Flodden 1513 m. ② Archibald Douglas Earl of Angus 1557

HENRY VIII 1491–1547 — ① Katherine of Aragon, d. 1536 — m. ② Anne Boleyn ex. 1536

James V m. Mary of Guise
d. 1542   d. 1560

Margaret Douglas d. 1578 m. Mathew Stuart, Earl of Lennox d. 1571

MARY I, 1516–58 m. Philip II of Spain d. 1598

ELIZABETH I 1533–1603

Mary Queen of Scots ex. 1587 m. Henry Stuart Earl of Darnley murdered in 1567

Charles Stuart Earl of Lennox d. 1576 m. Elizabeth Cavendish d. 1603

Henry Fitzroy Duke of Richmond (illegitimate son by Bessie Blount) d. 1536

JAMES VI of Scotland (James I of England) d. 1625

Arabella Stuart d. 1615

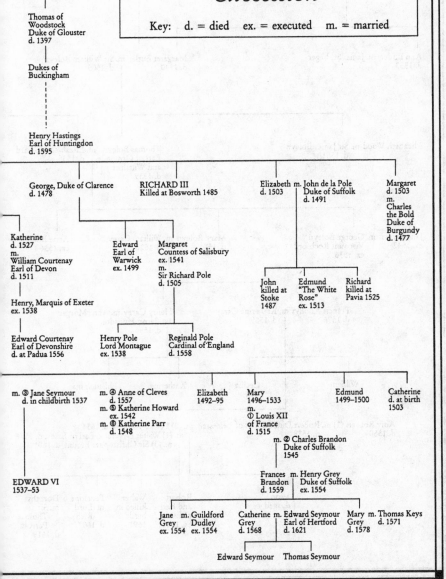

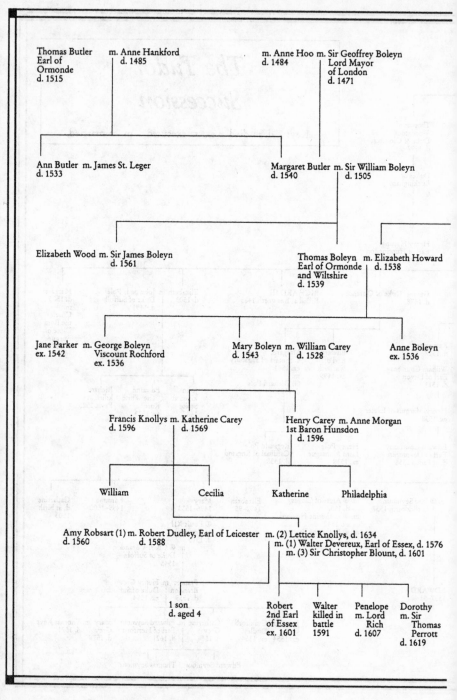

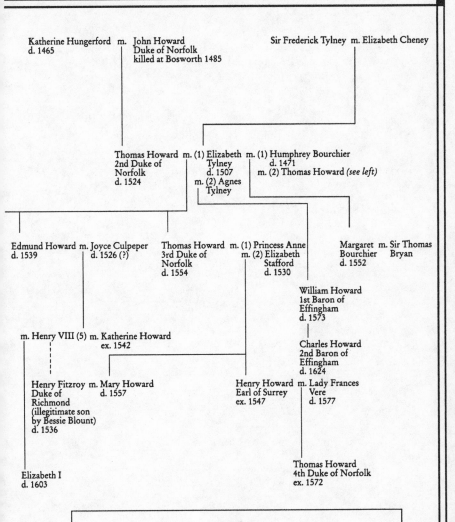

Katherine Hungerford m. John Howard
d. 1465　　　　　　　　Duke of Norfolk
　　　　　　　　　　　killed at Bosworth 1485

Sir Frederick Tylney m. Elizabeth Cheney

Thomas Howard m. (1) Elizabeth m. (1) Humphrey Bourchier
2nd Duke of　　　　Tylney　　　　d. 1471
Norfolk　　　　　　d. 1507　　　m. (2) Thomas Howard *(see left)*
d. 1524　　　　　　m. (2) Agnes
　　　　　　　　　　Tylney

Edmund Howard m. Joyce Culpeper
d. 1539　　　　　　d. 1526 (?)

Thomas Howard m. (1) Princess Anne
3rd Duke of　　m. (2) Elizabeth
Norfolk　　　　　　Stafford
d. 1554　　　　　　d. 1530

Margaret m. Sir Thomas
Bourchier　　Bryan
d. 1552

William Howard
1st Baron of
Effingham
d. 1573

Charles Howard
2nd Baron of
Effingham
d. 1624

m. Henry VIII (5) m. Katherine Howard
　　　　　　　　　ex. 1542

Henry Fitzroy m. Mary Howard
Duke of　　　　d. 1557
Richmond
(illegitimate son
by Bessie Blount)
d. 1536

Henry Howard m. Lady Frances
Earl of Surrey　　Vere
ex. 1547　　　　　d. 1577

Elizabeth I
d. 1603

Thomas Howard
4th Duke of Norfolk
ex. 1572

The
Boleyn and Howard
Families

Key:　d. = died　　ex. = executed　　m. = married

I, ELIZABETH,
Being My History in Five Parts

Prologue
1

Book the First · LIBER PRIMUS · Bastard
5

Book the Second · LIBER SECUNDUS · Virgin
109

Book the Third · LIBER TERTIUS · Queen
239

Book the Fourth · LIBER QUARTUS · Bellona
373

Book the Fifth · LIBER QUINTUS · Gloriana
461

Epilogue
546

THE PERSONS OF MY HISTORY
553

PROLOGUE

He will make a good death, they say. The better for him, for he could never make a good life. Nature made him a king among men, and offered him a king's fortune too. But Cecil, always the wisest of my counsellors, called him "the Wild Horse," and true it was he never could be backed or broken.

They knew I loved him. But none knew how, or why. When he threw away a thousand pounds at a game of cards by casting all his hearts into my lap, or when he tilted at the ring with my favour on his sleeve, they saw "England's Darling," as the ballads hailed him, and thought him mine. But I knew, none better, that he was born to love himself above all others—that he was wedded to his own will and rutting for mastery, till in his fury he swore that he would no longer serve a bastard and a woman . . .

Axe and block is not a bad death. There are many worse. Even after all these years, I can never feast the death of a traitor with crown of beef, sucking pig and baked swan, as my father did, but must choke on the reek of guttering tallow and the screams of dying men. My thoroughbred tomorrow meets the mercy of the headsman, not the courtesy of the butcher's cleaver, in spite of that foul insult. I a baseborn woman? It was nothing but a beheading that made me a bastard, when my father—God rot his soul!—rid himself of "the French Whore" my mother sixty-odd years ago on this selfsame block.

My father . . . The people called him "Good King Henry" and "Harry the Great," worshipping their great beef-faced bashaw like the sun in splendour. What did they know of those days when he . . . ?

My father . . .

Was it my father he recalled to me when first he came to Court in the Earl of Leicester's train that winter so long ago? Eighteen he was then, and the lustiest lad of his length in the whole of England—the youngest and poorest, too, of all those who hoped to make their fame and fortune at my Court, for all he was heir to the ancient and noble house of Essex. Leicester himself it was who brought him to me, my Robin, ever faithful to my service even to the point of supplanting himself in my eyes with a newer, fresher cavalier.

And mine were not the only eyes he caught in the snare of those rich tumbling curls halfway between brown and gold, those bright black eyes alight with hope and mischief, that smile flashing out to bring sunlight into the chamber even on the darkest day. Yet he was still young for his years and ill at ease in the foolery of Court fashion, his fine French hose too high-breeched for the loose length of those horseman's legs, the starched and goffered ruff too stiff about his soft neck. He chafed, too, under Robin's patronage, ill content to be no more than "my lord of Leicester's boy."

All this my Robin saw and was well pleased—for his plan had been merely to try the lad out, to see how he was fitted for the Court. Now, like a master cook, having given me the merest savour of the dish, he knew how to delay the delight of the taste. Late that year, when winter gripped the land in its iron fist and the rivers were as hard as roads to travel on, when Robin left for the Netherlands, groaning under the lion's paw, his entourage was richer by one, and that one above all I would have kept back. "Fret not, madam" were Robin's last, wicked words. "I do but take away the boy—I shall bring you back the man."

Never was truer word. The man who strode in Robin's train into the Presence Chamber two-odd years later in that May of '87 was a May lord indeed, and in his presence no other lord—no, not Robin himself—could hold a candle to that flame. Something of his boyishness lingered yet in the swift bright gaze, the ready smile, as it has all his life. But the girlish glance had become an eagle's glare, the tumbling tresses had been cropped till the red-brown curls lay to his head no bigger than buds of marjoram. Now the jewel at his ear proclaimed him a maiden voyager no longer, but a privateer full-fledged, trafficking the high seas of the eternal love-trade between women and men. Alas, pulchritudo virilis, *the manly beauty that the sages sang! I was lost—lost—and saved.*

Once again, just as I had with Robin that summer twenty-five years before, I was up with the lark to take horse for the fields, to catch the dew still glimmering on the grass and the speedwell opening her blue eyes to the sun. Once again I had found a man whose vigour could keep pace with mine, who, like me, never tired however long or hard the gallop, who could match me mile for mile through the forest rides from dawn to dusk, then pace me step for step through a night of revelling till once again the sun called us out into the fields and woodlands . . . all day, every day, all summer long.

But he was no mere centaur, half man, half beast, but a knight in the saddle, a cavalier in the chamber. He could hold up a fair hand at cards, yet in the freedom of his nature he cared nothing for winning if he could throw away the game with a laugh and a wink. He loved to dice, yet his favourite throw was ever ames-ace, the single spot that others take as ill-omened and the worst of fortune. A man made his own fortune, he believed, by the way he lived—and so, in the end, did he.

In the beginning, though, he loved me—I was adored once. He would watch out the night with me when I felt the silver creeping fingers of my mother's bane, the white night, when sleep will not come, sitting at my side in the silence of perfect companionship, through no more than the simple desire to serve my need. He would read aloud fair trifles to divert me, or softly sing airs of such sweet melancholy that the leaden hours were minutes, and darkness became day. Night after night he came not to his own chamber till the birds were singing, yet after the briefest of toilets, scarcely allowing his man to shift his shirt or persuade him to a fresh doublet and hose, he would be back again at my side, declaring himself "entirely Your Majesty's—at Your Majesty's will and pleasure."

Such was his love then that he would not share it with any man, would not permit one glance of mine to fall on any other. I raged at his presumption, grieved at the wounds he both took and gave. Yet in my heart I joyed, joyed with a joy the like of which I had never known.

Then—how it was then, the world remembers. And now?

Now I freeze, I burn, as ever I have been condemned to do from the moment I saw him, whether he was with me or far away. Now he goes to it, as we all must—we owe God a death. Does he know, I wonder, that this is his last act of love—an act of love for me so great that it will cancel once and forever all the passages of jealousy and hate?

Save one. Does he know, can he know, that his last insult, that final barb, will not die with him, but lives in my heart raw and bleeding as the moment he first stuck it there? I a mere bastard woman? It is a gross lie: I was no simple bastard, but a bastard three times over! Yet still no baseborn creature in reality, only in the eyes and hearts of men—bastard men.

As you shall hear.

Oh, you may trust my tale, for it is the word of a queen, yes, and a great one too—the greatest of all the rulers of Christendom. For now I hold the balance of their kingdoms and empires in my hand and sway the world with the smallest of my smiles. Now do the ships of little England bestride the seas, and her armies take and rule lands where she pleases—where I, who am England, please.

Yet it was not always so. Now he is gone, now I roam the rooms of memory, I have room enough both to wander and to wonder at the steps that brought me here. And I long to be delivered of my burden of knowledge, to tell my tale.

For I shall be much talked of when, like him, I am no more. And like him again, *precious little of it will be the truth. "What is truth?" that jesting fellow Francis Bacon, that follower of his, used to demand, and for all his wit, never had an answer. But I know what I know, and none knows it as I do. They say now (for I hear their every whispering) that I forget. And forgive, you ask? Why should I forgive? Now as his soul trembles on the brink and mine strains to follow after, what do I have to forget or forgive? Judge you, from what follows.*

BASTARD

Book the First

-LIBER PRIMUS-

of My History

BASTARD

Book the First

LIBER PRIMUS

of My History

Some are born bastards, some achieve bastardy, others have bastardy thrust upon them, as the fellow said in the play last Shrovetide—or would have done if he had made his bow on this great stage of fools as I made mine. My birth came under the last of these three heads. I was thrust into bastardy willy-nilly, since those who were so intent on making a whore of my mother Anne Boleyn would hardly lose the opportunity of bastardising her child as well.

Anne's fault was simple: she had caught the eye of a married man who had tired of his wife. For King Henry's once-doting Queen had turned into a termagant who could not come into his company without flying at his throat. Queen Katherine it was who first named her rival Anne "the Whore," and more besides: "the French Whore," "the Great Whore," "the Concubine," "the Harlot," "the Witch," "the Punk from Satan's Stews."

An evil wife is a scourge of God, they say. Henry needed his freedom —from Katherine's fury, and from God's. And more and more, as time went by, he needed a son. With a son, even one, Katherine would have been safe. With only a daughter, the puny Princess Mary, no more than a sickly sliver of Eve's flesh, she threatened to throw England back again to the bloody strife of civil war. Her day was done.

"A *daughter!*" Henry spat the word in the Ambassador of the Holy Roman Empire's face.

But Chapuys was a brave man. "It seems that God has shown us, my lord, that the succession to the throne of England will come down in the female line."

Henry laughed in scorn. "Think you so, Master Ambassador? *I know better than that!*"

For a woman could not inherit—all men knew that! A woman could not rule. All she could become was the catspaw of kingmakers, the power-brokers of a new reign who would use her as they pleased while they carved up the body of poor bleeding England.

All Henry's occasions came together at a stroke on the day when his mistress Anne Boleyn, pale with fear and pride, plucked at his sleeve and whispered that she was with child. Henry had waited for this, prayed for this. Too long perhaps—at least for Anne.

From the time that Henry first saw the new maid of honour, fresh home from France and garbed all in green, to the time when he made her, in one fumbling swoop, his wife, his Queen and the legitimate mother of his child, was seven long years. No passing lust, then, but a longing that withstood wind and weather; and she no mare of the night but a thoroughbred, one fit for a king. Yet time enough for the slowest tongues to be set a-wagging, for the juggernauts of Church and State to grind life, love and all to bonemeal.

The first Papal Bull declaring me null and void came with the first whispers that "Madame Boleyn" was *enceinte*. How Henry sweated then to make his child legitimate! Harder than he had sweated in the making of it! But bastard his babe became, and while still in the womb too— bastardised by a Bull from the highest authority in Christendom, the Holy Father.

That was the first time I was decreed a bastard—and that time, the King my father was on my side. Within the hour a mounted messenger was spurring west from the royal palace of Greenwich to York Place in Westminster, where Cardinal Wolsey lay.

"A divorce, Wolsey!" Henry ordered, before his chief minister had scarcely dismounted from his mule and rustled his red silks and ample frame into the King's presence. For now the long-awaited Prince was on the way, Henry was on fire to be married.

"This is a great matter, my liege!" said Wolsey, aghast, his mind nervously revolving the enmity of Spain, and the wrath of the Holy Roman Emperor, who was Queen Katherine's nephew and staunch supporter. Nor did he forget his own good Papist hate of Anne Boleyn, who, he feared, would be as lax in religion as she was loose in her love.

"No matter!" commanded the King. "Go to it!"

Desire now went hand in hand with dynasty as Henry strove to ensure that his son was born with a true and legitimate claim to the English throne. That meant a wedlock child. "No King since the Conqueror has borne the taint of bastardy," Henry reminded Wolsey.

Wolsey went to work. His clerks' candles burned early and late in the Chapterhouse as the documents were prepared. Again the fastest, trustiest royal messenger took horse, this time south, for Rome and the Holy Father, to beg a divorce from Katherine, to free Henry to marry Anne.

The Holy Father? A strange heresy, no, to make a childless male virgin the Father of us all?

And all in vain.

For the Emperor Charles, getting word that Henry had already supplanted his ancient aunt, flaunting Anne openly in Katherine's jewels and royal style, flew into a Holy Roman rage. From London his man Chapuys fed the imperial fury. Chapuys's spies were everywhere.

"The Harlot vomits every morning," Chapuys wrote in coded missives to his Emperor, "as I hear from the churl who attends her Groom of the Stool. Also, from a seamstress in Cheapside, word of a gown she has sent to be let out in the waist . . ."

Charles acted, and the Pope returned to the attack. That Bull reached England as Anne entered her last trimester. "King Henry VIII, of England, France, Ireland, Scotland, Wales, &c., &c.," so the proclamation ran like wildfire round all Europe, "lives now in whoredom and illegal cohabitation with Mistress Anne Boleyn, the Great Whore of England. The child she bears is thus bastard-born, and bastard beyond redemption."

Bastard twice over, then.

Not many can say that.

And as soon as it became known that God had denied Henry the son he craved, and that "the Great Whore" had thrown nothing more than an unwanted girl, I was honoured with yet another title, one that mocked both her and me together: "the Little Whore."

I make light of it now, you say? Now I am safe. Now none dares speak of it—who even remembers it?

But then—then . . .

So much for us—the two whores, great and small.

But what of the whore-maker?

King Henry my father—the monarch, the spouse, the man—what of him?

I

He was a man in his prime and a stranger to the word "no." He had looked upon the world for forty years, over twenty of them as a king. His tall body had filled out with age, indulgence, pleasure and action to give him a huge and powerful frame, on which his rich velvet coats and satin doublets, puffed, embroidered and slashed, hung like the royalty he was.

In every group he towered above other men. He bestrode the world, straddling the earth foursquare, as if he owned it, his jewelled dagger swinging carelessly beside the thrust of his great curving codpiece, and in his green and gold, purple and white, scarlet, silver and fox, outshone them all.

I speak of him like a lover, no, my father as I first remember him? His splendour, his danger, his might? Perhaps I was—in spite of everything—at least a little in love with him then, for so all the world was too.

Now I was ten years out of my nurse's arms, and he ten years nearer his grave—years that had dealt him a hard hand of suffering, sickness and betrayal. Yet was he looking, as he stood at the altar, magnificent in gold and rubies, in furred crimson surcoat and plumed hat, as handsome, as glorious as ever—and as cheerful as any man may, for what he was about to do.

The occasion was his sixth adventure into wedlock, his sixth attempt to make a marriage that would withstand wind and weather, to find a woman who would please him, and a pleasure that would last. The bride was Dame Katherine Parr, rich, religious, and comely in cream brocade, the three months' widow of the late Lord Latimer, and of another rich and aged husband before him. Squinting at the couple between my fingers as I knelt at prayer, I pondered on the mystery of marriage, and why my father still chanced his fortune on such rough seas.

This was the only one of my father's weddings to which I came invited. The first, to Katherine of Aragon, the Infanta of Castile and pride of Spain, was long before my time, when Henry himself was only eighteen. At his second marriage, to my mother Anne Boleyn, I have to own I was present, though unbidden and unallowed; indeed, I was the cause of the hasty and secret ceremony celebrated hugger-mugger in that January of 1533, for Anne had found herself, like many a maid before, with a child in her belly before she had a husband for her bed.

The third of the King's weddings, to plain Jane Seymour, was likewise a private affair. The fourth, to the Princess of Cleves (another Anne), was pitched as low as decency permitted, since the King, disliking her on sight, wanted to be as little married as possible to the woman he called "the Flanders Mare," with a view to unmarrying himself as soon as possible, as he was shortly to do. The fifth, another Katherine, his girl Queen of the Howard clan, the King could not wait to wed and bed—another costly lesson on the old text, *Marry in haste, repent at leisure.*

Only with this marriage to Madam Parr, the most motherly of all his women, did the King decide to make it a family affair. Beside me in the Chapel Royal at Hampton Court that day knelt the oldest of his children, my sister Mary, surrounded by her women. By her white knuckles and pale mumbling lips, Mary was praying hard enough to satisfy both God and man—but not, as all there knew, to satisfy the King, since she clung with all the fury of her nature to the old Catholic faith of her mother Katherine of Aragon. How would she fare, the Court whispered, under the new Queen, Katherine Parr, a woman as devout in the Reformed Religion of our Protestantism as Mary was absolute for Rome?

On my other side knelt the son for whom Henry had broken with the Pope and Rome, my brother Edward, whose pale, over-solemn face flushed with smiles as he caught my eye. He wriggled his small body nearer to mine with a confidential air.

"Shall we have comfits after, sister, and candy-things?" he whispered hoarsely. At once he was silenced by his governor Lady Bryan, while mine, my trusted Kat, though all ears, winked a blind eye and continued serenely with her prayers, confident that at my great age of ten, I for one was better schooled than to chatter in church. But I gave Edward a secret smile and a nod, for I longed for him to be more like any other child of six summers, instead of the infant Solomon all expected of the heir to the throne.

Within the chapel it was as cool as a cave, though high summer blazed outside. Here the only radiance came from bank upon bank of rich wax candles, the only sound from a small cluster of the King's Music sighing away sweetly in the shadows behind the reredos. At an unseen signal, silence fell like a cloud. The Bishop of Winchester approached the altar and the ceremony began.

". . . to join together this Man and this Woman in Holy Matrimony, which is an Honourable Estate, ordained for a remedy against Sin, and to avoid Fornication, for the mutual Society, Help and Comfort that the one ought to have for the other . . ."

My child's mind wandered, drifting away with the fine white smoke of the candles, high above the humbled heads of the tiny congregation.

Where were my father's other wives now? Were their spirits here with us, to hear him make again the selfsame vows that he had made to them? And why, since he was all-powerful, so fine, so wise, so good, had they all failed him?

I bowed my forehead to my hands and with all my young heart earnestly besought God the Father to bless this marriage for the King my father's sake.

Afterwards in the King's privy apartments, at a reception for the closest of his courtiers and councillors, there were all the comfits and candythings, jellies and quinces, possets and peaches and pigeon pies that my dear Edward's six-year-old heart could desire.

A visit to Court, the chance to see my father and the great ones, was a rare treat, and not to be wasted clinging to my governor Kat's skirts. Strange how men full grown pay no heed to a child, especially a girl. I had slipped away from Kat for once, she being deep in conversation with Lady Bryan on the trials of caring for the royal young.

I was standing now by the arras in a corner of the chamber near a group of the King's lords. In truth, I was lurking there to pluck one special lord by the sleeve, since well I knew that whether he was Archbishop of Canterbury or no, Thomas Cranmer was the kindliest man at Court and would always have a fair word for me. With him in conversation were two lords of the Privy Council, Sir Thomas Wriothesley and Sir William Paget, its Secretary.

Wriothesley was a short, angry, strutting man, shifting his weight restlessly from foot to foot as he spoke. "So our lord the King plays the farmer, going to market one more time!" He laughed unpleasantly. "And fetches back neither Flanders mare nor hot young Howard filly but a fair old English cow!"

"Not so old, my lord," interjected Paget smoothly, swirling the thick golden wine reflectively round his glass. "Our new Queen has seen but thirty-odd summers—"

"—and with God's grace may see many more," added Cranmer gently.

"Well may she see another thirty before she brings home what we most need!" said Wriothesley fiercely. "Money and land she brings him, I grant you, from her former husbands, a dower fit for a queen. But not a child from either of them—never has she cropped, though the earth twice tilled! I fear my lord King will get milk enough from this cow, yet never a calf—the golden calf we pray for, the god of our idolatry—another prince, to make all sure!"

"We are blessed with one prince, my lord," said Cranmer, looking fondly across the Presence Chamber to where Edward sported with the Queen's lapdogs under the care of his uncle the Earl of Hertford. The Earl looked sad, I thought—as how could he not, remembering on a day like this the King's marriage to his sister Jane Seymour seven years before, and her death giving birth to Edward so soon after?

"Hertford looks sour!" put in the sardonic Wriothesley with a greedy gulp of wine, waving for a passing servant to recharge his goblet. "As well he might if the new Queen's kinsmen are to be grabbing for places as fast as he and his brother did!"

"Truly, the Earl is not the only one of the Seymours to feel his nose put out of joint by this marriage," added Paget with a faint smile. "I hear that brother Tom had caught the widow's eye and thought to have her—or her wealth!—before the King popped in between him and his hopes. And now the rogue finds it politic to travel abroad until her heart returns to its rightful place in her new husband's bosom!"

"Yet Dame Parr may surprise us," said Cranmer reflectively, covertly studying the new Queen's ample frame as she moved about the chamber. "There looks to be no hindrance to childbearing on her side. Remember she has only ever before had aged men as bed partners—something that smiles not on the work of generation."

"And now—how is the difference?" came Wriothesley's sharp sneer. Together the three men turned their eyes to the King where he sat on his chair of state, leaning heavily on his gold-topped staff of ebony, the only wood, his master carpenter had told him, that could now support his weight. Even then I could read their delicate silence as it hung in the air. *The King is old . . . in his embraces Madam Parr will not bear nor bring forth . . .*

Now they were looking at Edward with a scrutiny I could not read.

"Take heart, my lords," rallied Cranmer gently. "God is love. Our Prince is forward for his years and likely to thrive."

There was no reply. My attention wandered. Across the chamber my sister Mary was locked in conference with a group of clerics around the Bishop, still robed in his ceremonial finery after conducting the wedding. With them stood the Duke of Norfolk, a dark-faced man of policy I had always feared, even though I knew he was distantly kin to me, and his son, a young warlord a mile above my head, the Earl of Surrey.

As if she felt my gaze, Mary twisted her small body towards us and peered shortsightedly in our direction. "Sister?" she called, for if she could not see me, she could make out my bright new scarlet gown. "Elizabeth, come and know my lord—my lord Gardiner, the Bishop of Winchester!"

As I moved away, Wriothesley's last gibe travelled with me: "If Popish Mary cleaves to Gardiner now, he will bear watching . . ."

Behind Mary, dominating her low form, stood a weighty figure, a bishop's cope and cross distinguishing his rank. Behind him a bevy of lesser clerics fanned out in silent ranks awaiting his command.

"Is this the child—the Lady Elizabeth?" Bishop Gardiner's air as he glowered in my direction was one of unspeakable arrogance, and his deepset eyes did not deign to meet mine. His face was swarthy, his nose hooked like a buzzard's, and his rough demeanour more that of an alehouse brawler than a man of God. His ragged frowning brows and pitted skin gave him an ugly fearsomeness, but the red mouth beneath his coarse moustache was as soft and spiteful as a woman's.

He must have known who I was! Why, then, this rude pretence? But Mary was gazing at him with an admiration that left her oblivious to anyone else. With difficulty she now gave her attention to me. "My lord Bishop has been instructing me, sister, on . . . on many matters . . ." Again the glance of adoration, which the proud prelate received as nothing more than his due. "Know him, Elizabeth, I beg of you, for your soul's good!"

"Souls, madam?" snapped the Duke of Norfolk, his left hand angrily gripping the hilt of his sword. "All was well enough when the care of souls was left to His Grace the Bishop here and his people. Our business is with bodies! If the King means to make these wars on France, we must have men—men and money! Or else the Netherlanders . . ."

I moved slowly away, so that no one would notice me. My father's marriage, my new stepmother's chance of childbearing, Mary's love of God—or was it for the Bishop?—I had food enough for one day, and more than enough for a ten-year-old mind to digest. Much of it, I confess, I laid by to think of later, and forgot. Soon afterwards I was sent from Court once more and returned with Kat and my women to my quiet life at Hatfield, deep in the Hertfordshire countryside. And there did the Fates, knowing what was to come, let me sleep out the last of my childhood, the sleep of innocence from which we all too soon awake.

II

He came on Lady Day that March, in the year of Our Lord 1546. Spring was early that year, breathing into stale, arras-hung chambers and cold, forgotten corners, and never more welcome after a cruel winter. Snug on its hillside, Hatfield turned a shining morning face to the newborn sun. Now, with the death of winter, new life was stirring, and out in the byres the bulls bellowed for the cows by day and night.

Within doors, too, the red blood was raging for God's human creation. The peace of the old manor was often broken now by the sound of deep whispers and soft laughter, and another maid of my years might have been sighing her heart out for her own true love, or at least for a dream of him on St. Agnes' Eve. But my head was in other clouds as I ripened towards my fourteenth summer, and old Dame Nature's games held no delight for me.

My books were my love then, and with the joy of a lover was I hastening down the dark passageway to surprise my tutor by being before him at my lesson, with a headful of knowledge crammed since yesterday: *"The might of Rome in those days was so great that many evil men plotted to grasp for themselves the supreme sway. Among them was Catiline, a man of many virtues, but fallen to a great hunger and greed for power . . ."*

The black figure hovering silently against the window looked like a creature from the nether world. I stood on the threshold, my eyes dazzled by the sun, and willed it to depart. I have no fear of spirits: they are no more than ourselves as we shall be.

Instead, it uncoiled like a snake and began to move towards me. I closed my eyes and hugged my books till the brass-bound edge of the Psalter dug into my chest. *Conserva me, Domine . . .* Save me, O Lord, for in Thee have I put my trust . . .

"My lady Elizabeth?"

Still ringed in early-morning fire, the figure of a man garbed all in black stood before me. Black, but gorgeous: a courtier, and one of rank, judging by the gleam of his gold-worked satin and the sheen of his silken hose. His black eyes held the same cold lustre, like the film on stagnant water.

"Sir?"

I did not know him. But it was a good while now since I had been at Court, where there were always new men. This magpie would glitter in any company. Around his neck he wore a rope of brilliants, and a table-cut diamond the length of a little finger flashed from the hat he swept now from his head. His bow was fulsome, but somehow careless too. His voice had attended the University, but had not learned its malevolence there. A pair of lizard's eyes in an old-young face never left mine.

"I am sent to bid you to Court, madam. You leave at once."

"To Court? But my governor Mistress Kat knows nothing of this! My household cannot uproot itself at a moment's notice. My gentlewomen—"

"Mistress Ashley has been informed—she is about it now. Likewise your women and the gentlemen of your household." He paused, and looked at me again with that strange hint of insolence and malice.

I could feel my blood rising. "Sir, I protest—"

His reply killed all defiance in me: "You would not advance your will above that of the King your father?"

"The King—?"

"—has expressly ordered haste. When great ones command"—he treated me to a saturnine grin—"underlings obey. And you, Mistress Elizabeth, situated as you are, would not be well advised to flout the King's wishes."

Something caught at my throat. *"Situated as I am . . . ?"*

He shrugged. "Madam, who would be so discourteous as to recall the taint of your mother's treason—and the form her treason took . . . ?" Another pause. "Yet are kings and great ones, too, subject to events, to a power none can resist . . ."

Around him the sunlit motes glanced through the air, and the sun, warming the polished gold of the old oak wainscotting, breathed the sweet honey smell of beeswax into the chamber. My gorge rose in fear. At the window, black like my visitant against the sun, a small fly buzzed helplessly against the greeny glass. Outside the casement the early-morning light poured across the park, glazing the windows of the great east gallery with gold and tipping all the buds in the orchard beyond with fire. Out in the fields the first sweet shoots were breaking free of the loamy earth, and the waysides were spangled with celandines as bright as fallen stars.

In a corner of the window frame a great black spider, its web newly spun, glistened for the fly. Sensing her peril, she flapped more frantically against the glass until at last, through her own fear, she tangled herself in the fatal threads. Now the spider uncranked his long black hairy legs and began to move up for the kill.

Domine, conserva me . . .

I reached out to the casement and broke the web, setting the small fly free. Opening the window, I watched her soar away into the clear blue sky. Then I turned on my black-coated visitor and, straining every nerve, favoured him with a smile to match his own.

"We are all servants of His Majesty," I said piously, folding my hands in maidenly submission. " 'When I forget my sovereign, may my God forget me!' as the Bible teaches us. It shall be as my lord the King desires it." I added a deep curtsey to complete the effect.

He blinked, discomfited, and then recovered his composure. His hat described a perfect black parabola as he made his bow. "Then I shall follow you, lady, to the Court."

"Your name, sir? That I may honour you as your due?"

"My name, madam, is of no account. I am nothing but the go-between of greater men—and Your Ladyship's ever-humble, ever-devoted servant."

There it was again, the suggestive drawl, the familiar, lingering glance. The very waters of my soul congealed. He dared to put himself above me, above the daughter of the King? *What did he know that I had yet to learn?*

"Farewell, mistress." He turned to go.

"Sir?" I tried a careless laugh. "What news at Court? How does my father the King? And Madam his Queen?"

His dark face assumed another false, fleeting smile. "As you shall see, my lady."

I could have killed him. "But do you bring no Court gossip for us, sir, buried here in the country?"

With infinite care he placed his hat on the side of his head and thrust back his lank, black curls. "Buried no longer, neither you nor yours." He drew on his gold-embroidered gloves, flicking their long beaded fringes into place. "As for news, Madam Elizabeth"—suddenly the chamber was full of his menace—"that shall be as you find it—*or make it!*"

He turned on his painted heel, and was gone.

The space around me was as cold and void as if the Devil had passed through. I gripped the corner of the table as my visitor's tapping heels died away down the dark gallery, and tried to fight down the fear now raging at my heart.

The treason of my mother . . . and the form that treason took . . .

Moments later, surging through the doorway, came my trusted Kat. Behind her, his gown flapping, strode my tutor Master Grindal. Neither seemed to want to meet my eye.

"How came it, Kat," I demanded, steadying my voice, "that this . . . this courtier bearded me here alone and unannounced, without my chaperone or any of my women?"

Kat's sweet round face showed both anger and fear, and her small body was aquiver with outrage. "Madam, he would have it so!"

I could not contain my rage. *"He* would have it so! And who is he, Kat, that his word commands my household?"

"Madam, he bore a warrant from the King!"

"In the King's own hand?"

"Permit me, Lady Elizabeth." The tall, lean figure of Master Grindal took a step forward and bowed stiffly before me. "Both Mistress Ashley and myself"—he nodded at Kat—"examined the warrant, lady, of this dawn messenger. It was authenticated surely—with the King's own stamp."

It was true, then. None could have signed the warrant but the King himself or one of his closest counsellors.

"Oh, my lady!" Knotting her plump hands, Kat looked as pale as death.

I could not have her suffer. She had proved her loyalty a thousand times in the ten years she had been my governor, teacher and more than mother to me. Only a year ago had she bound herself to me more tightly by marrying a cousin of my mother's, and my senior gentleman, John Ashley. Latterly I had lengthened both in leg and in body, following my father, and was startled, less than happy now, to find myself looking down on her. But never would I wilfully overtop her or deny her governance.

"Well then," I said as gaily as I could, "we have the King's warrant, and with it his will. To Court it is! When may we depart?"

Kat's anxiety now made off in a new direction, and her sighs had her tight lacing straining again at its moorings. "He says at once!" Her hand flew to the bundle of keys at her belt. "But I have a hundred things to see to first! Today I must go over the accounts with Master Parry, and afterwards—"

"Then so tell him, Kat." My calm voice surprised me. "You are the governor here, not he. We leave at your say-so, not his. That is my wish. So tell him."

Kat's woebegone face brightened at once.

"Tell him"—I pondered for a moment—"tell him, *I am my father's daughter in all things.* Tell him, further, that as my father forgets not me, so let this fellow not forget himself—*at his now-and-future peril.* Say him so."

Kat nodded, her eyes alive now with righteous anger.

"And tell him last"—I smiled defiantly at Grindal—"that I will not miss my lesson! And until then, Master Grindal and I will be roaming with Cicero and the wicked Catiline in ancient Rome!"

Kat dropped her curtsey, and was gone. Grindal came forward and placed his satchel down on the table. The sunlight played over his worn scholar's gown, his dusty cap, his absentminded toilet, which had left one side of his hair smoothed down, the other innocent of a comb, today at least.

Yet seen against the other black-gowned creature who had last stood there, he had the beauty of an angel in my eyes. As he always had: for with great care and dedication had he directed my studies for the last three years and, through them, guided the footsteps of my mind. He taught me to think, and with the spirit of enquiry; he abhorred blind faith instilled by violence, such as that visited on sister Mary, brought up according to the Spanish fashion and whipped every day. Dame Katherine Parr chose him for me when she became Queen. She wrote to tell him everything I should read or study, as he, too, corresponded with his own tutor Master Ascham from his Cambridge days. Along with Kat, he was a portion of my soul; more, one of its charioteers. I would have trusted him with my life.

Now, though, he seemed strangely wrapped in his own thoughts as he opened his satchel, carefully conveying a packet of letters to the inside of his doublet. Then he drew together all the paraphernalia of our working days in the schoolroom: goose quills, inkpots, hornbooks and even my old slate, still kept there for trivial writings. I seated myself, opened my last night's text and eagerly began: " 'As Sallust tells us, when the great Cicero was Consul of Rome, there arose a vain and wicked man, called Catiline. This Catiline was contemptuous of law and good government, and greedy only for power, which he sought through cunning, force or blood. He wooed the common people, then mounted an attack upon the sovereignty of Rome itself. His vile ambition—' "

"Power always attracts!" interrupted my master in a low and urgent tone. "Brighter than reddest gold, subtler than the lure of any woman—always—everywhere!"

This was no secret to a young girl who had read as much history as I had. "Master?"

"Always! Vain, greedy and ambitious men seek to win power!" He combed his hair with one distracted hand. "They gather around every throne. Even here!"

Here? Did he mean our strange visitant? Or at the Court? Who?

He read the question in my eyes. "Enough of Sallust!" he said hurriedly. "You have your *Fables,* my lady? Of Aesop?"

My fingers fumbled for the familiar little leather-bound volume.

"The fable of the aged lion, the King of the Beasts, as he lies near to death . . ."

The King . . . old . . . near to death . . .

I could not find the page. Suddenly Grindal's thin hand came down over mine, his voice no more than a whisper. "Put the case, madam, that the old lion, the dying King, has whelped but a small litter. And now the whole of the animal kingdom waits to see how he will leave his throne."

Beyond the casement window the soft sounds of morning came and went. High above, a lark cried in the clear morning sky. But in the bright schoolroom the silence was as deep as under water.

"The first of his brood, a young lioness, he sent out into the wilderness because he could no longer abide her dam. But out there alone for so many years, she found friends and gathered many round her who had pity on her plight. Now her party waxes strong as she prepares to claim her rights."

Mary. My older sister Mary. My father had divorced her mother, then disowned Mary and put her away.

Mary waxing strong—against me?

Fearfully Grindal glanced over his shoulder. Behind the door the winter arras hung swagged back to the wall; as I knew from Christmas revels, it could easily conceal a human form.

As I watched, it seemed to move. I turned to Grindal, but he kept his eyes fixed on the table, on the feather-stippled gold flakes of the grain of the oak, and muttered on. "Say that the old lion has another female cub, younger than the first, dearer to her father and closer to his ways."

Myself.

There was no other.

"She, too, has her own party, those who care for her and the New Faith. But as her sister waxes strong, so her people are put in fear. Their letters are read; their very words are used against them." His hand fluttered to the packet at his bosom. "So they see now, as through a glass darkly, in ignorance and confusion. There is order given that the friends of the little lioness must . . . abandon her . . . *or betray her.*"

The low murmur of Grindal's words died away. Then from behind the arras came another sound. I rose to my feet, smoothing down my gown, my palms sweating against the rasp of the rough velvet as I moved towards the door.

Betrayed . . .

At the door I trembled, but my hand still reached out for the arras. Whoever was betraying me, I would know it, if it meant my life.

Each his own Oedipus, said Sophocles, born to riddle out our own confusion.

Fool that I was, the space was empty! A small grey mouse ran scratching by: that was the sound my fear-infected ears had caught. I rejoined Grindal at the table and took up my Aesop again to still my shaking hands. "You were saying, sir. *The little lioness! Will they betray her?*"

Silence. Grindal sighed, reached forward, pushed aside the silver-fili-gree hornbook that had been Kat's gift for my baby primer, and picked up a book of maxims. "Let us construe, my lady." His bony finger stabbed at a Latin verse: " *'Si labat fortuna, / Itidem amici collabascunt: fortuna amicos invenit.'* "

"Plautus," I guessed wildly, and began to translate: " 'If good fortune falls away, / So also do your friends: yet good fortune finds friends again.' "

Was this Grindal's message to me, that he was my friend only as long as Dame Fortune smiled? Others were of no account. But Grindal—?

"One lesson more, Lady Elizabeth." He reached out for the slate and chalked crudely, even angrily, three words I had not seen before, in glaring Roman capitals:

VIDE AMPLIUSQUE ETIAM

I had not been used to such simple Latin since I began the language with Kat, ten years before. I turned the phrase once in my mind and dashed off a hasty translation: " *'Vide ampliusque etiam?'* Why, sir, 'See, and see again.' "

"Wrong! *Wrong!* Repeat! Repeat! Again!"

His feverish gesture as he pointed to the phrase left me in no doubt of its importance. Urgently I tried again. " 'See more—and see more again'?"

"*Yeesssss. Yeeeeesss!* Just so!" He closed his eyes and muttered under his breath, "Remember, my lady: *'See-more and see-more again.'* " Suddenly he opened his eyes. "And now for our last today."

Bunching his long trailing sleeve, he scrubbed the slate clean, careless of the white dust streaking the threadbare black. Then concentrating fiercely, he drew two shapes, side by side. I grasped the slate between both hands and stared.

A heart and a river—or a stream?

Softly my master leaned forward and laid his finger on his lips. "Remember, my lady." Intently he described a linking movement with his finger from the heart to the water. *"Remember!"* His voice was calmer now. "And remember, too, the words of great Cicero as he waited for the conspiracy of Catiline to reveal itself—for the poison to gather to a head, like a boil full of pus, until it could be lanced."

"I remember, master," I said huskily. "From my last night's study. *'Vide: Tace,'* Cicero told his friends. 'See, and hold your peace.' Well then, sir, let *Video et Taceo* be the watchword for me: I will see and be silent, never fear!"

He bowed, rose, gathered his books and left. Outside, the tower clock in the gatehouse struck the hour. Eleven o'clock! No more?

O Grindal.

He had as good as told me that he had to betray me.

Et tu, Brute? *You too?*

The dinner hour came and went, the sun left the chamber, and I remained frozen there, in a chill that gripped me now without and within.

III

The chill I felt was mortal, the birthright of any motherless child: for when a mother dies, her child catches an everlasting cold. My mother's life was short—so short it scarcely touched on mine. Yet if the evil that men do lives after them—well, we all know that women are Eve's daughters, born to sin, the children of God's wrath.

No wonder, then, that even in the grave her sins would not sleep but must come back to haunt me. And as I wept and wrestled, knelt and prayed all that livelong day, I felt in my bones that she was at the back of these fearful new events. Her death had infected me with her soul's plague, and now I saw I never would be free of it. And I wished her safely dead, even if that doomed her to an eternity in purgatory, rather than risen to torment me thus!

I showed little pity of her then, you say?

But what love or pity had she shown to my father when she betrayed him?

For I knew her story, I knew her treachery, I had known it all my life. I was not three years of age when Sir Thomas Bryan came with the news. Visitors to Hatfield were rare, and the slumbering peace of our warm hillside hollow hardly ever disturbed. That day, though, the sharp clatter

of hooves and the cries of men in the courtyard betokened a mighty
event.

"Within, there! My lord comes!"

"Call for my lady!"

"My lady Bryan, ho! Have her make ready the Lady Princess for audience with my lord—at once!"

"Anon, sir!"

"Make haste, fool!"

"Sir!"

He knelt before me, still in his great riding boots, all beslubbered with
journeying, the rank smell of his man's sweat mingled with that of his
gelding, for it was late in May and summer was on the wing. Beside me
on the chair of state in the Great Hall sat Lady Bryan his wife, for she
was my governor then before Edward was born, and Sir Thomas had
been sent as much to bear his wife up in the face of what he had to tell as
to break the tidings to me.

I can still see her face beside me a blank mask of shock, her back rigid,
her hands restless, writhing. And more: for the first time ever I remembered it, that thin scent in the air, sourer than vomit, sharper than cat's
gism, the reek of which can never be forgotten, never disguised—the
smell of fear.

That same smell filled the air, as leaning on his knee, hanging his head
like a broken man, Sir Thomas told me that this very day had Queen
Anne Boleyn, my mother and the King my father's former wife, been put
to death.

Where?

"On Tower Green."

How?

"She had her head cut off."

Why?

"She was a traitor, my lady, to the King her husband."

A traitor?

"She committed treason. And for treason, the price is death."

So.

A traitor. Treason. And death.

All this, not strange to say, served well enough for the child I was. For
as I had no understanding of what the words meant, I felt nothing of
their shame, nor of my curse.

And I knew nothing of the woman she was, the mother I had lost. The
miniature Kat kept by me in the drawer beside my bed was a picture of a
lady to me, nothing more. Soon after my birth the King my father had
given me Hatfield for my hearth and home, my place, my palace, my little

kingdom. At three months old I had been taken from the Queen's household and despatched on the first of my royal progresses to my new home far away from Court. And though I saw her once or twice thereafter—

Yes, yes, I saw her. I remember her, however fleetingly—eyes as black as coals, with little firelights deep within them—I remember her, and more, more than I ever wish to remember—wisps of memory that fret at the edges of my waking days and stalk unchallenged through my sleepless nights . . .

Yet was she no more to me then than any other great lady of the Court, and less, far less than she who cared for me, good-hearted Margaret Bryan, or my second governor, Mistress Kat.

Kat came to me when I was four years old, to take Lady Bryan's place. Poor frightened Bryan, whose horror on that day was so much worse than mine! She had her own reasons for retiring from her post with all speed, since before her marriage to Sir Thomas, she was related to Anne Boleyn on the Howard side. All Howards, all Boleyns, now stood compromised by Queen Anne's fall, and Bryan was not the only one to feel her head a little looser on her shoulders. From Anne's great-uncle to the husband of her sister, most of those who had known her now went swiftly to ground. Yet the Bryans were too shrewd, of course, to run like rats for cover. They let time roll by, and when it was clear that all Howard hopes had died with Anne, they bowed out of Hatfield and hitched their fortunes to the new Orpheus ascending, the baby princeling and heir to the throne, my brother Edward.

The King, however, required one last service from Sir Thomas ere he and his lady were permitted to give up my governorship. I was four summers high and more now, and a great lady, in my own eyes at least: for was I not the Princess Royal now that my older sister Mary had been put out of her place in my favour; was I not the only true heir of the Tudors, and the Princess of Wales to boot? No matter that I never came to Court, that the King never sent for me: all knew who I was. And none approached me but on their knees, none addressed me save with their head uncovered and every mark of respect.

Once again Sir Thomas had come fresh from Court. Once again I sat to receive him on the chair of state in the Great Hall, with Lady Bryan at my side. But now there was a difference. This time Sir Thomas in my presence did not kneel. Nor could he meet my eye as he made his bow. "My lady Elizabeth—"

I did not understand. "How is it, governor, that I was yesterday 'my lady Princess,' and today but 'my lady Elizabeth'?"

"There you have it, madam." Sir Thomas was not a man to mince words. "His Majesty the King your father has given order that as his marriage to the late Anne Boleyn your mother was no marriage, you are no true child of wedlock. You are therefore but a bastard born—and as such, therefore, no princess."

No marriage to my mother?

No true child?

No princess?

A bastard, then—bastard-born, the child of a woman who conceived out of wedlock—and what was the word for women such as that—?

Sir Thomas was still speaking. "All this is done out of the King's great love for you, my lady. You are no longer any daughter of the traitor Anne Boleyn, but now to be known only as 'the Daughter of the King.' And His Majesty bids me say, 'What is "Princess," "Heiress of Wales" or any other title to compare with that?'"

Again I swam in a sea of incomprehension, again I did not feel the barb of my injuries. My father loved me! That was all I knew.

What else could I know? I was but four years old. Bryan must have been heartily thankful that he had only a poor infant to contend with, and that after leaving the requisite orders as to my correct form of address for the future—"the King's Majesty's Daughter, the Lady Elizabeth"!—he could terminate his distasteful duties so lightly.

Leaving the place to Kat, my beloved Kat, who alone became my rock, my lighthouse, my pilot and my guiding star through the still rougher seas that were to come.

Kat. My Kat, my Kit, my consolation, my tib, my tabby, my queen of cats.

Kat had come as fresh as the curds off the whey to King Henry's Court. No Boleyn cousinage, no Howard heritage, clouded her history: nothing but an honest Devonshire girlhood of milk and cheese, and strawberries and clotted cream. Also an education that made her the boast of her brother, a gentleman in the King's service, who sang her praises until the King himself commanded this paragon to appear at Court. "For," said he, "we have need of learned maidens to learn our Court maids, and one above all."

That "one" was the royal me.

"My lady Princess" was Kat's soft greeting in her gentle Devon burr. "For so you are, though I must henceforth call you 'Madam Elizabeth.'"

"Mistress Katherine—" I began, steadying my tongue for an attempt upon her Devon surname, "—Champernowne?"

She checked me with her sweet, twinkling smile. "My lady, you may call me 'Kat.'"

And Kat she so became.

Four years old I was, and due to begin Latin. Like all those who loved learning, Kat was also passionate for Greek. And geography, and Italian, and a little Hebrew, and mathematics, and grammar, and rhetoric, and astronomy, and architecture, and more, much more. She was a library in herself, a universe. Laughing, she promised to teach me "all the answers to all the questions in all the books of the world!" Through her I learned both to trust and to think, and so we continued in a paradise of innocence like that of the first Eden.

The chill winds of the outside world touched me lightly, if at all. My father's new wife Jane Seymour died before I knew her, and to a four-year-old her death seemed a fair exchange for a brother like my darling Edward. Then came the Princess of Cleves, a lank and bony old thing with the worst clothes I ever saw, who smelled as if she never changed her nether garments, and spoke not a word of English. One visit to Court, one feast in her honour, was all I knew of her as wife to the King before my father found the way to retire her safely to Richmond with the rank of "the King's Most Honoured Sister." I cared for none of them. What I loved was the journey to Court, when for days on end I would be carried through the country, waving to the people who turned out to see me pass. And when they shouted "God bless King Harry's bairn!" and "God save thee, little Bess!" I was still child enough to think they cheered not for him but for me.

Yet next time I came to Court, who should be seated beside my father beneath the great canopy in the Presence Chamber but a laughing girl I knew well from times past. She was my cousin: for in the tangled web woven by my grandfather Boleyn when he married into the Howard clan, my grandmother Howard was Katherine's aunt. This Howard cousin of mine was then eighteen summers to my seven. She was tiny, vital, plump and pretty, with bright black eyes and spirits as high as my own, and like the King, her doting bridegroom, I adored everything about her.

For the best of reasons—to a child, at least. "I shall spoil you, Elizabeth!" she announced.

She gave me treats and trinkets, she took me for rides in the Queen's barge, she had me to stay with her in the fine riverside manor at Chelsea dowered to her by the King. Above all, she had me with her at her greatest feast, the first time she dined in public as the Queen of England. There in the Great Hall of Hampton Court we sat beneath the King's arms and her own, swagged in pink silk and gold, bearing the motto that the King had chosen for her himself: A BLUSHING ROSE WITHOUT A THORN. Small wonder, then, that I came home drunk with delight to my sweet safe refuge of Hatfield.

But there is no rose without a thorn, no pleasure that is not paid for without the prick of pain. One day of winter that same year, I was confined to my closet by a cold rheum on my chest. Snug and reading by the fire, I paid no heed to the giggles and whispers of the two maids making up my bed in the outer chamber. I had heard them before: they only ever talked of love nonsense and silly things, and I was all of eight now, and serious for my age. And I did not like the maids. They always brought kitchen smells with them, if not worse, and they would look at me strangely, whispering behind their hands. These two today thought I was in the schoolroom, and I was happy to let them think so.

Until I heard one say, "But is it certain she has to die?"

"No question—and at once, the carrier says. She's doomed for sure."

"Can she not beg for mercy?"

"She has done so! They say she 'scaped from her apartments at Hampton Court and ran shrieking down the corridors to beg the King's forgiveness. He was at Mass—she thought if he but saw her face again, he never would have the heart to kill her."

"And would he not forgive?"

"They caught her outside the chapel before she could come to him, and stopped her mouth. But she had no hope of mercy. 'Tis treason, what she's done!"

"How treason?"

"She's a traitor to the King. And for that"—the second voice dropped in ghoulish relish—"they'll cut off her head!"

"Like—? Like—?"

"For sure! Like my little lady's mother! Just like her! 'Tis the price for such as they—traitors, fornicators, adulterers and all. Look you, if a common whore can be dragged naked at the cart's tail round and round the town and whipped till her back be all hanging off in bloody shreds, what punishment for a queen?"

There was no answer. Chuntering together softly, they moved away.

I knew, oh, I knew then, that the serpent had come into my garden, and like Eve at the morning of the world, I awoke to the nakedness of my ignorance. How had I slumbered so long unknowing? Kat had promised me answers to all my questions, and I had lost myself in Greek and geography, Boccaccio and the Bible. Suddenly there was only one question I had to ask —something that had been growing inside me unfelt and unseen like an abscess I must now burst, or die.

Now at four o'clock day was done, and the night approaching was as black as the waters of the Styx. And I was not blue but grey of cold and sorrowing in the window seat when Kat came, flanked by candle bearers, to bring me to supper.

One glance at me and she drove the little maids at her heels into a fury of activity. "Dorcas, a fire here, fetch coals at once! Send Peter up from the kitchen with a brazier too, to make more warmth. At once, do you hear me? Look to it! Joan, a posset for my lady, quick as lightning, and piping hot, see you, or your ears will pay for it!" Then falling on her knees at my feet, she took my frozen hands. "What ails you, sweetheart?" she demanded tenderly. "May you speak of it?"

So many times before, we had hugged the fire together, Kat and I, by rushlight or tallow, in a companionable coze when our day's work was done. Now, though, everything was changed. The fire made, the posset brought and placed between my cruelly tingling hands, the maids sent away, and a great silence between us, the hour had come for another kind of story.

"Kat."

"Madam?"

I gathered my forces. "My cousin Katherine the Queen . . . the maids were talking . . ."

Kat drew a heavy sigh. "I had thought to spare you this, my lady."

"I want to know."

Another great sigh. "Only this, from this afternoon's carrier. That Madam Katherine your cousin is to die for treason—she has been proved a wanton. She had one lover when still a girl in her grandmother's house, and they say another now as Queen—admitting him to her privy quarters by night and denying him nothing."

"Is it all true?"

"Her lovers have confessed it, every detail."

"Like the last time?"

"The last time—?" Kat's voice bespoke her alarm. She was not prepared for this.

"The last time, the chambermaids said. *'Like the last one.'* I know what they meant."

Kat seemed turned to stone. Only her eyes, as wide as I had ever seen them in the leaping firelight, and her light, panting breath betrayed her apprehension.

"My mother—is that what they meant? *That she was like Katherine?*"

Kat seemed to fall into a silence deep as a well. At last she spoke. "You know already, madam, that the Queen your mother was accused of . . . of betraying the King."

"What is 'betraying'?"

"It was said she plotted against him, against his peace of mind. That she joked about the King's manhood, that His Majesty was not . . . not always a man as others are, after the way of the flesh."

I felt a rope of steel tightening around my head. "Kat, is this treason? *Did she die for this?*"

Kat's face was as white and bleak as a winter's day. "Queen Anne was charged also with whoredom, lady. That she won men of the Court to her carnal lust and adultered with them in her own chambers, in the King's very palaces."

As Katherine had done.

Go on.

"Who—?"

"Three young gentlemen of the King's Privy Chamber, one of them the King's dearest friend, Henry Norris—"

"And—?"

"And her musician, my lady—a lutanist, Mark Smeaton."

"And—?"

"And—her brother, madam. Your uncle Viscount Rochford."

We sat, Kat and I, like marble effigies or women turned to stone. I had it, then, all I wished to know.

That was the first of my white nights—the first night of my life that I slept not at all.

And that was the first chill of the first fear, afterwards always with me, no matter how deep I tried to bury it under my piles of books, my manuscripts, my mountains of learned facts. And now, with this summons to Court, with this sinister courtier, it was here with me again, lurking in the corner of my chamber: it was part of me, crouching in the corner of my soul.

And the day had begun so well, my soul lamented, that Lady Day, when spring seemed come and the sun had painted Hatfield in pink and gold. Now all night long, despite Kat's faithful ministrations, despite more blankets, more coverlets, down beneath and down above, and a log fire so high up the chimney in my bedchamber that the room was as bright as day, I could not get warm.

For the cold I shivered that night of childhood with, and now shivered with again, was not the wanton kiss of Jack Frost, but the charnel-house embrace of mortal fear.

Of fear?

Two fears.

That the King, for all his goodness and his great love of me, might one day—one day soon, even now—turn against the daughter of his traitor-wife. The text ran in my head like a dirge: *Should your father, or Our Father which is above him, ever minister to you as your sins have deserved, how mighty were your misery, how sharp the sentence, how rigorous the revenge.* That I might come to remind him of the woman who had so vilely betrayed him—a danger that must grow greater every day as I grew to that womanhood which must, like every daughter of every mother, show my kinship to her.

And the second, the greater fear, deeper and colder still: *If the sins of the mothers are visited upon the children, according to God's word, am I to grow up tainted by her sin? Will my corrupt Eve's flesh, the flesh that every mother gives to every daughter, betray me, as hers did her, into woman's foulness, woman's frailty, woman's lust?*

If I am to be like her, will my life be worth the shoes that I stand up in? Or has she infected me to death, and am I now to pay for it? Has this dark visitant, this courtier, this messenger from the King, done no more than come to call me and my mother's still-roaming spirit, her still-living desires embodied in my flesh, to our last account?

And how to pass through the dark unknown sea of the night ahead before I should find out?

IV

We parted before dawn of the next day, in the darkest hour of a starless night. The air was thick with frost and foul vapours, as if yesterday's spring had never been. In the great courtyard of Hatfield the mole-brown pack mules, poor sterile beasts, were shuffling their small hooves against the ice on the cobbles striking through to their tender flesh beneath. Behind them the gentlewomen's palfreys were whickering mournfully, sour and unhandy at being awoken so harshly before their hour.

I gripped my cloak tight to my throat against the cold as I came down to the courtyard at Kat's side. All about us the people of my household ran to and fro, shouting and swearing, fetching and carrying, loading carts and wagons in a frenzy of haste. Meanwhile the carters screamed and cursed and lashed about them, taking their fury out on their two- and four-legged underlings at will. Along the walls the chamber grooms emptied pot after steaming pot of reeking night soil onto the slimy dungheaps. The noise, the flaring torches, the vile stink, made it a scene from hell. Yet it was not so distant from my mood.

All night long, hour by moon-washed hour, my brain had been running with Grindal's riddles like a rat in a trap. The conspiracy of Catiline—was Grindal telling me there was a plot against the King? Or merely warning me, now I was going to Court, to beware of the men of power gathering round the throne?

The Aesop story he had fabled me—yes, my father was ageing, fifty-three, nearly fifty-four now. But did not the King his father live till the age of—?

Fifty-two! whispered a voice from I knew not where.

Yet my father was strong! So huge, and healthy, he was nothing like an old, sick lion at the end of his life! And "the lion's brood"—what was this talk of "lionesses"? Neither Mary nor myself was of the least importance in the Tudor line. *For a woman never yet ruled England in two thousand years,* I should have said to Grindal, *and never will!*

Yet there was one truth in his fable that now struck me to the quick. Of the malice of my sister Mary, suddenly I had no doubt.

Mary—the very name means "bitterness." Did those who named her know that God had fated her to drink her cup of gall and wormwood to the last drop, yes, and beyond?

I was shaking, but not with cold.

Enough!

Time to put on a better face than the ghostly thing I glimpsed in my glass as I left my chamber. The courtyard was alive—I must be on my guard.

Yet as ever, all had a smile and a curtsey or a good-morning word for me.

"Greetings, mistress!"

"Give you good day, my lady!"

Two of the principal gentlemen of my household at Hatfield, the brothers James and Richard Vernon, sons of a local squire, bowed as they shouldered past weighed down with horse harness. Beyond them was Ashley, Kat's quiet and steady husband, standing ready to depart with Sir John Chertsey, a young knight of the shire whose father, old Sir John, had placed him in my household shortly before he died.

Farther off, in the flare of the torchlight, I could see my black-clad caller of yesterday making himself important among the grooms and ostlers as if he alone were due to take horse today. Even at this hour of the morning, with a hard saddle-day ahead of him, he was agleam in burgundy, cased like the snake he was in a skin of silk, satin and velvet, the perfect popinjay. I hated him, fur and feather, and I feared him, and I knew not why.

"His name is Paget," declared Kat with a stout toss of her head in the fine one's direction. Kat had recovered all her natural bounce in the wake of countermanding him yesterday with her mistress's royal command. "Which, madam," she had told me gleefully, "he dared never gainsay, though he glowered at me like any tavern bully!"

"Paget?" My interest quickened. "Son to Sir William Paget, chief of the King's Lords of the Privy Council?"

"Not son, no." Kat's voice dropped a notch with every step we took towards the center of the courtyard, where my travelling litter awaited, with Paget himself standing by to receive us. "But a relation, he reports himself—a trusted instrument. I say, rather, a hanger-on, and an abortion of a true gentleman—a cloak-twitcher too, I'd not be surprised . . ."

"My lady Elizabeth!" He was before us, with his morning flourish. "And Mistress Ashley, as ever was!"

If our curtseys were both brief and chilly, that could only be put down to the frost of the morning. "Your servant, sir!" we chimed coldly in unison as Kat assisted me into my travelling bed and smothered me with coverlets.

"Sleep now, sweetheart," she soothed as she plumped up the last of my pillows and dropped a kiss as sweet and firm as a summer cherry on the end of my nose. "By sunrise we shall be in Eastcote, and I shall have a little something there to cheer your stomach, never fear."

Then came her comforting, gurgling laugh as she drew the heavy brocade curtains rattling together on their wooden rings. "As for him"—she chucked her chin at the stiff figure of Paget stalking off through the hurly-burly to find his own horse—"may Jack Frost have all his extremities, not forgetting his privities too, saving Your Ladyship's reverence! Sleep well, my lady!"

Sleep, sibling of death, is never far from a travelling litter. The rocking motion, the soft clopping of the horses all around, the jangling of the bridles and brass trappings, the low snorts and whinnies as the beasts share the burden of the journey with one another, would lure even a sleepwalker into the dreamless land.

But with sleep came not peace but torment. I dreamed I would die if I could not fathom out the riddles of Grindal. So in the playhouse of my mind the evil Catiline circled the old King's throne, knife in hand and dripping with blood, while the old King watched, powerless to move or resist, like a death-wounded beast. Meanwhile a female lion, her fangs likewise bloodied to the chops, drew circles around a younger lion, small and weak, with death hissing like Pluto's darts from the glare of her yellow gaze.

In the heavens above, wild rolling eyes hurtled through the skies like flaming comets, while Grindal's voice kept time with them, chanting *"See-more! See-more!"* in the tones of some mad priest at a dark sacrifice. Then came a flood, and a hart seeking to ford it to find safe haven on the other side. But there was no ford, and the flood overwhelmed the hart, and so it sank and drowned. *And the hart, like the little lion, was I.*

I knew I would die if I could not fathom out the meaning of the riddles. And I would die even more quickly if I did. Whenever I opened my mouth to scream, a dark fist in a dark gauntlet stopped my throat, cramming my gorge with loose, powdery flakes of ash, mummy, soot and withered flesh. And when I fought myself awake, the taste in my mouth was death.

Care-charmer sleep, brother to sable night . . .
   "My lady?"
Relieve my anguish and restore the light . . .
   "My lady? How do you?"
   The black shapes were gone, no more than a bad memory in my mouth; the litter was on *terra firma,* the sun warming my nest; and best of all, my dearest Kat was drawing back my curtains with something I never thought to see . . .
   "Kat, what's this? Fresh milk? White bread? And eggs in butter! How on earth—?"
   "This?" She tossed her head, and the Devon burr of her home country broke through as it only did when she was deeply pleased. " 'Tis nothing, madam. Only to know where to find provender in such God-forsaken holes as these, which be not accustomed to the care and comfort of a princess!"
   Curiously I peered out through the looped-up hangings. We stood in a large and tidy farmyard, with the last of the hayricks still standing well against the weather, and plump hens nipping sprightly to and fro to evade the early-morning attentions of the cock.
   "Madam?"
   With a curtsey that would not have dishonoured the Grand Sophy, my lady-in-waiting Blanche Parry appeared at my side. If I loved Kat for her closeness, I loved Parry for the opposite, the formal seriousness that never varied from Court to cow byre. Both she and her brother Thomas, now the treasurer of my household, had left their beloved Wales to come to me at the same time, becoming then, along with Kat, the family I never had and, because of them, never missed.
   Now, attended by two little maids sailing behind, Parry gave me her good morning. "And are you minded, madam"—she paused, delicately placing her question as a request not to be taken as coming from herself —"to be *seen?*"
   "Seen?"
   "The people of the village hereby, my lady: they have seen your train— the litter—and they beg leave to pay their respects. They have been waiting, in all this cruel frost, most patiently."
   "By all means!"
   Passing the remains of my breakfast to Kat's little maid, I took the travelling mirror Parry now handed me from my toilet case, and watched

closely as she combed down my hair. "On this side—there—yes, thank
you. My earrings, Kat? No, no, the great pearls. And now my hood—the
russet velvet. So."

In the smooth circle of beaten metal a wan face peered back at me.
Too pale for my taste! Roughly I scrubbed my cheekbones with my fist.
Now, with two perfect rings of carmine on my cheeks, I looked the image
of a wooden-headed doll.

"My lady!" Parry was scandalized. "There should be no *red* in a lady's
complexion, it is not becoming! A princess holds no peerage with a . . .
a donkey woman!"

A donkey woman! Kat could hardly scold for laughing, or laugh for
scolding. *Red!* Parry made it sound like a dirty word. Protesting, I submitted to her urgent ministrations with rosewater and powdered eggshells
till the hectic in my cheeks had been smoothed away.

Now I looked as I should have done if God had made me a great
beauty. And my "ivory look," as I called it to myself in my vainest moments, chimed far better than rose or carnation with my mermaid's hair,
which flashed now red, now gold, as the sun and clouds played hide-and-
seek, making it shine like an angel or deepen to unpolished copper. I was
vain of my hair, let me confess—and today it was gleaming like strands of
woven sunlight. I smoothed down my overgown, settled myself in my
furs, adjusted myself into a more princess-like stance, and was ready.
"Bid them approach."

In a corner of the farmyard a handful of my gentlemen stood together
with the men-at-arms, all stamping their feet against the bitter cold.
Waiting patiently beside them, huddling their hands into their armpits for
warmth, or blowing on their fingers' ends, blue already from the morning's bite, were a cluster of countryfolk: the farmer of the holding, by the
look of his buff clothing, weather-scarred face and rough brown leggings;
his men and maids; a scatter of children, from ten summers or so in age,
down to the baby in its mother's arms; and a gnarled grandfather, resting
on a stick.

Excitedly I prepared to greet them. I loved to meet the people every
time I ventured abroad. When they cheered my father—adding, as they
always did, "And bless thee too, Harry's little maid!"—I felt a pride of
belonging so rare I could hardly compass it.

Suddenly I felt a violent jolt: "En route, Madam Elizabeth!" It was
Paget's voice. "We have no time to spare for these farmyard clowns, my
lady. His Majesty's word was 'haste'!" He paused. "And for your health
and comfort, Your Ladyship would wish for your *privacy,* I think." He
reached up to untie the hangings of my litter, cutting me off from the
outside world.

He gave me orders, he banned me from the sight of the country people, he decreed that I must travel invisible, as if I were a prisoner of state.

How dared he?

And how much longer till I could discover how he dared?

"One moment, sir, if you please!" With a furious Parry hard astern, Kat tacked violently across Paget's bows. "In the daylight hours, when the noisome vapours of night are no longer to be feared, my mistress travels with her litter open," she said firmly, tying back the hangings Paget had just loosed.

"There is more than one kind of health, Mistress Ashley," murmured Paget, his charcoal eyes aglow. "It is not healthful for Her Ladyship to expose herself to the danger of the common people."

"My lady in danger from the people of England?" Parry could not stand by and let this pass. "Sir, you know not what you say! Why, they adore her, they have done since her infancy! Not one of her progresses but they turn out to see her pass! And not a soul in England would hurt a hair upon her head—no, not the paring of her petty toes!"

"Yet is it better," Paget said vengefully, nodding up two or three of his men-at-arms, "for the Lady Elizabeth to travel enclosed."

The soldiers lumbered forward. Paget smiled a victor's smile. "I have my orders," he said softly.

"Your *orders,* sir?" An inspiration struck me. "Orders that I must travel enclosed and unseen—is that so set down in the King my father's warrant?"

A dull anger mantled his cheek, and I knew I had him. "Not in so many words, madam. But I deemed it better—"

"And I deem it better, sir, to obey my governor Mistress Ashley—after my lord the King—in everything." Once again I played the modest-maiden card for all it was worth. "If she decrees it, we will travel open—we shall be seen."

Kat's eyes flashed triumph, but she knew this was no time for drums and trumpets. Paget's voice, tight as a weevil in his throat, spoke for him. "As you wish, my lady. To horse! You there! Away!"

He was my enemy, that was now clear.

When would I know why?

The cries of men, the straining of horses, brought my litter shuddering to life. Across the yard Ashley, Chertsey and the Vernon brothers were taking a hasty leave of the farm people and making for their mounts. On every honest, frozen country face was written bitter disappointment. My heart burned. I leaned forward urgently.

"Kat! Kat! I beg you, send to those people! Say I grieve to have no chance to speak to them, but our lord the King commands us haste, and his will must be done. Give them my greetings, and thank them for their kindness. Tell them I will not forget Eastcote and its people, its good milk and bread, and the warmth of its welcome!"

Briskly Kate despatched the last of the maids to convey my words. Off went my litter, step by ponderous step. The farmyard was receding now, the people getting smaller, with every pace. But as the maid reached them, I could see smiles break out among the little party like sunshine after rain. The farmer pulled off his cap, followed by all his men, and waving lustily, they raised a farewell cheer: "God speed you, Lady Princess! God save thee and bring thee to joy of thine own!"

Fervently I acknowledged their cheers, the warm tears of delight pricking my eyes. Riding ahead, Paget scowled and turned an evil face. Suddenly one of the straggle of farm children broke away from the group and came skimming towards us at full pelt. Swearing under his breath, one of the troopers moved to head her off; and Paget, too, reined back his horse, reaching for his sword.

Would they attack a child? "Put up your sword, master!" I shouted furiously. "Do not hinder her! Let her come to me!"

With shining eyes the child ran up alongside and with a sure aim tossed something into my lap. It was a posy of the first of the spring flowers: glossy celandines, a few anemones nodding their ivory heads, primroses as pale as lady's hands, and four or five bold cowslips with vermilion-spotted throats. The girl herself was no more than eight, her pinched face yellow with cold, her greasy hair half in, half out of a ragged headcloth, her rough working hands, little more than paws, cracked and blistered with broken chilblains. But when I gave her my thanks, her smile was a wonder to behold.

Behind me I could hear the rattle of Paget's sword unsheathing and the tread of approaching troopers. "Go now!" I whispered to the child. "And beware of these men!"

Nodding, she slipped away with a final smile. I could feel the air about me now heavy with menace, and knew that this would be the last I would see of the countryfolk today. But still as we journeyed through village and hamlet, the people there could not mistake whose progress this was, nor was the little wench the last to see her Princess that day.

V

This time of trial seemed without end. Every dawn now broke bitter and damp, every nightfall fell early and colder still. And in between, the going was so foul that we never knew a day without a mule foundering or a waggon overthrown. When would we come to our journey's end at the Palace of Whitehall, where the King kept Court still, even though the Law Term was over and the men of Parliament were scattered to the shires?

Young James Vernon had a ballad, a thing in the minor key that did little to raise my spirits:

> *The Court's a fine and bonny place,*
> *Where men kiss hands, and more, they say,*
> *But none I think do there embrace*
> *A quiet mind, for all betray . . .*

And on, and on, heavy heart keeping pace with heavy going, Hatfield to Eastcote, Wild Hill to Woodside, Bell Bar to Water End, Mimms to Green Street, making no more than a few miles a day.

And I was no nearer a solution to my vexing anxieties, no matter how I combed my Sallust for any light it might throw on Grindal's dark mutterings. Maybe at Court he would open his mind to me. And there, too, I would learn what was buzzing in the King's hive—who supped the honey now, and who the gall—and whose sharp sting I must beware of, at peril of my life.

At last there came the word I longed to hear.

"Courage, madam!" called old Francis Vine, my gentleman-usher, as he urged his reluctant cob, a horse equally as ancient and cautious as his master, alongside my litter. "We shall make Court tonight!"

Courage, yes! In London all confusion would be banished. At Court I would have answers to my questions. No more brooding alone, unwilling even to turn to Kat for comfort. No more sleepless nights, with only the cold-faced moon for company. And above all, no more Paget!

For he was still with me, still a thorn in my mind's side. Today he was more gorgeous than ever in a new rig of bottle-green. But his reign would be ended as soon as we made Court. And if no more Paget, no more fear!

No more fear. How I dreamed of that, when sleep would not come.

Whitehall.

Over the gleaming highway of the Thames, dotted as always with little craft no bigger than walnut shells, the sun was westering in a blaze of fire. As we came down Cockspur Street and turned towards Whitehall, all the white towers and glittering pinnacles of the palace were bathed in red and gold. Whitehall's hugeness, its vast splendor, gripped me once again with a pride so fierce it burned like a hot iron inside my ribs.

My father made all this! I wanted to shout. *Great Harry built the greatest and most beautiful palace in the whole of Christendom!*

For it was common knowledge that the Palace of Whitehall covered twenty-four acres, when all other palaces of the world's lesser kings took up no more than two. And its size, spreading like a great oak tree, was the least of it. The King had scoured Europe for the finest masons, the truest builders, the most gifted gardeners, the best artists of every sort to make the building in his fancy come to life as the palace of his dreams.

And all sought to find their own dreams in this mart of hopes and promises: dreams of riches or glory, of honours or royal service. This was a city of dreams where every day almost two thousand hopefuls jostled for place, for preferment, for one sign of the King's favour.

What were my dreams?

I knew that as a girl, ordained by God to have her life shaped by others, there was little indeed that I should dare to dream.

And yet . . .

And yet . . .

The good Vernon brothers had ridden hard ahead to give warning of my approach. Now the Royal Guard lined all the length of Whitehall in a solemn avenue of scarlet surcoats and glittering steel. Among the ranks of men were countless solid, loyal faces, as English to my eyes as ale and roast beef, familiar from my last visit and from years before that. Again I felt the surging pride of blood—Harry's blood, Tudor blood, royal blood since time immemorial, time before time. Yet for all that, I knew I was no longer what I had been before. If nothing else, Paget had taught me that.

Yet let me not be changed too much, Lord God, I prayed, *not too much changed . . .*

For I loved my childhood world, my Hatfield world, and I had no wish to leave it.

At the great twin-towered gatehouse with its wide brick arch of red and yellow, the Vernon brothers awaited me. The long train of horses, waggons, riders and mules came slowly to a halt.

"Ho-oa! Ho-oa-hoh! Hoa there!"

"Take the reins, boy, damn you—the reins!"

"Permit me, madam."

"Very kindly, sir!"

All around, the mounted gentlemen unhorsed to help the ladies, the waggoners climbed down to begin uncarting, the maids and boys tumbled whooping out of the carts at the back, and the mules and horses planted their feet in the dust and drooped their heads as if to say, *Not an inch farther!*

"Welcome to Whitehall, my lady."

Bowing low, Richard Vernon on one side and James on the other handed me out of the litter, my ordeal at an end. Now the flourish of my personal fanfare proclaimed to the Court that the Lady Elizabeth had arrived. While the silver trumpets were still ringing through the courtyards, the Lord Chamberlain, master of the King's household, came bustling out, his retinue on his heels. I could feel Paget moving up beside me to see without being seen.

"My lady!"

"Lord St. John!"

The Lord Chamberlain was an old man now, his dancing days long done. But what his bow lacked in grace and sprightliness, he made up for in devotion. Lowering himself on one creaking knee, he kissed my hand in greeting. "Most dearly welcome to the Court, fair lady."

I could barely suppress a smile of triumph as I returned my thanks. So I was not *persona non grata* to everyone at Court, despite what Paget had tried to make me believe! I turned. He was no longer with us. *Gone to make his report!* I laughed to myself. *To his uncle Sir William—or whoever else is his master here!*

So much for Paget, Sir Snake of the many skins! He had had his day with me. Soon now I would know his game—what he played for—*and why!*

"This way, my lady."

Courteously the Lord Chamberlain led us forward through the gatehouse and into the palace courtyard. Lord, I had forgotten how lovely Whitehall was! And how much bigger and grander than I remembered it! Suddenly I felt like the proverbial country mouse—or worse . . .

How will they treat me? I held my breath as the Lord Chamberlain spoke: "The King His Majesty has given orders that you be lodged in the Queen's household, Madam Elizabeth."

In the Queen's household! With the Queen—Dame Katherine Parr, as all still thought of her despite her marriage to my father three years or so ago now. This was good news, the best! She had always been kind to me, keeping me and my beloved Edward with her whenever she could, and always writing, always sending, when she could not.

I could not hold back. "When shall I see Her Majesty?"

St. John smiled. "Sooner than you think, my lady. Queen Katherine means to come to you this evening, as soon as she hears that you are recovered from your journey."

Bowing, he ushered me through a small knot garden, then along a cloister of slender columns to an open space beyond. As we emerged into the evening light, I gasped at what I saw. The King had been building again, for adding to his "White Hall" was a passion with him. Now, like everything else in his favourite palace, what his workmen had wrought was the finest in the world, brand-new and beautiful beyond compare.

We stood in a fair, flagged courtyard. In the fast-fading silvery light its perfect symmetry and the delicate carving that adorned every surface gave it the grace of a chapel. Yet the stone leaves on the stone trees graven on the walls around us almost lived, so true to life were they, the stone birds in the stone branches seeming on the point of taking flight or settling more sweetly onto their stone nests for the night, stone heads tucked safely under stone wings.

It was a magical place. Lapped in the glimmering dusk, we could have been standing in a petrified forest. Ahead of us, sheltering the courtyard within its two extended arms, stood the Queen's House, warm light glowing from every mullioned window, its lofty frontage blazoning its status as a palace within a palace, a dwelling fit for a queen.

The Lord Chamberlain escorted me to the door, of monumental oak as tall as two men, its massive panels deeply carved with scenes of Bible stories. Here, surrounded by Job, the Prodigal Son and Daniel in the lions' den, he paused. "The Queen bids you welcome to her new house, Lady Elizabeth. Her Grace bids me tell you that she hopes this will not be the last of the pleasures you will enjoy here at Court."

My young heart leaped at this. "What, are there treats and shows planned? Pageants? Mumming?"

"You shall see, my lady."

He raised his hand. The door flew open, and a gentlemanly steward came forth to make his bow. Behind him stood the servants, homely shapes against the candlelight within.

"Welcome to the Queen's House, my lady Elizabeth," he said respectfully. "Queen Katherine bade me say that all here is yours, and all hers is yours, from the moment you step under her roof. She has appointed you the finest lodgings at her disposal, on the first floor above. She has or-

dered refreshment for you and your people, and bids you command anything within my power she may have overlooked."

My cup was overflowing. "I thank you, sir. Pray tell Her Majesty I give
God thanks for her great goodness, so far beyond my deserts."

I could hardly speak. If the Queen herself was caring for me, protect-
ing me, what need I fear from a waggonload of watchers like Paget, with
his evil ways?

The steward bowed. "This way, my lady, if you please."

"Kat! Kat! What d'you think of this? Oh, do look! Is it not wonderful?"

Kat was ordering the arrangement of my Privy Chamber when I swept
in and pounced wildly upon her, hugging her well-covered figure in my
excitement. A rapid tour of our new quarters had shown me at once how
well favoured we were. From the door off the wide corridor, a large anteroom led into a spacious, well-lit chamber hung with French tapestries
and snugly fitted with gleaming wainscot, so new it still breathed beeswax
and linseed oil.

My bed was a fourposter in which I and six other maidens could have
romped at will. The bed hangings, of red, pink, cream and crimson silk,
were embroidered inside and out with carnations so luscious that in
dreams you could breath their summer scent or pluck them for a salad.
Below the yard-deep valance of the coverlet, the oak boards were covered not with everyday rushes but with a woven carpet of the finest
damascene, a luxury unknown at dear old-fashioned Hatfield.

On a table beside the bed stood the promised refreshments, enough to
tempt a sparrow appetite: a country pastie, golden brown and crusted
like a castle; half a dozen pike in a galantine of glistening calves'-foot
jelly; capon breasts in a yellow thyme-and-parsley cream, with plates of
filberts, quinces, marchpane and wafers; and sweet, rich hippocras to
follow, a cordial strong enough to restore any failing stomach.

"Look at this, Kat!" I exulted. "Truly we are at Court! I think we are in
heaven!"

*It is well said that ignorance is the mother of all rashness. But how was I to
know?*

"My lady! My lady!"

It was Parry's voice, shrill with disaster. A second later she came hur-
tling through the door, her customary calm thrown to the winds.
"Madam, the Queen! The Queen is coming!"

"The Queen?"

Into the shocked silence came the faint sounds of an approaching
train, the stamp of men and cries of "Way there for Her Grace!" "Back!
Get back!" "Out of the way!"

"They said she would not see you till you were ready, and now she comes!" cried Parry in an agony that the Queen would catch us weary and travel-stained, my gown unchanged, my face innocent of her cherished arts, my ears, neck, wrists and fingers naked of adornment.

"But queens may change their minds!" I laughed. I had no fear of the Queen's scrutiny. I clapped my hands. "Quickly now, both of you, quick, quick, *quick!*"

With every second the sounds outside were getting nearer, and more important.

"Way for Her Grace!"

"Go before and bid them open, fellow!"

With both my women working like Turks, I made what hasty toilet I could. "Smooth my hair, Parry! Kat, my cap—yes, that will do. My face, Parry, is it clean? Oh, spit on your sleeve—this is no time for daintiness! Kat, my dress—"

They were outside now. "Knock there and gain admission!"

"Within there, ho! Open! Open for Her Grace!"

We had done all we could. My travelling gown, a loose russet velvet, was no more than serviceable, but it would have to do. Hastily smoothing and straightening ourselves, we hurried out into the main hall of state. All my ladies-in-waiting and gentlemen attendants, clearly quite unstrung by the Queen's unexpected descent, fanned out around me. I glanced round. We were as ready as we would ever be.

Bang! Bang! Bang!

The rapping on the door tore through the air. Eagerly I gave the nod to old Francis Vine, my gentleman-usher. He waved my doorman forward. Slowly the huge door swung open on its great strap hinges. I dropped my eyes, lowered my head and swept into my best and deepest curtsey.

"Most honoured are my people and your humble servant by this visitation, Your Grace."

Formalities done, I raised my eyes to greet the Queen, my heart already reaching for her embrace. And instead of Katherine, found myself looking straight into the blazing eyes and yellow, quivering face of my dear sister Mary.

VI

"The Princess Mary's Grace!" bawled her gentleman-usher. Suddenly the Presence Chamber was abuzz with bright cloaks and rustling gowns, full to overflowing with Mary and her followers. The King had always kept her poor, to punish her for her Papistry. How had she come to be so grand?

And her train! My people were fifteen or less—hers, at a guess, more than forty. I read the minds of the Vernon brothers, Ashley, Chertsey, Parry, Kat in every face. In a world where numbers spelled status, we were outnumbered by the enemy.

By the enemy Mary—

Mary my senior, my sister, my blood, my kin.

Kin indeed, but as I saw in her face, a little less than kind.

But why "enemy"? Why unkind? I had to shake off the fear instilled in me by Grindal's riddles and my evil dreams. Mary had shown me kindness enough before. Presents all my life: on my sixth birthday, a yellow satin kirtle I cried with joy to get, and once, when I was sick, a still-treasured set of silver spoons, each one bearing an apostle's face. I had not seen Mary since the King's wedding to Madam Parr three and more years before, the last time my father had summoned all his children together, when all had been love and goodwill. She had kissed me warmly then as we met, and we had parted well enough too. True, she had caught me by surprise today with this unexpected descent, the more so as I had no idea that she, too, had been sent for and would be with us at Court. But child that I was, I thought of the sweet-faced holy men bright-shining on her spoons and schooled myself to give her a true welcome.

As was her due. For she was my father's daughter, however stubbornly she stood out against him. She was my senior by a good seventeen summers, so I owed her my respect. And like all who ever came there, I needed friends at Court. Would Mary be my friend?

"Sister!"

Her hands were gripping mine, assisting me to rise, her look of white-lipped tension gone, her eyes glowing in a delighted face. Clearly she had taken the deep curtsey I meant for the Queen as due to her alone. So be it. The salutation of "Your Grace" that I had made could serve for either, and my people would never betray my mistake. I kissed her hands. "My lady Princess!"

How Mary had changed! In the three summers that had divided us, she had aged ten winters. Her small, heart-shaped face showed now all skin and bone, with a peaked chin and hollow pouches of dark flesh beneath her bruised eyelids. Her narrow lips were now pale as lead, and her small pebble-brown eyes, never her best feature, looked more mole-blind than ever.

Yet still was she transformed from our last meeting. She was resplendent in a finer gown than I had ever seen, the sleeves puffed and slashed with ivory-coloured silk to match her milk-white kirtle, her dark red velvet overgown glowing like garnets in the candlelight and trimmed at collar and cuffs with pearls as big as peas. Her smile invited me to rush into her arms as I had always done before. But something made me hold my tongue till Mary should speak first.

"So! Madam Elizabeth!"

She held me at arm's length, blinking at my sober travelling gown. "Quite the little Puritan in dress, I see. Yet not so little these days, neither!" She laughed her small, harsh laugh. "By heaven, sister, I swear you overtop me now!"

"In no thing, madam, would I so presume."

Yes, of course I was lying—through my teeth, through lips and all!

Yet what could I do but dissemble? I was a head taller now than her short, squat frame, for nature had shaped her after her mother, who never reached my father's armpit, by all accounts.

Her worn face blazed up again as she replied. "Yes! You speak the truth! You will never outpace me, and I am glad that God in His goodness has brought you to the understanding of that! For God sent me before you into this world to guide your footsteps! To save you, sister, from the errors of the past, the words and deeds of those who would lead you by the primrose path to the everlasting bonfire!"

Clasping her hands together before her as if in prayer, she paced agitatedly to and fro, waving aside the gentlewoman who hastened to her assistance. "Fret me not, away! Sister, you are not to blame, God knows, for the King's great sin in breaking his marriage to my mother, in order to serve the lusts of yours—well, well, Our good Lord punished both her and him for that! But now you are of mature age, you must be mistress of your own soul. Remember, sister, the word of Our Lord: 'As you sow, so shall you reap!' Think upon this, I urge you, for your own salvation!"

Somewhere behind me came a hiss of sudden anger and the sharp release of breath. Then fell the kind of silence no one knows how to break. I was choking with shame and rage—my mother to be so spoken of! Yet greater still was my fear, a fear shared by all there present—and it was mortal.

For this was heresy—and treason besides! The King had long ago forbidden all dispute over his policy of religion, all discussion of his divorce from Katherine of Aragon, on pain of death. Men—and women too—had been burned alive simply for standing by to give ear to such stuff, let alone for daring to speak it. As the daughter of the King, Mary had been spared the worst of the horrors that befell others who clung to the Romish persuasion. But now I feared she vaunted the Old Faith at peril of her soul and body—and talked of it to me, at mine!

"Your Highness—" I began.

"Fear not!"

Her stone-brown eyes blazed with a peculiar triumph, an incandescence I had not seen before. She laughed. "You fear that I walk in the shadow of the stake even to talk of these things? And that I would draw you thither too?"

My silence was agreement enough.

"But Elizabeth, you know not of the miracle that has befallen!" Her exaltation was heated, unnatural, like a hard fever. "Almighty God in His wisdom has softened the King's heart and inclined him to our side! He turns away from the Reformed Religion, from the new learning, from the proud falsehoods of Protestantism, and at the last stage of his mortal pilgrimage, returns now to the Old Faith, the true faith in God!"

The King turning against the Church he created with his own hands? And its believers . . . ?

I smelled death again, just as I had at Hatfield.

"The King my father? Is he ill?"

Again the white, incandescent smile. "Never better, sister, never better! For now is his soul in health, as it has never been since he fell from grace in the union with your mother!"

I drew a deep breath and took hold of my rage. "Your pardon, madam. All men know that the King's marriage to *your* mother was the cause of his soul's sickness: for the Bible expressly forbids any man should take unto himself his dead brother's wife, as my father was forced to do in pity when your mother was left widowed!"

Mary's strange good humour vanished like winter sun. Now it was her turn to rage. "Beware, lady, how you speak so, in these new times!" The threat was unmistakable. Then her mood veered round again. "Oh, away with that whey-faced stare! Fear not, dear sister! You are but a young child, and will not be held to blame for the foul heresies and mistakes of the past!"

Another change of weather: another gleam of winter sun. "Yet not such a child neither. As I thought, a woman grown!" A smile that on any other woman might have been roguish broke over her sallow cheeks. Like a skiff when the wind swings about, she was suddenly, wildly, sportive. "How think you of marriage, lady? A maid of your years must be wearying St. Winifred of the Virgins every night to bring you a handsome husband!"

A husband?

Dear God!

Where was she now?

Light running footsteps, a young girl's howling scream down an empty corridor, echoed through my mind.

Marriage?

On guard! I warned myself as I steeled myself to cut and thrust in return. "Any maid might dream, my lady Mary, who was free to do so. But my hand, like yours, is in our father's hands, our will must be his will. And as you are the elder of us, sister, we all know your marriage must come first."

"My marriage!"

Touché—a hit so palpable I cursed my cruelty for making it. Suddenly the tight mouth trembled and collapsed, and beads of tears started unbidden at each corner of her mud-coloured eyes. "Marriage! Yes, little sister, well may you taunt me with that—for I have despaired of it! Long have I known that the King in his wisdom has meant to keep me here unwed, the unhappiest lady in Christendom!"

In all the crowd around, none dared move, hardly even breathe. My heart went out to her, and guiltily I fumbled for some words of consolation. "Yet the longest day ends at last, sister. Soon may you be married—and well before me, I trust!"

But Mary had the pride of all the Tudors. She wanted no man's pity, least of all mine. "You forget, sister, I have been many times 'married' already—as have you—in the King our father's games of diplomacy with foreign powers. All that wanted in each case was but the luxury of the bedding!"

And with the Tudor pride went Tudor danger, and the desire to wound. Her eyes were glittering, and the scent of blood was in the air. "But you —what would you remember of this, as the daughter of a most notorious bed swerver, a whore who would not know what bed she occupied, a trull whose adulteries ranged free before and after her marriage to my father? Is it a wonder if you forget your previous trothplights—and in the process, forget yourself too?"

Somewhere to my right I saw both Vernon brothers reach for their hilts. For myself, too, I knew that if Mary had been a man, she never would have left the chamber alive. But as a girl, not even yet a woman, what could I do? I bowed my head to hide the tears of shame and rage pricking my eyes.

None spoke or moved, like creatures under a spell. From far off in the palace, a sound of movement, the tramp of marching men, broke in upon the silence. Mary tried a laugh. "And now, I think, at thirty years or so, with or without the King's decree, I may soon choose a husband for myself!"

With or without . . . ? What was this dark hinting about my father . . . ?

Outside the Queen's House now were men laughing, men calling, and the flare of torches glimmering greenly through the glass. I tried to challenge her. "Soon, you say, madam? *Why soon?*"

She swept on. "But I also have a care for you, sister, greater than you think. I would not have you waiting for a husband as I have done, wasting the best of your virgin years."

Husband again! I felt my backbone stiffen. "I do not think to marry yet, madam—not at these years."

The sounds in the courtyard were louder now, and there was no mistaking their direction. Mary seemed oblivious.

" 'At these years'!" she cried in mimicry. "Many of your years are old wives long married, yes, and mothers too! Why, fool, our grandfather Henry had never lived, had not his mother been wedded and bedded in her twelfth spring, for only six months later was her husband dead. And had not that young lass the Lady Margaret then been brought to bed, thank God, of a son, our house had perished with him! It is the first duty of a Tudor to marry—even the women! Especially the women! What else are we ordained for?"

I put all the force I was capable of into my answer. *"I do not think to marry."*

Footsteps were approaching, a group of men by the sound, drawing near my door.

"E-liz-a-beth."

Mary bore down on me with every syllable of my name. I could smell the incense from the Mass lingering in the folds of her gown, see the pitted surface of her bosom like old tallow. Her breath was foul. "Remember: Man proposes—*God disposes.* We obey His will. And the husband He has ordained for you may be drawing nearer to you, moment by moment, day by day, step by step, even as we speak!"

And pat on cue, like some crude Christmas mumming, came three thunderous knocks at the door.

"Within there!" came a cry. "Give access, ho!"

Mary smiled, her eyes on fire with hidden purpose. At her signal one of her gentlemen thrust aside my gentleman-usher and threw open the door to the anteroom. In a voice of sickening coyness, Mary called out, "Are you there, my lord? If it be you, pray show yourself at once and come within!"

VII

" 'If it be you . . . ?' " demanded a sardonic voice. "Who should it be but your servant of Surrey, Madam Mary, honoured to attend your commandment here?"

He was sauntering through the door as he spoke, with a grace that made the punctilious Paget look like a kitchen scullion. He was supremely tall, taller than any of the liveried retainers who pressed about him, taller than my Vernons, taller than any man in the room. Yet he had a languorous looseness that drew all eyes his way.

"My lady Princess."

He was greeting Mary with great courtesy, but also with something more. His doublet and hose, a bright, burning ochre slashed with silk as brown as beech buds in March, finely set off his thick confusion of shining curls, echoing the fierce flecks of gold in eyes the colour of sherry wine.

"And my lady Elizabeth?"

His hat, jewelled and plumed like a prince's, played teasingly in his hand as he bowed low before me. His glance was lazy but caressing too, and I could not meet his eyes. He carried himself like a king; suddenly it seemed that I was the humble handmaid, he the royal-born.

And all so received him. At his entrance the room seemed to grow brighter, the very candles seemed to blaze with more conviction. He was smiling now, and I knew his gaze was bringing up the colour in my cheeks. His eyes flickered up and down my form, dowdy in its travelling robe—*God, why did You not give me time to change my gown?*

He was . . . he was . . .

"Henry Howard of Surrey, my little lady, and your servant ever."

He looked into my eyes. I could not speak.

"Know my lord of Surrey, sister Elizabeth!" prompted Mary sharply. I knew she thought I had lost my breeding. The truth was, I had lost something else—lost far more.

Of course I knew him. I knew him from long before as the heir of all the Howards, son to the Duke of Norfolk and the young hope of their clan. He was even a distant connection of mine through the vast Howard cousinage, for his father was kin to my Howard grandmother. But how was it I had remembered with indifference one who seemed so different to me now?

"My lord." I curtsied, and dropped my head to hide my face.

Mary nodded in satisfaction, then turned her attention to Surrey. She smiled, mistakenly showing her teeth, decaying like tombstones in the graveyard of her face. "We were talking of marriage, my lord!" she said, again with that strained playfulness that sat so ill upon her. "My sister says that she will never marry—what do you think of that?"

Again his arrogant gaze flicked me like a whiplash. He laughed. "It says little for us poor men, madam, if not one has ever stirred her heart enough to make her want to!" He paused, surveying me coldly, but his slow smile and sensual stare gave an extra sting to what followed. "Nor—forgive me, lady—stirred her senses."

Now he was speaking to me directly, his low murmur for my ears alone. "For the life of a virgin is a hard discipline, mistress: the faith of the flesh is a far easier one to follow . . ."

The faith of the flesh . . . ?

I was on fire, from my hot cheeks down. "You mock me, my lord!" I whispered.

He laughed again, lazily, into my ear. "Not so, lady. But what do I know of virgins"—his voice dropped to a whisper—"since I rather choose the company of those I may help to divest themselves of that garment of maiden modesty . . . ?"

"What are you saying, my lord?" cried Mary gaily. "Does he be-rhyme you, sister? He is a poet, did you know that? Will you make her a verse, my lord?"

Truly she was in a high good humour in this man's presence! He shrugged. "All men are poets at your father's Court, madam. And in the presence of such beauties, a mute himself would be moved to sing your praises. Say rather that I am a soldier proud to take arms in the King's wars, be they in Scotland or France, honoured to bear arms for him, for his divine daughters and all that he calls his . . ."

His flattery was so gross it would not have fooled a child! But Mary simpered like a natural. Her small hands made another sly expedition to pat his sleeve and playfully tap his shoulder . . .

Of course! Fool that I was to be so slow to see it! She meant to marry him!

And why not? He was of her age, or near enough—some twenty-eight

or thirty summers, as I guessed, like her own. Man enough to my unformed eyes for any princess, indeed of a rare manly beauty that his
princely air did nothing to diminish. His blood was of the best, for his
father Norfolk was a royal duke. After our royalty, then, his house stood
next to the throne, and he numbered among his forebears Plantagenet
kings and even St. Edward the Confessor.

But Mary wanted more than man alone. In her eyes, as I guessed, he
was a true son of God. For though like thousands of others the Norfolks
had conformed to the new religion on the orders of the King, all the
world knew that secretly they clung to the Old Faith. There I had it! A
Catholic, or as good as; a prince of the blood, or as good as; and of the
right age so that she would never have to stand up at the altar with a
twenty-year-old young enough to be her son.

And if my father was ailing, as I now feared, and losing his powers,
perhaps at last Mary could choose for herself. No wonder, then, that with
her own man chosen, she could not resist the chance to play a hand or
two of marriage games for me!

And in the meanwhile she was using me as a pawn in her pursuit of
him! I felt a fury of resentment simmering in my breast. What must *he*
think of me, forced to stand by in my ugliest gown and endure Mary's
foolish flirtatiousness? I could not look at him.

"What say I, my lady?" Smoothly he turned her question aside. "Only
that I am blessed among men, being at the bidding of not one princess,
but two. You bade me to attend you here, Lady Mary; my lady Elizabeth
whispers in my ear that she wishes me to wait on her here again, that she
may get to know me better"—his eyes, flickering with amusement, defied
me to contradict him—"and I her. And this evening I serve also a lady
higher still: the Queen's Majesty has ordered me to attend my lady Elizabeth to the royal apartments, as soon as she is ready to greet her mother
in love."

*My mother in love. My mother-in-love. Yes. Dame Katherine Parr had
tried to be a mother to me since she married the King. She at least I could
trust to deal honestly with me if I was to have these choking vapours of fear
and ignorance blown away.*

Later that night I stepped out under the escort of my lord of Surrey as
coolly as courtesy permitted. Now I was ready to face him, for in the
interim I had been dressed and dressed again until I was fit to meet the
Queen of Sheba, let alone of England. My hair had been combed till it
shone like beaten copper, and parted in the middle to cascade down my
back, the perfect mark of virginity. A proud, heart-shaped headdress
held it off my face, a wondrous thing of purple satin trimmed with pearls
and amethysts in the shape of Michaelmas daisies.

The little gleaming flower clusters of pearl and violet also edged the neck of my deep purple velvet gown and blossomed again all down the low-cut bodice, whose stiff, pointed stomacher made it impossible for me to bend, or sit, but only stand to attention like one of my father's guardsmen. My arms likewise were rigid inside the great sleeves of my overgown, padded with a rich, figured gold brocade, the same fabric as my kirtle. And after lacquering my complexion with "the merest *hint* of carnation, madam," as her final inspiration Parry had perfumed me with wild violets, whose sweet pale mauve fragrance has seemed to me ever since the very breath of maidhood unawakened and pure innocence.

"And thus it was, mistress, that the Princess your sister proved to hold all the cards in the last hand, and scooped the pool!"

My lord of Surrey's conversation was light and perfectly judged as we threaded our way through the labyrinth of Whitehall, his every word designed to set me at my ease. But I could not shake the weights from my tongue, nor quell my fierce suspicion of him and the turmoil he aroused in me. Yet I would not have had him stop talking for all the world . . .

Suddenly we were no longer alone in the dark night-time universe. Through a cloister before us appeared a party torch-lit like ours—from the great throng of people, the gentlemen and retainers of a great lord. In their midst strode a tall figure muffled from head to heels in a heavy cloak. They passed by and were gone.

Beside me Surrey drew in a swift breath. "Your Ladyship sees who goes there?" He tried to laugh. "A great man of our time, and one who has grown greater, I think, since your ladyship last came to Court. Lord Lieutenant of All England is his title now, and few believe he will content himself with that. Truly the Earl of Hertford flourishes like the green bay tree! As does his brother Seymour, proud Tom! Why did the King grant them the honours they have been angling for? To be the uncle of the Prince your brother should be honour enough for any man! This world of ours was a better place before ever the Seymours came into it!"

The torches flared, smoked and danced away through the night. Surrounded by his men, the tall figure of the Earl stalked away into the dark, oblivious to our gaze.

Hertford, new grown in power till all England was his fiefdom! And all believing that he was not satisfied even with that, but would aim higher still? Was he, then, the "Catiline" I had been warned against, the proud, ambitious man of Grindal's riddle?

Seymour . . .

Seymour . . .

The name hissed and echoed inside my head. What of the dark Earl of Hertford's brother—"proud Tom," as Surrey called him? If he were as ambi-

tious as Hertford, yet without his brother's role in government, might he, too,
feel the spur that drove Catiline to his doom?

Yet even as my lord Surrey spat out the hated names—"Hert-ford," "Sey-
mour"—his own pride could be seen leaping and snarling like a lion in
chains. How many Catilines now crowded Henry's Court?

"Let him go, the proud Lucifer!"

With an effort Surrey collected himself. Now he smiled with all his old
sardonic humour, and his face in the torchlight took on a vivid, diabolic
gleam. He reached for my hand and raised it to his lips. "Cold, madam?"
he murmured. I shivered at his touch, and he smiled again, deep into my
eyes. "I must dream on some device to warm you. But not now, I fear.
For here, madam, alas for me, is the bourne of our present journey. The
King your father is retired to bed, but Madam our Queen awaits you
here, in the royal lodgings."

After the dark of the courtyard outside, the royal lodgings blazed with
mellow light. The red-coated guards, the richly liveried servants, even the
hangings on the walls, trumpeted their bright colours to my tired eyes.
The vaulted Presence Chamber rang with the buzz of tongues, and a blur
of faces turned to challenge me, raking me coldly with stare after curious
stare. After the quiet of Hatfield, it was all too much. And where was the
Queen?

"Elizabeth—my dear!"

From the heart of the press, the Queen rose from her chair of state
with open arms. Her broad, unruffled brow, her brown hair neatly parted
beneath her familiar gable hood, her warm, welcoming gaze, were just as
I remembered. It was all I could do not to fall onto her soft bosom and
weep like a child. Stiffly I made my deepest curtsey and arose with my
Court smile firmly on my face. But she was too quick to miss the subtle
signs of weakness. The chamber was thick with people: Lady Hertford,
the wife of the Earl; Mistress Herbert, the Queen's sister, and the Marquis of Northampton, her brother; and Sir Anthony Denny, one of the
King's great councillors, in conversation with his wife. But with a word of
thanks to Surrey and a general good-night, she gave sign to her Lord
Chamberlain to clear the Presence, and we were alone.

"Here, child!"

Taking me by the hand, she drew me out of the chamber and through
into her private apartments. I knew at once the faint dark green scent of
juniper, the Queen's favourite chamber fragrance, and her constant companions, the brace of dainty greyhounds dozing by the fire beside their
evening bowl of milk. On the table lay my last New Year's gift to her, a
small book of devotions I had covered with a piece of my own embroi-
dery in yellow and purple heartsease.

A huge fire roared a welcome on the hearth. "Sit you down, sweet-heart!" Tenderly the Queen tipped my chin up to the light spilling from the great sconce by the wall. "Let me look at you. Speak now, unpack that heavy heart. What ails my Elizabeth?"

The first fear first.

"Madam, the King—how is he?"

She hesitated. "Not well, I fear. The ulcer in his leg rages afresh with the coming of spring, and he is much in pain. Nor does he grow any lighter, to reduce the weight his suffering leg must bear: for as you know" —she gave a wry smile—"it is death to him to be dieted! And his appe-tite—alas!—seems to grow with his wound. But I have taken his care into my own hands. Look you—from my apothecary—"

Rising swiftly, she crossed to an inlaid marquetry cabinet. Within stood a veritable pharmacy of medicines, in pots, papers, boxes, bottles and jars, all neatly labelled in the apothecary's Gothic hand, enough to physic an infirmary. The Queen smiled. " 'Cinnamon Comfits,' " she read. " 'Licorice Pastilles,' 'The King's Own Cordial.' Rest assured, my dear, I have everything here to make him better. Plasters for the spleen, fomen-tations for the leg, binders for the belly—not a part of him escapes the ministrations of Doctor Katherine!"

I laughed with relief. "Then he will recover? All shall be well?"

With a light sigh, she returned to her chair. "Indeed, you may soon judge for yourself: for the King intends to keep the Presence Chamber himself tomorrow and commands your attendance. You shall see he is not . . . not as he was. Prepare yourself for the change." She looked steadfastly into the fire. "But we shall not lose him yet! I am sure his hour is not yet come!"

We shall not lose him yet . . . My heart was lightened of its greatest fear. "But madam—my summons here to Court—it came so abruptly I feared the worst—"

She shook her head. "The King grows impatient with the years. When he desired to see you, his haste commanded speed."

"But the messenger—he used me like a servant, a nobody!"

She nodded heavily. "A Master Paget, was it not? Alas, he acts with the power of his uncle Sir William Paget, the Secretary to the Privy Council, now a mighty force among the King's Lords."

The questions now came tumbling from my lips. "Yet why would Sir William Paget or the King have given orders that I should be brought here almost in secret, travelling like a traitor, my litter closed and the people forbidden to come to me?"

The Queen was very grave. "The King is mortal, and begins to give much thought to the succession. At nine years old, your brother the Prince is still a child. Should the King die, he is resolved that none must be allowed to disturb Edward's right to the throne." She paused, and fixed me with her level stare. "You are much loved by the people, from your earliest days, when your father had you carried through the streets of London and shown to all as their trueborn Princess."

Trueborn then, bastard now . . .

How so?

But another time for that.

"But how could I endanger Edward's right? Women cannot rule—I could not take his place!"

The Queen's voice was light. "It is not so set down in the laws of England. This is not France, with its Salic Law against our sex."

"But there has never been a woman on the throne of England! The lords would never stand for it—the people would not have it."

"They might choose it in preference to civil war—rather than return to the Wars of the Roses, which bled our country for so many years."

"But if a woman may succeed, the elder must come first. My sister Mary—"

"Becomes then a force in her own right," conceded the Queen sombrely. "And so she is. Five years at least must pass before the Prince can marry and father a child of his own. Tudor men marry young, we know—your father at eighteen, his brother Arthur three years before that. But Edward is only nine. In the six years before we might hope for a prince from his loins, Mary stands next to the throne."

Now I saw how Mary had become so grand, courted by Surrey and his ilk, dressing herself royally and behaving so too, no longer the cast-off daughter of a cast-off wife but a power in the land! How she might use that power, though, was a prospect not to be borne. I blurted out my fear. "But if Mary ever came to the throne . . ."

There was no answer. The Queen gazed at me, and in silence we shared the same thought: *If Mary has the power, she will bring back the Catholic faith. She will overthrow all the work of reformation and root out all the new learning and new thought, all that we hold dear.*

Among the embers at the edge of the fire stood an earthenware jug. The Queen poured a measure of the hot mulled wine and handed it to me. "To bring some colour to your cheeks," she said with a rueful smile. The heady smell of cinnamon and allspice rose from the sweet rough vintage as I tried to bring some mastery to my fears. "But Edward may not be our only Prince, madam . . . if you and my father the King . . ."

The Queen's pale hazel eyes serenely met mine. "There is no hope of that, Elizabeth—none."

There was no doubting her. Doggedly I pressed on. "But if the throne comes to Edward while he is still a child, a child may not rule."

"And so the vultures gather," said the Queen heavily, "and the factions form. I told you Master Secretary Paget is grown a great man on the Council. He is not alone. Strong on his party are the Duke of Norfolk and his son the young Earl of Surrey."

Surrey!

My lord of Surrey . . .

The wine must have been heating my blood. I put my hand up to my scalding cheek as the Queen went on. "They are for the old ways, the old aristocracy, and above all—however thinly they disguise it under false observance—the Old Faith. They seek to turn the King from the path of Protestantism and persuade him to burn those of our persuasion as heretics. With them are Mary and the Bishop of Winchester, the lord Gardiner." The Queen's face darkened. "Their bully-boy is another great lord, Sir Thomas Wriothesley, a trusted ambassador of the King in recent years and now Lord Chancellor."

I had not forgotten the wrathful, strutting Wriothesley from Dame Katherine's own wedding day, nor his silken co-mate, Sir William Paget. Deliberately I kept my voice level and cool. "And do they prevail with the King?"

The Queen looked deep into the fire, where the hungry flames were gnawing at the coals. "They do. In his old age, and near the closing of his circle, the King fears for his soul. He has turned to burning heretics now, as he hanged Papists before, to pave his pathway to salvation."

No secret, then, as to Mary's newfound vainglory, and the shadow I was under! Her claim to the throne now advanced to next of place, her party waxing strong in Council, her faith triumphing from the ashes of its destruction to strike back and destroy the New Faith in its turn—no wonder the foul Paget had been under orders to remind me I was a bastard and a nobody!

And she and hers counted my lord of Surrey as one of theirs?

"For God's love, Elizabeth, you look paler than ever!" exclaimed the Queen. "Take heart, dear child!"

"But whom may I trust, madam?" I would not let my voice sound weak and small. "Before I left for Court—when Paget came—my tutor Master Grindal . . ." The last of my anxieties now came tumbling out in a long, disordered tale.

"Ah, Grindal!" The Queen smiled. "In these times the wise man speaks in riddles. But Grindal is one of us, and that is why I chose him for you. When he comes to you again, I have told him to tell you plainly who is for us, and who against."

"And who—are they?"

The Queen's smile held a certain triumph. "Tomorrow you shall see for yourself when the King keeps the Presence. Ranged against the Pagets, the Norfolks and the Wriothesleys, all the old guard on the Council, are those they scorn and despise as the 'New Men': John Dudley, Earl of Lisle; Thomas Cranmer, the Archbishop of Canterbury; and their leader, the Earl of Hertford."

The good Cranmer I knew, and Dudley too. Attended everywhere by his five sons like spaniels at his heels, Lord Dudley had been a well-known sight at Court as long as I remembered. But what of the "proud Tom" Seymour sneered at by Surrey in the same breath as he scoffed at the Earl of Hertford? The Queen had not mentioned him. "What of my lord Hertford's brother, madam?" I enquired.

Now it seemed the Queen's turn to feel the heat of the fire, or of the wine. One hand rose to her cheek, and her tone matched the warmth of her face. "Sir Thomas Seymour, yes, admired by all as a soldier of great renown! He is only now back at Court from affairs overseas, and so is not on the King's Council. But he is at one with his brother in everything else."

Was this the man they all spoke of from my childhood as the man she had once loved, the adventurer and the rogue? Covertly I studied the Queen over the rim of my wine goblet. Her face was glowing, yes, but as serene as ever. Her learning, her mind, were as renowned as Lord Seymour's boldness, her piety confirmed, her honesty impregnable. She was not the sort of woman to be harbouring a tenderness for that kind of man. No, it was evil gossip and nothing more. I would dismiss it from my mind.

Of far more importance now, nothing was clearer, was the Earl of Hertford. For he had been elder brother to Jane Seymour when that plain maid had caught the King's eye. He had received the first of his nobilities when his sister gave King Henry the son he had so longed for, my brother Edward; and in the fullness of time, he could not fail to be uncle to the new King.

Then if Edward became King while still a child—and a boy moreover who, as I knew, adored the uncle who was always with him, who played with him, talked and toyed with him—then, indeed, would Hertford have a card in his hand that neither Paget, nor Wriothesley, nor Norfolk, nor my lord of Surrey, not for all the beauty of his might, could ever hope to trump: for the card was the King . . .

If . . .

If . . .

So many ifs and buts . . .

Suddenly the wine, the dancing fire, the efforts of the day and the warmth of the chamber came together and began to overwhelm me. Through heavy eyes I saw the Queen smile fondly, then rise to her feet.

"Two things more, tired one, and then good night indeed. Did my Lord Chamberlain tell you that I have a surprise for you? I have two." From the table beside her chair she took up a little book and pressed it into my hands. "Newly come from Europe—by my special command. Read it and learn, for it will teach you much." Moving towards the door, she clapped her hands. "Who's there?" she called. "Send for Mistress Ashley, ho, and the Lady Elizabeth's men!"

Then I felt her arms warm round my neck as she whispered, "And now my second piece of pleasure for you. Get a good sleep tonight, little one, for tomorrow you will see not only the King your father but your dear Edward—for the Prince like you is come to Court! All the lion's cubs will be here to pay homage to their sire! Until tomorrow, then!"

At last I was in bed, my weary body sliding thankfully into sleep.

And as I slipped away, I thought I dreamed the answer to Grindal's riddles.

VIII

All Fools.

I awoke on that April first with the sure sense that just stalking out of my dreams was a tall, shrouded figure who held the key to all I had to know—if only I could recall who he was or what he said . . .

Dreams, enchantment, magic, spells . . .

I caught myself up. What was this foolishness, like a village moppet! No more of it, not even on this day of fools and all-licensed folly. At least I could rely on Kat, Parry and the rest to spare me from the old tricks and jests of All Fools' Day (salt in the sweetmeats, frogs in the bed, God save us!), for I always hated those clumsy country pranks and tomfooleries. And today, on this day of *poissons d'avril*, I had other fish to fry. For today at last I should see my father, and my Edward besides!

Yet still when I reached under my pillow for the present the Queen gave me and out came *The Speeches of Cicero Against Catiline*, inscribed in spidery gold along the spine, for the first time in my life I was disappointed in a book—not that I would have wanted songs of love, or the latest little sonnets, the *amoretti* from the Italian . . .

But when I stepped forth from my lodging later that morning, love was nowhere near my mind. All I could think of was my father, all I could see was that huge swaggering figure as he was on his wedding day, all I could feel was dread of what was to come. Whatever paint could do, or jewels and fine dressing, had been done to help me. Today's gown was the red of ruby wine, slashed and sleeved with cloth of silver, and my women had made my hair shine like gold beneath a circlet of rubies and topazes. Round my neck and at my waist hung ropes of matched rubies the size of quail's eggs, from my shoulders a ruby-red cloak like a train, while the members of my household marched all in red both before and behind. Yet still I felt myself sick to vomiting as we passed the red-coated ranks of the yeoman of the guard into the heart of the palace, the King's quarters. Thank God for tight lacing—the only thing in the world to hold up a quailing stomach!

The Presence Chamber gaped before me, as large and gracious as I remembered it, rich with its moulded ceiling, massive hangings and the fine figured carpet sweeping up to the pillared dais and canopy over the throne. The room was seething with a multicoloured mass: courtiers in their hundreds, ladies and lords, clerics and councillors, ambassadors, petitioners, messengers and attendants. Around the walls the Gentlemen Pensioners, the King's special guard, were magnificent in black damask swagged with gold, and their fearsome halberds towered over every head in the hall. Yet still my eyes were drawn at once to the tall figure lounging by the wall, and the sight of him eclipsed all else for me.

Against the meanly built and undershot wretch Wriothesley, groomed and befurred and gowned, Surrey had the grace of simplicity and the air of a prince. He was dressed today in royal style, his French-blue velvet cap sprinkled with silver blazons, silver spangling his blue-and-gold doublet, a wide gold buckle at his narrow waist. Both men bowed as I drew near, and Wriothesley's pale eyes gleamed as he lurched into conversation.

"Well met, my lady—and lady you are become indeed since last we met!"

"I thank you, sir," I returned coldly. *When last we met?* Had he recalled the child hanging by the arras and overhearing his harsh speeches at Queen Katherine's wedding?

"You will not remember, madam," he went on, oblivious, "our former meeting, for I was out in France a good while after that. But when my lord the King sent me to you to bid you all joy of the season, one Christmas years ago—"

"On the contrary, my lord!" I cut across him. "I remember well. I was six years old. We talked of His Majesty my father, and I sent him my good greetings from myself and all at Hatfield."

"Why, so it was," replied a nettled Wriothesley. "And I had to tell the King that you conducted yourself with as much gravity as if you had been not six but forty years of age!"

A low laugh came from my lord of Surrey. "Why then, my lady Elizabeth has been reversing the course of nature, growing down instead of up, into the loveliness of maidenhood she boasts today!"

"You are pleased to jest, my lord." *He need not think to advance his suit with Mary by flattering me!*

Again that piercing glance. "I do not flatter, lady. I speak no more than truth. For your beauty"—again his low-pitched voice dropped into my ear alone—"any man would live in your heart . . . and die in your lap . . . could he but dare to hope . . ."

He was playing with me! I burned with shame and anger till my face matched my dress.

A meaning leer stole over Wriothesley's coarse face. "Madam Elizabeth was always a picture of loveliness, I do assure you! Look you, I had the privilege of escorting the French ambassadors to make assessment of her, back in '34, when His Majesty was in mind of making a match for her with the King of France's son. The French messieurs demanded to see the child all naked, to ensure she was free of blemish. As she was . . . both before and behind . . ." He snickered suggestively. "You were six months of age then, my lady. I warrant you would not be so displayed for inspection now!"

He was loathsome. And all this greasy prattle before the sardonic Surrey, whose amused eyes had not left my face! I fought to keep myself from trembling, but could not drain my voice of all distress. "I would not be so displayed, my lord, for a king's ransom! Because I would not be so disposed of now, given abroad in marriage like a slave girl of the Turks, without my knowledge and without my consent!"

Wriothesley looked first startled and then, grinding his jaw, enraged at my rebuke. But Surrey cut him off, his pale face ablaze. "Marry abroad? Why should an English princess languish out her life in foreign climes? The King sought an alliance with France then—now we are at war! What hope, then, for any English rose forced to flourish among French thorns, to embrace her country's enemy!"

His passion swelled up as he spoke, his hand restlessly stroking his fine soft beard, his bright brown eyes burning into mine. "And see you, my lady, if there are not men in England here worthy to wed a princess— men of blood as good, as red—nay, and as royal too!—as ever the Frog-Eaters could boast, for all their pride!"

Wriothesley was stuttering now, not with anger but with a real unease. "Beware, my lord! The King . . . the blood royal . . . you tread on forbidden ground . . ."

"A fig for your 'forbidden ground,' Wriothesley!"

Were these men of the same party? They were glaring at each other now like gladiators in combat. I might not have existed. A strange fury swept through me: how dared my lord ignore me thus? Yet a moment ago I had wanted to freeze him with my disdain . . .

"My lords." I curtsied and moved away, my train with me.

Across the Presence was Mary, hugger-mugger with the sour-eyed Duke of Norfolk and the Bishop of Winchester once again. Nearby my Hatfield enemy Paget, finer than ever in sable silk, could be seen in colloquy with his uncle Sir William. The Queen spoke true of the factions, then! There were the old guard, all lined up against the wall—almost, it seemed, in open declaration of their intent.

As I came into view, both Pagets turned their eyes on me—the younger with undisguised hostility, the older with a more curious, urbane regard. Clearly his nephew's report of me had given Sir William food for thought. Master Secretary, his hand reflectively toying with his heavy gold chain of office, seemed on the point of crossing the chamber to speak to me. But I had had enough of the Pagets for the time being! Across the chamber I could see my old friend Cranmer in his archbishop's garb: my next greeting should be for him.

"My lady Elizabeth!"

Cranmer's welcome was all my heart could desire. His tired, sad, scholar's eyes and kindly mouth alike expressed delight at my arrival. Warmly he grasped my hands and drew me towards him.

With him in quiet conference as I approached was a neat, grave-looking man, less than thirty summers as I guessed, but seeming older from his lawyer-like garb and withdrawn manner. His mild blue-grey eyes rested on me in what seemed like gentle approbation as Cranmer spoke. "My lady, may I present you Master William Cecil? He is newly come from Cambridge and the Inns of Court to serve the Earl of Hertford. I commend him to you."

I started. "My lord Hertford? Is he here?"

Cecil nodded and bowed. "He attends my lord the Prince, and will be with us shortly."

Edward here! I laughed with joy.

"The Prince! His Highness the Prince!" Just then came the cry from outside the Presence Chamber. "The Prince! Make way for the Prince!"

Eagerly I surged forward, Chertsey and the others helping me press through the throng to the front.

"Make way for my lady, there! Room for my lady Elizabeth, the Prince's sister!"

And there he was! Edward, my beautiful, my forward baby brother, whose life and love had been more precious to me than my own. Blinking a little at the buzzing crowd, all around jostling and straining to see him, he stepped towards me, a smile already starting on his pale, oversolemn face. I had not seen him for so long, since the last time he and I were in the Queen's House together, enjoying with the gentle Katherine the nearest to a family life that we ever knew. And now he was so tall! It seemed I had lost that child forever and must now greet a strange young man!

Yet tall as Edward was for his age, he was dwarfed to boyhood again by the two tall men who walked beside him. My lord of Hertford, rich but subdued in a dark velvet gown, I had known since he carried me in his arms at Edward's christening, and I needed not the sight of his long pale face, his well-shaped features and keen grey-eyed gaze, to remind me of his close kinship to my brother. But the other, princely himself in red and gold, I could not be sure of—as tall as Hertford but with the build of a man of action: a fine leg, a hawk-like mien with a bold stare under dark, hooded eyes, which seemed at war with his open, flashing smile. This must be Sir Thomas Seymour, Surrey's hated "proud Tom," brother to the greater Lucifer, Hertford himself.

"Sister!"

With tears in his eyes, Edward raised me from my curtsey and insisted on kissing me before all the Court. Forgetting protocol, we clung together for a moment as we had done all our lives: both motherless, both children who lived from day to day as strangers and afraid in a world we too little understood. Did Edward know, I wondered, did he see, did he feel, how his life was now so much more than the sum of his nine years, his four-and-a-half-foot frame, shapely, strong and sturdy as it was? That he was the trump card of the Seymour party, a card they could not be playing more openly, nor throwing down more challengingly, if they had hired a Herald Pursuivant to trumpet their claim to power in the lists?

Beside me now Mary was making her curtsey to Edward and receiving her greeting in her turn. Across her bowed head I could see Surrey, ranged against the wall with his father Norfolk; Wriothesley, his recent adversary; and Sir William Paget and his nephew, my tormentor of Hatfield. Surrey's handsome face was contorted in a scowl of fury, which seemed to pierce my heart. I stepped back to be private. *Oh, my lord,* my random mind threw up, *my lord, my lord* . . .

"My lady Elizabeth?"

Before me stood a young man of my own age, but half a head taller. His fine light hazel eyes looked hesitant and questioning in his fair face, his elegant body gravely inclined as if unsure of his reception.

"Robin! Oh, Robin!"

My heart was in my voice. He grinned to hear it as he waved his cap in an extravagant flourish. "How do you, my lady?"

"Well—oh, well enough, I suppose. I am glad to see you here!"

"Here and everywhere! The Dudleys are come up in the world!" With an ironic nod he indicated the stout, hot-eyed man close behind Hertford in the Seymour entourage. "My father follows the Earl now, to some advantage—I am no longer the poor knight's son of your old acquaintance!"

Robin a poor knight's son? Never poor to me . . . How long now had I known him?

Time out of mind. He had been my friend since we found ourselves children together about the Court, a place not easy for the young. We had played together, and ridden and hunted, gamed and sported, in free companionship. But now the words I sought dried in my throat. He was no longer my friend of childhood—nor I a child now, any more than he.

Oh, Robin . . . Robin . . .

He felt it too, I could tell, the gulf, the awkwardness between us. His features were harder now than I remembered, his nose more aquiline, his brows more arched in that questioning stare. Suddenly he started. "My father leaves! I must attend him."

"Robin!"

He had already turned back and was gazing at me with a strange, uncertain look. "Do you ride still of the mornings, as you always did?" he demanded urgently.

"Of course."

"Then ride with me? Tomorrow, be it."

"Not . . . tomorrow."

"Wednesday then! Or any day you wish!"

"I will."

Another noise outside, lower and deeper—a murmur in the chamber growing louder every second. Then came the tramp of guards and the heavy step of men struggling, as it seemed, with a mighty burden, one too great to bear.

And then the sound I had longed for, prayed for, dreaded: "The King! The King is coming!"

IX

"The King!"

  "The King!"

  The King . . . !

The crowd pressing about my brother Edward parted like the Red Sea. Into the space between poured the King's black-clad Gentlemen Pensioners, forming a guard of honour to keep back the crush. Behind them came—what?

Four huge porters like the beef-bearers of Smithfield market, two aside, in pairs like a four-in-hand, behind them another four similarly disposed, all eight labouring to bear forward between them a great canopied contraption of swagging, quilting and tawny velvet.

I closed my eyes. I did not believe what I saw. Between the shafts of this great padded, covered frame was a mammoth chair, padded too, like a throne, and on this was a form for whom the word "mammoth" was a puny insult.

He must have weighed thirty stone. He was as big as the biggest of beer barrels, those in which vagrants sometimes make their homes. His head alone looked like a great bladder of lard, his cheeks were slabs of sweated cheese, his eyes mere slits that never now would open, but neither could they close. Like grey gimlets they peered furiously and suspiciously about from a face sunk between furred shoulders, his tight, twisting, toothless mouth expressing the same malice and desire to hurt.

On his hands, which could no longer meet across his bloated belly, his rings were lost, embedded in wreaths of fat as white and waxen as a stillborn child. From his protruding leg, padded like his chair, swathed and bound in damask linen and white velvet, jutting stiffly forth like a gross caricature of a human member, came the foul sweet smell that had entered the chamber with him, even before him: the smell of death.

My father the King.

You shall see he is not as he was, the Queen had said. *Prepare yourself for the change.*

I had heard her warning. But now I knew I had not heeded it.

Stolidly the porters hefted their burden to the top of the chamber, where, with a mighty struggle, they positioned the chair on the dais under the canopy in the place of state, removed the oaken shafts and withdrew. Ahead of me, first Edward and then Mary were approaching the throne and paying their devoirs to the King. What should Elizabeth say? *On guard!* the warning throbbed inside my head. *On guard! Once more on guard!*

Yet still was he as magnificently arrayed as ever I remembered him. His beard had been brushed with saffron to recall the days when once it gleamed with its own golden brown, his hair trimmed and tucked away neatly out of sight. On his head he sported a fine velvet hat in the fashion he always favoured, the black outline moulded to frame his face, the front edged with scrolls of pearl and gold, the top trimmed with a white plume descending to a curl above his ear. Beneath a surcoat of orange-tawny velvet ruffed with fox, he wore a sea-green doublet, puffed, wrought, padded and slashed until the very fabric seemed tortured out of any resemblance to nature.

And still the famous codpiece kinged it over all. Larger than ever to keep scale with the rest of his vast bulk, it thrust and bulged and curved and soared as if to boast an organ of generation befitting a giant, let alone a king. Hot and angry in flame-coloured bombast, it vaunted life over death, proclaiming a manhood that would never flinch or falter, never be put down. Yet my beloved Katherine, if she spoke true, would no more get a child from this than from the village maypole. There was as much truth in this bold show of manhood as in the bragging of any other vainglorious upstart or superannuated warrior. How hollow it was, then! Hollow in promise, hollow in reality!

"My lady Elizabeth!"

The usher was urging me forward. I fell on my knees. Beside the King on the dais now stood Edward and Mary; to his right and behind were Queen Katherine and her ladies, who had entered with the King's chair. A great white hand appeared under my nose, the fingers swollen as if with dropsy, cold with the weight of diamonds and sapphires. I kissed it with lips as cold, and a heart colder still. *How had he come to this?*

He was reaching for me now, pulling me up and drawing me towards him. "Come, kiss me, child, embrace your father!" he ordered.

At close quarters the smell was terrible. Even his voice was old now, ruined and collapsed. I bent to brush his cheek in a haze of nausea. And Katherine had to share a bed with this: had to permit . . . to endure . . . even to mingle flesh . . .

My mind flinched. Yet what else could she do? She had promised—I was there! . . . *to love, to honour and to obey . . . in sickness and in health . . .*

This is wifehood, I thought. *And this is the punishment for that offence.*
"Well? Well, Mistress Elizabeth?" The piglike eyes were hot on mine.
"How fares life with you?"

A decade of Kat's strictest training, coupled with a newer, sharper
instinct, came to my aid. "All the better, sir, that I see Your Grace in
health and strength, no less a model of manhood than of majesty!"

He snuffled with delight, like a truffle hog in spate. "Well said, maid!
Here, come and stand by me!" Then he raised his head and roared to the
courtiers pressing close around, "Hear you, my lords!"

On his orders, I repeated the whole exchange again. Again came the
wheezing bellow of delight. "Hear you! And judge you whether this maid
be her father's daughter in word and wit, or no!"

Beside me I felt Mary stiffen, but whether at this or at what we all now
saw, I never knew. Through the press of brightly dressed courtiers and
their gaudy ladies, the lords Hertford and Seymour, Surrey and Norfolk,
Wriothesley, Sir Paget and his toady nephew, Dudley and the Bishop of
Winchester, now came carving three or four plain, small, sturdy females,
town women by their dress of the plain Protestant style, the leader holding out a scroll. "Mercy, Lord King!" she cried as they all threw themselves down in the rushes before the throne. "Mercy for your true subject
and Christian believer, Anne Askewe, condemned to die for heresy!"

"What's this? What's this?"

Henry leaned forward, growling and pointing like a foxhound, as
Wriothesley stepped swiftly into the fray. "Foolish women, idle women of
no account, Your Grace!" he snarled, snatching the petition and waving
up the Captain of the Guard. "Take them away!"

"A moment, my Lord Chancellor! As you well know, our laws still give
the humblest subject of this land the right to petition his sovereign."

Queen Katherine's unexpected intervention, her voice clear and firm,
halted the captain and Wriothesley together. She leaned down to the
women, and her ladies Herbert, Hertford, Denny and Tyrrwhit closed up
in sympathy. "Say on, my mistresses. Speak to your King."

First the leader, then the others, began in turn to speak. "My lord,
Anne Askewe is a woman without evil, she deserves not the fire . . ."

"Through her teaching and preaching, she has helped many poor people to a greater love of God. As to her life, she is as free of sin as she is of
all suspicion of it . . ."

"She adores Our Lord Jesus Christ, His Father and the Holy Ghost
like all good Christian women . . ."

"She has suffered much, for in the questioning they have racked her
joint from joint till she can neither stand nor walk; she has had punishment enough!"

"We crave only mercy for her, my lord, and pardon, pardon, *pardon!*"

No one stirred. A praying silence like that in church stretched to the roof beams. On the throne the half-reclining King rumbled to himself like a slumbering hurricane. At last he thundered forth with a passion that shook the Presence. "Yet does she deny that in the Mass we are feeding on the body and blood of Our Lord Jesus Christ! She will not accept that the bread is changed, the wine is changed, by God's miracle, into Christ's flesh even as we eat and drink! Will she recant? What says she, yea or no?"

A whole communion of looks flashed like lightning between the women, a soundless litany of the damned. At last the leader spoke, raising her head with the pride of one who knows her cause is lost. "She bade us say, my lord, if it came to it, these words: *'I have not come so far, now to deny my Master.'* "

"Hear the heretic!" howled the King. "Her doom out of her own mouth!" He flapped at Wriothesley. "No mercy! No mercy to heresy! Let her burn!"

"My lord King!"

Again Katherine's intervention took the whole Court by surprise. "My lord, grant me leave to add my voice to these: to raise my prayers, too, for this poor woman. Her errors and follies are grave, God knows, but her soul may yet be saved from everlasting torment if we can but find the way."

She had the King's attention. Closing my eyes, I prayed as hard as ever in my life: *May your words find favour!*

Below the dais of the chamber the dread Wriothesley was trembling behind the women like a greyhound on the leash. From Mary's grim face and glaring eyes, I guessed that she was raising the opposite prayer from mine: *To the flames with the whole pack of them! Thus perish all heretics. We shall drive them pell-mell from the land, consume them with fire, bury their bodies in the depths of the sea!*

Katherine's voice flowed on. *He is coming, the King is coming!* my heart exulted. *You are winning him, do not falter now!*

But I had reckoned without Wriothesley. "My lord King," he interrupted with a good attempt at an easy, scornful laugh. "Does a King's Majesty sit by to dispute of God's word—and of his own royal will—with *women?*"

Henry jerked as if he had been jabbed with a dagger, and struggled to roll his gross bulk upright. "No!" he shouted furiously, like a child rising to a playground taunt of weakness. Then he turned, ranting, on Katherine. "Away, hold your peace, speak no more to me! Doctor my body you may, but Doctor of Divinity you will never be—no, nor no woman never shall be, neither! A good comfort to me in my old days to be taught thus by my wife!"

White-faced, Katherine fell on her knees and tried to speak again. "My lord, spare this woman, as we all hope to be spared at our own Day of Judgement—"

"Away!" screamed the King, trembling with rage. "Speak no more— on your life!" His great gross body floundered in the chair, his chest heaving like the sea. His hands flapped out of the mammoth sleeves. "Porters, ho! My guards! Bear me hence! Enough of this! *Enough!*"

All leaped at his commands. But with another imperious wave he stilled the Court once more. He was enjoying his power, there was no mistaking that. His eyes were truly alive now for the first time, glinting with relish, and his tongue flickered round the edges of his suddenly red mouth. Softly he began to speak, looking down on the women at his feet as the cat regards the mouse.

"For these women, away with them." He nodded at Wriothesley, who could not suppress a glad quickening in response. "For the heretic—the woman Askewe—she has defied her husband, her King and her God. To the fire with her!" He paused, and even smiled, showing black stumps of his remaining teeth. "And build it slow. Let her feel the flames lapping her one by one—for every pang will serve God's work to burn out the errors buried deep in her foul-tainted flesh!"

No one moved. The King waved to his porters. "On!"

Numbly the Queen rose to her feet to follow, Lady Hertford and Lady Denny hastening to her aid. But Henry arrested her with one terrible word: "*Off!* Be off with you, madam! Come not near me! Remove yourself to the Queen's House: from now on, I keep the Royal Apartments alone. Remain there until I send for you. That is my will! Away!"

The porters heaved and strained, and the King was aloft. Slowly the great juggernaut of the chair ground away down the length of the chamber through an awed and frightened Court. Slowly and stiffly Katherine moved in its wake to take to her quarters and begin her sentence of banishment. And swiftly, and with the greatest satisfaction, did Wriothesley, Norfolk, yes, and my lord of Surrey too, set about five small women whose demeanour, as they left between the three great lords and under heavy guard, still suggested that they were entering a world not of shame and punishment but of pride and honour—and above all, of love.

X

Anne Askewe died that day in a slow green fire and in great torment, but
with a spirit so serene that she seemed not a sufferer but a soul in bliss.
And all who saw that great soul of hers shining forth from her so-man-
gled body thought that they witnessed the martyring not of a heretic but
of a saint. So she died, and her followers with her. And I lived, in growing
pain of mind, beset by thoughts that were hardly to be borne.

My father sending this woman to the fire . . .

The dreadful hunger of his anger . . .

Who else would it strike down . . . ?

In the great stately bedstead I twisted and turned with all the comfort
Anne Askewe found on the rack. At last, as dawn washed the casement
in a flush of grey and gold, a light knock, a rustle of petticoats and a hand
drawing aside the bed curtains announced the blessed arrival of Kat.

"To break your fast, madam."

Laying before me a plate of fine white bread and a pitcher of small ale,
she briskly stirred up the maids on the truckle bed with the toe of her
shoe and despatched the sleepy, stumbling pair to the kitchens for their
own breakfast. The smell of the beer turned my trembling belly, and I
pushed the food aside. "Kat—not now."

In a second she was beside me, her hand on my brow. "You are sick,
my lady?"

"Not sick, no—but—"

"Sick," Kat averred firmly. "Of yesterday."

She was right, of course. Ever since childhood I had felt every grief,
every trial, in my stomach. Sometimes my head would join in the consort
of megrims with a blinding pain. But my *viscera,* my *venter,* were my weak
vessels of distress, nausea a companion from my cradle. Kat took my
hand. "May you speak of it, my lady?"

Speak?

Oh, God, where to begin?

My silence was a speech. Kat nodded. "Worse than we thought, lady,
worse than we feared. I hear from the housekeeper here, whose youngest

brother serves a groom of the Privy Chamber, that the King's ulcer is through to the bone. So he festers within—"

Yes, for truth . . . he festers within, body and soul . . .

"And now is he quick to anger from the torment he is in," Kat went on. "Like this flying out at Madam the Queen! No one at Court, they say, has ever heard the like. And now all are in fear here, all the people of her house."

I knew what fear they were in—the fear of what had happened twice before to an unwanted wife of the King . . .

My stomach rose again, and I furiously knocked it down. "Yet can the Queen never be accused of the . . . the treasons of the others!"

Kat shook her head. "Yet there are more ways than one of betraying a king—above all, one like your father, who demands complete devotion of mind as well as of body."

"Kat, think you the Queen stands in any danger?" As I spoke I knew this was the creeping dread that had been with me all night.

"All stand in danger of the anger of a king, lady—especially of—"

She broke off. But I could hear meaning—*especially of a king like your father . . .*

Never would I have thought that I could be ashamed of him. Henry the adored father worshipped from afar, the hero of my childhood days? I thought of yesterday and that gross apparition, more like a pageant player mumming greed and gluttony than a real man. *How had he come to this?*

"Kat, how—?"

"He eats and eats, they say. His hunger rages like his pain, and he gorges to the death," she replied simply.

"Yet I remember him so differently . . ."

"And so he was." A strong squeeze of my hand confirmed my childhood memories, my childhood love. "He was the handsomest man in England, lady, in those days—and the *bel homme* of all Europe too! So tall, so fair, so fine. An eye for a lady or for a work of art, a hand for the lance or the bow, a leg for dancing, running, riding—the glory of the country and a wonder of the world!"

But now—a bag of putrefaction and a bladder of ill will, a monstrous deformity and a Turk of cruelty . . . ?

Enough! I schooled myself. He was my father still, and still my King! He knew more of the realm, of the people and our religion, than I would ever know. Many things are hidden from the eyes of lesser beings. I must not judge my lord, my ruler and the author of my being. I would see and be silent. I would feel for the pain he suffered now, not for the suffering of the woman Askewe, who was by this time, please God, well past hers.

I looked at Kat. "He suffers much, you say?"

She nodded. "Very much, madam, and as much from his doctors as from his disease. For daily they have to open him, and cut to the quick of his ulcer to release its poison and drain the evil out."

I saw a glimmer of hope. "Why then, he may forgive the Queen sooner than we look for! For she alone is trusted now to dress his wound, she is sole mistress of all his remedies."

Kat smiled in sympathy. "Then all shall be as it was again! And we may yet have the mirth and merriment we came hoping for, with Easter on the way!"

We laughed a little like girls together, and my heart rose again. "Forward, then, Kat! First let's to Mass, then let us send for Grindal, for the Queen tells me that he's here about the Court. And have your good man Ashley or one of the others convey our morning greetings to the Queen, will you? I dearly wish to know how she does today."

"It shall be, my lady."

Rising, Kat moved about the bedchamber sorting and tidying in the early-morning light. "Parry says the green velvet today, madam? Or if you keep your apartments here to study, shall it be the loose grey chamber gown?"

I yawned, stretched and considered. "The grey to begin with and the small pearls for my hair. Then perhaps later, the green gown."

Kat threw aside the coverlets and assisted me to rise. The air struck cold on my naked flesh, and I shivered into her arms. "Madam," she said, suddenly vague as she wrapped me in my chamber gown, "who spoke with you yesterday—yesterday noontide in the Presence Chamber, before the Prince and the King your father came?"

She knew quite well who had spoken to me—she had been not two feet from me the whole time. "My lord of Wriothesley, the Lord Chancellor," I said slowly, "and my lord of Surrey, the Earl Marshal Norfolk's son."

As you well knew, Kat.

So . . . ?

A pause. Then in an offhand tone, "What think you of my lord of Surrey, madam?"

So that was it! Kat had seen, as I did on the first night we arrived, the way my sister Mary was angling for my lord. *My lord? No lord of mine!* I caught myself up angrily. Like me again, she had seen the way the lord himself was angling to take sister Mary's hook. I knew Kat's mind and all its ins and outs. She never ceased to think of my advantage. If Mary were to marry, Kat would want to ensure for me the place of honour as the chief bridesmaid, to assert my position, especially now I was under a royal cloud.

I smiled teasingly. But the eye that met mine was as sharp as any eagle's, bringing the carnation pinking to my cheeks without any of Parry's aid. "How do you like him?" she probed.

I laughed, then replied as truthfully as I could. "Well enough for a man —much less for a brother-in-law!"

"A *brother-in-law,* madam?" Kat burst out laughing in my face. "No, no, the wild geese fly not that way! He is minded to be married, I warrant you, and Mistress Mary means him for a husband, that's for sure—but the bride she wants him for is not herself, my lady, but *you!*"

My lord of Surrey—marry me?

I clutched at my stomach and stared like a natural.

Kat's laugh broke the silence. "Why, of course, madam! Your sister is too proud for a mere lord! For herself she will look higher, to Spain would be my guess, to her mother's country for one of their royal blood. But for you, her little sister, to have you wedded into the Old Faith, secured to one of her party and persuasion . . . is it not plain enough?

Marry? "I do not want to marry!" I wailed in anguish.

Kat smiled an ancient smile. "What, not to him?"

To him? To his fair face and long length, to his grace and cruel beauty, to his cold stare that heated up my blood, to his teasing wit and strong, arrogant will . . .

Married?

To him?

"Oh, Kat!"

With a hasty knock, one of the maids bobbed into the room. "My lady, Master Grindal presents himself. If you will study today, he attends your leisure."

Study? I could not: nothing would do but to escape from the suddenly small and stuffy lodgings. With a silent Grindal at my side I crossed Whitehall and led the way into the King's park of St. James, my maids and gentlemen chattering like birds freed from cages as they brought up the rear. The sun was glowing like butter in a perfect April sky, the dew was lifting off the grass, and we had the early-morning world to ourselves.

"So, master," I challenged him harshly, "what put you in such a riddling humour back at Hatfield, that morning Paget came?".

"Letters, madam," he replied simply, his plain face transparent with truth. "You know I correspond with the Queen, and others too—my old masters from Cambridge, Sir John Cheke and Master Ascham, all strong in the new learning and devoted to the New Faith. Sir John hears much from Europe, from the Protestants there, and as your brother's tutor, is near the heart of state affairs. From all sides I had heard the same evil news: that the 'old' men were prevailing with the King, that our faith was under threat as the King turned back the clock, and that in their witch-hunt against 'heresy,' to strengthen their own position they were poised to strike at the highest in the land—yes, even at those nearest the King himself."

"And then Paget came?"

He nodded gravely. "With a summons of fearsome speed. I knew young Paget was the tool of his uncle, a man of the Old Faith in league with the heretic-hunter Wriothesley. I feared they might have sent orders to entrap you—even to catch you out, through me. And these fears were not misplaced, madam! I have been with the Queen. She had reason to fear that faction then. She has even more reason to fear them now!"

"They move against her? How?"

"The King fears heresy now as he feared Papistry in the days when he saw the Bishop of Rome's hand against him in everything. If my lord Wriothesley can poison the King's ear against the Queen, convincing him that she harbours heresy"—he paused, and a look of wintry bleakness settled on his face—"then her life lies at the level of his fears . . ."

"Her *life?*" I was terrified. "Master, no! The King would not take her life! What, a woman so beloved, his wife, his Queen . . . ?"

I could hear my voice dying away.

He would.

He could.

He had done so before. Two queens before.

We walked in silence then, blind to the beauty of the day, each locked in our own world of dark thoughts. At last I groaned aloud and turned to him. "Master, may I read you back your riddles now?"

His long, lean face fixed anxiously on mine, his hands tucked monk-wise inside the sleeves of his black Cambridge gown, he nodded solemnly and I began. "The King my father—I have seen how sick he is—"

At once he stiffened. "Forgive me, madam. But since coming to Court I have heard there is new legislation passed through Parliament touching the King."

"New legislation—?"

"That now to speak of the King—in certain ways—is treason sure, and with it, death."

"What 'certain ways'?"

Grindal stared at the ground, then raised his eyes to the heavens. "Put the case," he said rhetorically, "that you were to say to Mistress Kat, *Grindal is sick, he must die*—that would not be treason."

I was with him at once. "But no man now may even *speak* of the King's illness? Nor of his future course of life . . . that like all men, he must go the way of all flesh?"

"Exactly, madam! For fear that those who speak of it may be led to hasten it, to bring it about . . ."

I nodded grimly. I had seen the King's suspicions in his eyes. "Back to our fables, then—Aesop, and the old lion. I see clearly now the state of the old lion. But I see, too, a cub who was not in your Aesop, the young lion"—*Edward my brother*—"who cannot rule alone but must have older princes of the pride to do his royal work."

Grindal nodded.

"And until he does, there is another contender for power." *My sister Mary.* "And therefore swell the parties on either side." I had seen the factions drawn up like battle lines. "For the young lion, there are two bold Seymour uncles who will 'See-more' and 'See-more' until they grasp at the throne itself?"

He smiled. "You construe well, my lady."

"And the elder of the 'See-more' brothers, my lord of Hertford, has the 'heart' to 'ford' any river, to win his way?"

Grindal nodded. "And to beat down any obstacles in his path."

"Such as the party of the older lioness?"

"Exactly, my lady."

"The Old Faith versus the New."

"The conservatives against the new thinkers."

All was falling into place for me. "The old blood of the aristocracy against the 'new men'?"

"The war party, fierce against France and all for Spain and the Hapsburgs, versus the peacemakers, who stand for league with all and free trade with Europe."

"One question, master, and good night to this. *Catiline? Who is he?*"

Grindal's voice was heavy. "There is more than one great Lucifer about the Court now, lady, as you have seen. But the Catiline who threatens to pull all England down to smoking ruin is my lord of Surrey."

My lord . . . my Surrey . . .

"How? And why?"

"He bears Plantagenet blood. From this he thinks himself a prince and swears that only blood as old as his should be about the throne. He loathes the Seymours as lowborn newcomers and vows that none but himself and his father Norfolk should have governance of the Prince. He moves with Wriothesley to strike at Hertford and the New Faith, even at women too. And all say he would not flinch from bloody revolution to win his way."

It was a long time before I could speak. "What can we do?"

Unsleeving his hands, Grindal plaited his long fingers to and fro. "Think on this, my lady. Two factions, two parties, two faiths." He paused expectantly.

Catholic and Protestant, Mary and Edward. "Yes?"

"Two policies, two loves, two hates."

My nerves were breaking. *"Yes?"*

He looked full in my face for the first time that day. *"And three lion cubs. Three offspring of the old—dying—lion."*

Overhead, from far away in the trees, I heard the far, faint call of the bird forever unwelcome, though its song be never so sweet.

"Cuckoo! Cuckoo! Cuckoo!"

Cuckoo . . .

I was the third of the old lion's cubs, and as such, I had no natural party of my own. The Seymour faction and the champions of my faith already had Edward. Did they need me when they had the Prince, the heir to the throne? And the Catholics, having Mary, the one true heir in their eyes, needed a Protestant claimant like a kiss from the Devil's dam.

And this very week Mary had taunted me with being a bastard and the child of a whore. True, only yesterday the King had boasted himself my father before all the Court. But Mary for one did not believe it! And how many others might be sneering behind their hands about my mother's treason—that I was the child of her lutanist—or of her brother . . .

"Cuckoo!" mocked the bird in the distant copse. "Cuckoo!"

Cuckoo . . .

I was the cuckoo in the nest.

Coldly I paced on through the park, and coldly I took stock. I lacked information, and I lacked advice. I knew nothing of my rights, my status or my claims, either in law or out. But I knew what I needed.

I needed information, and I needed advice.

And I knew where to get it.

XI

What is love?
It is a thing,
It is a prick,
It is a sting . . .

I could be brisk with Grindal, and crisp with Kat—I had brushed aside her determination to talk about my lord Surrey with a firmness equal to her own. But I could not be as ruthless with myself when the truth of what was happening could no longer be hidden from my eyes.

Whatever love meant, I loved my lord of Surrey. Whatever the great lovers of the past had felt, Dido for Aeneas, Cressida for Troilus, Hero for Leander, I felt for him. I loved my lord . . .

I loved him for his looks, his terrible pulchritudo virilis, *that manly beauty which is more than beauty, more than man. I loved him for his godlike form, his lofty languid shape and well-turned height; for his slender waist, his narrow horseman's hip; and for the length of his leg. If I had seen it, I knew I would adore the very roundel of his ankle bone, the hollow of his foot. I loved his eyes as bright as amber, his curving lips, his hawklike glare. And I loved most—Oh God! Tell it not in Gath, I lamented to myself in the Bible's confession of undying shame,* publish it not in the streets of Askelon—*I loved his princely arrogance, though well I knew that it might strike at the true Prince my brother's throne.*

Alone in my bed, with the maids snoring on the floor, I shivered with longing. I loved him. But what of him? What did he want with me? *Marriage,* Kat had said. What if Mary urged this marriage on the King, as she must surely do? To silence Kat, whose Protestant soul hated the Lord Surrey as strongly as she suspected that there was no such hate in mine, I swore with a vengeance that I did not think of marriage, that I thought nothing of my lord. But in truth I thought of nothing else. I could not eat, nor sleep, nor lie straight in my bed for thinking of him. Above all, I thought of his last words to me: *Any man would live in your heart . . . and die in your lap . . . could he but dare to hope . . .*

I knew little enough of men, God knows, and even less about the deed of darkness and the making of mankind. But I had heard the Hatfield maids giggling with the village girls about the work of generation. I knew that a man and a woman together made the beast with two backs; I knew that the philosophers called the act of love *le petit mort,* "the little death"; and I knew that a man who promised to *die* in a maid's lap did not mean to end his life . . .

How dared my lord tease me of country matters? I shivered with a sick sense of shame. Yet the fever I now felt was not all anguish, but a burning, burning through me, reaching down to my deepest vitals, a heat, a glow like nothing I had felt before—*enjoyed before—longed for, and longed to escape from, before—*

I must break free of this! What if I rode with Robin? Would I find relief from troubled thoughts and the endless spinning circle of my cares?

Robin—the very thought of him brought some small comfort, the sight even more. He was ahead of me at the palace mews when I arrived with Chertsey and the others, ordering the horses for the ride with an authority I had not seen before.

"No, no, the palfrey for my lady, the dapple-grey, you clotpoll—not that cart-horse! I ride the great bay. Then for Sir John the chestnut gelding, for Master Vernon the roan . . ."

How clever he was as he matched mounts to riders, and how willingly the grooms ran to obey him! As long as I had known him, Robin could handle any horse: now, it seemed, he had the manage of men as well.

As I mounted, my heart rose too. Grinning like a stable lad, Robin assisted me with a few brisk instructions—"A new mare, madam, and a fine ride. I sent for her myself for you, from my father's stables. Light in the mouth and needs no spurring; she'll not disappoint, I promise you that!"—and we were away.

How my heart eased as the line of riders clattered over the cobbles towards the open park! Once there, out in the kind of sharp yet tender morning only found in a sweet English May, I clapped my spurs to the side of the little mare in hope of a good gallop over the beckoning green ahead.

"Whhhnnnnnmmmmmmm!"

Robin was right—no spurs! With a high-pitched scream of rage the little mare stood back upon her hocks, reared, pawed the forward air, then leaped like Pegasus from the springing grass. As we took off across the chase, one by one our followers were strung out and left behind. Only Robin kept pace with me, his great striding bay easily measuring mine, his laugh echoing my own until we had put five miles between ourselves and the gates of the palace.

At last the mare, her pride restored by her high show of speed, broke time from her furious thrumming gallop down to an easy three-paced canter, and slowed to a walk. Ahead of us was a small spinney, a random clutch of oak, ash and thorn. With a nod Robin turned the bay's head towards it. As we arrived he vaulted from his horse and, grasping my reins, secured our two mounts to breathe, rest and graze.

"Madam?" His hands at my waist, his face flushed with the wind and his breath still coming short from the wild gallop, he swung me to the ground. "How like you the mare?"

I laughed with delight. *How well he knows me,* was the joyful thought. "She will do well," I teased, "when you have taught her how to make a little speed . . ."

He burst out laughing and protesting in the same breath. "Lady, you do her wrong! And my poor gift to boot—"

"No, Robin, never!" I broke out, suddenly in pain. "God knows there are wrongs enough already in this world!"

"Wrongs?"

He was regarding me with a curious sideways stare. Grindal's words came back to me with a sharp pang: *I feared they might have sent orders to entrap you . . .*

They?

Who?

I had known Robin since I was no more than eight, when first he came to Court with his father and was chosen to attend upon my brother. Such was the bond between us that he at once extended his allegiance to me. When I was at Court, there he was too, always there for me . . .

I had thought of him as mine, mine without question, like Grindal, like my Kat—those who in this world of quicksands and deceit I needed more than ever.

Yet could I trust him now?

Why should I?

"We must return," I said stiffly. Straggling towards us across the heath, still far distant, were the rest of our companions. I was alone with Robin and unchaperoned: an evil mind could make mischief out of that. Coldly I drew away.

He saw the change at once, and his face flushed with sudden anger. "I have offended you, lady? Be assured, you have nothing to fear from me!"

I stared at him, and he stared boldly back. His face was pale now with a strange determination.

"Robin . . . what would you say?"

He hesitated. "You fear for . . . recent events?"

I nodded, misery enfolding me like a cloud. He probed on, with a delicacy far beyond his years. "You fear for the Queen . . . because the anger of the King still rages . . ."

"I do! I do!" Furiously I tried to quell my trembling heart. "For they plot against her, as I hear—against all of us!"

"True enough!" Robin gave a bitter laugh. "And Wriothesley and his crew, they have the ear of the King. Yet against that, the Seymours have his trust. As uncles to the Prince, they would defend his right with their life blood, and the King knows this. It is for this that my father inclines upon their party. He wishes to rise with the rising sun! And that is my lord of Hertford!"

I saw a ray of hope. "Would your lord Hertford speak for the Queen? Or if you asked your father to take the Queen's part—to beg the King's forgiveness—"

"Oh, madam—" He sounded sick to the heart. "Madam, bethink you! Would the Earl of Hertford, or my good father either, lift a finger to save one who may by now be doomed to death already as a heretic and a traitor?"

"A *traitor*? The good Queen?"

A rook was cawing high above our heads with a harsh, mournful cry. A swarm of furies buzzed about my head, a plague of locusts settled on my mind, gnawing, gnawing.

What is a traitor?

One who commits treason.

What was my mother's treason?

She was a traitor, madam . . .

A sound came from me that I hardly knew. *"What is her treason? There is no evidence!"*

He sighed again with the same bitterness, the same reproof, then leaned towards me with the awkwardness of that first day in the Presence Chamber. "Madam, you know well—none better—that the anger of a king is a law unto itself! And when that fire rages, there are those about him who will find 'evidence' enough!"

"I know? None better? *How?*"

He held my gaze without speaking, yet his glare meant more than any speech. The day was hot now, hotter than I knew, but my hands and lips were cold. Something was cracking inside my head; I could not hear what he was trying to say.

He looked over my shoulder. Across the park the riders of our company were drawing near, Chertsey trailing Richard Vernon as they raced to reach us first. Their laughter carolled through the pearly air, their noise and shouts putting the rooks to flight high in the trees above us.

Robin began to speak, the words tumbling from him. "I hear much now, my lady, as I wait upon my father while he waits upon the Earl. They talk of the King's wives, for the former Queen Katherine Howard was of the old blood and the Old Faith, while your mother Queen Anne was of the New."

The cracking and tearing inside me were unbearable now. I could not breathe in the still, thick noonday air. "Yes . . . ?"

"Queen Katherine Howard was adulterous, lady: she did confess it, and her paramours confirmed it. But your mother was innocent of all she was charged with." He paused, breathing hard as one running a race. "Innocent of all but one thing—the crime of which our Queen Katherine now stands condemned—that of arousing the King's mortal hate."

Oh God—oh Jesus—

The earth was shifting, I was stifling, swooning. Dimly I heard Robin's anxious cry: "Some help here for my lady! Cut her lace, the heat overwhelms her!"

They were hastening towards us, they were almost here. Bearing up my weight, Robin supported me against the harsh tree bark. "Forgive me, lady, for this shock and hurt," he murmured brokenly, "but as God lives,

I swore on my soul that this truth should be yours—for I knew that no one else in the world would dare it for your sake!"

The truth . . .

Leaning between Robin and Kat's John, I submitted to be brought back to the palace like a lost child upon a leading rein, craving for nothing more than the peace, the solitude, to make this truth my own. But as we made the ante-room of my apartment, a wild-eyed Grindal burst through the door. One glance at his tear-stained face and I knew what he had to say: "Madam, the Queen! The King has given orders—she is to be arrested for treason and taken to the Tower!"

XII

For those of us who live in little rooms, it is the worst of sounds—feet running, like one flying from the face of God, and a voice howling, "My lady! Oh, my lady!"

They see me in my panoply of state, a leading player on the world's vast stage. But most of my life was lived in little rooms.

The Vernon brothers and Ashley were fighting to hold him back. But he fought too, as if the seven devils of hell had taken possession of him. I found my voice. "Let Master Grindal go! And speak, master, speak!"

Like a torrent released, the tale spilled from Grindal's stricken lips. "Anne Askewe—they entrap the Queen through her! Because the Queen showed her favour when she came here to Court, and pleaded for her when her life was forfeit, she is now judged a heretic herself!"

I gasped with shock. "Did Anne accuse the Queen?"

"Madam, the opposite!" Grindal wept hopelessly. "It was for this that the Lord Chancellor Wriothesley racked her—to drag the Queen into the selfsame fire. But even with two men throwing all their weight upon the levers, Anne would not condemn her. Yet with the Queen's disgrace, the lord Wriothesley deemed it time to strike. He has had a warrant drawn against Dame Katherine, and the King has signed it. And they are even now coming to the Queen's House with a guard of forty men to take her to the Tower!"

The Tower . . . How much time now could there be before they arrived? I tried to clear my head. "Who brought word of this?" I demanded sharply. "How is it known?"

Grindal struggled to collect himself. "The King's physician, madam, Dr. Wendy, was with the King when my lord Wriothesley came. He heard it all and, as a friend to the Queen, slipped on ahead to give word of it here."

Even as he spoke, we were hurrying through my lodgings and out into the Queen's House beyond. Now I could hear a terrible, soul-chilling sound, peal upon peal of great slow screams, each followed by a silence like the grave. "It is the Queen!" said Grindal fearfully. I could have screamed too: I had never heard her cry before, never even seen her shed a tear.

At the door to the Queen's apartments, no guards were in place, only a quivering half-wit boy clutching his wrists and gaping like a mooncalf. Where were the stately gentlemen of former days? We pressed on, following the noise ahead, till we came to the Queen.

She knew not where she was. Prostrate on the ground, she loosed off scream after gasping scream, great heaving, juddering cries. Her headdress lay fallen beside her in the rushes, her faded hair—brown only at the roots, where she had painted in the inch that would show—grey and elf-knotted like a witch's as she tore and tangled it, pounding her temples in torment, as women do in childbirth. Only one word was audible in her great shapeless cries. "No, no, no!" she was groaning. *No! No! No!*

Ranged close beside her, helpless with weeping, were her sister Mistress Herbert and her ladies Denny, Tyrrwhit and the rest. One glance at their blanched faces told me that they were to be arrested too: the Lord Chancellor intended a clean sweep of this nest of heretics. And with the Queen out of the way, his influence and Paget's over the King would be complete. What a hero! What a man, to strike terror into a pack of helpless women!

Kneeling by the Queen, chafing her wrists and loosening her ruff, was a small, stout man I had seen before among my father's train. "Dr. Wendy? What can be done for the Queen?"

He shrugged helplessly, his plump face lined with dread. "I do not know, my lady."

"But something must be done! Unless we are to abandon her to her fate!"

He spread his hands before him in the age-old gesture of defeat. My grief exploded along with my fear. "Think, man!" I raged. "Oh, God, we must help her!"

"My lady?"

It was Katherine's sober steward, who had welcomed me to the Queen's House on the night of my arrival. "If the King could only see her like this! He could not help seeing that she was innocent."

Another Katherine had tried this—my poor cousin, when she ran screaming through the palace to reach out to the King, thinking that if he saw her he could never take her life . . .

The steward was still speaking: "Or, madam, if you would undertake to speak to the King—plead for her life—" *As Katherine did for Anne Askewe?* He broke off hesitantly, his plain, sensible face clearly showing how little hope he had.

Yet surely there was something . . . I pounced on Dr. Wendy. "May the Queen be moved?"

He shrugged again. "As any woman may, madam, whose pains are of the mind, not of the body."

"Please, let us try your strongest cordial, then, sir—I beg of you!"

Beside me now was Mistress Herbert, Katherine's sister, her ruined face taking on a gleam of hope. "My lady Elizabeth, would you speak to the King?"

I grasped her hand. "If we can bring her to him as this gentleman suggests, I shall not need to." I glanced at the steward. "What means of conveyance do you have to hand?"

He was ahead of me. "A litter here, some of you, *now,* if you value the Queen's life! But to the courtyard gate, not the front entrance, mind!"

I turned to Mistress Herbert. "Mistress, if you and the Queen's other ladies—"

Her face quickened. "Surely, madam! Take up the Queen!" she shrilled to the other women. "Quickly now, her gown, her hair—"

They gaggled together chirping like starlings: "Witch hazel here, and borax and whites of egg, some colouring, and the Queen's fragrance—"

"But with speed!" Mistress Herbert begged frantically. "Make speed, I beg you—*all God's speed!*"

Ten minutes later her gentlemen attendants half-walked, half-carried the Queen out through the courtyard gate at the back of the house, even as Wriothesley and his men-at-arms tramped in through the front.

Slowly we traversed the maze of Whitehall's courts, all Katherine's people praying in our wake. But none prayed harder than I did, that this gambler's throw would bring us all success. At last one of my gentlemen hastened up with the best word we could have hoped for. "We have found the King solitary, keeping no company but his own, in the knot garden by the River Walk."

———

In Whitehall's small walled knot-garden by the Thames, the King dozed with his attendants amid the scent of thyme, sweet hyssop and new camomile. Katherine went to him all alone, while we lurked silent and watchful, peering through the gate.

But when she came he was at once awake, sharp as a beast caught napping outside its lair. Between his slits of eyes he saw her falter, stumble and then fall at his feet, for she could scarcely stand. He heard her weep, throw herself on his mercy and beg his pardon for offending him. He felt her terror and her self-abasement, tasted his triumph, smelt the burnt offering of her soul's sacrifice as it lay roasting on the altar of his pride.

And found it good. "Say you so, then?" he enquired with a newfound greedy joy in her, for all the world as if his hand had not just signed away her life.

"You are my lord!" she wept. "My head, my governor, my sole anchor under God and the keystone of my faith—I crave no more!"

A flicker of his old suspicion came alive in the sore flesh-pits of his eyes. "Not so, by St. Mary!" he swore. "You are become a Doctor of Divinity, Kate, in your self-pride! You want to wrangle, to debate, to overrule the one set by God to rule over you!"

"My lord, my lord!" she murmured through her tears. "Knowing of your Majesty's great learning—your matchless knowledge of all things divine—I only sought the comfort of your soul and the distraction of your body's pain by debating God's word with you—"

A small smirk broke about the corners of his mouth. "Even so?"

"—that I might learn from your most royal lips what the true doctrine was!"

That was the winning card, to flatter his vanity in his learning, as I had ventured as we were carried here. Now, watching from afar as my spells worked like witchcraft, I marvelled how I knew so well what to say.

"And is it even so, sweetheart?" he asked softly. She nodded her head. Drawing her to him on the sunlit bench, he knocked the tears from her cheeks with a rough hand. "No more! I do not like you thus!"

We had been right, then, to array her finely, for I knew he loathed a woman to be less than perfect for him, no matter what she suffered.

Now he was in a fine humour. "Come, kiss me, sweetheart, for I swear to you we now shall be as perfect friends as ever we were before!"

Huddling behind the wall, we wept for joy—pale rejoicings shot through with fear of what might have been. And as we stood there, peeping through the archway and wondering when to approach, who should sweep past us into this Garden of Eden but the great serpent, Wriothesley himself.

Not for nothing, though, did he hold his place as the King's first man of policy. On sight he knew that he had lost the game. To see the Queen ensconced beside the King in the rose arbour, the royal couple paired like our first parents Adam and Eve in perfect amity, showed him that the tide had turned against him with a vengeance. To watch his face working with this knowledge was to see a dancer on the wire as he strove to keep his feet.

And Henry gave him little time to dance. "See you, my lord!" he roared furiously. "You would have had me put away this Queen—this paragon of womanhood, this wife whose only joy lies here in me—and give her to the fire!"

"My lord—" began the Chancellor.

"Give me good reason for this, Wriothesley, or by God I swear—"

Any other woman would have seen her chance to turn upon her enemy. But Katherine kept her eyes fixed on the King, like a cow saved from the slaughter, and never said a word.

"Beast! . . . Fool! . . . Villain! . . . By God's body, blood and bones . . . !" The King's oaths flew like missiles, while his threats and curses rained down on Wriothesley like molten lead. Saint that she was, Katherine herself at last held up her hands to plead for the great villain, angering the King still more. "Oh, you poor soul!" he groaned. "You do not know how little he has deserved this kindness—for on my word, sweetheart, he has been a cruel knave to you, a deadly foe!"

Yet even now Wriothesley did not flinch. Indeed, he grew strangely calmer under the fusillade, till at last he even smiled.

"Well?" screamed the King.

Wriothesley spread his hands and shrugged. "Lord King," he began, as smoothly as the Snake of Snakes, the Devil himself, "right glad I am that my lord of Norfolk and his son of Surrey were so mistaken in Her Gracious Majesty, our Queen . . ."

Was he lost then, though I knew it not? I thought I saw Wriothesley's game plain enough, to clear himself of the King's rage by shuffling off the blame onto another, like some creeping schoolboy. Did I see then all the rest to come? Or simply feel it, like a garrote at my throat, to choke away life and joy?

I saw the event but not the fatal import of it. Then, it was enough to know that the Queen I loved was spared. On that dread day of her great danger, all that we lived by, hoped for, trusted in, had stood, it seemed, upon the head of a pin. With the passing of the crisis, like a fever overblown and health restored, all breathed again and life once more went on.

And that year, never came summer more beautiful. By early June the bright strawberry flowers were as plentiful as stars in a clear sky, the grapes were ripening apace in the King's vineyards at Richmond, and the peaches and cherries at Greenwich promised a fair harvest. The Court moved now, more freely for the good weather, more often for the heat, for the great palaces with all their people, hawks and horses, maids and men, needed their "sweetening," as we called it then, far sooner in the summer than in the winter.

For along with summer's flowers, every year came the darker blooms of pox and plague, strange sweats, swellings and death. Now the matted rushes in the halls, packed with foul droppings, human and canine, would make each meal, each meeting time an ordeal with their choking stink. Now this lord would be struck with a bloody flux, these servants sent away for the weals on their faces, and the men of the Court would never stop and speak but wave their pomanders in greeting, holding them to their noses as they hurried by. Then it was time to uproot our lives again and commit ourselves and all our belongings to the trials of the road. For summer enforced daintiness and frequent progress from one palace to another.

And as the Court removed, so, too, would all the players, king and queen, bishop, knight and pawn, like pieces on a chessboard. Yet life went on as usual only on the surface. Beneath the thin skin of civility, the Seymours, the Pagets, were merely biding their time. And taking its cue from them, all our little world held its breath.

As I did too—for if I had learned anything from this time of trial, it was the force of Grindal's teaching: *watch, and wait*. Daily I wrestled with what Robin had told me, and every night now brought a dry-eyed interval of grinding grief before I could find sleep.

And as I lived from day to day, so, too, as I thought, did all the Court. What were they waiting for? I complained peevishly to Kat. My father was much recovered, loyally nursed by Katherine both by day and by night; indeed, she now slept like a maidservant on a truckle bed in the King's dressing room to be near him at all hours. He still had need of his great carrying chair, his "tram," as he called it. But as time went by, it lost its terror for me and became part of our lives, even another aspect of his strangeness and splendour, for no other king in the world had such a thing. Yet still the little muttering groups huddled in corners watching and waiting, the whole Court seemingly become a whispering gallery.

Yet what did I care for all or any of them? Day in, day out, however hard I laboured with my studies, rode to hounds or walked till Kat complained against me for self-punishment, in truth I only pined to catch what sight I could of my sweet lord of Surrey.

My love was humble then and sighed for nothing but to see him. Truly it was the love our Lord enjoined upon us, the love that suffereth long and is kind, vaunts not itself and seeketh not its own . . . the love that beareth all things, believeth all things, hopeth all things, endureth all things . . .

It is the only time I ever found such grace.

And the nearer he danced to the edge of death, the more he flourished in life and love. I saw him in the early morning striding through the dawn mists to the stables, or en route to the tennis court with his friends Wyatt and Pickering for hours of tireless play. The same group with other friends loved nothing better than to play by night as well, and as I lay sleepless I would hear them roistering back to their lodgings as the cock crew. That day Kat would be full of their scandals: "A raid on the city, my lady, when they locked the constables of the watch up in their own watchhouse and tipped the beadles into the kennels with all the garbage and dog-do! Then they took to the river and rowed up and down singing and shouting, waking the whole town with their catches and caterwauling, pelting the poor town drabs plying for custom on the South Bank with bird pellets!" Yet though I half loved, half hated to hear these tales (drabs?—what had my lord to do with those poxy Bankside whores?), still I feared that these boyish pranks were no more than a cover for my lord's darker ends, his ambition for the throne.

In truth, if I tell truth, I feared him altogether. He sought my company; I fled from him. Under his gaze I knew I could not hide my favour for him, or my fear. My only hope was to avoid that savage, searching scrutiny. And how could I of all women love, trust or forgive the man who with his father had conspired against the Queen, against the faithful Katherine, my only friend at Court? For he must at least have known of the plot against her and done nothing to oppose it. And in his hatred of the New Faith, he would, I thought, rejoice to see her fall.

And yet—although at times I fled him like the plague, at other times, I must confess, I sought him too. His love was like the poison of the old legend, that increased the longing for it drop by drop, even though the drinker knows it brings his death.

And all this I bore alone, telling not a soul, for what was there to tell? I hoped for nothing, expected nothing, demanded nothing. I knew not what he thought, what he desired, nor even if he favoured Mary over me! I knew, too, that when my marriage came, as Mary said it must, my feelings would be nothing when my father made his choice.

Surrey had loved once, Kat told me (she had it from his man), an Irish heiress who was given, cruelly against his will and hers, to an old rich fool while she was still a child. He never loved again. He was married now, she said, but men could be divorced as fast as need be . . .

And for himself, he always wrote of love. He gave me pieces from his pen, tossed in my lap as lightly as a flower. Were they meant for me? I wooed myself to sleep with snatches of his verse:

> *Alas! How oft in dreams I see*
> *Those eyes that were my food . . .*
> *Wherewith I wake on his return*
> *Whose absent flame did make me burn,*
> *But when I find the lack, God! how I mourn . . .*

And I woke every morning with but one hope, to catch sight of him, fleeting through the Court to take horse, to make merry with his friends or to adorn the Presence as only he could do.

But all the time, it seemed, I waited with a far deeper longing for another man. Not as a lover, for this was a man of middle age, all innocent of such stuff. But fate had made him the one man on earth for me charged with the satisfaction of a far fiercer need, my need for truth at last—the lawyer Master Cecil.

XIII

I knew as soon as I laid eyes on his kind, clever face that he was a man I could trust. But his life story was its own recommendation—a Cambridge man, like my dear Grindal, and a lawyer besides. His friendship with Cranmer was another mark of favour, for the Archbishop favoured and trusted very few himself. But the greatest recommendation William Cecil ever had was himself—those blue-grey eyes that could meet any man's eye, that unruffled brow, that unassuming air, all spelled one who would render no man evil for evil but devote his life to doing good.

At last he came on a mellow day of harvest, and a fair harvest did he have for me. I was in my closet in the Queen's House, for we were back in the King's beloved "White Hall" once again, and as soon as he was seated with his papers, rolls and scrolls, he plunged straight to the point.

"Lady Elizabeth, you asked me to look into the circumstances of your mother's death. And of your birth—how, if your parents were married, you could be made a bastard. I have searched the records and discovered much." He paused, and eyed me noncommittally. "Much, perchance, you may not wish to know . . ."

The long gold fingers of late-summer sun were idling on the wall, and I had a vain desire to stay their passage. "Say on."

"The King your father was married to your mother by the Lord Archbishop of Canterbury—Thomas Cranmer himself—and thus by the highest churchman in the land."

I drew a breath. "Yet my father later made his own decree that he had never been married to my mother, and so I could not but be a bastard."

"Yes." Cecil's bright, shrewd face took on a guarded look. "Which brings us to your second head of my instructions, lady: the desire you had to know about the Queen your mother's death."

I would know more of her life, master; but you cannot help me there.

"The circumstances are connected," continued Cecil in his dry lawyer's tone. "Queen Anne Boleyn was accused of divers charges—speaking against her marriage, bearing malice against the King—but none of these is a crime known to our law." He paused, peering at me curiously.

I had read much Roman law in my study of ancient history. "The charges against her were questionable, then . . . from the outset?"

He gave me a long, level-eyed lawyer's stare, and continued. "On the major charge against her—that she had committed five adulteries since her marriage to the King—she was not tried until after the men accused with her had already been found guilty." Cecil reached for his texts. "Sabinus, Ulpianus, Justinian, are all agreed: to try one person for a crime separately from all the others so accused is a wrong in itself. It is a question of natural justice . . ."

An iron hand was gripping at my gut. "The men—who were guilty with her—"

"They were *found* guilty," Cecil emphasised carefully. "All in fact pleaded not guilty, save the lute boy Smeaton. But as a commoner, he had been put to the rack, and other sufferances besides. The record shows that on the very scaffold every man swore to their innocence and the Queen's, on their immortal souls. Indeed, young Henry Norris, a close friend of the King, was promised a free pardon by the King himself if he would but confess and implicate the Queen."

"And—?"

"He would not. He proclaimed her innocence with his dying breath."

"But if they were innocent—*how, then, were they convicted?*"

Cecil spread his hands. "By gossip, rumour, hearsay, malice—that was the case *in toto.*" He coughed discreetly. "On most of the occasions of adultery named in the indictment, it appears that neither Queen Anne nor the alleged paramours were even near the supposed scene of the crime at the time in question."

"Then—"

"There were no witnesses. There was no proof. The charges were . . . unsubstantiated."

"The charges were *false!*" The blood was roaring in my head. "But why . . . ? And *who?*"

Cecil looked me full in the face. "We keep the King's peace here in England, Lady Elizabeth, and serve the King's justice. All his servants act according to the King's Majesty's will and pleasure."

And it was the King's Majesty's will and pleasure to have her dead . . . ?

The voice I heard was not like my own. "Yet if she were to die, master, why did the King need to divorce her as well?"

"The King had chosen a new wife in Madam Jane Seymour. So he sought to wipe the slate clean—for her and for her son. This was achieved by bastardising and disinheriting you. Not you alone, for the Lady Mary your sister was also cut out of the royal line at the same time, by the King's will."

It was the King's will . . .

So Mary and I had common cause, then, though our mothers had been rivals to the death—to her mother's death, and mine . . .

Anne died for plain Jane Seymour, then—to make her safe. For my lord of Hertford and his brother, the proud Tom. But most of all for Edward . . . for the child I had so loved . . .

"My lady?"

"No matter, Master Cecil." I raised my eyes. The sunlight fingers on the wall had moved a great way from where we had begun.

"One thing more, madam." Cecil delved into his satchel. "In my searches in Chancery I happened upon this . . ."

He put a shabby packet in my hands, oilcloth bound with soiled and tawdry ribbon. His patient fingers had already worked at the old knots, and it opened at my touch. Within, still gleaming after all the years, was a parchment lettered in a careful hand: "For My Daughter, The Princess Elizabeth, Princess of Wales."

I did not move. "It is your mother's will, madam," Cecil said gently. "In it she sought to leave you all her goods. Her titles too: for she held the marquessate of Pembroke in her own right."

I looked down at the parchment. "This is the Last Will and Testament of me, Anne Boleyn . . ." The instructions were clear, the document brief, the signature a final flourish: *"Anna Regina"*—Anne the Queen—*"Semper Eadem."*

There was a husk blocking my throat. " *'Semper Eadem,'* master?"

"Your mother's motto, madam—'Always the Same.' "

Constant in all things.

Yes.

I would be so too.

"And her goods? Her titles? My inheritance? What became of them?"

Cecil's shoulders shifted in a shrug. "All the possessions, deeds, titles and appurtenances of a condemned traitor revert at once to the King. That is the law."

"The law." I was beginning to learn the rules of this game. "A little more law, then, master, if you please. You say that the King's marriage with my mother was declared null and void. *On what grounds?*"

Cecil took another careful breath and looked away. "On grounds of consanguinity, my lady. A prior union of the King . . . your father having held fleshly relations with one near kin to the Queen . . ."

"*Consanguinity?* Union with whom? Who could my father have bedded? Whose blood was so close to my mother's as to destroy her marriage?"

He met my gaze now without faltering. "That of her sister, madam—her sister Mary Boleyn."

Her sister Mary.

My sister, also Mary.

King Henry, too, had had a sister Mary, who died young in the year of my birth.

And if my father the King had remained true to his first choice for me, I would have been Mary also, know you that? Only as the godparents were bearing me to the chapel did the King send word I was to be named not for his sister, nor yet to spite his elder daughter, but for his mother Elizabeth, the Princess of York.

"Mary" means "bitterness"—for herself and all around her. But God loves to jest. And Almighty or no, like the fool of the old pageants, sees no harm in repeating a good jest once, twice and three times. So three Marys, then, like those who gathered at the foot of the Cross, in the life of Henry the King. And bitterness for all.

Cecil was gone—supper refused—and Parry, gabbling maddeningly about gowns, sent packing with a flea in her ear as I paced out of the Queen's House with none but Ashley and a couple of pages in attendance. In truth, I knew not where I wished to go, but set my course into the westering sun like a benighted pilgrim, to walk until I dropped.

My father and Mary Boleyn . . .

Now a hundred small hints and whispers down the years, sly glances and giggles from men and maids swiftly frowned down by Kat or Ashley, came together to make maturer sense.

She had been a beauty, my mother's sister, Kat had said once, as fair and plump as Anne had been dark and slight. Together they had formed a piquant contrast, one soft and mellow as cream cheese, the other all air and fire. Mary had married a country squire, one of the King's trusted servants who died afterwards of the plague, William Carey, and like all those bearing the Boleyn taint, never came to Court. She had had two children by him, Henry and Kate. But she had died and they had married, and our lives had never crossed.

And what did I really know of this far-off, long-dead aunt?

Cecil did not mince words. Mistress Mary had served her apprenticeship to the sheets-and-mattress trade at the Royal Court of France, where she was known (both carnally and colloquially) by the French King himself as "the English Mare," and well horsed by His Gallic Majesty. Yet though Mary lived to be tupped by two kings rampant, and enjoyed without benefit of clergy by men of lower rank besides, she suffered not, Cecil assured me, under the brand of a whore. For she came of a good family, with noble blood and still nobler ambitions. Her mother had been lady-in-waiting to Queen Katherine of Aragon, her father one of the principal lords at the baptism of the Princess Mary.

What if her great-grandfather had been no more than a rich silk mercer of London? "Gold lends wings to any wooing dance," he told his sons. "Fly high!" Emboldened, his grandson had secured himself the eldest girl of the Howards as his bride, daughter of the Duke of Norfolk. True to her ducal descent, then, Mary had been placed at the French Court, where she had served with distinction as a *demoiselle d'honneur* to the Queen of France.

As had her younger sister Anne.

Wretchedly I tried to cling to Cecil's words. A royal male fornicates not for his own pleasure: this was God's work, the copulation of the King. God was directing Henry's course as he set aside his old wife Katherine and found the way to his new love Anne. God was revealing to His Vice-Regent on earth *Via, Veritas, Vita* . . . The Way, the Truth, the Life.

What else?

Much else.

For if nothing else on that fell day, Cecil made me see that my mother Anne Boleyn was no whore. Had she been, like her sister Mary, happy to play the royal doxy, to bare her plump breasts on command, spread her cushioned legs, or cock up her smooth round golden rump as an afternoon dish for the royal delectation, she would have passed through the King's arms and heart inside a year, then been palmed off on some complaisant courtier to become an honest woman and respected wife, as Mary was, and live to a ripe age.

Then she would not have died.

And I would not have lived.

Lived now to pace the riverside in a rage of heart like nothing I had ever known. Against my father. For all that he had done.

Time to return. Night was coming, and it was unhealthsome to be
abroad. On the opposite bank were a pair of swans at nest, their graceful
silver shapes glimmering through the falling dusk. I remembered them as
clumsy cygnets, squawking and flapping like mudlarking boys in their
prentice livery of dingy brown. How fast they had grown! As we were all
forced to do!

"My lady!"

John Ashley was at my side, his hand on my sleeve. Wordlessly he
nodded up the river walk, towards sounds of strangers drawing near,
high-spirited horseplay and the ringing laughs of men.

"Please you to withdraw?"

Ashley was right, of course. A night encounter of a royal lady with a
group of low Court roisterers was not a seemly thing. But flee as I might
before them, with my tight stomacher, heavy kirtle and countless petticoats, they would outpace me for sure. Better to meet them head on, if
meet them we must.

"Forward, Master Ashley!"

Ashley was better than his wife at concealing his disapproval. He
merely nodded and, with a signal to the pages, fell in behind.

A torch flared, and three faces leaped out of the dark, carved and
moulded by the flickering flame. Behind them loomed a body of their
men, their distinct liveries all but lost in the dim night. All three I knew
as men around the Court. One was young Wyatt, flushed, fair-skinned
and still laughing as he exchanged foolery with a broad, bold-faced
knight they called Pickering; and between them, silent and withdrawn,
his angel's face dark with some hidden grief . . . *who should it be but my
lord of Surrey?*

"Madam Elizabeth!"

The light that lit their faces caught mine too. After all I had reined in
since Cecil came, it was no effort to show nothing now. "My lords."

"Where do you make for, lady? May we escort you? Grant us but that
and we need no torches—your presence would light our way!"

He was the perfect courtier again, never more ready with quips and
compliments, flattery and fair words. Wyatt and Pickering brought up the
rear as he escorted me back to Court, Pickering still attentive and on
guard, Wyatt sullen as a baby in disgrace and heavy now with the sour
backwash of his wine.

Only once that night did my lord let slip the mask of careless, courtly
banter, when at last he brought me to the door of the Queen's House, all
quiet in its secret courtyard square. The other two stood by at some
remove, their men and mine farther off still. Within the courtyard no
breeze stirred to move the air that had been gentling there all day.

Floating low above the castellated roof was a wide harvest moon, round and warm, a paten of bright gold so near now that a hand's grasp would have pulled it down to earth. He glanced down, then frowned and looked away. Lifting his head, he stood scenting the air like a stag royal on the final run. He was so close I could trace every fine filigree of the silver scrollwork cresting his doublet, and scent every note of the fragrance breathing from the pomander round his neck.

Without thought or meaning I leaned into him, my body longing for nothing so much as to lie along the length of his, to fold myself into the warm dark void within his welcoming cloak.

He started, caught my hand and inclined towards me in his turn, his arm about me to support my trembling frame. "My lady?" he said, questioning and very low.

All eyes were on us. I knew what their stares meant—for him, but more, much more, much worse, for me. Yet his hand gripping mine, the hardness of his arm, the nearness of his strength, his leanness, were so sweet, so sweet . . .

A shudder ran through me, and I fought it down. I must not look at him. One glance now would strip my soul naked, betray my secret into his rough grasp. Then could I count myself within his power, as good as lost.

Far off in the woods a night owl called, one lingering mournful cry. I thought of the Greek maiden turned into an owl for spurning the god's love, condemned to lament forever her lovelorn virginity to the cold fruitless moon . . .

The air was velvet, and his fatal fragrance drowned my senses. I looked up. His eyes were fierce on mine, and his gaze entered me, took me, knew me, made me his. My head was swimming. I sank and almost fell into my curtsy. "Farewell, my lord," I murmured through frozen lips. "God speed you—fare you well."

He held my hand in a savage grip that did not loosen even when he had raised me to my feet. "No, madam," he whispered softly as he bent towards me to make his good-bye, "say not farewell. I shall see you again —for now you see I must."

XIV

Now all I could do was to await events, and that came easily enough that last long sweet September. I lived like a young postulant, a virgin novice who has made her vows and waits but for the call to begin her life of bliss. Each golden day passed in a state of high and breathless ardour, yet of holiness and humbleness too. I asked for nothing, I expected nothing. It was enough he had acknowledged me.

Enough? It was more than I had dared to dream of.

And he had given me even more than this, although he knew it not. His love had rescued me, had saved me from myself and all my recent torments—my father, my poor mother, even the knowledge about Mary and Anne, with the hot and shameful thoughts of their fleshly sins. Dreaming of him put all these demons to flight and gave me hours of sweet serenity.

Always before, I had been overjoyed by my rare visits to Court, and sad to have to leave. Now I desired nothing so much as to be left alone, or better still, back in the safe arms of Hatfield, to dream of what might be. But fate had one more scene of this last act still in store, and like a well-trained actor I played out my part.

And I played it alone. I could not speak to Kat: how could I tell her of this surrender to the enemy? And I had lost my other trusted friend, for from the moment she escaped arrest, I never saw the Queen again alone. She never left the King now, but made her life his service, as if to pay him back for sparing her from death.

Mary, too, I hardly saw, for she never came to our morning Mass or Evensong. The old guard waited on her still, I knew, led by the Duke of Norfolk, yes, and my Surrey too. Meanwhile her old friend the Bishop of Winchester was never far away, his buzzard's scowl locked ever on his face, his great paws borne before him at all times as if for fisticuffs.

And fisticuffs he got, from an unexpected quarter too. One day at noon Robin came to me in the Queen's House, pale to the lips, yet stiff with livid pride. His father had been banished from the Court—they would take horse and leave within the hour.

"*Banished?* For what?"

"For striking Gardiner—the Lord Bishop of Winchester, to give the villain his due!—full in the face."

"What was the cause?"

"A dispute, lady—in Council."

"A dispute of what?"

"Because my father is the Earl of Hertford's right-hand man, while the Bishop stands for Norfolk and the 'oldcomers'!"

More than that, it seemed, there was little to know. But with Robin's father swept from Court and Council, was the Norfolk party then winning the battle for power? Robin could not say. They left at once, and I wept to see my playmate part from me: for neither he nor I could say when we would meet again.

That same day came the summons I had looked for. "Here was a messenger from my lord the King," announced Kat in high glee, entering my chamber at the end of my morning's work. "You are bidden to supper with the King and Queen in the King's Privy Chamber—and tonight!"

Had my lord spoken to the King? What would my father say? I felt my life, my hopes, held in the hollow of that hand—yet still if I could please my father, I might win my way . . .

Supper with the King! I sallied forth that evening bedecked as for a bridal, in a gown of orange-tawny-red, figured all over with Henry's Tudor rose. It was a garden of roses: the leaves and flowers blossomed on the overgown and peeped out again in raised gold cutwork on the kirtle and oversleeves. The royal theme sang out once more in the rubies that garnished the neck and sleeves, and in the girdle of pearls and rubies circling my waist and spilling down to the ground. A great jewel at my breast and a headdress like a coronet proclaimed me princess from my head to my rose-worked-velvet feet—and a Tudor princess too, *sans peur et sans reproche!*

The idea of a gown to please my father had come to me on my first night at Court. If Mary could be fine, I would be royal too! And Parry had thrown herself into the creating of it with all the skill and artistry at her command, despite her worries about the cost and her fear of the disapproval of her brother my treasurer, happily far away in Hatfield.

In truth, I needed to feel fine without, for what I felt within defied all words. *He is the King, your lord, your God on earth,* my mind instructed me, day by painful day, *one who knows all, sees all and determines all. How could he err?*

He is a man, my heart would cry by night, *and full of sin—a tyrant and a murderer, a lecher and a hypocrite, a whited sepulchre, a false father and son of lies!*

Both voices were hissing now like snakes in my head as I passed through the cold, benighted court. Where was my love now, when I needed those frail dreams and hopes to keep me warm? Shivering, we marched along to the King's apartments, through the men-at-arms, the outer chambers, the inner guard and the anteroom. Courtiers, servants, soldiers, melted before us till we came to the last chamber.

"Madam, this way."

"Your Majesty—the Lady Elizabeth!"

The studded black oak door was slammed behind me, shutting out Kat and Ashley, Parry's smile of pride, and all my loving people. The air within the room was sick and sweet, the chamber fragrance mingling with the stink of pus and blood. Sick with anxiety, I hovered on the threshold, my gaze fixed on the ground. "Come hither, girl!" came the long-dreaded growl.

Slowly I raised my eyes. In a great padded chair my father lolled in state, with Katherine on a footstool at his feet, beside her Edward in his finest fig, his bright boy's face now beaming up at mine. He sprang to his feet, the very crinkles of his eyes alight with love. "A chair for my sister, sire—I may command it?"

A wheezing, rumbling laugh. "Indeed you may, Sir Prince!"

One of the King's Privy Chamberers emerged discreetly from the shadows at the door—Sir Anthony Denny; I knew him from the Presence— and I was seated before the King, with Edward at my side. Cold as I was before from the night air, now I felt all the fury of the great fire on the hearth, which ran half the length of the wall, devouring oak logs as big as a man. Around the walls, from floor to moulded ceiling, tapestried figures of Diana and Actaeon, Cynthia and Endymion, sported through wild woodlands or green glens alive in the fleckered rushlight, their lovers all in love, their hunters all ascending to the kill.

The room was large and low, shimmering away in dancing pools of light. Yet still he filled the space and seemed to knock against its corners. He had put off his plumed and moulded hat, and wore now a soft cap of kingly finery in velvet and gold. At ease within his chamber, he wore no doublet but a loose round gown of sea-blue velvet warmly furred with fox and faced with gold-of-Venice trimming. His hose hung loose about his mighty legs; his wounded limb was swathed in unchanged rags as it sprawled out upon the padded bench. The eyes embedded in their scrolls of flesh sped this way and that like darting mice, and his great face was larded with a film of shining sweat. Yet was he King indeed, and would be in a dung cart.

"Some wine, Elizabeth!" he ordered me. "For Kate has news for thee —good news indeed."

"Not I, my lord!"

I caught the fear flaring in the Queen's eyes. "This was not my doing, sire, but yours, all yours!"

He nodded complacently. "True, my heart. Though you did move me to it, mine is the power. Hear me therefore!"

I sat like stone. *What now? What next?* And then the old refrain: *On guard! On guard!*

"It is our will and pleasure—"

I felt the raging of the fire across my face. *It is the King's Majesty's will and pleasure . . . that this woman should die . . .*

"—that you be known henceforward as 'the Princess Elizabeth.' What say you to that?"

"Sister!" Edward's face was aglow. "Now are you a princess as I am a prince! What joy, sister, what good joy!"

"Princesss" again! Did that mean trueborn too, no more a bastard? Or merely Bastard Royal, the Bastard Princess Daughter of the King? Oh, God! Why could I not be thankful? Princess was no mean thing—and better always to have half a loaf than no bread at all!

But still I heard within my soul's lament: *Will fortune never come with both hands full?*

"Well, girl?" He was growling now, a warning shot that he was not best pleased. "What, have you lost your tongue? Speak!"

"Give thanks to our father, sister, do, oh do, for his great goodness to us!" I could hear the fear in Edward's voice.

"Speak to the King, Elizabeth!" Katherine frantically seconded.

"Nay, if she will not . . ."

The threat was unmistakable. I rose and dropped before him, cradling his feet. The stench was sickening; my head began to swim. "I am quite overcome, my lord," I whispered. "I owe you everything. Your gracious goodness will be in my prayers morning and night for all my natural life."

"That is well said, maid!"

A hand like a white pudding appeared under my nose and flapped at me to rise. I could hear the soft outward breath of both the Queen and Edward as goodwill was restored.

"And Mary?" queried Edward with the openness of a child. "Is she now Princess too?"

The King's face in the ever-changing light flickered with an angry gleam. "So she is!" he owned, his fleshy fingers roaming irritably through the stubby saffron beard. "For one goes with the other. But she will never stand in my grace and favour while her stubborn soul still clings to the Old Faith! Chewing the Pope's cud of relics and indulgences, mumbling her Latin *mumpsimus* and *sumpsimus* instead of greeting God in our own tongue—I'll not abide it!"

So Mary's star had fallen—how was that?

And if her favour had declined, what of her party?
What of my lord?

"Yet under your correction, good my liege," began Katherine with a hasty upward glance, "the Princess Mary has submitted to your will, owning you her lord in all things—"

But even this timid plea was too much for the King's temper. "Yet still she popes it in her chamber!" he shouted. "As I hear from those who know her ways! With copes and candlesticks, and chasubles and Romish renegades! Better she had not been born than not to have pleased me better!"

Who had turned the King against Mary? For sure she had been riding high here, merely weeks ago. Who had turned against her, informed on her to win the King's favour . . . and against her party too?

He brooded like the great sea beast in the bestiary, floating half-submerged on the surface of his rage, with one glaring and one drooping eye, rumbling and spouting to himself while we sat frozen in a tableau of obedience. "You, fool!" he roared. "Whoever is without there! Bring us some food here, before we starve to death!"

Within moments a trestle spread with damask appeared, and all the trappings of a splendid feast for twenty men or more.

"Who sups here, sire?" I murmured in plain wonderment. "Who sups tonight with Your Majesty?"

He rocked with laughter till his body shook the chair. "King Henry sups with King Henry!" he roared. "No greater gourmand nor more valued guest than we ourselves—with our good family! Bring on the vittles!"

And on they came in a procession stately as the opening of Parliament: salads of damson, cucumber and lettuce, sparrows stewed and carp in lemon sauce, partridges in lard and stork in pastry coffins, oysters with bacon, eels in galantine, pheasants with cherries, pears with caraway, cheese in sugar, and quince with clotted cream; and on, and on, until I had lost count. And as we had begun with wine, so we swam in it, the servitors ever attentive to the King's great thirst, and pressing more on me and my poor Edward than I thought fitting to his tender age. With the wine all through the meal came bolts of bread, not fine and white as befits a royal table but the coarse rye stuff of the common folk, black-brown and chewable as leather in brine, which the King tore off in tranches with his own two hands to wolf down.

"Bread for the Prince!" he ordered, his mouth full. "And the Princess too! Eat bread!" he urged us. "Eat! It is the staff of life!" He waved for a servant. "More bread! More wine!" Slowly he turned his glass against the light. The wine within glowed red as any blood. "Bread," he mused, "and wine." A brooding silence fell. "I have been thinking, Kate," at last he resumed, "of what you used to say."

"What I, my Lord?" Katherine started. "Not I, my lord, if anything displease you!"

"Nay, Kate, you recall what you argued! That the Mass should be simpler, more a communion between man and God than a false ritual pretending to His presence there."

I could have thrown up all my food in fear. To say that God was not present in the Mass had brought death to Anne Askewe, and to others too! Even to say "Communion" and not "Mass" . . .

Katherine bowed her head. I swear she thought the doors would now burst open with a troupe of armed men. But the King spoke on. "I have it in my mind to reform the Mass to make it more like a feast of bread and wine, like a good feast of friends—a feast of faith—"

"Oh, yes, sire! Surely God guides your steps!"

The voice was Edward's, his whole being now alight with moral fire. Where had he learned such zealotry? I felt the shock, and something worse. Who did he look like, what was the echo in my mind . . . ?

God help us, it was Mary!

"Say you so, my son?" The King whickered softly, like a broken horse. "Hear you, Kate? *'Ex ore infantium* . . . Out of the mouths of babes and sucklings . . .'"

Katherine was quick to take her cue. "'And a little child shall lead them . . .'"

The King frowned. "I fear he must, Kate, I fear he must!" A great sadness trembled in his face, and his eyes filled with tears.

"Lead who, sir?" Edward bounced gleefully. "Who must I lead?" He thought it was a game.

"Two strings of hounds," the King said heavily. "Two packs of hunting dogs, each yoked with their own, but far readier to turn and rend each other than take soil of the fox." He paused, and studied Edward's face. "You hear me, sir?"

Edward turned very pale. "I hear you, my lord father."

"You are the huntsman, and they are your dogs. Never forget that. The fox is England's bane—or England's good. It is their duty to hunt that for you—with you, but under you. And you must leash them in or let them go, just as you list, not at their lust or liking. Hear you, sir?"

"My lord, I hear."

He listened, Edward, that was true enough. But I heard too, and I heard more than he. For I had seen the factions, seen the hounds, and knew the strength of young Edward's arm—he could not rein them in.

My father read my thoughts, or spoke his own. "No matter, though," he muttered to himself. "I'll spare you that, be sure. I shall pluck down

the proudest of them all, that Lucifer who seeks to take your light and
rule for you! That at least I can do!"

That great Lucifer . . .
So had my lord of Surrey called the Earl of Hertford.
Hertford to be plucked down?
I saw it now: the King meant his death.

XV

My lord of Hertford grown too powerful.
The King feared he would threaten Edward's peace.
His fate was sealed. No one could save him now.

I had no love for my lord of Hertford, the brother of plain Jane—Jane,
who stole Henry's heart away from Anne and so made me a bastard! But
neither did I wish to see the King about his grisly work of taking heads
from shoulders. My heart leaped then at the King's next command: "You
may leave Court, Bess, and take your brother with you."

My relief was in my curtsy. So my lord of Surrey had not yet spoken to
the King? He would—he must! And I could wait. With me to Hatfield
came Edward, and our world rolled back to its golden age, when we had
larked together as children and laughed to our heart's fill. Then came the
day the King willed Edward to return to his own house, the manor by old
Berkhamsted. I, too, was bidden to remove, to lodge in the King's house
at Enfield till Hatfield could be sweetened after Edward and his train.

"What, not keep Yuletide together as we have done before?" Edward
felt it badly and, parting from me, wept his heart away. I wrote him
letters almost every day, and straightway set to work to embroider him a
shirt with fine white stitchery and golden thread, as his New Year's gift
when we should all be back at Court, together once again.

Enfield was dismal, and the weather worse. An evil east wind peeked
about the place, rattling in at casements, rippling the rushes on the floor.
The heavens themselves that year darkened against us: a foul November
wept itself into dull, drear December, and never once did we catch sight
of the sun.

I heard from Katherine more than I wrote, for in my heart I liked her much less now for grovelling to the King. But I was glad to have her news of my father or of the newcomers to Court, for two of the Grey daughters were now in her house, my cousins through the sister of my father, the Princess Mary who died young in the summer of my birth.

But Edward's were the letters that I prized, and one especially struck me to the heart:

Change of scene did not vex me so much, dearest sister, as your going from me. Now I am alone, I long for every letter from you. It is some comfort to me that my Chamberlain tells me I may hope to visit you soon (if nothing happens to either of us in the meantime). Farewell, dearest sister—write, with all speed, to your loving brother Edward.

Poor lonely Edward! I looked up from the parchment. Before me stood one of my brother's gentlemen, a fair young squire I knew by the name of Lacey. "How does my brother?" I demanded.

"Madam, he's well, and overjoyed to hear from you. He returns your love and greetings a hundredfold, he bids me say, and wishes you were with him—now of all times."

Something in his tone gave me pause.

" 'Now of all times,' sir—?"

He leaned forward urgently. "We hear strange rumours from Court—that some dire change is pending. Some great man is foredoomed, or so they say, because he has given the King an anger that will not be borne. One man at least, or more. The Court flies buzz themselves to distraction with it, but none knows where or when the blow will fall."

"And nothing more is known?"

"Only that the King keeps his chamber and will not be seen. In the Privy Chamber he will have none serve him now but Sir Anthony Denny."

Denny! Thinking of that quiet man, I could see why the King would choose him now. "And in the Council?"

"Two men reign supreme there, governing with the King's voice, even as the King—Sir William Paget, still Secretary, and Sir Thomas Wriothesley, the Lord Chancellor."

Wriothesley! And Paget! The chief politico and his right hand! They were of Norfolk's party—Norfolk, who opposed the Seymours to his last breath. What hope, then, for my lord of Hertford, that proud Lucifer? Was his fall certain now?

"And my lord Hertford?"

"Still about the Court, it seems, but denied the chance to come to the King now the Prince your brother is away."

Without Edward to uncle it over all day long, Hertford would lose his main hold with the King.

And also his life?

I could not grieve for him. It would be hypocrisy as hollow as my father's.

"And heads will roll, you say?"

"That is the word, madam."

"I thank you, good sir."

I sent him on his way with thanks and gold for his good intelligence. Yet like fairy food, the news he crammed me with left me fretting like a weaning child and hungering for more.

And not for news only. I pined hard for my lord of Surrey, and matched my pining with hard penances: hard riding, walking, study; fasting, too, to purge my foolishness and clear my thoughts. When would he ask my father for my hand? What would the King say? My hand—what schoolgirl silliness was that? My hand was never mine, neither to give nor to withhold. And even were it, would I—should I—choose him?

No, said my reason.

Help me, said my heart.

But no help came. Kat watched me narrowly and conjectured much, but ventured little, and that little easily ignored. We made some merriment as Christmas came, with holly and ivy and the old wassails to bring the Christ Child in and keep the Devil out. But the festal over, our dull life went on. As did my restless hunger, yet the food I sought was all too soon approaching.

And so it came, in that dead blank of time between Christ's Mass and New Year, when earth itself stands still and time runs backwards into endless winter. No visitor was expected there at Enfield, even the weekly carrier now hard-pushed to drive his wretched beasts through the clogged ways. That day the early dinner hour was come and gone, daylight was on the wane, and Kat had just decreed not five minutes' stitching more if I still prized my eyesight. Then through the crisp air came the sound of hooves and the rough shouts of men. Who came to break in on our peace?

Within minutes a breathless page was at the door. "Madam, your brother—the Prince Your Brother's Grace—"

I started to my feet. "Speak, fool! Not—"

Not—dead? I dared not say it.

"Not anything, sweet sister!"

And there he was, the precious imp, skipping in at the door in his travelling cloak, as if he had just left me. I could hardly speak through tears of joy.

"Edward! What brings you here!"

He laughed, his face pink with travel and the glow from the fire. "To visit you, dear sister, why else?"

"But—"

He nodded, wreathed in glee. "You did not look for it! No more did I. But hear you, 'lizabeth, these are jostling times. I have such things to tell you of Court deeds, things you will not believe! A traitor found, and his nearest kin too, right next to the throne, and put to death, our father strong as ever to root out such evil against us—"

My mind was leaping on ahead of his pelting speech.

So the Earl of Hertford, the dark lord, went to his death, and "proud Tom" too, just as my father had foreseen and promised. A welter of emotions pierced my heart—relief that he was gone if he had threatened Edward or any of us, and yes, pride too, pride in my father, that his strength and cunning had waned not a bit with his body's decay. He still had the power to protect us from the prowling wolves! Long live the King! And Edward, and us all!

I took young Edward in my arms, stopping his headlong tale by hugging all the breath from his thin body.

"A moment, my lord Prince, and let me look at you!" I ordered playfully. "We will have time for that! I must give order for a feast tonight. We shall make merry and dance, and have some foolery—what do you say to ticktack or hoodman-blind? The old year closes fast. What shall we do to bring the New Year in?"

"Nay, sister, I may not—"

He broke off, glancing fearfully over his shoulder at the door. "I may not give orders, nor make promises, so my lord tells me."

"Lord? Which lord?"

Now I could hear low voices in the room below and the sound of armed men.

"Edward—*who brought you here?*"

His face was very white. "Who but my lord?"

Who but my lord. Fears, hopes and phantoms pelted through my head. *Who should it be but my lord . . .*

Think—think hard! If Hertford now was dead, who would take his place as Edward's chief lord and guardian? Not Wriothesley. Would it be the Duke of Norfolk? Or my own lord, his son my lord of Surrey?

Men's feet now on the stairs, the heavy tread of soldiers, yet with one sound leading the rest—the click-clack of a lord's wooden heels upon the naked oak. Edward's face was drawn in fear.

"Who brought me here? Why, sister, here he comes."

He motioned towards the door. My eyes were strung out, burning to see who should come through.

And here he comes. A dark shape, tall, and dim in the dusk light . . .

One wrapped from head to foot in a dark cloak, dark hat about his face . . .

It could not be, not he. What, could he rise from the dead? I shook my head and tried to will the ghost away.

But there he stood—that same Lucifer, the great lord of darkness, the Earl of Hertford, armed, with forty men.

"Edward!" I gripped hold of him and clasped him to my heart. *I must save him from them! They come to take him prisoner, to take us both; they want us together like the Princes in the Tower; they seek our deaths!*

Yet who were "they"? The dark lord was alone, no brother with him. And the men at his command looked cowed and sad, and clustered at the door, reluctant to come in.

And if dark Hertford lived to lord it here, who then had died? Who was the traitor my lord King had put to death so that we all might live?

Dread understanding like a sea of ink lapped my mind's shore. The Lord of Hertford hovered in the doorway like a bird of ill omen, with a strange and mournful gaze. Then he stepped forward, plucked off his hat and knelt upon the ground. Bareheaded, on both knees, he bowed before us, silent as in prayer—*and I knew then what he had come to say.*

So, too, did Edward, for his face was death, his breathing half-suspended in his frame. It was a silence when the world stands still to hear souls crying, or the angels weep. The Earl's voice when it came rang like a trumpet in the soundless room.

"Sire, God has called your father to eternal rest. You are the King, our lord and governor. Please you accept my life as yours, my service to command?"

THE ENVOY TO MY FIRST BOOK

I wept, of course: a river—nay, a sea—of stinging tears. And Edward too: the child howled like a dog. But were our tears for Henry, for the father we would not see again? No. I wept for my lost lord, my lord of Surrey, my lost lord of love, for at once I knew him gone, although I knew not how he died. If Hertford lived, Surrey had lost—there was no room for two such stars in the same sphere, and Surrey's had burned out. And Edward wept for shock, for fear, for his lost childhood and what lay ahead. But however the tears

*came, our King and father's memory was bathed in brine, as was his royal
and his filial due.*

*The rest was swiftly told. Edward was King by right of his inheritance—
and by the King's will, for that prince of self-pleasure, my will-full father,
could not go to his immortal crown without making his great will still king
here on earth. He willed the throne to Edward—see the arrogance, to think it
his to leave, like his close-stool!*

*He named me, too, in the line to the throne, my lord of Hertford said—
and sister Mary, once the only heir. After the King, until His Majesty King
Edward could have issue, were to follow in due order the Princess Mary,
then myself, as Tudor heirs. "But it is to be hoped," said my lord of Hertford,
"that God in his great goodness will spare us from so great a calamity. You
are entered in the will, my lady Princess, you and your sister, to lend your
weight to the King your brother's right: not meant to rule nor govern, for such
things cannot be, a woman over men."*

*Strange how the unthinkable, a woman holding power over men, becomes
thinkable when otherwise it means the loss of power. Even my father at the
end would rather leave his throne to a despised daughter, overthrowing the
thousand-year-old rule that the rights of inheritance only applied to men,
than see it pass out of his Tudor line. Yet still none thought that it would ever
be.*

"Oh, spare us that!" I cried hysterically—and wished him dead.

*For I would have had him strung up that instant, hearsed in a cart and
coffined at my feet, if his death could have brought back my lord of Surrey.
For he was dead, fallen foul of the King through opposing Hertford and the
Seymours, whom the King had chosen as Edward's champions to defend
him to their dying breath. The King feared civil war if the Norfolk party
challenged the Seymours for power over the boy King, and resolved to strike
first.*

*And my dark lord—not Hertford now but Surrey, my lord of darkness and
too early death—my lord Surrey had played into his hands. To show that he
and his father had the better claim to govern the young King, Surrey had
boasted of his royal blood, calling himself "Prince" and quartering his arms
with those of ancient royalty. Given a king tortured by fear that his son
would be cheated of the throne by false pretenders, and by his dying fury that
he would not live to save the boy from traitors, that was my lord's death
warrant.*

*He was detained in my lord Wriothesley's house—yes, our friend
Wriothesley, a fine irony that, no?—that very same who a few weeks before
had been so hot upon his side. I had not known, so far away from the
Court's house of whispers, that my lords of Paget and Wriothesley, too, had
turned their coats against the Norfolk party, against Mary, Gardiner, Surrey,
the whole pack, as soon as Wriothesley's move against Queen Katherine*

failed. That showed them, as I saw with perfect hindsight, that the King meant now to favour the New Faith and the new lords. When Wriothesley put the blame upon my lord that day in the knot-garden, that was when the ground began to shift beneath his feet, though he saw it not.

He fought, they said, fierce as a lion at his trial, brave as a prince, and made a fine defence—and it was true, for he was royal, he was of the blood! But what was truth when his judges were his enemies—my lord of Hertford and his brother Thomas Seymour, new made a Privy Lord in the King's last days, and his Judases Wriothesley and Paget, along with Robin's father Dudley and all the rest of Hertford's men? He was condemned without one voice to speak for him, and met the headsman and the block soon thereafter.

He died a week before the King did: had fate hastened my father to his grave, my lord would have lived, for a king's death cancels all treasons. His father Norfolk was likewise accused and likewise condemned, but unlike Surrey he had cheated fate when the King died before him, and lay now at leisure in the White Tower. The old Duke drew some comfort, it was said, from the word that my lord of Surrey's wife—his wife! God, how little any of us had thought of her!—his despised wife had given birth to a son . . .

But all the rest of Norfolk's hopes and schemes lay now in ruins, his associates in disgrace, scattered to the winds. My lord of Winchester was in eclipse and gone from Court, Mary sent off to some mean manor somewhere to hide her Popish head and think again of where her faith should lie.

Edward was safe, then, both in will and deed. Myself and Mary too: we were both thought of by the King, who left us money, manors, royal dowries both. Yet of the one great question that would bear for all our lives on both our marriages and our inheritance, in all the wordy pages of his long last testament, he said not a word. Am I or am I not a bastard? *my soul screamed after his departing spirit. And answer came there none.*

In truth, I think now that he did not know. His matrimonial morasses, with first this woman and then that declared the one true wife, till she was found either false of heart or false below the girdle and so to be divorced or done away with—could he now remember all that fine legal argument, that hairsplitting, that duplicity? Like all about him, we were his pawns in death, as in his life. He used us both, Mary and me, as he used all about him: both bastardised by his great will and pleasure, but both now used to prop up and support the claims of Edward to the Tudor throne.

Well, so be it. He went to his last reckoning without deciding which of his marriages was legitimate and which a fraud. Which left me bastard for all eternity. And "Little Whore" to boot: for my mother's false arraignment and her death were both eternised too, now he and he alone who could have righted that cruel wrong was gone forever. And with his going, willy-nilly I came into a third title yet: to add to "Bastard" and "the Little Whore," I now was forced to write the sad word "Orphan."

Here Ends
the First Book
–LIBER PRIMUS–
of My History

VIRGIN

Book the Second

-*LIBER SECUNDUS*-

of My History

Orphan I was; yet my loss was my gain. For now I was no longer "the Daughter of the King" but "the King's Most Honoured Sister," and level with the throne. We would not rule, Mary nor I, all men knew that. But even the naming of me gave me honour in men's eyes. Yet still the honour of being "Sister to the King" was my greatest joy back then.

And now suddenly I was marriage-ripe: along with sister Mary, I was one of the most valuable virgins in Europe. Virginity, though, what was that? A better state than bastard, take it from me, yet on its own a poor, sad, one-eyed state of things.

For virgins have no lovers, take that for sure however you take its meaning. *"Virgo intacta, vincere scis, victoria uti nescis,"* sang that rogue poet the young Catullus: "Virgin, virgin, you know how to conquer, but not how to use your victory!"

"Yet you know how to sell yourself," he sneered—*"Uti foro scis"*—for he thought all women whores. Still, he spoke truth of those virgins who cast line for a man without knowing what they catch. And as a great womaniser himself, that Catullus, a notorious whore-maker and scourge to maidenhead, he knew of what he spoke.

Yet every whore was a virgin once. Even my aunt Mary Boleyn, the "quean" of two kings, as they called a whore in those days, and *cocotte* of commoners besides. Named after the Virgin herself when she was baptised in the days of her virgin innocence, this Mary lived to be rechristened "harlot," "strumpet," "daughter of the game."

And Anne watched Mary's transubstantiation from madonna to whore, Cecil told me, and saw another future in her stars. As maid of honour to the Queen of France, she had learned that *noblesse* need not always *oblige*. And though the King of France himself, having relished the buttery delights of Mary's body, had desired to taste "that little dish, her sister," Anne had prized her slender person above a place between the shafts as the King's hackney, and had put him off with such pert grace that he swore he had enjoyed Anne's rebuff more than the taking of Mary.

For though her suitor was a king, to herself Anne was no less a queen, a queen of hearts. Back in England she caught more than a king's eye— she caught Henry's heart in her strong toil of grace.

For after fifteen years of wedlock husbandry, Henry had had hard harvest. There was no sign of the male fruit for which he hungered, no matter how hard he laboured in his Spanish vineyard. Every year of his marriage he had planted a child in Queen Katherine's womb, and every time he was cheated of the crop. Instead of the fair, fat boy he craved, Dame Nature doled out stillbirths, miscarriages, abortions of nature, and babes who lived a few hours or days. His pasture was poisoned, his toil was all in vain.

And he was tired—tired of a matronly body worn out with childbearing, tired of a love from which all desire had flown. Small wonder, then, that he gave ear to the word of the new young whore come ramping home from France—France, the very land of lust!—a sloe-eyed piece, they whispered, whose gaze could wanton with a man's mind faster than the rustle of her flame-coloured silks could set his body on fire.

A fair whore, a virgin whore, fresh and unfingered, yet versed in love tricks that were old when Cleopatra was young. A lady-in-waiting—waiting for her price, for her man.

And those eyes, glowing like coals in the face of the fair, fresh, young French whore . . .

She was no whore, of course, Anne Boleyn, though the King wanted to believe so—first, when the hot thought of it tickled his jaded lust and gave a necessary assistance in what was later revealed as "the King's Incapacity"; and last, when he was frantic to rid himself of her at all costs.

Men in love, men out, will say anything—like all women who have ever loved, I have this carved upon my heart.

But whore? Only in yielding to him, the great whoremaster!

For Henry knew his will. And though she twisted and turned in the love hunt, slipped the net when he thought he had her fast, broke and doubled back like the subtlest hind of the chase, Henry knew his power.

He knew, too, how closely hunt together those twin furies *eros* and *thanatos,* love and death. And though he hunted her with a passion, he stalked her like the King in the old story who pursues the unicorn knowing that once he lays his golden chain about her neck, it will be his death —and hers.

For the King was in love, for the first time in his life, and fathoms deep. The marriage of his youth seemed now but a dream of Anne, he confessed to his soul in broken lyrics and snatches of love song, a shadow of the passion he felt now. A lifetime had passed since he had complimented the little Spanish bride of his boyhood with love shows and gifts. Now the royal jewellers, the goldsmiths, the miniaturists, even the gardeners, were pressed into service as he rained love on Anne in a shower of gold.

"I send a rich gold bracelet, a garden of roses, and my portrait set in rubies and diamonds," he wrote her, "hoping, sweet maid and mistress, that they will find favour in your eyes."

What craven wooing, no, for a man like him—and for a king? Yet king or no, the very thought of Anne made him as bashful as a boy. "I pray you, madam, give me leave to hope!" he begged her when she had refused to walk aside with him into a honeysuckle bower at Greenwich, spurning him before the eyes of all the Court.

"To hope for what, my lord?" she breathed, her eyes like black almonds tilting briefly up to his before dropping again to the ground.

He groaned. "Only this: that I may one day find a lodging, be it never so poor—nay, the meanest tenement—somewhere in the region of your heart."

"How has she bewitched him?" screeched Katherine in a frenzy.

"Who knows, madam? But fear not, God is good; it will pass, it will pass!" her women soothed her.

But behind their backs they made the old sign to ward off the evil eye—and to avert, too, the bold black eye of Mistress Anne Boleyn, in whose glances the King now lived and died.

Did she know, though, what befalls those the gods love? Or that the ancient peoples all believed that only the woman who keeps her virginity can save herself from mischief?

Certainly she guarded her chastity for years, keeping the lion at bay, cherishing her cherry above all the rubies and rewards he heaped on her. Like Henry, she waited for the divorce, the magic dispensation whereby the ugly old witch Katherine would be made to disappear in a puff of papal smoke, and the true Queen step forward in all her glory to take her place.

Yet no man waits forever: least of all him.

"Lord Henry is a man of rare appetite, and his desires are infinite."

This word from Mistress Mary, now comfortably settled in the country on a complaisant husband, a former squire not merely happy but honoured to be a king's seconder, proved to be both a promise and a warning. When after seven long, lean years, therefore, the Pope at last dared to say "No," Anne knew now that she must dare to say "Yes."

Here, if anywhere, see the boldness of the girl! With no divorce, a lesser woman might have abandoned hope that the marriage she played for could ever be hers.

Yet Anne, with her high heart, knew at once that Pope Clement's "No" would catch Henry on the raw point of his pride—would compel the longing, lingering lover to raise the stakes. No Papal Dispensation? So be it, then, no Pope!

Then in the brave new world rising like a phoenix from the ashes of the old, the King would truly be free, and she would truly be "the Queen," no more "the Concubine" or "the Great Whore" of the Romans. For what would their insults matter or their condemnations count when their whole faith, with all their idols, relics, rubrics and rituals, even the very words of their Romish Mass itself, had been swept into the sea?

How—when—where—did she first yield her maidenhead to him in the great gamble to win a crown and get a son? No one knows—only that she was bewhored with words for years before she came to the King's bed, years while she was still a virgin, still no more than the virgin queen of Harry's heart, and he schemed to make her Queen indeed.

Yet to be virgin—and Queen . . . ?
To have the power without losing the power . . . ?
Would that not be a rarer, finer thing . . . ?
Mark how I learned that a maiden should keep her head.

XVI

The King was dead.

No—the King stood before me, mastering his tears, drawing himself stiffly out of my arms, the mantle of royalty descending on him with every second. Even as I looked, Edward grew straighter, taller, stiller, and the pale eyes staring at me now held a new strangeness, a new distance. Like the Lord Hertford, I, too, fell humbly to my knees, and remained there in prayer and weeping, refusing all food, all ministration, long after the King had withdrawn with the dark-faced Earl to his own chamber.

They left the next morning at dawn on that last day of January in that year of Our Lord '48, when a leaden sky hung like a pall over the house, and all the earth below wore widow's weeds. I, too, directed by the Council to join the Queen Dowager in mourning, was on the road soon afterwards with all my people and a guard of armed men, the horses pacing blindly into an east wind now sleeting with ice. Edward was taken at once to the Tower, and there proclaimed. Meanwhile my father made his last voyage west, sailing like King Arthur of old into the setting sun. And so he came to Windsor, where in St. George's Chapel he was laid to rest with high solemnity, and all his officers of household and of state broke their staves and hurled them in his grave.

Within a few days was my Edward crowned, though neither my nor Mary's presence was deemed necessary for the occasion, in the worst of February's chill and rheumy yellow fogs. Yet nothing could dampen the delight of the people in their new Tudor King. In Cheapside a boy no more than half his age leaped out to speak a ballad newly coined for the occasion:

"Sing up, heart, sing up, heart, and sing no more down,
But joy in King Edward that weareth the crown.
To have it much meeter, down had been added,
But up is more sweeter to make our hearts gladded,
So sing up heart, and sing no more down."

There were eight more verses of this limping, driveling doggerel. God be thanked for the shortening of the ceremonies due to Edward's youth, else would he have been forced to abide another forty!

That night, there was a treat after his childish heart, I knew, for as he sat at his Coronation banquet with his new-made boy-sized crown about his brows, Sir Edward Dymoke came riding into Westminster Hall on a great charger, clad from helm to heel in armour of white and gold, vowing to fight to the death any man from the four corners of the world who would not take Edward as his lord and King.

"I pledged him then," Edward wrote me in his best italic hand, "in a cup of gold, and thanked him for his pains." Reading this, I knew that he had acquitted himself like a Tudor to his toenails.

Yet already the words of the Good Book were ringing round my head: "Woe to the land where the King is a child!" Now I saw the fear that had plagued my father when he purged the men of dread from Court and Council to leave Edward in the power of his two uncles and a council of regency composed with utmost care.

Yet feared as Henry had been in life, who fears the dead? Before he was yet cold in his grave, the moths of state were nibbling at his dispensations. It needed no skill in divination to read between the lines of Edward's letter: "At the Tower I was informed that my uncle of Hertford, by the great desire of the Council, is to be made my Governor by law, and Lord Protector of the Realm."

Is he now? I pondered in alarm. This surely was the power Henry had sought to avoid falling into the hands of any one man? "And though our father set it not down so in his will," Edward continued innocently, "yet the new Lord Paget, who was Sir William, gave me great assurances that this was the wish of the King. For as Secretary to the Council, my Lord Paget received His Majesty's dying command that all his promises and intentions in life should be honoured after his death, whether they were set down in writing or no. Thus it seems our lord and father desired to honour my lord uncle Hertford by giving him the dukedom of Somerset. My lord uncle Thomas Seymour is to be Lord High Admiral; Lord Lisle, who was Lord Dudley, is to become Lord Lieutenant of the Kingdom; and Chancellor Wriothesley, the Earl of Southampton. Master Secretary Paget has made all the dispensations."

Paget! Paget again! Oh, well played, Master Slippery Secretary, to

abandon his former allies, the "old" men of Norfolk's party, and slide so
sweetly from the wrong side to the right just at the turning point of
power!

And whose was the device, I wondered, whose was the inspiration to
create this convenient clause of the King's "promises," the King's unfulfilled deathbed "intentions," which must be honoured now? And which
naturally none but my Lord Paget had been privileged to hear? Why, it
was no more than a licence to say or do whatever they liked!

Whose scheme was this? As the chief man in the kingdom, the Earl of
Hertford must have been the prime mover. But Master Secretary Paget
was clearly vital to the design. Wriothesley, too, would be needed as Lord
Chancellor to lend these rough proceedings some semblance of law; well,
as the Earl of Southampton he had had his reward. And the proud
Hertford's prouder brother Tom was also translated into new greatness!
Soon he was jousting at the Coronation celebrations as Baron Seymour
of Sudeley, so Edward pictured him to me in his letter, with all the
beauty of an angel and, I felt sure, the strength of the Devil himself.

Only for the rise of the new Lord Lieutenant could I feel any flicker of
delight. Now my old playfellow Robin would become a lord by virtue of
his father's elevation, along with all the sons of Dudley, and I knew how
that would thrill his heart. But still I saw these men as butchers plunging
hot and reeking hands into the still-living body of our State, tearing its
vitals out to feed their appetites. Woe to the land where naked greed
holds sway! And woe unto the child King in this den of savage beasts, my
poor brother, yet a child no more!

All this I brooded on huddled inside my litter through the long, slow
journey to Queen Katherine's house at Chelsea. The going was so heavy
that we made no more than a few miles a day. Yet no one urged more
haste or cried the horses on. We were like people in a trance, struck
dumb and fearful by the force of this great change. The King had been
the pillar of our universe—now a new world gaped, the world of catch-
as-catch-can, where the weakest go to the wall.

Would that mean me?

And how swiftly was great Harry overthrown at last, his very corpse
not even laid in the grand new tomb he had commanded, but despite the
high pomposity of the ceremonial, in reality bundled away alongside Edward's mother Jane in her existing grave! For all his golden glory, was he
now revealed to be no more than mortal man? I cursed his vain presumption as I wept for his defeat. How he had deluded himself to think his
writ, his will, would enjoy an afterlife when his body banqueted the
worms!

The worms fed well that winter: for besides the over-rotted King, that fat old stag who had hung too long about Death's larder, they had fair flesh and rare younger meat, the best of a long season. How I grieved for the butchering of my lord of Surrey, no man knew—no, nor woman neither, though Kat was never from my side, pressing on me food and love, comfits and consolation, none of which could my stomach undertake. I could not, would not be comforted for his death, and lay through the sick grey hours all glassy-eyed with grieving—not for my father, as they all thought, but for my lost love, my last love, as I swore to honour his great memory—though hardly even my first.

And as for that old devil, that rotting hulk of venom, guts and bile, my father—that vicious tyrant, bloated bully and plain murderer, that killer whale who called himself king and thought himself a god, to doom or spare whoever he so willed—that man, that king, that father, that vile butcher who must pluck down the brightest and the best, the most beautiful of all, a poet, courtier, soldier, scholar, the rose of our age, the hope of the State, my love . . .

To kill so, so to destroy, to take a young man's life because he was an old man dying, and knew it . . . ?

"Ho there!"

A shout ahead rose above the plodding train. From the front of the line, Richard Vernon came galloping up, his face masked with distaste. He waved a gauntletted hand towards the horizon. "Ahead lies Dead Man's Common and Gallowtree Cross, mistress. Half a dozen wretches last week danced there their everlasting dance, and hang there still, just where you will pass."

"We might go round about," offered another of the men. "By Ponders End, or by Arkley t'other way, and see it not."

Yet dead men may be treading air in Ponders End or Arkley, objected my thoughts. "And at that crossroads," Richard added, "people are gathering to greet Your Ladyship. If you go round about, their effort is in vain."

My decision was made. "Forward, Richard—over Gallowtree Cross. And call Parry to me—with all speed, I beg of you . . ."

At the crossroads a grey gloaming lay like lead upon the land, a dark drizzle curdling the blood of man and beast alike. The cold had pinched my flesh to the colour of putty, but thanks to Parry and her attendant sprites, I could at least put a fairish face on things. And there it was, black against the skyline, like an engine from hell, a huge, three-legged gibbet, holding many more poor wretches than may be turned off on the one-armed gallows of the marketplace.

How do men harden to the gallows and the foul fruit of that tree? They hung there blind and black and grinning, their black familiars flapping about their heads—for all the crows of the common, having had their eyes, were now feasting on the rest of the fleshy titbits cooked for their consumption by death and decay, by wind and rain.

Of the six, one of them had had his neck half torn off by the drop. He swayed there, head on one side, looking with his vacant grin like a mad jester trying to raise a laugh. One of them was a child, clad only in a shirt. One of them was a girl hardly more than a child herself, yet from the swell of her belly, with child too. And all hung swinging that heavy, mortal sway of the hanged, their lifeless trunks already a mockery of the thing called man, already more than half way back to the clay from which they came.

Even in the biting air, the stench was sickening. Furtively I felt for my pomander and worked the wholesome scent of orangewood and roses under my nose. Not for the world must the people waiting there see me flag or look faint.

Huddled together against the raw March dusk beyond the gallows tree, a good group of countryfolk had turned out to see the procession pass. Even the waggon master at the head of the train received a ragged cheer as he doffed his soiled headbinder and cracked his whip over the heads of his mules in salutation. Each of my gentlemen and ladies was greeted in turn with rising glee, every jewel, feather, hat or cape, however be-draggled now in the drizzling sleet, being hailed with open and admiring comment.

My litter, though, brought the keenest response. The shouts were deafening.

"God bless thee, my lady!"

"Save you and keep you, Princess Elizabeth!"

"May Our Lord and His Mother smile on Harry's bairn!"

My heart was overflowing. Not the dark memory of what we had just seen, not the cold, killing sleet, nor the burden of sadness I still bore could spoil my happiness. Here was love, love indeed, and the fullness of joy beyond compare. Warmly I returned their greeting.

"Thank you, good people! God's blessings on you! I thank you from my heart!"

Suddenly an aged woman broke from the group and darted towards the litter, her eyes boiling with rage. To my horror she ran right along-side, spitting and clawing at my wraps, the talons of her age-crumpled hands striking at my face. "Curse thee!" she shrieked. "Curse thee for a whore, and a daughter of a whore!"

Slash, slash went her hand. I sat upright and unbreathing, gripped in a rigor so deep it was like death.

"A black whore!" screamed the old cracked voice. "A goggle-eyed whore, she was, Nan Boleyn! Through her the Old Faith perished!

Through her we lost God's goodness—the blessed brothers and sisters of the holy orders scattered to the winds—"

"Mother, mother, mother, mother, MOTHER!"

The anguished cry of a younger woman cut through the old crone's screams. As Vernon and Chertsey with a couple of men-at-arms fell on the old woman and dragged her aside, her daughter, a sturdy country wife, appeared at my litter's side, her work-worn face streaming with tears.

"Forgive her, my lady!" she begged, almost on her knees. "She is mad, my husband says, mad as the March winds—all say so—but she is three-score years and more, and if her wits wander, who am I to beat her for it? Forgive, lady, forgive!"

"Do not fear," I said, as calmly as I could. "Go your ways—we do not take poor aged women for whipping."

"They beat her now, lady, see you!"

Within seconds some of the men had laid hands of violence upon the old woman, hustling her towards the gallows, while others ran ahead, knives at the ready, to cut down one of the ropes. The ringleader, a vicious brute with only one eye, had them in a frenzy. A man who was evidently the daughter's husband, an honest brave soul, fought like a Trojan for her, but in vain.

They were at the foot of the gallows now, and the rope was round the old one's neck. My gentlemen and people were standing by helplessly, like mutes at a mourning. I found my voice.

"Hold! Do no harm to this woman!"

They wavered, but no more. I nerved myself to shout again.

"You there! I command you! Leave off this hanging!"

There was a great silence: my own people had never heard me speak so before.

"Release that woman! And you"—with my most imperious air I summoned the daughter and her husband—"take her home, keep her close. Send for a physician to ease her malady." I waved for Chertsey. "It shall be at my charge—this lord will see to it."

Chertsey bowed, and hurried the couple and the old crone away.

A final thought struck me. "Have a care you keep her well! I shall look to see her in this place at my next passing through. No more attempts upon her life!"

At Vernon's sign, the men-at-arms fell into line, the horse master urged on his steeds, and my litter was under way. A few angry murmurings came from the crowd. But others of them seemed relieved, even proud, that their witch had been granted the attention of a great lady and received the care of a princess.

Slowly we moved away. Then at my side was the daughter again, eyes and nose running in unison, her raw red face blubbered with relief.

"Gracious lady, for your mercy, God ha' mercy on you again! She's no witch, mother, only a mad old thing. Take no mind to what she said, Princess, there be those in England would die for you—I for one of them! And my man there, for another!"

With a final snivel, she melted into the dusk. As Kat, Parry, the Vernon brothers, Chertsey and all crowded round the litter to see how I did, my last thought before a shivering ague seized me was this: *Though Henry has died, his legacy lives on. And I must live down this birthmark of the whore, or lose all in this land.*

XVII

I had not seen the King's manor at Chelsea since I was eight years old. One joyful spring and summer, misted now in memory like old glass, I stayed there as my cousin Katherine's pet while she was still Queen. Would the cherry blossom still drift there in the spring, the summer lavender perfume the evening walks, the roses still run down to the river where we rode in that great barge? Now the trees bloomed only with great flakes of snow, and the earth was clad in a veil of sleet and slush as we turned into the courtyard, where I felt my legs so dead with cold that I could hardly stir.

My spirits were numb too, and tinged with dread. How would I find the Queen? She must be stricken with bereavement, aged with her grief and loss. And with her reason for living gone, what would be left?

And how long must I stay imprisoned here, keeping this mourning while the Queen declined? To be the prop of a wretched widow would be nothing but life in death! Heaving myself stiffly out of my litter, seeing the black funerary swathes darkening the doors and windows, I sighed with burning sorrow. If only I could be at Court with Edward! I might as well be buried alive as walled up here in a dark house of mourning!

"Welcome once more to the Queen's House, my good lady."

Katherine's sober-suited steward, the same who had served her at Whitehall, knelt in deep reverence on the broad-flagged doorstep. At least they knew my state! Stiffly I suffered him to usher me in. Now the bright warm tapers clustering by the wall and the great fire on the hearth caught my heart by surprise and thawed me near to tears. If only I could be alone!

The good man read my wishes in my face. "This way, my lady."

We stood in a good-sized upper chamber, warm and well lit like the hall below—well enough, I thought mournfully, for the few people I now had. Still, I felt sullen and unsatisfied. "A wretched lodging!" I grumbled fretfully. "Why do they stow us here?"

"Come, madam, come and see your chamber now!" Kat came bobbing up. "You'll not regret that the Lord Protector Somerset sent us here." Triumphantly she flung open the door to the Privy Chamber and drew me inside, slamming home the oak. "Princess, how like you this?"

The room was wide and low, deep-carpeted and curtained against the night. The hand of Katherine was everywhere, in the hangings with their scenes from the Old Testament, in the applewood fire now scenting all the chamber, in the box of sweetmeats on the bed, and of all delights, a bowl of winter roses, pure and white. Kat patted the great bed with a look I could not read. "Pray you, madam, sit and rest awhile. The steward tells me you are bidden to join the Queen's household for supper in an hour or so. And before then, I have something I must say!"

"What about?"

Mellowing, I suffered to be coaxed out of my cloak and settled on the bed, my hands and feet chafed back to painful life, my frozen face buffed up by Kat's firm knuckles. Then Kat planted the comfits in my lap and herself down on the bed. "With your leave, my lady," she began. "The time was not ripe till now, the King your father's death throwing us all at sixes and sevens . . ."

I nibbled a sweet candied violet as I sourly eyed the hanging by the wall, where a fat Esther, prone before the great King Ahasuerus, worshipfully gazed up into his pompous face. Why were women always depicted so? Slowly Kat's words worked their way through my mind: "I would speak, madam, not of mice but of men: for you are now of age, and men will come at you, nay, you've been sought before . . ."

Her lips were parted, and her breath came fast and light, like women too tight-laced. I placed the comfit back within its box and stared her out. Surely she would not dare to speak—of *him?*

She dropped her eyes and hurriedly ran on. "I speak not of the late, lost Lord of Surrey, he who back at Court I thought was angling for Your Highness. I never liked the man, nor thought a Papist, be he never so well-favoured, fit for my lady's grace! And bear me out, my lady, never have I spoke of him since that first time, when you forbade me—you'll vouch for that."

Yes, I'll vouch for you, Kat.

"Say on."

"But now that we are here, so near the Court—and now the Lord Protector holds the reins—and all the world knows Your Ladyship must be married—"

Must?

Yes. If it is so decided, I must obey.

"—now more than ever, while your brother is yet young. Your place in the succession—"

Demands it.

Yes.

I know that.

"—and the King your father took account of it. No, not when he used you to beguile foreign ambassadors with hopes of treaty! But when he looked about to choose an Englishman, a good man here at home, a great man too, one any woman could love, one fitted for Your Grace's hand in marriage—"

Kat's eyes were bright with feeling as she ran on.

Love and marriage?

No more!

I do not wish to hear.

"Kat—enough of this idle chatter! Hold your peace, say no more!"

My voice was harsher than I meant it to be. But this was nonsense! What could she be dreaming of? I mourned a love and quailed under a hate: my mind was black with brooding on my father and my lord. Love nonsense now was—no, away! I could not think of it!

"My lady!"

She jumped to her feet and bobbed a furious curtsey. I shook my head. "Spare me, Kat!" I pleaded. "I am worn out with travelling, sick at heart and fearful of the Queen. And you know too, there can be no marrying, nor any talk of marriage, while we are still in mourning! I beg you, send for some hot wine to put heart in my belly and colour in my cheeks against this supper, or I'll not stand up to it!"

She curtsied and withdrew, her very farthingale as she retreated quivering with resentment. This was not like Kat. Why did she want to talk of lovers now? *Oh, Kat, you know I may not marry where my heart desires! What is this maids' talk of my own true love?*

The supper hour loomed. I must stop thinking of myself and try to think of Katherine! My task here was to comfort her, to respect and console her dreadful loss. So I had myself dressed with special care: even my mourning, of the deepest dye, I had trimmed back in deference to her state. My pearls, though black as only fitting, were small and hugged my ears, and my black gown, though fine, was not of richest three-pile: Katherine was still Queen, and hers the greatest grief.

The steward had sent word the Queen would join her household to take supper in the Great Hall. *Who will be here now?* I wondered as I came down the wide stairway. Some of her ladies would have left her service as soon as the King died: Denny for one, I had heard, was gone back with her husband Sir Anthony to their house in Cheshunt. But some would surely stay: her sister Mistress Herbert without doubt, and others, too, I would be sure to know.

And as the steward bowed me into the Great Hall, I felt the foolishness of one whose fears have been wide of the mark. So far from the meagre, muttering groups of grief-oppressed mourners I had imagined, the chamber was aglow. Among the little groups of Katherine's ladies and her gentlemen, the talk was sober enough for any Court still in full mourning. Yet the smiles, the warmth, the sense of ease and pleasure that they shared, were something new to me. A small cold thought went wandering through my mind: *Could this have happened in my father's time?*

I stepped forward to receive another shock. Standing together with others not far from the door were two girls I had never cared for, and least desired to see now. I should have loved them, for Tudor blood ran strongly in their veins. We were all near in age, and all bookworms too, in love with our studies. But we could not be friends, and as I spotted my cousins Jane and Catherine Grey, I knew again why not.

Jane was the elder, and she set the tone. She wore an air of such importance that it seemed perverse of fate to have made her so short: her head hardly reached my nipples. Ill-favoured too, as Catherine was, for they were both cursed with small clenched features crowded around a vilely freckled nose. Jane in particular looked like my sister Mary, except for the plainness of her dress. And like Mary again, they were both the wrong kind of Tudor: their pallid faces and dull rust-brown hair had too little of the Tudor fire to light their skins and lift their locks to red-gold like mine and Edward's.

Catherine, the younger and the duller, aped her sister Lady Jane in everything, always hoping, as I thought, that some of the praise lavished on Jane would find its way to her. For Jane's piety was a wonder of the world. "A child," I was sick of hearing since she was four years old, "who more delights to read her New Testament, in Greek, than Boccaccio or any merry tale." I, too, loved Greek, and my Bible too. But surely virtue can also take some joy in the things of this world? My faith was firm, I thought; hers, bigoted. And her puritanical dress offended me: in her plain dismal grey, she looked like a poor relation, not a princess!

Why did the poor child bring out such spite in me? No, not because she

made me feel like a giantess; most women did that now! It was because I
feared her—feared her pale fire and unbroken soul, her zeal for purity and
her faith in truth, the truth she thought alone revealed to her.

But here they were, and we must be cousinly together.

Like three old dowagers we greeted one another with frosty ceremony,
yet without regard. Beside them now I saw a group of girls, all around
our own age. I nodded at the others. "Will you present me?"

"As Your Highness pleases." Jane pursed her little mouth and began
in her schoolgirl voice, hissing her sibilants. "Your Ladyship knows Jane
Dormer, as I think."

Dormer. I stared hard at the narrow face now glancing up from a deep
curtsey. Dormer . . . so I did, or the family name at least. In her pert
gaze lay rank hostility, and I knew why. Her mother had been chief lady
to Katherine of Aragon, and a fierce Papist. This one had been born
deep-dyed in that bad blood. She could not care for Anne Boleyn's offspring if I had been an angel.

"Mistress Jane—" I made my curtsey short enough to indicate I did
not give a fig for her favour, fair or foul.

The others were soon done, the four daughters of a friend to the
Queen, the Greek scholar Sir Anthony Cooke. The eldest, Mildred,
brought them all in line, then all four curtsied like bob-apples in a barrel.
Against sharp Jane, dull Catherine and spiteful Dormer, Mildred's plain
but wholesome face had a rare sweetness and intelligence, and alone of
all of them, I wished to know her better.

I knew the Queen had favoured Lady Jane as she had me, by encouraging her studies. The others, too, I knew she must have helped. Suddenly I saw that we were all the children Katherine must have longed for,
and never would have now. "So," I said, determined to be gracious,
"shall we have here a school for learned virgins with the Queen?"

"God's own academy," Jane put in with that maddening pedantry,
"where we shall study the Word, and obey the Word in all our doings!
For God knows, we walk always in the eye and sight of Him—He sees
into the bottom of our hearts . . ."

Oh, God-a-mercy! Already she was preaching! An imp of mischief
seized hold of my tongue. "I have a better idea! Why do we not study to
form a Court of Love, as they once had in France . . . ? And choose
our lovers freely like the queens of old Provence, only if they please us,
nothing else?"

Jane, Catherine, Dormer, Mildred and all of them were staring at me,
and past me now like rabbits caught in lamplight. Behind me I could hear
the rising buzz of servants' clamour as they prepared for supper or some
such thing, but I paid no heed. Behind me, too, Kat gave my sleeve an

urgent tug, and I shook her off. I was enjoying scandalising the over-zealous little Jane, and no one was going to stop me.

"Say, Jane, and Catherine too, would we not have good sport as queens at our own Court of Love?" I laughed at Catherine's goggling face and all those pairs of frightened eyes. "If I were Queen at least—"

Behind me a low laugh curdled my blood. "Yes, my Elizabeth—*what would you do?*"

I could not speak. It was the Queen herself, who had slipped in unan-nounced, and with so little ceremony I took it for servants' flurry.

The Queen, yet not the Queen—never was woman so changed. This was not Katherine, not what I thought to see.

Where was her sorrow? Only in her widow's weeds did she resemble the grief-crushed relict of my grim foreboding. Her eyes were bright with some mysterious fire, her face pink and well-favoured, her step as light as if she had shed ten years. What had made her so happy? Her smile was always sweet but now was glowing, and her high spirits would insist on welling up in joyful bubbling laughter as she spoke. "Fear not, my dear!" She laughed at my stricken look. "We shall have love, and play, and joy in full, both in our work and lives. For truly, Elizabeth, Heaven deserves our joy—God is a marvellous man!"

"Yet men are marvels too, not so, my lady?"

I had not heard him come. Like all there he wore mourning black, but his alone was slashed with scarlet, the flickering tongues of red leaping up his doublet and round inside his cloak, so that he seemed a devil writhed in flames. His face was instinct with vitality, his eyes like a pan-ther's sideways in regard, yet knowing, piercing, till they stopped my breath. He grinned a wide white grin. I had never seen him smile so before; but then, I had never truly looked at him before. And though I knew him as the brother of my Lord Protector Somerset, now I knew I knew him not at all.

"My Lord Admiral!"

I made my reverence. He took my hand and pressed it to his lips, his forefinger caressing my inner palm as Katherine glowed on. Then they moved off, she to greet her guests and he attending her as was her due. Behind me came a stealthy hand on my elbow and Kat's voice trium-phant in my ear. "Well, madam—*what think you of your husband?*"

XVIII

My husband?

I could still feel the hot kiss of his finger branding my palm as Kat rattled on in my ear. "One that adores you, lady, I have it from his own lips! And one your father deemed a worthy match. And more—much more—oh, lady, such a man, such a bold hawking eye, such a leg, a hand, a heart. And now, now more than ever, may you hope to have him, he you were promised for, before the old King died—"

I made a feint of smoothing down my gown to still my twitching hands, and stared ahead.

The proud Protector's prouder brother Tom.

The new-made Lord of the Admiralty.

Back from the wars, where he had won great fame. Back from long exile too. What was it Paget said, on the day of my father's wedding—that brother Tom had caught the widow's eye and thought to have her—or her wealth— before the King popped in between him and his hopes?

Was that it? Had he loved Katherine then, or she him? Or had he simply seen what could befall young men of power too close to the throne, like my lost lord of Surrey, and prudently gone away?

He stalked on down the hall, tall and erect, not leaning down to others, as my lord of Surrey did, but throwing back his strong and well-shaped head in constant mirth or banter. His hair, cut like a soldier's, still grew thick and long, the candles by the wall still finding little fireworms of red-gold within its dark brown depths. His beard was redder yet, red as my father's . . . and his laugh my father's . . . and the look within his eye my father's, as he lived . . .

I know what you would say. My Surrey, Seymour, Leicester, even my late last lord, my Essex—all tall and lithe, all bold and bright, all fair, red-gold, well-favoured; and all abundant with that special thing that women always seek—forgive plain speaking, I am no virgin-mouth of fifteen now—that thing that makes them men . . .

Were they all mirrors of my father, then, all those who cracked the glass of my indifference, all those I loved?

Too easy, in all truth, to dismiss them thus. Never forget, all men were like him then, as later on, all women followed me when I was all the fashion. Suffice it say that my lord Seymour was half Harry, half Beelzebub; but the warlike grace, the nerveless swagger and the way with women, they were all his own.

What was Kat saying now? Keeping a pleasant air as I nodded around, and smiling lightly as if faintly bored, I hissed into her face, "What *husband?* Say what nonsense you do speak!"

"No nonsense, madam!" Her eyes were laughing, and her chubby chops were bursting with her news like squirrels crammed with nuts. Dropping a pert curtsey, she savoured her revenge. "Only that which I tried to tell you before, but you refused to hear me—the husband meant for you by your late father."

"Kat, how do you know all this?"

Her eyes went wide. "I have it from himself, lady. He told me all."

"When did you learn his mind, and the King's too?"

Her secret welled up like a spring newly struck. "In Whitehall first—when I was walking in the gardens, he came upon me to make talk of you. He had approached the King, he said, who pledged him you were his! He praised you to the skies, my lady, and for that alone I loved him from the first."

"But you spoke not of it then!"

"He bade me hold my peace till the time should be right—as you did, lady, at that selfsame time, over my lord of Surrey."

"And now?"

She passed her little tongue between her teeth, still panting like a cat. "Now? Bethink you, Princess—why are we sent here?"

"By order of the Council."

"By order of the ruler of the Council, the Lord Somerset, my lord Seymour's brother, who means by this to speed your courtship!"

"Kat, hold your tongue! And not a word of this to any other soul, you hear me?" The word struck terror in me.

Courtship, was it? Was I ready to be courted? Or worse still, married! Was there no escape?

And yet . . . if it were him . . . a man like him . . .

My mind moved wildly round it. "Say again: he told you that he loved me, sought my hand, and that the King consented?"

"He swore it, lady!"

"And then my father died . . ."

"And now Lord Tom is uncle to the King, who will refuse him nothing!"

Could it be? I stared down the chamber. Still poised by Katherine, still he seemed more the heart of the Court than she, the Queen, even with her newfound joy, her special glory. Life crackled from him with every laughing shout, every bold gesture. His eyes, his face, his teeth, all flamed with life, and lust for life—to which all flocked, to warm them at his fire.

As I looked down he looked up, and his mouth widened in a flashing smile. Half listening, still half talking with the man beside him, he laughed and saluted me. Both men now held my gaze until a word, a look I could not read, passed between them. Something inside me shifted, and the hand at my face grew hot.

And Kat had heron's eyes even for the smallest fish. "You like him, madam, I can see you do!" she exulted. "Oh, it will be a match, I feel it in my bones!" Then she was serious, and her face even sad. "If I could live to see you married once, and bedded too, to know such joy as I have had with my man Ashley here, then Princess, I'd die happy!"

He was there again in the Great Hall the next evening, clad in satin neither black, nor grey, nor sable, but coloured like the very thought of night and darkness everlasting. I had passed a wretched day after a wretched night. Only as dawn was creeping did I catch a little sleep, when in bounced Kat, warbling a love song.

I could have cuffed her. "Kat!" I groaned. "No more, I beg of you!"

"That's what all maids say, madam, when it comes to it!" she rejoined cheekily. "You'll soon learn to cry, 'More, more, good man, more, more, I beg of you!' "

"Kat!"

She noticed my cold pallor and at once busied herself with bundling me into my nightgown as I stepped bare and shivering from the bed of state. "I speak only of the rites of nature, which God in His goodness has ordained for us!"

"Not without holy wedlock and the sacrament of marriage! And that may not be!"

"It may be, lady, and within a week!"

"Dear God, what do you mean now?"

She was suddenly grave. "My lord Seymour has only to go to Court, half an hour's ride away, to speak to his brother, then to yours, the King, and it is done."

I knew she spoke the truth, for we kept no long betrothals then. "But my father's death—it would not be allowed while the Court is still in mourning—"

She shrugged. "It only needs the King's goodwill—and then a bishop's licence, given on grounds of your ill health—greensickness, say, my lady, a maiden's malady—some such thing . . ."

"And what of me . . . ?"

I never saw her tenderer. "Aye, sweetheart, what of you?" She kissed my face. "Could you not love him? Could you not indeed?"

I could, indeed I could. Already I was taken like a hard fever with hot liking of his fair length, his strong hand, his bright eye, his bold sun-browned face, his . . .

I knew not the word, and blushed even at the thought—but that thing, too, I loved, that thing that makes them men—for the first time, in him.

And with him too—as you shall hear, too soon.

After this day's beginning, I made no speed with Grindal in our morning's work, and that poor man's patience never was more strained. In the forenoon I pleaded a sick headache to avoid "the school of learned virgins," for I had been told that Jane my cousin and the others would all work on their Greek, translating Bible texts. I could not bear it, much though on my own I loved translating as a pastime. Today my mind was porridge, worse than porridge, curds and whey. One thing ruled the remnants of my thoughts: the summons down to supper . . .

Night came, and he was there, watching the door as I came stepping through. My toilet had been a nightmare, for as Parry wailed, "How many changes can one make in mourning, madam? Black is always black!" But now I wore my best black gown, and pearls as black as grapes in a rich double drop from either ear—perish the Queen's best right to mourning precedence, I was bent on making an appearance! With them went a girdle all of pearls, a rope that circled my waist and swung down to my feet. My headdress after fifty separate tries had been arranged at last to let my hair loop just a little, so, softly across my temples, then full loose down my back. My colour was Parry's perfect peach, with a mere hint of coral, and my scent was bergamot of Padua. Accoutred to the hilt, I felt I could do battle with Old Nick.

As I now have to do, my senses thrilled. *This man is danger's brother, danger's older brother Tom.*

"Princess! My duty to you!" The candles by the wall danced in his eyes as his bow swept the floor.

My curtsey lost nothing of the same magnificence. "And my Lord Admiral!"

He took my hand, and once again his bold index finger wooed my inner palm. A fierce scar, old now, gleamed across the back of his brown sword fist. He looked into my eyes with a hot stare. "How do you, lady?"

My skin was prickling all inside my shift, but I would not let him force me to look down. And thus I caught a glance from him to Kat behind my shoulder. *Have you yet broken my intent to her?* his eyes were now demanding. *What knows she of my suit?*

Kat would be saying *Yes—oh, yes, sir, yes!* with every bone in her round pliant body. I braced myself to discourage all his hopes. "You are back from the wars, as I hear, sir?" I said as coldly as I could. "Against the French?"

"The French, the Scots, you name them, I am needed!" he replied with a laugh. "And with those shag-haired kerns of Ireland on the prowl about our western gates, I could not break all your fair ladies' hearts by leaving England now!"

God, he was arrogant! Some chaste rebuke was called for, some reminder of my virtue, for I had not forgiven his freedom with my hand. "What do you think of the Queen's school of learned virgins here at Court?" I resumed loftily. "Is not that a fine thing? And may not men learn a good deal from it?"

"So fine that I hear it was too fine for you today, my lady," came the smiling thrust. "But perhaps you were otherwise engaged—with your own Court of Love, of which you spoke last night—and which, I pray you, give me leave to join, as your true servant!"

His eyes pierced mine. "My servant, sir?" I blustered. "Why, what's that? The merest groom that services my chamber can call himself my servant."

"Not as I would serve you, lady." The hot meaning was unmistakable. He stepped close. "Put me now to the test of a man's service: prove me."

The gold- and red-enamelled pomander about his neck was swinging before my eyes: my senses swam in the strong scent of musk and manhood. The eyes now burning into mine I seemed to know—they were . . . they were just my mother's in my dreams, brown like molasses, black in other lights, but shining, shining, like a wolf in heat.

I was trembling, and could not hold his gaze. To my shame and fury, I could hear him laugh.

A step and he was closer still. "Lady—and mistress?" He reached out for my hand.

Hold back!

Hold back!

Yet how could I hold back what I longed to begin?

The ushers were crying at the door, "Make way for the Queen! Prepare to greet the Queen!"

I hid my flaming face in a deep reverence. My kirtle as I curtsied made a pool of black I longed to drown in.

"My lord?" It was the Queen's voice. "Where's my lord, my lord of Sudeley?"

"Here, Your Royal Grace—ever the Queen's servant, Your Grace's to command."

And he was gone, and I was left repining.

Then came the strangest time. Night after night he wooed me as no man ever after was to do. For I was not the Queen then, but a green virgin of no great account: so his was the power, his the whip hand. At thirty-odd, he had seen more than twice my years, and had known the world, and more. When I protested at his bold attack, he brushed me off. "I am a soldier, madam, and have learned that women like rough wooing."

Wooing? He wooed, he courted, he taught me love's warfare, the endless game of advance and retreat. And I fought back, I flirted like a tiger. But only till the Queen appeared, for then he was all her man. She was the Queen, he said. All men were bound to serve her above all.

And when he talked of love and spoke of making me his, I even came to think again of marriage, to wonder what it would be like—above all, what it would be like with him . . .

I wondered more and more as my cold maid's blood was heated more and more by his strange alchemy, all through that wanton spring . . .

One day of April all the world burst out in life and love, after winter's death. The fields round Chelsea made a tapestry of daisies and buttercups as I danced through them glad in body, heart and soul. That night the Queen did not descend to the Great Hall, and I had my lord to myself. He was quiet, even sombre, and a new feeling for him filled my being. *He could be my mine,* I thought, *and I could be his wife.* Never was I more happy.

That night at bedtime, Parry was in raptures. "Never better, madam, you were never better! The gown, the headtire, the jewels, the complexion—"

"Thanks all to you," I rejoined none too graciously, for I was tired and longed to take my bed. "Here, off with this—and this—and then rub my head."

Her hands were deft as ever. "And all the lords admired you, I could see, madam, one above all, the great Lord of Sudeley, Baron Tom—"

I smiled to myself. "That lord—what do you think of him?"

"As a lord well fit—" Her nails stabbed my scalp as her hands stiffened. She broke off nervously.

"Well fit for what? Speak, Parry, do not fear."

She liked him, sure, and favoured him for me. That was good . . .

"I think the lord well fitted, then, to be Your Highness's brother—or your stepfather, as the honour may fall out—"

My guts heaved. I pulled my shaking head out of her hands and swung round. "Brother? *Stepfather?* Parry, you rave, you drivel! What on God's earth are you talking of?"

Her large eyes collapsed with woe like a sick cow's. "Pardon me, Princess! Only what I have heard just this day, from my brother at Court—my brother Thomas, now as your treasurer busy there about your father's will—"

My head was bursting. "Yes, yes—well, what of him?"

Parry picked up my fear, and her voice quavered. "Only this, lady, Court gossip, nothing more: that the Lord Tom was asking his brother the Lord Protector to wed the Princess Mary—"

Mary!

Oh, my heart!

"—or else to marry then the Princess of Cleves, your father's third wife, your stepmother still and a rich dowager here in England—which would make him Your Highness's stepfather—"

My ears, my face, my guts, were all on fire.

Fool that I was, to think he cared for me, when all the time he was fishing in another pond! Another two! And two old women too, nothing so young and fair and fine as I!

I raged and would have wept, no, screamed with grief. He loved *me!* Me, not Mary, nor that old bag of bones Anne of Cleves! *Anne!* She was a fright even when she was young, a veritable broomstick, no, a witch—except too stupid even for that! How could he—even for money—do this to me?

But the next thought came like lightning: *Yet am I still the one, his best beloved, the love that he seeks now, the one he always sought. He had to make show of wooing them only for protocol, to free himself for me, the Princess junior to them by so much.*

My mind was clear at last. I would have him.

I loved him, he loved me, and all was fitting. A wild and wicked thought took hold of me: *We shall have such fine children, tall, red-gold, fair-favoured, and bold fighters all . . .*

The fantasy was so fine it filled my mind and closed my eyes and ears. Parry's words came to me slowly, as noise reaches those trapped under-ground: "And now, it seems, his lordship is despatched, for rumour has it, in a few days will he now be wed . . ."

. . . in a few days will he now be wed . . . will I now be wed . . .

". . . and no happier woman will be in the world, they say, than that poor woman who has waited so long, when she walks down the aisle as Seymour's wife . . ."

. . . that woman . . .

What woman?

"That woman? Parry, who? Whom do you speak of? *What poor woman?*"

"Why, our Queen Dowager, Madame Parr as was—Queen Katherine, my lady—who else should it be?"

XIX

That was the first of my great megrims, when the pain blinded my head and left me sick and staggering. A week I lay inside a darkened chamber while a thousand painsmiths worked inside my skull to make lights flash like meteors, dull drums pulse like dead marches, and raw hurts indescribable. At last, by daily cupping and starvation was I drained of blood and all foul humours, and could be myself again, though weak.

Or so they told me—for I was left heartful of melancholy, choler and black bile—for in that week he married.

Yes, marry her he did, to my soul's fury: and even more to Kat's. Her anguish would have made the stuff of a fine comedy, had she not felt it so. She was a woman wronged, a woman scorned, every bit as much as I. She had of course fallen in love with him—all women did—and being pure of heart and true to her own marriage, for she loved her man, she wanted him for me.

Ashley had warned her, as I later found, that the Lord Admiral would never marry where he pleased, but only where his purse would grow pregnant by the deal. My inheritance was small, while through her three late husbands, one a king of royal largesse, Katherine had become the richest woman in England—who could compete with that?

And the Queen herself? So much for the saintly Katherine! Now as I wept with jealous rage in Kat's warm arms, I saw what had been staring at me all along. "She was no grieving widow!" I wailed to Kat. "She wanted him the second the King died, and always meant to have him!"

It was all true, of course, what Wriothesley said when he sneered about "the widow Parr" and her soft spot for "proud Tom." She had indeed loved him before and planned to have him when her second husband died. But then in popped my father, and she thought better of it than to resist the King's will, for her own and Seymour's sake.

Yes, yes, I knew how she had suffered in that marriage from the King's tyranny and cruelty, his turning against her even to take her life. And then his vile gross bulk, that festering hulk of evil-smelling lard, his rotting leg—as welcome as a slug's his bed embraces must have been! . . . .

So now, could I begrudge her? At thirty-six, as she then was, knowing at last for the first time in her life the love of a man—"and what a man!" wept Kat with bitter admiration, "a lusty long one famed in field and camp, in Court and city, for his prowess between the sheets!" With such a man, could I begrudge her?

Yes!

So they were married, and my world turned black with his betrayal. The wider world went reeling too, aghast at his presumption. For as I learned from my sickbed, the Protector had furiously forbidden his younger brother even to think of aiming at a royal bride. They were all, he said, queens and princesses destined for matches on the world's stage. But to a man like my bold lord, such denials were nothing but a challenge. And though the Lord Hertford, Protector Somerset, knew and feared his brother's fierce ambition, he knew not how to check it, for it would out, like murder, in the end.

As so it did. The wanton Lord Tom sought and received his nephew's blessing on his match with Katherine. And if the King was pleased to give consent, Lord Somerset could do nothing. But this made bad blood between the brothers and set the scene for darker doings still.

Dark doings, and dark thoughts: no darker, though, than all I suffered as I lay abed. And not only from my sickness.

"How does Her Highness?" From behind the curtains I could hear my cousin Jane's prim enquiry. "Tell your mistress I will pray for her."

Go pray, girl, pray, I thought in royal rage, *but not for me, not me! I would rather have loved and lost than live like you, forever trapped on the cold side of virginity!*

Grindal came too, the dear man, and spent hours by my bedside reading Greek to cheer me. " 'Αἰδὼς τοῦ καλοῦ καὶ ἀρετῆς πόλις, Πρῶτον ἀγαὸν ἀναμαρτησία, δεύτερον δὲ αἰσχύνη,' " he chanted. " 'Modesty is the soul's citadel, its beauty and its strength: the first of virtues is a trusting faith, the second, feeling shame.' "

Feeling shame! I felt shame, twice over—once for my folly in trusting my lord, once for my body racked now with self-disgust. From now on, I vowed, I would live like a nun, in study, prayer and fast. No one should come at me again like that, no man, no men, no, no, no!

A week I had been sick when I awoke and felt my fever gone. It was not yet much past four in the morning, the cock crowing, the church bell chiming from the nearest tower. Soon Kat would draw the curtains . . .

Then I heard the chamber door burst open, and a cry of Kat's, and then the hand upon the hangings in the dawn light flashed a pearly scar across its hard brown knuckles . . .

How long had he been living with the Queen in Chelsea, where we were? When they first were married, so doubtful was it till he won the King's consent that he only came by stealth at dawn, striding across the fields from the riverside, and no one knew he was there at all. But then when all was known, he moved himself, his men and maids, his horses, dogs and hawks, from Seymour House in town and came to live. And the next day he was there.

He was there, he was with me in the bed, leaping in like a lion, face and teeth agleam. I almost died of fear: I knew not who it was, save that it was a "he"—a maleness filled the air, for like all Toms he carried his own scent. In my fright I fell back to the side and fought to scramble free. But as I wore no nightclothes, I could not leave the bed without some covering for my nakedness—my nakedness now open to his view.

His hand was at my breast, where I was clutching the rough linen sheet. I screamed with fright. Behind him the bed maid set up a cater-wauling of pure terror, and behind him, too, brave Kat was hanging on his arm, beating his back and screaming in his ear, "My lord, my lord, for shame! Oh, my poor lady! Fie, my lord, leave off!"

I cowered in the corner weeping, trapped. Would it not ruin me if this got out? Betray me, destroy me—what more could he do? A flame of fury blossomed in my heart—how dare he, *dare he?* Yet beneath that sunburst of my rage, a newer, slower burn . . .

Kneeling up on the bed, roughly he took my hand and tore it from my bosom. What, would he strip me naked? But he gently raised my clenched hand to his lips and whispered softly, "Fear not, Princess. I only come to bid you a fair good morrow and swift return of health—no more, no less."

Kat was still in full cry. "Shame, sir, shame on you, to soil my lady's honesty and honour! Be off! You'll ruin her!"

"Who, I?"

Now at last he seemed to catch Kat's voice and the maid's howling. "Peace, you slut!" He silenced the girl with a fierce blow that brought blood to her mouth, then turned on Kat. "Hold your tongue, mistress!" he flashed out violently. "D'you dare to suggest a man may not call on a maid he now calls daughter? Fie on your foul imaginings! And beware!"

To see Kat's face now she was put so badly in the wrong! Within seconds she was abasing herself to him in humblest apology. "Forgive me, lord, and do not punish me! I meant nothing by what I said—only I must protect my lady—"

"And so must I, as her new father now!" he said magnanimously, turning her away to send her packing with a hard slap on her rump. As he did so, he turned his face towards me and, behind Kat's chastened and now-chastised rear, gave me a look so full of meaning that the burning fear and hate I felt before melted to a new fire—a fire now deep in neither heart nor head but moving down my body, through my breasts, within my belly, deeper, deep within . . .

And he was to turn the flame higher. For "father" or no father to Kat's face (and now she was again in love with him), in secret talk he wooed me once again, and once again I listened. All through that breathless spring, as the blossoms drifted like sweet flakes of snow along the river walk, he laid siege to my heart. And as summer ripened into a rare autumn, then dwindled to December, ruthlessly, patiently, one by one he breached all my defences.

Judge me, but blame me not—unless you heard him, saw him—loved him —as I did . . .

"My marriage is one of convenience only!" he urged me. "I married her to be near you, my true heart's mistress!"

Trust me, he said, as men have ever done. And as all women do, I trusted.

He serviced the Queen's body, he promised me, only as man was bound to serve his wife, and took no pleasure in it.

And yes, I did believe him—would not you?

He might take no pleasure from their amours, but she did, as all around could see. She blossomed now from nightly cultivation—daywork too, for she was often seen all flushed and drowsy with dilated eyes at noon, at forenoon and after noontide too. She clung to him as tenderly as a child; she could not bear to have him leave her side.

Yet he still had his way in everything. That day was the first of many a dawn "prank," as he called it, when he would invade my chamber and romp, and roar, and play the tiger, all the while playing a deadlier game. To set aside suspicion, he even brought the Queen into my chamber, to tease and tickle me from time to time. All was but fun, he claimed, and she believed him. Yet he knew it crazed me with excitement every night I went to bed, wondering if he would come the next day or not.

We locked the door against him, but he had access to all Katherine's keys. I filled my bed with maids, though I hated the smelly creatures being so near to me. He simply plucked them naked from the sheets and tossed them right and left, howling and screaming, till he had me alone, then kissed my hand and went away. Then came Kat, fully clothed, to sleep at my bed's foot—at which he bade her hop and leave the room or he would strip her too, like a plucked chicken! And hop she did . . .

Only by rising while it was yet dark could I forestall him. Then he would descend bare-legged and naked beneath his nightgown to find me at my prayers, the very image of virginity. Then he would swear and scowl and stalk about, and go away at last in an ill humour—until the next time . . .

Yet amidst all this roughest of rough wooing, still he called me "Princess," and so treated me too, whether naked and cowering in my bed sheets or in the full Court with our people all around.

Yet still he worked on me with looks and words, bold jests and soft suggestions, till I was as nervous as a filly foal. In Court I kept my countenance and was cold and haughty to his face. But in my lodgings when he came to call, I knew that all my people saw the blush his name brought to my cheek as soon as my usher Vine's staff struck the floor with the cry "My Lord Admiral to wait upon Your La'ship!"

And as he worked his way into my mind, so he did the same to my body— from that first most intimate caressing of my hand to a campaign of conquest, planned as soldiers plan the capture of a city, quarter by quarter, and then street by street, until they take the prize. We were not much alone, for much as Kat loved him, she loved me more, and even when sent packing, would return at once, for she knew she must preserve my good name at all costs. But as that year went by, the moments came when her guard was relaxed, when he distracted her, or I did too, such was his hold on me. Then would he smile like fatal Lucifer and touch my hand, my hair, my sleeve close to my breast, even till my lacing choked me and my ruff stifled my throat—so little does it take to stir a virgin's blood, as he well knew . . .

The old year turned, and found us at his castle, the ancient seat of Sudeley, wrapped in the hollow of an English shire. There he set up for Katherine her own Court of royal splendour, with fifty waiting gentlewomen for her, and a hundred ladies-in-waiting and two hundred men besides to wait on her, and him.

Only the most devout, though, could be found at daily morning Mass in the Queen's Chapel. These January mornings every flagstone on the floor glistened white with hoarfrost, it was so cold—even within the house. But Jane and her "learned virgins" never missed, and they were now firm in favour for their piety. And I, too, was among them as a rule, atoning for the bed romps with my lord by praying hard at his wife's devotions. On the sixth day of January came the feast we call Epiphany. Katherine went first to take the bread and wine, and as she knelt before the altar, with a soundless cry she fainted dead away.

"The Queen! Send for my lord! A doctor! Oh, dear God, spare us the Queen!"

A mortal terror now seized every soul. For as the Queen languished, within a week sickness had gripped the house. First to fall were half a dozen servants, of which three soon sweated their way to meet their Maker. My lord dispersed the household, those who had not fled, all but a handful needed to make fires, bear water and prepare our food. And we all kept our quarters, where we tried to live as if Death were not knocking at our door.

All suffered, each alone, in his own way. Kat, Richard, Chertsey, and old Francis too, faced it out stoutly, daring Death to touch them. Parry waxed grim and Welsh, muttering in corners, prattling of charms and amulets, sharks' teeth, weasels' privates and rabbits' feet, all save the last in poor supply in Gloucestershire in the dead heart of winter.

Of all my people, Grindal felt it most, his keen imagination feeding him with thoughts of death. His tall lean frame grew leaner, his pale face more waxen by the day as he prayed and fasted and encouraged me in our joint studies with a renewed devotion. One afternoon, about a week after the Queen's first illness, he laid down his Plato and begged leave to try again tomorrow: "My dull brain will not serve me today, I crave Your Highness's pardon."

"Tomorrow, then, good master"—for in truth, all through that year I gladly slipped my studies to think and dream of *him* . . .

So do our dreams bleed our true lives of reality. I never saw my dearest Grindal go, made no farewell beyond that brief good-bye. No sun saw the tomorrow that he spoke of, and the hand that thundered at my door that next dawn was not Grindal's but my lord's: who came in on me like an angel, yes, in his man's beauty, but with death in his face, darkness in his eyes, all deadly in his pallor.

"Leave us!"

His harsh command sent them all packing. I leaped up from my toilet, my unbound hair tumbling around the shoulders of my nightgown. The smell of death was on him; I could tell he bore the worst of tidings.

Why were we alone? I wanted Kat, I—

"Madam, prepare yourself."

I gripped the table. He was taut as a bowstring, and I trembled too. Then his voice faltered. "Lady, if I could but spare you this sorrow—"

I could scarce whisper. "Sir, is it the Queen?"

His eyes flared with alarm. "The Queen? No, God forbid! Good Master Grindal last night laid him down and never rose again. His body sleeps below, his soul is with God."

My heart was drowned in sorrow. Tears dissolved my eyes; I could not speak. Through my soul's rainfall I saw nothing till I felt him very close, smelt his man's musky nearness. His doublet brushed my face. One strong arm bore me up about my waist, the other circled my shoulders as his hand cradled my head. His fingers smoothed my hair, my forehead, then my weeping eyes . . .

His hand beneath my chin turned my face upwards. Through my tears I saw the face I loved descending on mine and—half in grief, half in joy —surrendered to him.

XX

So we were lovers: on that day my maidhood ended.

Not that he took my jewel, by no means: no man was ever more circumspect, no Lord High Admiral subtler in circumnavigation. But as I felt his fingers fluttering at my neck, into my bodice, down over my breasts, as I hung panting on his arm, choking on his nearness, drowning in his deep kisses, then I lost my soul's purity and knew myself a woman.

How does that wretched snatch of love verse go? "I freeze, I burn, and in love's height I die"?

I cannot now recall it.

Freezing and burning, though, I still recall as though it were yesterday— and to my precious bane, I feel it still today. He was the first, though, to wake my body to those dear delights, and he merited my maid love just for that—for all his spotted soul . . .

And Katherine, what of her while he and I played on the virginals? She was not sick, she lay not at death's door! Her malady was of the kind all women catch who lie down with a man.

Cranmer, the good Archbishop, was proved a prophet now for the words he spoke the day she married my father. "Yet may a young man's love be what is needed," said kind Cranmer then, and he spoke truth. My father was not that man, but her next husband was. Within a week of her first falling-sickness, Madam the Queen was greening in the morning and calling in midwives to divine the blueness of her breasts. Yet it needed no divination to wait out the course of nature, to show for certain she was now with child.

Her joy then was so piercing I could scarcely look at her without a pang of fury. Not that I envied her at all herself—her big body, never lithe or fair, now bloated and ungainly, her hair and skin grey and staring, as the child within took all her goodness. But in spite of it all, she was radiant as never before, transfigured like a saint.

Was it for this that he turned from her bed and sought my company? Not for pure lechery, for I was virgin still—and there were whores a-plenty round any Court back then. Rather, he had to have one female soul in which he still was king, one whose heart would always race at his approach, whose day would pass in thoughts of him and only him, while Katherine day by day grew closer to her infant, and her God.

And I? How could I so deceive her?

How could I not?

For I could no more call my soul my own. My lord's spell over me made my body his even as my mind said "No!" Suddenly I saw a new reflection of myself in the bright flattery of his silver tongue: lips like coral, hair not hair but filaments of gold, eyes not stars but constellations. And with that skill in women that was his greatest talent, he found my weakest point and lauded up my mind till he had softened it to his own will and pleasure.

And I was never happier.

Nor did he feed me only love talk, but would speak of statecraft to me, flattering my wit and judgment. Then I saw the envy in his heart that had grown as the Lord Protector grew in power. "What think you, Princess, of these Scottish wars my brother needs must make?" he would say angrily, drumming his fingers on his sword hilt as he spoke. "Your father had a better policy when he betrothed your brother to their Queen of Scots, the infant Mary. Now my lord brother harries them so hard they will marry her to the Devil himself sooner than our young King!"

"You will not go to war?" I demanded, much alarmed.

"Fear not!" He laughed in anger. "My dear brother holds me back here at home!"

"He has a care for you, then, and does not wish to lose you."

Another savage laugh. "My brother? Sure I think my brother is wondrous hot in care of every man save me! He rules the King; he rules *as* King; what cares he for the rest?"

At other times, late in the evening when the lights burned low and all except we and a few sleepy servants were in bed, his grief would burst out plain. "Why am I Jacob to his Esau, born to second place? Hear me, Princess, guard your inheritance and your birthright! Let no man make you second to his will!"

I stand in the line of inheritance? This was the first time I dared think the unthinkable: that a woman might inherit, a woman might rule. So he showed me my own true prospects, through the glass of his false hopes. For he himself was now in line for nothing, and he felt his honours nothing, despising what he had. Fretting in idleness, fooling with me, his pride grew

*with his frustration—and I fed that pride with my adoring, for I was a
princess of the blood, the youngest, fairest, cleverest of them all, and I
adored him, even to distraction . . .*

*What word of Edward, say you? What of Mary, Robin, Cecil, all the
people of my world?*

*Why, nothing of them, for they ceased to be. Only when there was talk of a
new tutor for me did I bestir myself to choose one dear to my poor Grindal
as his successor, in honour of his memory. Yet I was in no hurry to resume
my bookwork. For all that time, I lived only for my lord: for the thought of
him, the touch, the hope of him, and then the doom of him.*

*After my mother's fate, this was the second of my life's great lessons,
though it was not as yet even halfway through. But when I think how nearly I
threw my maidenhood, my throne, my life and all away, by putting myself
into those careless hands . . .*

*Yet still the thought of his long sinewy hands, so rough and brown and
hard as they then were, that white scar on the knuckles of his sword fist—
and still I feel that fatal stir that first he taught me to feel.*

And all that time we were lovers then, from Grindal's death until that
Whitsuntide. Our trysts were few and short, but each occasion was a feast
to feed on till our next encounter. Now my eyes, my lips, my breasts,
were his, my body all his, to the waist at least. Did I care nothing for
maiden modesty, for my good name, for the sin of fornication? Truly, no:
love had outrun them all. If he had ever wanted to storm the citadel, he
would have found all my defences down and all the populace imploring
him within!

Yet still I made great play of holding him off and aping the coquette,
for I knew even then not to seem easy, not to seem won. And he would
swear that between a pregnant wife and a cold mistress, a poor wretch
could go hang until his manhood rotted and dropped off! I took great
glee at that, for it pleased me hugely that he was not Katherine's now.

I knew he spoke the truth: they could not have coupled, not as she was.
Some breeding women carry all behind, spreading like brood mares in
the rump. Katherine to her discomfort bore all before, and was now so
vilely fat and splayed that she could hardly walk. And though all promised her a goodly boy from the child's great size, it made her weak and
tearful, even more clinging to my lord than before.

And thereby hangs the thread that ravelled out our tale, and cut that
tangled web, and broke—and saved—my foolish virgin's heart.

One summer morning when the sun was hot at only ten o'clock, I sent
Vine to tell my lord I would walk in the gallery. It was a favourite meeting place, for while our people waited at the door, we could stalk that
fair, well-lighted space like gods above the petty earth below, looking

down over the green sweep of the park from the great mullioned windows. And at end of the long gallery was a small oriel where the window jutted out over the moat beneath: there we would sit and talk, and steal our embraces alone and unseen.

He never looked more handsome, his face flushed from a dawn ride, his fair skin already browning in the hot May sun. His eyes were full of love, his mouth spoke love, his hands reaching for mine were love, all love. The year's long mourning over, he had blossomed that day in velvet green and gold—*green! I should have known!—the true colour of betrayal, the very hue of perfidy!*

Stop—do not hurry me—my heart, my heart . . .

Yet the hardest tale is always best told short.

He came where I awaited him within the sun-shot alcove—and with no word of greeting, seized my shoulders and bound me to his chest. I threw my arms about his neck and pressed my lips to his for my soul's food; and all was swooning, surging, rushing, roaring then, as it always was in his embrace . . .

Had I been listening I might have heard—no sound, but a great silence from the gallery door—and would have known that when ten or fifteen servants, ladies, gentlemen, usually chattering as they hung about the doorway, were in an instant silent, something was amiss. But all I knew was the sudden tread of a not-so-light foot now on the oaken floor, and the brushing of the hem of a loose gown suddenly upon us—

Then Katherine's voice—*yet not her voice*: "My lord? Dear Jesus, what—? My lord? My lord!"

She stumbled and half fell, clutching the curtain by the alcove and sliding to her knees. Behind her at the doorway I could see Kat, Parry, Vine and my lord's men and mine, frozen in a tableau of absurdity, terror in every feature.

I could not look at her. I reached out for my lord. But with a violent motion he shook me off.

"Sweet wife!" he mouthed in an ecstasy of passion. "Thank God you've come to save me from this girl! She lured me here against my will, in her rash wantonness! God in his goodness has brought you here!"

And throwing himself upon his knees before her, he wept like a crocodile until she wept too. Then throwing her arms about his neck, she thanked God for such a lord and such a man, who loved her and his honour better than all young temptresses and their lusts of the flesh.

XXI

Yet Katherine was a lady still—and more, a queen. Her only word to me was "Go to your chamber—I will speak to you by and by." When "by and by" came and she sent for me, I had no wish to speak, for what was there to say? On her daybed, shifting and twisting beneath her dreadful belly, she watched me kneel but did not bid me rise.

"A time upon your knees," she told me sombrely, "will be much-needed medicine for your soul. My lord swears on the Blessed Virgin's grave there was no more between you than I saw. But I fear the heat of your young blood and mean to take it down."

Take down my blood? When hers had been hot enough for the same man? I bowed my head and cursed her for a saintly hypocrite. But not as much as I was cursing him—cursing myself . . .

"I will pray God to forgive you," she went on. "I know I ought to think no ill of any girl who could not help but love a lord like mine, however little he encouraged you." I studied the great Bible by her bed, breathed in the chamber scent of juniper and pondered on how women will believe lying men.

Katherine's large empty eyes came to rest on my face. "My lord makes one confession," she said with a great coldness. *Oh, God, what now—?* "The blood of Anne Boleyn runs in your veins, as my lord now reminds me—bad blood: loose blood. He says he should have taken account of the stock from which you spring."

Oh, fine! Oh, noble, manly dealing, to dig up my dead mother, to brand me a whore!

Was this the man I loved?

Yes, this was he.

But Katherine was still speaking. "And my lord tells me more—that once before, he saw you in the gallery in the arms of another man."

My rage spilled from me. *"Another* man? Who? There is no 'other man!' No men but Grindal and my lord your husband ever came near me!"

She waved a weary hand. "Who knows? But my lord counsels well.

You are in danger here, both from your own blood and the temptation that he seems to be for you."

Her swollen left hand came to rest beside her swollen thigh. Her wedding ring—*his* wedding ring—bit deep into the flesh, as deep as his betrayal cut my heart.

He scorns me and my mother, defames me through his teeth about "another man." Just as he lied when he swore he was mine, then married her.

But third time pays for all, the proverb says. Twice I have trusted him, and twice been betrayed. The cock has crowed its last: no man from now on ever will deny me.

Katherine's voice was reaching me as through a mist. "You will recall the late King's gentleman, Sir Anthony Denny? A grave and discreet man, one wedded to your family and its good name. I have directed letters to his house by Cheshunt: he and his lady will give you welcome."

We left at once, no leave-taking allowed. At the last, though, she wept and clung to me, refusing to say good-bye. I made my adieus with a mouth of sawdust and eyes filled with sand.

We came to Cheshunt, deep in a woodland valley, as the last light faded from a day of June. A pewter sun swam low in wreaths of evening mist, and a bronze moon rising hung like a pagan mirror in the sky above the hills. As we arrived at the old stone manor, Sir Anthony was at the door with all his people, and from his deep reverence I could tell he knew nothing of what had happened. As he knelt with his lady beside my horse, taking off his hat to touch his forehead to my dusty stirrup, my sore heart dearly felt the respect of his welcome.

The next morning while the dew still shimmered on the fields, he called on me. Still the same small dark silent man I knew from the King's Privy Chamber, soft-padding in his walk, soft in his voice and manner. But his little eyes were chips of pure bright understanding, and his calm air was that of undisguised authority. Would he remember that night at Whitehall when I had dined with the King, the last time I had seen my father alive? From the warm light in his face as he entered, I saw he did.

Again the formal greeting, kneeling before me. "My lady Princess, I am heartily sorry that the sickness in the Queen's House has enforced your flight to mine . . ."

Sickness—yes, well enough: for my lord was a disease, and I took the fever hard.

I looked around the low, cool, airy lodging, its rich hangings and well-furnished rooms fit for a reigning monarch, let alone a damsel in disgrace, and tried a smile. "We are all most grateful for your hospitality."

He rose and stepped towards me. "Madam, the joy is mine. Would it please Your Grace to walk within my gallery to view the paintings I have there?"

I stifled a harsh laugh. *Another gallery? After the last time?*

Yet he meant well. And what else was there to do? "As you wish, sir."

He led me from my lodgings through the Great Hall to the wide solar above. And there before me hung the portrait of a face I knew, though I had never seen it. Sunk between rounded velvet shoulders, it was the careworn image of a pale and thrifty pursekeeper, more like a small businessman or shopkeeper than that of a king—and King of England too.

"Your grandfather, Henry VII, king and warrior!" Such was Denny's tale. "For it was a man of destiny, Your Grace," he insisted, "who ventured against Richard the King, the usurping Duke of Gloucester, at Bosworth Field that day—who staked life and all to found your mighty line."

He waved up a servant, pressing wine and dainties on me, his sweets as welcome in my mouth as his words were balm to my soul.

"Then came your father, lady—what a man!" He drew me to the next bay, where sunlight flooded a larger than life-size portrait of my father, his trunk-like legs akimbo, his massive body and bull-necked head in its familiar plumed and moulded hat thrusting at the painted canopy above. In Denny's face, pride fought with sadness. "He brought us glory and magnificence, made England reckoned with throughout the world!" He sighed. "And now—" He broke off.

"And now, sir?" I prompted him.

He paused, and looked me in the eye. "You are your father's daughter, madam. As I was his, so am I yours, to use and to command."

What was he saying? "Sir?"

He stroked his clever mouth. "We may not quarrel with the will of God . . . or I would have bargained with the Almighty for one great favour: that the King your father had been spared a few more years. For until your brother can be wedded"—*and well bedded* was in both our minds—"to bring another prince into the world—until then—"

"I and my sister are the only heirs."

Now all old Denny's love and his concern made sense to me: he had served Harry, he wanted Harry's bairns and Harry's stock to rule in England —not the Lord Protector, nor any others not of the blood . . .

"Not you and your sister—but your sister and yourself, my dearest lady," he corrected gently. I felt a redness mantling my neck. Fool that I was—of course Mary came first! She always had, and always would; that was the way of things. "And thereby hangs a tale. England has no queens regnant, people say. And yet—after Edward, there are none but females: your sister Mary, then yourself, and afterwards your father's sister's line, your cousins Lady Jane and Catherine Grey. And even if we honour, as some say we should, the claim descending through his older sister Margaret Tudor, who married the King of Scotland—why, her only descendant, your cousin Mary of Scots, is another female, and most female, by all reports!"

See the fatal legacy of the Tudors, just as my lord had said—the weakness of the males! The boy children all died, the girls all lived . . .

"There is a son," Denny went on, "of that Scots Tudor line, the boy Henry Darnley. But he is of lesser blood, and a Catholic too—and only his mother, the ambitious Countess, ever thinks he could be King."

Darnley. Yes, I had seen him when his hard-faced mother brought him to Court, a lanky, smiling fair boy, Tudor at least in height and colouring.

A new fear came to me. "Is he now a pretender to the throne?"

Denny smiled. "No more than the other 'Prince' whose claim the dreamers play with. You have heard of Edward Courtenay, the last of the Plantagenets?"

Courtenay? The name came back to me from Kat's endless tales.

"The only surviving descendant of the House of York?" I asked.

He nodded. "His mother was the daughter of that great Edward they called the Fourth. He is only a child. But still his blood runs pure Plantagenet. And your father in his wisdom saw fit to keep him and his mother away from any mischief: they have been locked up for ten years in the Tower, as prisoners of state."

I shivered. What a price to pay for the sin of royal blood! Denny was staring at my father's picture again. "No, lady, as it stands, until God blesses us with another prince, only princesses now bear up the Tudor line. And you must carry it on. *With the right marriage!*"

Denny's eyes, his words, were urgent now. "Beware all wooers, lady—I might even say, beware all men! Cherish yourself as the Princess you are —refuse all advances! For they could bring our country's ruin with your own. They could also cost your life. For it is treason for any man to court you without the express permission of the King and Council—treason for you too, madam, to admit his suit."

Had my lord thought of this? He must have done! And if not, how carelessly was he risking my life and his own!

I could take no more. I begged the good Sir Anthony to excuse me and withdrew into my quarters. As I gained the sanctuary of my chamber, one thought gave me some comfort: until the last reminder of his wooing, I had not thought of my perfidious lord for all of half an hour.

It was a brief respite. All summer I was sick and suffering despite the best that Kat could do. The doctors came and went, but none dared name my disease. *Because for that sickness,* maladie d'amour, *the only*

*healer is Doctor Time, who works with killing slowness, and gives no cor-
dials for the pain.*

I knew I had to make my own attempts to raise myself from this bed of
nails, this endless, ceaseless round of *Why? Why, Lord? Why him—why
me?* One bright morning as my breakfast came, I sipped the warm milk,
chewed on a little bread and sent to seek out my new schoolmaster.

"Roger Ascham at your service, ma'am!" came the booming Yorkshire
bass as he entered the chamber. Like Grindal's, his grooming was of the
sketchiest, his uncombed hair cut like a cowherd's, his long scholar's
gown showing a green-black patina of antiquity. But against the careless
gilded peacocks of the Court, his appearance was the one that showed a
truly lordly disregard. Under a fustian cap his honest face, fierce questioning eyes and nose as snub as Socrates' had no truck with fashion or
favour: he was what he was, and showed it.

I held out my hand. "Master Ascham, I have sorely neglected my
books. Now you must be my taskmaster, and treat me with all strictness
when I lapse."

His thick black curls tousled still more as he shook his head furiously.
"Not I, madam, never! I am not one of your punishing pedants, your
domineering dominies, your wretched arse-warmers! True learning
comes not from suffering but from love!" His black eyes were shining in
his broad red English face. "I will show you the book—the books!—of
love, all those you loved before—your Cicero, Sallust, Aesop—and more
again. Look, lady, see here!" From deep within a dusty long black sleeve
he hauled up a battered text. " *'Quod petis, hic est,'* " he read with passion
in his rich brown voice. " 'What you seek is here,' says the poet Horace:
take it, madam, read!"

Startled, I took the book and held it close. "Here?" I turned the page.
In the furrows of the rich loamy Latin I could feel my feet on God's good
earth again, even catch the scent of spring. "Yes, master, you speak
truth."

Slowly, slowly then, as the seasons turned, I found the strength to take up
life again. I sent for Master Parry, my old treasurer. "Sir, when you next
go to London to see about my estate, beg the King that I may come to
him—or at least return to Hatfield, to my own home."

The good old greybeard puffed up with his mission like a turkey cock.
Importantly he rearranged his heavy gold chain of office as he took his
leave. "Madam, it is done!"

I returned to my books, and with them found some peace. Yet peace is
a shy bird, and a migrant too: she never stays for long.

It was a fair, fine fall that year, mild and golden. Harvest home came
early, and the church bells rang. A fat moon as red as Leicester cheese

smiled low over the empty fields, and all the barns and rickyards bulged
with God's blessings. All that summer I had made headway, step by step,
against his memory, as the wounded of love's wars struggle to walk again.
But my strength was not of the greatest—as I was to find . . .

I was reading in my closet when a manservant, an ugly, clubfooted
churl, came on me unannounced. Servants were hard to get deep in the
country: Sir Anthony Denny kept about him all sorts of crippled and ill-
favoured things we never would have had in royal service. I did not like
to have such men about me. I liked it even less when he pointed and
mumbled, "My master—in the gallery—"

Never had Denny sent like this before: always he came to me. I found
him in his favourite spot beside my father's portrait, perusing letters in a
packet, his face unreadable. His voice was very cold. "News from London, lady—perhaps as good as you would wish to hear."

My heart leaped. "Am I to go to Court? To keep Christmas there and
see the King?"

"Not that I hear of. But as a loyal subject as well as the King's sister,
you will rejoice to hear of plans for the King's happiness."

Yes, yes, say on!

He tapped the packet he held. "They speak of marriage for him."

"Edward? But he is still too young!"

"And not only for His Majesty the King."

Oh, God—what was he saying?

"Tell me, Your Grace." He leaned towards me like an inquisitor. "How
stands your disposition to be married?"

X X I I

Mine?

How stood my disposition to be married?

My gut contracted. "Very badly, sir. I never think of it." I felt my anger
stir. "And why does it concern you?"

He was very still. "It seems the Court rings with it: marriage is in the
air."

"Not mine, I do assure you!"

He seemed to disbelieve me. "Yet it is said at Court that a great marriage—of one you know, and know well—is in the making."

I laughed. "Well, who are to be the happy pair?"

"Madam, who but my lord of Sudeley, Baron Seymour, and his chosen bride?"

So I learned Katherine was dead, that her child had cost her life. Her pains came on her as her quickening had, at early-morning Mass. For days and nights she laboured, sweating blood and her life's liquor, her old body not able for the work it had to do. And when the "great boy" she was promised made his appearance, he proved—like me, like sister Mary, like Mary of the Scots, like cousin Jane and all the little Greys—no more than an unwanted daughter after all. They named her Mary. Three days later Queen and child were dead.

God is just, if not always kind. Katherine died festering of childbed fever, like my grandmother Elizabeth of York, like Edward's mother Jane, like so many women who lie down with a man and find his name is Death. The purple in her blood made her wits wander as the fever raged. But in her final moments, my lord Tom (my lord, her lord, any woman's lord and yet his own lord always) asked her to say that he had been a good husband to her. And gathering all her forces for her last words on this earth, she nailed her eyes on him and, rattling in her throat, spat out "No!"—for he had given her many cruel hurts! And though he tried to force her to recant, she would not take it back.

So she died, and he lived—for like all toms, he had nine lives.

And now he would be married.

Did I convince Denny as I strove to show no more than a passing interest? "So my lord of Sudely thinks to marry again?"

Denny's eyes never left mine. "Indeed he does. Nay, he plans a royal wedding! He has bought the wardship of your cousin Jane—"

Jane? He would not marry her, she has no money!

"And it is said he'll marry her—"

No! It must not be! Not Jane!

"—to your dear brother, to the King your brother. So he has promised her father, who has given him two thousand pounds to do it."

Edward and Jane? What a neat knot that would be! Two Tudors, and two afire for the New Faith! Why did I not foresee this? But what of him?

"And my lord himself? Who does his eye light on?" I asked.

Who could it be? He once made play for sister Mary, it was said. And the old Princess of Cleves was still alive, with all her moneybags. And there were other heiresses too, young ladies who held half the North, or great estates in Wales or Ireland—which would he choose?

"My lord?" said Denny strangely. "Nay, madam, the game they play at court is 'Find the Lady.' "

We stood there stiffly, my breath coming shorter and shorter as my fear rose. Why was he treating me like this? Where was the reverence, the regard, he had always showed before? "Sir Anthony—*what do you mean?*"

"These are dangerous times." *Where was he leading now?* Again he tapped his paper. "The news I have here—strange news, lady."

"What news?" My voice was far too high.

"That you are the lady, that you are to be married."

"*Married?* This is sheer nonsense! What, without my knowledge or consent?"

He spread his hands.

"So then, to whom?"

"Madam, who but to the Lord High Admiral—the Protector's brother, my lord of Sudeley?"

Who indeed?

My lord again.

He had more lives than a tomcat to menace mine.

I put all the force I had behind a furious laugh. "I marry the Lord Admiral? Mere London news—which has not reached the bride-to-be at all!"

Denny surveyed me shrewdly. "Yet he will marry—and he would think you, Princess, of all women the most fit to take his late Queen's place."

"I—marry him? I'd sooner marry a . . . a . . ." I took hold of my voice. "And will he, nill he, his will does not count! My father's will determines what I must do."

At last a glimmer of warmth broke through Denny's cold shell. "Forgive me, lady. But the word, they say, is all over the Court. And after we had spoken of the need you have to guard your name and situation—I feared you had been"—he paused delicately—"induced by that same lord—"

Say "seduced," man, if that is what you mean!

"—to forget your own position—the King's will—"

I met his eye. "I know it—and the price for all who break it."

"Yea, madam—death! For all! No less than death!"

And what man is worth death?

Now I learned of Katherine's death from my lord's own brazen lips, in fulsome missives dwelling on his grief. He begged me pray for him in his hour of need. It was as if the way we were had never been.

And another memory just as short was to be found nearer home. Kat came upon me as I lay in bed, her pigeon bosom heaving, her lips urgently forming "Madam, great news!" I had not seen her like this since

. . . since . . . Oh, Almighty God! One man alone could bring that bloom up to her cheek.

She was like a child brimming with secrets. "Madam, I hear today that since the Queen's death not a one of all her lords and ladies, maids and men, has been laid off. 'Tis proof, they say, that my lord Tom will marry a lady of royal rank, one who will keep the same state as his Queen." Kat's whole body was trembling. "And lady, it could be, at long last! He is free again, he could be yours now! Think of it, madam!"

Think of it? I could not bear it! "Kat, bethink yourself! Have you forgotten his treachery—did that never happen?"

"Oh, my lady!" Her eyes were full of tears. *"What else could my lord do?"*

She wept for *him!* My fury knew no bounds. I screamed with rage and drove her from the room. The doctor and the apothecary from the village were both summoned to succour the fit that followed. But Kat knew what had provoked it and did not speak again. And though I was sick, sick to vomiting for days on end, suddenly I knew myself well again.

For I was free of him, free now of all taint of that first foolish love, that greed for touch and kisses, that fine fever felt in the blood, and felt along the heart, and felt most strongly deep within a woman's softest and most secret parts.

I knew not how it went—his wife died of her fever, and I almost of mine —but I survived my crisis and the malady burned out. Oh, I writhed in pain to lose him, and to lose him in that way. Anne Askewe had her fire and I had mine, and neither was deserving. But thanks be God, gone that love one day was, and gone indeed—neither his memory nor his handwriting on a letter, nor even his scent of musk upon the parchment, could move me at all.

"Your Royal Grace!"

Master Parry fell upon me as I paced the park. The grounds at Cheshunt lay snug in their valley, the broad walks round the house shaded by beech and oak even in leafless December. As Parry kissed my hand, I felt him trembling. "Well, sir, what is your news? Do we go to Court?"

His hands plucked at his chain of office, and he shook his head. "Madam, I did all I could! But the Lord Protector—"

"Would not have it so." *So it was true, as I feared: Edward had no power. The Lord Protector ruled.* "And what of Hatfield?"

"You have the Council's leave to return whenever you choose."

Some gain, then. Back in my own house I could begin to be my own woman again. Thanking Parry, I bowed and turned to go.

But speech burst from him. "The Lord Protector's brother, madam, my lord Sudeley—"

May God damn him!

"—sent a word for your ear. He bids me say that he offers you his services in the settlement of the lands your father left you. For some, it seems, are next to lands of his, and more of them might be so—"

"What are you talking about?"

Parry pressed on. "My lord suggests that your two estates, lying together, could best be run as one. It is a fine offer coming from the Lord Protector's brother—such a great and mighty gentleman in the land . . ." He was beaming with delight now. "And might mean further good news for you—great news even!"

So my lord had wrought upon Parry as well! Was there no limit to his spellbinding?

I lashed out in rage. "My lord has taken a most kind interest in my legacy! He could not do more unless he planned to join our lands together!"

"And if he did, my lady—if he found the way to join you both together as man and wife—how would Your Highness take it?"

After all this, he still believed that I could marry him?

Now like a lightning bolt in a black sky, I saw it all. First he would marry Edward to his ward Jane, then he would twitch the chain that he must think still held me and marry me too. Then as the owner of the boy King's wife and husband of his sister, he would have the power he hungered for in his hand. And thus he would be revenged upon his brother, whom I knew he hated more than he could ever love a hundred foolish virgins such as me.

Truly, proud Tom lacked none of his old nerve, sending my own man to woo me! Parry had been mad even to listen to such stuff. I burned, I shivered. Some poor ghost was walking on my grave. The sooner this was dealt with . . . for the very thought of it ran death rings round us all!

I fixed my eyes on Parry's beaming face. "Sir, this is dangerous meddling, and could bring danger on us all! For both King and Council now must know of and approve all such approaches, even the slightest murmur, on pain of death! I will not hear of this—now, or ever!"

I clapped my hands to call up a servant. Parry's eyes, like rabbits', quivered their dismay. He had meant no evil to me: indeed, the opposite. I smiled him my forgiveness. "If we may go to Hatfield, let us do it! I have a woman's longing to be in my home for Christmas! See to it!" He scrambled to obey. "And there we'll be as merry as the merriest at Court —the cheer we'll keep will make the very crickets on the hearth bless the name of Elizabeth!"

So we left Cheshunt as we had arrived, in haste, but in much better spirits. I ordered Parry to write as coldly to my lord as his welling Welsh heart could manage, to rebuff all his suggestions. The same icy resistance I displayed to my host Sir Anthony, begging he would convey my disdain of this unwelcome offer to all his friends at Court. We parted on the fondest terms of love and admiration, and I had no doubt that I had put an end to my lord's outrageous suit.

No doubt in my mind: yet who could rule his?

How dared he come at me again like this? I neither knew nor cared. My heart was set on Hatfield now, and I could not wait to see my house again.

The December days were short—it was no month to travel in, when even the boldest rooks kept to their roosts. But after such an autumn, the ways were dry and we made rare good going. All our hearts longed for home, even the mules, it seemed, pulling hard towards the west, where Hatfield lay. And as we paced, with Kat beside me, Parry just behind, my James, my Richard, Chertsey, Vine and all my people round me now, I felt myself more myself again than I had been since before my father died.

Hatfield was like a beloved returned from a long voyage, familiar yet strange, and even more beautiful than I remembered it. How joyfully did I play house that Yuletide!

On Twelfth Night, the last day of all the festivities, when at last Kat tucked me up and stole out of the room in the thin light of a pale sickle moon, I thought myself as happy as a girl had any right to be. I thought of my lost lords, of Surrey and of Seymour, without grief or rancour and resolved in this New Year to make a fresh start and put it all behind me. Even the death of Katherine did not bring the tears it always had: I thought of her now seated in all bliss beside the Virgin, tending the Christ Child in His heavenly manger, serene in motherhood for all eternity. And in that vision I slipped into sleep and dreamed of nothing but white peace and sheer contentment.

So I learned another of life's lessons, that the times of greatest peace should warn us to be most on our guard.

That January made a year since Grindal died. I had not seen my lord since Whitsuntide, a good six months and more. Less and less now did I think of him. Yet still he thought of me—and to no good purpose.

The year having turned, the days were growing longer. Although it was still January, that fatal morning dawned as bright and clear as spring. My heart was light, and my wits never sharper. My lessons sped by till my tutor Ascham fell back chuckling and declared, "Madam, no more today! You run me to the ground!" After he left I sat on in the schoolroom, lost in the history we had started on. At last the hunger in my belly could no longer be ignored. I wanted something light—just cheese and bread—so I could read till darkness drowned the west. I raised my head. "Who's there?"

A moppet from below stairs popped her head in and made her curtsey. "Here, madam."

"Send for my women or for Mistress Kat—to order up my dinner."

Off she scurried with a servile bob as I took up my book. How long I read I know not, but all at once I saw the shadows on the wall. Time had gone by again, and no one had come to me. I lifted up my voice in some unease. "Who's there?"

To call out into silence is to feel a fool—and worse. A creeping fear began to gnaw me. "Let me have service here, I command service—!"

Yet silence still. Now I knew fear indeed and, standing up, found my legs trembling. Not since my birth had I been unattended. Where were my ladies, where the maids, where all my men, where Kat? Suddenly at the door there stood the maid. I could scarce make out her mumbled, choking cry: "Madam, Mis' Kat is gone—she can't be found!"

I gripped my chair. "What are you saying? How can she be lost?"

"Not lost, mum—taken! Taken now, today!"

"Taken, you idiot? Who has taken her?"

Terror had made her wits wander: she could hardly speak. "Them, ma'm . . . below . . . all of them . . . when they came . . . now . . . here . . . today—"

I slapped her face. "Speak, fool. Who has come, and why? Why should they take my mistress? Speak, or you'll be whipped!"

I thought to bring her to her senses, but she fell into hysterics on the floor, clutching my skirt as if she were a natural. I was frantic. Kicking free, I made for the door. On the threshold I was halted by the sound of running feet.

In a great household no one ever runs. It means the breakdown of all order: it spells chaos, calamity. My nerves were cracking.

Moments later and a heavy figure burst into my view. Parry? Parry it was! But never as I'd seen her, face all of wax and sweating with wild fear, her hair about her ears, her skirt held up in one hand so that she could run, the other grasping—what? A loose chain of heavy, clanking gold?

Her breath came heaving, sobbing, like a broken horse at slaughter. But behind her came another, deeper sound, heavier and deadlier yet, the sound of men—

"Madam—my lady—oh, God, save us all!"

She almost threw the gold object in my hands. My grasp knew it quicker than my eyes: it was a chain of office—the chain of Master Parry.

"Madam, they've taken him—and Mistress Kat—and now they've come for—"

For me.

"For you, my lady Princess."

A man it was who spoke. I saw him enter by the door, but hardly recognized him as the Denny I'd known. Attended by a dozen armed men, whose tramp had been the sound my ears had caught, he stepped into the room like a black angel bent on punishment. His face was bleak as the far reaches of a frozen hell. He struck such fear in me I could scarce stand, I could not hold my knees from violent trembling. I tried to speak. "Why, sir, what is this? What—?"

"Speak not to me, madam, for I may not hear." He held up a scroll. "Lady Elizabeth, I am ordered by the Council of our lord and King Edward VI to seize upon you and your minions. By the power vested in me, I do arrest you now on charge of highest treason."

XXIII

A thin scream bubbled in my throat and died. I saw the face of death—mine, Kat's and Master Parry's. What had I done? I knew not. Yet I felt guilty as sin, as hell, as death itself.

Now came the scream again, and this time it found its way out of my choking throat. "No! I am innocent! How can I be charged with what I have not done?"

He smiled. Never had I seen open contempt in any face before. "Thus say all traitors, lady, all criminals and guilty ones. Yet have your say. Now you are charged, you may speak your fill. Indeed, you must: for I am here to get the truth of this—upon my life—*or yours.*"

More than the threat, his scorn stung like a scorpion. How had I lost his regard? The last time I had seen him, he had knelt and kissed my hand. Now the gaze I saw was as cold as that of any judge dealing out death. I saw the faces of the men behind, some flickering with curiosity or pity, most dull and brutal like the barnyard beasts. I saw their weapons, swords and pikes, all turned, it seemed, towards me. I saw myself at bay, heard my low whimperings, felt my gut turn to water, tasted the green bile of dread inside my mouth. My knees were giving way. The pale sun dying on the wall behind melted like mist before my failing eyes.

Yet I must not faint! That would seem proof of guilt. I clutched the nearest chair. "Sir Anthony—"

He gave a soft command. The armed men fell back, shuffling and clattering their way out of the room. Parry was hauled away, and then the maid, both weeping piteously, but Sir Anthony had eyes only for me. He bowed. "Be seated, madam."

I stumbled into the chair. He struck at once. "I did not think to see you of all ladies in such a plight."

"What plight? What have I done?"

"You have deceived me, lady."

"I? No!"

"You gave me your assurance at Cheshunt that you knew the late King's will—that you would never marry except with the full knowledge and consent of King and Council—"

"So I do!—and have not—"

"No?" He smiled a mirthless smile. "You deny it, then?"

I could no longer contain my hopeless tears. "Deny what? How can I deny charges I do not know?" He was playing with me, torturing me to break me down, I knew that. But I did not know how to stand against him. I forced myself to speak. "I have done nothing wrong."

"You say so? Sadly for you, your paramour—husband-to-be, I should say—my lord Sudeley tells us otherwise."

O my prophetic heart! My evil genius, my dark lord and demon lover, come to drag me down! What hope now? What chance?

A babble of denials rose in my throat and fought for utterance through my welling tears. "He? No! No, never—if he says so, he lies. Oh, God, God be with me—!"

Did God hear me? For suddenly I seemed to hear, *Speak not, say nothing, weep till you collect yourself or you will weave your death warrant out of your own mouth . . . Silence is golden, pay him in that coin . . .*

And so I wept and would not be consoled. Nor bullied, nor entreated, though he tried all three by turns. Around and round he went, with questions, questions, tormenting me yet telling me nothing, baiting me till I was drowned in tears, yet still I wept. If all I had were women's weapons, I would hide behind my waterdrops till nightfall came, and all night too, sooner than betray myself. Or *him*, Lord Tom, the author of my downfall, for all his wicked folly—or Kat or Parry or anyone at all.

It took all day, a day of tears and fasting—not so much as a glass of water did my jailor allow to pass my lips—but at last in a cold fury Sir Anthony owned himself beaten and abandoned all his questions.

Back in my chamber, by the light by one poor candle, attended only by one maid, a tongue-tied dimwit from the village I had never seen before, I struggled to make sense of what I knew.

It centred on my lord, that much was clear. He must have committed some offence, been arrested and interrogated, and then told the powers-that-be that he and I had planned to marry—or even that we now were married, man and wife.

I ran with cold sweat, even in my bed. If he had said that, and if they believed him, then he and I were now as good as dead! And even if they thought I had agreed to it without their say-so, that was my death warrant too! Oh, he was Death, his name was Death, no doubt about it! Like Katherine his wife, like every foolish woman that ever was, I had lain down with one whose name was Death, who now came for the maiden!

Yet so it was, the one who had endangered me came to my rescue—the lord who put me in this plight was he who saved me. At the darkest hour, when all around was black, my chamber black, my bed within its hangings black as inside a tomb, I heard my lord of Seymour's voice, clear as a bell inside my aching head. *Think, madam, think!* I seemed to hear him say, just as he always had. *Think with your man's mind, sharp as any razor, not with your wandering womb full of idle vapors. Think now! Think Think! THINK!*

And think I did. *This is a game of wits, I urged myself, and only that will save you—not your innocence (for Anne Boleyn was innocent!) but your skill in self-defence and counterwarfare too.* The first raw light of dawn came stealing through my window. If only I could think . . .

Waiting itself is torture, as they know whose work it is to torture. From early-morning half-light before seven o'clock, when I was ready, I waited all day long. The forenoon came and went, and brought no food for me, though I sent three times to demand it. Mid-afternoon the first candles appeared, and still the summons did not come. My sufferings began again as I sat there, and once again I wept.

Yet when at last they came, I had regained a measure of control. Head high, I left my chamber when commanded by the Captain of the Guard, a stocky, neat-made man whose ruddy face hinted a sympathy he dared not show as we marched downstairs. What I saw as we went gave me no comfort. The house was full of soldiers, tramping men-at-arms, coming and going just as they pleased. Not a maid or man of mine was to be seen. What was the reason Hatfield had been garrisoned like this?

Now with these men about, the house stank. No longer sweetened with applewood fires and my chamber fragrance of English rose, it was rank with droppings on the floor, the smell of horse-worn leather and the reek of soldiers' bodies. My gorge rose as they closed tightly round me—as if I would even think of trying to run from them! Still I tried to show some spirit as I was thrust into the small withdrawing chamber on the ground floor. "Tell Sir Anthony I am ready to receive him. And send for Mistress Kat—I have need of her."

But my control was fragile, and the "that's as may be" smirk that passed across the captain's face destroyed me quite. Behind me I could hear the door clang shut. I heaved with anxiety. Two paces brought me to the window: out there in the glimmering dusk, even the rats were free, while I was shut up like an erring dog. The foolish tears threatened to rise again. I buried my cold face within my hands, stiffened my spine and held my shoulders down.

"You are true mistress of yourself, my lady."

I had not heard him enter, and I did not know the voice. Slowly I turned, stifling a new fear.

Before me stood a man of middle years and more than middle height, plainly but richly dressed, and with the air of one accustomed to command. He wore no hat or cloak, and from the documents on the table and the papers in his hand, he was established here and quite at home. Yet in his narrow face and raven's eyes there was an air of hungry sharpness that gave a thrill of terror. He was a bird of prey, a carrion kisser who would tear live flesh, and I was his next victim—all this I felt in the first second we met.

He saw this, and it pleased him, I could tell. With a crooked smile he drew up a chair and bowed me to it. "Sir Robert Tyrrwhit, sent here by the Council, and at your service, lady."

At mine? I braced myself against the hard ebony of the chairback, plaited my fingers in my lap to stop them quivering, and did not speak.

"Sir Anthony is gone: you are now in my charge," he resumed pleasantly enough. I took some satisfaction in hearing of his predecessor's defeat. It was not hard to work out why Sir Anthony had been sent away. It would be known that he and I had talked of my lord's marriage bid when I was at Cheshunt—I had requested him to convey my disdain of it back to the Court—and the Council must have hoped I would confide in him and make a full confession. Instead, he had wrung nothing from me, only tears.

This made me stronger. I even smiled at my new inquisitor. "If I am in your charge—what is the charge? The poorest person is allowed to know what they are charged with. What is my offence?"

His smile was congealed urine. "You tell me, my lady."

"I have committed none!" I spoke more boldly than I felt.

"This marriage that my lord of Sudeley speaks of—when was it agreed between you?"

His tone was quiet, conversational. But I saw the trap yawning before my feet. "Never!" I gasped. "He never spoke of it to me!"

"To those about you?"

Another terrible trap! I thought of Kat and her fond prattle; Parry, too, had been fool enough to be drawn in. Neither of them would betray me, that I knew. But how much was already known? Did they know of last year's indiscretions, when my lord would come into my chamber and make free with me in bed? Oh, God forbid I should be shamed with that! I shut my mouth in fear and saw he noticed it. He smiled again. He was enjoying this.

I tried to win back the initiative. "Bring me to my people and you shall see there is no guilty knowledge between us!"

He smiled once more. "Why, madam," he said softly, "if only that were possible . . ."

Again that look of pleasure on his face. My words dried in my mouth. *If only it were possible . . .*

I could no more control it. *"Where are they?"* And yet I knew, I knew before I spoke.

"Where, madam? Why, where should they be? Where your betrothed lord and husband lies, where you will shortly join them, where all traitors end their evil lives—*where but in the Tower?*"

XXIV

They say that virgins' tears have a rare virtue to heal and cure, like pearls discovered in the sea by light of a full moon. True or not, my tears came like a fountain all that time, when there was nothing else to save us. Even to think of being taken to the Tower, where my poor mother met her dreadful end . . . where my lost lord of Sudeley lay . . . where my last lord lies now, even now, tonight . . .

How I wept then, for Kat, and for them all!

Yet this time there was to be no escape for me in tears, for now the game began in earnest. Against Sir Robert, my old friend Sir Anthony Denny had been a novice in the art of inquisition.

"The Tower?" My new adversary feigned a yawn of boredom. "Yes, they are in the Tower, where they have been singing their hearts out, as caged birds do." Carelessly he stirred his papers and flashed two of them before me. "Here they have made full statements of all that took place at Chelsea between yourself and the Lord Seymour—I know it all, for they have told me all." Another wintry smile. "And signed their names to every word of it. You know their signatures?"

As well as my own—but could they have done this, betrayed me like this?"

"So tell me, lady, how you can deny that you were troth-plight to the Lord of Sudeley, when you openly permitted him the liberties a man takes only with his wife?"

Not all, not all, but all too many now . . .

"Freedoms? What freedoms?"

It was a fool's defiance, and it played into his hands. He reached for the nearest paper with that smile I now knew to dread. "Why, to allow him to come to you"—he pretended to read what he already knew—"naked in your bed in the early morning . . . and then to take the covers off you . . . and to touch you . . . to see you and to handle you in ways forbidden to a man with a true maid . . ."

His small black eyes were glowing hot now with lascivious excitement: I knew he saw me naked in my sheets, felt his own hand reaching to uncover me, his fingers itching to make contact with my flesh. My nipples burned, my bosom and neck flamed in discoloration, as I smarted with the shame. I dropped my eyes and wished him burning too, in the ninth ring of hell.

But he was off, taking another tack. "And did he not, this wayward lord your husband, once chastise your own Mistress Kat, striking her on the buttocks when she displeased him—by this, showing the freedom any man may take to punish his wife's servants?" A dry laugh. "And for the chastisement—now how was that? Did he command her to prostrate herself, to lift her skirts the better for him to come at her—"

Oh, he was vile! How could he? "No! No! No!"

"No, he did not do this?" His face was all mock innocence. "Not at all? But Mistress Ashley says herself he chastised her!"

"He . . . he did, but not like that!"

"Like what, then, lady? And how did he—touch you? As man will touch a wife?"

Oh, how his web of words entangled me! "I was not his wife then! He was still married to Queen Katherine!"

"So it was later, then, he made you his?"

"No! He never did so! Then or afterwards!"

"Come, madam, come!" He laughed. "I can see it in your face that you are guilty! But say you could be innocent"—he leaned in for the kill—"then how do you explain—your interesting condition—?"

My blood curdled. "My *condition?*"

Now he gave me the selfsame look that I have seen bestowed on the lowest of the whores as they are stripped and whipped and carted through the streets. "Yes, madam, your condition. Tell me, my lady, when do you expect delivery of your child?"

My child?

The earth, the sky, stood still, the room swirling and darkening round my seething brain.

My child? A rage so deep I was bereft of words took hold of me, shaking me as a terrier shakes a rat. And that was my salvation. A raging fury forced me to my feet. "Call for a midwife—any hag you like will certify me virgin! Bring my lord to claim he took my body and I'll throw the lie back in his teeth! And you—make sure you have some proof of this, or else withdraw it, yes, and grovel your apology, or you'll pay for it! You forget, sir, I am still the Sister to the King, the daughter of our late, great King, and you yourself commit treason with your slurs against my purity, my body, against the blood of a royal line of kings, when you dare even to breathe a thing so wicked!"

His eyes, his stiffened back, betrayed his shock. When he resumed, a change was on him. "Madam, it is only a rumour—"

I seized my chance. "One I demand the right to have put down! Let me write to the Lord Protector Somerset to clear my name"—I took a deep breath—"and to intercede, too, for my lord of Sudeley, whose offences, these lies about me apart, cannot be very grave."

In truth, I was fishing in the dark, for I had no idea of his offence. Sir Robert nodded grimly. "You think so, my lady? Hear some good advice. Write on your own behalf to the Lord Protector if you so choose. But do not name his brother—the very name of your lord is anathema to the Protector now. You cannot save him—God above could not save him!—and the wise man"—he paused and favoured me with an ironic glint of pure appreciation—"or the wise *virgin,* as it seems that I must say, lets go her hold when a great wheel runs downhill in case she too gets caught up in its ruin."

"Its—ruin?" *Was there no hope for him?*

"He is a fallen star!" said Tyrrwhit with a savage emphasis. "Outcast and damned, the villain of the kingdom!"

Outcast and damned? My terror was renewed, for the greater his crimes, the greater stood my danger. "What has he done?"

Sir Robert laughed. "What has he *not* done? Let me tell you, lady . . ."

He had been laying a conspiracy since Katherine died. But he needed men and arms to seize the supreme power. One evil stroke of fate then sealed his doom—for until then his great conspiracy had been no more than castles and kingdoms floating in the air. He was informed that the Master of the Mint, Sir William Sharington, was coining for himself and growing rich.

So Satan tempted my rash lord: and so he fell. He saw it not as criminal corruption, but as sign from heaven that he should have the money that he needed. He forced Sharington to coin more cash and give it all to him.

Yet time was running out, and Satan came for him. The Lord Protector, hearing talk and wild rumours, ordered his brother to London to make account of it.

My lord refused—but now his hand was forced to one last desperate throw. He planned to seize the King and rule through him. He gained the Privy Staircase in the heart of Whitehall Palace. There he fobbed off the guard with false commands and prepared to take the King. But a little spaniel, Edward's chamber dog, rushed on them furiously, barking the alarm. And with his pistol my lord shot him dead.

The gunshot roused the palace, and all rushed upon him. He was arrested and taken to the Tower. They searched his house and found proof of all his misdeeds, along with all his booty, no less than two hundred thousand crowns. Yet in defeat he lost none of his lordly pride, demanding freedom and a safe conduct to France, denying that he ever planned or plotted anything against the King, the Council or the Lord Protector. And there he lay, a fallen Lucifer.

Would he now bring me down too, to fall along with him—as in ancient times, to be the virgin sacrifice that always accompanied the death of a great man of the tribe?

Never, while I had even one of my five wits about me, and a tongue in my head!

How we fenced now, Tyrrwhit and I, now I had found my strength!

Yet the subtle Tyrrwhit still believed me guilty of something and was determined to track it down. But I would have none of it. I was innocent of treason, and so were Kat and Parry. All I had to confess was that my lord had been familiar with my person. I had to own up to his rash horseplay in my bedchamber and abide by that humiliation.

And oh, how Tyrrwhit loved it! Hours and days were spent on how and where my lord had come to me, seen me, touched me, struck me, how much of me had been revealed. But though I writhed beneath his hot-eyed prurience, feeling as if his fingers probed my flesh, groping for cracks and fissures in my story, still I felt a little martyrdom was a small price to pay to keep my head on my shoulders and my body from the fire. And at last Sir Robert, like Sir Anthony before him, had to admit defeat.

The day he rode off with his clattering train of men-at-arms, I ordered music, made a feast in spite of Lent and danced with victorious glee. *So perish all the enemies of the virgin warrior,* I pledged myself, the innocent young maid!

Now to reclaim my life—my single life, for I was still my own woman, even more so now I had survived this ordeal and come safe through. Now I could resume my reign at Hatfield and queen it on my own hearth if nowhere else, all safe again!

Yet not until August did I get Kat back. My old treasurer, too, had aged a hundred years in his time of trial, and ever afterwards made such faults in his bookkeeping that I had to check all the household accounts after him, initialling every line.

But far worse than all I had to bear was my lord's death. For die he did: there could be no escape. He died as he had lived, rash and raging, passionate in self-love to the last. He spent his last night writing secretly to me, a letter scratched out with a metal tag taken from his clothing, for he could not write openly the things he wished to say.

Do you see in this the last flare of our love's strong passion? If you do, then you deceive yourself. Let me tell you that his last letter breathed no word of love nor any grace nor sweetness, nor even fear of death and hope to find salvation, but was instead a furious exhortation to overthrow his brother and have the Lord Protector kiss the selfsame block.

Let me tell you that he wrote the same letter to Mary—to my sister Mary!—word for bilious word, and that he could not even triumph with this last grand gesture, since the servant under orders to smuggle the letters out to us in the sole of my lord's velvet shoe promptly abandoned him even as my lord's head left his shoulders and brought the letters straight to the Lord Protector, to the very brother whose death my lord had sought, whose ruination had been his last black thought and prayer . . .

So he died dangerously, horribly, guiltily—and his fall entangled others and brought them down.

But not myself. He was the first great danger I had lived through—such a hard lesson that I live by it still.

So he was gone, and that was the end of him and the end of the affair!

Not of its consequences, though; and our recovery was slow. After the strains and torments of that time, when I swear to God I felt my own head wobble on my neck, I succumbed once more to a greensickness, and vile headaches too, till I hardly knew myself. I could keep no food down, and thinned down to my bones; my woman's courses, never strong or regular, ceased altogether for months, and that made me sick too, and full of humours that I could not shed.

But sick or well, I never ceased to pester the Lord Protector for my Kat's release and that of Master Parry. Only when my sickness took such a turn that the doctors swore my death would be on his head did the Lord Protector relent. Within the week there came horses to the door, and there was Kat, being lifted from a litter by men of the King's guard, her man Ashley close behind.

We did not speak a word, but gripped each other hard and clung close, too close even for tears. She seemed to have grown shorter, and had lost so much weight that I could feel her little bones. "Oh, lady, lady," came a broken murmur. "Can you forgive me? Or must you send me away?"

I was too happy even to raise a gentle laugh at her expense. "As long as you will promise never to try to marry me off again!"

A spark of her old brightness crept into her eyes. "Not if I were to be pulled limb from limb by wild horses!"

We mended slowly, for we had all passed under the shadow of death's wing. But my sorrow was a mourning and a learning too. Now I could see how little I had heeded the lessons of Grindal—how nearly I had played into the hands of those who strive for power around a throne. With my love for my lord Seymour, I could have fed a rising that might have cost my brother his crown and undone all our line!

The look of pure contempt Sir Anthony had given me when he thought I was unchaste was with me still, and still tormented me. Never again, I vowed, would I subject myself to such scorn from any man.

So I bade Parry shut away my gowns and jewels and all her colours and complexions—she made no fight on this, for she like all of us was shaken to the marrow of her bones. I ordered new gowns in the modest style, laying by all my old finery. I was determined to appear the perfect virgin, nay a veritable nun, to kill all gossip and rumours about my chastity.

So I wrote again to my brother—letters that, like my appearance, were the complete model of the pure learned virgin, modest and discreet. I did not ask again if I could come to Court: I was convinced that the Lord Protector never would permit Mary or me to come there while he ruled. But I could work on winning Edward's heart. And I had an ally in this, my old friend Cecil, who had risen with the Lord Protector Somerset and shared his success. Cecil now was made the Secretary to the Council, and he sent to me from time to time words of encouragement and cheer that showed me he had not forgotten our last meeting, just as I had not forgotten the good service he did for me when alone of all the world he gave me the truth about my mother's death.

My chief delights at that time were my books and my tutor Ascham. His keen, bright intellect, his patience and his love of what he did flowed over me like the waters of the Jordan, cleansing and healing me back to new life. We made such progress that he swore no maid could read so much as I did in so many different tongues.

"Say you so, master?" I would demand: I loved to hear him flatter me! I now had Latin, Greek, a little Hebrew, French and Italian, and some Spanish too—but still I would fish for his commendations, then work twice as hard to win his praise still more. So we fell into a restful country rhythm, and might have slumbered on so, undisturbed, until we slipped into our last sleep. But unseen by us and even by herself, blind Fortune turned her wheel.

It was mid-October, when the mellow kiss of autumn hung on the woods and fields, when the moss-covered cottage trees groaned with the last and biggest of their apples, and when the pigs were truffling around every oak tree for their beloved acorns, fattening themselves as nature bids them against the winter. On those days of golden October warmth before the sun dies into November, I could not be indoors.

On this day—it was a Tuesday—we had roamed the park on horseback and now were drawing homeward for a late dinner hour. As we rode slowly back in the failing light towards the low red outline of old Hatfield, I saw a horse and rider racing along the highroad, then turning off for the house. Straight as an arrow, he ignored the path and cut across the rough ground at a furious pace. The going there was bad, as I knew to my cost, with tussocks, rabbit holes and hidden swamps, and only the best of horsemen could hope to keep his seat at eventide upon such tricky ground. The horse was stumbling too—even at a distance the poor beast was overworn with galloping and near to collapse.

"Ride, ride to assist him, Richard, and you, James," I cried out in alarm, "or he will fall!" But even as I spoke, the unknown rider picked up his beast's head with consummate skill, outspurred all chance of their pursuit, and gaining the outer wall of Hatfield, vanished into the court-yard. We raced home after him.

To one side of the cobbled yard stood the new arrival's horse, a mighty bay, steaming and shivering as they rubbed him down. This was a lord's mount. *One of the Council?*

Was it my fear, or was the air growing darker? I tried to hide my tremors as I strode up from the base-court into the Great Hall. Vine was awaiting me with candlelight as I came in. "Oh, my lady, a messenger from Court—"

"Why has he come?"

"He will say nothing but for your ears, madam."

I gave a bitter laugh. "Who is he—will he say that?"

"An emissary from His Grace the Duke of Northumberland."

"Northumberland?" There was no Duke of Northumberland: only an ancient earldom, long since lapsed. Was this a trick? "Do you know of him, Vine?"

I could see from his face that his ignorance was as great as mine. "Attend me!" I commanded.

"My lady comes!"

I stalked as confidently as I could into the dark room. They should have brought more candles! I could hardly make the stranger out against the light. All I could see was a tall man leaping to his feet, pulling off his hat and making a low bow. "My lady!"

I would not demean myself by peering at the gold-brown head now bent before me. "So, sir, what is your message?"

He raised his head. So tall—and that face in the gloaming . . . His eyes were questioning, smiling, impudent. Suddenly I saw my mud-stained habit, reeking of the hunt, my sweated boots, my red face, my hat streaked with leaves and lichen from pelting headlong through the woods. I could hear the suppressed chuckle in his voice. "Your Highness appears . . . rather unprepared to give me audience. I crave a fitter time than this to tell you all in full—"

He dared dictate to me? Comment on my appearance? My fear flared with my anger. "Speak now, sir, or by God I'll have my people—"

He was laughing! *Laughing!* My fury broke. "John! James and Richard! Take this rude interloper, throw him from my house—!"

I turned to go. Then his voice, laughing still, made me a statue where I stood. "Madam! Princess! Why, Elizabeth, do you not know me?"

XXV

Robin! I might have known, from the fine horsemanship the stranger had displayed! I felt like tears, and laughter—I felt a child again. "Oh, Robin!"

He grinned a proud correction. "Lord Robert—at your service."

"But you've changed so! And grown—!" I broke off. "So tall—"

And handsome—a man now—boy no longer . . .

"As have you, lady—without flattery—"

"Oh, spare me not!" I laughed. "Flatter me, flatter, do!"

"I speak no more than truth," he said slowly and wonderingly, his eyes hard on my face. "Your slender frame, madam, your form and carriage now, your fine skin—"

I had to drag myself back to duty. "But Robin, what brings you here?"

His smile vanished. Now with a sudden ceremony he reached into his doublet and produced a parchment rattling with seals. "A letter from His Grace the Duke of Northumberland, Princess, telling you all."

The vellum in my hands was smooth and cold. "Northumberland? Who is he?"

He took a deep breath, flushed and braced himself. "John Dudley, madam, formerly Lord Lisle and Earl of Warwick—and my father."

A chill crept over me: I felt a great gap opening between us. *"Your father?"*

How was he now a duke? A duke was highest in the kingdom under the King: there had been only one duke on the Council in all my brother's reign, the Lord Protector. What had become of him?

And what of Edward?

He guessed my fear. "Madam, your brother's safe, and the Duke of Somerset too, the former Lord Protector."

The former . . . So . . . ?

Robin coughed. "But there have been—changes. The King, your brother has no Protector now—"

So he is not protected?

"—but has decided to govern solely with the advice and help of his appointed Council—"

"—A Council now led by your father, perhaps—His Grace the new Duke of Northumberland?"

He bowed agreement as he flushed again. Blood was always blood: he had his blood, I mine. *"Tell me of Edward."*

He threw his head up. "Your brother, madam, had far more to fear under the proud Duke than under my father! There have been riots and rebellion around London all summer long—the people discontented, many desperate, suffering under his misgovernment."

"So you mean that through these troubles, the Lord Protector lost power?"

Robin nodded. "He was too weak! He would not put these vile rebellions down—he wanted to be loved of the poor people, yet they it was who suffered! Then when he knew the lords had turned against him, and he was to be relieved of his high office, like his brother the Lord Sudeley before him, he tried to seize the person of the King."

"Oh, my poor Edward! How—?"

"By a night flight out to Windsor, where the King lay. My father could have stormed the castle, had the Duke killed! Instead, he talked him into a fair surrender, with no loss of life."

No mean achievement, I could grant the new Duke that. "What has become now of the Lord Pro— of my Lord of Somerset?"

"He lies now in the Tower while due consideration is taken of his future. My father of Northumberland and the lords have no desire for his death. They merely wish for change—"

"Change? What change?"

His face lightened. "They wish to put more power where it should belong, into the hands of the King. His Majesty is ready for it, as you will see!" His smile broadened. "For there are other changes now, not least for you, my lady! The new Duke wishes that His Majesty may be more with his sisters: so I am sent to bid you come to Court!"

And come to Court we did, in time for Christmas. All the way I dreamed of the reunion I had prayed for. I had not seen Edward since the night we were brought together at Enfield to be told of the King our father's death. Almost three years! How much would he have changed?

And he had to see that I had changed too. This would be my first appearance at Court since the rumours of my unchastity—God! and my pregnancy too! At least time had showed what a foul lie that was! Still, I must take this chance to lay to rest all the bad things that had been said about me. All the way to Whitehall I was planning what I would wear, how I would act and speak.

We came in late and over-travelled, soaked with November rain and sleet, tired to death and chilled through to the bone. But I was still awake and fretting long before dawn.

As we set forth from our lodgings when the summons came, I was racked with anxiety. After three years as King, how would he greet me? And what would he think of the new Elizabeth, the modest, plain-dressed maiden I now was?

For in place of my beloved headdresses encircled with two and three deep rows of gold and jewels, I wore only my own hair, drawn back off my forehead and flowing straight as rainfall down my back. Gone were my earrings and my finger rings; no rope of pearls circled my waist, no necklace graced my neck. I wore no scent that might lead men by the nose, seducing lustful thoughts. My gown was all one fabric, simply cut in dove-grey velvet up to the neck, the bodice high and chaste, even puri-tanical. I knew it made my pale skin glow like porcelain, like purity itself.

Yet my pallor was not all artifice, for I was suffering. As I glided calmly through the ranks of armed men in the outer chamber, I felt the pressure of a thousand eyes. Within the Presence was a denser throng, and mo-mentarily I faltered: where was my brother? I could not even see the canopy beneath which he would sit.

"Make way! Way for Her Highness the King's Most Honoured Sister!"

Make way!" Gentlemen of the Presence now came forward to clear my path. The crowds melted away. At the end of the room I saw a burst of colour, lords and ladies in bright satins and shining silks.

Yet not as I remembered. Court fashions had moved on: never had I seen such finery! Now all the women wore their hair teased up in furious curls or swagged in fretted golden snoods bedizened with pearls and opals. Beside the throne one was resplendent in a gown shimmering like a rainbow, with a ruff of gauze like gossamer, while her companion lord flashed out like sunshine after rain in gold and silver over fine brocade.

Now God help me! I wished the floor would open and admit me. How had I misjudged this appearance! So far from looking like a modest princess, I would look like the merest country wench, a bumpkin! All would despise me, and my brother most! Rage and tears fought within me, but there was nothing for me now but to go on.

I glanced up at the throne and fixed my gaze on it as I walked forward. The figure on it had to be my brother. And yet—and yet—? I stopped as was the custom, far away from the high dais, and fell upon my knees, bowing my head. "Approach, we give you leave." I heard his voice. I rose and, nearer still, knelt once again.

Could this be Edward? The tall boy, almost a young man now, coming down the steps to raise me up and fold me in his arms? His legs in their silk hose seemed twice as long as when we last had met. And could this be a king, this sober-suited, black-robed person, clad more like a young clerk or steward?

Yet there was no mistaking the joy shining in his eyes. "Sister, most dearly welcome! How my heart has longed for this moment!" Then turning to the courtiers all around, he said aloud with all the authority of a king, "Give welcome, all, to the Princess my sister—my sweet sister Temperance, I may call her, whose dress and demeanour set a fair example to us all!"

All day he kept me by him, as he kept his state under the eye of Dudley —now Northumberland, but just the same as I remembered him, a tall, stout, red-faced man, with eyes like popping coals, hot and everywhere. In the press of people, I greeted and was greeted by this one and that, by my father's Privy Lords, who now served my brother, by the Court ladies once attendant on Katherine, now out of service till the King took a wife. Among the crowd I caught sight of my old inquisitor Sir Robert Tyrrwhit, but by mutual consent we kept the distance of the chamber between us. And all the while I prayed to have my brother to myself.

Yet I had to remember that he was still the King. When the word came to withdraw, I hovered on the threshold of his Privy Chamber and neither entered nor was seated till he gave the word. His people bustled around with candles, sweetmeats, wine and every comfort, till at last he dismissed them and commanded that we should be alone. Now we could be brother and sister again, now I could tell him all that was in my heart!

His face was charged with meaning—clearly he also had much he longed to share. "Elizabeth—" he began.

I leaned forward eagerly.

"Tell me, madam," he said abruptly, "how do you think the state of our religion stands now in England?"

Our *religion*?

Edward, little brother, I want to know how it has been for you—how you have suffered in this change of power between the dukes, if you were frightened for your life in the mad midnight dash the Lord Protector forced you to make—?

I caught my breath. "I am quite ignorant about the state of religion, sire, living so quietly in Hatfield."

He nodded. "Yet I cannot avoid it! My uncle the former Lord Protector"—oh, how coldly he spoke!—"stirred the people up by forcing new forms of worship on them. They have been calling him the Antichrist, there has been rioting—"

"New forms of worship? Should we not follow the religion as laid down by our father in his will?"

His eyes blazed. "By no means! There is great need of reform! But it must be far-reaching, and imposed with strength, no mumbling resistance allowed!"

What could I say? I fumbled for the words. But like all those blinded by their own convictions, he took my silence for assent. "I see your mind is at one with mine on this question, Elizabeth," he said approvingly. "I see it from your dress and your modest demeanour—such purity is what we need now in our faith, as you have in your soul."

My soul? If he only knew how sin-spotted that had been! I blushed, which doubtless he thought more proof of my innocence.

"And now I see how wrong were the rumours of your dishonour, the unchastity that the former Protector once feared of you, through the sins of his most erring brother, my late uncle of Sudeley."

How coldly did he speak of the late this, the former that! Where was the Edward I had known, the happy, laughing boy?

He mused a little, staring at the fire, then took up his tale. "I hear the same virtue, the same purity, of our cousin Jane. Her true zeal for the faith is said to be a model of the new religion—the new wave of Protestant devotion by which we shall conquer and eradicate the last traces of foul Popery!"

I could not speak. He turned the pale eyes of a burning faith on me. "What do you think, Elizabeth? Should I marry her?"

Marry Jane Grey? I thought that plan had perished with my lord! It caught me floundering. I groped for words. "Do you like her?"

"Like her?" Nothing, it seemed, could be further from his thoughts. "She has much to commend her. She is of our blood, of the blood royal, and high up in our line. The late Protector has lost me my promised bride the Queen of Scots, through his bad policy: she has been sent to France to make alliance with our Catholic enemies there. And unlike her, Jane is of our faith, of the true faith. And that is under threat!"

"What, here in England—?"

He sprang up in passion, striking the carved oak arm of his heavy chair. "Yes, here in England, even here in the heart of this Court!"

"From whom?" But even as I asked, I knew the answer.

"From Madam Mary! Do you not know of this?"

"I beg you, tell me, sir."

"Our sister Mary, and the first lady of the land until I marry, has been setting all our people a fair example!" His face was bright with anger. "On all her estates she keeps Roman rites and Roman worship, she houses priests and shelters recusants, she foments dissension and disobedience with all her powers! My Lords of the Council have now sent for her to answer this; we meet tomorrow. And I shall hack it out, yes, root and branch, in God's name, by the strength of His arm!" He turned towards me, and for a second he was a boy again. "Will you be there, Elizabeth? I want you there!"

That night I wept into my sheets and found no comfort. Who had done this? Who had turned a loving child into this ranting bigot? He had been Somerset's puppet—was this the dark lord's training? Or had a lonely, clever, bookish child, unmothered, simply consoled himself with the chill discipline of dogma in the absence of warm love? I knew not. But I knew now how he thought. And I saw, too, that the Lord Northumberland, in giving him his power, unstoppering that bottle, had let out more than an unformed boy.

The next day drove that knowledge home indeed. The page was at the door before the dinner hour. "Word from the King, Your Highness. The Lady Mary has arrived, for private audience with the King and Council this afternoon. Please it Your Ladyship to attend?"

No, it did not please Her Ladyship! I had no wish to be the standard-bearer for the new religion, nor the supreme example of how pure a Protestant could be! So I dressed carefully in a gown of Mary blue, the colour of the Virgin and the very hue of chastity, yet not among the wan shades of the extreme faithful.

In the small Audience Chamber I found the King and his Lords of the Council, some new to me, some faces from my past. There was Wriothes-

ley, who had helped bring down my lord of Surrey, the Earl of Southampton now, yet as angry-looking as ever. I knew, too, another scowler,
Henry Grey, the Earl of Dorset, father of Jane and Catherine, talking to
the mild Marquis of Northampton, brother to the late Queen Katherine.
Most of the others, too, had held their offices in my father's time.

Foremost among them was the new Duke of Northumberland, attended by his sons. Nearest to him were John and Ambrose, Robin's
older brothers, then Robin himself and the younger boys, Guildford and
Henry. Robin looked pale, as if his father's new pre-eminence did not yet
sit easily with him.

Yet here, too, there were signs of the changes Robin had spoken of.
Standing unnoticed by the arras with his page was a dark, watchful man
in his middle years. Like the old sour-faced Duke of Norfolk, I knew him
as a Howard, and therefore kin to me: he had been my mother's uncle.
This Lord Howard had been one of those who quietly took to his estates
after her fall, and for years had shunned the Court. That must be why he
was free and in favour today, while the old Duke still languished in the
Tower! Yet one glance at the page standing nervously beside him and I
could see that Lord Howard had not disowned his family connections.
Young as he was, with his pale protruding eyes, long nose and heavy chin,
the child was instantly recognisable as a Norfolk. Kin to the old Duke—
had to be his grandson—which meant he was the son of my lost lord of
Surrey . . .

Oh, how the ghosts walked! And how they trod upon my grave!

I was shivering. Why did not Mary come? The chamber throbbed with
restless anticipation as first one lord then the other muttered behind
their hands. On his throne my brother sat like a statue, his long pale face
as motionless as marble. Outside the window a dismal sleeting rain
pecked at the glass and wore away our nerves. And still we waited.
Where was Mary? Surely she could not be refusing to attend upon the
King?

"Room for the Princess Mary!"

At last she came. After Robin, after Edward, I was prepared, I
thought, for any change in her. I knew she would not match my sixteen-
year-old height, nor even Edward's, though he was but newly turned
twelve. But where we had grown so tall, she seemed to have got smaller,
till she looked almost like a child, as undersized as Jane. And how she
had aged! At thirty-three she was an old woman. Her face had shrunk—
had she lost some of her teeth? Her skin was coarser now and yellowing
to a muddy brown, her wrinkles deeper, her frown creased like a scar
between her heavy brows.

Blinking piteously about, blinder than ever, she did not see me. Her
look of suffering went straight to my heart. But she was not there to win

pity. The scene was short and violent. "My lord the King commands me ask you, lady," began Northumberland, smoothly enough, "will you conform—?"

"And deny my religion?" she shouted in her deep, mannish voice. "No, I will not! And you, my lord, cannot make me!" Then turning to the King, she said bitterly, "Is this your will, sire? Do you know what they do in your name?"

Staring at her as if she were Medusa, Edward rose to his feet. "If you intend to follow your own faith and deny ours, you are in mortal error!" he shrilled hysterically. "And we will see that our laws are obeyed! Be warned!"

He waved her away. The lords closed round her, and she was swiftly hustled, still protesting, out of the chamber. Edward beckoned me to him. "You see her stubbornness!" he said, still in the same high, clear, unsettling tone. "How can we root out such wilful persistence in her Romish heresy and idolatry?"

Never would I have thought that I would plead for Mary—for the woman who still called my mother "whore," whose faith made me a bastard and denied me my place, my status and my rights of blood. But this hounding, this persecution, went to my weakest part. I was trembling. "I do not doubt, sire, but that the Lady Mary—"

Edward's face shone even paler, and his voice took on a deathly coldness. "Do not defend her, sister—*or you may give us cause to question your own faith.*"

I heard the voice of power, the expression of pure will in the accents of my father, and a gulf opened at my feet.

XXVI

Oh, how I wept for my lost Edward, for that lost boy child! And how I feared the man he was becoming!

Yet he could be a child again at times, for he still loved to run and play as all boys do. The next dawn, all the scene with Mary seemed like the memory of an evil dream, when he knocked at my door.

Kat was beside herself. "The King! The King is here! And we have not even emptied the night soil from the chamber!"

"Sister, come!" He bounced in like the twelve-year-old he was. It was as if the other Edward, the cold boy tyrant, had never been. "You must see how I ride now! For my lord Northumberland permits me exercise more than my uncle ever did!"

We followed him out to the tiltyard and saw him ride at the ring. He had grown fast and skilful, spearing the hanging circle at full pelt far oftener than not. His long legs gave him a natural advantage in the saddle, much like those of Robin, who had taught him all he knew. And every day the three of us rode out together, careless of fog or sleet, even of snow.

And every day Robin took some small pains—a nosegay of pomandered winter flowers, or a bell for my bridle—to show me that he was still my friend and never would forget our childhood bond. And yet, when he would take my hand in his strong fingers, or with his easy grasp circle my waist to swing me from my horse, or look up at me with his bright laughing gaze, then I would be reminded that we were not children any more . . .

Nor was I now the disregarded girl hidden away in Hatfield as I was before. With Mary banished to her far estates for spurning the King's proffered olive branch, I was become the premier lady of the Court, and all deferred to me. To show his displeasure with Mary, the King increased my state: my train was borne up now by duchesses as I went into chapel on the day of Christ's nativity or made procession into the Great Hall to dine with the King. I still observed all protocol, falling on my knees six times as I approached him and declining even to sit under his canopy. But all knew who I was, and my pride and pleasure swelled accordingly.

Northumberland, too, strove to win my support, choosing to govern with the goodwill of the King and those around him, not through fear as the Lord Protector had. He won my gratitude by settling my estates, transferring to me in two months all the moneys, lands and holdings left to me by my father, all of which the uncaring Somerset had not resolved in two long years.

And he would much have liked, so Robin told me, to win over Mary too. "She is the Princess Royal, the King's sister and the eldest of the royal family: her place is here at Court!"

I could not but agree. "And surely, persecuting her will only win her sympathy?" I cast a glance of interrogation at my master Ascham, for Robin had come upon us as we left the schoolroom.

Ascham nodded. "This treatment of the King's makes her a martyr, or at least the focus of all Catholic hopes and Catholic discontents." He reflected. "Were I a politician like your father, my lord Robert," he rumbled sagely in his rich brown voice, "my instinct would be that the lady would be safer here at Court under my eye than festering in Norfolk, where all too many of the folk still cling to Rome, openly or in secret, even after all this time!"

Ascham was right, of course—how right, we all were yet to learn. But armchair politicians always have all the answers: in real life, even the greatest Machiavel finds his hands tied. Northumberland promised Mary that he would wink an eye at her private observations, even at her holding Mass for twenty people in her chamber, for the sake of reconciling her with Edward. But the King would not abide it. And neither he nor Mary could give way, for their immortal souls. So Mary was ordered to keep away from Court as if she were a leper—she who once had been the greatest lady there.

I will confess, though, that when I heard she was in disgrace, I was child enough to take delight in it. And others took heart, too, from the New Faith in the ascendant and the old ways overthrown. One day in the great court I met my kinsman Lord Howard coming my way with two young men, the taller big and blond with a bright, innocent face, the other some years his senior, lean, dark and reserved.

"Madam," Lord Howard hailed me, "we were on our way to you. May I present two gentlemen newly come to Court—and two of all that you may wish to know better?"

He had never called on me before. Now he gave me a smile that seemed to mean more than he said. Why should I want to know them? I searched their guarded faces. Both of them kept their eyes on me and did not say a word. I turned to the older. Nervousness made me sharp. "Sir?"

He plucked off a hat that clearly owed more to country fashions than to Court, and made an awkward bow. "Francis Knollys, of Oxfordshire, my lady. My father served your father—before your time, madam."

His friend stepped forward, even more awkwardly, his fair face flushing under his thatch of hair. "And Henry Carey of Buckingham, at your service, Madam Elizabeth. I—"

Carey . . .

My mother's sister Mary Boleyn—as fair, Kat said, as Anne had been dark—had been married to a squire of Buckingham, a Master Carey—

"You are my cousin!"

He gave a relieved laugh and pointed at Francis Knollys. "And so is he, my lady, for he's married to my sister!"

They had long hoped to make their way to Court, they told me. Now with the new reign burying the past, they felt their time had come. Above all, with the rebuff of Mary, there would be no one to recall the old days of Boleyn disgrace and the family taint. How I rejoiced in my two new-found cousins, and the goodwill of Lord Howard to bring them to me!

For sure God smiled, to advantage me by Mary's banishment in more ways than one!

For in her absence I could queen it, and after so many hurts and slights and fears, queen it I did till I thought my heart would burst.

But still I kept my plain and modest ways among all the great state the King commanded for me. No frizzing of my hair, no painting of my face —not for me the layers of white lead and ground coral, borax, beeswax, madder or gloss of egg, but only the glow of health and exercise. And now I saw a new look in men's eyes, of admiration, yes, but of respect and wonder too, as like a pale star I blazed in my rich setting through my looks alone, naked and unadorned. And others that I did not see watched from far off, through the veiled regard of their ambassadors and agents, assessing me for their own purposes.

All this I learned from Robin, who, by virtue of his place next to his father, was now become another set of eyes and ears to me.

"I hear you are to marry, lady," he would tease. "The French Ambassador seeks you for the Prince of the house of Guise!" Or else he heard of a suit on behalf of the King of Denmark's son—"by whom in time you would be Queen of Denmark—a great Dane—"

"Am I a bitch, then? And what did old King Alfred fight for if an English maid must be subjected to the Danelaw?"

"Well, what d'you say to the son of the Duke of Florence? He's forward for his eleven summers, so they say."

"Is he yet out of diapers? It would be cradle robbery! I'd have to kneel to kiss him. Must I sink so low?"

"There is talk of the son of the Duke of Ferrara—he will be eighteen months at Pentecost—"

"Robin, I swear I'll cuff you if you try to bring any more babes-in-arms to bed with me!"

I could afford to laugh—I had no fear that Edward would dispose of me so lightly. For I was continually with him, and he clung to me. "Do you miss Hatfield, sister?" he would say as weeks, then months, went by. "Truly, sir," I would reply, "not so much as I would miss Your Majesty if you sent me away." And he would nod, satisfied.

So we followed the royal round from palace to palace and from place to place: Richmond and Greenwich, Whitehall and Windsor, Woodstock and Enfield and Hampton Court. I was young enough then to relish the adventure of constant royal progress, not to resent the upheaval as I do now!

And life went on, with good news for my friends as well as me. My Cecil, rising with the dark Duke of Somerset, had fallen with him too, loyal to the last. But it was known he had no other choice. Early in the

New Year he was released from the Tower and restored to all his former
duties. How I rejoiced at that! And not for his sake alone: as a woman
now of property, I had sore need of one I trusted to oversee my affairs.
In a brief, happy meeting I besought him take on the post of my sur-
veyor, and to my satisfaction he accepted, for a fee of twenty pounds a
year.

Now was my life set fair.

My only cares were clouds on the horizon, the concern I felt for Ed-
ward's newfound zeal and the same fear of Mary's fiery devotion to her
Roman rites. But with me at Court, and under the less harsh regime of
Robin's father, Edward seemed to lose his chill fanaticism. And he loved
Robin, who teased him, rode with him, treated him as a friend not as a
royal stranger, just as he did me.

Halcyon days! The first of spring saw us out racing through the last of
the snow, royally splattering the laggards behind. Or I would watch with
the other ladies from the leads above the tennis court as the men went at
it as fierce as gladiators below, stripped down to their shirts, contending
like Greek gods.

One day of April, Robin set a match with one of the King's men, a
cheerful rogue called Perrott. He was a man of action, hard as iron, and
in his late twenties; he had ten years over Robin. He also had a fox's
cunning and a will to win. But Robin had that too—he was a son of
Dudley! And Robin's skill was greater, for he had God's gift for all things
physical. The bets went to and fro, for none could guess which would
prevail.

My money was on Robin—a friend bets on a friend. That day I was the
first to climb the Ladies' Tower over the leads of the great tennis court.
Around me were as ever Kat and Parry, and the ladies of the Court I now
called friends, the Marchioness of Northampton, Lady Browne and Lady
Russell, with others of their circle.

Next to us stood the lesser women, wives of country knights, and
squires and gentlemen of no rank. Among them, eyes and mouth round
as a baby's, was a girl I had not seen before, short, pudding-plump and
countrified beyond redemption. Her face was sunburned, her nut-brown
hair was far too dark for fashion, her fat breasts were swelling like a
pigeon's bosom over her too-tight bodice. I turned to Browne. "Who is
that mammet?"

Browne squinted at her. "The daughter of a squire of the far shires,
Leicester or Norfolk, my lady—Roberts, as I think, or Robson—newly
come to Court, to catch a lord, as I daresay she hopes!"

"Ha! Little chance of that, when she looks as if she was found under a
haystack!" put in Russell smartly.

"Or when she looks like the haystack itself!" added another with a malicious laugh. I laughed too and then forgot her as the match began.

The game was hot and hard, and for long enough victory could have gone either way. Never did Robin look finer, his long, lean body quicksilver around the court, his heels winged like the god of speed himself, his fair sculptured face glowing with fervour. As he walked onto the court, he threw a glance up at the Ladies' Tower, started, and seemed to look at me with a strange surprise. All through the game his eyes would seek the balcony, and more and more his attention was drawn in my direction till it seemed as if he could hardly look anywhere else.

Never had he stared so before, never had he looked that way before, as if he saw me truly for the first time. And as I felt his burning, searching glances, a feeling in me stirred, and flowered, and woke to certain life— *he loves me.*

For he had the bruised look of a man now in love for the first time, and winded, blinded by it. I could not breathe for the shock—and then came delight. My heart was singing—

Robin! My true friend, my friend for so long, a man I knew and trusted, one who cared for me as I was, not as a pawn in the great game of power; one who shared my pastimes and my pleasures, who was beloved, too, by my brother . . . and who was, besides, a young lord in his beauty, a lord of life and love, as fine a long man of his length as Kat could wish for me . . .

As he played on, locked in a violent tussle, I sat above in a dream of wonderment, counting his charms. His finely modelled face, so fair and open; his strong yet chiselled nose and wide, determined mouth; his fresh English skin; his eyes as blue as skies in springtime; golden brown hair— *oh, Robin, Robin!* My heart thundered his name, my blood whispered it, hissing in my veins.

As his did too, I guessed, for looking up, he missed the ball on one crucial shot, and though he fought gamely after, he had lost the match. Sighing and chattering, the ladies all dispersed, but I came down to wait for him outside the court. With all the certainty of love newborn, I knew he would be longing now to see me. What I would say to him I did not know, for it was all still so fresh, and strange, and frightening. And yet I knew that it was age-old too, and predetermined, like all true love . . . Calm and confused, then, serene yet trembling, I awaited him.

He was not long. In a fresh shirt, shrugging into his doublet as his man scurried alongside vainly trying to complete his master's toilet, Robin strode out of the courtyard and came up to me. "Madam, let's walk," he said abruptly, snatching his hat and waving off his man. We set off across the grass towards the Green Park, our people falling back obediently at his signal.

The sun was up, the ground warm to our feet. The first of the daisies were venturing their white heads above the earth, and in the air the birds were singing love songs. We reached a scattered spinney of young beech trees, their leaves as green and delicate as Flora's bridal. Never was I happier, for I knew I was about to hear the sacred melody of love revealed—a declaration of devotion that I could now return.

He stopped abruptly underneath a tree more sheltering than the others. His scent was wonderful, his nearness almost too much.

His first words came so low I had to strain to hear them. "Madam—my lady—"

"Yes, Robin—?"

"I do not know if I may venture this—"

My voice was trembling. "Oh, Robin—nothing venture, nothing win."

He took a breath. "May I—speak of love?"

My pulse was racing. "Speak, I pray you."

"This may seem all too sudden—"

"Let me be the judge of that."

"—so sudden that you may not believe it."

"I would believe you, Robin, in anything."

"Then believe this, I beg you, lady, if I am to find happiness in this world."

He turned and faced me. I leaned back against the tree, out of sight of all our people.

"Speak, Robin," I commanded him on a soft breath.

He leaned his forehead against the rough bark and groaned like a dying man. "I am in love!"

"I know."

"And all my bliss depends on you."

I felt my woman's power. "Speak—ask—demand me anything." I glanced up and met his gaze, fierce now with unshed love. He was very close. I closed my eyes. He must now venture at least one chaste kiss upon my forehead—and after, if not now, later, when we could be alone, on my cheeks, my lips, my neck, and then . . . and then . . .

Even to think of it brings me to that slow burn I always loved—though I loved more the satisfying of it—which never came often enough for me . . .

I burned, I trembled, then I heard his voice. "The lady by you in the tower today—the brown-haired maiden—do you know her name? Oh, madam, help me to her, help me to win her, or I swear I'll kill myself!"

XXVII

Kill himself?

I could have killed him—I leave you to imagine how I felt. Not only for my hurt pride, and the vanity that led me to believe his eyes sought me, when all along his fancy had been caught by that fat bedbug from Leicestershire—but for the love that might have been between us if he had loved me then instead of her . . .

Oh, I know, I know, she was a sweet girl, a simple country girl: everyone told me that, both then and since. But I could not forgive her animal dumbness—worse, her rank sensuality, easy as any cow's, and like her dumpling breasts, quite irresistible to men—while those of us whom God has made to think and feel, who are strung out like harps along the wires of our own nature, why, we are rarer music and must content ourselves with smaller audiences.

Still, I put my pride deep in my pocket, for I had to cover my own folly, and did as he demanded. "Her name is Amy Robsart," I informed him coldly within a week or two, "the daughter of a Norfolk gentleman, the Parliament-man for the shire." I made him wait—any man who uses a princess of the blood as a go-between must expect events to take her time, not his. Nor did I see fit to let him know that she was her father's only heir to a fair estate round Framlingham, running from Crown Corner by Wetherup all the way to Pixey Green. And the girl herself I caused to vanish back to Norfolk—the merest hint through one of the Court ladies that her appearance pleased not the King's sister had the desired effect. I hoped to kill his passion. But it was not to be.

"Amy! My *aimée*, my beloved!" he raved. "And what after?"

"Robsart," I said with all the scorn that I could muster.

"And she has come to take 'Rob's heart'!" he rhapsodised. "And she stands just as high as my heart, I would swear!"

Too short for him, then, I thought with venom, and could not help observing, "You will have stunted children if you breed with her."

"No matter if the children are all small like her!" He was waxing lyrical now, forsooth! "Or if the girls are all as tall as I am, and the boys as short as she is herself—for then they will be like herself, perfection!"

I despaired. And truly there was no saving him, for he rushed helter-skelter into his wooing, and within three months they were wed. He was eighteen, she fifteen, not too young to be married, but too young, God knows, to make the world-without-end bargain that marriage has to be. The lucky Amy was in a daze of joy, which quite took from her the teaspoonful of brains she ever had. Even on her wedding day, leaving the altar on her bridegroom's arm as all the choir sang anthems, her gypsy face, still with its faint moustache—*had they not heard in Norfolk of salts for bleaching, camomile or oil of lemon?*—showed that she could not believe that she had landed the best catch of the Court.

I hated it, and her, and most of all him, and straightaway afterwards, pleading home affairs that needed my attention, I contrived to leave the Court and fell back to Hatfield, to lick the deep wound to my *amour-propre* in a six-month sulk.

But much though I loved Hatfield, now I saw one thing most clearly—that I could not live there now. In the last year I had become a lady of the Court, and that was now my home. I stayed away till Christmas, then I wrote Edward for permission to return. For answer he sent a troop of the King's Guard, with stern orders to despatch at once! Thus I returned this time in royal style, escorted by a guard of honour of two hundred men, to a palace of my own, quartered as I was in St. James, across the park from Whitehall.

To me, then, life at Court was life itself, and I rode harder, danced higher and laughed longer there than anywhere on earth. After the first fierce pangs, I did not miss Robin as I feared I would. For now ambassadors came calling, and great ones too: I was much sought after. And there were always my cousins Henry Carey and Francis Knollys, whom I liked more and more the more I got to know them, not to mention the other men jostling to take Robin's place.

Robin came once to Court with his new bride. But as he dangled her around, flaunting his new plaything for other men's admiration, as all men do with the woman who first gives them command of what they bear between their legs, she simply stood there, the poor clotpoll, her arms hanging like a puppet's, cow's eyes dimly working in her face, mouth open and panting like a thing in heat, till he was obliged to take her away again. How long their rural pastimes and country delights would have the power to hold him, I did not know. But I shame to say, I took a satisfaction in the thought that those who make their beds must lie in them!

Another spirit present in her absence was Mary, who was now more estranged from King and Court than ever. Another summons calling her to account had brought another, fiercer battle, as Edward tried to force her to submit and Mary defied him. Then in fear Mary had caused her cousin Charles, the King of Spain and Holy Roman Emperor, to threaten all-out war on England if his close relation were not allowed her Mass. Edward had wept, and backed down, under pressure from the Council, and now Mary was a heroine of the people, as the saviour of everything that was old and good.

"And not just in religion," Cecil confided in me with a heavy sigh. "I fear the country has been much unsettled by the shift of power between our two great Dukes." And now that Somerset was free again, and back upon the Council, there was deep concern on all sides. "Who rules the country?" wayside preachers, malcontents or drunkards would demand. "Two bad Dukes or a king?" And all this time Mary sat tight and queened it in her Norfolk fastness, and every day won more hearts to her cause.

I saw this all too dimly at the time, for I was myself too busy queening it again at Court as the first lady. I knew that as soon as my brother married, I would have to relinquish my unofficial crown, but I could not bear to think of that. Above all, I could not stand to think of Edward ever marrying Jane Grey. To have to give way to Jane, to walk behind her, curtsey to her, carry her train, attend upon her every whim once she was Queen of England—no! I could not bear it! Anyone but Jane!

You see from this I thought that I held life then in the palm of my hand. I was the star of the Court, and I did not know that stars may have a fall. The whole world danced to my tune through day after day of pleasure and privilege, days devoid of care. But when life's drum beats at its highest, then the wisest virgin learns to hear another sound, the soft pulsing of the dance of death.

The first to fall was Somerset, who had fallen once as Lucifer and risen again as Lazarus, so that all thought he was reborn by God's will, or Northumberland's, and was therefore safe. Now the dark lord was said to be plotting against the Council—more, against the very Lord Northumberland his rival, who, having spared him once, was in no mood to be bitten again by the same dog. Yet men of wit suspected that Northumberland had had a hand in the plot against himself in order to be rid of his great adversary. And who would risk repaying him in that coin?

Death came for "the Good Duke," as the ignorant still called the former Lord Protector, early in Our Lord's year of '52. His trial and sentence just before Christmas threw a pall of fear and melancholy over all the Court. Edward and the Protector had not been close: he was closer far to his other uncle, my bad lord, Lord Tom, who always cheered and charmed him. But from this time, Edward was not the same.

It came, as do so many fatal things, at first unnoticed. Edward had been the healthiest of children: from his birth, he had been so protected that the maladies of childhood passed him by. Was that his undoing? For though now a youth full grown, he took a child's bout of measles the next spring. Recovering from that, he fell into the small pocks and was confined to bed while he threw that off too.

Like all his English subjects, I prayed for the King's life each time I went to church. But I never feared his death: he was young and healthy, and only babies died from having measles, or weaklings from the pocks. Fatal omission! His pale eyes saw further, as did Northumberland's. And both had much to lose.

One day of the King's sickness, reading in my closet, I was surprised by Robin, who had been a stranger to Court for many months. But the Robin who now entered my apartments was not the man I knew. Pale, haggard and aloof, he seemed to have aged ten years. And when he knelt to greet me, he would not meet my eye. "Why, Robin," I rallied him with nervous jocularity, "how are you? And how goes married life?"

"Forgive me, madam—let us not speak of that."

What, was the gilt already off the gingerbread? Oh, my poor Robin! "To business, then," I said as briskly as I could. "What brings you here?"

"His Grace the Duke my father sends you this." He waved in a servant from the corridor, bearing a polished brassbound box. Wondering, I opened it. Within, enscrolled in lawyers' Latin, were the title deeds to an estate and house . . . "the Manor of Hatfield" . . . And others too . . . "to the Dwelling in the Strand known as Somerset House" . . .

"What does this mean?"

"The Duke of Somerset let you believe, my lady, that Hatfield was yours. It was not: it was his. He held the lease, and could have put you out at any moment. Now my father gifts it to you. It is yours in full—in absolute ownership, in perpetuity. And with the King's assent, he grants you, too, the late Duke's own town house, the mansion on the Strand."

"And why should he do this?"

"You are the King's Most Honoured Sister, and His Grace wishes—"

I knew he was repeating like an actor lines that he had to say. "Oh, Robin, I beg of you—*what does this mean?*"

He hesitated. "There are—changes planned," he said stonily. "If you will but cooperate—lend your support—or at least, remain in quiet at Hatfield—"

"What changes? And why must I be at Hatfield? Why not at Court?"

"You will know all, in time."

I stared down at the title deeds, then up at this cold stranger. "And if I refuse my—cooperation?"

"A litter is prepared: it waits at the door. On the King's orders you leave Court at once."

"I will see the King!"

XXVIII

His face was thinner; he was very pale. I had thought him no more than indisposed. Now I saw sickness in his eyes and his pinched, purplish mouth, I smelled it in the odour of his chamber. And more: once again I saw the Edward I so dreaded, the chill fanatic of my first day at his Court.

But his first words were friendly, though their tone was cool. "So, sister, you are now a lady of more property! Hatfield and Somerset House, and as I think, a manor or two besides. Is that not so, my lord?" He half turned to Northumberland, hovering attentively beside him, who spoke at once. "It is indeed, sire."

I gathered up my strength. "Sir, I would be pleased to know how I have now deserved this generous bounty at Your Majesty's hands."

He eyed me sombrely. "The King our father left you Hatfield in his will. You never had it. Better, I think, to regulate what should be while we still can—while we are alive—so that after we die the Devil cannot take advantage of our sins of omission, since we are already bound to pay for those we have committed."

What lay behind all this? I tried to rally him, and myself too. "I hope Your Majesty has no thoughts of death! We all pray daily for your health, and I am glad to see you so much recovered."

He stared me full in the face. "Yet must we all die when God pleases: I as much as any." His eyes were blank. Lying bloodless against the linen pillows in his white shift, his legs and arms straight and stiff alongside his still body, he seemed not of this world, a marble effigy.

I stood as one upon the edge of an abyss. *If Edward died* . . . But even then I could not think the unthinkable.

Northumberland, sharp as a terrier, leaped into the breach. "His Majesty makes these gifts, madam, only to show you the power of his munificence—"

And his power over me?

"—to reward those who honour him and his God-guided policies, who undertake faithfully to follow all his dispensations—"

"And obey my laws!"

Edward's own voice cut like a surgeon's knife. I felt the blade: somewhere I was bleeding.

"We all obey you, sire—you are the King."

Yet a King may be mistaken—as my father was . . .

I forced myself to speak. "And we are bound by God to obey you—*in all things lawful, and according to God's word . . .*"

Northumberland suppressed a violent start and turned to the King. A spasm seized Edward: he began to cough. Glances like bolts of lightning passed between them, a thunderous dialogue went to and fro, but neither spoke a word. My heart misgave me, but I blundered on. "Not that Your Majesty would ever deal in deeds unlawful . . ."

I stumbled on into unbroken silence. Then I knew that Edward now was bent on travelling a road I could not follow: that he would shrink from nothing to achieve his will. *And Northumberland must be his guide, his pilot, for their interests are now one. Without the King, or some arrangement continuing Edward's rule, the Duke could not survive.*

But what was Edward planning? I could not even guess. *Retreat!* my frightened heart was shrilling. *Save yourself, retreat!* I had been out of Court when the Lord Protector had lost his footing in this game of power, and so I must be now. I fell to my knees. "Sire—if I may leave you now—withdraw from Court to see about my properties, your most gracious gift . . ."

I left that same day. Did I know then how much the world would change, and how much for the worse, before I should lay eyes on Court again? That never in this world was I fated to see Edward more?

I knew so little, and how could I ever learn what was happening when I was buried in the country far away? And soon, too soon, my whispering fears received the worst of confirmations. First I heard that Edward was recovered of his pocks, and his old self again. More, he passed through the streets of London in full armour, and afterwards tilted and jousted as hardily as ever. But underneath the new facade of health, his frailty lingered. By that November he had a new companion, and one destined never to leave him: a high cough that shook him night and day.

Now the seeds of rottenness took root deep in his lungs. Pained observers noted that his frame was racked with spasms, then that one shoulder now stood permanently higher than the other.

When I heard that, I changed my daily prayers to hourly observations. But worse was to come. "Now is the King's mind known, or feared at least," wrote Cecil—newly made Sir William for his services—for it was he who had become the eyes and ears that I had left at Court. "His mind is bent on nothing but saving his realm from Popery and the rule of Rome. So he studies the succession, who shall rule after him."

When did the painless knowledge "We must all die" give way in Edward's mind to "I must die, and before I have a chance to sire the son that England needs?"—a "must" of such desperation that all his actions took on the madness of a runaway horse, screaming and galloping faster as it races towards the edge of darkness ahead?

Alone in Hatfield, I brooded night and day. How ill was Edward? Bland assurances from Court officials were full of falseness, never to be trusted. But even sick to his soul, surely Edward would not tamper with the ordained succession, with the King our father's will? And if he did, what changes could he make? All men would have chosen a male heir, certainly—the worst of men, however idle, ignorant or vicious, would be preferred to Mary or me or to any of us, so long as he came equipped with that which makes them men. But there was none, not one! For after Mary and myself, the next heir was yet another female, Lady Grey, the daughter of my father's younger sister, mother of Jane and Catherine. The next claimant by blood, to Catholics the one true claimant above the whole Grey line, was none other than the infant Mary, the little Queen of Scots, even now being bred up in all Romish rottenness at the Most Catholic Court of France—she never could be heir, that could not be!

Like a feather on deep waters, I was tossed to and fro. One grim November day after a night of torment, I knew my mind. I had to see the King. I dared not write him for permission to return to Court: I felt sure Northumberland would refuse me. So I sent for Richard, trustiest of my gentlemen. "We leave for Court tomorrow—no litter, just a handful of your fellows to keep me company. I'll ride the roan, for she'll go farthest without flagging. Tell as few as possible—see to it."

The men he chose I trusted with my life. And even Kat knew nothing of my plan till the last moment. But someone watched, and others rode ahead, faster than we ourselves. For Northumberland's eyes were still upon me, even in my own house. We had not covered half the way to Greenwich, where the King lay, when, cresting a hill, we saw them—an armed troop spread out across the road, barring our way. As we drew near, the leader rode to meet us. "Your Grace, you must return to your own house."

His words were courteous, but the scroll he bore spoke for itself. I did not need to see the seal, the hand, the words of Edward: I knew what it would say. Was this his doing, or Northumberland's? Did it matter? Like a defeated galleon, all sails pulled down as she limps back to port, I turned around and, weeping silently, trailed back to Hatfield.

Cecil's letters now became my only lifeline as I hungered for news. Yet as the scene at Court grew darker, information became more sparse and dangerous. All winter long I watched the starving birds pecking about for crumbs, however meagre, and felt as one with them. Then on a day of January, when a grey mist had enveloped all the frozen fields from early morning, a fellow greyer than the mist itself arrived at Hatfield and was brought to me. I knew who sent him even before I saw the badge of Northumberland on the side of his cap. "Your message, sir?"

His words were conned by rote. "His Majesty the King has drawn up plans to alter the succession to the crown. On his death, the Lady Mary is disbarred, on grounds that her mother's marriage to the late King Henry was unlawful, and no bastard may succeed to the throne of England . . ."

No bastard may succeed . . .

The blood in my ears roared and grew black. I knew the rest before he uttered it. One stone brings down two birds. "So is the Lady Elizabeth likewise excluded on the selfsame grounds of bastardy"—he had the grace to falter there—"for His Majesty decrees no bastard may succeed, no heir of the half blood may ascend the throne of England—"

Nor no woman neither? Had the King set that down too?

"If you will recognize the King's right to regulate the succession, and abandon your false claims to your title to the throne, then His Majesty will admit you back to Court, make much of you and assure you of your unassailable place as Sister to the King."

What, like Anne of Cleves, another cast-off and inconvenient woman? No, I was not made of that same pliant stuff! "Tell your master to convey to the King, that while my sister Mary lives, I have no claim or title to resign! Nor is she a "claimant." She is the heir, under my father's will! And tell him further, I will never give consent to overthrow the late King's dispensations, which were agreed by Parliament with all the force of law. I will not yield to anything unlawful—so help me God!"

Of course I saw the horns of the dilemma Edward had speared himself upon—and me! He could not disbar Mary for illegitimacy without excluding me too, as both our mothers' marriages had been declared null and void by the King, and by Church and State. Yet I of all would have been Edward's chosen heir! Northumberland's too: as a Protestant, and one whom he had favoured, one who he knew had been close to his son Robin, and might be so again . . .

Wheels within wheels, plots within plots . . .

With Edward dying, Northumberland would be forced to play the King's game, yet to play his own hand too. Was that his scheme: to allow the King

*to disinherit Mary, then to slip me into place, when Edward died, as the true
Protestant heir?*

*But he and Edward were both gambling-mad to think that Mary would be
so easily disposed of—as all found . . .*

*And failing me and Mary, who was to be Queen? Why, who but little
Jane? My cousin Jane, whose fate had thrust her forward for this role from
the time she was first broached as a bride for Edward. Put forward, then cast
off, she was now picked up again by Edward in a last grim mockery of a
courtship: his own handwritten will, which he called his "Device for the
Succession," named Jane as Queen over her own mother, over all of us.*

A kiss from a man dying all too often proves to be a kiss of death. And
now the dance of death at Edward's Court moved into its last wild jig.
From January was he rotting in men's eyes as his consumption galloped
apace. His lungs were suppurating, his body torn with seizures, all his
skin a mass of ulcers, his poor back pitted with bedsores. His shaven
head and empty belly swelled till they seemed a matching pair of melons,
yellow and bursting.

And if the torment of his body beggared belief, he suffered more in
mind. As he grew worse, he sank into a fearful sadness, varied only by
bursts of weeping, heart-stricken grief. Yet even then there still were
glimmers of his old sweet self. He sent Mary the richest table diamond of
his treasury, set with rubies and a pendant orient pearl, as testimony that
though he moved against her as a king, he still loved her as a brother.

And as his star sank into the last goodnight, so Jane's brief meteor
blazed. In mid-May her father Lord Grey, newly ennobled as the Duke
of Suffolk, acquainted Jane with her new status as the Queen-to-be. He
told her, too, that she would have a king—none other than the youngest
son of Dudley, my Robin's brother Guildford. To their horror and her
eternal credit, Jane declined both of these honors and begged to be
allowed to live alone with her virginity and her books.

But virgins, unlike bastards, can be refashioned into forms more fitting. Jane's father and her ever-loving mother took turns to beat her till
she changed her mind. At Whitsun of Our Lord's year '53 were she and
Guildford married. Then with the King's will and Northumberland's dynasty both now secure, at last poor Edward could be allowed to sink. On
Northumberland's orders, all the stimulants that had maintained his life
were now withdrawn.

All that remained for Northumberland was to gather the last pawns of
the game into his hands. In June my summons came: "His Majesty commands your presence at the Court." But Cecil's shadow was not far behind: "Feign sickness, do not go!" the warning came. "Your sister Mary
likewise is sent for, and she has fled to Suffolk." Next came the word I

dreaded, and yet prayed for as a relief for all his sufferings: "Your brother the King died peacefully today: the Lady Jane is proclaimed England's Queen."

Poor nine days' wonder! My last messenger came openly in royal livery, the Tudor rose triumphant on his breast: "The traitor Queen is overthrown, the foul conspirators in custody. Her Majesty Queen Mary sends her greeting to her most beloved sister and bids you ride for London, to give thanks for her deliverance and yours!"

XXIX

Bastard and virgin—how those twin themes played and replayed themselves in my life's history! Even my own brother, my loving brother Edward, found fit to bastardise me in the same terms that my father had, God shrivel him! Now I was once more subject to another's man's dying will, the will of another dead King of England.

And those around "Queen" Jane knew that they had to blackguard the true inheritors to shore up her flimsy right to rule. Before my brother's corpse was cold, Northumberland and his lackeys had myself and Mary proclaimed as bastards from every pulpit—yes, the leaders of the Church, the bishops themselves, preached against us—Ridley at St. Paul's and Latimer at Westminster, the very seat and throne of England's monarchy!

And England's new Queen, my co-sufferer from this stigma, my sister Mary, what of her? A woman who had herself been bastardised in my honour, reduced to the half blood by my father so that the sons of Anne Boleyn could reign—would Mary ever be the one to take this slur from me?

Bastard again, then, was I?

So be it.

There are worse things.

Some great men have been bastards. Our Lord Jesus Christ was a bastard and his mother no virgin, said that blaspheming playwright, you remember him, the scribbling spy that my old spymaster Walsingham had killed when his loose talk grew dangerous, when was that? Years ago now, back in '93 or thereabouts. What was he called? His name escapes me. Christopher, I think —and Morley, was it, or Marlin? Marlowe, was that it?

And was Christ of the half blood? My brother burned a madwoman, Joan of Kent, for preaching that Christ had not taken flesh of the Virgin but had passed clear through her body as through a pane of glass. If Jesus, then, did take life and form half from one human parent, half from one divine, and the human half herself a halfling, eternally half mother, half still maiden, was He not then half-blooded, like the best of bastards such as I?

And would he not cry with me in the words of the old Greek comedy, "Now gods, stand up for bastards"?

Yet still I had my other title, one I could be proud of—and in a dwindling hand, the virgin card was all I had to play.

I played it well, no? For who now remembers that I was not the only royal virgin of the time? That there was another, one greater far than I? And though I later won all hearts and minds as "the Virgin Queen," who now recalls that there was one before me who was both virgin and queen? And that she was the first in all our history?

And who now knows as I do that if Mary had remained a virgin, she would have queened it longer, and with the love of all her people—which, instead, she translated into vilest hate, as you shall hear . . .

The very sun seemed blazing Mary's triumph that July of '53 when her commandment reached me. The order was for Wanstead, to the east of Waltham Forest, there to meet the Queen and all her party. Even before the King's death, her supporters had been gathering. Now as we descended on the town, we were part of a great flood of people laughing, praying, singing, chanting, all giving thanks for the true Queen's succession, for the power of Harry's blood.

"The Queen!"

"God save the Queen!"

The Queen! So at a stroke the terror all men feared, the rule of a woman, had become reality. And if nine days' Jane had served no other purpose, her reign had shown that blood, even in a woman, true Tudor blood, was all that counted—indeed, it could raise a woman to the level of a man. And Mary was now the undisputed Queen.

What would that mean for me?

Only with a great effort did my gentlemen carve out a passage for me and my women through the stinking, heaving mass to the house where the Queen lodged.

Oh, God, how would she receive me? All through her disgrace I had queened it shamelessly in what was rightfully her place at Court. Would she now punish me for that? Her reasons to hate me went back twenty years. Now she was Queen, in absolute power, would she not want revenge?

For Mary's wounds, her injuries, beggared belief. All were now fresh in my guilty mind after the long ride from Hatfield: I had thought of little else. Kat used to have an old song that she sang at Eastertide, a ballad of Christ's mother at the cross:

> *The sorrows Mary suffered.*
> *They were one, two, three and four.*
> *When counted these be, lordings,*
> *Count the many more . . .*

I never heard this without thinking of my own Mary. How could another heart number her sorrows, even know where to begin? And all her sufferings had come through me, even before my birth.

For she was always a creature of no account. Never was boy more longed for, more desired. "Pray God send us a prince!" had been in every mouth for generations. I was to be that Prince. And then all Henry's suffering, the seven years when he bedded neither Katherine nor Anne, the pain of "the Great Schism," when he broke from Rome—all, all led nowhere but to my birth, a most unwanted girl.

God had made him the butt of an Almighty joke before the face of all nations. Someone must pay. Even Henry, the cruellest man I ever knew, would not punish a newborn child. But who better than a defiant daughter who might even by her prayers have brought this about?

So Mary was put out of all her honours and declared a bastard. How she smarted under the bar sinister! She who had been not merely Princess, but the Princess of Wales, now lost at a stroke her lifelong titles and rank as heir presumptive. Now I was "the Princess Royal," Princess of Wales, and she no more than "the Lady Mary." And as plain "Lady Mary" she had been stripped of the royal respect she had always known. From having two hundred servants, she was humbled to a handful; from having a palace of her own, she was now ordered to the worst apartments at Hatfield to attend on me, a three-month baby, as no more than one of my women.

And always she was kept like her holy namesake God's mother in perpetual virginity, although she begged my father for a husband: for the King would never tolerate a Catholic marriage, and he knew he could not force her into a union with a Protestant.

Then last and worst of her wrongs: to be kept from her beloved mother for the rest of Katherine's wretched life, divorced from Katherine as surely as Henry had divorced himself, forbidden to be with her even as Katherine lay dying, hastening her end by crying hopelessly for Mary night and day . . .

Just how cruel Henry could be, only another who suffered under him could ever know.

And all in favor of me! All this was for me, so the King claimed, to defend my precious rights. No wonder that she hated me! The wonder is that she did not find occasion to do as her supporters had long whispered in her ear—a moment's sleight of hand with a soft pillow, or a drop or two of poison—to dispose of a whore's brat, no more than the spawn of Satan.

Wonder? Rather say a miracle! How could she not hate me? And who could blame her for hating her heart out?

To me she seemed one of God's unloved, unloved and unforgiven, all her life, for all her godly life.

And I feared to see her, as the murderer fears the ghost of his victim, even though I never meant her any harm nor showed her ill will.

"Admittance for the Sister to the Queen—here on the Queen's command!"

I shuddered as we stepped out of the sun into the cool of the house. *Now God be with me!* Yet she had loved me once! In spite of all, she had loved the child I was. At my waist now I wore a prayer book cased in silver filigree, my only ornament on my pale grey gown, a gift from Mary when I was five years old and treasured ever since. Could she still love me? I could love the old Mary, I felt sure, given half a chance. And I was truly glad and proud for her succession, for her triumph in our father's name. Would she trust me, and believe that?

Domine, conserva me . . . O Lord, save me . . .

"The Princess Elizabeth, sister to Her Majesty, most humbly craves audience of the Queen!"

The door gaped wide before me. The great chamber loomed long and low, the blackened roof beams stretching out into infinity. My heart was in my stomach, my stomach in my mouth. I could scarce breathe inside my lacing, in the stuffy, airless, overcrowded room. I had foreseen advisers and supporters, even an informal council attending upon Mary, to confer on what should be done. But the chamber was alive: the new Queen was holding Court!

To my left as I stepped over the threshold, I could see Wriothesley, the Earl of Southampton, and his old ally Paget: they had lost no time in finding their feet again in another change of power. Huddled nearby were the Earls of Bedford, Winchester and Pembroke, all senior lords and members of great weight upon the Privy Council. With them deep in frowning conversation stood the Lord Shrewsbury, President of the Council of the North: he would have brought the loyalty of all the northern shires along with him. Among the lesser men, I recognised Sir Nicholas Throckmorton, who had been my brother's gentleman, with my kinsman Lord Howard. Further along stood Lord Clinton, Sir William Pickering, once my lord Surrey's boon companion, Sir James Crofts and the Earl of Derby, all known to me by sight from Edward's Court. If all these had declared for Mary, her title was secure. But where—and what? —was Jane now? What had become of Northumberland—and his sons?

Travel-stained messengers raced in and out, while seated at side tables a small army of clerks and scriveners struggled with parchments and proclamations under the direction of none other than my old friend Cecil. With him was William Thomas, who had been Clerk to Privy Council under Edward. Mary was assuming the reins of government— where did that leave me?

All turned towards me: I could have wept with fear. I fell to my knees, praying inside, choking my terror down. But the small blinking figure who stepped forward from the throng of burly lords was far beyond vengeance, almost beyond joy. She took me by the hands and showered me with weeping kisses, too full even to speak. "Oh, sister, God is good!" was her first, tremulous greeting as she raised me up.

I hardly knew her from the frail beleaguered creature I had last seen at Court. Shining like sunshine after rain, she had shed ten years or more. And surrounded by her lords, in the busy press of clerks and messengers, servants, squires and soldiers, amid it all, rich in rubies and red velvet, she was every inch a queen. I wept with her until at last I could speak. "How did Your Majesty escape—how were you saved?"

"By the hand of God!" she said huskily, "—or that of a good man!" With a dry smile she threw a sideways glance to an alcove in the window where Cecil sat immersed in papers, seeming all-oblivious. "I had a warning from a well-wisher not to come to Court when the Duke of Northumberland sent for me. And by the time he came to Norfolk to arrest me, I had gone."

"Thanks be to God!"

"Yes, sister!" Mary's face, her molelike eyes, were working with strong passion. "For this is proof that He has spared me for a greater work, to save our country and to bring her back to Mother Church!"

To save our country . . . ? I brushed aside misgivings. "The Duke? What has become of him?"

Mary's face saddened. "Alas for him! All turned against him when he came to take me. He was himself taken in Cambridge when his army fled."

"Pity him not, Your Grace!" It was the bluff Lord Bedford, himself an old soldier. "He was sole architect of his own downfall—which otherwise would surely have been yours!" Mary nodded and convulsively crossed herself.

"And the Duke's sons . . . ?" My voice trailed off.

"All stood with their father in his traitorous course," put in Lord Pembroke, "and all now lie with him in the Tower."

Oh, my Robin . . . I choked it all back. This was Mary's hour; nothing must mar it.

"And the Lady Jane?"

Mary sighed and brought her clasped hands to her mouth. Pembroke vented a harsh laugh. "The nine days' wonder who thought to rise to the throne has merely crossed Tower Green, my lady, from the White Tower to the traitors' jail. She had been lodged there for her Coronation—now she will lack a head to wear her crown on, just as soon as the law takes its course!"

Mary's clasped hands grew tighter beneath her bowed head, and she drew in her breath. Behind her shoulder I could see the Earl of Shrewsbury give Lord Pembroke an angry glare, which plainly said, *Tread softly! Do not press Her Majesty on this!*

Mary raised her head, breaking the awkward silence with a luminous smile. "With God's grace, and her own sincere remorse, we shall yet save her! When sin finds true repentance, then we do God's work—then there is joy in heaven, and all the angels weep!"

I looked around, but not a man of all about her met my eye.

We rode for London the next day, myself accorded the place of honour just behind the Queen. Towards seven at night, on a clear, cool August evening, we entered by the Aldgate. Never before had I seen anything like it. The streets were carpeted and garlanded with flowers, children danced beneath streamers and bright banners to the music of wildly shouting crowds, choirs singing anthems and peal upon peal of bells. Through it all Mary shed smiles and tears in equal measure. "I thank you all! Thanks be to God! Thank Him and pray to Him, good people, I beg of you!"

Yet Mary was still Tudor enough to know the value of a public demonstration that God stands up for Tudors! As we approached the Tower, there came forth a small procession—even from a distance clearly prisoners by their manacles, their ragged dress and hungry, haunted eyes. Chained to one another, they fell in the dirt before us.

One sour and aged face at the back arrested my attention—yes! the Duke of Norfolk, father of my first lost love, my Surrey. He had escaped the block his son had kissed, only to languish in the Tower all through my brother's reign—for who would risk releasing such a stubborn Papist? Now with Her Most Catholic Majesty Queen Mary in the seat of power, the wheel of fortune had turned for him indeed!

In front of him stood a couple, oddly matched. The woman was well aged and weeping piteously, her skin pale and crumpled like old flax, her body bent with years of imprisonment. Beside her, smiling, was a fine young man, tall and unbowed, and handsome as an angel. Even without his bright red-gold hair and long Plantagenet limbs, I knew who he must be. With a painful mixture of guilt and gladness, I knew I looked on the last sprig of the White Rose, Edward Courtenay, and his mother, imprisoned by my father fifteen years before for their taint of royal blood, buried alive ever since then, and quite forgotten.

Mary's deep voice rang out: "Strike them free!"

Rubbing their wrists, some shaking their heads as if in disbelief, the little party struggled to their feet. Now a new face stood out, one forgotten since my childhood—ferocious as a buzzard's, rough and swarthy, with a ragged beard and yet a woman's spiteful, soft red mouth . . . my old adversary from my childhood at my father's Court, the hated Bishop Gardiner, another crypto-Catholic put aside by the fierce force of Edward's Protestantism.

"My lord Bishop of Winchester!"

He stepped forward, his dull eyes gleaming. "You bring me God's deliverance, Your Majesty."

Mary's eyes were brimming: I remembered now how much she had adored him. "But not to a life of ease, sir! For I here appoint you my Lord Chancellor."

He bowed, I noticed, but without surprise: all Mary's plans had been well laid. Mary looked round and raised an arm to encompass all the group. "We bid you all to feast with us tonight—a feast of thanksgiving and celebration! Follow us within doors!"

As we moved off, she reined her horse back and summoned me alongside. "And at supper, sister," she breathed, "look out for that young Courtenay—tell me truly what you think of him!"

Think of him? What could I think of him? Only one man was in my thoughts as the horses picked their way over the cobbles into the Tower, where we would lie until the Coronation. Yards only now divided me from Robin, pent up in the Beauchamp Tower along with his four brothers, one the nine days' King. Guildford, who had been Jane's husband and a pawn like her, was surely doomed to lose his head. But Robin? Could there be any hope of mercy for him? I knew there could be no answer during this period of rejoicing—what could disturb Mary's unearthly radiance, her rare state of bliss?

And yet—and yet—no matter what I thought of Courtenay—*why should the Queen, Mary the Queen, be thinking of him?* The answer came to me that same evening as she banqueted him and his mother, one on either hand. As a great-grandson of King Edward IV, he was of royal blood. A Catholic too, of Mary's faith, and tall, and handsome, golden and fair as any man in England. Most of all, he was no stripling, having spent most of his life in jail: at twenty-seven summers he was nearer to her age than most men still unmarried . . .

Did she then mean to marry him?

And if she did, would there then be a child? Though she had worn out almost four decades here on this earth, with a young, lusty husband, as I had seen when my lord Seymour bedded Queen Katherine, such things could be . . .

XXX

All August long the sun shone with the promise of better things, after the queasy, quarrelsome reign of the two Dukes and a run of rotten harvests. Few grieved for Northumberland when he paid the price for all his machinations that same August. And Mary's mercy shone like the sun on his five sons, and even on "Jane the Queen," with the hope and pledge of peace.

A promise of good things—but as the sun burned on all summer long, its scorching rays, its fierce and unrelenting heat, the fires that blazed up unwanted in every field and town, gave fearful warning of what was to come.

So at her accession, Mary joyfully wedded herself to a rejoicing nation, and not a heart in England but prayed for her long life as England's Queen. And joyfully, too, did the tongues wag of yet another wedding when the Queen would take a husband: Courtenay was the hoped-for name in every mouth, and Mary pleased still more by favouring him.

Yet even before the Coronation, all the signs foretold the honeymoon was fated to be short. First came her order for our brother's burial. All this time he had lain above the earth in a sealed lead-lined coffin, for his poor body had all but putrefied before he died. Now his hour had come: he was to be buried, Mary decreed, with full Roman rites of the Popish Requiem Mass.

God! To think how this would torment Edward's spirit, wherever it was hovering! The Council warned against it: Londoners, they knew, would rise against a Mass in Westminster Abbey. But still the Queen would have it, if only in private. So my Edward went to his last rest with all the stinking superstitious foolery of Rome, the asperged incense, guttering candles, chant-

ing monks, and priests mumbling their idolatry. And as I knelt there in the
Queen's Chapel, I prayed for his forgiveness—and for God's.

And I had need of both, for now Mary's work of reclamation began in
earnest. Now she was God's virgin, sent to cleanse the temple of all
England from its newfangled devilry; now every pulpit thundered with
denunciations of the New Faith, and leading Protestants were taken for
questioning almost every day. Foremost among them, I was shocked to
hear, was the name of Cranmer: for querying the enforcement of the
Mass, he was sent to the Tower. So a new name was added to my prayers,
along with Robin and his brothers and poor wretched Jane. And every
day brought more.

And as the arch-mover and the architect of "God's holy work," Mary
had the strength of seven devils at this time. She rose before dawn and
spent her days in labour among her papers, till as midnight neared, her
poor purblind eyes could hardly see the candle, let alone the documents
over which she pored. To fortify her soul for this great struggle, she
would hear six or seven Masses every day, and of course wished to in-
clude me.

Of course I feigned a bilious fit, a greensickness, to avoid going to
Mass! But how many megrims can a woman suffer in one day? Within a
week, as soon as the Court was settled at Greenwich to avoid the heat of
the city, my tactics had been noted.

"Be wary, madam!" Cecil warned me privately. "These are dangerous
times. You must placate the Queen!"

It was sound advice, I knew. I begged to have some private time with
Mary. Even as I entered the Privy Chamber and made my deepest curtsey, I could see that the newfound warmth between us had vanished like
winter sun, and would not return.

The reason for it stood at the Queen's elbow dressed head to foot in
black, a small, suave creature, olive-skinned, with eyes like olives too,
hard and black and shining. "Madam Elizabeth, give greeting to His
Excellency Simon Renard," Mary began abruptly, "sent to me by His
Most Holy Majesty the King of Spain."

I dropped another of my deepest curtseys.

Spain! Well, well, it had to be. All through Mary's years in the wilderness
the Spanish King, her mother's nephew, had been her only friend. And with
the King's man now at Mary's side, Spain could—and must—claim the
reward for its support.

And did not the King of Spain have a son? Dear God, could that be where
the wind was blowing now . . . ?

And this Renard—Renard the fox? A true Spanish don from his black
gleaming pate to the curved dancer's heels of his fine leather shoes, he had

*not the appearance of a fox. But fox he was, if I knew anything. And what
was I but a defenceless lamb? Yet I must out-fox him—out-fox them both!*

"Sister, I wish you to consider well your actions at my Court . . ."

Mary knew how to bully, for she had herself been bullied by a champion. I must attend Mass at her side, be seen in public making Roman devotions after the high Romish rites. I wept and pleaded, wriggling like a fish upon the hook. "Is it my fault," I sobbed, "that I was never taught the doctrine of the old religion? How can I go to Mass without belief?"

Mary smiled her burning smile. "If you go to Mass, belief will come!"

I sobbed harder. "Time, madam, grant me time!"

I could see Mary wavering: she hated to cause pain. But then a light touch on her sleeve, a whisper in her ear from her companion, and her backbone stiffened. "Beware her, madam," I heard him breathing in her ear, the glance he gave me showing that I was meant to hear. "Remember, she is the daughter of the Whore, one who adultered with her lutanist! And I detect in her a spirit full of enchantment, against you and the true faith."

Mary flushed. He had sounded her darkest fear and waked her deepest hatred. "Just like her mother!" she said wildly. And my fate was sealed. "This Sunday is the thirteenth after Trinity, the Feast of the Nativity of the Blessed Virgin Mary, and a holy day for both of us, God's sacred day for virgins," she ordered angrily. "It is my command that you attend my Mass, here in the chapel at Greenwich. Defy me at the peril of your soul —and of your body!"

I saw Renard's eyes light on me in the blackest irony of high amusement as I bowed out—what would I do?

What could I do? "Oh, Kat!" Back in my quarters I relieved myself with a great burst of tears—true tears this time, not like the waters of the crocodile I had splashed forth for Mary. Then I had to school my anxious spirit for what lay ahead.

That Sunday was the day after my birthday—"Twenty years, madam!" Parry rejoiced with Kat—yet could I take no joy.

Though Kat and Parry tried their best to cheer me, I grew more and more desolate as the hour of the Mass approached on that dark Sunday. What could I do? I had to go. And yet for the sake of my own faith, I had to show I went unwillingly—and yet again, not in a way that might draw down the wrath of Mary . . .

What could I do?

Not for the first time in my life, Dame Nature came to my aid. I woke with a vile colic gripping my guts, and by the hour of the Mass as we went in procession to the Chapel Royal, I could fairly claim to need relief and support. "Oh, help me! Rub my stomach!" I begged good Lady Browne, who walked beside me, while Kat and Parry held me up behind. From the quick glances and smothered grins of all around, I knew my far-from-dumb show had not gone unnoticed. And I knew now that the word would spread far and wide, that though the Princess Elizabeth had been forced to go to Mass, she had gone most unwillingly, and the very thought of it had made her sick!

And my ploy found success. Mary was so pleased with my "conversion" that she sent me a diamond and ruby brooch and one of her own rosaries, most exquisitely carved in pure white coral. And praise God for his mercies, her warmth towards me continued until her Coronation. Once again she made me the second person in the realm, showering me with diamonds to wear in her procession, ordering for me royal quantities of a rare white samite from Jerusalem and cloth of silver, to make me Coronation robes almost as rich as hers.

As rich—but not as regal. Whereas I was proclaimed by my pure vestments as the Virgin Princess, pale and untouched, Mary was magnificence itself in royal purple, rich as King Solomon or the Queen of Sheba. On her head and breast she blazed with jewels—her small crown, newly made, flashing and glittering in the sun. On her gown, rubies and diamonds like fallen stars clustered shoulder to hip across her ceremonial baldric, amethysts and rose stones gleamed from every fold of her full embroidered skirt and huge padded velvet sleeves. The very finger rings crowding her hands tapped out the tune of triumph, that the new religion, the pure self-denying Protestantism, was dead, and the old indulgence, with its rituals of shameless luxury and self-glorification, was back to take its place.

Back with a vengeance?
In the burning sun I shivered and grew cold.

XXXI

I had delighted Mary by attending her special Mass: England's Virgin Queen and her Virgin Princess had been seen side by side in worship on the Virgin's day. I had also satisfied my own beliefs and my supporters, those who were staunch in the New Faith and could not cut their consciences at will to fit the new season's fashion.

But my triumph was not without its price. For if the Queen's sister had been forced to bow her head, all men could see which way the wind was blowing. With faces of defeat my cousins Francis Knollys and Henry Carey came to take their leave. "This is no place for true believers, madam!" whispered Francis harshly as he wrung my hand in bitter farewell. Henry wept openly and begged leave to write to me. "Though what I may be able to say freely, lady, I do not know . . ."

Now in place of these and others who had been friends to Edward and me, all Mary's Popish people crept out from their hidey-holes to flaunt their victory. Chief of the thorns in my flesh was the old Countess that Denny had warned me of, the mother of the only Tudor son, young Henry Darnley. With the long-legged twelve-year-old in constant attendance, the Countess Margaret of Lennox never missed a Mass, sweeping in ahead of all except Mary and myself in her determination to vaunt her royal blood. Her very look was like the kiss of a toad, she stank of incense masking something fouler, and I loathed her with all the passion that she vented against me.

And the respite I had contrived with such an effort was all too short-lived. When the next Sunday I feigned illness to avoid the Mass, Mary punished me shrewdly by downgrading me at Court. Now on her orders I had my place as the Queen's sister quite denied, and was forced to give way to lesser women of the royal blood! To scrape and curtsey now to such as fat old Frances Grey, my far-off aunt and the mother of the convicted traitor "Queen" Jane besides, and even worse to have to defer and curtsey to the triumphant Countess and her wretched son, were poison to my pride, and Mary knew it.

And worse was to come. The next month, pushed through by the Spanish Ambassador Renard and her Lord Chancellor, the hated Gardiner, the first Act of her Parliament repealed her bastardy, while confirming mine.

Bastard again . . . how many times now?

And each sting of the lash the worst.

Yet in all the other matters Mary sought, Parliament refused to do her bidding. For all men saw how Renard had wormed his way into her confidence, how she turned to him for counsel. And all knew as I did that His Most Catholic Majesty the King of Spain had a most marriageable son, the newly widowed Prince Philip . . .

"She *would* not, *could* not do it, marry a foreigner and a Papist!" young hotheads could be heard raging in corners. Yet all knew that the Queen would marry—all her long, lonely, barren spinster years she had longed for nothing else.

And not only that she would: more, that she *must*. "There have been no queens regnant in our history," Cecil lamented to me privately—God, would I never hear the end of this refrain? "And such queens consort as have held sway have brought disaster with them!"

"Disaster?" I did not like his word.

He shook his head helplessly. "Even the fierce Matilda could not secure the throne: all she bred was civil war and cruel anarchy. Then in the wars of Lancaster and York, the two queens consort then, she-wolves both, usurped the power of men until our country ran with blood! Never again! No, the Queen must marry—we must have a prince! And for that, we must have a king; but not, please God, the son of the King of Spain!"

Alone, I brooded on it. Courtenay was Catholic, if it only were a matter of her faith. But a ruler must weave more than one strand into the cloth of state. She had promised Parliament she would take no foreign husband, she would not marry out of the kingdom. Courtenay, then? I did not envy her decision. And at thirty-eight now, her sands were running down, faster than any knew, yet still not fast enough to spare the rivers of blood, rivers of fire to come . . .

Beset by problems like a swarm of bees, Mary yet found time to wrestle with the Devil for my soul. For weeks we stormed and struggled while she blandished me with diamonds to submit and threatened me with banishment, and worse, if I would not. Powerless at Court, I knew my only course lay in retreat. As she ebbed to and fro, I clung to one refrain: "I pray Your Majesty give me leave to withdraw to my own house."

At last she yielded, and I left for Hatfield. Another winter journey did nothing to raise my spirits. Mary was the rising sun—was my star setting? We struggled back to Hatfield like a band of beaten soldiers who must recover their fighting strength or lose all in the attempt. Yet Hatfield was to prove no sanctuary for me from the toils and perils of the web of Mary's Court. Not a week after I returned, I had a visitor.

"Sir James Crofts, at your service, Princess!" he announced himself with a loud public flourish.

"Sir James?"

I had last seen him among those gathered at Wanstead to salute the Queen's accession. A little, wiry man, he was a courtier who had served my brother; other than that, I hardly knew him. But as he knelt and kissed my hand, he squeezed my fingers and stared into my eyes, whispering, "Dismiss all but your most trusted people, lady—what I have to say is for your ears alone!"

Was it the memory of my lord of Seymour's boldness with my hand on our first meeting? Suddenly I felt a coldness stiffening every bone. Even in Hatfield, walls had ears. I bowed. "Let us walk in the park."

Outside the day was dry, the sun making a valiant play to reach us through the clouds, and none could hear us as we paced along.

"Now, sir?"

His voice was hot with fury. "Your sister has announced her marriage choice. She has betrayed her promise given to Parliament: England's King Consort is to be Philip of Spain!"

It was the worst news, for all English hearts. I could not speak. He rushed on furiously. "Our country, then, becomes subject to Spain and to the Pope—an outpost of the Holy Roman Empire and a petty fiefdom of the See of Rome! England will not endure it! It is not to be borne!"

My lips were stiff. "What must be, will be."

"There is a remedy."

A remedy.

But not for Mary, I heard in his tone.

What, a plot against her, with me as its pawn? "Whatever happens must be as God wills."

He flared up again. "Yet if men stand for their rights—take arms in a just cause—is that against God's will, or His command?"

I knew deep water when it swirled around me. "Speak no more!"

"Hear me, madam! If you were called to rule—to be the saviour of the New Faith against the evil of the Old—"

"God may call me, as He has called my sister—I leave all in His hands!"

I broke away, and would not hear a word. I smelled conspiracy, I felt the cold draught of its fatal wings as it brushed past me, coming near, too near! Even to talk like this was treason, if my guess was right.

An unsought secret is as welcome as the touch of an unwanted lover. I could not, would not, plot against my father's daughter and the rightful Queen! But was I safe in my ignorance? No—I had to know. The day after Crofts's visit I despatched my trusted Chertsey to follow Crofts. He was to sound him out discreetly and then bring me speediest word of it.

Within two days a grim-faced John was back. "Sir James has secret rooms in London, in a mean house off the Poultry, far from Court. Gentlemen came there to see him by twos and threes, all muffled up, their hats down over their faces. But all of them I knew."

"Yes?"

"They are William Thomas, the Clerk to the Council in your brother's time: a devout Protestant who fears the triumph of Popery in our land. Sir William Pickering speaks as one who served as our Ambassador in France: he fears Spain's domination. Sir Nicholas Throckmorton loved and served your brother when he was Gentleman of the Privy Chamber, and says he will not suffer to see the good young King's work perish. And Sir Thomas Wyatt fears the Spanish marriage: no good came of the first one to the Princess of Aragon in his father's time, he swears—and he swears, too, madam, that on his father's life, he will now see the daughter of Queen Anne Boleyn rule in this land."

Wyatt.

"He is the leader, then?"

"Lady, he is."

Wyatt!

My heart convulsed: how my life's tale went round and round! I knew this Wyatt—I could still see him roistering with my late lord of Surrey and William Pickering that night beside the Thames. But I knew still more of the Wyatt who came before him: for his father, as all men knew, had loved my mother.

And this young Wyatt now desired to vindicate his father's lost love by placing her daughter on the throne of England? "When is this planned?" I murmured through stiff lips.

"Palm Sunday, madam—the day chosen for the Prince of Spain and all his entourage to arrive in England. All our people will be on holiday, and the roads will be clear enough to raise rebellion, and then march on London. But I do fear—"

"Yes?"

"This plot leaks like a sieve!" Chertsey spoke out violently. "We are now in December—this will not hold till March and none get wind of it!"

He spoke the truth. We had no more than a scant three weeks' grace—if "grace" can be the word for anxious days and troubled, fearful nights. Then the news came to me by a messenger, half falling from his horse, come nonstop from Whitehall from the same trusted source as when Edward died: "It is over—*and they have lost.*"

The tale was swiftly told. The Council getting wind of the conspiracy, the plotters were forced into swift action, too soon for success. And this in spite of two great new names on their side. First was Lord Henry Grey, the Duke of Suffolk, who saw one final chance to set his daughter Jane upon the throne. The other was none other than the slighted King Consort, Edward Courtenay, who now saw himself as King in his own right, but with another Queen—none other than myself.

So—Queen Elizabeth, wife to King Edward?

I had to grant the beauty of the scheme: to unite the last Plantagenet with the last Tudor would have been a distillation of the royal blood of England to its finest liquor—a chance worth playing for. Yet who would have ruled, myself or Jane, if the rebellion had succeeded? No man knew.

And now? My informant turned his muddied hat in his hands as he replied. "All men proved loyal to Queen Mary, and the risings are put down. Sir Thomas Wyatt, Courtenay, the Duke of Suffolk and all the lesser lights are in the Tower, and the hunt is on for their secret co-conspirators."

Co-conspirators.

I had not conspired. But as the centre of a traitorous plot, that would not save me!

Now I knew fear indeed, fear like before when my lord Seymour had entangled me in his black treasonous schemes. Shaking, I called for Kat and took to my bed.

But even then I knew, that even though I crawled into a mousehole, they would seek me out.

And so they did. The whole house could hear the tramp of armed men coming from ten miles away. With them came Mary's high commissioners, all Lords of the Council, charged to bring me then and there to London. I pleaded illness; Mary had sent her own physicians to forestall me. I begged for time to set my house in order; it was refused, with such uneasy glances passing between the Lords that I seemed to hear them say, *Do not seek to know when you will see your home again.*

Now was I sick indeed. My body swelled with waters, I could not sit a horse. No matter: the kind Queen had sent me her own litter. "May it please Your Highness to prepare for London—*at once?*"

Now I knew that I was their prisoner, every bit as much as cousin Jane. We parted the next morning, just as dawn was breaking in time with my poor heart. And as we turned onto the highway, I dared not look behind, for when would I see Hatfield's beloved face again?

As I came into London that drear February, another soul was leaving it, one whose innocence had saved her so far but could not spare her now. Poor, wretched, helpless Jane: simply for being named by her too greedy father as the Queen again, she now had to die.

Yet even then Mary struggled to pardon her, for she would never kill for her own sake, only for God's. Would Jane then cheat the headsman? Installed that night under an armed guard in Whitehall's grimmest lodgings, I was half-dead with my own sufferings. Yet as I wept, I could only think of Jane—for her fate as queen-pretender could be mine . . .

Chertsey brought me the word as he attended my service at supper. I pushed aside the dish of dressed rampion Kat had placed before me, and gripping my goblet, stared into the blood-red wine. I saw the fact in his face. "She died, then? How?"

His voice was like winter husks. "Most bravely, madam—unlike her husband Guildford, who had to be carried sobbing and screaming to the scaffold. So small and thin, they say, that she looked no more than a lost child, stumbling blindfold through the straw and casting around for the block. But she died like a—"

Like a queen . . .

Could I die like that?

And would I have to?

If they could prove that I had known of Wyatt's rising, that would be enough to send me after Jane before her blood had dried upon the axe! First to try was my old enemy Gardiner, the bully Bishop and Lord Chancellor who ruled Mary's mind in Council as Renard did in her private counsels. As he came into my lodgings, I saw his tongue circling his teeth and fat red underlip, and I knew he almost felt me in his jaws. His smile invited me to my own graveside. "So then, Madam Elizabeth—*shall we begin?*"

Christ, how I feared him! Feared him and hated him. And how he loved his work! He cat-and-moused it with me day in, day out, and all the while I knew that in the Tower they were towsing Wyatt joint by joint to get him to implicate me. And then came the day when Gardiner, eyes alight with glee, triumphantly informed me, "The traitor Wyatt has confessed that you knew all his plans and supported them!"

I was prepared for this. "Men on the rack say anything. I am innocent!"

He was deaf. "All that remains now is for you to throw yourself upon Her Majesty's mercy—"

What, like Jane?

"—and crave forgiveness for your most foul crime."

"How can an innocent person ask forgiveness for what they have not done?"

And on, and on. How could I blame Wyatt? With or without his word, even without a shred of evidence against me, I knew we were not safe, nor free, nor likely now to be.

For now the shadows darkened every day. As Wyatt went to trial, the people openly cheered him, while broadsheets and ballads on the streets of London hailed him as a hero and a martyr. In Eastcheap came a miracle when a talking wall—God knows who was behind it—bellowed aloud, "God save Queen Mary!"

No answer came.

"God save the Lady Elizabeth!"

"Amen, and so be it!" was the reply.

"What is the Mass?" the voice then cried.

A groan: *"Idolatry!"*

"Beware idolatry!" came the final horrid warning. Then it cried "The

Spaniards are coming! The Spaniards are coming!" till all the inhabitants fled the place for fear.

Worst of all was the dog. A dead mongrel, clad in a mockery of monk's habit, with its head shaved in a tonsure, was hurled by night through the window of Mary's Privy Chamber, and the fright and disgust felt by the Queen alone at prayer caused her to vomit till she fainted. Now it was plain to her that Antichrist and his dark minions stalked her land and she must struggle harder still to drive him out.

Northumberland and Suffolk, Wyatt, Jane and Cranmer: with all her other heretic opponents dead or defeated, I alone stood out. And with her "husband" hourly expected to take ship for England—for Mary had married Philip in her heart the moment she decided that God meant her for him—she wished to give him welcome to a Holy Roman land, not a foul nest of heretics.

And all those weeks, locked in my Whitehall lodgings, my world grew darker, darker with fear and dread. I lived on the dull buzz of rumour and stale scraps of gossip; I chewed on these dry bones night and day in lieu of other food.

"The Bishop Gardiner is determined to entrap you and bring about your death!" would come one day. "For he sees you as the Devil's stumbling block to the Queen's work of restoring the Old Faith." But then I would be whispered, "The Queen wants you alive, to show Prince Philip that even the greatest heretics can be brought back to Mother Church!"

What was I to believe? Would it mean life or death? All I knew was that I did not want to die! Despair was my everyday companion now as I faced the worst. Yet still I was unready for the moment when my enemy Gardiner strode in flapping like a great black bat.

"Remove the women!"

Kat, Parry and the maids were hustled out. Behind him came a body of the greatest lords of the Council, the Lord Treasurer Paulet, Lord Bedford, the Earl of Sussex, Lord Paget and even my kinsman the Lord Howard, with a dozen more.

The room was full of men, furred, hatted, booted; the smell of power crowded the air. They had the gait of executioners, and the same eyes. Gardiner's hour had come. His triumph burst from him; he was swelling with the joy of his own venom. I felt his fangs feeling for my neck. "It is the Queen's high will and pleasure that you be committed to the Tower."

XXXII

Conserva me, Domine . . . *Save me, O God, for in thee have I put my trust . . .*

Jane cried out the Miserere as she gripped the block, Chertsey said. So pray all lost souls: Miserere mei, Deus . . . *Pity me, pity me, Lord . . .*

And you, black hat, black heart, black Bishop, the psalmist had words for you: Quis gloriaris, tyranne saevissime? . . . *Why boasteth thou, tyrant, that thou canst do mischief?*

Gardiner stalked away. My voice trailed after him, stripped down to a whisper: "Let me see the Queen."

The Lord Treasurer Paulet broke the silence. "Your request the Queen herself anticipated, and denied."

I looked around the gravestone faces for one spark of pity. My kinsman Lord Howard met my eye, and his sad gaze seemed to say, *I cannot help you.* Beside the Lord Treasurer stood Lord Sussex, beside him Paget, the slippery Secretary from my father's reign. Were these the men who had conducted Jane on her last journey? A shaking seized my hands. "Then let me write to her."

Paulet shook his head. "The tide is rising, and the Tower barge is standing by for you at the river stairs. You may not write."

The Earl of Sussex shifted heavily on his feet. "My lord! It is the right of any—"

Prisoner at the bar?

"—of any subject to approach his King!"

There was a general murmur of assent. I sat down at my desk as they filed out, and took up a pen. My life depended on what I should write now, but what was there to say? All my defence lay in my innocence—which no one now believed or I would not have been committed to the Tower.

Yet what else could I write? *Spare me, sister, for the love of God! I do not want to die?*

I wept then, a good while.

Then a faint notion seized me. What time was it? If I could delay the time of leaving, we would miss the tide. A night's reflection then might touch her heart and change her mind . . .

But if I wrote, would she even get the letter? Ghosts whispering *No* came crowding in upon me. My lord of Seymour, doomed by his own brother, as I now was by my sister—I knew for certain his last letters never reached their destination.

And a still sadder ghost—that of a woman not out of her twenties, just as I was, who had made this journey before me, never to return.

Lord Howard was my mother's uncle—was he thinking of her too?

I could hear the voices of the lords outside in the entrance hall. Winchester sounded pleased with the day's work. "When all's said, the lady's safest in the Tower."

"Safe from her enemies, it is to be hoped, as well as from any rumour of conspiracy!" came Lord Howard's neutral tones. He still had some family feeling for me, then, if he could see the danger I was in.

"Yet we must tread with care." Sussex of all sounded the most troubled by what he had to do. "She is of the blood royal—and who knows, she might be our next Queen!"

A soft laugh from Paget. "That's as Queen Mary finds harvest in her marriage. If she bears a child, our young lady here is no more than an afterthought of history."

Sussex was undeterred. "Yet is she still the daughter of the King."

Paget snickered. "The Queen does not believe so!"

Was that it? Was it for that I had to die? If Mary truly now believed me the daughter of a lutanist and a whore, my cause was lost!

Enough! I would at least try to act like Harry's daughter! And as I had hoped, by the time I finished the tide had turned. I could not now be taken to the Tower until tomorrow. Would that give time for Mary to relent?

That hope died the next day as soon as Paulet and Sussex stepped hard-faced into my chamber. "So far from softening Her Majesty," Paulet reported heavily, "your letter has inflamed her to a fury. As a punishment all your people are now dismissed, except for two or three of your gentlemen. For your body, a few of the Queen's own women henceforth will attend you."

Jane was so stripped of her own women, leaving her to face the block with none but strangers' hands to take off her gown and bare her neck for the blade . . .

"This way, my lady."

Numbly I suffered to be led out to the dark barge waiting at the pier. The afternoon was fading, and a steady, sullen drizzle, thick as my soul's grief, blanketed land and water. From Whitehall Stairs the eye could see no more than fifty yards; from where I stood to the world's end, it seemed, all, all was dark, dark and devoid of hope.

Was this how Anne had felt on her last journey? Time hung suspended in this formless world, but yet I felt the steady rhythm of the pulsing oars, beat upon beat, stealing my life away. And still it rained, as if God himself had opened all the gates of heaven as He did at the Flood, earth and air merging as the walls of water washed down the dying sky. Now the Tower loomed like a leviathan out of the mist, a black and deadly monster lying in wait for me. And now there, dead ahead, low in the water, was the Traitor's Gate, its jaws agape, its deadly iron teeth hovering above and ready to close behind me like a trap!

The Traitor's Gate . . . the last glimpse of the world . . .

A groan burst from me. "I am no traitor! I will not enter there!"

Lord Paulet shook his head. "Lady Elizabeth, you may not choose."

Crabwise across the water, the men backed up the barge and shot across the tide to bring us in. Under the portcullis we floated in the slimy sucking surge of the inner landing stage. Flotsam and jetsam trapped within the walls seemed like the very image of my life, adrift and sinking. A dead dog, sightless, hairless, purple, stinking, knocked against the prow. After the sodden journey, I had thought myself chilled to the bone. But as I set foot upon the stone steps leading up from the water, I felt a chill like death itself and cried aloud in fear.

Seeing with my feet only, for my eyes were blind with tears, I climbed the stairs. Above me at the top a dark arch yawned upon the yard beyond. The stones were black and gleaming: in the dim light they seemed to sweat with the blood of all the wretches who had suffered there for the last thousand years.

Lined up at the back of the walled square stood a troop of Tower yeoman with the Lord Lieutenant, their coats a bloody crimson in the gathering gloom. Like any animal dragged to the slaughterhouse, I smelled the smell of death. My legs betrayed me, and I stumbled weeping to the ground.

Behind me I could hear a shocked intake of breath. "Madam, what ails you?" one of my gentlemen called.

I could not hold back. "Only my innocence!" I cried. "I am as true a subject as ever landed here. God be my witness, for I have no other friend!"

The Lord Lieutenant of the Tower, a courteous, knightly man, hastened towards me. "Madam, I beg of you, get up, come in," he entreated. "It is dangerous to your health to sit here like this!"

"Better sit here than in a worser place!" I burst out. "For I think that I will catch my death inside the Tower sooner than out here!" And I lifted up my voice in hopeless grief.

Suddenly from between the armed guard my usher Vine was beside me kneeling on the flagstones, bareheaded, weeping with grief. His thin grey hair, his black silk hose, were slubbered with rain and mud, his old face streaming with tears. "Oh, madam, madam, if my life or my poor body's pain could be exchanged for yours," he wept, "I would lay it down now beneath your feet!"

Alas, the poor old man! How could I hurt my loyal friends like this? Stiffly I struggled up. "Do not weep, good sir!" I ordered him as firmly as I could. "The time to weep will be when you know I have deserved this—and that will never be! Follow me, come."

The Lord Lieutenant bowed. "This way, Your Highness—to the Bell Tower." *The Bell Tower. Robin is in the Beauchamp, the next tower along the wall . . . Oh, Robin, if they move now against Protestants, how long will the sons of Northumberland be allowed to live?*

As we moved forward, one by one the men-at-arms broke ranks till all were kneeling. "God save the Lady Elizabeth!" came a hoarse cry, followed by a ragged cheer. Briefly my heart revived. But then before me rose the Bloody Tower—beyond it lay Tower Green—and there! See there! A huge black structure in the gathering dark! *Oh, God, save me, I do not want to die!* I saw the raw frame of the scaffold, and I knew the great machine of death had not yet run its course.

Then the cell door clanged behind me: I was a prisoner.

"Mortem ubi contemnas," *wrote Publilius Syrus,* "viceris omnes metus: *"When you can despise death, you have conquered all fears."*

Now I can have the last laugh on the old scarecrow, the old skeleton with the scythe whose terrors and embraces I have so many times escaped, whose bony kisses I have fought off for so long—but then . . . Oh, God, then . . . ?

Daily I walked with Death, he now became my one familiar. He it was who haunted me by day and lay with me by night, draining my courage as he suckled at the teat beneath my breast, the breast nearest to my ever-failing heart. And while Death courted me, Mary wooed life. Now she made ready for her bridegroom, now at nearly forty summers she knew a mad, late-flowering lust for life and love. She was in love with love, and here lay my great danger: for only if she put me to death, both Gardiner and Renard scolded her daily, would her new husband come safely to her arms. For while I lived, and while the people loved me as my father's daughter and the sole surviving beacon of his faith, the Queen herself, they said, was not secure.

As slow as any spider, Mary moved to clear the way for Philip. No wonder that every day I feared for my life, when other deaths fattened the February winds and fed the March airs with blood! Jane's father and her uncle trod the scaffold outside the Tower walls, as one by one all who had believed in him died for Wyatt's wild and wicked dreams.

Yet one thing gave me a frail thread of hope. Mary spared Courtenay; she would not take his half drop of royal blood. So the would-be King, my almost-husband, was banished from England to roam and die abroad. Like Plantagenet, like Tudor, then? Might I yet be saved?

But from my window I could still see the unrelenting scaffold. And when I begged the Lord Lieutenant to know why it was not taken down, he only said, *"It is not done with yet . . ."*

Now locked in night and day, I saw none but the Queen's own servants —servants, or spies. The women Mary sent me were hostile Papists all, ugly and venomous, who killed me with Catholic kindness, sickened me by praying loudly all day long for my repentance. One had the face of a rat in a drain, another a nose so eaten away with pocks that it had crumbled like a piece of cheese; a third was so old and gnarled she knew not if she was a man or woman, and so was nothing, like an old tree root. And they all stank of the Mass! Only Mary would have kept such loathsome hags about her!

My gentlemen still attended me, but never alone: not so much as a whisper could they offer me unheard by my jailors. I craved for word of Robin, or at least the comfort of believing him near me. But was he even still alive? I knew not.

For I knew nothing beyond these four walls. The cramped stone-vaulted chamber where I had been shut up the night of my arrival was all my world now—or my tomb—and God alone knew if I would get out of it alive!

Six women and myself, locked in a cell together night and day—God, think of it! Then with the addition of my gentlemen and the gaolers— besides the still-malignant Gardiner and his train, who came to bait me whenever he could—in the first week the air, the place, grew foul. Even three privies in the garderobe, which ran the length of the wall at the back, would not meet our needs. By noon each day the closestools were overflowing, urine and excrement puddling on the floor, till my shoes, my gown and petticoats tracked it up too. And I who had always loved clean linen almost more than anything . . .

The stink in the cell was as bad as the town midden—it invaded everything. Though I would have every window opened even on the bitterest day, the cell was so foul that the North Wind itself could not have sweetened that lodging.

April came joyfully for the seagulls winging upriver from the sea, for the swallows I could see on Tower Green, for the new buds, for the meanest blade of grass growing out there in freedom—but not for me. Sicknesses seized my stomach, megrims my head, while the pain of my confinement invaded the very marrow of my soul. Almost daily I begged my keeper Sir John Gaze, the Lord Lieutenant of the Tower, to let me out to take the air. Always his answer was the same: "My lady, I dare not."

Now I spent much of my day in bed. One noontime I awoke from a sick doze to find Sir John at my bedside. *Oh, God, has he a warrant for my death? Has he come for me? Is this my last hour?*

I gasped: my breath came choking. But his voice was kind. "News, madam, and good news for you, if not for him. Sir Thomas Wyatt yesterday went to execution. His last words were, 'The Lady Elizabeth was never privy to my rising—she had no knowledge of anything I planned!' "

"Now God be thanked!" My eyes, my head, were swimming as I struggled to sit up. "For now you see I am innocent!"

"I do believe Your Highness," he said slowly. "And if you wish to exercise tomorrow, I will give orders that you may walk upon the battlements."

Oh, the blessed smell of the air, the feel of it about my face and neck! As the turnkey heaved open the small door at the top of the garderobe passageway, I gasped upon the threshold, reeled and almost fell. I had to reach back to my women for support, so heady was it, like the finest wine. Unsteadily I took a step, then two, and edged out of the door. Ahead stretched out the long reach of the battlements, undreamed-of freedom! And there was the Beauchamp Tower, its slits no more than blind and winking eyes—could Robin see me, even if I could not see him? Or was this a fool's fantasy, of a man no longer still alive?

I had taken no more than a dozen yards before a child appeared before me, so unexpected that he might have been an angel or a messenger of God. The morning sun burnished his copper curls as he bobbed his head and, blushing, thrust at me a clump of flowers.

He startled me. "Who's this?"

The turnkey grinned. "One of the gaoler's sons, my lady. He has free run of the Tower."

I bent my head to the child to take his garland, a thick bunch of wildflowers roughly clutched in his small earthy fist. "Your flowers are precious to a prisoner, sir. Tell me, what are they?" The primroses I knew, and the sweet violets, and the unopened daffodils, their small snouts just poking out of their pale brown papery hoods. But others came from lowly woods and water meadows where I had never been.

"What they be?" He stared up at me with his solemn seven-year-old eyes and pulled my sleeve to draw me down beside him. "Primroses, that's for maidhood; purple pasqueflower for Easter suffering; white buds of blackthorn for the truth amid trials; and them's lady smocks for a lady—so the gentleman learned me say."

I started violently. *"What gentleman?"*

He nodded confidentially. "Him." At the center of the nosegay, a clutch of pink-red flowers nodded their ragged heads. I swallowed. "Forgive me—I do not speak the flowers' language—what is this one called?"

"That? 'Tis ragged robin!"

Robin—ragged Robin. "The gentleman in the Beauchamp Tower?"

He nodded vigorously, swinging his small body from side to side. "Him. Lord Robert. With his brothers. He give me money, every week since you come in, to hear if you be let out on the walls, and bring you this."

"You have been keeping watch?"

"Listening. And yesterday I heard them in the wardroom, that the lady of the Bell Tower was to be let walk today. So I went over Fenchurch fields at dawn an' found what my lord said."

Oh, Robin, Robin—what would I send you, if I had flowers to send? Pansies for thoughts, for I have thought of you. And rosemary, that's for remembrance—pray, love, remember . . .

Forget-me-not . . .

The child was gone—I did not see him go. No matter, I told myself as I paced the walls. He would come again, Robin would see to that. I walked the leads till the late afternoon dew chilled my bones, for in my absence the Lord Lieutenant had promised to have the maids sweeten my cell, cleansing every corner. And when I returned, all was as he had promised. Not sweet, but sweeter than it was. I stepped up to the window with a lighter heart than I could remember since I was first imprisoned.

In the window lay a fan I had been using to freshen the air. I picked it up, then saw something beneath. My little messenger of hope must have slipped in unnoticed with the women, and what he had brought me was a gift beyond price—small, pale, brown-speckled and still warm to the touch: a robin's egg.

I sat within the window, cradling the fragile treasure in my hand. A black shape flapped across the casement as one of the Tower ravens came to rest on the stone ledge outside. It was so near that I could count its blue-black feathers, feel its gimlet eyes with their oily sheen and baleful gunmetal leer. I started back and saw beyond the bird a line of moving men. They moved together across Tower Green to mount the scaffold, each with a bale of straw. Slowly they began to open the bales and shake out the wisps to cover the dark-stained boards.

They were making the scaffold ready . . .

. . . ready for use . . .

. . . for use on the next day . . .

I could not move or breathe. Into the silence came a sound I had learned to know, all, all too well. From beyond the Bell Tower, beyond the Bloody Tower, coming from the wharf by Traitor's Gate, I caught the tramp of armed men. Now they came pouring through the archway onto Tower Green. I could hear others in equal numbers taking up their positions at the rear of the Tower, surrounding it on all sides. I saw them lined up by their officers, facing my window, the Queen's own guard, her best men, five, ten deep.

Wild laughter moved inside me: *How many men are needed to lead one woman to the block? Or does my sister take me for a witch, with powers to charm them all asleep and fly away to freedom over their heads?*

I trembled to my feet. "Send for the Lord Lieutenant of the Tower! I would speak with Sir John!"

One of the women stumbled to obey, another fell to her knees on the nearest prie-dieu and began noisily babbling her prayers. We waited in a silence worse than torture. At last came feet outside the chamber, and Vine entered, or the trembling ghost of him. His voice came like the shadow of a sound: "Madam, the Lord Lieutenant of the Tower!"

But the man who entered now was not Sir John. Clad all in black, short, ramrod-stiff and stern, he scraped a bow and did not drop his eyes before mine as he said, "Sir Henry Bedingfield at your service, Lady Elizabeth."

"Where is Sir John?"

He stood foursquare before me, grey and precise. "You are my prisoner now."

I knew a new commissioner always came to take charge of the condemned. *"For how long?"*

"As long as may be." He paused, and stared. His small eyes looked right through me. "I can only follow the orders that I have. And I am ordered by the Queen to bid you prepare yourself for your last night in the Tower."

XXXIII

He had his orders, and he lived by them.
  Now I would die for them.

All night I prayed. I could not weep—I was all done with weeping—
and now I prayed God only to spare me from the sin of mortal rage, that
I could die so, like a dog, untried, unjudged. Now God must judge me—
and my fellow men. I wrote no letters, struggled to compose no last will.
My life must be my testament. That was all I had to leave.

My women were withdrawn: I was alone. At dawn, I knew, would come
the only jury I would meet, the inquisition of matrons, like a flock of
ravens, empanelled to see that I was not with child. Jane's childlike body
would have had to bear this last indignity. But she was already violated,
her body had been given to a husband—not so mine! As I lay there I
thought that I could feel the coarse hands and horny fingers of the old
wives probing my tender parts, and all the fundament of my body loosed
and clenched in sick and violent spasms. Among my prayers I prayed for
strength to withstand this.

The ravens began calling before dawn, just as my women came. I dressed
with care—all virgin white, down to my shift, the whitest that I had, then
a pure white overgown of simplest maiden cut, no jewels but my prayer
book, and my hair loose on my shoulders. When I knelt to kiss the block,
it would be my last veil, to shield my face.

Sir Henry came in armoured and clanking, twenty or thirty men at his
heels. "If you are ready, my lady Elizabeth . . ."

"I am ready."

"Then pray you descend."

"Am I not to have the comfort of my faith? May I not see a priest?"
He frowned. "It is not so ordered."

"For pity's sake!"

"The Queen has not allowed it!"

*Strange . . . when she set on her own Popish chaplain to torment Jane's
last moments with his efforts to bring her back to Rome . . .*

At least it seemed that she would spare me that . . .

"If you are ready, madam . . ."

Two of the men stepped forward and seized me by the elbows. I felt a wave of terror take me—my head was floating, I could not feel the ground. My ears seemed out of tune—I could not catch what he was saying.

". . . your litter is below. If you need a priest, there will be priests at Woodstock—"

I could no more than whisper. "My litter—?"

He nodded tetchily. "Lady, of course! To convey you to Woodstock! The Queen has given orders to discharge you from the Tower: you are to go to Woodstock."

Woodstock . . .

Never was there happier sound in all my life than that one word.

Not that I truly heard it, for I swooned at the mere name and knew no more till we were under way. I later found from my dour gaolkeeper Sir Henry who the wretch was for whom the scaffold was prepared: it was the last of the Wyatt's co-conspirators, poor William Thomas, the staunch Protestant and former Clerk to the King my brother's Council, and not myself at all. The heavy guard of the Queen's men had been ordered only to keep the peace as I was taken from the Tower. All the people were to be kept well away, so none would see me go.

For Mary was in sight of her earthly bliss and now raging to make all sure. The day that I left London was the day Philip set sail from Spain. By the time he landed, she was all but crazed with pent-up love and hope. They met at Holy Cross at Winchester, and there they were married, she hastening to his arms like the most longed-for bride, though all the Court knew that the love between them grew on one side only. When they met, he took her in his arms and stoutly kissed her on the mouth. But the young lords around him could not hide their horror and dismay. "She is so old!" one gasped. "So ugly, and so small!" whispered another. "And badly dressed—and flabby— and so yellow—and half-blind—much worse than we were told!"

But through it all Mary knelt rapt at the high altar, her eyes fixed on the Host, weeping with joy.

Why do I dredge this up? Oh, I had time for this and more! From the day I left the Tower till I was free again was ten long months—a more-than-pregnant period! And now that sister Mary was a wife, I had full cause to brood upon her marriage and what chance there was of children from this union of Spanish loins . . .

As Mary now did too. She had no doubt of issue, for she daily saw God's signs and blessings on her newfound bliss—an angel, flying by old

St. Paul's; a birth of triplets, all alive and well, to a woman over fifty; a
fair summer and a brimming harvest all through her land. Me, I besought
God nightly for just one sign from Him that I was not forgotten!

For in Woodstock, Mary had chosen well the place to bury me, so far
from London that all must think me dead!

God, my life there was a living burial—let me hurry over it! Old Bedingfield did his stiff-necked best, but the truth was I was a prisoner,
locked in day and night, on the Queen's special orders narrowly re-
stricted in everything I did.

And most of all, I was starved for any word of the world outside. I
hoped and prayed Robin still lived. I dreamed of Kat and her soft touch
at every lonely midnight. I even thought of Mary and her walnut-shriv-
elled soul.

Now her precious Mass was everywhere enforced. The people murmured, but Mary was inflamed with her belief. If only they could choose,
she thought, they would all turn against the New Faith and come back
with open hearts to Rome! But how could she force them to embrace
what in their souls they hated?

And now I saw what I had seen before no more than through a glass
darkly: I now knew how near I stood to the throne.

And so I dreamed until the autumn day when Bedingfield, good Papist
that he was, came hastening to my side with the joyful news that the
Queen was with child.

And then the burnings began.

Punishment by fire is as old as time itself. Mary was called "Bloody,"
but in truth she shed no blood. No, her desire was always to burn the
devil out. In her devil's work she had two able seconders, two hearts of
ice whose fury for the fire equalled her own. The lesser was my enemy
Gardiner, ruling the Council now and raging to destroy. But the great
Lucifer of Mary's road of light, that pathway of pure terror lit by the fires
of hell, why, he came from the Devil himself, the Pope of Rome.

This Papal Legate, Cardinal Pole, was a man Mary had prayed to see
in England almost as much as she had hungered for a husband. And once
he came to subject the harlot England to her Roman pimp, then her
punishment for the years of wantonness and self-pleasing could begin in
earnest.

How cruel the punishment, none had foretold. Now day by day all over
England they went to the fire, men, women, children even, the blind, the
lame, the simple, young maids and boys driven mad with torments till
they confessed to anything. Some were with child—one laboured and
brought forth there in the flames, tied to the stake, and her infant

dropped down between her legs into the faggots and was thrown back to burn with her. Some were seen still to be moving after four hours in the flames; others were still conscious and howling, screaming, begging for death after their legs, their arms, even their lips, had burned off.

And Mary thought to bring our people back to her God by this? Yet the higher burned the fires, the stronger burned their faith. I wept to hear that the bishops Latimer and Ridley went to the stake in Oxford, though they had been my enemies, had proclaimed me bastard at St. Paul's when Jane was made Queen.

At the last, poor Ridley faltered when he felt the flames, and cried out in agony. "Be of good cheer, Master Ridley," Latimer called back, "and play the man, for by God's grace we shall this day light such a candle in our England as shall never be put out!"

Before their poor remains were cold, this word had run like wildfire through the land. And all the people wept and marvelled that the Queen could burn such men. If the hand that held this taper, lit this fire, was that of the Mother Church, the old Church of Rome, she was a monster and no mother, and all shrank from her with loathing. Yet still Mary drove her purpose on, feeding the flames with living, quivering flesh to welcome forth her son.

The Queen had quickened in September, and a boy it was, for certain —doctors, midwives and astrologers were all agreed. In thanksgiving for this bounty, the Queen had pardoned all her enemies, and now made war only on God's.

Because of this, Robin still lived, though still a prisoner like myself, still in the Tower. And Kat, my faithful Kat, kept up, I heard, a steady stream of letters to the Queen begging to come to me again. Cecil, too, contrived to send me twice his shadowy messengers, men grey as ghosts who melted up to me and were away before any had time to notice one too many among the servitors. Each time the message came in just one word: "Madam, *conform!* If you love life, *conform!*"

Conform.

Conform.

It was the one word in the Queen's mouth.

No message could be simpler. Renounce your faith, attend the Mass, make your Communion and Confession after the rites of Rome—or grasp your crown of martyrdom in both hands and prepare your soul to die!

My soul I thought I might in time prepare, but not my body, not to die that death, not death by fire—oh, God, spare me! And since even now I still lay in my bed at night and shook when I remembered how close Death's scythe had passed me by that last night in the Tower, I could not even dream of his long fingers and his bony sightless skull coming to-

wards me wrapped in sheets of flame, calling me through a wall of searing fire, without screams shaking me out of my fitful sleep.

All through that year, then, Mary waxed in motherhood, swollen like a
maybug by the blood of martyrs. And her husband Philip stood by at
Court to await the birth of the Prince before he had to leave for his lands
abroad. As he waited he had time to think; and not surprisingly, he
thought of me. His thoughts came to me in the bluntest form when
Bedingfield knocked at my chamber one fine April noon with the star-
tling words: "Madam, we leave tomorrow to attend the Queen at Hampton Court. It is the King's will that you join your sister for her lying-in."

That day was Passion Sunday, and I fell prey to every passion known.
As I endured the slow march of the south-bound litter, round and round
went my thoughts like rats in a trap, frantic for freedom.

For the Queen's lying-in . . .

What would my future be when I was nothing but the aunt—though
hardly even that if Mary still denied that we were sisters!—say, then, the
bastard aunt, of the young Prince?

And why had Philip sent for me? Was he moved by statecraft, the
shrewd desire to have the younger sister under his eye in case Mary died
in childbirth? He would then be Regent for his son. But another rebellion could still put me on the throne and cheat his child of his inheritance.

But when at last we reached the Court at Hampton, there were few to
notice and still less to care. Even the gatehouse stood unattended save
for one poor lad, who could sing but one tune: "The Prince, the Prince is
coming! The Queen is fallen into her labour, and the Prince will come
this day!"

The Court was in an uproar, none in their places, all rushing to and
fro, servants stinking drunk from the barrels already cracked and flowing
in happy anticipation of the rejoicing to come.

"Where must we go? Who takes the Princess now?"

In the chaos Bedingfield almost died of his anxiety. Only when I wea-
ried of his folly and offered him my most solemn oath that I would not
flee away did he stop fussing and go to see where we must lodge. My
quarters were not grand, but after Woodstock they seemed like the palace they were: a suite of rooms decent if not gracious, with a rolling view
across the water meadows and Hampton's unrivalled park.

Of course, the ever-present men-at-arms took up their places outside
my door as soon as we arrived. But now, in the heart of the Court, that
did not terrify me as in the Tower. Here no one could make away with
me under the eyes of all my father's lords and those who knew me. And
once installed, all I could do was wait.

As Mary waited, for her Prince to come. She laboured for three days. I prayed for her night and day, but no news came. Then one forenoon, a flurry at my door, Vine scrambling up too late to do the honours, and in swept Susan Clarencieux, the Queen's first lady and her dear right hand.

I could not say what struck me more, her face or what she carried. Despite the name she took from her Norman ancestors, Clarencieux was English to her bones, from her long horse's face to her air of arrogant reserve. Now the heavy jaw and chin were grey and set like granite, while above, her purple eyes and swollen lids bespoke hours of weeping. Across her arms she bore a gown of royal purple: royal richness too, and obviously the Queen's.

"Madam!" I murmured as I bowed my head. I was afraid to speak.

"My lady!" With true English breeding Clarencieux dropped an immaculate curtsey.

I took a breath. "How does your lady—how is the Queen?"

She raised her head. Her eyes were desolate. "Well enough, madam, I thank you. It is her will you wear this gown tonight, when she will send you word of her further pleasure herein."

Clarencieux was gone, and I was left alone to choke on curiosity till it killed me.

But Mary was still Queen, and still to be obeyed. I was to wear the gown? Well, I would wear it.

No matter that not one of the clumsy Papists she had set about me could dress my hair, or fix a sleeve, or see to a train. A train? It was all the hateful hobgoblins could do to sort out a clean shift. And the dress, being Mary's, cut into my armpits, strained across my bosom and was woefully too short, however hard they tugged it down and swore "It does well on you, madam!" But still it was a gorgeous gown and in a wondrous colour; and as I stroked down the fine rich royal purple, feeling the tickling velvet kissing my palms, a rogue thought took possession of my mind like an unwanted tune: *If I were Queen* . . .

"Madam, the King! The King is here to see you!"

It was almost too much for my poor Vine, to see the King of England and the Most Holy Catholic Majesty of Spain walking unannounced and almost unattended into my lodgings. I was shocked too, I will confess. I thought that Mary had sent the dress to make me fine for her—how much more like her to want me fine for him, for the man she loved, the man whose love she was still trying to win!

But he—what was he doing here? What was he thinking behind that dreadful Hapsburg jaw and those small pale unfeeling eyes? I sprang to my feet and sank into a curtsey as he approached me down the entrance hall, where I sat obedient to Clarencieux's instructions, awaiting Mary's command. "My lord King!"

He stepped forward. With him, besides two men-at-arms, was one I knew must be his close adviser the grandee Feria; behind Feria was a fine young don who might have been his aide. These two outclassed Philip in both height and bearing, as horses do a goat. Yet still something about him drew my eyes and—

—yes, yes—why should I hide it?—heated up my blood.

Alas for my rogue body! Though I always loved a man of length, fair, tall and well-favoured, yet sometimes a man with nothing more about him than that hot look in his eye could light the flame in me—as he did then . . .

I knew he saw it, though I dropped my eyes in the same instant. Above his neat forked beard, the smallest smile shadowed his meagre lips. He bowed, and took my hand. "Good evening, lady!"

His Spanish accent was as thick as the fat pink tongue that seemed to fill his mouth. As he raised my hand to his lips, his moustache lingered on my fingers. As I tried to draw away, he would not let me go. He nodded to Feria. "My Ambassador! He speak you English!"

Now the Ambassador was smiling at my elbow, as smooth as olive oil. "His Majesty desires me ask you, madam, *habla español?* Do you speak Spanish?"

I put on a woeful face. "Alas no, sir, not a word!"

Philip grunted in satisfaction. *"Muy bien!"*

What would he say, then, that he did not wish me to hear?

His thumb played with my fingers—was it accident, or did he mean to stoke the fire between us? I returned him a long pale stare, as cold as chastity. He released my hand, muttering to Feria, *"Muy calmada*—she is very calm."

How could he stand there making small talk? My impatience broke its bounds. "Your Excellency Señor Ambassador, forgive a sister's anxious care—I mean no disrespect to my lord the King—but I beg you: *how does the Queen?"*

A swift glance at his master, a rapid exchange in Spanish, and Feria was authorised to answer. "Well enough," he said guardedly. "Under God's will. Her labour is suspended, God be thanked—for had the Prince come now, he would have been only an eight months' child and less likely to thrive."

Good news or bad? No Prince yet—but no abortion of nature neither, to clear the way for me . . . Hush, perish the thought, for Philip now was speaking, and I could understand him. "It was told me she had a spirit full of incantation! But now I see beneath her calm she has a woman's passion . . . and all about her, a brightness like sea fire . . ."

Feria bristled. "It is no wonder, for she is a harlot's daughter, the

Queen says, a child of wantonness, of her mother's wildness with the lewdest men—"

Philip clenched his heavy jaw. "The Queen's a fool!" he ground out heavily. "A one-eyed man could see that this is Henry's child—see her natural royalty! Otherwise a man might take her for a changeling . . ." He laughed uneasily, shifting his stance. "You will think I am in love with her!"

"No, no, sire, no!"

But I could hear the language of his eyes—I knew he was.

XXXIV

If he could read my eyes, I could read his. And more than his mean hot eyes, I could read his stubby body straining for mine like a terrier after a rat, the subtle shifting of his legs again, as a third, unseen leg now stirred between them . . .

Yet there was more, and that called to me too—his serpentine intelligence, his cunning spirit versed in duplicity from the moment when the Jesuits first taught him to say "Sí—e también, no." Above all, I was drawn to the deep well of sadness in him. I had yet to learn the cause of that vast sorrow, but I felt it like a spell he cast between us. And all women want to heal the sadness in their men.

What did it mean, this interest of the King's? All knew the Queen might not survive her childing—did he have designs on me, to keep England under the heel of Spain?

Philip would be my death as a husband, I knew that. But could I use him now to save my life?

For I was still in danger. I had thought that if the Prince arrived, I would be safe. But now I saw that once the Catholic succession was assured, I was dispensable. For then the Queen could afford to make an example of me—to send the strumpet's bastard to the fire!

Yet now fate had favoured me with Philip's interest; now I had a new card to play . . .

I wrote to him, a flattering, fulsome letter full of learned cleverness. A pity that I could not twit him with one of my favourite Spanish proverbs

—Nace en la huerta lo que no siembra el hortolano, for instance: More grows in the garden than the gardener knows he has sown! But still, with a light touch of Tertullian, a hint of Hipponax, and an obscure ode from Ovid, I contrived to tickle his fancy to the height of my desire. It is the world's most simple truth that every man is led by the tip of that which makes him a man, just as every ass is led by the soft end of his nose. Yet each man keeps his manhood in a different place, and the sharp woman finds out where it lies. Men like Philip keep it in their brains and in their pride of learning. And that is how they are led.

And my letter, my calculated courtship of his self-esteem, paid off at once. The same young don who served the Ambassador Feria arrived the next day in a cloud of officiousness and Andalusian pomade, his nose, head and ruff high in the air, but his eyes far from aloof. "His Majesty bids me inform you, Serenissima, that you may now receive."

What a triumph! At a stroke I was no longer banned from company or shut off from the Court. What though my first visitors in a twelvemonth proved to be Gardiner and his canting Catholic crew, the earls of Arundel, Shrewsbury and Derby? What though I knew Gardiner was still pressing for my death, he and the Ambassador Feria? I feared him no longer, not with the King behind me!

I greeted them boldly. "My lords, I am glad to see you, for I have been too long alone!"

Gardiner flamed with rage as he fought back. "We are come here to confess you, not to bandy words! You must admit, madam, your guilt in the conspiracy against Her Majesty!"

I laughed in his face. "I will stay here forever before I will admit to such a falsehood!" So the old stinkard stormed away. But the lords left with glances of admiration, and I thought I had won them to my cause.

And now I could receive, to me came others—open and covert overtures that made my heart rejoice. One ancient dame of the Court, so vacant and twittering that the soldiers laughed behind her back as they admitted her, proved to be both sharp and shrewd as she breathed to me a secret word from none other than my old friend and ally Cecil.

"Sir William is far from the Court now," she murmured, "for he quit the Queen's service when the burnings began. He begs you to hold fast—the time will come . . ."

Then came a lusty lad from the Hampton ostler, to inquire if I would need new horses when I was at liberty to ride. I had to say that I could not ride till the Queen had given me leave. But the hat he waved about him in farewell bore in the hatband a great clump of the small pink nodding flowers the boy in the Tower had taught me to call ragged robin . . .

Robin.

When would we ride together once again?

And what of Philip, Philip, Philip . . .

What was he thinking, planning, scheming in that sleepless brain behind those shallow, stone-cold eyes? His game—his gamble, rather—turned entirely on Mary. His hopes of dynasty, the future of his empire, stood on two casts of the dice: if she brought forth a prince and if she lived. And solamente lo sabe Dios, *as he would repeat: only God knew, only God could say.*

And Mary his unloved wife?

I prayed for her, but I prayed more for myself. And the next evening there again was Clarencieux, the Mistress of the Robes, as she was mistress of all else about her mistress, with another gown—short as before, but now a heavy sculpted Florence satin, a rich Catholic red with the whole bodice blazoned with gold and jewels, so fierce in its finery that it stood up by itself, a gown fit for a queen. Again I was to wear it, and again await the Queen's pleasure.

Five hours I sat a martyr to that whalebone, the miserable bodice biting my breasts, the stomacher cutting into my thighs, the sleeves crushing my armpits, till she sent for me—at dead of night. *Now the Court is asleep,* I realized sourly, *and none can see me as I come and go, now she sends for me!*

For May, the night was cold and starless too. Hugger-mugger I was conducted shivering through the black courtyards till the Privy Stairs of the Queen's lodging gaped before us. A flight of steps, a growing smell of incense and oppression, an unobtrusive door, her guards and women melting away in silence—and there she was, before me in the small and stifling chamber, on her knees at her prie-dieu, turning to greet me with staring eyes like one possessed awakening from a trance.

And after our long separation, despite all my best breeding, my eyes were staring too. She wallowed towards me like a great beached whale, but her belly under her loose gown was not as I had ever seen on a woman with child before. She was all splayed out and fallen around the hips; she looked like a cast mare. I dropped to my knees and mumbled the old greeting: "My life and service to Your Majesty!"

She fell into a chair. How she had aged! She looked a hundred, no, a thousand now, her yellow face ingrained with age, her small mouth almost collapsed inside itself. Yet the fire that had made the martyrs burned in her eyes with an eerie incandescence, and when she looked at me, her rage broke out like lightning. "My Lord Chancellor, the Bishop Gardiner, came to confess you, and you gave him nothing but bold, offensive words!"

"Only that I am innocent! I never plotted against you! That is the truth!"

"The truth!" She gave a harsh, barking laugh, and her eyes roamed wildly round. "As to that, madam, *Dios sabe!*"

God knows—in Spanish? Was Philip hearing this?

Of course! He was here! But where was he, then? As Mary spoke, her eyes moved to a hanging by the wall. It did not move or twitch, but I knew he was there.

Philip! A secret watcher, then, an overhearer, an arras twitcher, a lurker in the dark? I stared at Mary in horror. What must it be like to be married to such a man?

But Mary was elsewhere. "You talk of truth! Let me tell you a truth, my little sister, greater than all of us! See here! Come here!"

She was upon me before I knew it, wild eyes, sour breath, the sickly smell of incense. She caught my arm and pulled me forward, plunging my shrinking hand into the side of her belly. Even through the soft folds of her chamber gown, I could feel the slacker folds within.

There was nothing there! Nothing but soft old flesh, half-rotted like an orange in decay, and no new life at all. Except—something deep within, hard like a kernel, a thing without warmth or life, dead as a stone.

"And here!" To my horror, she unripped her bodice and heaved out one small, sunken, ancient breast. Feverishly she kneaded the grey doughy surface, punishing the nipple as if insensible of pain. "Here! See here!"

Not daring to show shrinking, I bent my head to look. On the extreme end of the brown wrinkled nipple, dry and mildewed like a shrivelled grape, stood a small pearl of liquor. "See my milk!" she crowed. "Milk for my infant, the new Prince of Wales!"

I was terrified. "So be it, madam, and may God be thanked!"

"I shall bring forth! My son is in my belly, my breasts prepare his milk! The house of Hapsburg shall reign in this land! And then my lord the King will stay with me, with his son, with his sons—for I shall bear and bear again to make the true faith safe in England. And *that* is the truth, Madam Elizabeth, and you must bite on it, chew on it till it breaks your teeth and your proud heretic heart!"

She fell back gasping. Suddenly she clasped her side and gave a violent cry: "Call for the midwives—and my women—for the Prince will come tonight!"

How have women endured childbirth through the ages? She screamed like Katherine on that dreadful day when she foresaw her death—and screamed, and screamed, and screamed . . .

In rushed her women led by Clarencieux, followed by her Spanish doctors and their English rivals, the midwives and their maids, and all the

attendant riffraff short of a pox doctor's clerk. And as her pains began
again, so did our heartfelt prayers.

A prince . . .
God send us a prince . . .

*Oh, the curse of the Tudors! Only my grandfather, old King Henry, ever got it
right!*

By which you gather that the curse of the Tudors claimed Mary too.
For the Prince never came. There was no prince, her swelling only
dropsy, her belly empty of all but wind and water and something darker
too.

Her grief was terrible, her shame even worse. May lingered into August before at last she could admit she was deceived. And by then Hampton was a sewer, an open sink, festering in its own garbage, its every
dunghill a mass of flies and maggots, a breeding ground of plague and
every disease. I felt for Mary. But I could not help rejoicing when I had
the word I prayed for: "The Queen's sister may remove from Court and
take to her own estate once again."

Back to Hatfield! I wept aloud for joy. Truly the hand of God brought
my deliverance!

And I saw, too, a human hand in this, for Philip continued to protect
me. Now that the Queen had not brought forth, I was the heir again. And
if I died, the next in line was one of two other women: either the next of
the Grey sisters after Jane, or the descendant of my father's eldest sister,
the young Queen of Scots.

As to the Greys, Philip knew the country would never stomach Catherine instead of me. And the Queen of the Scots, that Mary who was once
pledged to my brother, she was now betrothed to the young Dauphin, the
Crown Prince of France. In Philip's mind, to let her accede would be to
give "his" England into the hands of his greatest enemy in Europe! To
Philip, then, even a stubborn Protestant, an unmarried girl, was prefera-
ble to France! So he gave orders I was to be set at full liberty once more,
and accorded the rights and honours of a princess once again.

Poor Mary! How she gnawed on the bone of bitterness, forced by
Philip to forgive me! And in her darkest hour, for now Philip left her too.
He made her bring me right to the quayside to bid him farewell, though
she had begged to see him off by herself. And there he favoured me with
a fleshly kiss full on the lips—till the young lords of his train openly
lamented that the King had not had the tilling of the fresh virgin soil of
this "New-Found-Land" in place of the overfurrowed, overfallow earth
of poor old Mother England!

Now Mary had no heart to keep me with her, and I won permission to
leave at once.

Hatfield! I paced the cold and dusty unaired rooms alone, in tears and trembling. I could not believe I was back home again after so many perils. I give you leave to guess whom I sent for first! Some three days after my messengers went forth came hooves in the courtyard, a small plump flying figure, flurries of curtsies drowned in floods of tears, and there again was Kat, my darling Kat . . .

A mere half a day of sighs and smiles and whispered confidences, and with us now were Parry and her brother. Ascham my tutor bounced back next and had me at my Greek within the hour. Ashley, my dear Kat's man, had like so many gentlemen been forced abroad, but now he could return. Before long some of the ladies I had befriended at Mary's Court —Browne, Russell and the Admiral's wife the Lady Clinton—came to see how I did and stayed to rejoice with me at this safe homecoming.

And still the burnings went on.

Indeed, they now went even faster as Mary, mad with grief, convinced herself that God was angry with her for the slowness of her work.

"I have reigned for three years now, and still the sin of heresy in England is not yet rooted out!" she cried to Gardiner. So the shortest day of the year was made longer by the light of burning bodies, and the tapers that flared for Christ's nativity were the torches of living flesh. Candlemas followed, the Feast of the Purification of the Blessed Virgin Mary, and with it human candles lit the February sky.

Of all who died, one grieved me beyond words. I have the letter still that brought the news.

Lady and Princess,

Before you hear of this great loss from others, I set it down, although I can scarce write for weeping. This day died Thomas Cranmer, your father's Archbishop of Canterbury. Brought low by suffering and his long years of lone confinement, he was induced once to deny his faith. But then his God returned. As he approached the fire he said, "This right hand shall burn first: for with my signature, this hand has offended." He met the flames in glory, with all the patience of that great spirit of his, and the world is poorer for his parting. We shall not look upon his like again until we meet in Heaven, if it please God admit us where poor Thomas surely triumphs now. There is a ballad that the people have made of his story: if you listen out, you will hear it. Pray for his soul.

Your ladyship's servant ever,
William Cecil

That night in the graveyard hour I did hear it, a woman's voice singing across the marshes away to the east:

> *"When constant Cranmer lost his life*
> *Then streams of tears for him were rife,*
> *When Popish power put him to death.*
> *We prayed for our Elizabeth—*
> *When children now are done to death,*
> *God send us our Elizabeth!"*

Yes, Mary's power, Mary's persecution, would give me England, her England, now more and more my England, on a plate.

But when, oh, Lord—when?

XXXV

And now another spectre came to stalk my days and nights—that bugaboo called *husband* . . .

If there was not to be a child of his own loins, Philip now resolved to find another way of putting a Catholic king on the throne of England—and a son of his own blood. As a sop to my pride, he also offered a selection of Europe's eligible Catholic princes. But his choice for me was plain.

"Which do you favour, madam?" Kat ventured nervously as I sat brooding in my window early one morning with Philip's letter in my hand.

I snorted. "Favour? All of them—to be consigned head-down to the nearest dunghill, there to kick their heels for me!"

"But this offer of the King's son, the Prince Don Carlos—" Kat tried a smile, but I knew she was afraid.

"Never fear, Kat!" I rallied her. "Don Carlos may be his father's darling, but neither for Spain's nor England's glory can they force me to take a boy of ten to bed!"

We laughed then, Kat and I. But Don Carlos! Had I known . . .

I knew he was the son of Philip by his first young wife, a Portuguese princess who died in childbirth. So I thought of him pityingly as a motherless boy. In truth, he was a foul abortion of a child, deformed in mind and body. A hunchbacked cripple, he weighed no more than eighty pounds. His plea-

sures were to torture horses and roast hares alive for the delight of hearing the creatures' screams.

From childhood he liked whores' flesh even more than horseflesh, and his servants swept the Spanish brothels for poor sluts who could be whipped to death. It was his pleasure, too, to let them escape halfway through, then redouble their torments by pursuit and recapture. But God is just. While he was playing this game, his palsied legs betrayed him and he fell down a flight of marble stairs, cracking his addled head like a bad egg.

He should have died then. But Philip his father ordered him trepanned— perhaps he hoped that when the surgeons entered and probed his skull, they might be able to reorder what they found there. But leaving nothing to chance, Philip commanded, too, that for his recovery Don Carlos should be bound to the mummified corpse of a local cook renowned for performing miracles. For two months Carlos lived strapped to a withered body night and day. No wonder he was mad! Yet they would have married me to him, to keep England under Rome!

This was Philip's sadness, this condition of his only son. This was the cross he had to bear, the great sorrow I had seen in him at our first meeting. And he had not yet drained this chalice of poisoned fatherhood to the dregs. The time would come when he would curse the miracle-working mummy for saving this foul life: a time when this son Carlos would plot to murder him, to take Philip's crown and violate his new and adored young wife—when Philip himself would have to have this Minotaur his monster-child walled up, and then come by night in secret, with men and monks, to end this death-in-life . . .

And that was to be my husband! But in my ignorance I was not much feared of him. A stronger challenger was another Catholic Archduke, the soldier Emmanuel Philibert, Duke of Savoy. Letters from Mary demanded to know if I would take him: Philip wished me to marry, and Mary wished whatever Philip did.

Yet if I was vulnerable, so was she too. Now plots against her came thick and fast. In Sussex an impostor claimed to be my erstwhile "husband" Courtenay, the last of the Plantagenets and the man whose name was so often linked with mine. This mountebank raised a rebellion in my name, to put himself and his "beloved bedfellow the Princess Elizabeth" upon the throne! My wishful husband was soon mounting the scaffold for his foolish efforts to mount the throne through me! But the more Mary cut the conspirators down, the more they flourished like the Hydra-headed monster. To increase terror, she stepped up the burnings. And the more burnings, the more plots there were.

"And just as long as Her Majesty refuses to name you as her successor," Ascham noted heavily, "it will—it must—continue!"

He was my anchor then, that sturdy Yorkshireman, and my books were my salvation. Now the news from London worsened with every post. My old foe Gardiner died, raving in terror of God's judgement; but before his corpse was cold, Mary had replaced him with another fire-raising bishop, so cruel that Londoners called him "Bloody Bonner" for his delight in death.

And slowly, slowly, all eyes, all hopes, turned towards me. Only the brave dared speak—and even then, not words but nods and silent pledges were the order of the day. But of Mary's lords, Sir Nicholas Throckmorton, who had served my brother and narrowly escaped with his life in Wyatt's plot, contrived to convey his loyalty to me in a pair of perfumed gloves; as did Lord Paulet, the venerable prop of the Privy Council, who had served Edward and my father too; and Clinton, Derby, Bedford, Pembroke, Sussex, all great lords and vital to the State; and not least in my eyes, my own great-uncle Lord Howard—all looked, all nodded and all bowed their heads, as I did too, to wait.

And now Philip returned to Mary, fresh from the coupling shops of Amsterdam, where gossip said he had taken refuge and refreshment after long service with his dry and dusty wife. And the word I dreaded reached me at Hatfield that September when Mary wrote to me in the words of Elizabeth in the Bible: *"Yet though I have been barren and stricken in years, yet has the Word of God leaped in my womb*—rejoice with me, sister, for I am with child!"

" 'My soul doth magnify the Lord: and my spirit hath rejoiced in God my saviour.' " Numbly I muttered through the Magnificat at the service of thanksgiving that followed, palely repeating the Virgin Mary's psalm of praise. And inwardly I was raging, my soul mutinying against God.

If Mary had a child . . .

If she had a son . . .

Oh, God, what have I done that You discipline me with these savage strokes?

And so the whole tragicomedy began again. Back at Hatfield, I groaned, wept, prayed. But would the Prince come? Was she even with child?

And while Mary lost herself in motherhood, the country drifted down the path of war. Now daily I had news from my new friends and supporters at court. "The French threaten Spain's borders, and the King is bent on war," Throckmorton wrote, "but English hearts have little stomach for it." Cecil likewise had objections that rang just as true: "Not enough men! Not enough money! Not enough silver! Not enough gold!"

Cecil was right, as he so often was. Now Mary, borrowing, selling, pouring all the money she could raise into this war she made to win her husband's love, found herself almost bankrupt here at home. I had to watch my allowance dwindle to a trickle, just when I needed money more than ever.

It had started as soon as I returned from Court. The next morning at Hatfield a stranger was waiting in the hall. "My lady!" He fell forward on one knee.

He caught me by surprise. "What do you want, sir?"

He lifted a face as open as a child's. "Service, my Princess," he said simply, "and with you."

Now every day they came, gentlemen, commoners, squires and knights —and women too, ladies and laundresses, milliners and maids. I was the rising sun, they turned to me, and as the sun must shine, I had to have them. One thing made it possible, a little missive whose double bounty had me on my knees in tears of joy.

Dearest lady,

The bearer of this has money for you, all I have raised by the sale of the land left me by my mother. I am free of the Tower but banished to far Norfolk, to Framlingham. I pray God for you with my every breath, and for the day when once again I may lay at your feet the service of

Robert Dudley

Was God at last turning His eyes my way? I hoped and doubted, for the pains I saw all around me beggared belief. The whole country suffered for Mary's mad love of Philip, for when there was no money, there was no bread. One man was taken up starving at my door, and when asked when he had eaten last, could only mumble, "Wednesday'll be a week—I had a handful of dried acorns, if't please Your Ladyship." A young woman with three bairns scarce toddling, another in arms wailing at her dried-up breast, was whipped through the parish as a vagrant, all the while screaming, "A penny for two eggs! That's a man's daily pay! And my man's dead of hunger! A penny for two eggs!"

And with the cold came sickness, a great plague of running, festering rheum that came in with the wounded coming back from France. Hundreds died, and then thousands, till the credulous crossed themselves every hour and swore that Death himself now stalked the land. But worst of all that winter was the news from France.

For we had lost, lost all, lost the war, lost men and money, lost our good fighting name—and most of all, we had lost Calais.

"Calais! Calais is fallen, fallen to the French!" The word ran through the country and the rage of England knew no bounds.

Mary told them, "When I am dead, you will find Calais carved upon my heart." Like every soul in England, I would myself have joyfully done that carving, letter by letter, herself alive and bleeding at my feet.

Did Calais kill her babe, as she believed, or was he, like his brother before him, only the angel-child of her fond fantasy? For as in her first phantom childbearing, no prince ever came. "A child who can count to nine upon its fingers could tell Her Majesty that there will be no infant," Cecil wrote to me. But the growth that I had felt in her the time before, then only as big as an unripe plum, had now swelled to a gourd, a gourd of deadly matter. "The Queen's health now gives serious cause for concern" was Cecil's word.

I clasped the letter as I paced my chamber. Mary had been sick so long —was she now losing the battle?

Her lords thought so. Yet she could not accept it. When they pressed her to name her successor, she cited her son the Prince, and after him Philip her husband. Philip! He was now known to be openly cavorting with the whores of Holland while his wife fought for her life.

Yet still she tried to will the throne to him. To a Spanish interloper, a Hapsburg usurper—how little she knew our people!

Her other inspiration at that hour—*may God forgive her, she was at least consistent in her unflinching hate of me!*—was to leave her throne to Mary, the young Queen of the Scots and Catholic through and through. Mary of Scots rule England—foreign-born, French-raised, and a Papist to boot? What could our Mary be dreaming of?

Nothing—for there was only now the final nothing and descent into nothingness. When the first of August came and even she could no longer hope for the miracle of a twelve-month babe, Mary let out one wailing cry that raised all hackles for ten miles around. Then she lapsed into sadness, and then slid into madness. "She neither eats nor sleeps," I heard from Cecil, "but roams her chamber by all hours and cries continually on God." Others wrote me that she had dwindled into a frightful terror of her life, hiding in corners, wearing armour to ward off the assassin's secret knife, and keeping by her night and day an old and rusty sword to defend herself in any mortal combat.

But her own combat was mortal now, and nothing now could save her. And step by step I moved towards the unseen future. My stream of followers became a flood as more and more flocked to my door. But of all my people, foremost in my cause was William Cecil. With Master Parry as his second, he began sounding out both lords and landowners great and small to see where they stood. From Wiltshire came a pledge of men and money from a knight who vowed to set me on the throne or die beneath my banner. From Berwick, a lord himself and ten thousand fighting men. And this from the North, the secret home and heart of the Catholic faith!

Yet for all Cecil's care, an armed revolt of Papists against me was not my real fear. I simply lived, walked, ate, slept, prayed in a white fever of anticipation—and a black mist of dread.

For now it was approaching, almost here, this thing that had shadowed me for twenty-five years—how was it now, to be almost the Queen?

Now? I craved for it so violently that I slept to dream of it and woke to taste it, feel it, live it. Yet I was sick with dread that even now fate might be playing with me as it had done for so long. And I made this vow night and morning with each prayer: Now not Mary, no, not even God Himself, should cheat me of my time. I would be Queen! Nothing would stop me now!

So I rose every day before dawn, after night upon sleepless night, and began my work. With the aid of Parry, Ascham and my newer recruits, no letter but was answered, no suitor but was kindly dealt with—yet for all my busyness, days crept like weeks—weeks, months—as we made all ready and yet still had to wait.

One event broke the strangeness of that time when Kat and Parry, Ascham and Master Parry, and all of them and I would eye each other and hold our breath from the moment we awoke until the last candle was out. Although Philip was refusing all Mary's frantic entreaties to come back to England, he did not want to kiss good-bye to the kingship as readily as he would bid his wife farewell. In the last week, then, of Mary's life, England, Hatfield and I had an unexpected visitor.

How I remembered the first time I had seen him when he stood at Philip's elbow all in black to translate his master's words! Now he was sombre in a deep olive-green doublet of three-pile velvet, his fashionable long hose a perfect match in cut brocade. Still with him were his young attendant don, and his sneering, slippery smile. I received him in the withdrawing hall as soon as he arrived, and rejoiced at my new importance, that now he waited upon me. "Señor Ambassador Feria, most welcome to my house!"

I almost added *and to my kingdom* . . . but this was no time for mischief.

"My master's greetings, lady!" he began with all pomposity. "The king salutes you! He pledges you through me that he will champion you in every way until he can be with you to aid you in person . . ."

I gave him back a smile as false as his own. "I pray you, tell your master, *that when we need his help and counsel, we will ask for it!*"

Feria caught his breath and blenched with shock. I felt a surge of triumph: I would be Queen here! I, *I* would rule, without Philip, without any man—except my Cecil!

Now every day was torture as the world waited for Mary's death. I prayed to God to shorten her sufferings, but even more my own. I ordered Cecil to convey to the Council to send no word until it was definite. More than all, I had to see the ring from her finger—see the Coronation ring from off her dead hand in the palm of mine.

November was fast ebbing. One midnight it came, through Throckmorton's truest man: "The Queen is sinking; she cannot last the night."

I did not sleep at all, but wept and prayed all through the cold and silver hours alone. With the first light of dawn I left the house and paced the park to the gates, taking my stance under an old holm oak, the very tree of England. There I could see the messengers turn off the high road the moment they came in.

For hours I waited, forbidding company—but what were hours now after twenty-five years? And there at last they were, four of my lords spurring towards me. I leaned against the oak to draw its strength, and tried to breathe. The leader knelt. "Your Majesty, please you to accept the throne and rule of England?"

In his palm lay Mary's—England's—ring—*now mine!* I could not contain it. "Oh, my lords—my lords—" The tears flowed then, and I knelt down too. "Now God be thanked!" I raised my voice in joy. "For this is the Lord's doing and a miracle in all eyes!"

Their shouts rang round my head: "The Queen is dead! God save the Queen!"

The Queen . . .
The Queen . . .
The Queen . . .

The Queen Elizabeth!
Elizabeth the Queen!

THE ENVOY TO MY SECOND BOOK

Queen . . .

No longer bastard, orphan, "Little Whore," but Queen at last, Queen indeed, and Queen of England now . . .

It was ecstasy, pure ecstasy, a surge of bliss. And with it came that rush of blood that my lost lords of Surrey and of Seymour had taught me, the blood called up in woman by a man. But not for them—for another, a nearer, dearer, deadlier man to me—

My father.

Was it like this for him when after all those years of no account, he, too, became the first person of the kingdom?

The cries hailing Henry as King went near to split the hammer beams in the Abbey roof, so they say. Henry was King—with God's love, and the people's.

Would they do the same for me?

Why should they not? For I had triumphed just as he had, and over more perils too. I had survived the malice of my sister Mary, and the machinations of her Spanish spouse. I had thwarted Henry's bastardising of me, yes, and the Pope's and the bishops', even Edward's too!

So I swore then, in the fullness of my soul, No man shall call me bastard, and live! *And now I live to see that oath come true, when the only man who dared to throw it in my teeth will pay for it, just as I swore then on the day of my accession.*

Bastard no more.

Fears for the future, then. But I had conquered the past, conquered my father and trampled him down, and all his evil legacy. Yet still I knew I would not have all this without him, none of it without him—I owed him that, and more!

For now I could admit it. From him I drew my height, my looks, my health, my gift of music, dancing, riding and all forms of action. From him came my impatience, my love of learning, yes, and of men too, and of the sport of nature, ever his favourite sport . . .

From my mother I had taken only my eyes, dark eyes that sorted so seductively with my fair hair, eyes to make ropes to catch men's souls . . .

And I was, like him, nothing but Tudor in my love of power and gold!

So then! I would use the best of him, take the best that he had left, and like him give the best of myself to England as her Queen. Standing in Hatfield's park, shivering in the raw November air, but not with cold, not cold, I saw my destiny high and aloof, but near and precious too.

For I was burning, burning with desire, ardent with love to give my countrymen, the people that I loved, all that I had to give. I would give them my heart, my soul, my spunk, my spirit, my love, my faith—but above all, my body should be England's till I could go no more.

Virgin no longer, then.

Married to England.

I would embrace my destiny like a bridegroom and hug it in my arms.

And every man in England should bear arms for me!

Here Ends
the Second Book
–LIBER SECUNDUS–
of My History

QUEEN

Book the Third

-*LIBER TERTIUS*-

of My History

Queen . . .

Regina Anglorum . . .

Queen of all England, in England's royal line . . .

And all men in England would bear arms, would break their hearts for me!

I heard the music of the stars. Bright shoots of bliss shot through me, swelled my heart and fed my bursting soul. I was Queen! I saw eternity in a bright, shining flash, bathed in its radiance, and saw too—oh, God! I saw my father and his father, and our line of kings stretching back even to the crack of doom.

And even then, at that most joyful moment, still I laughed at what I saw. For it was false, all flimflam, nothing but legerdemain, delusion!

Our line of kings was only two kings old. And our first and founder, the young Henry Tudor, had less good red English blood in his thin veins than any King of England since the French bastard William, the Conqueror of Normandy. Henry was a mongrel truebred, part French, part Welsh.

Gaudeamus igitur! Let us rejoice the more because of it, praise grandfather Henry for his sleight of hand, hand it to him upon a royal platter!

Mongrels and bastards, bastards and mongrels, the strength of our kingdom . . .

Now all are dead, I—I, Elizabeth—I, England's Queen—can say it: that my kingly grandfather Henry's only whiff of royalty came from the wrong side of the blanket. For his grandfather was no more than a steward risen to be Lord of the Lady's Wardrobe in the house of Henry V when the King died. And this wardrobe man had popped himself between the sheets of the grieving widow and then married her. At a stroke then became he Bed-Presser-in-Chief to Her Majesty the Queen, Head Steward of the Body Royal, Welsh Dresser of the Royal Meat, and Sole Stirrer of the Royal Stew— and all this By Appointment, royalty coming, like guilt, by association.

That cunt-climbing Celt paid for his presumption with his head. But his wooing of the widow, his voyaging in foreign parts (for the Queen was French), had served their turn. The son of that union also made a shrewd leap out of his league to land another royal bride, the last of the Lancastrians, and the Tudor line of kings-to-be was on the march.

Am I attacking grandfather Henry?

No—applauding—just as I applaud the choice of his future Queen, the one woman who could heal the wounds of the Wars of the Roses as the sole survivor of the royal house of York, my namesake-grandmother, the young Princess Elizabeth.

From her came the royal red-gold of the Tudor hair, the pale skin and fine-carved features of which, let us confess it, we are all so vain. And it was more than a marriage of convenience. "I love thee, sweetheart," he wrote to her in the springtime of their love, "and yearn for thee, more than heart may tell." There was more than a counting frame beneath that furred exterior after all.

And it was a good match, as he was a good king. He restored a land piteously ravaged by war and great ones. He put down rebellion till it became no more than the louse that lurks about the body politic. He fought against faction. He made no favourites.

And he kept his loins to himself, no minions, male or female, no Piers Gaveston, the beloved of the second Edward, no Mary Boleyn nor other whores for him. None of his children had to writhe under the lash of "bastard"—would my father had been as careful when he spilled his seed!

Nor did this Henry squander his gold any more than he squandered nature's harvest. He kept his coffers tight, "tighter than a frog's fundament," the Earl of St. Johan, his Lord Treasurer, was fond of saying, "and that's watertight!" So he left the State in credit.

And Henry was a peacemaker—he always pardoned more than he condemned. In twenty-four years of rule, our first Tudor made no foreign wars and never left his country. All he left was a clear conscience and a clean balance sheet. Not a bad legacy.

And not a bad lesson for a new-fledged queen. I vowed to learn it all. For I swear I saw him there that day at Hatfield, there before me, come to tell me this. And I swore to remember—to remember and obey . . .

XXXVI

"Have," "keep" and "hold" are three fine words, so the old proverb says.
   Have, keep and hold . . .
   And so I would.
   I was panting with joy. But even as my head reeled and my spirits stag-
gered in those first heady moments, my inner voice was whispering, " 'Have'
is but one part, the first and easiest, see now to 'keep' and 'hold' " . . .

I could hear my voice still gabbling on through the thin November air,
"Thanks be to God! This is His doing! Give out the news! Send messengers to the Holy Roman Emperor, to the King of Spain, to the English
Ambassadors, to Lord Robert Dudley, to the King of France, to the kings
of Denmark and Sweden . . ."

To Lord Robert Dudley? How did he thrust in there amid far greater men?
Ask me not, I know not.

The clammy earth was soaking through my stockings, chilling my knees
as I knelt on the ground. Behind the messengers, the people now were
pouring into the park. Their lordships grew alarmed: "Your Majesty,
pray you walk in!"

Majesty . . .

Was there ever a sweeter word?

From the great gallery I looked down upon the noisy crowd thronging
the courtyard below, my heart too full for tears. Across the hillside, peal
upon peal of church bells rent the air in a wild carillon while on the far
horizon a beacon flared, sending the news of my accession from hilltop to
hilltop across the land. Now the cellarmen were lugging out firkins and

hogsheads, and the cheering revellers were breaking out the bright, clear ale with ringing toasts.

And then from the heart of the crowd, a lone voice, pure and haunting, raised in song:

> *"When these poor souls were put to death,*
> *We prayed for our Elizabeth,*
> *When all these souls were done to death,*
> *God sent us our Elizabeth!"*

I wept then.

Beside me a speechless, quivering Kat clung to my hand, while Parry, newborn into fresh vistas of her own power and command, burbled majestically of gowns and jewels, headtires and complexions, stomachers and ruffs, and trains forty feet long. All my people rejoiced in their own way, Ascham pounding his fist into his palm as he quoted Greek, my treasurer Parry cackling in Welsh, while Chertsey wept openly on the shoulders of the mute and glowing Vernons. At the door Vine, aided by a handful of the houseboys, kept the raucous throng at bay. But one quiet soul was swiftly nodded through.

"My most gracious sovereign!"

A kneeling man, a gown of sober cut, a lawyer's soft black cap, a satchel of scrolls and deeds, and there he was—my Cecil!

Laughing and crying, I raised him up. "My dear, good friend!"

His shrewd grey eyes were smiling, but he shook his head. "Your servant, madam."

His words, the heavy bag of documents and his earnest air all told the same story. "Very well, sir!" I returned with a smile. "Serve me as you can!"

Thus within hours, within minutes even of my accession, did my work begin. Cecil's concern was not his alone.

We shared the same desires: prosperity at home, fair peace abroad, and plenty then for all!

He spoke to me as we sat huddling our feet to the fire that first day in my closet, more like a young girl with her tutor than a queen taking command. "We must make peace, madam, finish this war with France," he insisted, "defend our boundaries—and for that we must rebuild the navy—but keep our strength within them! For wars cost money, money we do not have, so plundered is the Exchequer. To do this, Your Grace must establish your own rule through your own Privy Council, and so on down through all the judges, officers, beadles and bum-bailiffs, clerks and catchpolls in the land."

I felt a breath of fear around my heart. *Can I do this? All this? All by myself?* He must have sensed it, for he smiled and added, "But first, your Coronation!"

My Coronation . . .

"Which your Privy Lords will help you to direct and plan."

My lords . . .

My Privy Lords . . .

My Council now . . .

In Hatfield's vaulted Great Hall they awaited me, the Lords of the Council, grave and wary, their faces blank like parchment awaiting my sign and seal. Gown, train and kirtle, top to toe I flamed in royal red from the rubies on my coronet to the rosettes on my shoes—but within I felt as pale as winter's dawn.

My heart in my stomach, my stomach in my mouth, I scanned the kneeling ranks: my great-uncle Lord Howard, attended by the young Duke of Norfolk; the Lord Treasurer Paulet, Sussex, Derby and Bedford; beside them Arundel, Hastings and Shrewsbury, three who had come with Gardiner every time the good Bishop came to bully me; then Clinton and Norfolk, Pembroke and Paget—Paget, yes, and at his shoulder the foul Rich, once the henchman of Wriothesley against Anne Askewe, though God be thanked Wriothesley himself had seen fit to retire from Court—and all their fellows in their finest fig to wait upon a queen.

Which of them could I trust?

The silence was mortal, the very air hung trembling between us. As well it might! Well might their lordships quaver in their noble insides, however boldly now they faced me out! The last time I had seen them in a mass, they waited on me to send me to the Tower. Could I or they forget?

And yet I must.

I must forget, and queen it—now or never . . .

The carved lions' heads on the arms of my chair of state were hard and cold beneath my hands. "My lords," I began. "God knows I grieve for the death of my sister—He has placed this burden on my shoulders, and I may not refuse. As God's servants we must all yield to His will. And if rule I must—rule, then, I shall!"

This was not the green girl, the maiden meekness, they had looked for. A quickly stifled gasp and wary eyes flickering in alarm gave me a pang of precious vengeance. My heart soared.

But I must heal the future, not revenge the past. *You must first choose your Council,* Cecil had said. My father's Council had numbered only a score of men; Mary's weakness and her desire to please her husband by honouring his men had swelled hers to nearly fifty. *Too big!* my instincts cried. Mine must be smaller, I was sure of that.

Who could I trust? All the half hundred who had been Mary's men now knelt before me, hats and hearts in hand, all beating faster now, that I was sure of too. For a place in Council, or a place at Court, was power indeed. And power was prestige, prestige money, money power, for those I chose to charm into my circle.

Who could I trust? What of Derby, Shrewsbury, Arundel, Northumberland, Westmoreland, great lords of the North, Catholic since time began, and hostile that long, too, to all that "Boleyn" stood for—would they now serve a heretic and a woman? I could not sweep away all Mary's men. But if I balanced them with men of my own family and faith—men like my uncle Howard and my cousins Francis Knollys and Henry Carey, who I knew were as strong in the New Faith as Mary's men were in the Old—would not that serve my turn? And there were other men I could make up myself. Cecil had mentioned his brother-in-law, a clever lawyer and a Parliament-man, Sir Nicholas Bacon—I must see him . . .

Some I knew must go—Paget, for one, and his toady Rich!

But the others?

They must wait!

"My lords!" I gave my sweetest smile. "You see me here, my lords, a simple maid, God's virgin and now guided only by Him. Multitudes make for muddle. I must have a Council I can deal with, one small enough for my most modest needs. And I shall soon appoint them. From you, my lords, I shall accept your services as I see fit. But you, Sir William"—I stepped forward and took Cecil by the hand—"I give you this charge, to be my Chief of Council, to take pains for me and all my realm. I know that you will not be corrupted by any man, but will give me always the advice that you think best. I know I can rely upon your secrecy, and I promise you mine. I give you liberty to negotiate at your discretion, at home and abroad, with friend or foe, and deal for me with all matters, all intelligence. And so I charge you."

Later my Cecil wrote, "Whatever secrets are kept between a Princess and her Secretary, these can be compared to the mutual affections of two lovers, undisclosed to their friends." And so it was with us: as in a love affair, albeit a high affair of state, a marriage of true minds. I knew his closeness, cleverness, integrity, loyalty, would never fail me. Now I must try his patriotism— and he mine!

Well indoors is well out: first set thy house in order . . .

Nibbling a cherry comfit, sipping a sweet gold wine, I struggled with another mighty task, the establishment of the Queen's household. Some appointments declared themselves: Kat and Parry to be my leading gentlewomen, Mistresses of the Maids, of the Robes, of the Queen's books and bijoux, of the Queen's peace of mind! But for the others—

"You must have ladies, madam, and fine ones too!" insisted Kat, now well into her stride. "There's Lady Catherine Grey, Your Grace's cousin; and Lady Jane Seymour, daughter of the late Lord Protector; Lady Anne Russell, the Duke of Bedford's daughter—all good Protestants, lady, and fit to be about a queen."

Catherine, cousin Catherine—every bit as meagre, pale and fox-favoured as Jane had been, but with only half her brains. And doubtless twice as self-important now she was the eldest of the family! What a dismal prospect, to have her attending on me, always around me, night and day!

Still, she was now the next in line to the throne—she was myself as I had been under Mary. Far better, then, to have her under my eye than left to her own devices! Yes, I would have her.

"Kat—"

"And others of your blood, ma'am, albeit a touch removed. There are young ladies related to your cousin Henry, son of Mary Carey—"

Or Mary Boleyn, as she had been . . .

Yes, I had not forgotten Henry. I would show the world that blood, when all is said, is blood, good Boleyn blood . . .

Kat was still chirping on. "And your cousin-by-marriage Master Francis Knollys, he has a young daughter Lettice and another they call Cecilia, by your cousin his wife, the daughter of your aunt Mary, and then there is another Mary, the young Lady Mary Howard, daughter of Lord Howard your great-uncle—"

How did she keep track of them all? "Kat, enough! You are now Mistress of the Maids, you choose for me! As long as they are young, healthy and handsome and sound in faith, I care not—but I'll have no creeping Papists round me now, nor ever!"

Not that this was the end of it—with Gentlemen and Grooms of the Privy Chamber, Ladies-in-Waiting, Maids of Honour, Gentlemen Pensioners, Esquires of the Body, and the Queen's own Royal Guard . . .

And I had inherited a family of fools from Mary's Court, Will and Jane Somers, dwarves from my father's time; an Italian jester; two Italian women dwarves, Ippolita and Thomasina; plus a tiny blackamoor clad like a monkey in baggy trousers and a jacket of black and gold tinsel . . .

What to do with them all?

Dinner hour was approaching, and I left the faithful Cecil once more at his papers to pace the gallery alone. My head was thumping, my ears ringing, my whole being strung out like a harp. The Coronation, the Treasury, the army and the fleet, France and Spain, were all beating like waves upon my mind. But one thought swamped them all: *Has the messenger yet reached Norfolk?* Of all my despatches to all of Europe's kings, none was dearer than this, sent forth by my most special order upon the swiftest horse . . .

How many miles to Framlingham from Hatfield?
When could I look to see him?

The evening air was glimmering red and gold, a wafer of pale moon hung in the air as the light faded from the hills. The roads were thronging still with people coming from miles around to offer goods, to seek employment or to rejoice with us. Yet even above the noise of those below, one sound rose clearly, the regular thrumming four-time of a horse in perfect balance, a horse galloping as to the end of the world.

And there it was, white as a spirit in the gloaming, a great pale stallion thundering down the highway who took the boundary wall in his huge soaring stride and dropped down in the park like Pegasus descending. Only one man in England could have ridden that horse, dared that jump—

And now he was here, just as I needed him, oh, God! dear God, he was here, he was at my feet, kissing my hands—

"Majesty!"

He was weeping, dashing tears from that fine narrow face, those eyes I never thought to see again on this side of the grave, except in dreams . . .

He was older, darker, both in face and colouring . . .

He was . . .

XXXVII

"Robin!"

My Robin.

He brought me oak leaves as his pledge of love. Robur *his name comes from, did you know that*—robur, *the Latin for our English "oak," for his devotion, for his heart of oak?*

And I had something long planned and promised in my mind for him, the perfect office for the perfect knight.

Thus when I rode for London the next day, beside me rode my new Master of Horse on his white stallion. Just behind came Cecil, none too happy to find his dismal palfrey some twenty inches lower than Robin's charger and my fine high-stepping mare. A thousand people followed us that day, swelling my train to London. And as I sat my golden chestnut in a gown of purple velvet flowering like Parma violets, crowned with amethysts, with a scarf of gold against the biting air, I felt myself a queen indeed with two such men to serve me.

Yet still when we came to the Tower, a shuddering seized me like an ague, and I could not hold back my tears. Here Jane had suffered and my mother died, here Robin had seen his father and his brother Guildford hauled out to slaughter, here I had lived my last night, as I thought, on earth. "Oh, God!" I wept. "Many poor souls have been cast down here from Prince to prisoner, few indeed raised as I am from prisoner to Prince! Almighty God, You saved me as You saved Daniel in the lions' den: all my life may I show myself thankful!"

Robin's father was forced to profess himself a Catholic before he died, did you know that?—forced to deny his faith, suffer that humiliation before all who came to sneer at him on his way to the block, to save his sons from the same dreadful death. Yet the oldest, Lord John, died in any case of his confinement. He was not past his four and twentieth year. Do you wonder then that Robin hated Papists, clung to me?

And that Christmas at Whitehall, Robin seized his chance to show the world that Popery was dead, "for the old Whore of Rome," as he impudently put it, "has lifted her skirts for the last time in this land!"

So we had masques and mumming with loud colours and braying music—priests and friars as old black greedy crows, bishops as fat as pigs and dull as asses, and cardinals as wolves ravening the populace of silly sheep. That was a fine dish for the Spaniards still about the Court to feed on! Feria's eyes bulged like a man in an apoplexy, but he had to endure it. Behind my fan, Robin and I laughed just as much at his discomfiture as at the antics of the masquers. And afterwards we danced, and danced, and danced, the highest, fastest, galliards that I think were ever seen at Court.

And what of Amy, poulter-breasted Amy, the nut-brown wench his wife? He did not say, I did not ask—voilà.

And then my Coronation—

Hush, I can hear it now, the bells, the royal salute, the roaring crowds, all England cheering itself hoarse, the four-part ringing cry "E-LIZ-A-BETH!"

One thing I knew, I must be crowned in state, and in such glory none would dare dispute my right or claim to rule. Already now the Romans, priests and laiety, were growing nervous, nervous and furious, fearful for their power and for the return of all our exiles, those like Ashley, Kat's man, and my cousins Knollys and Carey too, who had fled Mary's persecution and taken refuge in peaceful Switzerland.

"Sure, the wolves are coming out of Geneva, that sink of stinking Protestants!" they raged from parish pump and pulpit.

Then at Christ's Mass on our Lord's Nativity, a ranting bishop dared to elevate the Host before me, before his Queen, after the Romish ritual.

"Cease this mummery!" I shouted him down.

But he would not be silenced. And I knew that some would whisper, some say openly, that I was not the Queen, being bastard-born, and that the true claim to my throne lay with my father's eldest sister's line and the Queen of Scots, my Catholic cousin Mary.

So I meant to make my Coronation such that even my enemies would wonder at my majesty and power. "Leave it to me, madam!" Robin had begged. "As your Master of Ceremonies, I shall give you to your people as neither you nor they could imagine it. Only allow me!"

And so it was.

He would have nothing but the best, I would have nothing but speediest and soonest, and our people fell over themselves to comply.

"Your Grace, the cloth of gold is come from Antwerp, the crimson from Braganza and the ivory silk from Cathay—"

"Madam, it's gossamer, cobweb, angels' breath, butterflies' wings, I swear!"

God knows how they did it, but Parry and Kat had four gowns of state ready for me by mid-January. That was the date decided by a learned doctor Robin found for me, who cast my horoscope and promised me long life and Virgo still ascending, always ascending . . .

On the day appointed for the Coronation, Virgo arose having slept not at all, but in a state beyond fatigue, beyond all thoughts of the flesh.

"No, no cordial, Kat, no wine, no beer, nothing, I need nothing!" And reading the spirit luminous in my eyes, she let me feed on air and exaltation.

And indeed I seemed to float from the Tower to Westminster, first to the Palace, then to the old Abbey, where my father and my father's father had been crowned and buried. Through Eastcheap, past St. Paul's, down Ludgate Hill, up Fleet Street and along the Strand beside the Thames, I was borne up upon a seamless web of sound, the roar of the crowd, carolling choirs, bells calling from each steeple, cannon thundering like the crack of doom.

"You must be seen, my lady!" Robin had decreed. And seen I was, floating above the heads of all the people in a gown of gold and silver, enthroned in my chariot in a nest of white satin, reared up on eight huge white satin cushions edged in gold.

Gold? We swam in gold, we wore it, walked on it. I rode in a golden coach under a rich canopy of gold carried by four of my lords: why, even the mules that bore me were swagged and swathed in gold, gold brow-bands, gold saddlecloths, gold harnesses. Behind me rode Robin, himself in gold, on a black charger now, to set off the pure milk-white palfrey he led by a gold rein as the Queen's mount, should I have need of her.

A thousand horses came first as all my courtiers, judges, churchmen and civic dignitaries led the way. Before me went the Lord Mayor bearing the gold Sceptre, and beside him Garter King of Arms with the golden Orb. Behind them walked Lord Pembroke holding aloft the Sword of State, its heavy scabbard gilded by the winter sunlight and gleaming, too, with thick-encrusted pearls. All about my coach came a marching hedge of sergeants-at-arms, about them my Gentlemen Pensioners, about them my Yeomen of the Guard rich in new scarlet velvet heavy with gold and silver spangles, and behind them forty of my ladies gorgeous in cramoisie and cloth of gold, for we had plundered England, plundered the world, to make all fine.

And everywhere the people, oh, my people, I never loved them more! In their thousands, in their tens of thousands, pinch-faced and blue with cold they braved the early-morning snow, the ways made foul with days of sleet and slush, to cheer my passing.

"To see Her Grace!" one woman wept. "To see her blessed face!"

"Long life and joy! Joy to good Queen Elizabeth!"

"Bless you!" I called back, beaming. "And you shall see I shall be a good lady and queen to you!"

The posies and the nosegays of dried honesty, heather, thrift and thyme rained on my golden lap. Another ancient dame thrust forward with her offering, a spray of rosemary. Rosemary for remembrance—how haunting is that scent! *Pray love, remember?* I glanced back at Robin, and in his eyes I saw remembrance too.

"God bless Your Majesty!"

"God save you all!" I called back. "For I thank you with all my heart!"

"Praise God for you, lady!"

Blessings and prayers, welcomes and good wishes, showered down on me like golden rain. And gold did too: at Cheapside Cross the Lord Mayor of London gave me a crimson satin purse of a thousand marks in gold. Yet the richest gifts money could never buy, like the thin piping cry of one shrivelled ancient: "I remember old King Harry the Eighth: now shall England be merry once again!"

At Westminster Palace I changed my diaphanous gold and silver for a robe of royal velvet, red as the heart of the rose, as red as love, as blood. Cut high to the throat with a tiny ruff of snow-white damask, it was the promise of maiden modesty, of the rose unblown, and so I trod the purple carpet to the Abbey.

And now the time had come, I was weak, I was quivering like an aspen.

In the porch the thick pall of sickly incense that came forth to greet me almost turned my tender stomach. I trembled on the brink, a virgin shrinking seized my limbs, I could not take a step.

"Courage, Your Majesty!" came a gruff whisper in my ear. On either side the Earls of Shrewsbury and Pembroke held me up, and behind me their Countesses bore up my train. Still, I flinched as I came in the Abbey and the vast cold vaulted space exploded with light and sound, flaring with the fire of a thousand thousand candles and the heartfelt greeting of a thousand thousand throats.

But in the Sanctuary no one was present save myself and the old Bishop—*yes, and God.*

Yes, He was there, I felt His presence close at hand that one immortal moment!

You do not believe me? Do you not think that He has shown since then His blessing of me, shown He blessed my anointing, blessed my country and my reign?

He was there, I knew it, felt it, and He inspired me with my destiny. For now I would be Queen—now I had a lover's longing to embrace my fate, to give myself, surrender body and soul, be taken . . .

Piece by piece my women prepared me for that moment. Off came my little velvet cap, my ruff, my cuffs, my sleeves, my overgown, my kirtle, bodice, chains and earrings, all my petticoats, even my shoes. At last I stood before him in my shift, nothing but a film of lawn between my modesty and the biting cold.

Now even that was laid back as my breast was bared for the kiss of the holy oil. Augh! How cold it was on my forehead and my unprotected front! And it was rancid—how sour and strange it smelled as it trickled down between my breasts! I was panting, half with fear, half with possession. The old man's thumb, hard as a labourer's, dug the sign of the cross three times in my flesh, once on my forehead, once above each breast, carving and carving till my nipples rose against him, but he seemed to see it not, as on the wedding finger of my left hand he roughly drove the Coronation ring.

So was I married: so I gave myself, and so was I taken, for at that moment something possessed my body as my soul. Even as my feet, my hands, my head, grew cold as ice, my body's core, my deepest woman's part, thrilled through and through, and a warmth, a heat, suffused me—and I knew myself England's, married to England, taking her life as mine now, to be England's ruling spirit, guardian angel, mother and lover, wife and Queen. Queen . . .

I sobbed my joy in silence, as women do when we are most happy.

Now came the finest of my robes, my Coronation vestments, a gown of cloth of gold, a deep gold silk embossed in silver, with a ruff of finest

samite edged with gold. Round my neck and shoulders, on my fingers
and around my waist, I wore ropes of table-cut sapphires set with great
round rubies and pendant orient pearls. And over it all came the cloak of
royalty, matchless in grace, gold figured silk to match the gown below,
with an ermine collar twenty inches deep, and lined to the floor with
ermine. Over it all flowed my unbraided hair, worn maiden fashion quite
unbound and free, its bright red-gold the same hue as the shimmering
silk of the gown, and all in perfect keeping.

*All save my foolish virgin weakness—for my panting heart, my shaking
limbs, almost betrayed me to fainting, every second—*

And then at last the Crown of St. Edward, most ancient and most
sacred, was placed upon my head. Then at last came the crown I was to
wear for the rest of the ceremonial—

*How the ghosts walked that day! For the crown was Edward's, made for
his boyish head and now the right size for mine. And how beautiful it was,
with its four soaring hoops of pearls and gold, a wreath of pearls and diamonds and sapphires encircling it, and at the centre, underneath the cross, a
huge fair crimson gem, the ruby once the pride of the Black Prince and
called by his name.*

Trembling, I was led out of the Sanctuary, and in a voice of thunder,
Garter King of Arms gave tongue: "I now proclaim you Queen of all
England, France and Ireland, Defender of the Faith, our most worthy
Empress from the Orcadian Islands to the mountains of the Pyre-
nees . . ."

His words were lost in the high silver screaming of a hundred trumpets, drowned out by kettledrums, borne on the wind of pipe and organ
as the anthem swelled along with my bursting soul. Did the people take
me to be their lawful Queen, to honour me as their liege, to live to serve
me, to die for me?

Did they?

"Yea! Yea!" And "Yea!"

A bliss so bright it seared like a flame passed through me. I saw my
past and future becoming one that hour, and all my present moments
stretching out into eternity. I saw my father and my mother, and I
yearned for her that instant as I had never yearned in all my life.

"Yea!"

"Yea!"

And "Yea!"

All my lords roared their approval, all circling their coronets in the air
like boys at a half-holiday. And so they brought me back to the Palace
Hall, where we banqueted eight hundred peers and prelates for eight
long hours and ate, I think, eight tons of food per man.

For myself, I partook little of the gilded roasted swan, the boar's head stuffed with apple, the peacock in his feathers, the blackbirds in their pie. And I took a pleasure sharper than the wine in watching my people—*yes! my people now! my peers, my knights, my people!*—seeing them feast and gorge. The palace cooks had outdone themselves in Westminster's eighteen kitchens, each one surely a hell of heat and torment, yet still the source of food fit for saints in heaven.

And still the toast went round: "GOD SAVE THE QUEEN!"

My champion rode full-armed into the hall, his gauntlet of mailed steel clashing to the stones as sonorously he challenged any man not to support my right. And as we ate, the young Duke of Norfolk, in his first appearance as the hereditary Earl Marshall, and the Earl of Shrewsbury as Lord Steward, both caparisoned in gold-and-silver tissue as gorgeous as their horses, rode at watch and ward between the lines of the four-sprigged tables to ride out all unwelcome visitants lurking there.

So was I Queen, and queened it like the Queen of Heaven, supreme in bliss. And so I came at last into my chamber too tired even to raise my arms as my ladies lifted off the crown, the cloak, the heavy Coronation robes, until my women, Kat at the helm, carried me to my bed to fall at once into a deep and dreamless sleep.

It was the best sleep I ever had in my whole life, and the most peaceful.

And the last night of peace and innocence—for the next day Cecil woke me with the news that all had dreaded since the day Mary died.

XXXVIII

Cecil's calm voice belied his dreadful words. "Madam, the Queen of Scots has proclaimed herself the Queen of England. She now lays claim to your throne."

I stammered like a natural. "How—claims? How does she challenge my right to the throne?"

"By war, she says, if need be."

"War? Now God help us!" A cold sweat bathed my limbs. I saw screaming Scots kerns and gallowglasses breaching the Borders, enemy ships in London water, the armies of France pouring down the gang-planks as he spoke.

"Not by invasion, madam—at least, not yet!" Cecil said grimly. "But by proclamation, by bullying and bluster backed up with a show of arms to establish herself as the true and rightful Queen—"

Now I was screaming. "And I the usurper, the bastard interloper?"

He knew better than to agree. But he could not disagree as he withdrew, leaving me sick and shuddering in my bed.

My cousin Mary—how I hated her!

For whatever women have that makes men love them, Mary of Scotland had it from her cradle and kept it to the grave. I could make men fall in love with me. But Mary never had to—for with her, it was a force of nature.

God knows how! For she was mannish tall, as tall as Robin, two standing yards! And a black-eyed, clay-faced hoyden too, I heard, with a lump, a great wen, on the bridge of her nose, which came towards her chin in a real witch's droop . . .

What did men see in her? Not that I was jealous! Why should I be?

No, only her pretensions to my throne made her my bane. And in the end, black bane to all who knew her, to her cause, herself.

"This is her father-in-law's doing—this is our enemy Henry, not the young Queen!" the Earl of Arundel broke out angrily at the Council meeting later that morning. I looked up anxiously at his bulbous face, twitching with feeling, and his staring eyes. I knew he kept the old rites in his chamber, I could smell the incense above his body's smell in his fusty velvet robes. And old or not, he was still a man. *What, was he amorous too, as all men were said to be about her?*

Paulet threw down the despatches from Paris with a contemptuous lift of an eyebrow. "Henry's doing? Only to this extent," he corrected in his dry, pedantic voice, "that the King of France has commanded her to be proclaimed throughout Europe as Queen of England, yes, thus far it may be." He tapped the parchment with a disbelieving fingernail. "But the young Queen-Dauphiness, as we are told here, herself revels in royal mourning for the death of our late Queen her 'sister,' and prinks herself in the royal coronet of England at the French Court."

Cecil nodded. "For sure France thinks by this to frighten us and win advantage in the peace negotiations now in hand," he agreed heavily. "But the Queen of Scots herself would be less than a queen, less than a woman, if she could resist the hope of joining the crown of England to her titles of Scotland and of France."

"Let us send, then, to our peace commissioners and strengthen their hand," cut in Lord Clinton loudly. "Give orders that this peace may only be settled on terms that the Scots Queen abandons these false claims, or they shall pay for it. And since we know that the war between them has bled both France and Spain to the bone, then we know, too, that they both must treat, and soon."

My cousin Knollys took up the refrain, his dark eyes burning. "And we have no way but one against the hosts of Rome, these Popish pretensions . . ."

I sat there watching, brooding, as the argument dickered to and fro round the green baize.

For Mary was no common or garden pretender to my throne. Young as she was, she was a royal one, and doubly royal. And her claim, though false, was not without foundation. I could imagine the angry words of Arundel, Derby and Shrewsbury, all the crypto-Papists, when I was out of earshot.

"She is the senior descendant of the senior Tudor line!" they would be muttering. "And as such, she stands above the Grey girl Catherine, whose claim derives only through the late King's younger sister."

Then would old Bedford or Pembroke, staunch Protestants both, come back raging. "King Henry cut her out! As Catholic-born and foreign-born besides, never having set a foot within our kingdom!"

"Yet many now alive in England believe that hers is the blood right!"

Yes, and many more of our Papists and crypto-traitors would welcome a Catholic queen as if she were the Second Coming!

And of all the angry, troubled faces round the Council table, none dared say the words: *If Mary were to challenge you by force . . . how should we fare?*

And who, then, could I trust?

And that same week a messenger from Italy brought more ill tidings of the power of Rome. For all Robin's mirth at Christmas, the serpent of old Rome still pulsed with venom, still adored to sting.

"A Coronation present, madam, from the great Beelzebub, that villain of the Vatican!" snorted bluff Pembroke, who as an old soldier never beat about the bush. "His Great Unworthiness Pope Paul IV has laboured and brought forth more of his speciality of office, Papal Bull!"

My flesh crept—*would they dare to bastardise me again, now I was Queen in my own land?*

But the rat had taken a turn down a new sewer. Cecil spelt out the details. Inspired now by the cat—*or say, rather, the bitch*—Mary of Scotland, not bastardising but usurpation was the Pope's theme. Now he urged all who would listen to put me off my throne. That would be no sin at all, he ruled, but an act of God.

It was an open incitement to treason. But worse was to come. At the next Council meeting a falling messenger, a reeking horse, brought more news hot from Spain. "So the Spanish Inquisition, that bloody band of torturers, has a new Vicar-General!" Knollys burst out. "With a mandate from the Pope to purge all Europe of heresy?"

It meant the power of Rome resurgent, there was no doubt. We hardly dared look at one another. For, as Cecil quietly pointed out, we had our own inquisitors here at home, a still-strong rump of Mary's Papistry who would bring back the Roman fires in England if we did not establish our faith. And that could only be done through Parliament.

"The test, the trial of your rule, will come in Parliament," Cecil counselled me. "Your Majesty must win them—you must rule with their consent."

I nodded. "Yes, and more—*I must rule with their love!*"

Mary had packed her Parliaments, all men knew that, shamelessly ordering the sheriffs to send "none but such as be of a good Catholic faith." I would have none of that. None but Englishmen tried and true, hearts of oak come from the shires of their own will and with the good will of those who sent them.

Among whom, I was amused to note, was one Lord Robert Dudley, who contrived to get himself elected to his father-in-law's seat for the shire of Norfolk—though I was less amused that to do so, he had to leave me and return to that flat and clammy county where his wife was stowed.

For fat brown Amy was the lady of the manor, and through her he derived his title to the seat. Yet Dudley was in Warwickshire, was it not, and Warwick his father's and his brother's seat and title?

Not Norfolk, no.

He should not need to go there.

I must take care of it.

To London then they came, my Parliament-men, on foot and horseback, by mule and cart, battling for days, even weeks, through snowbound ways and roads mired deep in mud. The Commons I did not fear. But would the Lords stand with me now against the might of Rome, against the poisonous chalice I had inherited from Mary, in my work to root out the deadly legacy of Popery in the land?

God on my side had swept away some of the worst of Mary's bishops—ten of them died that winter, including, in the clearest sign of His good favour, her Archbishop of Canterbury, the Papal Legate who had been her fatal consort in the burnings. Perhaps he was even now feeding the flames himself! But the rump were all still there—and with my Catholic lords in the Upper House, the great ones of the North like Derby and Shrewsbury, not to mention Mary's still-surviving creatures, fierce Catholics like Lord Hastings and Lord Montague . . .

Who could I trust?

Who but myself!
Oh God, defend my right!

Like the knights of old I kept a holy vigil the night before the battle: I watched and prayed all night before that first of my Parliaments, and well did I have need of all God's strength that day.

I met it like my Coronation, in full sail, pennants streaming from every topmast and all spinnakers flying. "Give the people a fair show, Your Majesty," Robin urged me, "to show that you are Queen, going to your Parliament, to have your will and way—allow me!"

So out again under his mastery came the milk-white mules, the golden chariot, the gold and silver trappings, all the panoply of state. This time I blazed forth in scarlet velvet trimmed with soft white fox at the neck and wrists, framed by a high standing ruff of pearly silk goffered to perfection, with a collar of gold and pearls about my shoulders. On my breast I wore a pendant ruby the size of a pigeon's egg, and a cap of matching velvet dripping with pearls and golden spangles topped my freely flowing hair. On the steps of the Lords my peers all wore their Coronation robes as they waited to greet me, and Westminster once again seemed ready to give a loyal welcome to her Queen.

But how I was deceived! As the massive doors swung back, baleful with age, a low chanting hit me—plainsong, it was plainsong! And bearing down on me was a defile of faceless black shapes, hooded monks gliding forward two by two, a forest of crucifixes waving aloft, a swarm of censers swinging, each carrying a wax candle after the old high Roman fashion. Could I not open my Parliament without the aid of the malignant minions of Rome?

"Away with those torches!" I shouted in furious rage. "We can see well enough!"

"No Popery!" came the roar of the crowd behind me.

Yet among my entourage I caught a hiss of fury, and I knew that if I was going to rule my Church as my father had, it would not be without a battle royal.

And in the Commons they awaited me, two bands of wolves, the Protestants hot from Geneva and home now for revenge, ranged against the undaunted Papists, who would go down fighting before they gave at all. Enthroned at their head, I stared them round.

Many I knew by name if not in person. Here white-faced, red-lipped, black-gowned was the infamous Dr. John Story, yes, the man who had prosecuted Ridley and Latimer as far as to the stake. Story was speaking, the first speech of the Parliament. "Keep to the Old Faith, root out the heretics!" he urged, eyes blazing. "We must keep up the burnings, nay, Your Majesty will do well to increase them, for your soul's health and the health of all your people! Why, I myself," he boasted, "threw a faggot in the face of one of these earwigs at the stake in Uxbridge when he was singing psalms, and set a bushel of thorns beneath his feet—and I wish I had done more!"

The nauseous stink of incense throbbed in my nostrils, and my gorge rose. *There was no curing such men, no saving them, no dealing with them.* And inch by inch, speech by speech, we bested them, Cecil and Knollys and I, and Cecil's brother-in-law, whom I had appointed the Lord Keeper to aid in this, till at length all the Parliament came round behind me. And we thrashed out a law that all who would not stand with me in establishing a true and peaceful religion in our land in place of the Old Faith and all its cruelties should be sent out of office and if necessary stowed in the Tower till they had time to reflect where the truth did lie.

"A good Parliament's work, madam," Cecil congratulated me as I dismissed them.

I nodded.

"Good work, my lady," Robin agreed, then with a wicked grin: "And now for play? I have a gelding come from Ireland who craves a lady's hand upon his bridle, longs to feel your spur, the touch of your whip . . ."

I laughed up into his mock-innocent eyes. Yes, I had proved myself royal, now I could royally prove myself a woman.

And then my Parliament-men spoiled all for me by demanding their reward.

XXXIX

Quid pro quo.

Say, rather, *quim pro quo,* for no less were they demanding.

The price for this session's parley was, it seemed, my maidenhead. My Parliament-men, having given me my head in the matter of religion, decided to cut short my maiden voyage—to petition, no, to *require* me, to take a husband as soon as possible.

My Lord Keeper of the Great Seal, Sir Nicholas Bacon, came hot from the last sitting at Westminster and stood puffing before me with the offending petition in his hand.

His story was soon told. I must be married, and soon: they were all agreed. "They also desire Your Majesty to give thought to the succession —to name your heir, who now should succeed you—"

I stared at Bacon, a blubber mountain of a man but with a mind like a needle in the vast haystack of his bulk. He was Cecil's brother-in-law, and I knew that I could trust him.

But should I put myself at risk, the risk that I might die tomorrow, in order that their minds should be at rest today?

"Name a successor?" I raged to Cecil as he stood quietly by. "Do they know, have they forgotten, how I suffered under Mary? When all men knew that I was next in line, how I became the focus of all plots, of all unrest, and so nearly lost my life?"

"Not you alone, madam." Cecil strove to pacify me. "The first in the kingdom always feels his life in the hands of the second—why, the Emperor Tiberius in ancient Rome made away with all who stood near to his throne, and all those who had even a drop of royal blood, even if it were not of his own house . . ."

As did the English Tiberius, that tyrant my father, who cut down my first lord, my lord of Surrey, for the drop of Plantagenet in him; who butchered also two queens, a cardinal, a lord chancellor, a duke, a marquis, a countess, a viscount and viscountess, four barons and dozens of lesser fry . . .

And should I now make snares for my own feet and pitfalls for my path by creating successors and pretenders, when he had so considerately cleared the way?

But Parliament's main business was to sow the seed for a true successor, a new Tudor: to bully me to the altar, to hobble me and hamstring me with a husband, whether I liked it or not.

"The State requires it, Your Majesty," Bacon opined, accepting a cup of hot sweet wine and thrusting down a tranch of March-bread, "for we must have consensus! Rogue claimants like the Scots Queen show us that!"

"More wine, sir?"

He hardly paused to nod to the servitor. "The peace of the realm requires it—for we must have stability!"

Cecil's meaning look supported his every word: *No more wars like those of the White Rose and the Red, never again, no, no!*

"And the succession requires it"—gobbling off the last of the sticky loaf, the Lord Keeper made great play of wiping his fingers on a huge napkin, staring at the ceiling to avoid meeting my eye—"for we must have an heir in the shortest time, a prince of your royal line."

And there it was again, the eternal cry of all the Tudors: God send us a prince! A prince! The phantom boy child so longed for, so like the Shekinah in the Tabernacle, adored, yet never seen!

And I knew the fear he harked on—for short of the Queen of Scots, after me the next in line was the short Catherine Grey, and next her never-seen infant sister, an even more wretched creature, misshaped and misbegotten, one of God's outcasts not three feet high—a dwarf.

I sat in my chair of state and ground my nails into my palms as Bacon roamed on, for I also knew what all would be saying behind my back: that *I required it*—I, Elizabeth—*for no woman could govern without a man to bear for her the cares of government.* Why, all men knew that!

And that my health required it—*for without coitus, never broken by a man, women have no passageway for their foul flux and bloody humours, and are always subject to greensickness, to the rash motions of an unruly womb and to a constant, ticking lust.* All men knew that too!

But above all, they *required it—for being men, they never thought that I could live without one!*

And so they came, my suitors, in search of all. And at first it was a game.

"Give me some bread, Kat, and a slice of brawn to help me stomach them!"

Thus almost every morning with the new day's despatches over breakfast, I teased a laughing, frowning Kat, who dreamed of a great love in store for me, and a Parry who now thought in terms of a state wedding and dreamed of the best match for me in all my parish—which now meant the world.

"So many men, so little to choose between them—see which one you like for me!" I rattled through them like a maid at market checking off her wares. "Item one—the King of Spain . . ."

One brother-in-law, rather used now as a husband, thirdhand indeed and somewhat shopworn, yet who takes the credit for making the first proposal I ever had, when he offered for me even before his wife had died. As a husband, then, practically a bigamist, but who now wrote wonderful love letters to me—or someone did . . .

"Item two—the King of Sweden . . ."

Erik the Ever-Ready, for he had bid for me before, in Edward's time. Now he sent perfume and pomegranates, tapestries and ermines, and then his own dear brother the Duke of Finland as his proxy to plead his cause . . .

Successors now, they ask me? Why, that same Finland, Erik's heir apparent and successor designate, once back from wooing me, took his brother's throne, and then his eyes, and last his life and all, with a sharp poison . . .

And Philip of Spain's successor, the boy Carlos—how he planned to take his father's life till Philip was compelled to relieve him of his own, you will remember?

I will name no successors!

———

"D'you hear me, ladies? More bread here, Kat, and a sliver of that cheese. Items three, four, five: the Holy Roman Emperor, uncle of Philip, and his two sons, in one job lot—"

"Yet which does Your Grace prefer?" Unlike Kat, Parry took the game completely seriously. "The Holy Roman suzerain himself or one of the archdukes?"

"Parry, tell me"—I kept my face very solemn—"will England stand for it? After my sister's husband, what price another ugly, short, bandy-legged, undershot Hapsburg Papist as England's King Consort?"

"Madam, madam!"

"Nay, my lady, fie, do not speak so, *fie!*"

"And now item five, the Duke of Saxony . . ."

Of the world's royal males, easier then to say who was *not* on the list!

And there were homegrown suitors too, who saw their chance and took it. The first I knew was one day in the Presence, when the Earl of Arundel entered in green taffeta and yellow stockings, sprouting like a daffodil.

"For sure, lady, he's in love!" giggled Mary Sidney, Robin's sister, now come to be among my ladies on Robin's high praise of her wit and spirit.

I craned to see him. "In love, Sidney? Say, who with?"

But as the old goat approached the throne with a cow's grin, a bull's grace, an ass's reverence, and a new hat flapping its plumes like a hawk held by the feet, my sinking stomach knew.

"Your Serene Majesty!"

"My lord of Arundel, welcome!"

Welcome?

He was as welcome as a wet St. Swithin's: fifty if he was a day, a pithering Papist, bald, bulging, short of breath, short in the leg—short, too, on courage and even more on brain, as his blusterings in Council showed!

And so far short of another man, the man I—peace! Enough!

"Madam, give him fair greeting!" This was Kate Carey, sweet and sly. "For he has laid out above six hundred pounds among us and the maids—"

"To drop his name into Your Grace's ear, whispering sweet nothings of him as you sleep!" finished Kate's sister Philadelphia, almost unable to speak for laughing.

"What has he given you?" I hissed—for any gifts should have been mine, not theirs! And I made them yield to me the jewels besides that he had squandered among them—above two thousand crowns' worth!— gold clasps inlaid with mother-of-pearl, a rose made all of rubies, a collar of agates and a dozen pretty rings. The baubles pleased me, but the man not at all.

"For all his wealth and power, Kate," I breathed to Carey as he strutted round the Court, "it must be centuries since he made any maiden's heart go hop!"

And as if I would have taken a Roman Catholic, albeit of the creeping crypto-kind, to be my husband, even for a queen's ransom!

Yet other eyes were on me, and Kat, my Argus-eyed defender, never failed to notice them. Notice? She could read the future, like the Sibyl of old Rome. "Your late brother's Ambassador to France presents his compliments," she observed lightly one morning a week later as the maids dressed my ruff for the Presence. "Coming in late last night, he craves the favour of the speediest audience with you."

Returned from France?

"Still a good Protestant," Kat dropped out as she tidied the books beside my chair, "a good man, of good breeding, and ever loyal to your family."

If suitors are in fashion, she was telling me, *this one is worth a whistle.* I took a breath. "Bid him come."

Kat nodded up a Privy Gentleman. "Call Sir William Pickering."

"Sir William Pickering at Your Majesty's command!"

Pickering! Page to my father, courtier to my brother, and steadfast for Mary when others turned to Jane, yet turning against the burnings to support his old friend Wyatt in his rebellion. But before that, the bosom friend of that dear friend of my bosom, my lord of Surrey . . .

Would he remember that night by the Thames, the last time I saw my lord alive?

"Sir, you are dearly welcome. We will dine alone, and speak of . . . many things . . ."

"Your Majesty is too gracious!"

"No, no, rise, be easy with me, Pickering . . ."

I could have loved Pickering for that alone, for that love of ten years gone by. He made my heart ache with remembered pain, set that old scar throbbing till I longed to have him soothe it. And he was tall, with the looks I always favoured—fair, lean and well-set, for all he was past the first of his youth.

And my Parliament men liked him, liked the idea of an English prince. They liked still more the idea of a son of mine with his long limbs, dusty blond colouring and cool-eyed, careless, lordly air . . .

But an eagle mates an eagle, a lion partners one of the pride. As a royal princess I could take none but a prince, I could not mingle flesh with common blood.

And besides . . .

Pickering's visit unsettled me, though I could not say why. Fretfully I turned the whole conundrum over in my mind. Of course I had to marry —I knew that! And I knew that somewhere in the world must be a man that I could love.

Yet how often did true love and marriage go together for those of royal blood? As long as I could remember, I had known that choice was the one luxury denied to me. For all my riches, privilege and power, the meanest milkmaid with her pail on her arm had a freedom in love that I could never have. I must choose for England, not for myself!

X L

Should I marry?
  Could I?
  How could I marry when I was in love—with life, with England, with my crown, myself?

The days lengthened, winter melted into spring, the fires sank down the chimneys, and still I brooded. If I had to marry, I would much rather *be* a husband than have one! For I had seen at first hand with Dame Katherine and sister Mary what it was to be a wife, to be subject to a man and bound to obey his will. *In marriage men gain, women lose!* I raged. For I had learned one thing above all from my last lord, Baron Tom: *women lose in love because we always love, we cannot choose, and men can, and do!* Must I, then, marry? And without love?

For the right marriage, I would have to—a queen could not marry like a cowgirl. *But a wife's part,* my flesh protested, *in a marriage without love is the same as the trade of the trulls of the street.*

Yet if a woman felt that stirring, that heat in her loins, men thought her a whore indeed. And for whores, as the daughter of Anne Boleyn well knew, there was only one punishment.

Who, then, could I in honour marry?
  None!

I am married to England, my heart cried, *and every day sees me about my wifely duties!* Furiously I turned the black-and-gold Coronation ring upon my hand. On my Accession Day, Cecil had set my feet upon this path, and there was much to do. The State I had embraced was rotting, like an oak, from the heart outward. And the heart was money.

Never enough. The curse of kings, wars and money!

Never enough money!

And debts! Mary had left debts all over Europe, at rates of interest that were the cruellest folly: money, money, money . . .

We worried at the money question night and day, Cecil and I. Then Cecil found him, Sir Thomas Gresham, a moneyman of Europe but with an English heart of oak, albeit one with a silver tongue and fingers of pure gold, the very man to help us. How Cecil's quiet competence soothed my spirit—nay, he was like my own spirit to me, and so I told him: "Where should I be without your unseen hand, your invisible presence, Sir Spirit!"

Within days this Gresham made his first report. "Your Grace, you must restore the currency! So debased is it, the very name of England is degraded with every dubious coin. If you wish to restore our country's credit, here and abroad, this is the only way."

To avoid war, said Cecil, *we must defend the realm.*

To do that, we must buy arms and men.

And that meant money . . .

Money . . .

And Your Majesty must marry . . .

Marry . . .

Marry for money?

Yet who had any?

Lammastide came in weeping from dawn to dusk, and now I was brooding in Windsor, nursing the same concerns that had dogged me from Westminster and Whitehall. How I hated these dank days when I could not walk or ride but had to stay imprisoned in my chamber! Even with an out-of-season fire smouldering on the hearth, the place smelled like a crypt.

Marriage and money, France and Scotland, money and marriage . . . As I turned a listless solo hand of cards, beset by these conundrums, I could hear my ladies tittering and tutting over a packet newly handed in. "Come here with that!" I called fretfully. "What are you laughing at?"

Catherine Grey paced up on her short donkey's legs, proffered a redbound volume with a curtsey and stared straight at me with her shallow sandy eyes. Cousin or no, she had precious little kindred spirit, that one! Yet the airs she now gave herself as my nearest kin, boasting of her rights in our royal line, never failed to grate on me. I scowled at her.

"Books from the stationer's," she began in that maddening schoolgirl voice, so like Jane's. "One in particular, come from Geneva—against Your Majesty—"

"What? Against me?"

"A lunatic Scot expelled from his own country, no more than a wretched, ranting hedge-priest, please you, my lady," hastily cut in Kate Carey, who could always tell when Catherine was ruffling me, "a rogue preacher known as Knox, who has sent forth a most ridiculous pamphlet—"

Anne Warwick helped her out: "—which he has most ridiculously entitled *The First Blast of the Trumpet Against the Monstrous Regiment of Women*—"

I grabbed the book. "What does he say?"

Catherine could not resist it. "He says the rule of women is against nature, my lady—more, that it is against the will of God."

I could not contain myself. "So myself and my sister, and my sister queens of the world—has God divinely blundered with us all?" I flung the cards at Catherine's head, and the book into the fire. "Fool! The man's a fool!"

Fool that he was! How could I have come here as Queen but by the will of God—who spared me from my enemies and called me through a thousand perils to this place?

But here once more was the same theme as that of all my counsellors and suitors: I could not rule, I must have a man.

God damn them all!

Catherine was still parsing her way through the argument as a terrier shakes a rat. "In nature, as he says," she puzzled on pedantically, "no lion lies down before the lioness, no beast so low but the cock rules the hen, the ram the ewe, and the male the dam. Thus a queen ruling degrades all men, making them less than beasts!" She paused. "But if Your Grace were to marry—"

"*Jesus God!*" I screamed aloud in rage. "Hold your presumptuous tongue! I swear I'll have you sent to the Tower if you say another word!"

A queen ruling degrades all men . . .

"Do I degrade you, Robin?" I pouted.

Robin was never one to flinch from a jump, no matter what the drop on the other side: "Degrade me, madam? Such a hope of heaven lies far beyond my dreams. *Would that you did!*"

At least I had one friend! And the more my burdens multiplied, the more he proved himself a friend to me. When I came from the Council meetings wrinkled deep in worries—Scotland, the French, the currency, my marriage, the succession, chasing their tails like cats inside my skull—he would be waiting in the antechamber attended by his men, his bright face and flashing smile a beacon of delight after the hours spent with their grey old lordships, bearing with their beard-clutching hesitations, fears and compromises . . .

It was a summer of . . .

You blame me?

Hear what happened first, and how easily, oh, how sweetly . . .

Then blame me, if you will.

"Exercise," Robin swore, "is the only antidote to the poison of high office"—the long hours in close-fumed chambers, the late conferences when my only nourishment was hot air, night vapours and cold candle snuff. So he had always his hawks and hounds at the ready, the archery butts set up or a new ride to show me, a new colt or filly foal he was trying out for the Queen's Horse.

"Love your four-legged subjects, madam," he insisted, "for they all love and serve you."

And so I got to know that secret world of blood and fire, of jades and jennets, nags and dobbins, as he called them—for we kept above three hundred horses in my own stables, let alone the heavy chargers, court gallopers, chariot horses, pack animals and wagon mules, and the great beasts used for the tilt and jousts in the Queen's Lists.

"Majesty, come!" he would command, as if he ruled and I was no more than his maid. "For my man tells me a wild boar was seen in the low coppice, and a stag with hinds in the far forest an hour's ride away."

"An hour as we ride, Robin?" I quizzed him laughingly. "Or at the pace of those snails who follow us and call themselves riders too?"

"Madam—*whose pace but yours?*"

When I came out of a difficult audience, he was there. When I stepped into the Presence, he was there. When I woke in the morning, he was awake before me, his page at my door to know how I did today, and he never closed his eyes in his own lodgings till he knew from Kat or Parry that I had closed mine too.

He was not alone. All my lords, all the envoys and ambassadors, courtiers and servants down to the meanest potboy, paid me the same regard.

How I relished it! I fed on it, lapped it up like sweetest syllabub, and my enjoyment grew with every mouthful, every fleeting taste. Why should I give this up to make myself the property of one man alone? The premier dukes and earls of England knelt to me now, the Duke of Norfolk, the hereditary Earl Marshal; Arundel, my antique *bel homme;* and the dour Shrewsbury, lord of the northwest Marches—all prayed to kiss my little finger. Yet always in the Presence, Robin's laugh rang out above their heads, and his high spirits, bubbling like sherbert, sparkled over, overflowed their laboured attempts at courtship and gallantry.

Not that his wit pleased all.

"Lord Robert is a fair flatterer," I overheard Cecil murmuring as he stood talking with the envoys of the Hapsburgs, just within earshot. I laughed: I knew I was meant to hear. *Did I detect a note of sourness?* For with all his gifts, my Cecil had a leaden way with words, could never make them skip and gambol, float and soar and dive, tickling the mind, the ear and the heart with laughing joy, as Robin did.

Not that his wit pleased all.

"He talks too much!" growled the Duke of Norfolk. "Such petty prattle demeans Your Grace's dignity and abuses Your Majesty's ear!" For a beginner at Court, the young man took little care to conceal his opinions. Yet as I looked at his pale and ill-favoured face cursed with the Norfolk protruding eyes and hanging lower lip, I understood his jealousy. And this was at least said openly: behind Robin's back he maligned him viciously as "new blood, bad blood, sprung from a house of traitors, an upstart popinjay."

Just like all the Norfolks! His grandfather, under my father, had been furious against the Seymours as "new men," mad to defend his rank next to the King. Yet where were the Norfolks, where were all the Howards, when I needed them? *Clinging to Mary!* Robin was my friend, staunch in the darkest times. He was my man, not the Pope's, not his father's— *certainly not his wife's*—loyal to me, my most loyal friend . . .

The consort of viols struck up the entree to a slow pavane. With a sigh the woodwind took up the lilting air. Across the Presence Chamber I could see Robin, bright as a guinea fowl in a glowing doublet of tawny silk slashed with brown satin, the golden plume of his soft brown velvet cap just kissing the pearl in his ear. Now he was cutting a path towards me through the press to beg the honour of the dance.

Cecil's voice beside me was as quiet as ever. "Baron von Breuner of the Hapsburgs seeks to know how to describe Lord Robert when he writes to the Emperor Ferdinand of the persons of your Court."

"Lord Robert?" I watched the easy, springing step of Robin's lithe body now approaching me, saw the smile he seemed to save for me alone. "Say he is my friend."

"Your Majesty's friend?"

Cecil's pale eyes were empty, almost opaque. What a foolish question! What could he mean? "Of course, dear Master Secretary! What else could he be?"

"Madam, I know not."

I turned away. For the first time, Cecil girded me, and I knew not why. Could he not see the way things were between us?

Robin and I had grown up together, endured together, suffered under Mary in the selfsame way. Here was a man who had lain with Death as his bedfellow, just as I had in that fearful time, and in the same fearful place.

He had seen his father and his brother dragged out to the block. He had watched his elder brother John die of his sufferings, and his mother die of grief. And he had lost, too, his youngest brother Henry, last of all the sons of proud Northumberland, fighting at St. Quentin to restore the family name in the foolish war Mary had made against France.

Was it strange, then, that he was so in love with life, so enraptured by his freedom, so determined to burst each day like a grape against his palate, squeezing the pips till they cried out for mercy?

Now we had come through, he swore to me, now the sun shone on us, now, though he could not reel back time's rope of sand, at least he could cast line for life and love and freedom! And though we could not make the sun stand still, yet we would make it run!

I frowned at Cecil coldly as I took Robin's hard brown hand and moved towards the music. Robin loved life: that was all there was to it.

Yet still those pale grey eyes of Cecil's followed me with their unspoken question as I took to the floor.

If Robin loved life, life loved us all, back then.

"Amor gignit amorem, nescit ordinem, omnibus idem," said that great toga-twitcher of old Rome, the poet Virgil: *"Love begets love, love knows no rules, this is the same for all."*

And hear you, let me promise you, this was a time of love, a summer of love, a honeymoon of love . . .

The people loved me, for now the glassy mirror of the sky was never clouded with the smoke and grease of burning flesh. Now in their ancient mossy chantries and little churches built of golden stone, they could worship in their mother tongue, pray to God in our good English and know He heard them.

And I loved them, and I loved all about me as I flirted with Arundel, with Pickering, with Philip's Ambassador and the ardent envoys of Sweden and the Hapsburgs: from all sides I was sated with adoration, worshipped like a goddess.

"And like Diana, Virgin of the Gods, you live for the chase!" cried the gallant von Breuner, leader of the legates of the Hapsburgs, as he attended me in Windsor's Great Court, watching Robin as he assisted me to mount, then mastered horses, riders, hunt followers, hounds and men for a day in the saddle. Day after day found us hunting in the sun, falling from our panting horses deep in the forest alone, we had so far outdistanced even the fleetest of our followers in our breakneck ride, or picking at wine and dainties in the enchanted circle of a fairy ring, our people out of earshot.

All through England it was a lovers' summer, when the sun flew up the heavens every pearly dawn, and oh, so slowly—oh, so sadly—every scented dusk slid down a sky spangled with evening stars in a ball of glowing fire already promising a shining morrow.

But for me—

What can I tell you?

Oh, I could play the game of courtship to perfection, every opal evening, or each deep velvet night after supper in the Presence when all about me, their tongues loosened with wine, were piling Pelion on Ossa in their efforts to outdo each other in praise of me. But the next morning all my griefs were there in my chamber corner as I awoke, waiting to greet me like Katherine's faithful chamber dogs, her little greyhounds—but more and more, for me, they were hounds of hell.

Mary of Scotland, marriage, the succession, France . . .

Each one had teeth like a wildcat, and the jaws of a mastiff—which would bite first?

In the event, all bit together, the teeth closed on me as one. The first messenger that morning came even before the maid with the bread and beer. The bare words made my stomach clench like a fist. "Madam, your Secretary Cecil craves the earliest audience with you."

It had to be bad tidings—nothing else would bring him to invade my chamber.

I was gowned already, though not coiffed, my hair still playing freely over my shoulders. But Cecil was privileged, no ordinary man; and by the sound of it, this was no time for coyness. I nodded at Parry. "Admit him."

Cecil's grey face, his heavy gait and bundle of despatches showed the weight of his concern. "My lady, evil news. The King of France is dead, pierced by a broken lance as he fell while jousting, and Mary of Scotland is now France's Queen."

There was only one question now.

And Queen of England too, does she reach so far?

Within the hour we were in Council, I and Cecil and a handful of my lords hurriedly assembled.

My voice rang thin and harsh even in my own ears. "Will she enforce her claim against my throne?"

Lord Bedford growled, shaking his grizzled head. "As Queen of France, she now commands all the forces she would need for an invasion. And with a French garrison already in Scotland under her mother the Regent—"

"We are caught like rats in a trap!" I turned to Cecil. *"Will she invade? And when?"*

"Who knows?" Cecil leaned forward and tapped the table urgently. "But certain it is, Your Grace, that you must now marry! And at once! For as long as you are alone and childless, your throne, our safety, stands on one fragile pillar—thus you give the Scots Queen free rein to vaunt herself as your successor!"

Now the subject of my marriage came tumbling hot from every lip.

But Cecil raised a hand and sharply silenced the debate. "Her Majesty must make choice!" he said almost angrily. "And in the shortest time! For the Queen of Scots has another reason to press her claim—yes, and the best of all reasons—!"

I gasped. "No! She is not—?" *Yet I knew at once she was.*

"She will claim your throne, she may even carry war into our land to seize it now, not only for herself—but for her heir."

None of my lords moved. At last I was the one to speak. *"Her heir?"*

Cecil nodded savagely. "I have it from intelligence that she will give the world a bonny boy before the year is out!"

And I thought it was a game, no more than courtly ritual? What a fool I had been! Mary of Scots now Queen of France, and with child too? Oh, God, my hand was forced, forced now in earnest!

Yet must I suffer this? Was I to be put up against a wall in all the violence of haste, rushed to execution like the merest villain? *No! I could not bear it!*

I was beyond tears, beyond thought. Last night I had slept little, and the nights before that. *What comfort for the head that wears a crown? Even Cecil is against me! Who can I turn to now?*

My violent pacing of my chamber had brought me to the door. Without thinking, I passed through it. "Parry, come!"

Like a homing pigeon, followed at a distance by Parry and her page, I traced Windsor's warren of apartments till I found the door I sought.

"Knock here, and attend me!"

"Ho, there! Who's within?"

"Your Majesty!" Only the exquisite breeding of the manservant kept his eyes in their sockets as he saw the Queen herself, pale and trembling, on his threshold.

"Where is your master?"

"Off, man! Away, leave us, I will receive Her Majesty!"

Thrusting forward from behind, waving away our attendants, Robin took my hand and drew me into his lodgings. Awkwardly he gestured at his shirt and hose as he slammed home the door: "Forgive me, madam: I was still making my toilet."

I gripped his hard brown fingers, quivering at his touch. In the glass by the door I saw a white face crumpled with misery, set against another glowing from his dawn ride, and I did not know either myself or him.

The chamber was cool and low—the midday heat would never reach in here. But for the clutter of riding, hunting, hawking and shooting, it was sparsely furnished, a pure bachelor's apartment. On a table near the window a bowl, a sharpened razor and a discarded napkin bore witness to the daily ritual of men. At the small casement the early-morning sun knocked for admittance through the greeny glass.

Around the hearth two or three great chairs fronted the inglenook. Anxiously Robin seated me and knelt at my side. His face was still dewed with rosewater from his man's attentions, the hair at his temples damp, curling and brown like buds of marjoram. "Majesty, tell me—what brings you here? What ails you?"

Suddenly I could release all I had suffered for the last two hours. Now I was gabbling like a natural. "Mary of Scots—she's Queen of France now, and due to give them a prince—" I tried to collect myself. "It was a game! I took it as a game! But now I have to lose—lose everything!" I could not hold back the tears. "Oh, God, Robin—tell me, help me!"

"Lady, I am yours, you know that! Simply command me!" He was baffled: never had I acted like this before.

But now I could not stop myself. "I must marry, d'you hear me, I have to get married, all against my will! For England, Cecil says—and he says, too, that it must be the Hapsburg—for Europe, he says, to keep the balance of power—" The tears of rage started again. "So now must I be Europa, to be ravished by the Bull?"

He flinched with distaste, his face flushed with strong feeling. "Madam, do not speak of it! If I had my way—" He broke off furiously, dropping his eyes.

I leaned wearily into him. The scent of his pomade was warm and familiar, damask water and lime, myrtle and barberry, manhood pure and strong. "Yes, Robin—?"

He started like a thoroughbred, his eyes flaring. "Majesty, I must say no more! I should not have presumed to venture this far—forgive me—"

"Say on."

He gasped. "Madam, do not force me—!"

"Give me your thoughts! Must I marry? Without love?"

"Love, lady?"

His voice came from a thousand miles away. "What do we know of love?" His eyes were bright with tears. "What dare we know?"

What did I know of love?

How could I answer?

Amor vincit omnia . . . Love conquers all—I had embroidered that both on my sampler and on my heart, like any other little girl. And like every other little girl, I had soon learned it was a lie.

Other than that . . .

I had known my lord of Surrey and my lord of Seymour, the one air, the other fire, the one all spirit, the other ruled by his senses from his manhood *upwards: one love so pure that my love asked for nothing, fed on nothing, needed nothing, could live on nothing but sighs, tears and thoughts; the other so demanding that it grew hungrier with what it fed on till it demanded flesh, and fed on flesh, and fed my flesh, and fed my heart of darkness—was that love?*

Who knows what love is or how it comes between two people?

My father loved Katherine of Aragon for the joy they took together, Kat had said.

This was the love I had never known.

Not as I knew it now, now I had come upon its palace in the heart of a dark forest, stumbled through the briars and found myself in fairyland . . . no, in paradise, in bliss, in mutual bliss . . .

"Love? Robin, what are you saying?" I gripped his hands. He looked up, startled, and a vivid flush darkened his features.

"Who, I? I—"

He made to rise, and I held him down beside me. "Robin, speak!"

He bowed his head. His breath was coming short now and harsh, like a man in pain. "Pardon me, Highness—oh, God forgive me—"

"I command you—speak!"

My heart, my being, stood on tiptoe: I could not move. A ray of the rising sun filtered through the window and scythed the breathless air. Outside a skylark laughed and cried high in the blue.

"Oh, lady!"

He was weeping. "Of this your marriage, I have taken too little thought. For me, too, it was a game, no more than a game!"

"And now?"

"Now? Now, if I had my way—"

"Yes?"

"Your Grace—oh, may I venture this? For God's love, I will speak! If I had my way—Your Majesty's Most Beloved Grace—should take to her heart—*no man but me.*"

XLI

Within the hour it was all over the Court: *"The Queen has visited Lord Robert in his lodgings—she was above an hour with him in his chamber all alone!"*

At the noon Council meeting none of my Privy Lords dared challenge me, nor even meet my eye. But voices were higher, tempers were shorter, and they returned to the subject of my marriage like dogs to a bone.

The Hapsburg . . .

No Papists . . .

The King of Sweden . . .

What of a suitor nearer home—an Englishman . . .

"Yet say a *nobleman!*" Shrewsbury's sarcastic emphasis was not to be missed. "He must be noble, not jumped up and newmade—a man of blood, of old wealth and position—and ancient loyalty—"

Not Robin Dudley, he was saying, *son of a traitor and a new man besides!* And all their eyes were saying, *Hear this, madam—he speaks for all of us! No son of Dudley, not this lordling, never!*

I looked at their faces, anxious, angry, sneering by turns. Yet their disdain was powerless to burst the bubble of my joy. I felt like shouting, dancing, jumping in the air! Sitting there in Council I was rapturous, I was floating, I was in bliss, hugging myself with it, forcing myself to keep my dignity about me and my face Puritan-straight, while my heart, my mind, my soul, resounded with one refrain, *Robin, Robin, Robin.* And inside I was beaming like a baby, aching with reciprocated joy: *He loves me! Robin loves me, loves me, loves me!*

"Wait for me!" I told him when I had to leave.

His heart was in his eyes, his lips on my palm as he murmured, "Madam—*what else?*"

Now I was fleeting back towards his lodgings on wings of fire. His man at the door had obviously been given his orders—with a murmured "Majesty!" he vanished. Now I was laughing as Robin drew me in—now as he knelt before me, he took my hand and pressed it to his lips, his forehead, touching my knuckles to the hard line of his cheek, then kissing it again. Leaning down, I placed a trembling hand to his neck and felt him start as my fingers stung him. *Robin, all's well,* my heart cried out to him. *Fear not, all will be well!*

I wanted to live once again that moment of his declaration, now I could savour it to the full. *I will speak!* he had said. *And if I had my way, Your Majesty should take to her heart—*

To her heart . . . ?

"And to her precious soul—"

And—

"And to her bosom—for so I worship you—adore—and love you."

I looked into his eyes. Behind the wainscotting a little creature stirred in the trembling silence. Like two enchanted spirits we sat together, neither daring to move for fear of breaking the spell. His hands were heavy, warm and real in my cold, frightened grip. I could feel his warmth entering me, taking me, claiming me, restoring me. As my tears fell, his knuckles gleamed like pearls in the early-morning sun.

Was it a half-formed memory of my lord of Seymour and his silver sword-scar? Or was it all my new lord's doing, all his presence, all my sense of him?

But I gazed at his hands and knew I was in love, had always been in love, and now would be in love with Lord Robert Dudley all my natural life.

Now his face was soft and dewy to my touch—oh, God, how I loved him! He had had his man shave him again and now was sleek as his smooth satin doublet and his silken hose! He was in dark blue, the colour of the far horizon, of woodsmoke in the distance, the moody indigo of thought. Pearl clusters sprigged his breast and shoulders, and as he rose, filled all my gaze; around his neck he wore a chain of pearls and tourmalines glimmering like owl-light. His eyes were blue as lupins, he smelled like heaven descending, and in my eyes he was a god.

Wordlessly he led me to the inglenook and seated me with a deep bow. His strangeness hurt my heart. "Robin," I begged, "no ceremony! Sit beside me—please?"

He coloured, but obeyed.

Neither of us could speak—a great silence, a great purity, fell between us, both casting down our eyes like virgins at a nuptial, both afraid to say a word. I could see his long, strong leg, his hard, well-shaped thigh thrown out before me, his long-fingered hand lying tensely by my side, the other gripping the wooden edge of the seat. In the dim chamber nothing stirred but our souls, nothing was heard but our beating hearts. Through the warm air his scent reached me like a fox's, the strong trail of musk and barberry rose to my head and seized me like rich wine. His hand by my side drew me as adamant draws iron. Hardly knowing what I was doing, I brushed it with mine, then turned into him.

"My lady!"

Brokenly murmuring, he took my hand between both of his, as a man would touch something sacred, joyfully but in awe. Bending his head, he brushed my fingertips to his lips, then covered each finger with kisses, venturing joint by joint. The pressure of his fingers scalded my palm, and I could not hold back from him. "Robin—oh, Robin."

He raised his head. His eyes in mine were Greek fire now, fire and blue lightning. With a trembling hand I traced the outline of his hair, springing beneath my touch. My fingers brushed his ear, and again he started, the ready colour racing up his face. "Oh, my Princess," he whispered harshly, "my sweet Queen!"

He was kissing both my hands now, showering them with soft caresses like the rain in spring. Slowly we drew together, and when our lips at last became one, they met as sweetly as the kiss of our first parents at the dawning of the world.

And now I loved him, now it seemed I saw him for the first time.

Now I noticed how few men he had attending him—now I saw the little seamstress slipping out of his lodgings with the cloaks and doublets, even the hose he had commanded to have turned and turned again, when another's drunkenness or carelessness had spoiled them with wine or candle wax or worse—never his own, for he was fastidious beyond measure, so clean and proper that he was the model of a courtier and a gentleman.

Now I saw the tradesmen he dealt with knocking at his door or harassing his man in the attempt to recover at least some of the cash he had laid out on being fine for me, being fine as my Master of the Horse, being fine, fine, fine in his new role and office.

And now I saw him plain, I fretted at it. It was true what Norfolk said, he had nothing! For nothing remained of the ruin of his family with his father's death, even his mother's dowry being swallowed up in that great earthquake, that chasm of disgrace.

And he never complained of his poverty, he would not speak of it.

"Robin," I begged him, "tell me of your estate, how does it stand?"

He laughed. "I am the richest man in all the world! For I have access to a mine of gold and jewels. All my wealth is in Your Highness's eyes, where I can see a Milky Way of sparkling diamonds—no, I lie, Empress, I see sapphires today, from the sky's deep blue heavens—"

"Robin, no fooling! Hear me, you must have money, your position now demands it—"

"Lady, I have what money can never buy, your white hand in mine—"

And with a bow, a laughing flourish and the brush of my fingers to his lips, he would put me off.

But I would not be silenced. "Robin, see here!"

I gave him money, twelve thousand pounds in a great leather bag, just to see his face, laughing and weeping with surprise and joy.

And "Lady, see here!" was his riposte: for the first thing he commanded with it was a gift for me, a golden heart studded with emeralds and rubies to speak our love in the language of jewels—*E*meralds for *E*lizabeth, *R*ubies for *R*obin, and gold for love pure and everlasting.

And see I did: for he had Parry slip it on my pillow as she drew back my bed hangings, so that I awoke to find his pledge, his tribute, shining in my eyes. My eyes, his eyes—so close were we that we knew not where one soul ended and the other began.

And now, even more than ever, he saw with me and for me, he had become the eyes in the back of my head. "Your Ô Ô greets you, in all thanks for your most royal largesse!" now he wrote to me. "For so I joy to sign myself—your own two eyes, your own Argus eyes, ever vigilant for your good, till death claims him—R. Dudley."

Dudley.

That was all that he had too, the bare name of Dudley and the empty phrase, the honorific "Lord Robert" no more than a courtesy title come to him from his father's dukedom, now defunct along with him.

And that, too, I can repair, along with his fortunes! I breathed to myself.

And so I did.

I did it when I was rewarding others, among them Harry Carey, my ever-loyal cousin—I had pledged myself I would show them all that Boleyn blood was as good as any other! I made Harry Baron Hunsdon of Hertfordshire, with the lands to support his title. But the greatest honour was for Robin alone.

"Robin, kneel here!"

I made him a Knight of the Garter on St. George's Day. No villain in a pageant ever looked so fine, so fierce, so smiling-wicked as he did that day in Windsor, wrapped from top to toe in royal blue velvet, white satin hose hugging his marvellous legs, the sash of scarlet slashing his breast like a great love wound.

Windsor meant so much, for there we had found each other and ourselves.

"Robin, read here!"

The document was long, Latin, and loaded with seals and ribbons, but in a trice he took the drift. "Oh, lady—oh, my lady!"

I had made him Lord Lieutenant of the Castle. Kissing my feet, he swore himself my lord and my lieutenant, mine until death. But now he was a lord indeed in his own right, and king of the castle too.

And for our private times I gave him a house, a little manor of no more than twenty or so apartments, tucked away under a hillside at Kew, and lands to give him rents and tenants and men to draw on, men to serve him, as a lord must have. And because I could not bear to be apart from him, I would visit him in his lodgings, which I had had moved next to the Royal Apartments, or command him to breakfast or supper with me in mine. You will guess how the young Norfolk with his family pride hated it! And hated Robin even more!

He was with me every hour we were not asleep, yet still there was that reverence between us, a trembling hesitation. It was as if we were now strangers, strangers and lovers, surely, but yet strangers still. He who was always so bold, so confident, now turned to me for every trifling thing. "Majesty, I must have a steward to run my estates, watch over my household and see to my affairs—what think you of this man?"

"John Forester at your service, gracious Majesty."

I glanced at the dark-faced fellow now making his reverence. Was this the best man he could find, this sallow, stone-eyed creature with the hard edge of an ex-soldier and the soul of a bailiff, as he seemed to me? "But choose how, Robin," I urged him, "he is your man, and if he is loyal to you, you need not my permission!"

And I gave the man Forester with his dark stare no further thought.
Would it have made any difference if I had?

And yet it pleased me that Robin made this demand, sought my advice, lived and died in my approval—for so I did in his! Now I dressed for him, rode for him, danced, sang and played for him, and even in my reading, thought of nothing else but him.

For I still tried to keep up my Greek and Latin even in the midst of all my other labours. And though I worked daily now on my Spanish and Italian to deal better with the foreign ambassadors, yet the older languages still held more grace and truth for me. Ascham, still in my household, showed no surprise when I fretted at Pliny and bade him turn for a change to Ovid or Catullus. "Yes, all the best poets sang one time of love! But might I suggest, Your Highness, the lyrics of Meleager or the peerless Sappho, singer of Lesbos?" In his rich round tones he began to incant her lines:

> *"Love has unbound my limbs and set me shaking,*
> *A monster, bitter-sweet, and my unmaking . . ."*

What a comfort he was to me then, Ascham, till age and ill-health took him from my side into retirement, with his copious draughts of consolation from the immortals. And what a joy Robin was, even the thought of him . . .

But every Eden has its serpent: there is not joy without its share of pain.

I knew Robin had used some of his newfound wealth to bestow his wife nearer to Court—Cecil, who saw all through his own "eyes," saw that I knew of it. Courtesy of Norfolk too, dropped clumsily into the pool of Court gossip, where he knew it would be sure to swim to me, was the word of where—Cumnor in Oxfordshire, where he had also bade his new steward, the silent, stone-faced Forester, and his men to guard and keep her.

I troubled at it. What, under lock and key? Was she a caged bird now, a prisoner, now he was flying high and needed no fat poulter-pigeon wife to take his sky and crowd his soaring flight?

Why did I think of her? For her existence was immaterial to me. Indeed, she did me a favour, for it meant that none could misconstrue my friendship for Robin—nor could he be accused of having designs on me. He was married, I was considering marriage, there was no more to say.

Yet still Amy obsessed me—I could recall her still as plain as day, her little body, her half-open mouth, her upwards, beguiling glance, her plump brown breasts and russet cloud of hair.

Why did he never speak of her?

And more, and worse: why did I never dare to raise her ghost myself?

For she would not go away. Indeed, she would live to haunt us! For she lived, she throve, she was no ghost; she was real, and a real threat to my peace.

And yet I did not speak.

And still life went on. The more I favoured Robin, the more my Council pressed me to take another man. What could I say?

As I dithered, others saw other chances. One day in the Presence a new ambassador, one Bishop Quadra de Ávila, a fat, sleek prince of the Holy Church of Spain, billowing in black and red, presented his credentials and craved leave to speak.

"Speak, my lord Bishop."

His voice was mellow, gently accented, soothing to the ear. "His Most Holy and Catholic Majesty of all Spain greets his most loving sister, Her Most Serene and Imperial Majesty of England, and begs her good wishes on his espousement."

"His *espousement?*"

"To the Princess of France."

To the King's sister, Mary's sister-in-law! Was Philip now therefore against me too? I was trembling. "So much for your master's professed love for me—if he could wait no longer before snatching a princess when he might have snared a queen!"

Quadra threw up his hands and fanned his short, fat olive fingers, each speaking volumes of his master's regret. "Yet alas, dearest Majesty!" He pursed a sorrowful mouth. "The King must have a son—Spain must have heirs—and time will not wait."

Time will not wait . . .

"The Hapsburg!" chorused Shrewsbury, Cecil and Derby.

"An Englishman!" carolled Bedford and the Protestants and the people.

"Me!" drivelled Arundel, and in a lower key, "Me?" queried Pickering.

But the man of my heart said nothing—and I knew why.

XLII

And at last I could bear it no longer: inward grief must out, or it ulcers all within. One day as I approached the Presence, I saw him standing as ever just within the door, to be first to greet me as I came through. All eyes as always turned my way: my cousin Knollys with big blond Harry Hunsdon and our cousin Lord Howard, and old Bedford, ramrod straight, arguing warfare with the Earl of Sussex, newly home from France. But Robin was deep in conversation with my unloved cousin, Catherine Grey, and the Earl of Hertford, a tall youth I knew as the late Protector's son, of a good body, but dull brain; I never rated him. But something of the way Catherine, pale as a primrose, now turned her face up to my lord—*"my" lord, d'you hear me, Catherine?*—and the way he hung smiling upon her words, caught me on the raw.

"Her Majesty the Queen!"

He leaped to attention at the heralds' cry—he was at my side. "Your Most Serene Grace!"

I could not help myself, the poison spilled from me in my passion. *"Non vien ingannato, se non che si fida!"*

Behind me my ladies Mary Sidney, Robin's sister, and Jane Seymour discreetly faded a few paces backwards. Robin's eyes widened in pain. Slowly he repeated, " '*None is deceived but he who trusts too much*'? You have trusted too much? Trusted me? And been deceived—by me? Lady, how have I deserved this?"

I was furious with him, and more with myself. "No reason! Command the music strike up! Bid them dance!"

He shook his head, still puzzling. "Surely Your Majesty—!" He glanced across the Presence at Catherine, now clogging the young Earl of Hertford even more closely than she had clung to Robin. His face darkened. "I shall return your proverb, madam, with another! *Chi ama, crede* . . . He who loves, trusts!"

" '*Chi ama*'—?" I burst out. "No, no, it is false! *Chi ama, teme!* . . . He who loves, fears! Always! Always, always!" And to my fury, I burst into tears.

Swiftly he stepped forward and gripped my hand. "Clear the Presence!" he called out to the Lord Chamberlain. "Her Majesty will withdraw!"

Surging forward, the Gentlemen Pensioners carved a pathway through the throng.

"Come, lady!"

Head up, nodding and smiling on all sides as if all were well, Robin led me swiftly through the throng and into the withdrawing chamber. "Give Her Majesty some wine, refresh a napkin for her with sweet water, and then leave us," he ordered the attendants. In a flurry it was done, and we were alone.

He came to my side and gently raised the heavy silver goblet to my lips. "Here, madam, take a little of this Canary—it will strengthen you . . ."

The wine was full in my mouth, his hand on my forehead cool and firm and sweet. My head was throbbing. Kneeling before me, tenderly he pressed the newly sweetened napkin to my temples. "Now, Majesty—my dearest lady—my queen of women—tell me what grieves you. Was it my talking with the Lady Catherine? You can have no fear of her! Why, you outshine her as a star does coal! Tell me, then, why are you jealous?"

A violent trembling gripped me, and my tears fell like rain. I knew I was cutting a sorry figure, but I knew I had to speak. *The 'why' comes in three letters—and it ends with 'y'!"*

His look was of pure torment. "Oh, my lady—Lady Elizabeth!—do not weep for that! Never weep for her—or me!"

How could I tell him I wept not for her but for us, for the two of us? "Robin—forgive me—*what of Amy? What of your wife?"*

A flash of pain savaged his features once again. "Madam, you must have seen—or guessed—how little she is to me now!" He shook his head in anger, almost derision. "But she is still my wife, oh yes, alas, my dear wife!"

His bitterness was palpable. I felt a perverse desire to punish him. "Yet you married her!"

He almost snarled. "At seventeen, eighteen? What does a boy of that age know more than the call of the flesh? And when I had done feeding upon her like a cannibal, gorging myself upon her, what was left?"

Carnal marriages may begin in pleasure, but they must end in grief . . . Cecil had spoken these prophetic words at Robin's wedding, and they rang down the decade hollow in my ear. Poor Amy. Oh, poor Amy. Sappho knew her story, wrote of her plight: *the doe that would be mated by the lion must die for love.*

I was overwhelmed with pity. "Was nothing left?" I whispered.

He laughed sardonically. "For me, the cold curds of a lust long left, as a dog leaves its vomit. For her, something far worse, a man she now disgusts."

His coldness chilled my soul; yet just as coldly it pleased me too. *Now he would be mine! For unless he had spoken like this, I could not love him —I could not love a man whose heart was spoken for, preempted, mortgaged and possessed by a prior owner, no, not I, Elizabeth, Elizabeth the Queen!*

One more probing of the wound, then like a surgeon I would try to heal it. I touched his hand. "God did not bless your union with . . . ?"

Robin took my meaning with a harsh sigh. "She might have kept a memory of our love if we had had a child. But none came of our early tumblings, my brief honeymoon with her body. And now—"

He broke off, staring out into the room.

I had to know! *"And now—?"* I prompted him.

He looked me full in the face, pain glistening in his eyes. "Now I never touch her," he said bleakly. "While she, poor innocent, still loves me! Better for her I had killed her body than so to kill a living soul!"

"Oh, Robin!"

He laughed furiously. "Nay, lady, do not pity me! She is the sufferer! In body and in mind. She has a malady in one of her breasts—growing within, from grief and inward sickness, her doctor says." He gave me a steady look. "He also says she has not long to live."

I caught my breath. What was he saying? *Wait, do not marry, I shall soon be free for you?*

I bowed my head and yielded heart and soul to the call of the serpent, the age-old sirens' song.

I did—and I did not.

For what I did, I did—and I did only what I chose to do. I could not lay the blame on Robin for what my heart and soul, myself, no other, led me to. If there were a serpent in our garden, it was not he, for he was Adam to my

Eve; together we were like the children in the first garden of God, and like our first parents we were without sin—for long enough, at least . . .

And I chose to forget her.

Yet had I spoken of her, what could I say? *Robin, how does your wife?* And would he reply, *She's dying nicely now, I thank you, ma'am. My man Forester keeps her tight and close, and she has every comfort . . . ?*

Every comfort except the one she wants, now in her last extremity, the man she loves . . .

Yet all knew that I loved him, and he took the blame for that. Arundel was furious, Pickering mortally hurt, and the Emperor of the Hapsburgs, as Cecil did not spare to lay before me, fell into a Holy Roman snit at the fear that he or his could be enmeshed in marriage with a loose-laced woman, a light-of-love.

I would have no truck with this, however. "Tell His Excellency," I defended myself volubly, "that a thousand eyes see all I do! That a camel could more readily pass through the eye of a needle than I encompass one sinful moment with Lord Robert!"

"As you say, Your Majesty."

Cecil was nothing if not true and trusting. Yet even his eyes—blank as coins unminted, like the weights they lay upon the eyes of dead men—called my bluff and oh-so-politely, too, called me a liar.

For the truth was I sinned every second I was with my newfound lord, and every other second too. Just to be with him was sin, to think of him was sin. The hairs glistening on the back of his hand, the turn of his neck, the way his ears lay brown and sweet against his head, the curl of his hair behind them, all or any of these could make my blood prick up in an instant and bring the colour to my cheeks, the warmth to my body.

And he, he felt it too, I was sure of that. At times in my chamber, the blue evening falling but the candles still kept at bay, a lute sighing in one corner and the pale voice of a page singing of pains that he had yet to feel, my lord would abruptly rise and, with a hasty bow, break from me, call for wine or cards, shattering the circle of our enchantment to let the cold world in. Yet the next moment he would glance at me or I at him, and we would be lost again, drowning deep, deep in that well of peerless love.

Yet we said little, and did even less. It was enough for us simply to be, to live, to dream. The end of summer rounded out like a full-bellied wench into a rich harvest: at Michaelmas the church at Richmond was groaning with the fruit of the season—ripe gourds, bulging in brown and yellow, carrots and turnips, apples and damsons and smooth golden pumpkins. At Court, too, my cooks excelled themselves to bring in the last of the sweets of nature before Persephone, fleeing to the Underworld, would take the summer with her, ushering in the cold and dark for another half year—so we had loganberries and hazelnuts, the last of the plums, plates of ripe quince and medlar cut in with our sweet, crumbling English cheese.

Winter came, and all life died around us. But other fruits, other strange growths, were flowering on other trees, and even in my paradise, my love retreat, I was forced to know of them. Now I did not attend each Council meeting, as I had done in those nervous early days—I knew I could trust my lords to debate for me, and Cecil to make sure that nothing passed me by. And all things came to me in any case: I had to see and sign all the decrees, acts, bills and proclamations.

One crisp day of December I had dallied outdoors to watch Robin, also playing truant, shoot at the butts. Only after the Council meeting had finished did I return to the Audience Chamber.

There Cecil awaited me, smoothing down his long gown of Burgundy velvet as he knelt to give me greetings. With memories of Robin's faultless archery fresh in my mind, I was never in a better mood. "And what do I sign today?" I plumped down at the table, reaching for the bank of quills. I was eager to get back to him. "Let us begin."

"As Your Majesty pleases."

Carefully I composed myself to the task—I was vain of my great, bold, flourishing *ELIZABETH R* and never wished to hurry it. One by one Cecil laid the papers before me, and as I finished with them, his scriveners took each one away to a side table to sand the thick black ink until it dried.

"Soldiers to Scotland, sir?" I frowned over the writ.

"Your Majesty will remember that the Council recommended the strengthening of the Borders, the Queen Regent in Scotland being so hard-pressed to hold her country quiet. And now the preacher Knox has dared his return from the hotbed of Geneva, and daily inflames the people against the Roman Church and their French masters. There will be rebellion, sure—but we must make sure it does not spread to England."

"Knox? The rabble-rouser who wrote against me, against the 'monstrous regiment of women'?"

"Madam, the same."

"Agreed then—all the men you need!"

I signed and moved on. Beneath the remit for the raising of the army lay a document I had not seen before. "A Warrant for the Arrest . . ." I read slowly. I never dealt with such trivial stuff.

". . . to arrest Mother Down of Brentford, and Hugh Birley of Totnes . . ."

Who were these people? "Master Secretary, what is this doing here?"

"That? What is it, madam?" He peered over my shoulder.

I stared at him. Cecil not know what was among his papers? I would as soon believe he had forgotten his own name! His eyes were clear and guileless, the grey of inland waters, with no malice in their depths. Yet as I glanced back at the warrant I knew he was deceiving me: ". . . for lewd and seditious behaviour, in that the said Down and Birley went about to say that the Queen was no honest woman, no better than the parish whore for her immoderate life—for that Lord Robert did swive the Queen, tupping her like a Turk—"

I found my voice. "A very foul-mouthed couple, as it seems."

Cecil stared straight ahead and simply nodded. I felt for my pen and signed the warrant with a vicious slash. "See to it that they pay the lawful price for their vile slanders."

"It shall be, Majesty."

I would not show the rage I felt at being subjected to the scorn of these magpies. Yet these pickers and chatterers, these caterpillars gnawing at my name and reputation, gnawing at Robin, stung me like an adder's bite. He had to know of this. When I told him he flushed and bit his lip, black with anger.

"Swive? They dared say 'swive'?"

I nodded, mute with shame.

He met my eye, his eyes like thunder on the mountains, and I read his thought: *If they only knew!*

For there was nothing between us, nothing of the flesh. Nothing, that is, but love too deep for words, daily becoming too deep now for tears. But love there was, and sighs and songs, and tributes and love tokens, and looks and mutual likings discovered more each day. And as with my second lord, my lord of Seymour, sometimes a stolen kiss in an oriel window or hidden embrasure, our people far apart, or out in the field, our favourite place of all, where like children of nature we could do as nature willed.

We rode every day. From early summer, when our horses would carve their way through bridle paths breast-deep in meadowsweet and ladies' lace, through the flat and fallow summer plains to the rutted plough of autumn, only the days when the rain came down in torrents or when the frozen earth would be too much for the horses' feet, ever kept us indoors. And even then Robin would blandish me to watch him ride indoors, where the best of his horses would display their "airs above the ground," and he his *maisterie* of them, as the French called this new and graceful art—and where, not least, I could not hide it, he would exercise his mastery of me.

He was the best horseman England ever had, did you know that? I never saw or found his like again. He was a centaur in the saddle, he became one with the horse—he could so sense its every movement, I swear he could read its mind.

And every day the sense I had of him deepened in me. His long horseman's body, his strong face, tanned like a gypsy's now, his white flashing grin, took hold of me till I could think no more. From Scotland came the word that the French were strengthening their presence, building up a hostile garrison on our very borders. I heard it, felt it with a spurt of fear and anger—*Mary! Now she queens it in two countries, bestrides my kingdom like a great witch, one foot in Calais, one in Carlisle!*—felt it, and then forgot it.

Then came the word that the Scots lords, sick of the French, of the Queen Regent, sick of their cardinals and of the Pope, had mounted a rebellion—they meant to turn their country from the Church of Rome and establish the New Faith there. And that Mary of Guise, the Scots Queen Dowager and Regent for her daughter, sick of her lifelong struggle, sick of a dropsy raging out of hand besides, and now sick of the task of beating off the Protestant challenge to her daughter's throne, had laid down her head, her life, her crown, and died.

XLIII

"The lords! The Scots lords have risen against the Catholic rule from France! This is good news for us, the best!" gleamed Cecil. "We must support them, madam, with men and money!"

All the Council were agreed. "Think what that would be, Your Grace," rumbled Sussex, mentally feeling for his sword, "to have the French, their Queen, the Pope and all driven from our island, buried in the sea!"

I snarled and quibbled. "What? Support a rabble of rebels against their anointed ruler?" I had not forgotten the nine days' rule of Jane, that traitorous attempt to overthrow my bloodline! I shook my head at Cecil and the little group of lords. "I would not aid a single soul on earth to take up arms against their ordained King. For who knows when the same rebellion might not turn against me!"

"Madam, think not of it!"

"Lady, you rule with the love of a good people!"

Of course, they all rushed to protest that none could strike at me. But I did not credit them. My grasp of my throne was hardly a twelvemonth old. All I had was the people's loyalty—and if I lost that . . .

This was the stuff of nightmares—the very stuff that had poisoned Mary's terrible last weeks as Queen, when she huddled herself in her foolish rusty breastplate and kept an old sword by her on her pillow—not that she ever slept! Now with the Scots in arms, I, too, knew what it was to fear for my throne, even fear for my next moment. Yet one look at him and that fear would be forgotten, all forgotten in the love of him . . .

Still, I could scarce believe in my good fortune, his love, our joy. And I could not speak of it, for all around me had their own reasons for disliking him. The jealousy of my lords I could tolerate; much harder was the silent obstruction of my faithful Cecil. The worst was, Cecil liked Robin, unlike Norfolk, who despised him as a "new man," vaunting his own "old blood" in Robin's teeth. But Cecil longed for the Hapsburg marriage to give us a friend in Europe, and he saw Robin as the stumbling block to that.

And Robin had an enemy nearer home, and nearer still my heart. While Parry had been glad to aid his wooing—"Such a lord, madam, such a *gentleman!*"—he had won her heart with that first heart of gold—yet my little Kat now showed her claws indeed, and hardly a day passed but I felt their needling barbs.

"The Lady Catherine was grumbling, madam, yesternight," she would begin while busying about, as if in gossip, "that Your Ladyship does not recognise her state as your successor, that you take no heed of her desire to marry and become a mother, after nature's way."

"Her state, forsooth!" *If they but knew my mind, my other cousin had the far older, better claim—not that wild horses would ever make me acknowledge Mary of Scotland—but Catherine Grey?* "Tell her from me, a fig for her, and for her 'state'!"

And I knew what Kat was up to! She thought to goad me with this talk of Catherine's marriage, Catherine's children, into thinking of my own. But all she did was to make me turn even more against that silly girl!

And why Kat could not love Robin, when every other woman worshipped the ground he trod on, when besides she had loved that false-faced, false-tongued lord, my lord of Seymour, I never knew. But she tried and tried again to turn me against him. "That lord of the North, the one new come to Court, Your Highness knows the man—Spofforth or some such—"

"Yes, I know him."

"Well . . . !" Her eyes were wide with feigned indignation as she oversaw the maid laying before me a dish of fish and figs, my Lenten supper. "They say he keeps his poor wife buried in the country, locked away out of sight, and never meaning to bring her to Court, makes love to another lady—what man would do a thing like that?" Finally it came out. "Oh, do not keep company with the Lord Robert, madam! Think of your reputation!"

And always, everywhere, the watching eyes, eyes all around us, eyes staring, judging, peering, prying, trying to pierce beneath the surface, foul eyes, questioning our every move, probing even to see if I yet retained that triangle of flesh, that sacred membrane, that precious jewel of women throughout the ages, my virgin hymen, or if Robin, along with my good name, had robbed me of that too . . .

Some of it we rode off in frantic flight, charging our horses through bush and briar, over brook and ford and fen and the roughest ground we could find till we nearly broke their necks and our own. Some Allemands from Germany and the great gallopers Robin sent for out of Ireland lived up to their names, and taxing us to the hilt, gave us some hours of joyful oblivion. But heavy and strong though they were, they were nothing so surefooted as our smaller native breeds, and riding them, as we well knew, we were riding for a fall.

One German above all, a monstrous bay the colour of bruised mulberries with a blue-black baleful eye to match, I misliked on sight.

"Beware that stallion, Robin!" I urged him as we mounted up. "He is a rogue, if I know anything."

"Lady!" he cried in mock offence. "Which of your servants has more skill than I with dangerous, high-bred, mettlesome creatures who will not willingly give any man control over them?"

I laughed at his impudence. "Nor no man has a gentler hand on the bit, nor better balance over rough going than your good self! But this ill-tempered nag will throw you sooner than you think!"

And I was right. Within the hour, racing behind him, I saw the huge beast slip a stride, shuffle and drop its shoulder, just as Robin was rising in the stirrups, leaning forward to urge it on. The viciousness of the thing! I saw him fall between the huge flashing front hooves, and be tumbled again like a dog by a bull between the scything iron at the rear. My breathing stopped—all I could think was, *Dear God, no! My love is slain, before he is my love!*

It was half a mile before I could rein back to aid him, my galloper was so strong. As I came up, he lay crumpled, white and silent, a thin line of carmine slicing his temple like lawyer's ink. I wept and prayed a good while before he opened his precious eyes and our people came up to help us. And when the tale got back with us to Court, we found scant sympathy. Even Cecil did not shrink from saying pointedly, "Thanks be to God Lord Robert took the fall and not Your Majesty!"

The next day in his chamber Robin had his man show me his wounds: great swellings on his back, on his side the tenderness of three or four ribs well cracked, and the bruise of a horseshoe on the white skin of his breast, blue as a tattoo. Another inch or two and the great beast would have trodden his throat and broken his neck—but thanks be to God . . .

All that summer, all that autumn, all year long, we were so happy—and yet . . .

And yet Amy did not die!

I cursed myself for even thinking this of another woman, an innocent woman, yet the truth was, I wished her dead!

Or did I? Did I truly? For while she lived, she held all in suspense. And I held myself away from Robin, did not yield him more than my hands, my lips, for the rarest of sweet kisses . . .

Yet how hard it was, God be my judge! Days followed weeks, weeks became months, and his nearness taunted me more and more. *How did I bear it?* you ask.

And how did he?

Partly I was helped because he stood so far off—he always kept the reverence between us. And my good Cecil chaperoned us too. Even with his papers, his committees, even with his dealings with the Scots, his endless efforts to make the treaty that would secure us from the enemy at our gates, still he made it his unspoken business to be always at my elbow. And then, with the men who more and more hung upon Robin as his fortunes grew and he became a great man in the world, with my women and my people of all kinds, my ladies-in-waiting, my maids of honour, my courtiers, counsellors, and ambassadors—not to mention my coiffeuses, my milliners, my dressmakers, my portraitists, my jewellers, my tiremakers, my stockingwomen, herbwomen, shoemakers and ruffmakers—the miracle was that we ever stole a moment alone.

As we did—of course we did! From that first kiss, that first day, he left my soul hungering. As his Queen I could have commanded it. But as his lover I desired him to command it, command me, to take the freedom of my lips—*and if I speak truth, of my body too.*

For now all that my second lord of Seymour ever taught me, every place he ever touched me, awoke and cried for Robin. Robin had only to take my hand and I was alight, he had only to kiss me and I was afire. When he cupped his palms beneath my instep to help me to mount, or swung me from my horse at the end of a ride, his touch made a hot girdle round my waist, and from my soul to my secret centre. I burned with love for him. And inch by inch, the love between us grew till it would not be contained.

Still, we were strange with each other.

"My lord, why do you start when I touch you?"

"Lady, may I speak freely . . . ?"

These and other questions hovered between us like shadows on the sun. But when he showered kisses like butterflies upon my hand, one for each finger, twenty for each joint, then slowly, softly, turned my palm to make love to that too . . .

When I raised my hand to his face and touched his hair, springing like bracken in August, smoothed it back from his ears, stopping to make love to them too . . .

When he blistered the insides of my wrists with kisses of fire and ice, until I did not know if I was hot or cold, awake or asleep, half-dead with love or twice as alive . . .

When I dared brush the cleft of his chin with my kisses, stroke the soft fox-gold of his close-trimmed beard, when I longed for more, and dreamed of more, and then awaked crying for more, I so longed for him, and cried for him, and pined for him . . .

Oh God, I wept in my night prayers, *what will become of us?* For now I loved the one man in the world I could not marry—a married man!

Yet would I marry him even if I could, seeing what marriage was, what marriage did, even to a queen . . . ?

Especially to a queen . . .

And yet—and yet—I could not give him up!

He gave me happiness, joy pure and simple—and I had had so little in my life.

Yet even then the worm at the heart of the bud was gnawing at our happiness . . . and we had not long . . .

Now the word of Amy's malady had got out, and the world and that evil-minded witch his gossiping wife made a meal of tongues of all of us. "Lord Robert has a poison to make away his wife so that he may marry the Queen!" was the least of the rumours raging around. I heard from Throckmorton, always my loyal supporter and now Ambassador in Paris, that the whole of France was revelling in the story of "the Queen of England, her Horse Master and his wife."

I could not bear it. "Robin, you must build up her household," I begged him frantically, "ensure enough good people around her at all times to prove you do not plot against her—to spare us from this wicked calumny!"

"Madam, I have done so!" he protested furiously. "My steward Forester and his family, his wife and sisters, live with her in the Cumnor manor, besides all his men. And with her also I have installed a friend of hers from schooldays, and with them an ancient lady of untarnished reputation, and all their maids, and boys, and women—she lives safely, I do assure you, surrounded by a full and busy household—and lives as well—"

He did not need to finish—*as well as any woman may do in her circumstance . . . a lady in waiting for the rough attentions of the bridegroom known as Death . . .*

Waiting . . .

We were all waiting . . .

Waiting is no good exercise. Nerves become strained, bodies pay the price. I suffered a great megrim late that summer when the pain in my face and eyes blinded me one whole day and left me weak and shaking. Afterwards Robin coaxed me out to try a game of bowls. It was a thin, chill September, not rich and golden as that month at Richmond so often was.

It was my birthday—how could I forget?

Robin had greeted my dawn waking with a consort of flutes and boys from the Chapel Royal piping like an angel choir outside my window:

> *"Dear, if you change, I'll never choose again.*
> *Sweet, if you shrink, I'll never think of love:*
> *Dear, sweet, wise, fair, change, shrink not, nor be weak,*
> *And on my faith, my faith shall never break.*
> *Earth with her flowers shall sooner heaven adorn,*
> *Heaven her bright stars through earth's dim globe shall move,*
> *Earth, heaven, fire, air, the world transformed shall view,*
> *Ere I prove false to faith, or strange to you . . ."*

I called him into my chamber, still in my nightrobe, for I knew the sea-green brocade with its collar of white fox, sent to me from the wild northern wastes by my Swedish suitor King Erik, set off finely the red and gold of my flowing hair. I did not scruple to go loose before my lord, and besides, I wanted some appreciation of the new washes of lemon and camomile Parry was trying, to improve the colour, my hair seemed so dull and thin these days . . .

I was moody, though, and he had to woo me. "I am an old woman now, a hag of *twenty-seven,* and soon I shall be thirty!"

"Yet Your Majesty is but a girl to me! I shall always be the old man, you my junior by so many—"

"Days alone, don't provoke me! For you know you are but two months older than I!"

"But two months? Madam, two lives—for that is how long have I loved you, unrequited . . ."

"Unrequited, say you? What satisfaction do you hope for?"

And so we knocked it to and fro all day, and by degrees he bantered me into good humor. And he showered me with gifts: a double string of pearls as fat as peas, both black and white; an ivory fan quite two feet long in the stem; a silver cabinet with tiny drawers of filigree from Venice; a 'pothecary's cup of holly wood edged in gold, to keep off the pains in my face. And there was more, much more, from all sides: gloves fragrant with frankincense; a riding whip of whitest bone and leather; pins and pens; and rings and things and love and largesse from all my ladies, all my courtiers, all my people of all sorts. As the day wore on so winningly, I began to agree to be wooed back to good cheer.

Late in the afternoon we made our way slowly back from the bowling alley to the Court. A rising mist was seeping off the river, its thin fingers reaching and groping like a lost soul falling, clutching in vain to find a hold.

Suddenly I was cold, violently cold and shaking.

"Here, Majesty! By your leave?"

Robin plucked the thick velvet cloak from his shoulders, placing it tenderly on top of mine. I gave him a wan smile. "I thank you, my lord."

But still the cold would not leave me—my heart was knocking in my frame, shuddering with it, and I knew not why.

Yet as we entered the Great Hall, I saw the cause of my heart's chill and knew the reason. His hat in his hand, his face a mask, Robin's steward Forester from Oxfordshire stood waiting. He fell to his knees in greeting, bowing his head.

"Well, speak, man, speak!" Robin's voice was high and harsh.

The man looked up, his dark regard as closed as a locked book. "My lord, forgive the bearer of bad tidings—may God strengthen you for what I have to say. I grieve to tell you—your wife is no more."

"Hah! My wife?" He had gone very white. "God rest her soul! She died peacefully? Her doctor with her, her priest, her women?"

"Alas, no, sir." His face did not change. "A tragic accident, my lord. The lady Amy, alone in the house, missed her footing on the stairs and fell to her death. Sad to relate, my lord, she broke her neck."

XLIV

I could not look at him.

My birthday . . .

Amy's deathday . . .

And all would say he had commanded it.

Without a word I left him and fell back to my chamber.

All my women were whey-faced with horror, Robin's sister Mary Sidney almost overcome, my cousins Francis Knollys and Hunsdon and all my gentlemen quite dumb with shock—none dared speak. Once within the royal lodgings, I bade them quit me, and shut myself away in my privy quarters. There I fell to my knees and weeping, began to pray: *Salvum me fac, domine . . . Save me, O God, for the deep waters are come in, even to my soul . . .*

I am come into deep waters, even till the floods run over me . . .

I tried to pray for Amy: *Blessed are the dead which die in the Lord, for they rest from their long labours . . .*

But the still small voice of dread and cold reproach would not be silenced.

Who has done this deed?

How has it happened? Who commanded it?

Never say he . . .

Yet if not he, who?

Cui bono, as the Romans said. Who stood to gain?

I dared not think of the answer. Only a phrase came floating back to me, thin and remote as fairy music from a distant hill: *Chi ama, crede . . . Who loves, trusts . . .*

But like all those who miss the elf music, their ears too dull and full of earthly clay, I could not hear this.

And I could not trust.

I had no reason to believe he knew of this. But no one who had lived my life could lightly trust again. And I could not trust now.

———

The slow hours passed, and my people knew better than to disturb me. An owl called grievingly across the dark. Now with the falling night I was cold to my bones, cold to my soul, and I knew nothing now would be the way it was before.

At last a knock, trembling and timorous, and Kate Carey's voice: "Your Majesty—"

"Let be, Carey, away!"

"Madam, here is—"

"Leave me!"

A pause, then another voice, his, yet not his voice: "My lady, I am come to take my leave: I ride for Oxfordshire tonight."

Leave?

He was going? Why was that word like a stake in my heart, when I did not want him here any longer, did not want him to stay?

What did it matter now in any case? "Admit my lord of Dudley."

He walked like a man well thrashed by a hard master. A gaunt shape in the gloaming, stiffly he stalked towards me where I sat candle-less in the window, and fell to one knee.

"Majesty, I beg leave to depart. With this news from Cumnor—"

I could not look full at him. But I forced myself to speak. "What is the news? How did she—"

His eyes flashed bitterly as he shook his head. "The worst way!" he said simply. "So much for my wish to protect her with good people! She was alone, last afternoon—the maids and women gone to the fair, the old gentlewoman her companion dozing in her chamber, the men about their business on the farm, all miles away and out of earshot—"

"All save your steward . . ."

"He had given them leave to go to the fair. The house was empty."

How it came to me then, I never knew. But in that instant I saw it all—the crime, the criminal and even the victim—Amy's small, wasted body, sprawled oddly at the foot of a flight of stairs, her head twisted around, her brown eyes staring at the ceiling.

The steward Forester.

A man to whom one little death was nothing after his time in the ranks, when men died all around him, and not a few before him too, choking their lives out on the end of his sword. A big-handed, strong-shouldered man— how easy for him to deal with one small, sick woman, taken by surprise, alone in an empty house.

A man who had grown impatient for his own advantage and weary of the game of waiting, a man who feared that if his master were forced to wait much longer for his freedom, then the prize he sought that would make Robin great for life—the prize not myself, but no less than England—would be lost to another lord, to the Archduke, to the King of Sweden.

A man clever enough to see the advantage of clearing the way for his master, yet not politic enough to grasp that this deed alone would ensure that his lord and I could never marry—not on this side of the grave . . .

No, we could never marry now, nor even be friends again. Because the taint against Robin was no longer his bad blood, his new blood, his less than royal blood, but the blood of a lost innocent upon his hands, the blood of his murdered wife.

Now for the first time I looked in Robin's eyes, dazed and grey-black with shock, and knew that he saw it too. He flinched at my gaze and said as stiffly as before, "I must to Cumnor—to take charge of matters there."

Suddenly it was plain before me, as a fork of lightning through a night of blackness. "To Cumnor? No! That will compound the scandal, set the tongues wagging harder! All will say that you had the business done while you were safe here with me in Richmond, then you took yourself back to clear up the traces!"

I could hardly see him now in the deep gloaming. He drew in a dry breath. "You think . . . they would say that?"

"Of course! The only hope is to send in men above reproach as commissioners to set in train a full discovery, a coroner's inquest."

"Oh, God forgive me!" Blindly he took my hand. He was on the point of weeping. "Lady, for her, I can hardly speak the depth of my grief—and for myself, pure loathing! But the worst of it is sullying you with this, dragging you through the muckheaps of Europe, the middens of the worst minds of the world!"

In the dim chamber his eyes glimmered with unshed tears. I reached out a hand. He started as ever as my fingers brushed the edge of his jaw, combed the hair tangled at his taut temples.

"Oh, my lady!"

"Oh, my Robin . . ."

I leaned in towards him, my hand on his neck. I could feel the sinews tight as iron beneath my touch, feel his resistance, feel it melting as I touched my forehead hesitantly to his. A great silence fell between us, and now I was weeping too.

At last I took his tortured face between both my hands and tried to smooth his brow with a chain of little kisses, kissing away the fierce furrows of grief, kissing the tears, kissing the warm and silky lids of his closed eyes. And at last I kissed his mouth, but haltingly, as a woman kisses who knows not if she should.

"Lady—oh, lady!"

He was beside me on the window seat, his hand on my shoulder, the other to my cheek. Tenderly he tilted my lips to his and kissed me as we had never kissed before. It was the kiss I had been hungering for, thirsting for all my life, it seemed—his lips sucked forth my soul, time slumbered on its wheel, the very stars stood still.

Our mouths were sweet together, like ripe fruit. Softly his tongue found mine, searching deeper and deeper as I responded. Now my tears were drying in a slow fire, a fire building and building with every touch of his lips, every movement of his hands.

His fingers gripped my shoulders. I felt myself pulsing with his rhythm, a rhythm growing steadier, stronger with each kiss. Now I unfolded to him, opened like a flower, took him and drank him in, with no thought but of his kisses and the next kiss . . . and the next . . .

His arm was about me now, crushing me into him, his hand at my neck, smoothing my cheek, stroking the line of my jaw, and down, and down. Surely and certainly he found the hard line of my bodice, his fingers tracing the jewel-trimmed edge. Beneath the stomacher of whalebone and stiffening, hard as sheet armour, my breasts ached for him, my nipples pricked at his approach, my whole body calling in silent, passionate reproach: *Why so long . . . ? It has been so long . . .*

And so long for him too?

It would not seem so. With the assurance of a man long practised, his strong fingers found the hooks at the side of my gown that held the stiff bodice taut against my breasts. He was laughing now with joy, very lightly in the back of his throat as he bent his head and kissed my cheek, my neck and the top of my breast, where my bodice now was opening at his touch.

I was craving for him, crying for him, my tears springing again as soft and sweet as flowers in the rain. The scent of him was gorgeous to me, marjoram, benjamin . . . Light as an elf-step his long fingers swept the heavy bodice to one side and slipped within.

"Lady! Oh, lady!"

His gasp and mine came together as his hand found my breast, cupping it reverently, brushing the nipple with his marvellous hard palm. Slowly he explored the circle of one areola, then the other, till my breath was coming like a milkmaid's and my breast, my bosom, my whole body, were one with his touch, yielding him mastery. And like a milkmaid I could hear myself crying, "Oh-Robin-yes-sweet-Robin-yess-oh-yes-yesss-yesssss . . ."

"Oh, lady, *no!*"

He pulled away. "What am I doing? God! May God and you, my lady, forgive me for this!"

I struggled to find my voice. "Forgive you, Robin? What is there to forgive?"

He hung his head, shaking it like a man dazed from a blow. "That I could so far forget myself—and *you!"* He scrambled to his feet. "I must go—I must go away—at once!"

"Robin—no! Don't say that—*don't go!"*

Even in my ears, it sounded like the plea of a lost woman, an abandoned soul. I stumbled on. "If anyone forgot themselves, it was not you! It was I—it was both of us—it was—"

He shook his head. "There is only one service I can do you now, Majesty—to leave at once. Then none can say that your Horse Master having disposed of his inconvenient wife, you kept him as your lapdog here at Court!"

I bowed my head, blinded with tears. "Where will you go?"

"To the Manor House at Kew. And wait there."

Until . . . ?

Who could know, who could say, which of us dared even to ask?

Before, he had never had to say so much as a farewell. Always it had been "Until noontide, Majesty" or "I will await you after your audience." But now he broke my heart with just one word: *"Adieu . . ."*

When sorrows come, said one of those rogue scribblers, those playwrights of the public stage, they come not single spies, but in battalions.

With Amy dead and Robin gone from me, as foolish as a milkmaid once again, I thought nothing could befall that could be worse. But the same scribbler, the same pen-and-ink man I could swear, once also demanded, "Who is it that can say 'I am at the worst?'"

For always there is worse.

And it was coming, worse was coming, coming even as I wept and raged and prayed for Robin, for Amy and for me.

Oh, the vanity, the selfishness of grief! I took not the slightest notice when Throckmorton sent from Paris to say that the new King of France, Mary of Scotland's husband, a poor youth her junior in years and size and everything save French self-conceit, was suffering from an ear-ache. All my thought was of affairs at Cumnor and my desire to know the truth there.

"Has the investigation yet begun? Has the Coroner sat? What is the verdict?"

Never had I valued Cecil's supernatural powers of discretion more than now, when with a neutral face and a voice purged of all meaning he replied, "Madam, all is in train: all is proceeding as it should be."

And with the—*death, I almost said, for he was dead to me now*—with the loss of Robin, other affairs came pressing in that I had neglected cruelly till now. And cruelly for me, most pressing, was the still-running sore of my marriage and the succession—for with Robin away, the wolves came ever closer, howled the harder round my door.

Marriage!

I could not think of it. And yet I had to.

For now the Emperor of the Hapsburgs showed a disdainful withdrawal: he began to pull away, for fear that "the Queen of England will marry her Horse Master, who has killed his wife to make room for her!" —as my sweet cousin Mary now sneered all over Europe. So now *we* had to court and flatter *him,* send gifts of perfumed books and jewelled gloves and rarest trinkets to keep the Holy Romans sweet; above all, make overtures to the young Archduke Charles, the only one of the three still willing to marry a woman of my age, a heretic, flyblown in reputation and now in all eyes a murderess as well, by intent if not by deed.

"Take heed, Your Excellency," the wags of his Court were teasing him, as I had to hear, "that you take not a mistress, nor turn your back on the Queen whom you would wive, or one or other of you will not get downstairs alive!"

It pricked, it stung, it stank in my nostrils! But my daily wear now was a crown of thorns, each with its own peculiar power to pierce and wound. Yet other hurts were brewing, blows I never had expected, even at the worst.

"It is said in France that the young King takes the blood of babies for his ear-ache," grinned Norfolk, who loved such gossip, "which is why his face and forehead are covered in crimson weals, all ensanguined, as they are said to be!"

But even as the whole Court revelled in this blood libel, the black-clad messenger was hastening from France with a heart-broken lament:

My lord, my husband and my King is no more. Plunged therefore as I am from the heights of happiness to the most wretched state of women, barren widowhood, I am resolved to withdraw from France to my own kingdom, and crave your leave, sister and sovereign, to pass through your lands that I may get to mine . . .

Mary of Scots

The King was dead. His ear-ache, Mary wrote, flowered into an abscess inside his head that burst apart his brain. And my brain, too, reeled under it.

"Barren widowhood"?

So there was no child of this marriage, as Cecil's spies had promised?

"At least she has not strengthened her claim to your throne, Your Majesty!" blurted bluff old Bedford. He did not need to add: *by putting forth the Prince that you have yet to give us.*

Treasurer Paulet gave a mirthless smile. "Yet she may—she will, she must!—marry again."

One thought was in all minds: *Which of our enemies will she choose as her husband?*

"And now she wants to come to England in all her Papist pride, to fly the flag of Rome in our despite?" groaned my cousin Knollys to the Lord Admiral Clinton.

Another queen in our small island—and a Catholic queen to boot, one who claimed my kingdom, challenged my right to rule?

It was the horror we had not foreseen.

"This is her mother-in-law, that witch of Italy Catherine de' Medici, this is not Mary!" protested Shrewsbury, ever loyal to his Catholic vision of Mary the Innocent. And true it was that Catherine the old Queen Mother, left as Regent for her younger son, was now the sun in splendour and could not help but eclipse Mary the royal relict.

"But think you," argued Bedford with a grin, "if the Scots Queen was ever born to be a dowager? To hide away in black, seeing no man? To carry her mother-in-law's train this week, who only last week was carrying hers? No, no, my lords, she would rather queen it in a kennel, that one, so long as the dogs were hers, then be a widow-queen in paradise!"

But should she pass through England?

I was distracted with the fear, tantalised by the prospect. For I longed to see her! All my life, it seemed, I had heard of her, her beauty, wit, intelligence, her languages, her music, her riding, her dancing, till she seemed the measure of all women, and I was mad with it.

Not jealous, no, no, of course not! Why should I be?

But I would have given a great deal to see her once, to lay eyes upon that famous hobbyhorse . . .

And who knows, had I seen her then, had we met then, might I have steadied her, with my words if not my example? Stopped her in that bolting course of hers, before she unhorsed her next rider, threw him, biting and kicking, and then was herself horsed by the worst of horsemen, the worst ruffians that our world could show, that she could ever find?

"She may pass through England, I would suggest, Your Grace, if she will ratify the Treaty of Edinburgh."

"The Treaty of—?"

Oh yes, the Treaty of Edinburgh. Cecil was justly proud of his handiwork there, to make all smooth between us and the Scots. Through hours of patient labour, paperwork, candle work, lawyers' work, he had got the French to agree to leave Scotland and to abandon Mary's claims to the English throne.

"If the Queen of Scots will agree to it, lady, then let her come here, and welcome!" Cecil said.

Let her come here . . .

Yet was there also a trick that I could spy and Cecil did not? "If I receive her here, greet her and welcome her, then I must do it with the finest welcome England can afford—"

"No less would be seemly, madam, for one who has been Queen twice over, of our two neighbouring countries—"

Yet who also would be Queen of this one too! Who was Queen already, in the eyes of all good Catholics, all those who hid their Papistry under the cloak of good observance, worshipping regularly with their hands behind their backs, their fingers crossed to absolve themselves from sin, and their eyes, toes, souls, I'd swear, crossed too, crossed, crooked and black as hell. Were Mary to come here—were she to be seen as my guest, welcome and acknowledged—would not that seem a clear establishment of her rights, or worse—much worse—an open invitation to all Catholics to rise up and place her on my throne?

"She may not pass!" I stormed at the Scots envoy. And though many demurred, with long faces and black looks—and none longer and blacker than my little Catholic crew, Norfolk and Arundel, Shrewsbury and Derby—no one dared argue when I shouted out my will in the full Parliament: *"La Reyne ne veult!* The Queen will not permit it!"

And Mary was no fool: she would not ratify Cecil's precious treaty, not even though the ambassadors had agreed to it and the French had been whipped from Scotland! Not for anything would she agree to give up her claim. "For you see, I *am* the next in line!" she insisted sweetly to Throckmorton in Paris, protesting, too, that she and I should meet and be great friends, "two queens in one island, two cousins of one blood and each other's nearest kin, one language and one heart."

One heart?

My heart was away.

"Is the word come from Oxford yet? Is the inquest done?"

"Not as yet, my lady."

I would not move from Richmond: all my other palaces were too far from Kew. Now the days were deadly drear and endless without him. I sent, he wrote, our messengers passed to and fro, and yet I did not dare to send as often as I wished, for I could not countenance him again until his good name—and mine!—had been restored.

As I longed for it to be—but even for him I could not openly tamper with justice. How to endure, though, its snail-like process. "Is nothing heard from Cumnor? Have the commissioners concluded their investigation?" *And who can tell me true what happened to Amy?*

At last he came, reeking of the road and his hasty journey, an apple-cheeked alderman of Oxford, with the verdict of the coroner and the commission. He told the story we already knew: a sunny day, the fair come to town, the women at play, the men in the fields, a lost figure tumbling unseen down the stairs. "Death by accident."

I was right, then: no witnesses; the man Forester acted alone, and knew what he was about. He must have been an old hand at this stair work and neck work, this one-way-to-heaven work—where I had no doubt Amy was now, and where he would never be.

"The search was thorough?"

The alderman bobbed importantly. "Your Majesty, all witnesses were questioned, no stone unturned, all found above board!"

So my lord's name was clear—and mine—as far as this could clear it . . .

I gave him my hand. His cheeks burned even redder at this signal honour. "You are most welcome, sir, and even more welcome for the news you bring." I turned to my Chamberlain. "See this good man well victualled for his return to Oxford."

" 'Tis done, Your Majesty."

I sat on the dais, lost in thought. Around me in the Presence my courtiers buzzed and flapped like gaily coloured insects, their thousand eyes on me, their minds awhirl.

So.

My lord found blameless.

Would they believe it?

Did I?

I had to!

Any man was innocent until proven guilty! There was no proof against him, no shred of evidence found from a true investigation. How could I have doubted him! He had been proved free and clear!

And must be seen so. My heart surged with love reborn. I would send for him, command his return, and when he came—

When he came! Oh, God, I was giddy at the thought, my heart leaped up my throat—when he came I would show the world faith in his innocence!

The next day I sent for Garter King of Arms. His answers left me triumphing: I could do this—I, Elizabeth! I could, and would!

"Yes, Your Grace has the power," Garter agreed.

But . . . ?

For sure I heard a "but" there! Yet it seemed not, for now he was reminiscing of "Good King Hal." "Your father made up many men, my lady—one above all."

"The Lord Protector, Earl of Somerset, the uncle of my brother?"

"He was much honoured by your father, true," Garter nodded. "Made Earl of Hertford, the title that still lives on in his son, and Duke of Somerset, and more besides. But you father's greatest creation was also his first—"

"His first?"

"His first minister, the Cardinal Wolsey. Yes, I see Your Majesty knows of the man—the greatest man of the time, his own progress from palace to palace in scarlet and gold as royal as the King's, so his enemies said." He cocked an eye at me for my response. "Your father made him—let me see"—he paused, then began to recite, ticking off on his meticulous old fingers—"the Dean of York, Precentor of St. Paul's, Bishop of Lincoln, Bishop of Bath and Wells, of Durham and Westminster, of St. Alban's and Worcester."

I gasped. "And was this all?" I begged ironically.

"Oh no, Majesty," Garter assured me earnestly. "Afterwards he became Archbishop of York, Cardinal of Rome and not least the Pope's Legate in all England, the greatest and the richest Prince in Christendom!"

"A fair haul!" I murmured. Why were we talking of this? "Truly my father was generous to his servants!"

"Royally generous—like Your Majesty!" He bowed, and I dismissed him, with no further thought.

Yet that night, why I know not, the red Cardinal returned to haunt me. It was a white night just like any other—Parry and Kat dismissed, the Lady Jane Seymour and my cousin Knolly's daughter little Lettice asleep on the truckle at the foot of my bed of state. A mere wafer of a thin late autumn moon rode in a sky as black and blank as the waters of hell, and I was in the window seat again, my head on my arm, my eyes fixed on the moon now racked with sulky clouds, pining for him, dreaming of him, planning for him, for the morrow when he would return and I would overwhelm him with the proof of my love, the new honour I planned . . .

And suddenly, unbidden, there the other was, so vivid in my mind I could almost see him in the room.

Wolsey!

The man had started life as a pigman's son of Ipswich! From a mere royal almoner, a poor beadsman paid to rattle through his rosary and mumble a few prayers for the royal dead, my father had made him with his own hand, made him the greatest man in the land.

Why had he done so?

Because he trusted him, needed him, loved him—as I did Robin . . .

Was I making Robin another Wolsey?

Not so, not so! Robin was no Wolsey! I would have no butcher's brawn to serve me! The men I would call mine were men of blood, albeit tainted as Robin's was.

And a ruler showed his own greatness by making others great—for princely generosity befitted a great prince . . .

My father's generosity? sneered my midnight demons. *Well might a man be generous to those who take on his burdens and so set him free!* I stared into the blackness and saw truth. My actions now would seem to reward and praise Robin for taking my burden by taking Amy's life, so freeing me—and him.

And none who rose so high fell so hard as Wolsey did, even though he threw as sops into my father's greedy jaws the peerless palaces he had created at Whitehall and Hampton Court. But even these were not enough to stay that great maw, which at last pulled him down and ate him up alive and screaming . . .

But that does not, observed my demons, almost conversationally now, for they could see that they had won their battle, *absolve a monarch, then, from the bloody business of tearing a man down, for though Henry ("Good King Hal," "Bluff King Harry," &c., &c., &c.) always loved blood sports and never better than when the blood was human, Your Grace's female stomach is nothing so strong—you will not relish signing the warrant to destroy your own creature the Earl of Leicester . . .*

"Majesty!"

The next morning Garter was before me, presenting the patent I had commanded. The black italics danced before my brain: "Patent for the creation of Lord Robert Dudley to be Earl of Leicester and Ashby-de-la-Zouche, Melton Mowbray and Walton-on-the-Wolds . . ."

Before me on the table a silver knife flashed in my eyes. And my hand caught it up and slashed the parchment, ribbons, seals, bindings and all, into a hundred thousand shreds.

XLV

Si en quelque séjour, soit en bois ou en prée,
Soit pour l'aube du jour, ou soit sur la vesprée,
Sans cesse mon coeur sent
Le regret d'un absent . . .

Wherever I am, in wood or field,
By dawn or evening light,
Without cease my heart feels
The pain of one who is not here . . .

He returned the next day, stalking towards me across the Presence as stiffly as he strode away on that last night, and I could see as soon as I laid eyes upon him that he knew of his lost earldom and the slashing of the patent. Now the poignant poem Mary had written for her lost lord and husband spoke to my heart even more feelingly, for my lord was here and yet not here for me, never to be mine again.

Now I knew I had been right to resist the urge to cover the blot on his escutcheon with new honours, right to greet him here in the full Court, before all eyes. For all eyes now must see all that he did, all that I did, and know that there was nothing between us—and that if anyone had planned Amy's death to clear the way for us, then rest her soul, poor soul, she died in vain.

For there was nothing now, I was sure of that.

Nothing left now. The sudden surge of love I felt when I knew there was no evidence against him had fled away. For few believed him innocent: the sneers and laughter of all Europe were now ringing round my ears. I could hardly endure it—and each day felt my love for him burned out by these searing flames of scandal and the sharp loss of my respect and reputation, just like my love for my second lord, my lord of Seymour.

Nothing . . .

"Your Majesty!"

He knelt before me at the dais clad in black from head to foot, everything he had endured etched on his features. He pressed the back of my hand to his lips, raised his eyes to mine, and I felt . . .

. . . *nothing* . . .

Winter came down—a mild fat December, as countryfolk called it, the air so warm it felt like goose grease on the skin—and a rash of unseasonable plagues fattened the churchyards. The year turned wretchedly, for now another ghost beside Amy's haunted my nights and filled my day's affairs, preoccupied my lords and led to angry, fearful words as we talked it to and fro.

For "What news from Scotland?" was the demand in every mouth. What we meant was "What news of the Queen?"

"For sure Her Majesty will get a cold welcome when she comes," Cecil said hopefully, "herself a stranger there since five years old, speaking no English and not a word of Scots, the Scots lords in the saddle, and the Church of Rome overthrown."

But I had heard too much of her winning ways to feel other than sick at heart. I knew besides that God's battle there was far from won. "And whatever befalls is no good news for England!" I argued furiously. "If she returns in peace, and her people accept her and her Romish rituals, then we have an outpost of the Vatican on our northern borders! But if she inflames the Scots to rise against her French ways and her Papistry, then we have an island rebellion on our hands, and war at our own gates!"

From France came the word that as soon as the great storms of winter had abated, she had taken ship, weeping and crying out, *"Adieu, ma France! Ma chère France! Je pense je vous ne revoir jamais!"*

In all my life, Mary was the greatest thorn in my side. But even I could not have wished for her the welcome she received into her kingdom.

"To be sure, Scotland is the arse of the world!" exploded old Lord Parr, the Marquis of Northampton, the late Dame Katherine's brother, when he heard.

As she came into Edinburgh, the vicious ranting Knox was preaching against her in the streets, gloating over the double tragedy of her recent loss, the deaths of her husband and her husband's father, crying out that "God has raised his hand to smite with blood and death the stinking progeny she mated with, one through the eye, the other through the ear!"

Once in her palace of Holyrood, she called for music: the coughing woodwind, squawking fiddles and screeching rebecks made her French attendants burst out laughing in dismay.

She tried to form a Council of Lords. I had thought myself hard beset with half-a-dozen crypto-Catholics out of my twenty, yet of her twelve, all twelve were solid Protestants, against her to a man. And on her first night in her own land, when she held a private Mass to give God thanks for her safe delivery from her watery pilgrimage of so many hundred miles, the filthy rabble rioted in the streets.

Yet the heart of the woman! Within days of her landing in Scotland, Cecil's "eyes" informed us—some of them saw her despatches even as she, or they, inscribed them—she was wooing the world in search of a new husband.

"She solicits—*who?*" I gasped, abandoning my grammar in the horror, the sheer absurdity of Cecil's revelation. "*Don Carlos?* What, the Infante, nay, the boy monster of Spain, Philip's heir?"

And my leavings, I could reflect with some savage satisfaction, for he was my suitor back in my sister Mary's reign. Now my cold porridge was a child no longer, but a youth deformed in mind and body, each worse than the other.

Did Mary know? Or care?

And Philip?

He had taken a French wife. Would he now take Scotland as his daughter-in-law's jointure and encircle us once again, as France had tried to do?

How these fears sickened me! And how alone I was, not turning to Robin, not to anyone . . .

And Mary was not wooing the world alone, but she must also make love to me. So who comes to my Court at Whitehall, sitting on a sober bay all the way down the Great North Road from Scotland till he knocked on my door, but her most special envoy.

"What's your business, sir?"

He had a silver tongue, Maitland of Lethington, and well he needed it. "My lady greets you as *la plus belle reine d'Angleterre*"—*while she is doubtless* la plus belle *of the rest of the world!* I noted furiously—"and begs that you will consider making a meeting with her—if not in London or Edinburgh, midway between your kingdoms."

York!

Meet her in York?

Why not?

That would avoid the danger of countenancing her here in London— enable me to tell her to her face that I would never name her as my successor for fear of making her my winding-sheet!—and feed my curiosity to see this girl Queen, this pretty widow of nineteen that all now prattled of.

And I could do what I had to do well in advance.

"Where is the Lady Catherine Grey my cousin? I will hunt today—command her with me—"

It was a fine midsummer, ripe for hunting. But my quarry now was not the hind or boar.

If I could build up Catherine, favour her, even let her marry or at least seem to consider it, this would show Mary and the world that when it came to successors, we had successors homegrown here in England, heirs of Tudor blood whom I could make up with my own hand if I chose, to put her witchy dew-dropped Stuart nose out of the succession!

"My lady Catherine is indisposed this morning, Your Grace," Jane Seymour reported.

"Sick? Of what?"

"Of eating apricots yesterday. She had a longing for them—"

"At this time of the year? They would not be ripe!"

"Just so, madam, she pukes her heart out—but swears tomorrow she will wait on you . . ."

"Hmmmmm . . ."

Who should Catherine marry? There were young lords about the Court, like Rutland and Devereux and the dull Earl of Hertford. But if I married her off, and if she then gave birth to the elusive son, the phantom Prince of the Tudors . . .

My brother Edward would have been twenty-five this October—two generations, then, since a Tudor prince was born . . .

And born to Catherine?

Perish the thought!

It was a strange summer, with marriage in the air. My faithful Viking, now more mad with love for all my shilly-shallying, sent his Chancellor from Sweden to press his suit. Here was a man to catch the eye of a blind woman, though Catherine, pale and sulking beside the throne, did not seem to think so. "Tell me, my lord," I quizzed him as he kissed hands, "are all the men of your country as long in the thigh as you, as fair, as red-gold?"

His bow swept the floor, but his eyes, the bright blue of turquoises, never left mine. "Madam, my sovereign is the handsomest man in Europe—and yours for the taking!"

I looked across at Robin. He gave no sign of having heard a word.

And with the lofty Landgrave came a gift of eighteen great piebald gallopers, each one matched to the others, all particoloured in great splashes of white and dun, their feet all fringed in silky feathers of ivory hair combed like a maiden's at her first Communion. I loved King Erik's horses—even more I loved the two shiploads of treasure that came with them, great chests of gold, diamonds like quails' eggs, an emerald like a carbuncle and fistfuls of pearls. How I gloated over them in my chamber—and they went some way to filling the hole at my heart . . .

And others, too, were wending altar-wards. My great-uncle Howard married his daughter Lady Douglas to the Earl of Sheffield. He brought his son to Court for the first time too, young Charles, shy but attentive and clever too, if I knew anything. He would bear watching. For the occasion my stockingwoman produced a miracle, hose of the finest silk that had ever been seen. And though these were unseen, they were another passing comfort.

And I had need of comfort.

Seventeen summers, young Douglas was, and even then not young for a bride, when maids of twelve went to the altar—and I a good decade older than Douglas—more, thirty now looming!—and feeling, too, a tooth on the side of my face, a pain to add to my pain . . .

At the wedding Catherine dutifully attended at my side, but what was wrong with her, I hardly knew. "Now, girl," I rallied, for I wanted to put some good red Tudor blood into those pasty cheeks, "what say we find a husband for you next?"

She tried to force her mouth into a smile. "I have no wish to marry," she said thinly. "I am happy as I am—as a maid in Your Highness's service."

What had got into her? And what had become of her former claims and boasts?

"Oh, pish!" I snapped at her. "Never say so! I will look out a husband for you, never fear! There, take some venison pie and a little of this good wine, put heart into your stomach!"

But still her frightened greensick eyes followed me out of church.

I would not think of Catherine. It could be no more than the high season working in her maid's blood—and the time of the year brought the blood rising in more veins than hers.

Although I had looked hard the other way, I knew that eyes at Court were looking at Robin. He was a widower now, handsome and rich. Would he remarry? Or would he take a mistress?

Why did I watch him?

What did I care?

He was always there, always attending, in the Presence, in my antechamber. He would speak to all, look pleasant, now and then even jest. But he was not the Robin I had known. When I hunted he would hunt in my train, but always in the rear. If I spoke he would leap to respond; if I danced he would dance on command . . .

But he no longer sought me.

And as I fretted with it, fought with it, in this sad Court another sadness struck when my poor Jane Seymour died.

Like Amy, it was another lost young life—she died in a day, of the small pocks. I wept for her, and on my orders two hundred mourners all in deepest black attended her to her last rites in Westminster, and all my other maids of honour, all my gentlemen and ladies, followed her to her grave.

I could not say if my own life then was life in death, or death in life. But I know I did not live. The summer turned on its wheel; we fled to Greenwich to escape the heat, but there was no relief. Day by day the thunder built in the sky like a boil gathering to a head.

Then came a day when darkness fell at noon. By midday heavy clouds had cast a pall of ink across the sky. From our refuge and vantage point the City lay below, all drowned in blackness. Only at evening did the longed-for storm split the great bowl of heaven with furious lightning flickering like witches' tongues.

"Madam, beseech you, come!"

Eagerly Carey, Anne Russell and Mary Sidney conducted me up Greenwich's highest tower.

"See, Highness, see, see you the fireworks?"

As the heavens opened, all the world could see St. Paul's punished by God in cracking, bursting thunderbolts. From their deepest vaults the heavens rained balls of fire upon all London, fire-balls falling on tree-tops, down chimneys, all as clear as earth's last day in the wicked, flickering light, in the livid fury of the skies.

"God is angry!" moaned Catherine beside me on the battlements, clinging to Lettice Knollys, green to the gills. "He sees our sins! He will repay!" She got scant sympathy from Lettice, who was growing into a bold, pert creature—she felt no fear, that one!

St. Paul's was burning now, the spire in flames. The very bells were melting, so fierce was the heat, dropping tonsures of molten bronze on the heads of those trying in vain to save them.

"God save us all!" mouthed Catherine, half-dead with fear.

"He will!" laughed Lettice, tossing her red curls. How could she be so sure?

It was a night of dread. I did not sleep, but as the sky lightened towards dawn, I fell into a doze. Yet more dread was the knock on my chamber door the next morning, just at dawn. None ever called so early. Why had the guard not barred the intruder's way? Scarcely awake, I could hear Kat's frightened voice. "Who is it? Who is there?"

"Pray tell your lady I must speak with her."

The voice of—a voice I knew better than my own.

"My sea-green chamber gown, Kat! And then admit my lord."

God, how I loved him! My eyes stung at the sight. His face so pale, so lovely, his look fixed on mine . . . Welcome back, my lord—I am a woman who has been lost to herself, since losing you. Yet what of all I had suffered because of you?

Yes, what of it?

My voice was very still. "Lord Robert?"

He paced forward. The carelessness of his dress, the doublet hastily thrown on, showed no sign of the attentions of his man. He had not shaved, nor by the heaviness of his eyes, slept all night. "Lady, I can put no pretty gloss on what I have to say."

My stomach turned. Oh God, what could it be?

"Last night, your guards will tell you a maid came to my chamber."

He had come to confess, then, before the swift tongue of rumour reached me, destroying him.

His shirt was undone at the neck. I could see the soft hollow at the base of his throat . . .

I could scarce speak for pain. "A maid?"

He hesitated. "Not a serving-maid, madam, but—a lady of quality."

"One of mine?"

He nodded.

"One of my maids of honour?"

He dropped his head. "Even so."

"And you were alone with her in your chamber—"

He flushed. "To say truth, above an hour together."

Now I lost all my pretended control. *"Above an hour? A good time, my lord, for—"*

He cut in low and calm. "Not too long, lady, for what she had to tell me, and to implore me to reveal it to you. The maid—or former maid, as I must say—is Your Majesty's cousin and nearest of kin, the Lady Catherine. And she is with child."

XLVI

Catherine with child.

I looked into his eyes. And I saw truth there, the honesty to me that he always had.

I was beyond speech. He knelt before me, sharing that endless moment, his breath suspended too. At last I found my voice. "Who is the father?"

"She says—the Earl of Hertford."

Hertford! *That numbskull youth she had been clogging when I thought her too familiar with my lord! Yet fool or no, one who through his father, the late Lord Protector, was cousin to my brother, cousin to a king! All would say therefore that he was kin to royalty, which, taken with Catherine's claim, would put their child strongly in line for the throne—even more if it should prove to be a boy . . .*

Still, as a bastard it could have no place in the succession.

Yet some said all my life I was a bastard—and my Catholic foes, if they could not have Mary on the throne, would certainly prefer a bastard child with a vain and witless puppet of a mother to me.

I found my fury. "Guard!"

Now my door guards and their captain, with two or three of my Gentlemen Pensioners, were tumbling into the room.

"Arrest the Lady Catherine, have her conveyed at once to the Tower. And the Earl of Hertford! But keep them apart, d'you hear me, under close arrest. *They may not be allowed to speak to each other, write or be together.*"

Eyes bulging with shock, tongues tied in astonishment, they scattered to do my will. "And one more thing: guard my door close! If the lady sends to me, I will not admit letter or messenger—no, not so much as one word or syllable from her!"

They clattered off. Robin looked up, a shadow in his eyes. "You will not hear your cousin, my lady?"

My fury burst its bounds. "Why, what can she say in her own defence? She knows as well as I do that as a Tudor she is forbidden by my father's will and Parliament to marry without the express permission of the monarch, the Privy Council and both Houses! What she has done is treason! If my father were alive, even my sister, she would soon follow where her sister trod—and leave her head behind!"

His voice was low. "Your Majesty would not have her put to death—?"

"Do not ask!" I laughed hysterically. "I cannot say now what I may have to do!"

And not least for her attentions to you, my lord . . .

I rose to my feet, roaming the chamber wildly as I clutched the chamber gown around my cold body, trying to hide myself inside its voluminous folds, burying my face in the rich fur at the neck. I burned with rage and, more, a kind of shame. *How had she come to this?*

"You say she came to you, and asked you—"

He did not flinch. "She came to me in my chamber last night just after I retired. First she tried to . . . to win my goodwill—"

By offering him that wretched spindly, stunted body of hers, more like a doll's than a woman's—even down to her bad legs!—and a body already gone beyond her pleasure, her own possession, being made God's vessel for another life . . .

"Which you so nobly disdained!" I flashed at him.

He did not rise to the bait. "Madam, I did," he replied quietly. "You may interrogate my man and his boy, who were within earshot, but under the worst of tortures, they could tell you no other." He gave a tired smile. "This was no tribute to my charms, lady. She was beside herself, she knew not what she did."

I shrugged it off furiously. "And then—"

"And then she besought my help in her extremity. She is now some six months gone with child and knows she may not conceal it longer. She saw the hand of God in last night's tempest, accusing her of her sins—"

"Vain booby that she is! Is she the only sinner in the world? Why should God speak to her? And more, my lord." I turned upon him. "Tell me one thing: *why did she come to you?*"

Why not another woman, why not Kat, the Mistress of the Maids, or another of the older ladies at Court, if she had to confess? Why Robin? Had there been a tenderness between them at that earlier time, when I had suspected her with him? Was it for that she had sought his help now?

He read my thought. A bleak smile lit his lips. "Because she said that of all the souls at Court, I had the best chance of breaking this to you, my lady—that I best knew you—and—" he broke off.

"Tell me!"

"And best loved you—and in that lay her only hope."

I turned away, my eyes blinded with tears. Best knew me—*and best loved me*—Catherine said so?

It was true.

As I loved—and trusted—him.

Beyond the casement the day was lifting in pale wraiths of mist like grief departing. My heart was knocking in my bosom, all the words in my mind seeming too heavy for my mouth. My back still turned to him, I spoke huskily. "Well, you have done a good office today, sir—"

For me, and for yourself, oh, my sweet lord!

"—for my rash cousin and her ill-expected bastard."

Behind me I could hear him catch his breath. "Her *bastard,* madam? Did I not tell you? Lady Catherine is married!"

Who is it that can say I am at the worst?

Mary scouring Europe for a good Catholic husband, Catherine well married and about to cast a good Protestant heir.

Domine, quid multiplicati . . . *Lord, how they are increased that trouble me, many are they that rise against me on all sides.*

But Cecil and the Lord Keeper Bacon, hastily sent for, confirmed that

I could do no more. "As the law goes," opined Bacon, eyeing the cheese and cold cuts lying with the pitchers of milk and ale untouched on a side table, "Your Majesty is best advised to keep the pair of them fast in the Tower, and wait."

Wait for the Prince—or wait to see if all she carried was yet another unwanted Tudor girl?

"And in the meantime," said Cecil, his gaze fixed artlessly on the mouldings of the ceiling, "we may take occasion to establish the circumstances of the lady's marriage."

I knew that tone of voice. I looked at him sharply. Was my "Spirit," as I still called him to myself, stirring below the surface? But his long pale face was as innocent as a schoolboy's with a satchel full of apples. I stared at him and nodded. "Very well, sirs, let us look further—and then wait and see."

The one crumb of comfort to be found in Catherine's folly was the thought that it would rattle Mary's dovecote! Now she would feel that the crown she saw descending on her brows was slipping sideways to a good English, trueborn Protestant heir! And as our envoys went to and fro to make our great rendezvous at York, I took what cold satisfaction I could from that.

But Mary had other schemes in hand, other fish in play, and in her former kingdom the turn of events was bad enough to keep us all at our midnight candles. In France, Mary's former mother-in-law the Regent Catherine de' Medici was struggling to wield the power of a king with nothing but the strength and cunning of a woman, and against mighty forces too. The tempests that had split our England under my father had now come to France. That Most Holy Catholic country had for long been blasted by the winds of Protestantism from both England and Geneva; now they blew hard enough to tear down the flimsy veil of tolerance in France and show what lay beneath.

One of Throckmorton's most trusted men, Walsingham, a young scholar fresh out of Cambridge, now stood before me dropping with exhaustion, twenty over-ridden horses between him and Paris. His dark eyes were burning in his face. "The perfidious Catholics are in arms, twelve hundred slaughtered Huguenots lie dead in the streets, and France is poised upon the brink of civil war."

I looked at Cecil, and the same thought came to both of us: *Time to recover Calais? To make war on France while she was racked with war? To attack a weakened beast already prostrate with internecine struggles—?*

To recover Calais! Oh, what a dear hope and prospect! Our candles burned to their sockets that night.

"That would be the best defence of all against the King of Spain," mused Cecil, "who otherwise would have us caught between France and Scotland: the Queen Regent of France being his mother-in-law, and if this match with Don Carlos goes ahead, the Queen of Scots his daughter-in-law: a fearsome union of Catholic powers—not forgetting, madam, Ireland, our western flank—"

"Ireland!"

Ireland.

What a bloody graveyard of hope and reputation! Why, my last lord, my Essex, and his father—but peace, no more of Ireland: we shall hear those tragic bagpipes in due course . . .

Only myself and Cecil knew of it. As secretly as he had dealt with the Scots lords to support them against their Catholic Queen and the forces of France, my grey eminence went to work again. We made a deal with the Huguenot lords of France to support their cause, sent money—oh, God, money! Money! More sleepless nights over that . . .

Never enough!

Never enough men and money!

The eternal refrain! But we found it—I made a sale of crown lands, a pretty monastery at Beacon's Bottom and an estate at Strumpshaw Fen, though to part with both was like drawing teeth—then sat back to wait.

Waiting . . .

It seemed to me that Robin and I were both waiting as the days wore on, though for what I could not say. When I rode out, he still rode behind me, but closer now. When I received in the Presence, he was always at hand, and his eyes never left me. And when the messenger came from the Tower, when the Lord Lieutenant himself, stiff with the weight of the news he had to impart, stood there before me, it was to Robin that I found myself turning, heard myself speaking, even before I knew what it was that I was going to say.

"My lord? No, no, Sir Edward, pray attend a moment—are you there, my lord?"

Catherine's child. He brought word my pestilential cousin had been delivered. Of a girl, pray God, a girl!

The Presence Chamber at Greenwich was low and airy, cooled by soft breezes off the river, newly sweetened, and fragrant with fresh green rushes and rosemary underfoot: we were not in the great glass-dazzled atrium of Hampton Court nor the solid walls of Whitehall. Why, then, did I feel breathless and fevered now? "Parry, please—my fan. Let us withdraw. This way, Sir Edward—and my lord—Lord Robert—attend us too?"

Trembling, I paced into the withdrawing room, Sir Edward at my heels, Robin in the rear.

A boy, or—?

What he had to say would soon be all around the Court, was known already, I dared swear, all over Greenwich in the courtyards and kitchens, where Sir Edward's servants, his groom and his yeomen of the guard would be busy scandalising our servants with the indiscretions of their betters. But I still had to hear. Composing myself, I took a seat, Robin moving silently to my right hand, as Sir Edward began to speak.

"The Lady Catherine, Your Grace's cousin, was this morning brought to bed. Her pains came on her early last night, and her labour—"

"God, man, were you the midwife? Spare us all this!" Robin broke in angrily. "Give Her Majesty the news she wants to hear."

The Lord Lieutenant stiffened, then at another glare from Robin, thought better of it. "The child was a boy."

A boy.

"And lives?" *Still he was speaking for me, speaking as me.*

The man bowed. "Lives and thrives—as bonny a bairn—"

"Enough, sir! Her Majesty thanks you. See that mother and child are cared for according to their rank; you shall have further orders soon."

As bonny a bairn . . .

"Very good, my lord." He bowed, hesitated and then began uneasily, his eyes on Robin but with a constant flickering towards me. "My lord, the lady's husband, the young Earl of Hertford, troubles me night and day for access to his wife. He tells me those whom God hath joined together, no man should put asunder. A young couple, sir, and much in love. And now the child is born, so fine and fair a mannikin—"

"Away, man! Her Majesty will take heed of this in her own good time. In the meantime you had your orders—it is her will that they be kept apart!"

"As you say, my lord. Your servant, Your Majesty." It was not what he wished to hear, from his frosty bow and back as he departed. But it was what I wished Robin to say.

Outside were all the Court, surely now a-slaver over this prime gobbet of raw news. Within, staring like statues, were Kat and Parry, Mary Sidney and Kate Carey, Kat's man Ashley, Knollys and Hunsdon and my Gentlemen Pensioners . . .

The dark panelled walls seemed to be coming towards me, and I could not escape their eyes, their eyes all staring at me . . .

Robin bowed, leaned forward and took my hand. "Majesty, will it please you to take the air? Please you to walk?"

Beside the river the air was cooler and the waters flowing sweet and slow. Great sweeps of bullrushes and spiky teazels clothed the banks, and careless of our presence the water birds, all fledged now in late summer, noisily plied to and fro. In the trees a small choir of willow warblers fluted gently down their scales. We came to rest on the river's edge, amid a clump of weeping willows, Robin waving our people off. He stood away, not speaking, but his eyes in waiting, ready for what I had to say.

"We must send men to France, not just money, did you know that?" I babbled. "The Huguenots have to defend Dieppe and Rouen. They promise us Le Havre till we can secure Calais . . . a hundred and forty thousand crowns, and then another three hundred thousand, all in gold, they want; ten thousand men they ask for—we might raise six if I sell more crown lands . . . We must set the fleet in readiness for their transport . . . And, of course, if we do this, then this is open war and I may not leave London to visit with my cousin Mary of Scots—so the York conference is lost—"

The voice of the Lord Lieutenant cut across the disordered ramblings inside my head . . . *A young couple, sir, and much in love* . . .

My chatter petered away.

So fair a bairn . . .

My tears began to flow in time with the river, and like the river, I could not stop. Still he did not speak, but his eyes grew darker every minute. Across the trees the sun stood high in the sky, and our shadows curled at our feet. I wept a good while before he broke the silence. "Madam—lady —tell me what grieves you, that I may try to put it right."

"Oh, Robin—" *I have been so lonely—all my life. Mary has had a husband and will have another, Catherine has a husband and a baby, and I have nothing—*

"Majesty, you have my life, my service, to command."

What, had he read my mind again, as he did before?

"More, madam—" he broke off, flushed beneath his gypsy-brown sunburn, then lifted his head. "I dare offer you the truth of my heart, make of it what you will. You have more than my life, my soul in your hand— you have my eternal love."

"Oh, Robin," I gasped like a baby through my tears. And folding into him, weakly giving at hips, ankles and knees, I swooned away.

XLVII

Was I asleep? Dreaming of this?

> *. . . Then think that we*
> *Are but turned aside to sleep:*
> *For they that one another keep*
> *Alive, ne'er parted be . . .*

Seconds later I was myself again. "Sidney, away, leave off my laces, they are not too tight. It was only the heat, nothing but the heat—"

The heat of my passion—of my joy—he loves me! How that song of joy went dancing through my head . . .

"Your Majesty is very hot to the touch, your brow is burning . . ."

Mary Sidney's sweet pale face hovered in my vision like a harvest moon. So like Robin—*was it Robin?* I could smell the damp smell of earth. I was lying on the ground. *Where was my lord?*

"A litter has been sent for. Your Majesty will be back in your chamber in no time at all."

Painfully I moved my eyes. There he was, kneeling beside me, his face a mask of angry concern. "Villain that I am, to lead Your Grace such a goose chase in the heat of the day!"

"No, Robin, no!" I found a surge of strength. "I am well enough, see you!" I struggled to sit up, and with his ready aid and Sidney's, found my feet.

Yet still I was glad of Robin's arm as we paced slowly back to Court— and glad of his hand fervently pressing mine—and gladder than I could say of what had passed between us—

For now I clearly saw my love for him was not dead, had never died, but had simply passed over the dark side of the moon, thrown into eclipse by the evil planets that had come between us. Now we were once more restored to our proper sphere; our love could shine again, and grow, and we could recover all we had lost, all we had gone without during this time. Now I could show him how I valued him—his truth to me over Catherine, his love that had waited patiently till now—

Yet why could I not feel it as I should? And why was my head burning every day—day after day no relief from this late-summer heat?

"Is Your Majesty well?"

Mary Sidney's anxious concern showed her attentive nature, but unaccountably provoked my irritation. "What else, Sidney, I am never ill! These dog days have tried me, that's all. And today is very warm for so early in October—very warm . . . Robin, come!"

A brisk walk back would soon set me right. Off we struck into the autumnal park glowing in gold and bronze, Robin's presence at my side all my fevered heart could desire, but still I could not shake off this strange lethargy, this unwanted heat. And the sun seemed to leave the meridian earlier than I thought, and soon I passed from heat to a great coldness. I began to shiver. I could see Robin's eyes on me now in puzzled speculation. "Faster!" I commanded. "Faster! I will soon shake off this cold!"

And by the time we had returned to my apartments, I had built up a very satisfactory heat. "There, you see!" I laughed at Robin for his long face. "I will now take a bath before supper and will greet you then as fragrant as a garden of Tudor roses—you will think the seasons have rolled back and June has returned!"

"A bath?"

This was Kat. "Madam, this is madness! Why, you had one less than a year ago! And after exercise too—it is not to be thought of!"

"Kat, a bath!" My voice was shriller than I intended. "I will have a bath! And bid the kitchen scullions make it hot!"

It was hot indeed. As I lay in the great tub of copper lined with brass, I saw my whole body flush from palest alabaster like the sky at sunset to an ugly mottled red. "Parry! Kat!"

They were there behind me, cool white napkins as big as tablecloths at the ready in the hands of their willing maids—but both now looking strangely at me.

"Your Majesty is best now in your bed."

Kat's tone brooked no denial. Why did she frown like that, so old and anxious?

I laughed, a light and tinkling sound, not like myself. "Kat, no! I am supping with Lord Robert. I want the table in my Privy Chamber set with bowls of firethorn berries and white Michaelmas daisies—not the blue—and the chamber scented tonight with lavender and oil of roses . . ."

Why was I so slow? I moved to my dressing table and bade Parry prepare my complexion. I could hear Kat and Anne Warwick muttering in a corner, and the noisy Lettice arguing with the new girl, Radcliffe, come to take Jane Seymour's place. How her voice hurt my head! I called up Mary Sidney instead. "One of the black gowns tonight, Sidney, tell the tirewoman—perhaps the Italian velvet with the pearl gauze and the new ruff from Milan . . . Why, who's this?"

Behind me in my glass a low-built stout man swam into my view. His face, jaw, beard and all wore a look of fierce concentration as he stared at me, his small round eyes boring into my face.

"Who are you? And why do you look so, sir?" Men did not stare at me like that! And why did he not kneel? I was furious at his lack of respect.

"I am a scholar and physician, madam!" he retorted proudly. "Of Heidelberg—visiting your London."

I loathed his light, clipped German accent. My head was aching violently. "London, perhaps, sir—but why visit me?"

He leaned forward and, without a by-your-leave, laid one hand to my brow, while the other pulled down my chin and peered into my mouth. "Because, my lady," he said tersely, "you are grievous sick. Of the small pocks."

A red mist rose before my eyes. "I?" I screamed. "You impudent German knave! How dare you handle me so? And lie to me so?"

"I a knave—a liar?" His face became almost as red as mine. "With Your Majesty's pardon!" And he stalked on his heel and left the room.

"Good riddance!" I crowed. "And now, Parry, your best fucus for my face—Sidney, the gown—and I will sup with Robin and the angels, bright clouds of angels floating on bright wings . . ."

Now I was in my bed.

How did I get here?

So cold—so cold and shivering . . .

I could feel the furs at my face, feel the weight of bedding loaded on my limbs, so heavy that I could not stir a muscle. I could hear all their voices far away—Anne Warwick, Sidney and Radcliffe, Kat and Parry, my great-uncle Howard, and was that cousin Henry—why was he here?

Urgent whispering now, one crying—who could that be?

"He is the only doctor for the small pocks. He came from Brussels to save the lady of the Laceys when all her body was pocks, no flesh in between . . . He must return!"

"He has been sent for to come back—he will not—he says not even the Queen of England calls him a knave!"

A man's voice—Robin's—that at least I knew: "Leave the vile knave to me!"

The door slammed. How long passed? Time suspended. Then many feet, men's feet, men's voices, a face not a yard from mine I knew at once, despite the vinegar-soaked muslin tied round his mouth and the pomander waving to and fro between us. "Master Cecil!"

"Sir William now, madam, a good while since, I thank Your Grace."

"Master Sir William . . ." I pondered. When was he made a knight? How long had I been Queen? No matter. He was here now. "Sir, my Master Secretary!" I was pleased with that.

"And here is your Lord Treasurer Paulet, your Lord Admiral Clinton, the Lord Keeper Bacon, your great-uncle Howard, your cousins Knollys and Hunsdon, your lord Bedford . . ."

On he droned and on. *What were they doing here?* I drifted in and out of what he had to say: ". . . Your Ladyship must name a successor . . . now with your dying voice, give your blessing to your chosen heir—"

Dying voice?

I laughed again. I was not going to die! And when I did—which, yes, was now—only one man could take my throne, govern in my stead. "You will appoint Lord Robert Dudley Regent of England for all eternity. He must have every year a pension of twenty thousand pounds—"

I heard a gasp—from the Lord Treasurer? "Yes, you are right . . . it is too little . . . at your discretion then . . . say, fifty thousand? A hundred? And a pension for his man."

"Dudley!" The seething fury had to be the jealous Duke of Norfolk. "Now we know the truth of his devotion to the Queen! He must have been her lover, for her to try to make him King over us like this!"

"No!" I protested piteously. Robin was being misjudged—I could not have that! "I call God to witness that I am as God made me! I confess I love Lord Robert—dearly, dearly!—that I always loved him and I ever will—but nothing evil has ever passed between us. I am innocent and he is spotless, or he would not be playing in the clouds now, see above us, in the sky, up there by the sun . . ."

"Madam, drink this!" It was a German voice. "It will bring the pocks out."

"Pocks?" I pushed the cup away. "I do not want the pocks out!" I protested fretfully. "They will make eyelet holes in my skin, make me old and ugly—"

"God's truth, lady!" he exploded. "Which would you rather, that the pocks came out in your skin and lose your beauty, or lose your life and all?"

"Swear at Her Majesty, you German villain, and I swear I'll run you through! Give her your potion, damn your eyes, and pray that it works!"

Why was Robin standing in my chamber with a drawn sword pricking the doctor's throat? The man leaped like a hare and tried again, his beaker to my lips.

The drink was red and warm and soothing, like a cordial of hippocras.

Greedily I gulped it down. Now Sidney and Kat were swathing me in
yards of red flannel and lying me before the fire.

Red drink . . .
Red flannel . . .
Red fire . . .
And at last it drew the redness out of me . . .

Days and nights it seemed I floated there, in a red dream. Then one
dawn waking, as I passed my hand before my face, I saw the telltale
pinpoints, and my voice, thin and unused, cracked into a scream. "The
pocks! The red pocks are come upon me!"

"Never fear, lady!" It was Sidney's voice. "Once the pocks are out, you
will recover. See, I have them too." I tried to look at her. It was like
looking in my own glass, for her sweet heart-shaped face was all pocky.
But then I saw I did not know her, for her sweet heart-shaped face was
hideous with scabs and craters, ruined beyond repair.

"Oh, Sidney!"

"Do not weep, my lady. It is God's will."

Dominus regit me . . . The Lord is my Shepherd, I shall not want . . .
Yea, though I walk through the valley of the shadow of death . . .

It was a long, slow climb back to full health. Like one who has taken a
violent fall from a horse, I had to learn to walk again. And learn who I
had to thank for my new life, for I had been through the valley of the
shadow indeed: death had possessed almost every part of me. First, who
but Robin? When the doctor had stormed out, he had galloped like the
devil to overtake him and threatened to slice him limb from German
limb if he did not return—adding, too, that death by a thousand cuts
awaited him if he failed to save both me and my beauty. Who but Robin?

And who kept the doctor there for days on end, refusing to sleep even
when he slept for fear the German would leave again, but Robin?

And who else watched by me night and day, feeding me liquid drop by
drop when my throat was too swollen to drink at all, but Mary Sidney,
who had paid for her devotion with an attack of the pocks far worse than
mine? Indeed, her poor features were all eaten away, scarred so badly
that her husband burst in tears when he saw the ruin of her face.

He wept again as he knelt to me and begged that she might retire from
my service. "For her face now so disfigured, she cannot but be a blemish
to your Court. And besides, madam, our son having taken the infection
too, she craves your leave to nurse him."

Oh, my poor Mary, and poor Henry too. Their only son, the adored boy
they called Philip, 'horse lover' in Greek, after Mary's beloved brother Robin
—so forward, so fair—

His mother saved his life, but not his looks. Like her he bore the pocks on his face till death kissed all away.

Robin and his sister did that for me in my illness, risked that for me, suffered that for me. Even his brother Ambrose had stood guard over me night and day and never left his post. And dullards scratched their heads when I promoted Dudleys? The riff-raff wondered why I loved him? He was called a murderer, and worse. Let the truth be known, he was my man—one who gave me his life, and now, when I was dying, gave me life!

And I could give in return, a hundredfold! Now I could show the world his value to me as my most constant friend—yes, and lover, but not as they understood it. Hark what I did! Oh, the joy of giving! To see his eyes as I whispered him what I had devised!

For his position: a licence to export cloth to the Netherlands, to ensure him an income equal to that of all other great men at Court. For a West Country fellow they called Hawkins, the mayor of Plymouth, was newly come to London with a hundred seafaring schemes, and many were making money from these trading ventures overseas. Hawkins was worth knowing, Cecil said, for he waged constant warfare with our shipbuilders. He demanded ever smaller and neater craft when they loved above all things to build floating palaces like those of the King of Spain—from whose coffers, travelling in those ships, it seemed, a good proportion of the Plymouth adventurer's profits really came.

"I fear the fellow is no better than he ought to be," said Cecil gloomily, "even a privateer. But he may be useful."

"A privateer?" I did my best to look shocked. "No, let us use him, let him overlook the fleet—we must keep it in trim." *And if this Hawkins finds that any of my ships might come in useful for a money-making voyage or two—well, need the world know that?*

For I needed money now for Robin as much as for myself! To keep up his position and reward his loyalty, I had to fill his coffers; and I decreed an income from the Civil List of those rewarded from the Queen's Purse, a pension of twelve hundred pounds a year as Master of the Horse.

And for his noble service at my time of crisis, I made him a Lord of the Privy Council, to be a young man for me against the greybeards, a man of action against men of talk, a soldier against the penmen, and new blood against the old.

You may guess how his enemy Norfolk hated that! But I offset Norfolk's bile, silenced his protests and balanced up the score by appointing him to the Council too—and for good measure, my cousin Henry Carey, Baron Hunsdon, to make up a third.

And now the war with France was out in the open, no more a hugger-mugger trade of secret gold sent to Admiral Coligny, the head of the Huguenot forces, or to the Prince of Condé, their leader in Orléans. With our six thousand men one of my lords would have to go as commander.

"Majesty, send me!" he begged me on his knees.

"Robin, I would not spare you for an hour! Do you truly think I would risk your life in action? Think how your brother Henry died in a French war," I rated him tearfully, "blown to pieces at St. Quentin! Do not make this demand of me. Do not think of it!"

Yet to show him I did not mean to spite him with my refusal, to honour him I chose the next best man. "Robin, what think you of my appointment for France—of the commander of my forces?"

He frowned. "Lady, I cannot say till I know who he is!"

"Oh, you know who he is! Almost as well as you know yourself! His name—let me see if you can guess—it begins in an "A," and ends in a flower . . . the flower of the Tudors . . . the flower of England . . ."

Recognition dawned like sunrise in his eyes. "Ambrose! Brother Ambrose! Well, well, madam, you bless our house!"

And to honour his older brother, I made Ambrose now Earl of Warwick, restored him to the family's lost title and parcelled out between them all their father's former lands lost to the crown when he was condemned and executed under Mary. To see them both kneeling before me in speechless gratitude, their sister Mary looking on with her dear husband Henry Sidney, in whose arms my brother died, was a joy too deep for tears.

Now each day I felt stronger. To show my recovery, I attended a full Council meeting dressed in pearl-white satin: my skin was still far from restored to its former smoothness, but no other colour took down the lingering redness better than white. And Parry's magic equalled the German's when it came to potions and lotions, so I thought I looked as well as I could hope to.

I had thought to receive my lords' fulsome congratulations, to reap my reward in love and devotion for the scare I'd given them. Not a bit of it! As delicately as only he could, Cecil sketched in the two poor alternatives they had faced when my life seemed in danger, the two candidates for my throne and crown. No, not Mary, they never thought of her—*was I glad at that, or angry that they had all rejected the senior line of my father's Tudor blood?* They had, they felt, to choose between none but Catherine Grey and the Lord Huntingdon.

"Huntingdon?" A worthy peer who did his duty, nothing more. *"Huntingdon?"*

"He has Plantagenet blood, madam."

"He? Hardly a jot—barely a tittle, and two centuries old! He counts seven generations back to the youngest son of the third Edward!" I was fuming. "No, if I am to be replaced, better one of your lordships—who at least are men of merit, men of mettle!"

One above all . . .

They knew that I meant Robin. Norfolk's eyebrows shot up into his velvet cap, and he scowled viciously. Across the table Robin coldly stared him out, and beneath the board the hands of both were on their sword hilts.

"One of ourselves . . . ?"

Cecil held the pause long enough for it to grow hostile, and my heart grew sore.

Oh, God, I had forgotten how much they hated Robin when I loved him before! Now he was once again in my favour, even proposed as my successor when I rambled in my fever and thought I was dying—why, the very attempt would have brought in its train all the old blood of England up in arms, and the death of England's peace, a bloody civil war!

And the same would go for any lord who tried to make himself primus inter pares, over all their heads. But if it could not be Robin, it most certainly could not be the dull distantly Plantagenet Earl.

"No, not Huntingdon!" I muttered, enraged for Robin, furious with myself. "Nor Catherine neither!"

Norfolk's long, thin sallow face composed itself into something like a sneer. "Then must Your Majesty marry! And give us a successor of your own!"

The succession, the succession! Now Mary was pressing again. "Disappointed of our York meeting, dearest sister," she wrote in her fine italic hand, almost as good as mine I was nettled to see, "we hope to have by your own mouth the promise of our rights." Or else, she added in a scarcely veiled threat, she would have to look to her husband to vaunt her rights for her.

"Her husband!" I scoffed to Robin. "Why, all the world knows that her vaunted match with Don Carlos, which might have given her the hosts of Spain to invade us, is as far off as ever!"

Robin frowned. "Could you, madam, persuade her to take a husband of your choice—one who would strengthen her rights to the succession—rather than an enemy?"

I looked at him. An idea flooded into my head, of such simplicity, such beauty. "Robin, yes!"

To give Mary a husband I could rely on, one who was man enough to keep

her under control—to have his child upon the throne of England one day—
our love was such now that—

I took his hand, my eyes alight. "Robin—shall I make you the King of Scotland?"

XLVIII

Robin marry Mary?

Was I ever serious?

She never thought so. "The Queen of England offers me her Horse Master?" she screeched at my envoy Randolph.

"He is a Lord of the Privy Council, a great man in England, and the Queen's dearest ally," replied Sir Thomas stonily. "And there is no man in the world Her Majesty would sooner see beside Your Majesty upon the throne of Scotland—*or of England.*"

That was bait enough for greedy Mary! She sent down her own man, the smooth-faced Sir James Melville, forging south through the worst of the winter snows, to probe my intentions. I received him at Whitehall, with smiles as false and civil as his own. I would show him, and her! "This way, Sir James!"

At least my new Gentleman of the Privy Chamber, a tall and handsome newcomer called Hatton, put the short Scot in the shade! We must teach these troublesome neighbours their true place! I led him through the royal apartments until we stood in my bedchamber.

"Sir, see here!"

Beside my bed of state, rich in its red silk hangings, stood a cabinet of finest marquetry, as high as a man. On the front it bore my *ER* blazoned above my coat of arms in tulipwood and blackthorn amid a flourish of Tudor roses and plump oak leaves, all inlaid with ivory, ebony and mother-of-pearl. I threw open the doors on their cunning brass hinges. Within were other doors, within those twenty drawers, inside them smaller drawers, all within and within.

"See here!" I cried in rising passion, throwing open doors and drawers for his inspection. I pulled out a perfect rope of palest pearls, a tree of gold with leaves of emeralds, a fistful of diamonds, a ruby sized like a tennis ball that my father had kept beside his bed—and more, and more. "All this will be your mistress's—in time!"

If she does as I want! I did not need to add.

But Melville's eyes were too sharp to be dazzled by toys, no matter how magnificent. And like a great stork, he could see a fish a mile off. He caught up a candle. "Why, madam, what is this?"

"This?" I tried to laugh. "Why, nothing!"

But before I could stop him, his lean hand had snaked into the cabinet and pounced. "'My Lord's Picture'?" he read in mock astonishment. "Why, lady, who may your lord be?"

There was nothing for it. As haughtily as I could, I took from him the little packet in its scroll of paper and opened the gold-framed miniature within. Melville did not even pretend to be surprised at the likeness he saw there. "A fine lord indeed, Lord Robert, and one well worth his place next to Your Highness's heart!"

Next to my heart . . . standing up, or lying down? How cleverly he sneered, to insult without insulting! I would not endure this! "Lord Robert is a lord for any lady—and has been no more than a dear friend and brother to me!"

"And my Queen would not take from you, Majesty," he purred, his eyes as seeming clear as water over pebbles, "the man you call your brother and best friend. She simply seeks what all know is her due."

Oh, these slithery Scots! *My lord—her due!* "What, does she spurn Lord Robert?"

Melville's smile was oil on water. "By no means, Your Grace! And as Your Grace's sister and next heir, my Queen wishes to make no marriage that would not content you! . . . But what is one man, when a queen as fair as she must have a thousand suitors pressing for her hand?"

Mirror, mirror, on the wall . . .

I could not resist it. "How fair is your Queen? As fair as I am?"

He coughed delicately into a cupped hand. "She is"—he paused—"the fairest Queen in Scotland as you are the fairest Queen in England."

Hmmmph.

"But is her skin as clear as mine?"

"She is of the browner hue, my lady—but still very lovely."

"But which of us is the fairer?"

Sir James sleeked back his silvery hair with a practised hand. "Paris himself," he said easily, "who made the famous judgement of the three goddesses, faced with two queens like yourself and my mistress, would not know which to award the golden apple."

Hmmmmph!

"How tall is she? Taller than I am?"

"Yes indeed, lady."

At last I had found a flaw he would admit! "Then she is too tall—for I myself am neither too high nor too low!"

"The easier, then, to match your good self with a man than my Queen, madam."

I shook my head. "I am not minded to marry. If I could choose, I would remain all my life as I am now, a virgin queen, and never change my state. But if your Queen thinks to frighten me with threats of a foreign husband, when she could be my lovingly accepted heir, then her undutiful behaviour might force my hand!"

He laughed, a surprisingly rich, fruity laugh. "Nay, madam, let my Queen do what she will. You do not think to marry! You have too much pride to suffer a commander: for you think if you were married, you would be only Queen of England, whereas now you are Queen and King both!"

I glared. He hastened to make amends. "But rest assured, lady, my Queen is not undutiful! She knows what she will owe to you, her kissing cousin, when you name her your heir!"

Some comfort, then. Sir James was saying that Mary would submit her marriage plans to me if I would openly recognise her as my successor to the English throne. Well enough—if the true heir would in fact be Robin's child! For I was of an age with Mary, give or take a handful of years. I would outlive her, I dared swear to that, and it would be for the next generation to inherit.

But to have her marry Don Carlos, to see the child of a Spanish marriage poised to mount the throne of England, that I could not bear. And if she would take Robin . . .

"Madam, you jest!" was his first, flat response, his face aghast, his eyes like milk pails in his head.

I held his hand and studied his long fingers, pale in the wintry light. "You say you love me—yet you refuse to do this little thing for me . . ."

He gasped. "Little thing? Madam—"

"Robin"—I laid my finger on his lips—"I must not let the Scots Queen marry an enemy of England." *But can I let her marry my best friend?* I looked away.

He burst out laughing. "Now I see the game!" he grinned. "My clever lady will accomplish much by this! While we sit snug in Whitehall, the snow at the doors and all warm within, by throwing me across her path you hamper the Queen of Scots in her husband-hunt, delay her marriage to another and keep her trotting at your heels like a little dog in the hope of winning your official recognition, your nomination for her right to succeed you!" He turned my hand in his and raised it to his lips. "I salute you, lady!"

"This is not all!" I pouted.

"By no means!" His smile flashed white as a pike sighting a minnow. "By offering me, you frighten off other suitors: for the King of Spain, say, will not readily cross the Queen of England's precious plan for her precious favourite to win a throne!"

His hand was warm in mine. Capriciously I played with his long fingers, fanning them out and stroking them one by one. "You think that, do you? Then you see that I do think of you, plan for you . . ."

"Oh, lady"—his mirth vanished, and he reached for my hand again, crushing it to his mouth—"believe me, lady, I see through your plans for me! By this you test my love as in a vise, turning the screw till you wring out the last drop of my devotion. If I refuse, you will say I am no true knight who will dishonour his lady's bidding when she calls on him—when I should be—what was your father's motto?—"Coeur Loyal," loyal unto death, be it the death of my heart? Yet if I agree and clamour for advancement—"Lady, yes, make me the King of Scots!"—I dishonour myself. For where is my love, then, where my constancy?"

Now it was my turn to laugh. Stroking his face, I tried to make him smile. "You read too deep in the book of my intentions! I only want to share with my dear sister of Scots the pleasure of your company."

He looked me hard in the eye. "I give you warning, madam, that I shall write to the Queen of Scots and tell her that you are using me as a mere stalking-horse—for do not think that my love for you has made me a tame snake!"

Did he doubt me? I would kiss his opposition away, beginning with the nail of his littlest finger. Instantly he seized both my hands in his, and alternating rough caresses with the gentlest kisses, moved by delicious, exquisite degrees over my hand, up my arm . . .

I could feel my passion rising. "All of which shows me what a splendid husband you would make for any woman," I moaned, moving to disengage myself.

Then, madam, why not you? his eyes demanded plainer than any speech. But aloud he flashed, "Is this to torture me? To test my fidelity? Is this a game?"

I turned away. I could not answer because I did not know.

Should I give up my scheme? While I brooded on it—*and on him, and her, the twin poles of my universe*—Sir James Melville and my own Randolph went about it, to and fro. Assisting Melville was another of Mary's favoured envoys, Maitland of Lethington, while my Cecil joined in the game on our side, as did the Earl of Moray, Mary's bastard half-brother and most trusted lord, on hers.

For this was not the only matter to resolve between England and Scotland. Many of our northern earls had lost lands to the thieving Scots, our light-fingered neighbours, in the Borders skirmishes, and now that the lairds of Scotland had made peace with their Queen and the French had been sent packing back to Paris to fight their own wars, it was time to reclaim them. And to muddy the marriage waters, a little more pressure on Mary from another quarter would not come amiss. I sent the Earl of Lennox, who had lost land on both sides of the Border, to Edinburgh to demand restitution.

Yet as soon as he was gone, I gave way to an agony of doubt. I sent for Cecil to lament, "Lennox we cannot trust! For with one foot in Scotland, one in England, who can tell which way he will jump!"

Cecil was struggling then with griefs of his own: his newborn son Robert, hoped and prayed for during eighteen long years of marriage, had proved a hunchback, a poor crooked pygmy and unlike to thrive. He gave a watery smile. "We may trust his wife the Countess even less, forgive me, madam."

Though he misspoke blood kin of mine in this, I had to forgive him. The Lady Margaret was an old enemy from Mary's time. I hated her then, and since she was a Papist, her temper was not improved by my accession. She also suffered from the same malady as my cousin Catherine, enough Tudor blood to give her vain delusions of importance, yet not enough to lend her any wit or common sense. As the daughter of my father's oldest sister, who was married into Scotland—as a foreigner, therefore, born out of England—as a Catholic and not least as a woman, she had been expressly debarred from the succession by my father's will. His Hoariness the Pope of Rome himself had scarcely less hope of getting near my throne!

But Madam Margaret had had that jewel of a thing, a live-born, healthy son . . . that Holy Grail, a boy with Tudor blood flowing, however thinly, through his veins, and on his father's side, that of Royal Stuarts too, by direct descent from the Scots King, James II.

She had always been ambitious for her son—in her birth throes she had cried out "His name is Henry!" before he had gasped out his own first cry.

"And now," Cecil said sombrely, "I hear she is dreaming of a match for her son with the widowed Queen Mary—to make him King there."

"What? No, no, it cannot be, it is impossible! He's only a boy, scarce out of diapers!" Surely I remembered him with his insufferable mother as a child at Mary's Court, just a few years ago?

Cecil shook his head. "Madam, he's nineteen."

Nineteen was it? Years younger than Mary! And as a husband for a woman who had been Queen of France, and even now was angling to be Queen of Spain by marriage to the Crown Prince, he had less than no

position—even his name, "Lord" Darnley, was, like Robin's, an honorific, not a true lordship. No, he could be no threat.

And yet . . . Cecil was rarely wrong in his intelligence. It would be
prudent to take down the boy's pretensions.

I had it! The very thing to build up Robin, make him fit for a queen
and throw the boy Darnley in the shade! And it was my chance to make
my lord—*for my lord now he was, and always would be, world without end*
—what I knew he ought to be, a nobleman.

. . . "And for your gracious goodness, we do pronounce you Baron
Denbigh and Earl of Leicester . . ."

*I never planned a ceremony in my life with more care than the investiture
of Robin. First, the title: it was always a mark of royalty, being given to the
youngest sons of the monarchy, as the Duke of York always honours the
second son. Then his manor: the ancient honour of Kenilworth in Warwickshire, with the great castle, one of England's finest, all the lands once his
father's and lying next to his brother Ambrose's lands at Warwick. And then
offices, and grants, and pensions—how I loaded him with wealth and
honours till he burst now like a shooting star into the highest ranks of the
English aristocracy and was truly a match fit for a queen.*

*And to proclaim his state, I ordered that as he progressed for his investi-
ture into the Presence at St. James, after a high and holy service in Westminster Abbey, he should have as his supporters my cousin Hunsdon, the Lord
Admiral Clinton, the Earl of Sussex and the Earl of Huntingdon—to show
that all the premier peers of my land, even Huntingdon, who some thought a
claimant for my throne, bowed before Robin, took him as their peer.*

*And to drive home the lesson, and throw up the contrast between my lord
and his base imitators, who should be the page carrying the golden sword of
honour before my lord at every stage of the ceremony but the youth Darnley,
who looked, as I intended, an overgrown boy against a man, a pale parody
of an English lord, a shallow stripling.*

And how well Robin looked, I leave you to imagine: kneeling before
my throne as Cecil read out the words of the patent, clad from head to
foot in white samite from the Holy Land, his doublet crested in gold,
white hose, white shoes with golden heels, white-and-gold leather belt
and buckler, white egret feathers tipped with gold in his white silk bonnet, a triple rope of whitest pearls set with gold bosses around his neck,
even his pomade today of lily and white honeysuckle—rising to greet me
as I leaned forward to invest him. First came the sash of honour, then his
own golden sword of ceremony girded across his shoulder, last of all the
heavy velvet robes of his new rank and estate.

As I fastened the gold cords to hold the cloak in place, my hand
brushed his neck. *Oh, he was warm . . . so smooth and warm . . .* I

could not help myself. Before I knew it, my hand had slipped inside his
snowy collar, his stiff ruff, to stroke his neck. He looked so serious, I was
tickling him to make him give me one of his Robin smiles, his darling
smiles—even in the presence of Mary's lord, Melville, and the French
and Spanish ambassadors, I did not care. He resisted long enough, but at
last his mouth glimmered in spite of all into a wicked grin. And his eyes
said to me, *You will pay for this in kisses afterwards* . . .

Now she could not resist him, I was sure of that! As the procession
moved away, I saw Sir James's eyes on Darnley and rallied him teasingly,
sure of the answer. "What, do you like more the look of yon long lad?"

Melville shrugged a shoulder, raising an eyebrow. "Madam, my Queen
is a lady of discretion, distinction too! How could she prefer a beardless,
lady-faced boy to a man such as your lord?"

I nodded in satisfaction. How indeed? Mary had been married to a boy
before, she must want a man now. And where was the man to compare
with my Robin?

And that same evening, as I feasted with him in my chamber, brought
more good news—my Archbishop of Canterbury, come himself upon the
weightiest errand.

I rose to greet him with both hands outstretched. "Welcome, my lord
Archbishop, welcome within!"

I gazed warmly at his cautious, furrowed brow, clasped hands and
tightly folded mouth clamped against indiscretion. Parker! Little Matthew Parker was my own appointment—dear in my estimation as a man
once chaplain to my mother, and more, still loyal to her memory when
others could not flee the forest fire of her devastation fast enough. But
never was he dearer than when he stood before me and solemnly pronounced, "The Court of Arches has met in urgent session, at the bidding
of your Secretary, Cecil, to consider a case matrimonial. The Lady Catherine, who calls herself Countess of Hertford, is merely Grey, now and
for all time: for she is not married."

"Catherine not married?" I gasped. My mind flew back to Cecil's innocent words on the day of her disgrace: *And in the meantime, we may take
occasion to establish the circumstances of the lady's marriage* . . .

That clever man! He had been right again! It was true, in fairness, that
Catherine had had evil luck, the very fates had conspired against her.
Her marriage had been an impulse, clapped up, it seemed, on the day she
had refused to hunt with me, and all the Court was absorbed in following
the chase. To keep it secret, they had used an unknown priest, pulled in
from who knows where, to do the honours—there was no record of the
service, and he could not be found. The only witness to the ceremony
had been Hertford's sister Jane Seymour, and she, poor soul, was that
young lady-in-waiting who had died of the small pocks. No church, no

banns, no priest, no witnesses, no documents of the ceremony, no register signed—where was a rightful, legal marriage in all this?

Catherine had a document, she proclaimed noisily to any who would hear her, a jointure from her husband that would prove they were married, a settlement he had made on her as his wife. Where was the document? The lady had mislaid it, forsooth! And the woman who could not even guard one piece of paper, be it never so important to her life, thought she could govern England? I laughed aloud!

Now she swore on her immortal—*her immoral!*—soul that a true Christian marriage had taken place. "A fig for her immortal soul!" I pronounced with satisfaction. "Give the Archbishop some wine. Let him set in train the process to get this "marriage" voided. And publish the bastardy of her son through every pulpit in the land. Another glass of wine! Here's to my lord and my Archbishop, not forgetting my Master Secretary!"

We were merry that night. But I never learned the hardest lesson of high office, that no joy is ever more than a minute long, that the black dog Disaster always trails his golden brother Triumph hard at heels. For soon cruel news from France drove Catherine from my head as no more than a pinprick—news of loss and death. We lost good money in that dreadful war, more than I can bear to remember. We lost Le Havre and with it any hope of ever winning Calais back again. We lost true hearts of oak, brave men and the good name of England, only a ragged remnant of our force trickling back to England under Ambrose's torn and bloody flag. I wept on Robin's shoulder and suffered a megrim that attacked my stomach and struck me in the side of the face, where another tooth was now painfully loose . . .

Did I, then, not listen hard enough, think hard enough, when the Earl of Lennox sent from Scotland to say that he needed his son to aid him in the struggle with the Queen of Scots to recover their land lost in the Border battles? Or did I simply give in to persuasion when on all sides they urged me to grant Darnley his passport for Scotland and let him go.

"What do you fear, lady, that the Queen of Scots will marry him?" laughed Robin, pausing to hand me carefully over the wet cobbles as we paced back from the Chapel Royal on the Feast of Stephen. "Sure, she has pledged that she will never marry without your consent—for that means she kisses good-bye to all hope of your making her your heir."

"But for sure she wants to look at him, consider him!" I objected, carefully skirting the late-December slush threatening my kidskin shoes and figured velvet cloak. "Marriage with him would strengthen her English claim through his Tudor blood, as well as her hold on her own Stuart throne."

"It is most likely," murmured Cecil on my left. "But even if she does care to consider him, it is in our interests to dangle as many suitors as we may before her. For even though King Philip makes no great speed with the Don Carlos match, yet the Queen Regent of France, Throckmorton writes from Paris, now offers marriage with the boy King her son Charles—"

"What, with her husband's brother?"

Shades of my father and his first Katherine, Katherine of Aragon, when he took his brother Arthur's widow, as is expressly forbidden in Leviticus, and the grief that all that brought!

"Ach, the French!" I was disgusted. I would not think of it. And I was sure, too, that Darnley was such a negligible youth that Mary, if she thought of him at all, was bound to reject him.

Let him go, they said.

Never was such a train of gunpowder ignited with three small words, when I let him go.

XLIX

> *When wert thou born, Desire?*
> *In pride and pomp of May.*
> *By whom, sweet boy, wert thou begot?*
> *By Self-Conceit, men say.*
>
> *Will ever age or death*
> *Bring thee unto decay?*
> *No, no! Desire both lives and dies*
> *A thousand times a day . . .*

How do men fall in love?

How do women?

Nay, ask me not, I know not. For I never fell: I never fell in all my life, not so much as off a horse, much less in love. When I loved Robin I awoke into love, a love that had been there for all my life, all around me like the air I breathed since we were children together in God's garden, before we grew into sinful human love after the pattern of Adam and Eve, our first parents . . .

But fall?

No.

What is it, love?

If not a fall, is it a hunger? The appetite casting around for strange meat not yet encountered, hungry for what it does not yet know, but will recognise at the first scent in the air?

I know one thing: no one tumbles straight into their greatest love, the great love of their life. For there are many kinds of love—maiden love, flesh love, flesh hunger, then the deepest love hunger—and all these must be tried, tasted and relished before the one great love.

I knew Mary's pride—I recognised it as scarcely less than my own! And I felt sure she was too much a queen to think of an untitled boy as her husband and her lord.

Yet for all that, Darnley would bear watching.

He came to kiss hands on his departure, and I took the chance to look him over once again. Yes, he was worth watching, for he would please any woman's eye. He was the tallest man in the chamber, overtopping even Robin, and his fine, well-shaped legs in his black woolen travelling hose, his graceful body, slender through the waist and broadening at the shoulders, could have been carved by a master sculptor, not rough-hewn like other men's by the hand of old Dame Nature. Perhaps the sensitive, heart-shaped face, with its straight nose, wide eyes and delicate mouth, was a touch too soft, too girlish for all tastes—certainly for mine! But his golden brown hair, fair skin and perfect courtesy, next to old Arundel or the glowering Norfolk, made him a young god.

Yet as a lady of the Scots later observed, there was more in him of Pan than of Apollo. Curiously I scrutinised his faunlike ears and the brilliant hazel eyes set slightly on the slant, and tried to read their meaning. Were they inscrutable, or merely empty? Did the blank windows of his soul mask hidden foes inside the house, or were they signalling no one within?

"Farewell, Gracious Sovereign!" His voice was coarser than I expected, loud and grating.

"God speed!" I waved him off, suddenly noticing the heat within the chamber. Where was my fan? A cluster of my ladies, Anne Russell, Lettice Knollys and Mary Radcliffe, were chattering with Kat below the dais. I beckoned Kat to come to me. How slowly she climbed the two shallow steps! A sadness smote my heart: *Why, Kat is old!* And in concern for her, I gave the boy venturer no more thought.

For with the talk of Mary's marriage had come a new upsurge of interest in my own. At holy service in St. Paul's to mark the new session of my Parliament, the rogue Dean spoke out against the single life and attacked me in person.

"If your parents had been of your mind," he demanded truculently, *"where would you be?"*

The villain! I could have struck him—the loud-mouthed preaching knave—to speak so to his Queen! But all my Parliament men were of his mind, and so with many a sigh I buckled down to play the marriage game once again.

Who did we have? The Hapsburgs we had kept dangling, with a few judicious baubles thrown their way. Now with the death of the old father Ferdinand, his son and heir the Archduke Maximilian was minded to bid again for "such a Helen," as he flatteringly termed me, "with such a dowry!" Would I consider his brother the Archduke Charles?

I responded, for as ever we needed friends abroad, weight on our side against Spain. Yet it would not be easy: already Maximilian was warning that "he would not have his brother led by the nose, as on the last occasion."

I brooded on this through a week of summer nights, when, two hours and more after all the Court was abed, the sky was still glimmering with that fairy light of a midsummer eve when it seems night will never fall again. Who could I use to counterweight the Hapsburgs, bring another suitor into play, give me room for manoeuvre, give me time?

I chewed fretfully upon some candied citrons Throckmorton had just brought me back from Paris. Then a wild thought made me laugh aloud.

Not—?

I could not!

Could I?

Yes, I think I could!

What if he was—oh, God help us!—no more than fourteen summers, whereas I—well, double that and add a few years more . . .

Where was my mirror? I peered into the glass. Even my kindly candle-light could not hide the crow's-feet and the faint marks of time that now showed through the best of Parry's complexions. But he would not wed me for my face! And as for him—well, my uncle Arthur married at fourteen, and all the world knew that the French led the world in matters of this nature . . .

A hint to the French Ambassador, a quick passage of royal letters in cipher to and fro, and I had another suitor—none other than Mary's young brother-in-law, the boy who had earlier been proposed for her, the King of France!

I should not have so enjoyed taking her beau, but I could not help myself. *This will teach her to turn up her nose at a premier peer of England —at my Robin!* was my gleeful thought.

Would I have given her Robin, if she wanted him?

No matter, that was for me to decide, not her!

She had lost Don Carlos of Spain: his father Philip let it be known the suit was cold. Now she had lost the King of France as well—soon she would learn that a bird in the hand was worth two in the bush!

And along with France, I still had Sweden: for King Erik had remained faithful to me and to his dream of uniting the two great Protestant powers of Northern Europe.

"Wait!" I told Robin, almost daily now. And, *Slower! Slower!* I told myself. For our love ran on wheels, and I was hard-pressed to avoid succumbing to his kisses, to his lightest touches—and to his blandishments.

Wait . . . yet what were we waiting for?

"Madam, as I am yours, so must I hope that I may make you mine!" he broke out at the wedding of his brother. "What, must all the world rush to the altar except we two?"

Marriage . . . It was the first time that the word sprang up between us. And once it had been spoken . . .

One evening on the river, we were with Bishop Quadra, the Ambassador of Spain. The barge was decked with early-summer flowers, the evening air was kissing the slow-swelling waves, and all the world was at peace. Behind us one of my people picked out a love melody on the lute, the sweet notes falling gently around us like summer rain. We lay half reclining under canopies of rose and honeysuckle, sweet Spanish wine, served in honour of the Bishop, like nectar in our mouths. "Now we are in heaven indeed!" I breathed in ecstasy.

Suddenly Robin sprang up and fell dramatically onto one knee. "Madam, I beg you, make my heaven on earth—marry me, lady! Here we have a priest to hand—this good Prince of the Church will tie the knot for us!"

What, marry a pair of heretics? Quadra puffed up like a bullfrog ready to burst. I giggled wildly. Robin was wicked to scandalise a man of such importance! I searched for a way out. "Sure, His Excellency does not know the words of the wedding service in English!"

"Oh, but *I* do!" Robin said softly, reaching for my hand. "Do you, Elizabeth, take me, Robert, to be your lawful, wedded—"

The caress of his strong fingers, the hard pressure of his thumb within my palm . . .

Oh, Robin, Robin . . .

Wait and see!

But while we played and waited, others hastened to get down to work. For now Desire and May met together up in Scotland, as soon as the devil Darnley got off his horse—yes, devil, for what he was, and what he became, though he looked like an angel!

Now as spring ripened, Darnley made his way back into my mind with a vengeance, via ever more urgent missives from the North.

"Your cousin Queen likes well of the young Lord Darnley," wrote Sir Thomas Randolph, my Ambassador. "No sooner was he arrived at Wemyss than he ran through the castle to dance a jolly galliard with Her Majesty till she cried out for breath. Now she calls him the tallest and best-proportioned long man that she has ever seen."

I read this as Parry dressed my hair for an evening reception with a Hapsburg Embassy newly come from Vienna.

Not good!

"Who's there?" I snapped. A page leaped into view. "Give orders for a rider to stand by to post to Edinburgh . . ."

"Return at once!" I ordered Darnley by royal warrant.

"I find myself very well where I am, and so purpose to remain" was the puppy's insolent reply.

The next command went straight to Sir Thomas Randolph, my man in Edinburgh. "Use your own men, accomplish it how you will, but see that our cousin Darnley returns at once to England!"

"The Queen will not permit it!" Randolph wrote back in despair. "She dotes upon Lord Henry: people say she is bewitched!"

Now of my forty riders standing by to take my decrees and documents to the four corners of the earth, at least half seemed to be flurrying up and down to Scotland.

"Lord Henry?"

"She has ennobled him, madam, made him Earl of Ross."

So Mary was in love, for the first time in her life? Would she have a hard fever, then, as her blood raged?

She would.

"She has laid all shame aside," wrote Randolph sombrely. "She is besotted on Prince Henry, and this matter may not be dissolved now but by violence."

How—and when—did Randolph foresee that? For no less than Armageddon was then a-brewing.

But all I saw from England was his meteoric rise. *"Prince* Henry?"

"She has made him, madam, Duke of Albany."

A title royal. Her meaning could not be plainer.

I ground my teeth and, in a third, last, desperate throw, sent a final messenger, no mere rider but the loyal Throckmorton, my Ambassador from France, and not to Randolph but to the Queen herself, with the best card in my hand: "If you will take any peer of my realm, any lord other than Darnley, I shall consider well naming you heir to all England."

But by the time my man was passing through the great gates of Holyrood, Mary was past caring.

He was proclaimed "King Henry" now.

And the next day they were married.

L

The sorrows of Mary,
They were one, two, three and four . . .

Marry in haste, said a wise man a long time ago, repent at leisure. Now Mary discovered the truth of the dour observation Cecil had made at Robin's marriage long ago, when Amy robbed his heart—Nuptiae carnales a laetitia incipiunt et in luctu terminant . . . *Carnal marriages may begin in pleasure, but they must end in grief.*

But Mary's marriage and any pleasure she may have had in it lasted not years, as Robin's did, nor months—*hardly weeks, some said not even days. Fragments of information reached me almost daily from the loyal Randolph, who tried with me to delay Mary in her headlong course. And even before Randolph was whispering to me that her maids whispered to him that the Queen of Scots was with child, all the world knew that the bride of May had been forced to sleep apart from her moody groom. For she had found that "the lustiest long lad of his length in all England," as she had dubbed him, also possessed the vilest lust and the longest reach of any man that she had ever known.*

For Prince or no, his manners now would have shamed a groom of the stables. Returned from Scotland, my Ambassador, Throckmorton, stood before me lost for words, his honest face a battleground of emotions.

"Tell me the truth, sir," I urged him. "This is no time to bite your tongue—speak out!"

"Madam, the King's a sot!" he broke out bluntly, tugging his red beard. "When he was here in England, it now seems, his good mother the Countess held him to the mark as she made him into the perfect courtier—and with his riding, fencing, dancing, his lessons at tilt, his French and Italian, he was kept to the grindstone. Now he is like a boy let out of school: he carouses to his heart's content, most days puking-drunk before breakfast and then drunk all day long!"

God Almighty! What a swinish vice!

"And—?"

"And in his cups he swears vilely at the Queen for not making her Parliament crown him as King Regnant—a power she does not have, her lairds are so touchy to resist her will in all things."

King Regnant—just the same struggle as dear sister Mary had had with our Parliament over her husband Philip, who likewise craved the title, fought tooth and nail for it, the official sanction of his royal status over his wife's.

Look at what befell the two Marys in the marriage mart!

And they urged me to marry?

I could see the rest. "He drinks, and abuses her—and so she bans him her company for his viciousness?"

Throckmorton grimaced agreement. "Which then excuses—in his clouded mind—his subsequent course of lewdness—"

"Debauchery too?"

Throckmorton's colour turned a shade, but he was a man of the world. "He seeks out the lowest whores, the trulls of the town's end, the Grassmarket and Cowgate—and for something he brought back to the Palace that he did not find there, the Queen bans him her bed and company."

I almost laughed aloud in savage sadness. So the fool had caught the pox! The man who had the swiving of a queen preferred her scabby sisters of the streets! What a foul end to a boy's dream of kingship and a queen's dream of love! A heart of marble would have pitied them.

Outside the chamber the last trees of the park were shedding their last leaves; a few survivors trembling on the high branches poignantly bespoke the death of summer and winter's fatal fall.

And with the New Year . . . ?

I nerved myself for the next question. "What of the child we heard of? Surely this is a rumour! Is it possible that a marriage so short and so ill-starred could bear fruit?"

I could see Throckmorton hated what he had to do. "Forgive me, madam, but I have it from one of the four Marys who have attended on her Majesty since she was five years old—it is true, she is with child!"

Oh, God—how you punish me!

Mary with child?

My mind raced like a runaway: *A royal, Catholic, male heir in the Tudor line . . . no hope of bastardising this one, as with that ninnyhammer Catherine Grey—and I as far as ever from either husband or child . . .*

New life—yet death to my peace of mind, death to my hopes for a child of Robin's through this Scottish match, which I might have made my heir, my godchild and my own.

Now fate conspired to drive the knife into this wound, deeper and deeper. As I stood the next day in my chamber, all my women about me to aid and advise on my next new set of state gowns for the opening of Parliament and the season's round at Whitehall, I saw Kat suddenly pause in the midst of sorting bales of cloth. "Here, give Her Grace the cloth of gauze, the silver," she directed Mary Radcliffe. Then she pressed her hand into her side, under her bosom. "And hold up the midnight velvet alongside," she told Kate Carey, "for herself and Mistress Parry to make judgement." She leaned a little on the table, as if to catch her breath, then went on as before. But the next day she was dead.

My Kat, my consolation, teacher, nurse and mother, how I missed you—how I miss you still!

Death and birth—how these two endlessly jar and collide like the great floating blocks of ice that mariners yarn of, far in the frozen seas! The very week that we went into mourning for my poor Kat, as I walked alone and grieving in Hampton's dying gardens, Cecil appeared at my side with the Lord Lieutenant of the Tower, Sir Edward Warner. For once my patient Spirit was neither calm nor controlled. "Speak out, man, tell your tale!" he snapped. "Never try to mince it! Tell Her Majesty what you have told me!"

The Tower Keeper was as pale as death.

What, did he bring, then, word of a death?

Was it a sin, Lord, that my mind leaped straight to Catherine and her son —and to quick-flowering hopes of a sudden gaol fever swift and fierce enough to cut off both those blossoms in their bud?

But Cecil's face said, *Vain hope!* His angry bearing added, *This could not be worse!*

What was it? I could feel the darkness gathering.

"Your cousin, Lady Catherine Hertford—"

"*Grey!*" I howled. "She is the Lady Grey, not Countess of Hertford—the Court of Arches has pronounced her marriage null and void!"

"The Lady Grey," he corrected himself hastily, "is . . . has . . . ." He stumbled to a silence.

"Spit it out, man!" said Cecil vengefully.

". . . has been delivered of another child."

My voice was pale as lead. I knew at once. "A son. Which lives and thrives, even as his brother does?"

How the new heirs were snapping at my throne! No mercy now for Catherine and her traitorous partner in crime! Whether they bribed their keepers, or whether the Lord Lieutenant had taken pity on "the young couple so much in love," as he saw them, I neither knew nor cared. But these lovebirds would not bill and coo again this side of the grave.

I spoke, and it was done—Hertford banished, and the royal broodmare Catherine sent under close arrest into the deepest countryside that could be found to bury her in.

Yes, of course I remembered my own life in death buried in Woodstock— Woodstock, the very name can still bring palpitations to my heart! But I did nothing—nothing!—to bring that fate down upon my own head. Whereas Catherine—ach, save your pity for those who do deserve it!

And that excludes my other lack-brain cousin, Mary of Scotland, like Catherine led by her woman's part, not by her wits; guided by what throbbed under her girdle, not by what grew beneath her wig. Now her lairds turned against their clown of a "King" and found a thousand ways to slight him, all of which drove him to wild bullying and a loutish violence more fitted to a whorehouse than a Court.

"For some imagined injury he split the face of an aged duke of the Scots from eye to chin with one ferocious blow," wrote Randolph. "And he demands royal obeisance even from those of royal blood."

Mary's half-brother Moray, and royal though a bastard, rose in rebellion. Mary put the rising down, and though he had been her dearest friend and supporter, she proclaimed him outlaw and, in old Highland parlance, "put him to the horn," along with all his followers.

The letters telling me this were full of despair, for all those forced to flee with Moray were the lords who were for England, who could be relied upon to fight our cause—insofar as anyone could rely upon the slippery, self-seeking Scots! And with her husband a spent force, her best lords and advisers gone, Mary now more and more relied upon one Rizzio, I was told by Throckmorton in our next closet conference.

"Rizzio? Who?"

"David Rizzio, a Savoyard, her new secretary—for she has fallen out with Maitland of Lethington, her former Secretary of State, and formerly a right hand as dear to her as Sir William Cecil has proved to your good Majesty."

"A man of parts, then, is he, this Rizzio? A lawyer or a scholar?"

"Madam, he's her musician. He won her notice as a fiddler, but no Nero he, merely a musical knave!"

O my prophetic heart! As soon as Throckmorton said "he's her musi-

cian," my mind flew back to my mother and the wretched Mark Smeaton—how she was accused with him of adultery, and the poor youth paid for it with his life.

I made my own music always in my chamber—yes, on the virginals!—or relied upon my ladies or boy trebles, for that closeness can give fodder to evil minds, breeding suspicion!

As it did in Darnley's puny, drink-degraded brain. Despised by the Court, cast off by his wife, jealous of the life now swelling in Mary's womb, "the King" devised a plot to restore his fortunes. Mary herself took up the tale in missives posted hot from her shaking hand:

. . . sitting at supper in my chamber in my palace of Holyrood, in bursts my lord the King with a gang of ruffians and dragged out my servant Rizzio to his death—above sixty dagger wounds he took to his poor body. Myself threatened too, a sword at my throat and a pistol at my belly till I feared for my child's life . . .

She need not have feared. For with the first show of foxgloves and before the moon daisies of midsummer showed their faces, on a June day hot enough to make her labour a torment even in Scotland, she was delivered—

Need you ask?

Yes.

Was God angry? Trying to punish me? To warn me?

The child was a boy, beautiful, fat and healthy, and likely to thrive. She would call him James, after her father and her father's father, and all the kings of her line.

I wept in Robin's arms when the news came. "The Queen of Scots is lighter of a fair son, and I am but barren stock!"

"No tears, no tears!" he soothed me, but there were no words to gainsay it.

At last, the Tudor Prince. Well-shaped and very forward, we soon heard, and so knowing that all swore he had been here before.

But born on the wrong side of the Border, the wrong side of the altar, to the wrong woman—all, all wrong. Now *if* he were not a Papist, *if* he could be brought up without her fatal influence, *if* the succession could skip a generation—too many "ifs." And already I was being bombarded with "buts."

"Never think to name him your successor!" my fiery Parliament warned me. "We will have no Catholic on the throne of England, nor no son of Scotland—the very stones of London would rise and mutiny against him!"

So be it. But I was to stand godmother, by Mary's express wish—too late she grasped again the value of cultivating me! I sent the Duke of Bedford as my proxy, with a magnificent font of solid gold, two stone in weight, as my gift for the child, and with it my sincerest prayers for peace.

But peace in Scotland?

As soon hope for quietness in hell.

"Scotland is a sewer, Majesty, a quagmire!" Bedford swore on his return.

Now with the birth of a son, the Scots succession was secure, and the man who would be King, the hated Darnley, was superfluous to requirements. Cecil's "eyes" saw and his "ears" heard and whispered the ways in which the lairds of Scotland now went about to rid themselves of this troublesome relic of the Queen's dead lust.

"The prime mover is Scotland's hereditary Lord High Admiral, Border Earl of Bothwell, the Hepburn of that ilk—but beneath the titles," Throckmorton warned me, "a murderous bully, a vainglorious, rash and hazardous young man." I tore the parchment when I read this—another Darnley, by the sound of it! And would he take Mary's fancy as the other did?

"No divorce!" warned Mary, for she knew that to cast off her lord would call in question the true birth of her son, would risk making him a bastard when the marriage was no more. Her lairds looked at each other and read the meaning hanging in the air—*if no divorce, how else to end a marriage, dispose of a husband?*

Yet though I lay down every night thinking of Scotland, I arose with other worries knocking at my door. The French pressed daily for an answer to their King's suit of marriage, and the young Charles wrote wistfully from France on violet-scented parchment, "You say you are anxious, madame, that you are too old for me. I would you were as content with my years as I am with yours!"

Meanwhile Cecil almost daily found the way to bring the Hapsburg Archduke, another Charles, to my attention, for he still cherished hopes of that marriage above all others as our armour against Spain. For now the Duke of Alva, Philip's first lord and chief of war, came from Spain and settled himself in Brussels. From Throckmorton's young man Walsingham in Paris came alarming news:

The Duke by degrees is bringing into the Low Countries all the might of Spain. Here he has built a force of ten, fifteen, fifty thousand men, Germans, Walloons and Italians, the very best of mercenaries: the like of which has not been seen in these lands since Julius Caesar brought his legions out of Rome. And this enemy force is poised here on the counterscarp of Europe, ready to break down England's door!

"How to hold back Spain, harry her forces, take down her ambitions, trim her swelling sails?" I groaned in Council and outside; it was my dawn greeting and my evening prayer.

Robin laughed. "May I propose a venture for you, Majesty, with the man Hawkins? It seems he is turning many a pretty penny for the lords and merchants who care to invest in him."

"Oh, venturers . . ."

Before me the Presence and the antechamber beyond swarmed with petitioners—a motley crew, clutching their rolls and scrolls, ready to thrust into any hand—and among them for sure were many venturers, dreamers and schemers after gold, who in their fantasies coined gold, slept on gold, ate gold, even fornicated gold. But this Hawkins . . .

"The Plymouth man, is it? The seafarer?"

Robin nodded. "Give him money, lady. Send him to the Americas, where the Spaniards find their gold. Let him make you rich and vex the King of Spain at the same time!" he urged. "Only one thing—give him good guns as well! He must be well armed if with his fleet of English cockleshells he is to sail under the bows of the great galleons of Spain and tweak the nose of your erstwhile brother-in-law!"

I loved him for his disrespect—and his daring! And I knew Hawkins now: he had made himself very useful with his advice on the fleet. But money, *money*, *Money* . . .

"How much, Robin?" I carped. "And it must be secret, not known to come from us . . ."

His white grin showed how he read me and my needs. "Leave it to me, sweet lady—leave it to me!"

Yet still Scotland lurked there on our borders—and always sucking at our ankles, at last drew us all down into its primordial bog. Not Sophocles, I wept in my late candle hours, nor any story makers of the ancient world, could have dreamed of a more fatal tragedy: how the gods made playthings of us, evil fed fat, and passions spun the plot. And Mary my sister Queen was at the centre of that web, from the very first, from the first thread the Fates began to cast . . .

"The King," as the wretch Darnley was still known, had become a stranger to his wife and child.

"He would not grace even his own son's christening!" the Duke of Bedford told me.

"A filthy sponge!" Mary had called him to his face in the full Court, at which only the Earl Bothwell's intervention had saved her from a blow. Then came a feast of civic dignitaries in staid Edinburgh town, when he stepped aside to answer, as all thought, a call of nature.

A call of his own bad nature at all events: he was discovered by her cries in an antechamber of the banqueting house, drunkenly ravishing one of the Queen's maids, forcing her fundament after the manner of a boy. Mary swore she never could countenance him as her lord again. And when he fell grievous sick of the pox, voiding and pissing blood, with daily fevers and great rosaceous weals all over his body, all men saw his punishment as dealt by God for his lascivious sin.

Yet now, Randolph informed me, Mary reconciled herself with her loose lord, forsooth, and blandished him to a house at Kirk o'Field, promising him that he might resume a husband's rights upon her body as soon as his sores were healed. And having tucked him up in bed, in the room below hers, what did she do but suddenly decide that she might not sleep there, but must return to Holyrood?

You know the rest: like Amy's murder, the sorry tale went three times round the world.

Towards dawn a huge explosion blew the house where "the King" lay to smithereens. The house—but not the poor impostor of a king. His body was found outside in the midnight grass of the February fields, naked and strangled, lying beside a chair and a long rope. Poor fool, he must have seen or heard his enemies gathering, let himself down from the window with the aid of his chamber valet, and been caught and murdered as he tried to flee.

"Madam," I wrote in icy coldness, not "Dear Sister"—*"Ma Chère Soeur"* —as always before, for my soul sickened at her,

I should not do you the office of a faithful sister and friend if I did not urge you to defend your honour, not look through your fingers and wink at taking revenge on those who have done you such a pleasant turn!

But even as I wrote, I knew she would not do as I did when Amy died, when I sent my lord away and set in train a thorough, legal search for the real truth. And she did just the opposite! Darnley's old father brought a charge at law against the Earl Bothwell, to seek justice for his son. But on the day of the hearing he found himself barred from the court in Edinburgh by four thousand Bothwell clansmen blocking the Canongate, claymore-clad, dagger-handed, dirks in their teeth, yowling and jeering. And how far Mary was from clearing herself from the darkness now defiling her like pitch was all too soon to emerge.

For now Mary's slippery slide gathered apace. Riding one day, she was waylaid—*kidnapped*, she later pleaded—by Bothwell. She went with him to his castle and there he took her—*by rape was the subsequent case for the defence*—and they were one. Within a fortnight had she married him, and all Scotland under Moray the Queen's half-brother was up in arms. "Those who did down Lord Darnley care even less to take the Earl

Bothwell as their laird and King," Randolph sent post to me. "But the Queen swears she cares not to lose her kingdom, England, France and all, but she will go with him in a white petticoat to the world's end ere she will leave him!"

Was any man worth this?

Now with Bothwell at her side, Mary took to the field to beat down her enemies. He fled, she was defeated and brought back in chains, muddied, disgraced, while all the people lined the streets to see her shame and scream out, "Burn the whore!" She was deprived of her throne and forced to abdicate, bereft of her son, and made a state prisoner in the grim island fortress of Lochleven, there to rot out her days repenting of her sins, while Moray and his Council reigned in her stead through James the infant King.

Now in England I sighed with relief while at the same time composing bitter letters to the lairds for deposing their true Queen.

"I shall consider well of revenging this insult to my cousin and sister!" I wrote huffingly—how I loved myself in that swelling vein!

And I huffed to some effect. To sweeten me to his Regency, Moray offered me the first pick of Mary's jewels at less than a third their value. Urged on by Robin—"Pearls are for virgins, madam, moon jewels well suited to yourself, Queen of our Heaven"—I secured six ropes of black pearls strung like a rosary, the nonpareil of beauty, each as large and lustrous as a grape.

Almost as good—nay, even better—was the pledge from Moray that the little James would now be free of every taint of Rome. He would be brought up a Protestant by the Scots lairds. He could now enter into communion with his English godmother, my gracious self, Moray promised—*and with my people?* was my own unspoken thought.

Yet even while they moved to dismantle all traces of Mary's queenship, the lairds knew that the lady herself would not be so easily disposed of. What would become of her? Not merely Scotland but the whole of Europe scratched its head. Something must be done—in time, for sure, all would become clear.

But Mary was too hot in self-esteem to wait out her life while others sat in judgement. She wrote me missives full of sound and fury demanding sympathy for her life in prison; "a daily crucifixion," she described it, of boredom and the death of mind and soul. She begged me to relieve her. "Have pity, oh, have pity," she implored me, "on your dear sister and cousin!"

Yet even as she penned these touching words, she had another of her whore's tricks up her skirts.

And my greatest, my still-undying torment now began with a gabbling messenger tracking me down in the depths of Windsor Forest on a pearly morning of the first week of May: "The Scots Queen is escaped, fled from her realm, set naked on your kingdom; the Governor of Carlisle holds her in custody and sends to Your Majesty for most urgent instructions what he should do with her . . ."

LI

What to do with her?

So simply began the question that was to poison the next twenty years— what should have been the best years of my life . . .

My heart was hammering against my lacing—I knew at once how bad this was.

"Fool, fool, triple times *fool!*" I wept in my fury. "Why does she flee to England? Why not stay and fight for her own kingdom? Or if she must, why not fly to France, for God's sake, where she has lands, and money, and Catholic friends to give her welcome?"

No answer could be heard from any man around the stunned and silent table. Beside me Cecil looked drawn and ashen with fatigue after a night of watching for despatches as they came. Opposite him Bedford and Sussex, disdaining parley, were rumbling for instant war.

Cecil demurred. "Yet to make war to restore a Catholic queen on our very borders—"

"If we do not, we let in the French!" Sussex protested in red-faced rage. "Scotland then becomes an outpost of France again, a French garrison, on pretext of restoring their Queen Dowager to her throne."

"And no doubt, 'tis better for England, she there in her own kingdom," put in my cousin Knollys, "than lodging at Carlisle here, here in the heart of our secret-Catholic North, to attract men's eyes and to foment treason . . ."

Was there a flicker across Norfolk's pale staring face at this? I could not tell—for my heart stalled on the last word, "treason."

From that time forth I never slept easy in my bed.

That was the gift my "dearest cousin and sister" brought with her to England for me.

And they say Mary was a saint, a Catholic martyr? She was the vilest wretch I ever knew. Of all women, she most justified the gross term that the vulgar give to all our sex. She was, in every sense of that capacious word—let me fall into French now, for greater delicacy, offering their three letters for our four—a "con." Sauf qu'elle n'avait ni la beauté ni le profondeur . . . Except that she had neither the beauty nor the depth, as the French say.

May, and the blossoms frothing the hedgerows should have been calling all hearts to delight.

May, and my world was darkening every day as the import of Mary's action dawned on every mind. Bolstered by Robin, I tried to find what crumb of comfort could be gleaned by scratching in the filth under the table of this feast of unwelcome news.

"At least the boy James her son will now be spared the taint of Papistry!" my bishops promised me. "Now he is in the hands of the lairds and his uncle Moray, he will be brought up a Protestant."

And Parker, my Archbishop, firmly agreed. "If the young Prince—nay, the King, as we must now say—is under the rule of the Scots lairds, I dare pledge Your Royal Grace he'll prove the keenest Covenanter of them all, even though he is scarcely a twelvemonth old! His first words will be of the revealed truth—for God be praised, he is too young to have learned the mumbling mongrelism of his mother's faith."

Yes, that was some consolation. If the young Prince, the heir of all the Tudors, could be brought up a Protestant, and if he could escape the influence of his mother—well, we should see.

"And with her faults and follies, she has played right into Your Highness's hands," pointed out my old Lord Treasurer Paulet, whose increasing age had done nothing to dim his sharp tongue and caustic wits. "Though she demands you set her back on her throne, by force if need be, the Scots as keenly swear to shed their blood to the last drop to block her return. And a queen who has shown herself so unfit to govern her own kingdom may legitimately be excluded from the succession to ours! Her claim to your throne then will fail in the eyes of all, save the fanatics of her own persuasion."

I watched the nodding heads around the table, Bedford and Sussex, Cecil, Clinton, Knollys and Hunsdon and my great-uncle Howard, and not least my lord of Leicester. Did the small group round Norfolk nod less keenly, agree more faintly? I did not see.

My lords and Parliament-men did not publicly cry "Hang her! Burn her! Drown the whore!" like her own loving subjects when they put her off her throne. But they pressed most vocally for her to be brought to trial for her complicity in Darnley's death—so hard that, albeit with a cousinly show of reluctance, I had to allow proceedings to begin against her.

Yet who knows who laughs last?

Unlike Mary, I had my kingdom, my freedom and my lord—Robin, my lord of love, my love, my life. But my beloved lord and Horse Master was a cause now not of joy but grief—or, rather, say grief and joy in equal measure. Now with each month, each season, our love grew till it outpaced both of its begetters. I loved him to the topmost mast of my soul, and I knew he loved me with the mainmast of his.

And yet a shadow lay between us—the shadow of time passing and love unfulfilled. Now we quarrelled too, and wept, and were reconciled—until the next time. And always those jealous of my love for him, like Norfolk, waited their time to strike.

For Norfolk harboured bad blood—he was as proud as his grandfather and his father, my first love, my late lost lord of Surrey, and like him, never could not endure the new blood, *nouveau sang, nouveau riche.* And he would fight against it: even in sport, his blood ran as hot as it was blue, while Robin's, as I knew from every one of his thousand kisses, ran all red, nothing but red, red, red . . .

One day at Hampton Court I set a match of tennis for my lords: a royal game, and I hoped a royal diversion from my endless cares. I could still see my father striding the court, racket in hand, for he adored the game, when I gave the command for play to begin. The day was hot; the leads, where I and my ladies sat above, thronging with people and with memories.

On such a June day, in this same place, I watched Robin play once before and lose—lose the match and his heart—

I shook myself.

Away with Amy's ghost!

"À la paume, my lord!"

Who cried for the victor of this game of royal tennis? Curiously I looked along the gallery. Flushed and laughing, red curls bobbing, leaning forward till it seemed her plump breasts would fall out of her bodice, was little Lettice Knollys, or Hereford, as she now was since her marriage to the Viscount, Walter Devereux. Beside her was my new maid of honour Helena of Snakenborg, a visitor from the Court of the King of Sweden—smiling, true, but showing none of Lettice's abandon.

I frowned down the line. Lettice withdrew with a bob curtsey, but not, I noted, looking too abashed.

I raised my hand in summons. "Parry, my fan—and a napkin cooled with rosewater, if you please. Then pray you, speak to the Viscountess of Hereford!" I ordered. "Tell her I do not like this hoydenish behaviour, especially in a young lady lately married!"

"Your Majesty!"

Like a great galleon, all sails flaring, Parry rustled off. Cooling myself with the fragrant handkerchief, I peered down into the court.

Yet before long Lettice and her boldness were nowhere in my mind. The match over and Robin victorious, I was descending to congratulate the players when Robin stepped forward to assist me down the last few steps from the gallery. As he did so, he took the handkerchief I was holding from my hand.

"By your leave, lady—"

It was not a question. With an expansive gesture he indicated his dripping brow, his sweat-stained shirt. "I dare not come before you in such foulness!" he explained. Laughing, he began to mop his brow.

No one saw Norfolk till his great hand tore the napkin from Robin and threw it at my feet. "You villain!" he stuttered thickly in his throat. "How dare you make so free with the Queen's Majesty?"

We were all struck dumb. Like a crazed bull, Norfolk raged on. "And I have heard that you enter Her Majesty's chamber as she dresses in the morning, even handing her maids her shift to robe her in!" he stormed.

Robin had gone very pale. "Vile and vulgar nonsense!" he said quietly. "And you insult Her Majesty even to speak it. Withdraw it now, you scoundrel, instantly, or I shall make you eat every last word!"

"A duel, then! My men will wait on yours for the appointment!"

And the idiot Norfolk looked at me all proud and puffed up, like a schoolboy who has triumphed at a muss.

"Leave the Court, do not dare speak to me!" I exploded in his long fool's face. "I will not have you behave so, presume so to take the keeping of my honour into your hands, sir, by God, I will not!"

Oh yes, he argued back, but I shouted him down, made him bow his stiff neck. But now I clearly saw again the black heart he bore towards Robin, how my love for Robin was his excuse to vaunt his own superiority, push his own power. Every day showed my love for Robin, the clear preference I had for him over my other lords—an offence they never would forgive. And to continue to love Robin would be to expose him to endless enmity, to undying hate.

Should I then give him up? For sooner or later I would have to come to terms with one of my foreign suitors, for England's sake.

Robin, God bless him, saw the opposite. That night, we lay on silken cushions in a summer pavilion at the river's edge, the light, lapping sounds of the water idly accompanying the lilt of madrigals and a distant flute. We bathed in the scent off the river and I floated in paradise until Robin sat up and leaned forward. In a strange new voice he said, "You see, sweetheart, my dearest lady, how I will never have respect or lift up my head—"

He broke off, staring sightlessly into the dark. High on the horizon, far above our heads, the star of Venus glimmered in the dark. I turned towards him. His eyes were filled with tears. He grasped my hand, and his gaze pierced my heart. "Unless you make me your lord, and not your lapdog—"

"Robin—do not—"

"—unless you marry me!"

L I I

Marry in May, repent alway,
Marry in June, you'll change your tune,
Marry in July, you're sure to cry,
Marry in August, suffer you must . . .

Marry Robin . . .

It was the moment I had dreamed of with all my heart—once, long ago, for an hour above the leads of the tennis court, when I first fell in love with Robin and foolishly fancied him in love with me.

But that girl, so far removed from power and with no thought of being Queen, was gone like that time, long, long ago. He—we—had missed that precious moment, and it would not come again. Was that why what he said hurt me so much now?

Round and round I chased it in my mind. How could I refuse him? Yet how could I accept? For I was married already—married to England from that moment in Westminster Abbey when I bared my breast to the cold, rancid oil and felt the chill kiss of England's ring upon my finger. And any other marriage would be adultery, fornication, blasphemy . . .

But still my flesh fought against it, fought me all the way. For I loved Robin, I was more in love than ever now with his darkly handsome face —what did I care that the bloodless Norfolk called him "the Gypsy" in his spite and jealousy?—in love with his bold hawklike profile, his bright, ironic gaze, his mouth—oh, God, his mouth!—his strong brown hands, his horseman's leg, his body—

Oh, leave off, leave off! He was a man of men, a man in his perfect prime

*of ripened manhood, and I a woman just then growing to the mid-height of
my womanhood, cresting my thirties, in my prime and salad season too . . .*

And I wanted to be his! There was no reason in the law or constitution
why not: as Queen I could marry whom I liked. And I liked, oh, I liked! I
could not resist him. Day by day that summer, our passions mounted.

"Do you desire to live and die a virgin?" he half wooed, half taunted.
"Do you not long to know the love of a man and children—?"

And then with a kiss in my palm, then inside my elbow, and one
behind my ear, his tongue inside my ear—*the love of this man . . . the
joy of my children . . .*

When he talked so, such visions filled my mind . . . How could I hold
out?

But already my royal suitors did not relish losing ground to a mere
English earl. French pride above all would not stomach it.

"The Queen our Regent cares to wait no longer to match her son the
King," the French Ambassador the Compte de Foix coldly informed me.
Before all the Court I threw a fit of pique and outraged damselhood,
then adjourned to my private chapel to murmur, "God be praised!" And
to my Court and Council I laughed it off: "Could I really have stood up
at the church door with a husband young enough to be my son?"

But now I must woo the Archduke of the Hapsburgs with a vengeance
—losing France, we dared not make an enemy of the Holy Roman Empire too! And with my head and heart full of Robin, I had to stretch out
this courtship as long as I dared, or England would be friendless in the
world.

"See how I adore your master's gifts!" I told the Hapsburg envoys,
kissing the agate-jewelled cuffs of a pair of ivory-blush kid gloves, pale as
my hands, on which I waved a winking Hapsburg diamond. "I long to
have His Excellency Lord Charles here in person!"

"He will not come unless to take Your Majesty to the altar," came the
reply.

"What, does he fear to come and woo in person? Should I rely on
portraits to choose my lord, my life, my bedfellow and the father of my
children?" I demanded dramatically. "Do you not think your master's
uncle Philip of Spain had good reason to curse all portrait painters when
he laid eyes upon my sister Mary after agreeing to marry her picture?
No, I will give my answer to the real man your master, in the flesh!"

I knew he would not come to be looked over, for fear of rejection. But
I could still insist I could only give him his answer after I had seen him.
This game would last a good while, buy us months and years of peace and
good will.

———

And while I struggled with this, others struggled to bring Mary to account. "How goes the case against the Queen of Scots?" I demanded of Cecil.

He gave a cautious nod, his long forefinger caressing his lips. "It goes well," he conceded. "For we have evidence—"

Evidence?

Oh, blessed word, "evidence" . . . !

Never was I better pleased that I had chosen a lawyer to be my eye and ears, my "spirit," my right hand of government.

". . . letters in a wrought silver casket belonging to the Queen, discovered after she was arrested and now sent to us from Scotland by the Regent Moray. They show that the Queen knew of her husband Lord Darnley's murder from the first. And that she was complicit in the plot— and amorous too—with the Earl Bothwell . . ."

My heart soared.

Proof! God smiled on us.

"We must send to Scotland, to tell the lairds we will proceed against her!" I announced. "Now who shall be our envoy?" I pondered carefully, then it came to me. I would give him more to think about than tennis! "Let it be the Duke of Norfolk, for with the late loss of his wife and son, he is sorely in need of the relief of some occupation."

He had ill luck in wives, and they even less in him. For he was their death, they all died in childbed, every one . . .

I meant it as a favour to him. I thought to change his life for the better. God, how You punish our pride, even in our good intentions!

Cecil cocked an eye. "The Queen denies the letters, calls them forgeries."

I laughed aloud. "She would, would she not? Oh, I smell triumph!"

And we won the day. Mary refusing to answer any of the charges, I was able to suspend the hearing without allowing a verdict against a fellow queen—a thing I would not do at any cost. "For if subjects, even those as highborn as my dukes and earls, ever call their kings to judgement," I expostulated, "then the monarchy is doomed, and anarchy must follow!"

"Yet the truth of the Queen's crimes being now exposed," Cecil advised, "we have every good reason to hold her in restraint. We should indeed move her south to Staffordshire, to your more secure castle-fortress of Tutbury."

For all the world knew, except her blinkered self, that I could never now set Mary free. None wanted her, either in England or Scotland, ever to have her liberty again. Released, she would raise an army to regain her throne, call in troops from their Catholic majesties of France or Spain, and bring back her paramour Bothwell from exile in Denmark, where he had fled to save his skin. And with the Scots lords pledged to fight both

354 I, ELIZABETH

of them to the death, that would bring civil war to these shores, to the heart of our island. Their boy King James was proving quick and clever, and with him they had peace. Why would they ever wish to see their Queen of Discord again?

And then a black-clad messenger, eyes on the ground: Catherine was dead, my cousin Catherine Grey—or Hertford, as she still called herself—of a congestion in the lungs, like my poor brother. No tears for Catherine, one who made her bed if any did, letting lust and love choose for her, where her head should have ruled. But now with her death, there was only one Tudor heir—one who many felt was already the rightful heir instead of me—

Mary.

Think of Mary with an army of her own, ranging our land? How could she resist the opportunity to turn her power on me, put me off my throne?

Already there were whisperings: prayers said secretly for "the true Queen" in the cathedrals of the North, tokens and pledges of old Romish relics smuggled to her in her captivity, and herself, shown a miniature of me, saying with a charming smile, "That is no good likeness of the Queen of England, for she sits here before you!"

No, she could never be free!

Yet simply by living she was an envenomed thorn in my flesh.

And always there was Robin with his sweet, endless refrain: *marry me, love me, marry . . .*

And to help his suit he put the word about that we would marry—that I was on the point of taking him—that we were married indeed. One day when I came in from a day's hunting alone with him, all my ladies fell to their knees and demanded to know if they must kiss Lord Robert's hand as well as mine, and kneel to him too.

I gave a nervous laugh. "Why so?"

Trust the pert Lettice to pipe up. "For we hear that you were married to him this afternoon—"

I threw him a furious glance. "You hear much that is not true!"

But would I refuse it if it simply happened—if I could be given in marriage like a village girl or drawn into it by impulse, as Catherine was?

In the tension, tempers frayed. One evening in the Presence, I called for music. Around the dais stood my ladies Carey and Radcliffe, Warwick and Snakenborg, my great-uncle Howard's daughter Douglas, Lady Shef-field, and not forgetting cousin Lettice—she would never allow anyone to forget her! With them were Robin, and behind, some of my gentlemen with my new courtiers Heneage and Hatton.

Heneage . . .

Yes, a fair-enough-looking man—not tall like Robin, but a well-jointed, purposeful body and a hard, smiling eye, a way of looking at women . . .

The music flared, and Robin approached the throne. The pavane was one of our favourites, "Come Back Sweet Love," a slow haunting air.

"My lady!"

As Robin bowed, an evil demon stirred. Coolly I turned to Heneage. "Come, sir," I commanded—and to Robin's rage, sailed past him on the arm of Heneage, where I danced till the silk soles of my slippers were worn through.

The next night I favoured Hatton—till to my fury, Robin took out Douglas Sheffield and then Lettice. Douglas I managed to ignore—*but Lettice . . .*

To see them dancing—her plump breasts bobbing, her full, slanting, sly brown eyes upturned to his, the way he swung her, lifted her—I could not bear it.

"My lord!"

My voice was high, too high and sharp.

He snapped round towards me. "My lady!"

We quarrelled, and the words that followed were fierce and unforgiving. But I brought my wandering falcon back to my side, for I could not do without him.

And that night in my chamber, the last candles guttering their black shadows on the wall, he left no inch of me unkissed as he urged huskily, "Marry me, madam, marry me—or set me free! For no man can endure this life in death, this monkish torment of denial—"

His hand was at my neck, playing along my clavicle as if it were a clavichord. I held my breath. "Robin, I suffer too . . ."

Set him free?

Never.

Was it my passion? Or was it the hidden evil swelling against me, even though I saw it not, that drew me to him, needing his strength, his comfort? Or simply his long service and my woman's need for love? But as a languid June warmed into a ripe July, every new day brought a quickening of the pace between us. His presence was the cloak I wrapped around me; his hands, his mouth haunted me; his eyes followed me like eyes I only dared to see in dreams . . .

All July and all August we spent hunting in Windsor, progressing to Oxford and then back to Richmond.

We were walking there in my vineyard when Robin plucked a cluster of grapes, pressing them to my mouth.

"No, no!" I waved them away.

Robin laughed, tearing the juiciest from the stem. "Does a lord take a lady's "no," or must he play the man's part and decide?"

Gently he eased the sweet ripe fruit against my lips.

I opened my mouth and looked into his eyes. "A man must decide."

Did I know then what he planned when he said, "Lady, September comes—let me feast you for your birthday!"

A week beforehand he withdrew from Court to his house at Kew to make his preparations.

The day dawned hot as June but over-mellow, a thundery fullness in the air. From the casement in my chamber I could see a pearly pink dawn burst into angry fire, with a slash of orange barring an indigo horizon tumbling with purple clouds. I clutched my side.

"Snakenborg, will it rain? I fear a storm!"

"Madam, it will not dare!"

Never did I take more care with my appearance. "No, Parry, no! Not that, another gown!" Mulberry and silver, royal Venetian and red taffeta, peach and saffron, followed each other into an ignominious pile upon the floor. At last I settled on a gown of palest ivory silk, its low-cut bodice demurely edged with bone-pale lace. Every inch was lovingly wrought with creamy leaves and roses, my ruff framed my face in a pearl-edged halo of finest gauze, and pearls clustered my ears, my neck, my every finger—pearls, my favourite of all jewels, pearls for brides, pearls for virginity.

And pearls for tears, they say—I had forgotten that . . .

Slowly we rode from Richmond to Kew, my mood strange and silent, my little train knowing better than to interrupt my thoughts.

It was still early morning, yet there were many people on the roads, and from each one I had a loving greeting. At farmyard corners women rushed to hold up their children for my blessing, carters pulled up their wagons, and one poor peasant trudging to market threw his load to the ground to tear his ragged cap from his greasy head and cheer himself hoarse.

Everywhere cheers . . .

Praise God, Pembroke had said, *you rule with the love of a good people . . .*

True enough, my lord. But I had ridden behind my sister Mary when she came in, and heard the people then cheer her to the hollow.

And could they not—would they not—cheer cousin Mary too?

In the newly shorn fields of harvest, urchin children were playing in and out of the houses of heaped stooks. At the meadows' edges, poppies and yellow hawkweed still proclaimed high summer, but the hedgerows, festooned with blackberries, sang autumn's song: in among the scarlet hips and haws and the bright bleeding crimson of bittersweet were chains of bryony and the last of the rosebay willow. And beside every cottage door, the rowan trees blazed with orange berries against their winter task of warding off witches from the warmth within.

I do not know what made me say, "Tomorrow is the Feast of the Blessed Virgin."

All those within earshot looked at me curiously, but none ventured to reply. At least Robin always had something to say . . .

And there he was! As we rounded the last bend before the approach to his house, there my lord was, rank upon rank of his men behind him, every one in a new livery of his familiar Leicester blue, flashing with rich silver. His horse today was a great white stallion, a Hanover by the depth of its chest and quarters, for all the world the brother of the Pegasus on which he flew to my side the night of my accession. And on his horse he shone like sun-bright Apollo, his doublet of gold slashed with red-gold, gold hose, gold hat and gloves, his breast and sleeves glittering with yellow stones—topazes, agates and citrines in clustering scrolls of gold.

"My sweetest sovereign!"

His bonnet swept his stirrup as he bowed. Leaning forward, he took my reins and led me in.

"God bless you, lady!"

"Long live our good Queen!"

The gateway to the courtyard was crowded with his people shouting and cheering, and the archway above was bedecked with red and white roses plaited to form entwined *E*'s and *R*'s. I laughed with joy. " 'R'?" I quizzed him. "For 'Regina' or for 'Robin'?"

His eyes flashed. *"Rrrrrrrrrrrrr!"* he fooled, growling like a dog. "Ask me not! A man so in love as I am cannot tell his 'R's from his elbows—only Your Majesty can hear what the flowers say . . ."

Within the house the Great Hall had been transformed into a bower of late roses, guelder flowers, vine leaves and dodder blossom. Across the length of the chamber a board swathed in white damask groaned with golden platters the size of cartwheels, loaded with veal and lamb, kid and mutton, capon and duck, quails spatchcocked on breasts of peacock, smoked eel and pickled coney.

"Oh, Robin!"

His eyes were dancing. "Your birthday gifts, my lady!"

A goblet of gold was his first present, a silver eating set his second, a plate of crystal his third. The sun dancing and glancing around them dazzled my eyes.

"Oh, Robin . . ." Was this all I could say?

"What will you take, lady? A little wine, with some salmon and few oysters? Or like Miss Muffet, nothing but curds and whey?"

Trembling, I tried the wine. But I could not manage more than a sip.
He was beside me, leaning down. His pomade was fresh as a May morning, strong as my love. I turned in to him.

"Oh, Robin . . ."

He read my longing. "Lady, this way . . ."

At his sign our people melted. Taking me by the hand, he drew me
through the Great Hall, through the bowing servants, into the room
beyond. The doors closed behind us.

All within was fresh and newly furnished, smelling of beeswax and
lavender. Instead of rushes, silk carpets kissed our feet, and rich hangings
adorned the walls. Here and there piles of bright cushions graced the
floor, while copper bowls of late lilies sweetened the air. At the high
mullioned windows, heavy curtains, half drawn, shaded the low westering
sun: we might have stood inside a jewel box of bright treasures seen
through air like amber, warm and golden.

Across the chamber was another door, and striding forward, Robin
threw it open. Beyond was a small room furnished like a chapel, an altar
bearing a cross and in front of it a robed priest, his hands in his sleeves,
bowing before us.

As if I were made of china, Robin stood before me and tenderly took
both my hands in his. "I do not know, my dearest lady—oh, my sweet
love!—if I may say I give you what I hold most dear after yourself, my
life, my love, my service—or if in giving, I seek to take, to win, to keep, to
hold *you* and your dearest self—"

I turned my face up like a flower to the sun. The priest bowed again
and withdrew, closing the door and leaving us alone. Robin drew me into
his arms. His kiss was chaste as ice, but his fragrance hotter than midsummer madness. Dreamlike as dancers in a slow country round, we
came together as if for the first time.

Wonderingly his fingers traced my forehead, his kisses brushing my
eyelids lightly as a hummingbird. Mine, in return, found the sweet kissing
groove above his mouth, the soft tuft of hair beneath his lower lip.
Roughly he stroked my neck, his hand moving surely down over my
bosom, down to my waist. Now his kisses were harder, hotter, kiss upon
kiss until both of us broke away, gasping for breath.

I was drowning with joy in the dim warm space, drunk with desire.
Hardly knowing what I was doing, I felt for the jewel clusters fastening
his doublet, I so longed to see him, touch him, *now* . . .

"Oh, madam—Elizabeth!"

Lithely he shrugged out of his doublet, tore the fine cambric shirt over
his head. His skin was smooth as silk, his body shapely as a hero's, as a
god's. Standing before him, I moved my hand to the stiff metal catches

notching the side of my heavy bodice down the edge of the deep-pointed V.

He laughed tenderly. "No, no, my love!" he whispered. "This is no work for a queen! I must do the office of your women for you." Patiently he loosed me from the prison of the tight lacing, slipping off my bodice, kirtle, puffed and padded sleeves, till like a maid indeed I stood before him in nothing but my shift.

His hands at my coiffeur skilfully found the pins, and my hair tumbled down.

"My love: my Queen, my mistress!"

Gently he drew me towards the welcoming cushions, and we sank into the soft down. Now his hand hovered over my breast, only the thin lawn between my skin and his hard touch. I was longing for him, my nipples pricking for his caress, his kiss. Pulling loose the ribbon at the neck, he slipped down the front of my shift, stripping it back till I lay exposed to his view.

"Ohhh . . ." His breath was raw in his throat. "Oh, see, sweetheart, see there . . ."

Always before, I had hated my small breasts, envied God's well-endowed, well-bosomed women like Amy and Lettice. But now to see Robin's love, his adoration . . . Slowly, slowly, he made love to my breasts till I was gasping, trembling, crying, but not for grief, not grief . . .

Now fear struck me and I tossed to and fro in his arms, and moaned in my throat like an animal.

"Hush, sweetheart—see—I am naked first, there is nothing to fear . . ."

He shrugged out of his hose. His body gleamed like marble, his beauty made me catch my breath—

Oh, a man's beauty, hot and firm and strong . . .

Now one by one he peeled away my petticoats and undergarments, slipped off my shift till we were lying on a froth of scented lawn and lace. Now he stroked a body swelling to his touch, rising with desire. I could feel his hands, his lips, moving on down my belly now, coming to rest in the tangle of pale golden hairs at the top of my legs . . .

I was panting, cresting a wave I did not know existed, nor where it came from—a raw power, a pure force of life . . .

His length, his man's length, smooth and sweet and hard . . .

And he came between my legs and entered me with infinite tenderness, murmuring, "My Queen—my wife."

I cried out once, in a sharp shaft of pain. But as I did so a deep shudder convulsed me and a darkness came before my eyes, a cloud of unknowing, joy beyond speech, beyond thought . . .

Love in a mist . . .

I lay in a white haze of joy, wholly at peace.

"My love?"

Beside me his eyes were pools of dark blue joy, wells of endless bliss, and I knew he was at peace too.

The die was cast.

I was his woman—as I always had been and now forever was.

And now—to be his wife.

Slowly we found our clothes, as sweet together as a country husband and wife helping each other to dress, not like a lord and lady who never knew what it was to fasten up one button. At last we were done. With a sigh I kissed his neck as I fastened his ruff, and accepted his kiss on mine as he clasped my pendant pearls.

"One last embrace in our unwedded bliss?"

He took me in his arms.

That kiss was long as all eternity . . .

And for so long has it had to last me, comfort me . . .

"The Queen! Where is the Queen?"

The cry came from the Great Hall, followed by a babbling uproar, the wild sounds of anger and fear.

Dread struck me motionless. "Oh, God, what is it?" I whispered. "Danger? Danger to the State?"

Robin shook his head, drawing me towards the chapel. "I know not, heed it not, lady, *come!*"

But I could not move. Like a stag at bay I glanced wildly around. On my one hand lay the Great Hall, where I was Queen, and called for; on the other, the little chapel in the chamber, where three minutes would make me Robin's bride.

From outside now the clamouring increased. "The Queen! The Queen! *The Queen!*"

"Lady—Elizabeth! I beseech you, come!" In silent agony he extended his hand. As I stood frozen, he began to weep.

But I could not find a tear in my dead and dying heart. Dry-eyed, I paced to the door and threw it open. "Who's there? What is all this?"

Hatton it was who burst through to kneel at my feet. "Majesty, we have word of a plot against your life, against your throne. The Duke of Norfolk is in league with the Queen of Scots, and your own Earls have raised the North against you!"

LIII

Why did I send Norfolk on that mission to Scotland?

All my life since, I have asked myself that question. But the real question is, *Why did he betray me?*

He was my premier peer, England's only royal Duke, Earl Marshal and the most powerful nobleman of all England—why did the fool not see that his interests were close kin with mine, that he should underprop my power as a pillar of his own? As a Howard he was my blood kin too, for his grandfather and my grandmother were brother and sister, and more, the blood of the sacred King, the first Edward they called the Confessor, ran in his black veins—did he give no thought to that?

And I meant to help him! I thought a journey to Scotland as my Viceroy, to treat with the lairds there on highest affairs of state, would shake him from the fixed melancholy he had suffered since he lost both his lady and the child who took her life . . .

But I should have known to fear those northern earls.

His dead wife was a northerner, Anne Dacres of Westmoreland. His sister was married to the Earl of Westmoreland, his other sister married to Lord Scrope of Carlisle, who had played host to Mary when she first crossed the Border . . . ach, they were all entwined together like a nest of serpents!

Was it the truth that like "the Mermaid," Mary herself, as song and image now depicted her in that eternal symbol for a woman who was neither fish nor flesh but through-and-through whore, I was blinded by self-affairs? Not thinking with my wits, but led by my love . . . ?

If so, then never again.

For I lost Robin then.

I lost my love, for England—to be not Robin's bride, but England's Queen.

When the time came to choose, I chose her, and not him.

And we both knew it would not come again.

Trembling, I faced Hatton. "Tell me the news!"

He was stuttering with shock. "Word . . . word of a plot . . . that the Duke is raising an army in the North . . . that he is in league with all the great earls there, all the hidden Papists, to free the Queen of Scots, set her on your throne, and marry her!"

I clenched my fists to still my shaking hands. "Let the Duke be sent for at once to answer this!"

"Madam, he was."

It was Cecil, all his young men around him, his face never paler, his mouth a thin grey line. "On your authority I sent for him in your name, before I rode from London to come to your side. And he returns word that he cannot come, he will come in a few days, he is sick now."

"But he was not too sick to ride at once to Kenninghall, where he can raise all Norfolk in revolt—Kenninghall, his private fiefdom, where ten thousand men bow to his will, where he commands six hundred square miles of ancestral land and revenues higher than Your Majesty receives from Wales!" The speaker was a thin, dark young man burning with pale fire.

Cecil passed a hand across his brow. "Your Majesty remembers Francis Walsingham—formerly with our Embassy in France, newly come to my aid in this most complex matter."

Walsingham's tense body spoke his bitterness; his narrow face was alight with the same passion. "This is your enemy in action, madam, this is the work of the Queen of the Scots!" he cried. "We have her own hand in proof against her, secret letters to the Duke, and her spoken words of treason too, faithfully reported by our eyes and ears among her servants. 'I am the Queen of England,' so she boasts herself, and more—'within the month the Mass will be said again the length and breadth of this land!' "

My stomach clenched to vomiting—if only I could spew out this poisonous thing sticking in my throat—

Mary! The very fount and source of treason, just as I knew she would be, as I had foreseen . . .

O my prophetic soul!

I forced myself to ask, "Who can we still count on? And who is against us?"

Cecil bowed. "The Earl of Sussex sends to say his men are ready, he awaits your command. The Earls of Derby and Shrewsbury hold aloof—though close to the Duke in Council, they are not ready to close with him in war. But your Earl of Westmoreland, the Lord Dacres and the Earl of Northumberland are all fled to their lands in the North and, as we hear, only await the Duke's signal to march. In London still, but under surveillance, the lords Arundel and Pembroke—"

"Pembroke? And Arundel?"

Northumberland, yes—easy to see why one of Mary's made-up Papist noblemen would turn against me. But Pembroke and Arundel? Not the bluff old soldier who had served my father and my brother and helped my sister Mary to her throne . . . and my former wooer Arundel, who even now might be my husband . . . ?

. . . husband . . .

I dared not look to my left, where the man who had been Robin stood still as a statue, silent as eternity . . .

Cecil nodded. "They both were seen in close conference with the Duke all this last week—"

My heart congealed. "Arrest them. Call the Duke of Norfolk to appear —on his allegiance! Fetch him on a litter if need be! Send the Earl of Sussex to garrison York and hold the region quiet if he can."

Walsingham leaned forward. "And the Queen of Scots?" he urged. "She should be brought south at once, to ensure she does not fall into rebel hands. Coventry Castle has a garrison, she could be held safe there in the loyal country around Warwickshire—"

Warwickshire loyal—loyal Warwick, loyal Kenilworth—

No more of that.

"Yes!" I cried. "And the Earl of Shrewsbury is to have guard and ward of her, so command him!" That would test his allegiance, force him to show which Queen he served!

"And Your Majesty must remove from here at once."

It was Robin, at my side. I could not look at him. His voice was dead and cold, impersonal as a herald or a sergeant-at-arms. No living soul would believe that I had lived, and loved, and become a woman, in the circle of his arms, not half an hour gone.

Oh, Robin . . .

"To Windsor, Your Highness—"

I knew why he said Windsor—*for Windsor is of all your castles easiest to defend.*

"I will give orders—set the horses in train—"

He bowed and departed. And my heart, my life, went with him.

On the scaffold, it is often seen that a man goes on living, even seems to speak, when his heart has been cut out of his body. So it was with me. Dead inside, I seemed to usurp my life. Now huddled in Windsor, I sat mute and motionless in the council of war as my lords sought to piece together what was known, and what feared.

"The Duke fell into the Scots Queen's toils when he first crossed the Border," reported Cecil sombrely, his face a strange mask in the candle-light. "When he treated with the lairds, one of her minions took him out hawking and—with no more ado, speaking for her—offered him her hand, and with it the throne of England."

"Offered him her hand?" gasped Knollys. "Fie, these filthy Papists! Why, she is still married to the Earl of Bothwell! Though doubtless she planned to rid herself of this husband as she did the last! She tempted him—"

"Showed him the world spread before his feet—and by giving ear to the tempter, so he fell," Walsingham swore bitterly. "And from that first betrayal of your trust, Majesty, all the rest sprang."

Betrayal . . .

I dared not look at Robin where he sat pale and still, his eyes fixed on the wall. I forced myself to listen, listen and think.

In truth, we had heard countless whispers of the Queen's wiles and overtures. We knew she had been searching far and wide for a husband ever since coming out of France—she had cast line as far as Don John of Austria, who was ever at the wars!—and like a fool jester, I had even tweaked Norfolk with this, warning him as a single man to watch his pillow before he lay down with one who had fallen into the habit of burying her husbands . . .

And he had seen her "Casket Letters," seen the written evidence of her love for Bothwell and the plot against her husband. So this recreant traitor had seen Mary for the adultering, murdering whore she truly was, stripped of her Frenchified ways to show her naked self, as they lay bare the drabs in the streets for whipping.

And still he planned to marry her!

And I had been fobbed off by his hot avowal that he would never think of it!

Fool!

Fool!

Fool!

And now?

With Sussex holding York, whom else could I trust?

I looked round the table at the faces etched like gargoyles in the flickering shadow-light. Cecil and Walsingham, Knollys and my great-uncle Howard, the old Lord Paulet, Robin . . .

Robin . . .

I took hold of myself. "Authorise musters—order my cousin Hunsdon, the Lord Admiral Clinton and Lord Warwick to raise their forces—at least ten thousand men. And empower Sussex to impose martial law, to press men locally; grant him what powers he needs."

They bowed and withdrew. A cowed Parry, Carey and Radcliffe assisted me to undress and then left me, Radcliffe to sleep across my chamber door in the anteroom, not at my bed's foot as was usual, for I

had to be alone. And alone with my candle I looked deep into the mirror
of my soul and, in the shadows there, saw what I saw.

No virgin now—a woman, just like others.

*But no wife like other women—no good man to call my own, lend me his
love, his strength, his arm, his comfort, to be close by me in my hour of need.*

*Yet an honest woman in my heart, for when I gave myself to Robin, I did
so in the thought that I was to be—that in all ways I was—his wife.*

*And now—oh, God, God help me—a mother? Though some women
were still childless after years of marriage like sister Mary, others I knew were
mothers after one lying down with a man.*

God, no!

Could it be?

*A madness gripped me. I could hear the gossip ringing around Europe—it
would be the choicest piece since my mother was made pregnant by my
father! The Queen of England has played belly-to-belly, and is with child
by the Lord Robert Dudley . . .*

*Would I then have to marry him? And he, jilted and spurned at the altar,
rejected when my choice, true love or England, came so starkly, would he
marry me—if I bore his child?*

Is that what I wanted? What I planned?

Oh, I would weep many more tears than this before I knew!

*Think! Think! When were my courses last upon me? My palms were
sweating, and I gripped the table edge to steady myself. Not last week, nor
the week before, for certain—nor all the week before that, I was almost sure
—so if my tail-flowers appeared in a few days, then all would be well.*

If not . . .

*These would be the longest weeks of all my life. Already I felt a year older
than the woman who had set out so hopefully only this morning. A day had
passed. One day. Could I believe so little time had divided me from what I
was, and what I now had to be?*

*I forced my fist between my teeth, biting my knuckles to hold back the
tears.*

*But if I lost my throne, found myself at Mary's mercy, how would I be
then?*

*And if I found myself threatened with the block, then like a woman taken
in theft and due for the rope's end, might I not be glad to "plead my belly,"
as they say, to get off with my life?*

Yet what life? I could not have believed there was so much pain. I was
like one who has lost his arms and legs; I rolled in a mist of pain, through
a maze of pain. And losing Robin, I scarcely cared if Norfolk triumphed,
if the North turned against me, if I lost life and all.

He came at last, Norfolk, riding to London just as Cecil sent an army to flush him out. The great traitor arrived protesting that he never meant harm to me, that he had sent messages to the North to forbid the Earls who were his fellow traitors to rise.

I would not see him—I would have spat in his face, the Judas! Betray me with *her?* I could have had him crucified! Instead, I gave orders that he was to be lodged in the Tower with all the pomp and circumstance due to a royal duke, and blood kin to the crown.

Now came an uneasy peace—all the harder to endure. I could not tell if it was worse to see Robin, or not to see that frozen figure, still stiff and bleak with shock. The whole Court fell into limbo, no word, no movement. September ebbed, the gold and red trees shook their leaves, and Dame Nature serenely disrobed herself for her long winter sleep. But my fear, like my grief, never slept.

"The Duke may be safe. But what of his brother-in-law Westmoreland, what of Northumberland and the Lord Dacres?" I wept to Cecil.

He shook his head. "Nothing."

Day in, day out, nothing.

At last I could bear it no longer. "Send to Sussex," I begged Cecil, "bid him flush out these hidden traitors, command them south in my name, to come here to Court to me, to pledge their allegiance."

Walsingham gave a dry laugh. "They will think Your Majesty intends to give them a straight passage to the Tower, there to lodge with the Duke until you find them narrower lodgings underground! They will not come."

Sussex, too, was aghast. "You will force on the very thing you dread, open rebellion!" he wrote. "For knowing that Your Majesty knows of their treachery, and fearing the block, they will have nothing to lose."

But I was past caring. *"Do my bidding!"* I sent back by anguished post. "Better by far to spring them from their ambush than give them time to perfect their treasons and grow strong against me. *Do it!"*

Now more war councils, more candles, less sleep, more tears. And now a man before me nursing a useless arm, his shoulder dislocated by a fall in his headlong flight. "The North is in rebellion, the traitors have struck! All the church bells ring backwards as the sign to raise the people. The treacherous Earls have led their armies as far as Durham Cathedral, where the Mass is said at the High Altar, all the English Bibles burned, and they swear by the rood to make a Pilgrimage of Grace, as in your father's time, to restore the Old Faith and put the Scots Queen on your throne."

One fire drives out one fire—one nail, one nail, they say.

That shaking terror, that skin-crawling fear for my life, for my throne, worse than the worst I suffered under Mary, put the pain of Robin a little from my mind—from time to time at least.

But fire or flesh—each holds seeds of pain that cannot be described.

"Why, sir, what's this?"

So tired . . .

"A candle, nearer, for Her Majesty—"

So tired . . . my eyes blinked at the parchment.

Cecil met my glance unflinching. One finger, stained with his recent endless toil of enscribing musters, war rolls, orders to and fro, traced the black-letter flourishes at the head of the great scroll: "A Warrant for the Execution of . . ."

"For the execution of the Queen of Scots?"

He nodded. "Merely a precaution, Majesty—in the event that the rebels push through as far as Coventry, show any likelihood of laying their hands on what must be the chief card in their game, the Queen—"

Even so had my sister Mary stared at such a warrant against me, when her bloody Bishop Gardiner and her Spanish advisers sought my life. Even so would Scots Mary reach eagerly for the quill if a warrant against me lay now before her. Even so my father . . . my mother . . .

I could not stop the screaming. "Away with it, I will not sign it, away, away, *away!"*

I could not even look at it.

But that was when it first came into mind.

But Sussex held, and the Earls broke, wandering south with a Papist rabble and no plan of campaign. Derby held fast, for all my fears, and Shrewsbury too, and the only fighting was between my cousin Hunsdon with his son George—God! Was that boy of his old enough to fight?— and the Lord Dacres, who carried his coward's guts as fast from the field as if the Devil were after him, to join his partners in evil over the Border in Scotland, whence most made good their escape to the Low Countries, France or Denmark.

We had won.

If a woman could be said to have won who had lost all.

And I slept no easier in my bed. For as one of the traitors, huffing brimstone, wrote from the continent, "This was but the first bloody bickering, and it will not be the last!"

Yet, for a while, it seemed we had cut off the snake's head. Norfolk wrote grovelling, begging off death with the promise of reform, and loud pledges that he never meant the treachery I saw in his hopes of marrying the Queen.

"And his actions fall short of high treason, madam," Cecil advised me. "For he held back at the last."

"What? Not treason?" I screamed. But I had to give way.

And I had no wish to kill him—I lacked something of my father's relish for the taste of human blood. The Duke had had a sound scare, as I thought—nothing like feeling the axe blade at your neck, and your neck upon the block, for recalling a wanderer to his allegiance! As Christmas came then, with the other traitors all despatched or fled, I lost the will to keep him locked up anymore. And in the New Year, when God knows I was praying for the hope of new beginnings, I allowed him out of the Tower to house arrest in his palace of the Charterhouse—one of the finest of London's noble homes, and therefore no great suffering.

And as February's end unlocked the frozen rivers and the icebound roads, I gave Cecil his reward: in a private ceremony I raised him to stand equal with my other loyal peers—Sir William no longer, but "Arise, Lord Burghley of Stamford Burghley, in the county of Lincolnshire!"

Yes, it reminded me of the same ceremony when I made Robin Earl of Leicester. But what was one more pain among so many?

Yet my heart dared not unfreeze with winter's thaw. For Mary festered still, her poison fixed in my side, the legacy of her deeds still bloodying her wretched country. That same month saw her half-brother and our ally, the Regent Moray, fall to a hail of bullets, his assassins a rival clan greedy to grip the Regency into their hands. At least my young godson, the six-year-old King James, had taken no hurt in the bloody struggle to gain control of him. But the whole of Scotland now was up in arms. Now Mary's faithful saw their chance to set their mistress back on the throne, and in a series of bold raids, the Marians, as they called themselves, struck to and fro until I was forced to send Sussex north again to fire the Borders and bring a plague on both their houses.

Pax nobiscus, Deus ultionem . . . *Give us peace in our time, O Lord, for thine only is the vengeance, thine to repay . . .*

Peace?

Fond hope when the Anti-Christ himself was stirring against us! Now in the sewers of the Vatican, the Romish rat twitched once again, the monster guts rumbled, the fundament heaved, and like a nightmare from my past, voided out the fragrant tribute of another Papal Bull.

Never was such a stinking heap of dung!

. . . Elizabeth, pretended Queen of England and servant of evil, has seized the crown from our true daughter Mary and monstrously usurped the supreme authority of head of the Church, reducing our land of the true and faithful to miserable ruin . . .

. . . therefore we call her a heretic and a traitor and do deprive her of her titles, strip her like a whore and hurl her into darkness, outcast and excommunicate her from all fellowship of God's Church . . .

And with this we do absolve her subjects of all allegiance to her, and forbid any to obey her laws. And those who disobey our will and Bull are likewise excommunicated and cast down to Hell forever.

"Madam, we have him!"

Waving the Papal proclamation, Walsingham flamed with his triumph. "We caught the Catholic traitor in the act of nailing this to the door of St. Paul's—they are racking him now!"

Oh, that Felton, he was a watershed! Until then I had tried to make no windows in men's souls—tried not to see Catholics as traitors, as my enemies, or enemies of the State.

But now . . .

He died bravely, that terrible death of traitors, and God be praised, even loyally too—on the scaffold he kissed a great diamond, the sum of all his wealth, and willed it to me. By doing that he left his widow destitute: I ordered her a pension to keep her from the streets. He had paid his debt. But he set in chain a process that would take legions of good men with him.

Oh, that rogue Pope—that Holy Farter, not Father, for whose foul flatulence good people died!—that cretin in his castellated cap, with his mitred head, muff ears and devil's delight in making *merde* into malice. Did the fool never see that nothing was more calculated to stir up hate against his dear daughter Mary than these dangerous diversions?

"Give me leave, madam," Walsingham urged, "give us more powers. The Catholics are upon us, we must search harder!"

He wore the look I remembered from the first time I saw him, when he brought the word of the Huguenots slain in France. He still saw, I was certain, the women screaming with their breasts cut off, heard the cries of mothers and children burning alive in their churches. For every one of those poor Protestant deaths, if he could help it, a Catholic would pay back in double pain. Yet he was the fit instrument to my hand now. I nodded. "Do what you need to, sir. Go to it."

A week later he brought an Italian to my chamber. "The Signor is a banker, Majesty, a native of Florence, and a man of parts—mark him, my lady."

"Signor, you are most welcome."

"Serenissima! Roberto Ridolfi kisses your hands, your feet, the hem of your gown . . ."

Ridolfi . . .

"He is a double agent," Walsingham whispered me as my new gallant's bow swept his silver buckles, "for the Pope, but now in our pay too—mark him!"

Oh, I marked him, and marked him the more when Ridolfi the double agent doubled again, doubling back upon himself and us, going between Mary the Queen and none other than that lost soul the Duke of Norfolk.

For now he was lost indeed—I could not save him. On the rack his secretary confessed that for all the Duke's lies and protestations, he had not once given up his dream of marrying "the Mermaid Queen." Letters had passed between them, in oilskin packets inside leather bottles. Ridolfi had borne missives from Norfolk to the Pope and to Philip of Spain seeking money and men, arms and support, and promising the Mass throughout England, and Mary to be Queen.

His peers sat in the House of Lords without rising from seven in the morning till eight at night, to sift the charges against him. He could not wriggle out of a single one, but on all the heads of all the dreadful charges, he had only the one guilty head to lay down. And now the warrant lay before me, and none but I could sign it.

Must I take his life?

Twelve good years I had had of my people's love.

Now must it be hate?

I wept and prayed, thrashing myself like a fish caught in a net as I tried to escape what even the Duke himself now accepted as his due. Three times I tore the parchment and would not sign, and three times my new Lord Burghley, every whit as patient as the old Cecil, brought it afresh. And on the coldest day of the summer, the first nobleman of my reign stepped onto the scaffold to give his life for his treason.

My father sluiced the steps of his throne in blood, so freely did he kill all those who stood near it—and I could not put an end to one who had plotted my death?

No.

For now Parliament was howling for another blood sacrifice, the head of Mary—"the dragon-scorpion who would sting your life to death!" she was called. Very true—but I could not do it.

Though she sought my death, I fought to save her life.

Had to fight, had to take up arms.

Lost my love.

Became a queen of war.

THE ENVOY TO MY THIRD BOOK

Only this.

Farewell, Robin.

Adieu, my love.

Now welcome a loyal friend, a true warrior in my cause—my cause of war, as we now saw it coming, growing from a cloud no bigger than a man's hand to a storm and tempest blackening all the world. Never did he fail me, in private or in public, never cease to treat me with shining devotion, as he always had.

And never did he reproach me for that day when I was his, and not his— when I took but would not give, and gave but would not take.

Never did he or I thereafter speak of it.

We never kissed again, flirted again, made love with our eyes, tongues, hands, voices or lutes—never played again upon the virginals nor on the man-dolin.

I know I always queened it in his heart. But on that day, I knew I had given up the right to know what was in his heart.

And the world darkened now down to destruction. Our sweet spring was blown away by the harsh blasts of war. I did not like now what I saw in my glass, and my teeth ached me now more often than not.

The doe that would be mated by the lion must die for love.

Farewell, love.

Here Ends
the Third Book
-LIBER TERTIUS-
of My History

BELLONA

Book the Fourth

-*LIBER QUARTUS*-

of My History

Bella, Bellona, Belladonna . . .

So love fled weeping, flew away out of my life. And in the place of Cupid came another killer boy, the young god Mars.

But before God came Magna Mater, the Great Goddess, the Great Mother of us all. And so before Mars came Bellona, the great war goddess, the mother, sister, wife and herald of Mars himself.

You do not know of her?

Pah, they teach children nothing in school these days! Bellona it was who heard the first whisperings of war wherever they awoke throughout the world, and called forth her warrior son.

To Bellona as Queen of War belonged the honour of the first footing on the field of battle. Bellona it was who readied Mars for war, handing him his sword and shield with holy spells and incantations to ensure victory through her magic, black and white. And Bellona oversaw the mourning for the fallen, aided by her priest-gladiators, heroes who had all survived untold battles to the death.

I was Bellona now.

And Mars was the only child I ever had—for yes, my courses brought the monthly blood-blossoms before the week was out, and no, I was not with child. Do I regret it? Only when my blood is low and my cold nights lonely, and my mornings hungry for small smiling company, not cheese and ale.

But I regret that my only offspring was this child called War—that I was forced to be the Mother of Battles, of the war between Spain and England, the greatest battle the world has ever known. That was another courtesy I had to thank cousin Mary for, for it was her work. She it was who sowed the dragon's teeth, she who pulled down the temple of peace around our ears, blind, blind and stupid as she was.

Stupid, but strong—as strong as Samson eyeless in Gaza, at the mill with slaves. For like the great Israelite she, too, had a supernatural gift, the gift of destruction. She was the daughter of Discord himself, born in time of war, suckled by Conflict like the incubus she was.

And she brought discord with her—it was the element in which she moved and throve and had her being. She would not, could not cease her plotting, cease trying to stir up the other Catholic kings against me. So my song changed from "Come Away, Love" to an endless chant of war.

For Philip still loved me, festering in Spain, and his love was death, hatred and death.

LIV

So Norfolk paid for his sins with his head, and so did I not pay for mine with my body. For through this treason I lost Robin, I lost my peace of mind in my own kingdom, and for the first time now I heard the evil whispering in my head: *Her life or yours . . . her life or yours . . .*

Would I have married Robin?

Like all lovers, I believed I could be mine and his. But I could never be both his and England's. And when England called, when she stood at the stake beset by dogs like Norfolk, vampires like Mary, whose blood should be given for her, whose nerve and bone and sinew should be cracked for her, whose heart broken for her, but mine, and only mine?

Any who say that suffering ennobles have never truly suffered. Now my world and all the people in it were ugly beyond belief. Now I saw them as if for the first time, the ugly, limping beggar, the one-eyed crone, the scarred, the toothless, the pockmarked, the dribbling naturals, the shit-shotten imbeciles, the plague-burst rats, the hanged dogs. Now I was sour, screaming or tetchy as the mood took me, veering from spite to grief like a weathercock. And in this state, to play the lovesick virgin, ape a woman in search of a husband? Could I do this?

England expects . . .

Oh, how hard it was! Yet my body had to turn again for England's sake, for with the new threat against us, the plots of the pox-brained Pope and Ridolfi his pawn, now I had to set to again to find England friends and partners in a Europe growing colder every day. And how could I do this except by going courting, soliciting suitors, the old marriage trick?

And this was not the least of my purgatory then.

"She sought your throne—your life!"

Through speaker after speaker, newly convened in terror of my death, Parliament was baying for Mary's blood—"that monstrous dragon, that mass of evil!" as they called her. Yet though I wished her dead, I would not be her executioner. And alone of all England, it seemed, I saw the danger, for in any death of hers I clearly saw the pattern of my own: those who pulled her down could do the same for me! Nor did they see, those self-opinionated, puffed-up men, that all their other schemes and devices to hit at Mary and keep her off my throne would strike at her son too—the boy James—on whom, for England's sake, I kept a more than godmotherly eye. Alone, then, I stood up amid the howling Commons, and amid their stinking breath and reeking regicide, I hurled their violence back in their teeth.

"What?" I cried, "would you have me throw to the hawks the dove that fled to my feet to escape from the storm?"

"Then marry! Marry!" they yelped.

Oh God, must I?

What could I offer? I demanded of my midnight glass, and flinched at its honest answer. A sad-eyed spinster, whose fortieth winter was creeping up this fall, her first bloom gone, her skin shadowed now with loss, sallowed with midnight weeping, showing the fatal *lignes d'amertume,* the bitter wrinkles carving their furrows from nose to mouth—a mouth now holding in the teeth of the left-hand cheek by scarcely a thread, the others now yellowing despite the best of Parry's cloths and powders, gold toothpicks and tooth washes of white wine and aquafortis, vinegar and honey . . .

Not to mention another disintegration, the condition of my heart. That night I had tried to talk to Robin. "Robin, I—"

But with an infinitely sad shake of his head, he laid his finger on my lips, kissed my hand and went away.

The next day came a true-love knot fashioned all of pearls—pearls for virginity, pearls for tears. I wept a river then.

And in this state, to go shopping for a husband?

Yet what did the future hold for all of us—for England—if I did not?

Was I only ever to be married to England? And was England to be merry at my expense?

They laughed already behind their hands, I was all too sure of that as I wept and raged in my chamber—laughed at my loneliness, now that Robin had left me.

Left me?

The bruised shadows round his steadfast gaze told me that in his eyes I had left him. Yet we walked, talked, debated in Council and outside, even danced as we did before. If the tears came for me, they came when there were none around to see. And all eyes were upon us now, day and night. None knew what had passed between us, but all could see that he and I were not as we once were. The ripening year saw us all on one of those wearisome great progresses that became so famous with the people —and the next summer took us roaming through no fewer than five of my counties, Bedford and Berkshire, Hertford and Warwickshire and even past Watford, as far north as Rutland and Leicestershire.

And Leicester who was Robin came in my train, though at a distance now. And even from a distance I could see he was not long unconsoled, with all the women of the Court fluttering about him like moths to his flame. The two pert daughters of my old great-uncle Howard, Lady Frances and the other one, the one they had named Douglas after her mother's family, she who had married Lord Sheffield—

And I—I danced at her wedding—how was I to know?

—she, the Douglas, and her sister too, that pair of little harpies vied with each other for his every glance, and I had to sit, to watch, to dance, as both played out their lines for him, played fast and loose for him, and were played upon in their turn by the ever-present, ever-more-hated hot-eyed Lettice, who now seemed to fancy herself queen of all the ladies.

And I—oh, I played too, longer, harder, freer, faster and looser, than even he could dare.

"Majesty, I beg—"

"Deign to give me the honour—"

"Lady, throw a dog who loves you one bare bone—a glance, a smile, your hand for the next volta—"

"Madam, I claim the right—!"

They were all round me now, my gentlemen, my Esquires of the Body and my knights, and I clung to them for comfort. Was it me they loved, my money and my power to reward, or my power over them? I knew better than to ask. And they knew better than to treat me as a money box! The front-runners of the pack were Heneage, my Tom, with his hard and watchful look, his hard and watchable body, and the young de Vere, Earl of Oxford, new up at Court from Cambridge, where he had been Burghley's ward and married his daughter. Oxford was a handsome, sly-eyed villain with a mouth like a scar and a tongue that ran on wheels of malice, but his gossip gave me at least a little diversion. After Robin he was the best dancer at Court, and to take his hand, to follow his sure footing as he threaded me through a lightsome reel or showed off a new step he had learned that dawn from his dancing master, was some salve to my poor aching heart.

And other hearts ached too, though I knew it not. That day at Kew when I parted from Robin, one faithful soul on his knees before me saw as much as any ever did. The next day he knelt at my feet again, a parchment in his hand, his brown eyes bright with standing tears. "Majesty, read!"

Wondering, I took the scroll from his trembling hand, and read the opening lines:

> *I saw my lady weep . . .*
> *And Sorrow proud to be advanced so . . .*

With the parchment was a jewel, a tiny love bud of rose rubies with emeralds for leaves, all set in chased gold. But to me the most priceless jewels were the diamonds standing in his eyes.

Oh, the comfort of a man's love! I had to have it! And who would not love a man who wept for your suffering, felt it in his blood, along his very heart? Before I knew it, my hand had stretched out to his soft dark auburn beard, stroking the jutting jaw, soothing the crinkled curls.

"Oh, Kit! My dearest Hatton . . ."

But though I could share his tears, no man must see mine. "Come, sir!" I cried with hectic gaiety. "Give me your hand, let's dance! And tell me your true opinion, shall I marry the French Monsieur or not?"

For now another of the sons of the old Queen of France, Catherine de' Medici, was beckoning me to the altar. First was the boy Charles she offered me, you remember, who became King after Francis, Mary's husband, himself still only a boy, died of his festered ear? Now the next brother, chafing at the bit, jealous and idle, was threatening trouble. At a small conference in my chamber, a handful of my lords pondered the overture.

"To marry him out of France, securing him a kingdom along the way, would be no mean policy for Madame the Queen his mother, if she could pull it off!" was my cousin Knollys's sardonic view.

"Yet he sounds horrid!" I objected like a schoolgirl, pulling out the report from our Embassy in Paris. "Debauched and viciously cross-grained, they say, going to whores to beat them afterwards!" Angrily I found another document in the pile. "And the holy hypocrite writes me here that he must have the right to Mass in public, yes, in our most sacred places, St. Paul's and Westminster too!"

Sussex gaped, his good red English face going even redder. "Why, he might as well call for bell, book and candle, and all the rotten flummery of Rome to be restored in these isles—if we pocket up this one, madam, give a good welcome to the Pope next week!"

"My lord?" I turned agitatedly to Robin.

But he bowed his head. "Your Majesty will do as she thinks fit."

What did I want of him?

Something—

Not that!

"Where is Burghley?" I demanded fretfully. "Why is he not here?"

"Your Majesty gave him leave to go to Bath—to take the waters for his gout . . ."

"Oh yes, oh yes," I grumbled. "Well then, there can be no decision until he returns. Tell the French so."

"As you command, Majesty, so it shall be."

But from the eye-work round the table, I could see my lords well knew that I wanted nothing of this French suitor, even if Burghley had been there to dance a jig on one tiptoe before me. And my Burghley, whose sure sleight of hand was no whit impaired by the grievance in his great toe, secured for us an agreement to agree, a treaty at Blois.

Robin came to me in the Presence with all the other petitioners, hat in hand, and a small, drab, pasty figure in tow. "A boon, Majesty. My nephew Philip now leaves the university—let him blood his spurs in your service, send him with your commissioners to Blois—"

Outside, the blossoms glistened like pearls, like tears, on the new springtime boughs, and the air gleamed fresh as the first dawn—

Philip—the son of my former lady-in-waiting Mary, the child who had taken the pocks from his mother when she took them from me—and Henry Sidney's child too, the son of my dead brother's most faithful friend. But most of all, Robin's nephew—

"Granted."

—for your dear sake, I did not say.

But as he kissed my hand, his eyes thanked me and loved me, and mine loved him. And though he was shy and tongue-tied before me, the boy did well, Burghley said, as did the treaty, which, for the meanwhile, was almost as good as if we had married England to France.

"Yet I favour the French offer of marriage, as before I favoured the Archduke Charles, my lady," Burghley told me gravely, "and for the same reason. For now more than ever do I fear the might of Spain."

As who did not?

Yes, I feared and fretted too.

How had I lost King Philip's love?

For gone it was, though I knew not how it went.

He had loved me once, I knew it—I had seen it. When first we met I felt his eyes upon me, lingering in my neck, fingering my bodice and feeling for my breasts, my belly, trying to probe all my most secret parts. He loved me then, I knew. How did his love turn to such a storm of hate?

He had his own love in that time, for he loved his little French wife the

Regent Catherine's daughter as any man loved woman, so I heard. But another loved her, too, whose love was nefast, the forbidden sin, the sin for which Oedipus was damned by all the world. God help him, Philip's own son, the monster Carlos, was now become his Minotaur: he had buried the boy alive in the labyrinth of his palace-cathedral, the Escorial, and what was meant as a living monument to God was now a living grave.

A grave to hide a Minotaur who was Oedipus too—for this sport of Satan had tried to ravish his father's wife, the beautiful young Isabella, who was then with child. And she, miscarrying, lost her reason with her child, and her dear life with both. And Philip went by night with a priest and a few men, and in full armour, with his own hands, for he would not put such a sin on any other, praying and weeping, took the creature's life.

Small wonder, then, that all his love, all his hope and joy, and whatever warmth of blood he had in his thin veins, now turned to ashes and diamonds: ashes of all his dreams, to dry up his life's river at its source; diamonds to deceive with flattering brightness and meanwhile cut him to death, the death of a thousand cuts.

And so, like me, Philip knew his Calvary.

"And like us, Philip fears France, madam," urged Walsingham, his dark face jaundiced with the inner enmity that always gnawed at him. "Though France and Spain are supposed to be on the same side of the blanket, as good Catholics all, yet the King of Spain fears the French are not true in religion, so strong are their Huguenots. He fears, too, the fiery temper of their fighting men, more savage than any he can call upon in time of war."

Walsingham's eyes were pinpoints of live coal. I nodded slowly. "Go, then, and see for me, sir, be you my eyes . . . ."

No, not my Ô Ô, not my "eyes," there could never be another Robin . . .

"Be my ears," I resumed huskily, and then, looking at his black burning stare and tawny complexion: "No, Francis, go and fight for me, be my Moor!"

He gave a thin-lipped smile. "And like the Moors of old, so may I prevail against the dread might of Spain! For their hostility is certain, madam—we may not escape it. Now God defend us, as our cause is just!"

One muttered word was thick in every throat: *"Amen!"*

So in huddled conclaves and furious debates, time wore away. That July saw a treaty of peace between us and Spain, but the unwritten codicil was *for how long?* And our fear fed on Philip's fear, and our hate on his hate. The war chief Alva and his massed legions menaced us only twenty miles away across the Channel: we stopped the money ships that fed his men, he closed the ports to English shipping; we harrassed Spain's treasure ships from the Canaries to the Azores, he murdered our hapless, helpless merchants in The Hague.

Yet how true Walsingham's words were we were yet to find. For on another sunless day of early spring, another black-clad messenger from France stood eyes downcast before me, just as he had when Mary's Francis died, and told me that my would-be husband, Monsieur the King's brother, was dead too.

I wept for Catherine—witch of old Italy though she was, how could she bear to suffer like Niobe the loss of all her children, one by one? Nor had Fate finished cutting his sickle swathe through her poor brood, as time was to show.

Yet the heart in that squat ugly body never failed its cunning owner. Dauntless as ever, she sent new word, defying death. "Yet have I another son, my Francis, the finest gentleman of France and now to be Duke of Anjou, who shall be yours, madam, if you like of him."

I smiled a grim smile as I read her *communiqué*. She would stop at nothing to place one of her brood beside me on my throne! But I could work that wish to England's gain. I had myself arrayed in a gown of glowing russet worked with gold and silver, a high-standing ruff and shoulder gauze of silver tinsel, with the finest porcelain complexion money now could buy and Parry's new device, hairpieces to bulk out my coiffeur crowned with pearls and Tudor roses, until I knew that I looked *la plus fine femme du monde*. What if my heart . . . ? Enough! England expects.

"Tell your mistress," I informed the scraping Ambassador, Fénélon, waving a hand so jewelled I could hardly lift it, "that I may well like of the Prince your master, if I may see him."

None of my suitors had ever dared to cross the seas to beg for my hand. Would this one now? I was gambling that French greed for this rich prize, myself, my throne and the wealth of my kingdom, would draw the fox from his lair. Would it do so?

What crossed the seas before him was a blow that killed my heart and almost killed all hopes of this union dead in my hand. Walsingham's fastest man, stinking of over-sweated horse, brought from Paris letters in hands that trembled, news in a voice that broke in stifled weeping as he tried to speak.

"The Queen ordered it, and the King agreed it . . . all the Huguenots, every man jack . . . and not just the men! . . . oh, God, madam, the babes, the children and the women! . . . never have I seen . . . you would not credit it . . . all, all . . ."

He could not speak for sobbing, and no wonder. But his papers spoke for him. On St. Bartholomew's Day, which the people call the Feast of Barnaby the Bright, in a hot June of madness uncontrollable, the French Catholics rose against the Protestants and from Paris all through France hunted and killed them with the cruelty of Satan. Women with child disembowelled of babe and all, men with their privities hacked off and stuffed in their mouths, virgins raped back and front till their innards ruptured and their fundaments split, infants spitted over slow fires—in every town were scenes from Purgatory itself.

"Remember when this happened once before?" Walsingham sent despatches flaming from the safety of his house in the fields at St-Germain-des-Prés. "That was a Whitsun ale-tide pastoral to this!"

"Full mourning—for all the Court!" was my one word before I shut myself up to weep and pray.

And when Fénélon limped in the next day to make his mistress's lame excuses, all he saw were solid ranks of black from the meanest guard to the Queen herself, a living wall of black reproaching that vast cruelty, that unspeakable shame.

"For which my lord the Duke of Anjou will come and kiss hands for his chastisement at your hands, make his *devoirs* on his knees in person to you," Fénélon declared.

Que voulez-vous? as the French say.

What could I do?

For if she had lost the English Queen through her vile act, Walsingham's best spy discovered Catherine de' Medici had another stratagem. Her son would marry Mary of Scots, get the throne of England by the back door, by dint of marrying the Tudor "heiress," then asserting his wife's rights.

"What? Marry *Mary?*"

My screams were heard from Hampton Court to Yorkshire, to the castle-fortress where cousin Mary lay. They shook out the tooth I had hung on to for so long that I thought it was safe forever. My megrims then and the pains in my face lasted the best part of a month. Yet for all that, in the end I had to put my pride in my pocket, bite my tongue and smile—for with Spain hostile and the Scots untamed, we had to have the French against the rest of the world!

And through all this I saw Robin watching me, always watching.

LV

Robin watching, all men watching.

I walked on a pavement of eyes, and what they saw, no man would tell. It did not seem to lessen, the pain of losing him.

And watching him watching me, the ever-watchful fox-faced Lettice, with the two silly Howard goose girls always tittupping around his elbows —*look at me! look at me!*—like the dimwits they were . . .

Yet I knew his love was unchanged!

I saw it every day in his eyes, in the thousand ways he strove to aid and support me. And that summer progress, when we passed by his castle of Kenilworth and he filled the moat with sea nymphs singing of love, I could almost fancy that I could still lean into that strong body now beside me on the dais just as I always used to, touch his face again, kiss him again, take him again as I had done before—

Almost—but not quite.

God, but my little body was aweary of the world!

And the world wagged on careless of me or my weariness. And others felt their own pace picking up and danced to its beat.

"Madam, give me your blessing or I—we—cannot thrive!"

"What are you saying, Snakenborg?"

After years of waiting, my sweet Helena, the love-pale Princess of the North who had come to me in the Swedish royal train so many years before, was to wed her old wooer, the Earl, now Marquis, of Northampton.

And wed him she did, and I stood gossip and supporter to the dear girl, and if old Parr, the Marquis her groom, made me think sadly of his long-dead sister Katherine, once my "mother-in-love," on this special day I kept it to myself. We had bride cakes and bride ale, teal and widgeon, shelldrake and shoveller, peewit, pigeon, partridge and pheasant, and as we dined, at each course trumpets and kettledrums made the hall ring. And afterwards we danced, I with my Hatton, Heneage and Oxford, and Robin with the Douglas—only from pity, I felt sure, since her husband Sheffield six months since had died, of a bloody flux.

I danced at that wedding too—what was I, Death? For Death was there among the guests for both these unsuspecting bridegrooms. Within six months of his marriage was old Edward Parr, who had served like Jacob six years to win his Rachel, dead too, of an apoplexy.

And summer or no, Death knew no long vacation like the lawyers. From the funerary rites I was called back by fastest horse to Whitehall, where the summer's plague-dead still lay rotting in the streets, because those dogs of Ireland were at their lords' throats again.

"The club-headed Catholic kerns are up again in fierce rebellion!" reported my cousin Knollys, in one of his dark Puritan rages. "No nation is more savage—who will Your Majesty send as your Captain-General and Lord Governor to put them down?"

"Oh, God—!"

I hesitated, and he pounced. "May I, Your Majesty, beg the preferment for my son-in-law?"

"The Viscount Hereford, young Walter Devereux?"

"He. A good soldier, madam, and as loyal as they come."

Lettice's husband. I needed no time to brood. "He shall go."

Then it was necessary to give him the honour to act for me in my place and name, to strike terror into the hearts of those foul Irish hobgoblins, those cormorant gobblers of my money and my men! As cousin Knollys had doubtless calculated, it must be an earldom—and I had a fatal fancy to make it Essex, make him Earl of Essex . . .

What was that whim?

The Viscount Hereford, who had been Walter Devereux, was of course the husband of Lettice, and a governor's wife would go with him to his new residence . . . Did I choose him just to get rid of her? But if so, why Essex?

At any rate, I chose him and I ennobled him, and so the rest ensued.

Now with Ireland up, it was more urgent than ever to sweeten France, to keep the French out of the weakened Catholic back doors of our kingdom.

"Where is my Prince? Does your master come?" I demanded of the patchouli-pomaded Fénélon. God, how his smirking stuck in my gizzard along with his scent! And all this with Robin looking on . . .

"He sends you his best proxy," Fénélon assured me with a *faux-gallant* flourish. "Our choicest courtier, and Monsieur's best friend, comes as his *courier du coeur*, the Lord Simier."

"*Coeur*, says he!" Hatton's laugh was harsh and too loud, his eyes glaring. "Better for England if our Queen kept her own heart here at home!"

"Kit, hush!" I chided him, laying my finger to his strong red lips. Yet I was pleased with his jealous protests. I made him Captain of the Queen's Own Guard, and to see him bedecked in black and gold, those fine long legs of his flashing in black silk, cheered me a little.

And with Robin gone, Hatton's love was a comfort to me, yes, even his jealousy.

"My lord of Leicester?"

"Hush, Kit!" I kissed my fingers and laid them to his lips. "An absent lord is no lord, you are my favourite now." After this, as summer warmed from May on into June, as the red cockle-flowers drove the white campion from the cornfields, so his adoration grew warmer and bolder too. Yet he knew too, as Robin never did, that I could never marry him.

And when I saw him kneeling before me, his neck bent, his brown eyes flecked with little amber lights about the pupils, his face all love close beside me in the quiet of my chamber, on a velvet evening when the air was warm with honeysuckle and I with a little wine, it seemed the only reward for his true love to take that strong face between my two hands and kiss that wide, deep mouth . . .

Yet the Lord Simier when he came, braving winter's mountainous seas the next January, black eyes snapping and fine flourishes two a-penny, made even my handsome Hatton look like a maypole rustic.

"Madame, *mon prince le duc d'Anjou* kisses your feet—I am sent to whisper in your ear his *chanson d'amour*—"

Amour!

Parlez-moi d'amour!

Encore!

Encore l'amour!

The very word in French sounds better to the ear, feels better in the mouth, raises the blood, stiffens the sinews of the heart. To look at Simier, a man supremely at ease in his own well-tended, slight but shapely body, his subtle, well-cut doublet of taupe silk making our English fashions with their peascod bellies suddenly out of style, his clever fragrance teasing at the senses with its hint of Indian spice, was to renew the excitement to be had from men.

"Ma belle dame, si j'ose . . ."

"Lady, if I dare . . ."

A poem in my glove, a rose on my pillow, a consort of music underneath my chamber window on a May morning—*chanson d'amour, plaisir d'amour, maladie d'amour, toujours l'amour*—he courted me, wooed me till I felt all the exquisite sensations of being loved. Oh, tell me I was foolish! An old fool too, the worst kind of all! What else did I have? If it was a charade, I meant to play it to the hilt. And if against all the odds I loved the Prince when he came, it was through the skill of Simier, the servant who had made straight the way for his master.

With consummate art—for if we on the English side were peddling porcelain a little cracked beneath the glaze, the French were selling damaged goods indeed.

"I fear Monsieur will give you no contentment of the eye," wrote Walsingham with magisterial understatement from our Embassy in Paris, "for besides being somewhat misshaped, and so undersized that his baptismal name of Hercule has had to be changed to his dead brother's name of Francois, he is so villainously pockmarked that his whole face is punched like leather, even to the tip of his huge inhuman nose."

And what, thanked be Jesus, my Moor had the tact not to say: Monsieur has not yet seen twenty summers, you, madam, forty-odd . . .

How was I over forty? How could it be, God help us! Or help me, at any rate?

"I like him not!" stormed Hatton, fiery as his scarlet satin. "If I must have a rival, let it be a red-blooded Englishman, not a toad of our old enemy, France!"

A red-blooded Englishman? There was only one for me. But what Robin thought I could only guess. He was away often from Court now, and when he returned, he seemed indifferent, and not only to me. I took a savage glee in seeing that he now grew cold to the silly widow Douglas, who, whenever he left Court, departed too, in a great huff. Yet to no avail in rekindling his attention. And she, instead of pining away as the ballads always have women do, lost her wasp's waist and grew of a sudden fat.

"What, does the Douglas eat to console herself?" I demanded of Kate Carey.

"She must do, madam," was the reply. Kate would not meet my eye. I understood. She must be as embarrassed as they all were now to talk of him—but I knew he still loved me, and I could guess now how he felt.

But from what he did, guessing was not hard. And as the Douglas begged leave to go from Court to diet herself back to health and figure, and so ceased to pester him, he had time to play cat and mouse with me!

And play he did. For days after the French delegation's arrival, to my annoyance I saw no sight of Simier. At last I sent for him. His excuse was plain enough: "Majesty, my lord of Leicester told me you were indisposed, and must not be disturbed."

A simple trick—but my lord had a thousand.

"Madam, my wish you know," said Burghley, leaning heavily on his stick to spare his sickly leg. "It is that Your Majesty may marry to give us joy of a child"—*before it is too late!* hovered unspoken between us—"and so make safe our kingdom. But my lord of Leicester foresees violent

disturbance, riots like those when your sister married the King of Spain
—he raises fears in Council, where he swears that the English will never
accept a Frenchman as their King."

I nodded impassively. "Says he so?"

Burghley gave a gouty smile. "Of course, my lord thinks merely as a
good Protestant who fears the return of the Papal Anti-Christ in our
truth-loving land."

"Of course."

And no more was said.

Robin now had a new dancing partner as another New Year was born in
an evil, treacherous, pinching, sleeting January—and it was another
widow, for the Earl of Essex was dead in Ireland, of another bloody flux,
like Douglas's husband.

Ireland! that deadly place . . .

"I commend my children to Your Grace's care and my Lord Burghley's
keeping," went his last, feeble writing, "my wretched body to the earth,
and all my hopes to God."

He had the finest of funerals, I saw to that. Afterwards I took coach
for Burghley's house by the Convent Garden, and a sad conference with
him. The well-proportioned chamber and roaring fire, the fine furnish-
ings and exquisite hangings, the warm honey-flavoured wine, sugared
suckets and other comfits, brought small comfort to me. "Another good
man gone! And the upbringing of his boy on you!" I sighed. "A heavy
charge!"

Burghley shifted his stiff leg and shook his head. "The boy will be
companion for my Robert—who, had I perished like the Earl in Your
Majesty's service, I would hope might find a second parent in your love."

I nodded. I had forgot his Robert, the poor misshapen thing who
against all odds had lived and even proved, so his father said, though
dwarfish, a sweet imp of nature, with a precocious wit as sure as Burghley's own.

"Will Your Majesty give the new Earl your blessing?"

"Poor child! Yes, willingly."

Burghley clapped his hands. I could not forbear a savage smile as the
three black-clad forms knelt before me. Like her or not, Lettice had been
a fair breeder!

"Your Majesty!"

"Majesty—"

"Majesty—"

"Arise!"

Of the fatherless flock, the two girls, Penelope and Dorothy, were a pair of golden beauties ripe for marriage. Behind stood a tall lad of a dozen or so winters, the new Earl.

"Come hither, boy!"

His eyes were bright, unfathomable, as he stepped up towards me on the dais. Beneath his soft black cap with its ebony plume, a streak of auburn hair glowed in the winter chamber.

So like Robin's at that age . . .

"Tell me, sir, what do they call you?"

He had the eyes of a hawk, proud, fierce and wary. "Robin, Your Majesty."

Robin.

I pulled myself up and laughed at his solemn face. "My lord Earl—it is customary, greeting a queen, to remove one's headgear!"

He stiffened, flushed, and with a furious glance, tore off his cap and cast it to the ground. I felt a strange compulsion—*for the sake of his dead father? Yet I neither knew nor cared for him*—and leaning forward, took him to my bosom. With a wild start, he shrank from me and turned his face away.

"Robin! For shame!"

It was Penelope, his elder sister, by her mortified look half-dead at the rudeness of her graceless sibling.

"No matter, my dear!"

And I, laughing again, released him, and dismissed him from my presence and my mind.

Should I have known then?

Too young for the university, he was sent back to his far estates. Then with the two beauties made wards of the Earl of Huntingdon, the widow Lettice was now single again at Court and determined to conquer all my lords' hearts.

One above all.

"D'you dance, my lord?"

All spring, all summer, night after night her bold challenge rang out. When a lady spoke, no gentleman could refuse. I laughed sardonically to see that she embarrassed Robin with her requests far more than most: how she outpaced herself!

For I had all faith in him. Without doubt, as I saw evening after evening in the Presence, my lord liked to be wooed, to lose himself in Lettice's almond-and-cinnamon eyes, her hot glances and beckoning, secret gaze—what man would not? But how she could grate!

"Lord, sir, how you prattle! Can you speak nothing but fine words and poetry?"

It was Lettice, setting about Robin's nephew, the sweet, clever boy

Philip, fluttering her tortoiseshell fan. I squinted across the Presence where the candlelight bloomed on her coppery hair, her unseemly rash of rubies, the great pearl hanging smack in the center of her low forehead, and tried not to hear her common, gurgling laugh as she turned once more to Robin.

"D'you dance, my lord?"

What could he do? I knew he could not favour the coarse charms of that fat-breasted pigeon, after me! And no sooner would he hand her to her place than he would be once more at my side in earnest conversation: "As I was saying, madam, my advice runs against a visit by the French Prince at this time, the people being restive in this high heat of summer . . ."

And all, I hoped, would see as I did what Robin said and did to block the Anjou courtship—the thousand tiny, almost invisible tares and snares he threw in Simier's way—and would know that all he did, he did and said for me.

I still could swear even now that he acted out of love—in his own fashion. But his own fashion cost us dear—God, let me not remember it . . . dear God, dear God . . .

For in Simier he was tangling with a master. Even at the time, I knew that there was nothing personal in Simier's revenge. The French are purely practical in these matters. As time ticked on bringing no progress for his master's suit, blocked now by Robin at every turn and side, Simier saw what he had to do, and did it.

Did it one June evening in the knot-garden at Greenwich, when the sun lay gilding the river, when the cool air off the water fell like a charm after the heat of the day, and the low sound of voices chanting to a *cor anglais* had just died away.

They were singing "O Faithless Heart," the little consort of boys and their master from my Chapel Royal.

Simier leaned forward on his cushions, exquisite in sage green and emeralds, his neat hand reaching for his wine. "Tell me, Majesty," he said easily, "what think you—of my lord of Leicester's marriage?"

LVI

You knew, of course—you knew he was married?

All the world did.

All except me—the poor deceived fools are always the last to know.

I had a fall once, riding, and a kick that wounded me so deep it stopped my wind. So now I gasped in a black flood of pain and could not scream, because I could not get my breath. Simier rose to his feet. "Help for Her Majesty!" his command rang out, and my women rushed at once to hold me up.

Robin married—oh, faithless heart . . .

They bore me to my chamber, where I raved and shivered, clutching Parry's hand. "On your honour, Parry—*tell me all you know of my lord of Leicester's marriage!*"

Her old face flushed an ugly mottled grey. "Madam, I may not!"

"Has he commanded you? Bullied or bribed you? Forbidden you?"

All three, by her broken look. "Lady, forgive me—I cannot—"

"Parry, *no!*" I howled. *"Someone must tell me!"*

Oh, God, that Kat had still been alive! Parry never could endure my tears and rages. "Oh—oh—ah! Ah! *Ahhahh!*"

Now she was in hysterics too, and my maids rushing about her with burnt feathers and smelling salts. Only when she had screamed herself into a swoon did the noise cease.

"Helena—Radcliffe—Carey—"

One by one they melted from me. After Kat, I never found a woman I could trust. And even she betrayed me when her foolish heart betrayed her to my lord of Seymour.

O faithless heart . . .

Now the commotion in the royal lodgings had spread throughout the palace. My Lord Chamberlain burst through the door. "Madam, what's to do?"

The pain in my side now: "Sussex—I command you—*tell me—of my lord of Leicester's wife!*"

The broad brow furrowed with concern cleared now to the watchful stillness of an upland lake. "As you bid me, madam," he said carefully, *"but which one?"*

"Guard! Where's my guard? Send at once, arrest Lord Leicester!"

The captain's face was a mask of horror, I snarled to see. *They all loved Robin, he was a man of action, one of them.* "Why, my lady, where may he be stowed?"

I laughed inanely. "Take him to the Tower!"

"Madam, 'tis impossible from Greenwich! The tide is falling, and the best of bargemen may not get there by nightfall."

"Tomorrow then! Tonight, hold him fast here!"

Still he stood gagging like a gomeril till my scream sent him spinning. "Away, you tick-brain! Obey your orders—unless you think to join my lord in the Tower!"

He hopped off at that, his fellow fools clattering after him.

"Madam, it may not be!"

Never had I seen Sussex look so grim, so distraught. "The Tower is for traitors, for high treason, madam."

My wail was thin as witch's blood, the last cry of the sufferers on the wheel as the torturers prepare to turn again, again: *"Why, so this is . . ."*

So Robin went direct to close confinement in the keep at Greenwich, and I went straight to hell. Did God want to punish me? For what?

Madly I roamed my chamber, muttering like a Bedlamite; madly I sought a reason for my pain. I could not marry Robin—why should he not marry where he chose?

I did not know—only that *I could not bear it . . .*

"He is in the keep they call the Tower of Milleflore, here in Greenwich Park," they came and told me.

Milleflore—the Tower of the Wondrous Blossom. Pain upon pain. My father built it for my mother in the first flush of their love, when she had been his wondrous blossom, and he had been her tree, her sky, her earth, her everything.

As Robin had been mine . . .

"Madam, it may not be."

Sussex, simple and true, had not become the man he was through yielding up the castle of perseverance and the citadel of truth. "What, lock a man up, take away that precious freedom that Englishmen have died for—and all for *getting married?* This is no offence under our law, nor under God's! Nay, lady, it is enjoined on us by God, it is His will, a holy sacrament ordained for two who love each other, to prevent fornication—"

"Enough, enough!" I screamed. "Talk to me not of their love!" *Still less of their fornication.* "Send for Hatton! No, no—let me speak to Burghley!"

He came hastening, his stick cast off, his gout forgotten. Speechlessly I fell on his old shoulder, wrung his hand and drew him to my side. But like his hands, his comfort, too, was cold.

"My lord of Sussex tells you true, Your Majesty," he said steadily. "This act of yours is all against our law, against our ancient rights. The Earl of Leicester has"—he hesitated but could find no other phrase— "committed no offence . . ."

My tears fell like a fountain. *"What has he committed? Will you tell me true?"*

Burghley let out a long light breath, the merest shadow of a sigh. "If you insist. But my dearest lady, I must first insist that it is no crime for a man to be married as often as he pleases—nor to father a child—"

A child.

To search a wound, the barber-surgeons say, go straight to the quick of the ulcer. Cut hard and deep, they say, and the pain is less.

They say.

They speak to me that never felt the knife.

And I called Mary blind!

This marriage-go-round, this morris dance, this making of babes, had been taking place under my very nose, and I had seen, and seen it not. The fair Douglas, with her pointed chin, chamber-cat's eyes and alley-cat's instincts, had caught his glance on our progress to Rutland—aptly named!—when his lonely loins had got too much for him and he had bedded her. Back in her own house, her cuckolded husband discovered his new horns from a letter she left lying, and parted from her instantly, to ride to London to seek a divorce.

And there he died—"Some said of poison, madam, but none dared challenge my lord of Leicester, so favoured by the Queen"—and left the lovers free to pursue their lusts. Thus when Robin went from Court, did she—*I thought she went in pique at his neglect, and laughed at her discomfiture!*—but they made assignation for a lovers' tryst, and in truth she went to be with him.

O faithless heart—

Cecil laboured on. "Now Madam Douglas was with child"—*yes, I had seen it, the rounding of her waist, seen and suspected not*—"and two days before the child was born, he married her—"

"The child—?"

"A son—"

"Called—?"

"Robert, Your Majesty."

What else?

"But then my lord fell out with his wife the Lady Douglas because she insisted on having herself treated and served as Countess of Leicester, served on the knee, under her own cloth of state—"

Oh, I could see it!

"—and he feared her boasting vanity would bring their union to light?"

Burghley nodded. "When he wanted above all to keep it secret—exactly so. And when she persisted in claiming her full rights as a countess and his wife, he had cause to look into the marriage, and it was found not legal."

I laughed aloud. "On what grounds?"

"A hurried secret ceremony—no true form of lawful wedlock—nor no witnesses as the law requires."

Just like the stolen marriage of cousin Catherine—no priest who could be found, no register, no witnesses, nothing—well, well, well . . .

"And now my lord being strangely in love again . . . ?" I demanded savagely.

A slow reluctant nod. "He cast her off. To marry—"

"Who?"

You know, of course.

And suddenly I did too.

All, all. And that meant—

God have mercy, surely they were not lovers before her poor lord died? That was another fortunate attack of the flux, then—for them if not for him!

I clutched my side, my heart bursting my laces, my scream splitting the air. "Deceiving whore! She must leave the Court at once!"

He raised a rueful smile. "She took the first horse when she heard Your Majesty had been informed."

I wept another waterfall. "Never—*never* will I allow her back again!"

"Madam, she knows that."

Oh, Robin . . .

I bit my lip till blood soured all my mouth. "As for my lord of Leicester—"

Burghley's cool tones flowed over the jagged rocks of my rage. "You must release him, madam. Let him retire from Court too, to purge his disgrace."

I wept a river now. "Very well. But give order he may not retire to be with *her*—wherever Lettice is, *he may not be!*"

Does it surprise you that I turned again to Simier—that now I pursued the French alliance with the fury of a mother whose child has been plucked from her arms? And within two months he came—my Anjou, my last hope of marriage and motherhood.

How I needed him! For my monthly courses were growing thin even as my flesh grew fat and slack, and worse, prone to shivering flashes and sudden violent sweats. If ever I was to bear a child it must be soon. Yet how I dreaded him!

"God's body, Parry, is that the best you can do? You've made a hag of me, an ugly old witch. Take off that red, it rages like consumption on my cheeks—"

"Oh madam—madam—"

Parry could not say, *My dear, you're forty-five. Your cheeks are hollow now with not one tooth gone but three on your left side alone. And grief's a canker-cake to be cramming yourself with day and night, while you take no other food. And wine without victuals may be sweet in the mouth, but it's sour to the belly and sourer still in the blood . . .*

"Parry, by God's body, blood and bones, do something, damn you, for my lord the Frenchman waits!"

For Monsieur was here, Simier had come himself beaming that morning to tell me, in such eagerness that he had barely been prevailed upon to take some rest after a nonstop ride from Dover. "Now will your Majesty see that my lord's heart, his bursting love for you, as far exceeds his outward parts as the first of May does the last of December . . ."

Que voulez-vous?

What can I say?

I wanted to be loved.

"The trumpets, ho! Sound forth!"

"Her Majesty! Her Majesty the Queen!"

"Call for Mounseer! Her Majesty awaits!"

Even the ushers of the Great Hall were in a frenzy. I took the throne all virgin, all queen, in a blaze of white: lily-white satin trimmed with pearls and diamonds, an ivory and osprey fan, and a perfect halo of a ruff with the sheen of alabaster. As I sat waiting, staring at the door, Walsingham's horrid warnings rang in my head: *villainously ugly, short and pockmarked . . .*

But when the heralds cried, and the guards stamped, and the ushers bowed and scraped, and he bounded through the door, he won me with his first simple throw. Yes, he was ugly, small—smaller than Kat—and worst of all, so young! God's blood, how young! My heart stopped at the sight of him. Oh, the pain, the folly of being an old hag over the midhump of my forties, faced with a boy of less than half my age! How the world would laugh at both of us! But the little bandy form, clad all in frog-green–gold from the feather in his cap to the rosettes on his shoes, stopped dead at the first sight of me, and turning to Simier, ringingly declared, *"On m'a dit qu'elle a quarante ans et plus—mais elle est plus belle que si elle avait une quinzaine!"*

Simier advanced, bowing effusively, smiling broadly. "Majesty, my lord says that he was told you were forty and more—but you are more beautiful than a fifteen-year-old!"

And a small shoot stirred in the desert of my heart.

Yes, it was gross, his flattery.

But then, so was my hurt.

Have you never seen the surgeons at work on a great wound? It must be packed with padding.

The next day, under a heavy August sky, we walked in the park. His lord did not ride, Simier had told me; he had not the legs for it. But on foot, the Prince rarely skipped along like the boy he was. Behind us prowled my lords, some, like my Burghley, determined to like him and the French alliance, others, like Hatton and Oxford, vilely surly and unsure.

By daylight his skin was swarthier, his nose like a piece of ancient crumbling cheese, his pockmarks bigger. With his wide grin, jumping gait and green doublet, he could have only one nickname: he had to be my "Frog." Yet he could charm the monkeys from the trees. He flattered openly, like a bold child.

"That tall lord—the dark one—so 'andsome—he mus' be one of Your Majesty's greatest dukes, no?" he demanded innocently, and my poor sulking Kit, born plain Master Hatton, suddenly thought "the Mounseer" a man of some discernment after all.

He had the right word for everyone. "You mus' tell me the secret of your English ships, those boats—so leedle—and your cockleshell warriors!" he enthused to my young cousin Charles, son of my old Lord Howard, Lord High Admiral, and as bold and forthright as his father was circumspect. "We French fight good on land, but we don' like to get our feet wet—how do you breed men like your Drake, your Hawkins, who can sail in the King of Spain's own waters—"

"Right up his Spanish nose!" guffawed Howard. "And take his gold!"

"Warriors, you call them, sir?" I leaped in hastily. "They are rogues and pirates! They get no help nor countenance from me!"

"Naturellement, Majesté!" He grinned. And the dear boy had the nerve to wink at me and, with the index finger of his right hand, pull down his lower eyelid in the age-old demand: *Do you see any green in my eye?*

Oh, my darling Frog! I loved him, small and ugly as he was. And I loved inflaming Hatton's jealousy, and even more flaunting the gifts, the kisses, all the paraphernalia of courtship under another nose, my lord of Leicester's nose. God, it delighted me when he stalked up to me in the Presence, and in fury begged leave to quit the Court.

But the people, remembering sister Mary and her union with Spain, and fearing cousin Mary, who had wedded Catholic France, could not be wooed to a foreign marriage. A mad Puritan, a fool called Stubbs—God blast his arrogance!—wrote pamphlets of sedition against me till he had to have his hand cut off, to see he wrote no more. Yet with the hand that remained, as they clapped the red-hot iron to the bleeding stump, he tore the hat off his head, waved it in the air and cried "God save the Queen!" before he fell down in a swoon. Now he was become quite the great hero, and my little Frog the cruel French tyrant who had cost an honest Englishman his hand. And the people's hatred of France, fed by these Puritan zealots, grew and grew.

And though absent, Robin was not idle: he had a rogue scribbler of his own, a university ex-wit he patronised, one Edmund Spenser, put out another calumny against me, called "Mother Hubberds Tale," God rot the fool! Worse still, his own nephew, Sidney's son Philip, chimed in with an open letter attacking the marriage, a broadside of more concern than sense. I sent the scribbling clown Spenser to Ireland—that would teach the would-be poet a little of real politics!—and Sidney away from Court to learn better manners than to lecture his Queen. But behind them both I saw the hand of Robin and knew not whether to laugh or cry.

And my Council blew hot and cold till the wind turned against me, my Frog and all.

"For sure he is a great lord, and a prince of France, and he loves Your Majesty even to distraction, as he tells me," began honest old Sussex gallantly.

Walsingham, back from Paris, laughed in contempt, brandishing a paper from his ever-present bundle of despatches. "Love? Yet is his country home now to a new nest of Papist vipers my intelligencers have lighted on, still in the egg—a seminary at Douai where they plan to train young men as priest-agents, missionary martyrs, Catholic spies and traitors to invade in secret, turning 'the Faithful' against your Majesty . . ."

A random flush invaded me—I poured with sweat.

"Oh, God—against me?"

"Against you, against the revealed truth of our faith, against us all!"

"Yet if it is so secret, my lord of Anjou may not know of this," Cecil quietly put in.

Walsingham's face twisted in a bitter sneer. "Then is he nothing but puppet, a pawn to his detested dam, the baby-killing Regent Catherine—and no mate for England's Queen!"

One, three, nine, fifteen . . .

Suddenly my sweat was an icy chill. I sat in the Council Chamber counting the nods, staring at the unforgiving faces, my hands angrily, vainly plucking the green baize. "So of all women I am to remain unmarried, childless, never to hold my own bairn in my arms, a child born of the joy of a good man's love?" I wept and berated them.

There was no reply. But when Monsieur had to leave to return to France, we all knew that he would not come again. I pressed a ring of diamonds on his finger, weeping and swearing I would wed no man if not him.

And that at least I was true to.

Was it all a charade, put on for England's benefit? Or was he truly my last hope of love, of a child, of full womanhood. Both, both, of course.

And now?

Now I am forty and too many more summers, the same age as my sister Mary was, growing death in her womb in her struggle to bear her husband's child, and with it win his love.

Now my women's courses are dwindling every month, I wax hot and cold like my Council, and I feel the onset of my climacteric. I will not bear a child.

Even the parasite Mary my cousin of Scots, born to grasp, to take, to suck the life blood out of all around her, even she has given back her self to nature, she has had a child.

As Douglas has.

Lettice has his love, Douglas his child—his only child, his son—and once again I am but barren stock.

Barren . . .

Barren . . .

Barren . . .

Did I drop into a slumber, or was it a waking nightmare when the cry came ringing down the passage and the hammering began on my chamber door: *"The Queen! Awake the Queen! My lord of Leicester's dead!"*

LVII

Lord, what have I done that I must suffer this?

"How dead, fool? Speak, or die!"

I had the gibbering idiot by the throat, a dagger—was it his own?—searing his neck, blood running down his ruff, and all around us motionless in horror.

"Spare me, madam," he blubbered in an ecstasy of fear, "have pity, I know nothing! Only that he was on his deathbed when I was bid to ride for my life to bring you the word!"

And the word is death.

"The horses, ho! Her Majesty calls to horse!"

"Madam, the ride is long!"

"On, fool, *on!*"

"What? No, I want nothing, I did not speak."

The groom reining in his horse beside me bowed. *A new man—did I know him?* "As Your Majesty pleases."

"When do we make Wanstead?"

He leaned forward to pull his cob's stout ears. "If the horses tire not, we shall be at my lord of Leicester's house by nightfall."

Under the heavy hangings of the bed, in the fading light Robin's emaciated frame lay like a corpse. The air was stifling, stinking, the very walls sweating in sympathy within the sweltering room. "Open these casements!" I cried when I found my voice. "Send to Court for my physicians! And fetch some broth or water for my lord! Who is in charge here?"

An ancient crone, frightened out of her one remaining wit, shuffled into view. What, had this foul, wrinkled, one-toothed thing still stinking of the privy, her hands crusted with filth, had the care of him?

"She is no more than the housekeeper, she says, Your Majesty," put in one of my gentlemen. "My lord came all unexpected, moving now round his manors as he does to keep apart from his lady—and then fell into this sickness. He commanded her to silence, till fearful of his life, she sent for you."

"Better to have sent for a priest!"

The low mutter came from somewhere in the throng. My people, swollen by his people—I turned on them. "Away! Clear the chamber! Give my lord some air!"

"Madam, it would be best—"

"My lady, let me—"

"Away! All of you!"

I closed the door, leaning my head hopelessly against the oak, and gave way to grief. Behind me came the ghost of a cracked sigh. "Lady—for God's love—do not weep for me."

I whirled to face him. His eyes were open, staring, over-bright. I leaped to his bedside. "Oh, Robin!" I blurted painfully. Tears and words fell in a jumble. "I cannot bear it—so ill—and *married?*"

His lips cracked like his voice as he tried to smile. "Of my illness, I may recover. Of the other, never."

I grasped at the offered straw. "Would you—if you could?"

He had unmarried himself from the Douglas. If it could be proved that he and Lettice—

He laughed harshly. "I am hard fast in this one, madam, married twice over. For her father Knollys, your puritanical cousin, so little trusted our first, hasty secret nuptials that he enforced a second ceremony with himself as witness to make all tight."

The hope died and with it another part of my heart. I twisted his hand cruelly. *"Why did you marry?"*

He turned his face away. "For the oldest and best reason. The lady was *enceinte.*"

"Lettice with child? But—"

"She miscarried at the twelfth week."

"Then could you have quitted her!"

"Lady—my love—"

His eyes were tightly closed. But in the silvery dusk, tears glinted along his eyelids. "Hear this—and then make judgement. I am the only hope of all our house. My brothers dead, Henry and John and Guildford, Ambrose childless in three unions, and she"—*he could not name her, that was a good sign!*—"she—Lettice—was ever a good breeder." His sigh rustled through the airless sick-chamber. "And I loved her son young Robin, as all who meet him do—"

"And you thought in default of an heir that you might make him yours?"

Was that when the thought came to me too? That I might make him—whatever I would?

Robin gleamed like a man in torture. "That was my thought. But all I have gained from this marriage is one piece of knowledge, one revelation of one truth"—his voice now was the merest husk—"that I am yours, that I must be yours and I will be yours, whatever you choose to do with me—and from the ends of the earth, where you may banish me, I will devote the end of my life to being yours."

"What, is it dawn? Yes, my lord sleeps—he took a little broth and slept sweetly all night."

The doctor swiftly placed a hand to Robin's forehead. Sick with fatigue, I moved towards the door. "Guard him well. I will sleep now." At the door I turned back, faltering. "Doctor, will he—?"

The doctor smiled. "Yes, madam. He will live."

Yes, yes, he lived—lived to bear my anger along with my joy: he had deserved it! There were bitter hours and words before we sailed again into calm waters. Lettice suffered too, for never again could I endure her near me; she had ruined herself at Court for me, now and forever. Of course, I paid for that! Paid for it in his outbursts of black anger, or his even blacker silences, when his heart swelled against me. Most of all I paid when he went from Court to be with her—and with their son. But at least I had him at my side as the Eighties set in and the plots began.

Oh, nothing at first—green plots, bye-plots, baby plots, a doubtful young man here, a suspect there. But my enemies were multiplying, putting on strength—and before I went to war with Spain by sea as Bellona now, I had to fight a nearer enemy by land at home, here in the heart of my own kingdom.

"Majesty, this is the man."

I never liked Durham House, on the dead cusp of the Strand there as it was, on the inmost bend of the river, where the dead dogs washed up and rotted, and always stale, always damp, even now in the height of August. Restlessly I peered round in the gloom. Did they not know it was midnight—why did they not bring more candles? At once the answer came: *because they do not wish to see what they are doing.* I was shivering beyond control as the door swung open and a troop of men half-marched, half-carried, a shuffling figure into the dark chamber.

So many men to one poor hapless wretch?

He could not stand, nor, when a stool was roughly thrust beneath his twisted haunches, properly sit. His shoulders were unnaturally wide, with the bones sprung from their sockets, his arms hanging at terrible angles. The hands he pressed together now in prayer had bloody sockets where the nails had been. His drawn face, uplifted in the shadow-light, was gleaming with an unearthly greyness, of a man beyond mortal suffering, already almost passed beyond this earth. The men behind me stirred with intense excitement, murmuring like dogs on the leash. I drew my scarf about my neck and turned to Hatton. "Kit, I know this man—"

He was the boy of Christ's Hospital, the scholar in his long lapis-blue gown and yellow hose, who spoke the words of welcome when Mary came into London, myself at her heels. Thirteen years on, he was the Public Orator who welcomed me to the university when I made progress to Oxford and heard him again there.

He was a jewel of our country, Burghley said then—and Burghley no friend to Oxford University, as a student and lately Chancellor of the other place, the college in the Fens.

"You know him? Not as well as I do, Majesty!" A big, raw-boned brute in a wolsey jerkin was thrusting forward now from the shadowy group behind me, making a crude bow. "For I know him"—a queasy snicker greased his lips—"as a man might say, intimately, nay, part by part . . ."

My stomach, my whole being revolted.

Who was this beast?

What he did, I could guess . . .

"Topcliffe, hold your peace!"

Walsingham was at my elbow in a trice. "Forgive your Master-Torturer, madam, his zeal outruns his judgement. And we have here a mighty prize, which is why your lords saw fit to bring you to him, the great priest-traitor Campion!"

And all the while the poor ruin sat on his stool as serenely as a man at his own fireside. I could not bear it. "Francis, this is no traitor, but a man of arts, of learning, a Latinist, one of the University!"

"Lady, bethink you!" The look Walsingham threw Campion was glittering with hate. "This man has come out of Douai, travelled your land forbiddenly, ministered to hidden Papists, given comfort to your enemies and set up their hopes of the Scots Queen ruling this land! The greater his God-given gifts to love and serve you and his country, the greater traitor he!" He turned to the prisoner. "And a great traitor's death you will surely die!"

Campion wryly moved his head from side to side. "Sir, spare your threats. The death that you would frighten me with, I was born to seek."

His calm insulted Walsingham more than his words. "And all for what, foul wretch?" he shouted wildly. "Tell Her Grace, for what?"

The poor death's-head before me broke into a smile of such sweetness that I could not look upon him. "For my Lord and Master in Heaven, sweet Jesus Christ—to whom I am no traitor—whom I hope shortly to see face to face, with whom I hope to live and dwell, world without end."

I leaned forward eagerly. "You admit Christ?"

He bowed, a painful inclination of the neck. "He is the Son of God."

"You accept that there is but one Christ, and one God, and all the rest is nothing but trifles?"

Another beatific smile. "On my soul, madam, I believe no less."

"And did you teach that the Queen of Scots should be Queen here, instead of me?"

His eyes were the only part of him untouched by suffering, clear as a child's. "On my soul, madam, no."

I cast wildly round the group of my lords, struggling to pierce the shadows. Where was our great lawyer, Sir Nicholas Bacon? "Lord Keeper, what is his crime? For what must this man die?"

Bacon shifted his vast bulk and prepared to speak. But he was interrupted.

"Majesty, by your leave."

I had not noticed him in the group of men behind Walsingham and Topcliffe in the shadows. Shorter than Walsingham and paler, as if he had spent his life underground, he had the same black and unyielding eyes. This unknown interrogator now stepped forward, lifted a candle from the table and thrust it uncomfortably close to the prisoner's face. His voice was very quiet.

"Your Pope's last Bull called Her Majesty here a bastard heretic and pretend Queen of England. It ordered all to cease from their allegiance to her, on pain of excommunication, of sharing the outer darkness into which she was consigned. Palter not with Our Lord, nor with God's holy name! Do you honour and obey the Pope's proclamation, or no?"

The blue eyes burned brighter. "I honour and obey my Queen, and bear no evil thoughts against her."

The little interrogator smiled. "Equivocate, Jesuit, till Doomsday if you please," he said mildly. "Simply answer me this: do you renounce the Pope—who is the Devil—and all his words and works?"

No answer.

The interrogator's voice was kindly now, almost caressing. "If the Pope sent armies against our Queen, who is your master? Which would you serve?"

Now it was Campion's turn for a twisted smile. "The 'Bloody Question,' sir? We have heard of this in Douai!"

I could see the trap—as he could, for his mind was finer than all of ours. With his eyes open, then he stepped into it. "God is my master—and I serve Him."

The interrogator scented the kill. "And as you believe, God's regent on this earth is not our Queen but your Pope!"

"I do affirm it." Campion bowed his head.

His face an inch from Campion's, the interrogator screamed. "The Pope! You serve the Pope!"

I could not bear it. *"Why must we make windows in men's souls?"*

Burghley, old and drained, shook his head. "The law seizes on what men do, not what they think. He has subverted your lawful government, suborned your people. You may not save him. This is treason, madam."

They racked him until his arms were hanging off his shoulders by their torn tendons, so that at his trial one of his fellow priests had to lift his hand to the Book to take the oath.

And still they came.

Though Campion's fate was told through all of Europe, still they came. They sang psalms as they were led down to Topcliffe, tried to jest with their torturers, went to death as to a bridal, in extremes of agony were heard to pray, "Lord, rejoice with me now, make me worthy of this I suffer in Your name."

"By God, and Christ, and all the saints in heaven!" I wept with fury to my lords. "Why must we kill such men? They are the jewels of our nation! Would God they were for us!"

"Madam, while the Devil your great enemy rules in Rome, that may never be." Sussex looked weary, wearier than Burghley. "This Douai, this seminary where they train the priests—in a life of voyaging, soldiering, I never heard the like. They say the young scholars sleep on beds made like the rack, in chambers painted with life-size pictures of the Boot, the Maiden, all the tortures devised by man, to prepare them for their fate! And they pray to die like martyrs in the cause." He shook his grizzled head. "I thought the Old Faith would die with your sister—or with old fools like me. Now I live to see new life, new birth in that great mass of error, that iniquity that calls itself the Holy Church of Rome!"

"Yet remember Mary! We must make no martyrs as she did!"

Walsingham laughed, a high sneering cackle. God, how he tired my nerves these days! "My lady, with a hundred and more young men in Douai poised for landing and praying to die as martyrs, we may not choose!"

And so the game went on.

And still they came.

LVIII

They came, still they came, we could not stop them.

And still they suffered, all those glad young men.

Not one was ever found with details of a plot against my life. Yet as long as Mary worked to rouse all my Catholics against me, they could not live. For she dreamed constantly of a foreign army—of France, of Spain, of the Pope, of who-cared-who—to come into our land and put me off my throne. After a decade and more of deposition she wanted her throne back, and now mine to boot, as interest for the delay.

She on my throne, on the throne of my father—!

A shallow, murderous whore, sick of self-love like all that tainted sisterhood!

No matter that the whole world now—even her own son, for so he had been taught—believed her an adulteress and a husband killer! And even worse, because queens both then and now have been both these things and still kept their thrones, she was known worldwide as an impolitic fool, one who carried all the brains she ever had in that open pouch at the top of her long legs, who sat on an ever-spreading rump not of wisdom and discretion but of lard and affectation, and when she felt any itch stirring, could not forbear to scratch it like a tavern cat.

And dodge as I might her demented dance, weave away from the web that she wove night and day locked up in her tower, I could not escape her—nor the blood wedding that she brought us to.

Walsingham saw it from the first. "There is no room for two queens in one kingdom, madam. Your Majesty will never freely enjoy your own while the Queen of Scotland lives. Remember the Duke of Norfolk! She will find other men to make tools of! *She will try again to take your life and throne!* Mark me!"

I could not stand his bullying. "Prove it!" I wailed.

"Madam, I will."

Within a month he had it all in place. "A new man inside the castle who has won the Queen's trust; a loyal brewer in the nearby village who will make up barrels with hollow corks; a double agent in the French Embassy, which receives word from the Pope—in short, all the machinery for a secret correspondence. The Scots Queen will betray herself, Majesty, I make no doubt. All we must do is wait."

Wait.

It is the hardest thing.

God, it was hard! For she had them all on her side now, all the Catholic powers—we were hemmed in! God only knew how it frightened me in my dark hours, my silver-white hours when sleep would not come. I was right to fear the weakness of our western gates: the ever-treacherous Irish gave welcome to an army of the Pope, recruited in Spain, God rot their traitorous hides! Only the fiercest struggle drove them out. In Scotland, Mary's French uncles the Guises had won the trust of her son the boy King James—what was he now, rising twenty? Boy no longer, then— and who knew how long we could rely on that young Scotch urchin? Meanwhile, across the Channel now, the devil we knew, the cruel Alva, was replaced by a worse, Philip's half-brother Don John the Bastard.

Bastard by name and nature, we soon found—we had to send one of Walsingham's right-hand men, the trusty Davison, armed with bags of gold, at once to hearten and bully the good Dutch burghers as they groaned under these cruelties. But Mary effusively welcomed him to her cause in one of the first letters to fall into Walsingham's hands. "I embrace you," she wrote to him, "and pray God for the day when I shall welcome you to England as England's Queen!"

"Treason!" cried Walsingham and Robin.

"Not enough for a court," lamented Bacon and Burghley. "As you are childless, she could simply mean that she expected to inherit the crown as Your Majesty's heir."

"You are a lawyer, Kit," I appealed to Hatton, "help me!"

He shook his head. "Madam, not since I danced my way into your service. Yet we may ask the views of the Inns of Court."

"Ask, then!"

He asked. And all agreed with my Lord Keeper—*not enough treason.*

That night once again I wept at my casement window, baying at the moon. God damn and blast Mary, blast her eyes! Curse her fine flowery phrases and her loose-sided mind, that even when she sought my overthrow, she could not say plainly what she thought and planned!

Yet if—

If we caught her red-handed, plotting to take my life, my blood upon her pen—*what then?*

I could not take her life.

For I saw, as none else seemed to do, that Mary must live. While she lived, I was safe from Philip—he would not wish to put me off my throne to favour Mary, who with all her soul would lean to his enemy France! Yet I was under no illusion how much he hated England, how he hungered now to put us down.

He sent a new ambassador, Don Bernardino de Mendoza, to warn me of his master's change in temper. From the vein throbbing in his temple to the black-gilt heels of his Spanish-leather shoes, I hated him on sight. And oh, the studied shallowness of his bow!

"His Serene Majesty, my great King, greets you through me as his dearest little sister—"

Hah! Does he now, the short-arsed pelican!

"—and he would have you know his twin desires, in which he counts on your cooperation. He looks to see the return of the true Holy Roman religion to the world—above all in his own dominions! Also he will have the shipping lanes of the Spanish Main cleared of those thieving wretches, Your Majesty's sailors, your privateers."

I sat in the Audience Chamber fanning myself to cool my blistered nerves. Beneath my fancy frontlet in the new deep-pointed fashion and my bodice spangled with sapphires and turquoise set in silver, my heart was hammering as fast as my mind.

"His own dominions"—that meant the Netherlands, his Burgundian inheritance, where all the states were growing ever more restive against his harsh and distant rule, where neither Alva nor Don John nor any other could hold back the tide of new belief as the Reformed Religion reached out to enfold them from both north and south.

But my privateers?

"Who preys upon the Spanish galleons, Don Mendoza, who steals your master's treasure with my knowledge? They are freebooters, nothing but sea beggars, pirates, land rats, water rats!" I blustered, sweeping from the throne to confront him face to face. God, his pomade was sickly as Papist incense, and his meagre chest flaunted a Romish cross half a foot long! I rapped the enamelled, bejewelled thing hard with my fan. "We do not countenance them, do we, Burghley?"

Burghley plaited his pale fingers in something like anguish at the very thought. "No, indeed!" he said earnestly. "We keep the rule of international law both here and in the international waters."

I chuckled to myself. That was true for Burghley, at any rate, one of God's law-abiding souls. But unknown to him, I had been keeping an eye on my merchantmen for some time now—and more than an eye, a finger if not a hand in their every pie. When Robin first persuaded me to invest in those West Country hopefuls, Hawkins and his kinsmen, I could not guess how useful they would be. But their raids on Philip's treasure ships plying back from his mines in the Indies had proved the neatest way of weakening him even as they enriched me.

But of course I chirped along with Burghley like innocence itself. "No, no, we know nothing!" I assured him virtuously.

"As Your Majesty pleases!"

Of course Mendoza, hissing with rage and leaving a trail of stinking bile as he stalked away, was not convinced. But what could he do, short of calling the Queen of England a liar? And God help liars, who should choose this moment to make London water but the rogue Francis Drake?

Drake! When they come to tell the story of my reign, his name will be there as one of my great heroes, I know it. Yet who will remember my good old greybeard Sussex, or my Lord Keeper fat Nick Bacon, both of whom served me daily from my accession, for a quarter of a century, both of whom died that fall, to my great sorrow. I was hard-pressed to replace Bacon above all and cast around a good while before I determined on the loyal Sir John Puckering. Yet Drake? I hardly knew the man. He was of use, that's all.

"Madam, the *Hind*, the *Hind! The Golden Hind* stands in the Port of London!"

London ran wild with joy, prentice boys playing truant, women and children, lords and merchants—all running to the docks to see the heroes, see the miracle.

"Drake! After three years? By God's lights," I swore to Robin when he brought the news, "he has been gone so long I had forgotten his existence!"

When he left England, I had not set eyes on Monsieur, my last love, and I still thought Robin faithful—

Enough of that! It was my birthday month, Virgo was once again ascendant, and let alone Drake, to have Robin with me was a good enough gift.

Robin smiled into my eyes. "You have loving servants, lady. His first question, as he made landfall, was 'How does the Queen?' And he begs you will visit his ship and take your choice of all his booty—for his prize, he says, is from the realm of fable."

Of fable? Of fairyland, rather!

He knelt to welcome me on his little ship, a short, ruddy man with eyes like the far horizon. On either side of his broad figure, huge chests of silver, gold and jewels gave me an open-mouthed greeting too. I threw back my head and drank in the salt air. "Now God be thanked!"

Drake jumped to his feet, pulling out treasures like a conjurer. "Majesty, see! Bullion bars galore, pieces of eight! Ingots of gold and silver, crowns and crescents, angels and escudos! And hold!" Like a child at play he dived into the chests up to his elbows, tossing the bright baubles like playthings here and there. "A necklace of water diamonds? Nay, too poor for a queen—what would you say to a collar of yellow diamonds and rose rubies fashioned like honeysuckle blossoms?" Another bijou flashed in the air, and his short, stubby fingers snatched it as a gull takes a waterfly. It was a ship of emeralds, tossing in a sea of sapphires, with pearls for sails. "Does this please you, lady?"

I could hardly speak. "It—pleases me."

His weatherbeaten face creased in a broad smile. "Then may I hope my gift will find your favour?" He bowed, and clapped his hands. Up popped a tiny midshipman bearing a tasselled cushion almost as big as he was, on which lay a crown of solid gold, studded with emeralds, the smallest longer than my little finger.

And then I could not speak at all. But by the time Drake came to Greenwich with a few more trifles—a great cross of diamonds, a gold-and-silver casket, a girdle of black rubies and a triple rope of pearls—I had found my voice. "And is it true, sir, that you sailed *right around the world*? You circumnavigated our terrestrial globe?"

Never did I hear more pride in any voice than the little man's as he stood foursquare before me on his sea-knotted legs. "Madam, in your name and the name of England, so we did! And God be praised, for the first time in the world!"

And now I found my sword of ceremony along with my voice: "Arise, Sir Francis Drake, new-dubbed and most beloved knight . . ."

"He has *how much* silver bullion? How much gold? A million and a half ducats? It is nothing but plunder, piracy, theft!" Burghley and Mendoza squealed.

"It is lawful prize, the law of the ocean, booty!" blazed Robin and Walsingham.

"We must return it!" Burghley—bless him!—cried.

"Never!" howled Robin, and I blessed him more.

And all the while Mendoza dogged my doors, furiously seeking audience to demand back his master's treasure. I sent to say that I was sick, that I was abed, that I had a toothache—and that at least was true!

And I also sent secretly to Drake, Hawkins and the rest of my seafarers the simple word: *Keep up the good work! Harry the treasure ships of Spain, keep their King poor and myself rich like this!*

But I could not keep Mendoza out forever, shrink though I might from what I knew he would say.

When he said it, though, I tried to stop my ears. "So, madam, you will not hear my master's words, you refuse to hear the all-powerful King of Spain as he speaks through me? Let us see, then, if you will listen to the voice of our great cannon, which will split your little England into a thousand parts and scatter you across the face of our fair globe!"

Was it then that I knew? Knew it must be war? I heard it in his voice, saw it in his eyes, Philip's eyes.

So was the joy of Drake's great triumph lost in the growing fear that like the gallant little Netherlands, we, too, lived now in the shadow of the lion's paw.

It was a long and sneaking approach to Lent, the plague unseasonably early this year and the lime pits not ready for the dead; no meat, bad fish, dried roots and old apples wrinkled like the skin around my eyes and shrivelled like my heart: Septuagesima, Sexagesima, Quinquagesima, all dwindling down to a dead Ash Wednesday. And ash was my mood, ashen my hopes, as I wound my way dully into church at Westminster that March day. Now a steady drizzle made the world grey as my soul. Even St. Margaret's, a church I always loved, its grey stones old when the Abbey was young, could not lift from my shoulders the cloak of impending dread.

In the chill void the voice of the preacher came like a cry from hell: "Turn even to me, saith the Lord, with weeping and fasting and mourning, rend now your heart . . . O Lord, spare thy people, give not thine holy heritage to reproach, that the heathen shall rule over us, that the people will cry out and say, *Where is our God?*"

The heathen shall rule over us—

Philip rule over us?

Papists all about us, traitors undermining us—

On the lead of the roof the rain was drumming like the restless hand of God. That day, I knew, two more of Douai's priests were doomed to go to it, the butcher-executioners even now sharpening their knives and cleavers for their dreadful work. My soul abhorred it. Yet how could I let them take away my land? In Spain, Philip's Inquisition, by his order, now burned alive any foreign visitor, let alone heretic, who did not kneel to adore the Host even in the street. Here in England a man could doze through a whole service and none presume to question the state of his soul!

God rot them all, I cried in anguish as the service ended, bringing me to no state of grace. It would be a long, lean Lent and a still longer summer, autumn, winter. My subdued cortège wound out to the church door, thronged as usual with blind beggars, lepers, cripples, Tom o'Bedlams with weeping, hideous sores. *Oh, God, why did You make Your Creation so ugly and so vile? Is this the price we go on paying for the great sin in the Garden, the sin of Eve?*

The wretched downpour had left pools of standing water all over St. Margaret's yard. Now a weak sun was silvering the scene as I stood on the threshold surveying a great puddle that had gathered where I had to tread.

"Your Majesty, permit me."

I started violently. I had not heard that soft Devon burr since my dear Kat had died.

Who—?

To say eyes are blue means grey or green or at best the watery azure of a rain-washed sky. These eyes were true blue, Mary blue, cornflowers in August—yet not so pure, the eyes of man who had looked on women and liked what he saw.

He stood a good six feet in his kidskin boots, and by my guess had seen no more than twenty-six summers. His curling hair and well-trimmed beard were all the blacker against those bright, deep blue eyes and pale gleaming skin. His doublet was the blue-green bloom of juniper, the matching plush cloak richly worked with bugle beading and lace of Milan. But for all this, he had a slightly raffish, ragged, desperate air—was this Sunday best his only best?

Pressing through the throng, he twitched the cloak from his well-made shoulders and, with a flourish I never expect to see repeated, twirled it through the air. Floating like an eagle, it settled slowly until it sank over the great patch of mud and water where I had to tread. As he pulled off his cap, the tangled curls tumbled about his face. His bow was lower, his finish finer, than even my French lord Simier's, yet with a tigerish grace that was all his own. "Your Majesty's most devoted servant, while I live and breathe."

And he was gone, leaving the slow languorous Devon growl hanging in the air. I turned back to my people. "Speak, one of you—*who is that man?*"

LIX

Now what is love, I pray thee tell?
It is that fountain and that well
Where pleasure and repentance dwell.
It is perchance that saucy bell

That tolls us all to heaven or hell—
And this is love, as I hear tell.

"A man of the West Country, madam," said Burghley, peering over my shoulder at the retreating form. "A kinsman of Sir Humphrey Gilbert who led your troops in Ireland, a poet of sorts, but said to be a doughty fighter: Raleigh, they call him."

"Call him back!"

"Bumptious upstart!" grumbled Hatton behind me. "Sure, he imposes on you, madam, with this trick, to throw away a fine cloak like that in the mud!"

Robin, at my other shoulder, laughed, a shade unpleasantly, I thought. "I'll warrant that young swaggerer will not take much calling back—Your Majesty will find he has not gone far!"

And Robin's nephew, the pale youth Philip Sidney, gazed at him as if he had said something wonderful. I glared my disapproval. But it was true, my gentlemen had the newcomer back before me in a trice.

"Well, sir—Raleigh, is it?" I laughed at the jealous faces all around. "By my faith, I have heard but *rawly* of thee!"

He laughed too, showing strong white teeth, not a whit abashed. "Yet I have done good service in Ireland—and will do more, much more, for such a Majesty!" Again that Devon burr, gentle and strong.

"You speak broad, sir."

His proud head flew up. "I speak my native tongue, madam. My mother was a Champernowne of the West Country."

"Champernowne? Then my old mistress, Kat—?"

"—was my dear mother's sister."

Oh, my dearest Kat. Trembling a little now, I looked up into those bold blue eyes. "Well, sir, you will need a new cloak now to serve me!"

"I would serve you, lady, to the ends of the earth, be I dirt-ragged and bleeding-poor!"

I laughed again. "Would you indeed? Then come to me tomorrow!"

Could I have shown more favour?

But see the arrogance of the man! He came not, but sent instead a gift, a crescent moon of gold, studded with seed pearls. With it came the poem above, the teasing question piece "Now What Is Love?" And with them both a letter:

I may not come at your behest, fair moon, nor dare my lowly star swim into such an orbit, until I have the new cloak I have ordered: for I shame to appear before a goddess like our Diana in anything unworthy of the kiss of her sweet rays.

I liked that.

I looked forward to seeing more of him.

And when at last he chose his moment to return, his reward was the largesse to fee three tailors for a year.

And still they came, the missionaries, the martyrs, with their strange gaiety, their terrible bravery, to face our terrible cruelty—and though our cruelty grew ever more terrible, still they came.

And still Mary wove her endless, traitorous webs, wrote her endless letters, casting line from the Spanish Regent Don John in the Netherlands, to her Guise kinsmen in France and Scotland, and from them to the Vatican, and back again to Spain. Silently and in darkness, unseen like Penelope, we unpicked her threads of treachery one by one—but still she spun and spun, by night and day.

And still Philip brooded in Spain, still he sought and prayed for the way to bring the Low Countries and England, too, once and for all under the Spanish heel.

And all three strands came together as the Three Gray Women, the ancient Fates, spun out the doom of all.

"Madam, a casket—left by Master Raleigh—"

"Perfumed sandalwood, carved with 'ER'! Pretty! And what's this inside?"

> *Those eyes that hold the hand of every heart,*
> *Those hands that hold the heart of every eye,*
> *That eye, that hand, that wit, that heavenly sense,*
> *All these do show my mistress' excellence.*

"Call him back! Run, girl!"

"Madam, he will not be gone far!"

Raleigh was the first of my favourites to love me in true poetry—yes, in the finest verse. Oh, others could carve out a quatrain or serve up a sonnet—any man could who had half an education, and most women too! But for the skill of words, to make them fly into my heart like kisses, hop about like little Cupids and gambol in my way, it was my Raleigh every time.

And that was not the least he did to make other men jealous. "Your Majesty's own laureate!" Robin dubbed him sardonically. "Yet if you want true poetry, lady, may I commend to you my nephew, whose rare gift—"

"What, Sidney's boy Philip? No, Robin, you may not!"

"You call this poetry?" snarled a red-faced Hatton, snatching up the parchment where this day's treasure was inscribed. In a mock-moaning voice he launched himself upon the second stanza:

"O eyes that pierce into the purest heart,
O hands that hold the highest hearts in thrall!"

"Enough!" I commanded sharply, eyeing him with disfavour. For already I had the lines by heart, and I needed no critique of their merits as long as they pleased me. As they did—especially the end:

The heaven of heavens with heavenly powers preserve thee,
Love but thyself, and give me leave to serve thee.

Yes! For I needed new servants now, in these new and trying times. Now the Netherlands groaned and wept under the firestorm of Spain's fury, and now at last the hour found the man.

The man of destiny: William the Silent, they called him—"a man of such fortitude, madam, that he would rather open the dykes and drown his land than see those painted Spanish heels treading it down!" said Burghley, marvelling. But he needed help—small though we were, the States, as they called themselves, were smaller—and yet—

You know already what I will say—what I said then till even my fondest lords were sick of my refrain—

Money! Money! Money!

Where are the men and the money?

Never enough!

Never enough men and money!

Yet we had to keep the hosts of Midian from our gates! If we let Spain rampage unchecked through the Low Countries, we were only hours away from our own doom.

"Thank God you have a navy you may trust to, lady," said Raleigh sombrely, pulling at his beard. Again the challenge of that hard blue stare. "But we must build more ships . . ."

"It must be war, madam," Robin said, passing a weary hand across his brow. "And we must build the army . . ."

Oh, God, money!

Amor et pecunia . . . Love and money . . .

Money and love are bedfellows, said Martial, and he said true; they swive well together. Raleigh won my love by using my money, given to him in love, to build not a town house but a palace on the sea—not a fine wardrobe but a fancy-trimmed four-masted schooner. He called it the Ark Raleigh, *and then, making a royal gift of it in my hour of need, renamed it the* Ark Royal.

Robin fought back with other weapons, with words, like Raleigh, but not of his own—he took on a troupe of players, called them Lord Leicester's Men and had them act for me pretty trifles and tomfooleries that served to distract me from my growing weight of cares—for the time, at least.

And for that I loved him again.

Did I love Raleigh then, you ask?

He pleased me, surely. What if he had not yet reached thirty summers, and I was trembling under the threat of my half-century? What if I knew he courted me for my money as much as my fine face? They all did that! Even Robin.

The skin of his face was soft against his curling, upturned beard, his hands hard, his laugh long, and his legs inexhaustible.

And he was nothing like my father!

And no matter if the world laughed behind its hand at an old woman's fancy for a pretty young man—it was the beacon fire at which I warmed myself in a world growing darker.

Ireland rose up again—*Ireland, always Ireland!*—and I had to part with Raleigh, sending him there with an army to make safe what he called "the King of Spain's back door." And Spain knocked, too, at the front: now our candles burned to their sockets all night again, just as they did when we feared the marriage of Norfolk and Mary—with more fear now of the legions at our gates. Yet they still had to cross that bright ring of water, our moat the Channel, the first, last and best of our defences.

"How stands the navy? We must make inventory! Who can we put in charge?"

Burghley bowed. "By your leave, madam—I have the very instrument to your hand. My son Robert, having left the university, craves the chance to serve you. May it please you to try him in this, see how he fares? I dare swear he will make a loyal servant—but only you can judge his value."

I flexed my aching neck and stared at him. Robert? That hunchbacked, crippled boy enter my service? Wonderingly I studied the light of pride that played in Burghley's smile. Truly a father's love is a marvellous thing! And yet, I mused, to stake his reputation on his son like this, Burghley must be sure the youth was worth a try. I patted his hand. "Let him come to me—at once."

"At once?"

Nay, sooner, it had to be!

For as we sat there in the sad guttering light, Burghley and I, I thought my ears caught—I thought I heard—

"What was that?"

The sound above all I had learned to dread, a running messenger panting with evil news: "The Prince of the Dutch is dead, fallen to an assassin, slain by a Catholic servingman suborned by King Philip!"

So William the Silent had been silenced for all time. God rot his murderer —and the King who ordered it!—in the lowest sluice of hell!

I closed my eyes, slid forward to the floor and tried to pray. Beside me I could hear Burghley's stiff rustling as he followed me down onto his poor old knees.

Oh God, my heart cried, *is this Your will? Why do You punish Your new saints like this, those of the reformed truth who struggle as he did to reveal Your light?*

We knew of course how Philip had schemed to have William killed. Six times at least the gallant Dutchman had survived poison, knife and pistol —once shot in the hand, once even through the throat, hence his eternal sobriquet of "Silent."

Beside me I could hear the low hum of Burghley winding up his devotions: *"Per Iesum Christum Dominum nostrum, amen."*

And I knew that he was praying as I was: *O Lord, take Thou this cup from our lips . . .*

For it was a bitter chalice, wormwood and gall. Decapitated now, the States of the Netherlands rushed to and fro for a new leader like a headless chicken. There were few contenders. Why should I, then, have been startled at their choice?

"What? You offer the rule of the Low Countries to *me?"*

I was horrified. The grave grey-suited burghers of Holland, Zeeland and Utrecht, standing as stiff and solid as one of their own dykes before me, bowed in high dudgeon and had to be appeased with feasts and flattery, in cash and kind. But I could not take the Netherlandish throne —I had enough to do with my own kingdom! Yet still I knew that without a leader the States must yield to Spain inside a year.

"We must hold them fast to England!" I burst out as they trailed disconsolately from the Audience Chamber, their tails between their legs. "Who shall rule them now?"

"If not yourself," urged my cousin Howard, son of my old great-uncle the Lord Admiral, "send our best leader, one as good as yourself!" Charles's eyes were now as clever as his father's, his nerve stronger, his sense of England true. I knew he was right. I brooded on it. *As good as myself?* Who, even now, was more myself than Robin?

He came to kiss hands as he took his leave, glittering from head to foot in a new set of ceremonial armour, for though he went as my Viceroy, he must be my warrior too. A full Court, on my orders, gathered to see him off. Yet as he entered with his entourage, his sister's son Philip Sidney and his stepson the boy Essex at his heels—was it a trick of the light (for it was late November) or my tired eyes (my sight was so dull now, nothing looked as things were) or the contrast with young Essex (boy no more, I was forced to see, but a proper stripling, tall and promising)?—

the next second I was asking myself, *Who is this stranger? When did his waist start thickening, his hair thinning, his bright complexion begin to dim? Where had it come from, that heaviness of tread, where once this man had leaped and cavorted his way into my heart?*

Beside me Raleigh, lean and coiled, laughing the laugh of less than thirty summers, signalled the musicians with a careless wave and sprang up to my side. "The music waits. Would your Majesty care to dance?"

His black curls gleamed and nodded, his eyes were already dancing, his hard young body breathed of lime and lavender—

Yes, Her Majesty cared . . .

Oh, I danced and he danced, I made music and he made poetry, I was finely courted, for my Raleigh well knew how to sing the birds out of my trees. I made him a Gentleman Pensioner and Captain of the Guard and granted him leases of fine manors, with the rents to keep them, and he paid me back for all of it in love.

And I took it greedily, like a starving woman. For I was fretful, angry, out of sorts.

"Your Grace misses the Earl of Leicester," whispered Kate Carey as she dressed my hair.

Oh, God, yes! I missed him! Missed the man he was, and the man he had been!

And I needed Raleigh all the more when the first despatches came from the Netherlands. "Your Viceroy holds Court here like a king, in all magnificence," they innocently wrote.

"What?" I exploded. "We are bleeding money, one hundred, two hundred, three hundred thousand pounds, and he keeps Court?" I turned back to the letter: "—and his charming Vicereine, as we hear, is shortly to join him, to share his pains and duties—"

A slow-burning grief, an agony of rage, spread from my very vitals. He had sent for *her!* They would play King and Queen—*at my expense!*

The goblet in my hand smashed to the wall and fell in a thousand pieces. "Command him back!" I wept to Burghley. "Strip him of his titles, throw him and that she-wolf Lettice in the nearest jail!"

"Majesty, no," said Burghley soothingly.

"Lady, forgive!" Robin wrote beseechingly. "If it displeases you, she will not come!"

"You are no longer to be my Viceroy!" I screamed by fastest messenger.

"Then let me be the lowliest of your servants!" he sent back faster, grovelling to my will. "Let me but keep your stables here, if only to rub your horses' heels . . ."

He had to stay, to keep Spain off our backs. And I had to forgive him. "Rob," I wrote weeping, grovelling in my turn, "a midsummer moon has seized my wandering wits, I know not what I say. I can only imagine I still talk with you, and therefore grievingly say farewell now to my two Ô Ô, my eyes that see all and watch on my behalf. I pray God bless you from all harm and save you from our foes, with a million thanks for all your pains and cares, ever the same, ER."

Now God help me . . .

But at least I had my Raleigh!

Was it to punish Robin, for I knew it would goad him sorely when the word winged over the water that I granted Raleigh a rich monopoly of wines, gave him a town house on the Strand and made him a knight? My new Sir Walter wept at my feet—and swore he would search out new worlds for me and call them "Virginia." Foolish talk, young man's talk, but I took comfort from it.

And youth and comfort now were in demand, for old age, or worse, seemed suddenly to have ambushed all about me. From France came word that my poor Frog, my last lover the Duke of Anjou, was dead of a seizure, and I wept for him. Even Hatton was now looking on forty, and Robin, God save us, was my own age! Which I would not so much as have whispered about me, but which now rhymed and chimed with what I also had to be in these hard times, *nifty* and *thrifty* . . .

Fifty!

How I hated it!

And all to do with it!

"Parry, the thing's a monstrosity, take it away, it has a life all of its own! Look you, it twitches like a wild boar's arse!"

Fanning myself furiously, I peered into the glass. Two anxious hands snaked forward, tweaking and prinking at the ginger curls. "Madam, such perruques are the height of fashion for the ladies of France—"

"Blast you, Parry, perruque me no perruques, call a spade a spade—the vile thing's a *wig!* Do I need a wig?"

If I did, was it any wonder, with griefs enough to make Job himself tear his hair out! Yet surely these thin itching patches on my scalp would clear away as soon as the spring came?

"It is but a small advance, lady, on the hairpieces we have used before to give a little aid to nature. And when the girl has finished your colour now and varnished your complexion—"

"It is too much!"

Too much of everything—heaped-up red ringlets bobbing above, carmine and cochineal, white lead and borax below, ground peach powder, shellac and gum arabic—but most of all too much to conceal, too many wrinkles, too many years on my face!

How I missed Robin now, how I longed for his return, for in the mirror of his eyes, I never saw my age. Now not a month went by but I was sharply reminded how I was hated—how my enemies fed fat their grudge against me, biding their moment, spinning their endless plots.

Throckmorton.

God! The very name can still bring tears to my eyes. You remember Nicholas of that same name? Sir Nicholas Throckmorton, one of the first to cleave to my cause, even under sister Mary, he who served me in France as my Ambassador, and then again in Scotland when Mary of Scots was still on her throne and first in lust with Darnley? When he died I swore to be a mother to his orphaned daughter, whom he had named after me, and the young Bess was newly come to Court. Think, then, what it meant—his closest kin, his brother's son, to turn against me and to plot my death!

It was so simple, how they caught him.

"All plots come from the Pope," Walsingham swore, "and from him through France and Spain. Let us but set a watch on their two outposts in our country—and watch, and wait."

And *voilà!* Throckmorton was seen leaving the French Embassy, and taken in his house vainly burning his traitorous writings. Walsingham himself oversaw his racking, with a committee of my Parliament-men, to keep all legal and above board. The traitor swore he would endure a thousand deaths rather than speak a word. But he told all—in the end. And a grim tale they got from him.

These were no ramblings of a small schemer like Ridolfi, but a grand conspiracy. The Guise dukes were behind it, Mary's French kinsmen, masters of dis-*guise!* They had never ceased to work for her, even as they tried incessantly to bring her son—the boy James in Scotland—back to the faith of Rome. One of them would invade from our south coast, the other down through Scotland; a third attack would come from Ireland with five thousand mercenaries; and the English Catholics everywhere were to rise up. Myself, I would be granted the courtesy of a dagger's point while Mary took my throne.

"The plot master is none other than your adversary Mendoza," Walsingham came hotfoot to inform me. "So much for his Ambassador's neutrality!"

I ground my teeth in fury, and the pain added to my rage. "Send him packing! Expel him at once! But search his papers first—find out who paid for this!"

"Madam, we know already from Throckmorton's lips!" Walsingham retorted. "Who but the Pope and the King of Spain?"

So the traitor sold me to my two archenemies—and all for Scotch Mary and the Old Whore of Rome! Did you hear his piteous weeping when they took him from the rack? "Now I have betrayed her who was dearest to me in the whole world," he blubbered. He loved her! She was dearer to him than I was, his Queen, his lawful monarch, the mother of his country! And for that treachery he justly met the drawn-out agony due to traitors. For burn my heart as it may, I would not lift an eyebrow to spare him.

And not all wished me dead. As the Court moved that month from Hampton to Whitehall for the winter, the people thronged the cold, mud-swollen roads.

I could not help shedding tears to see the lines of loyal English faces. "God bless you, my good people!"

"They love you, madam," opined the French Ambassador, riding beside me.

I laughed sardonically. "Some of them at least, as Your Excellency may see!"

But burn my heart for their love or Throckmorton's hate, it burned more for Mary, in this up to her fine-painted eyebrows. For who was Throckmorton writing to when they arrested him but "My dread sovereign Queen Mary II, England's most true and rightful Catholic Queen"?

"Now, madam!" Walsingham exulted. "Now we have her!"

No, said the lawyers.

She had written to him, true.

But once again her flowery French flimflam fluttered through our net.

And once again Walsingham was reduced to swearing, *"She will betray herself. Wait, madam—only wait!"*

L X

Wait.

How could I bear it?

But she was waiting too.

And I might have known that she would weary of the game of patience before I did.

When he came, then, the great traitor, she was ready for him, nay, over-ripe.

He fell in love with her, of course, as men always did. "Jesus God!" I raged to a shocked and tight-lipped Walsingham. "Do all the sons of Adam carry their consciences in their codpieces, their brains in their manhood as donkeys do?"

"Madam, he loved her chastely since his boyhood as a page in her keeper the Lord Shrewsbury's house!" Walsingham rebuked me—he was such a Puritan!

Yet still, like the ill-starred Duke of Norfolk, whom she entrapped before, like Throckmorton, too, who had never seen her, never met her, not one single moment of adult eye-liking had ever passed between them. He cherished a boy's fantasy love for a pretty young captive queen. Would he or the others have thrown down their young lives if they could have seen her as she was—a hook-nosed, humpbacked, double-chinned dowager rattling with Romish cant, silly with sentiment, stiff with vanity and self-regard?

"So unlike Your Beauteous Majesty!" Raleigh at least was there to remind me.

Yet still she had that knack of winding a man about her little finger—a word, a phrase, and suddenly he saw himself magnified ten times beyond his natural size in the glass of her flattering gaze. Just as she flattered this next fool in line! He wrote, she answered, and Walsingham's prayers were answered too.

My Moor's satisfaction then went too deep for joy, for tears, for anything but prayers of thanksgiving to his unforgiving God. When he came to my chamber, I never heard him speak so quietly: "Madam, I swear by Christ's blood that we have her now."

I clutched the parchment in a shaking hand. *God, give me strength to read this, for I have to see!* It was broad daylight, but the black scratches crawled like spiders before my eyes.

A curse upon this fading sight that makes evening at noon. I moved to the casement, opening the window to let in the sun. Had she at last penned a letter that could be used against her? I squinted desperately to see the words.

"I like well of the matter," she had written. "And when affairs are all in readiness, then shall it be time to set the six gentlemen to work . . ."

I turned, trembling, to Walsingham. " 'The six gentlemen?' "

"Those she agrees, Majesty, must take your life."

How long, O Lord, how long?

The silence in the chamber grew until it echoed like thunder in the book-lined space. In the tight circle of grave old faces, not a one flickered. At last the oldest and the gravest there laid down the document, shook his head, and spoke. "You have her, madam—there can be no doubt."

I turned my head. Behind the ranks of gray-wigged, black-robed figures, beyond the little window of the Temple, fresh white clouds scudding like rabbits' bobtails chased each other across a shining sky. On such a day of any other summer, Robin and I would have been ahorse, afield, chasing and racing too. But he was far away, and here I sat, a prisoner like Mary, who at last had brought me here.

To seek her life.

Beside me I could hear Walsingham release his breath in a hiss of satisfaction. The Law Lords murmured quietly among themselves and then fell silent.

The Lord Chancellor spoke again, his finger jabbing at the bold MARIA R. "We are all agreed. She has signed away her own life in agreeing to take yours."

How did it start, this plot of Babington's?

For it was he, he was the leader of the six, the so-called "gentlemen" who would take my life. There was a priest in it, the foul Father Ballard, and behind them all the old hand of Don Mendoza the Spanish Ambassador, who even from overseas never ceased to dream his blood dreams and scheme for my destruction. Under Babington the six were to poison me, pistol me as I rode or walked in my garden, stab me in the Presence or despatch me at my prayers.

And I dead, the gates of England were to be opened to Spain. Now we heard the first word of that terror that was to swell and grow until the darkness of it shadowed all our land. "The King will send an Armada to encompass your deliverance!" wrote Babington in ecstasy to Mary. "Not galleons, but floating fortresses!"

She approved both the invasion and my death—treason in any book. *Jesus God!* I laughed and cried aloud when I read this. "When was it?" I wept to Burghley. "Twenty years ago, it must have been, when I was courted to approve the selfsame plots against my sister's life?"

"Nearer thirty, madam." *God, he looked old, so old, leaning on the boy Robert, his hunchbacked son.*

"But I sent them all packing, Wyatt and Courtenay, all of them! I agreed to nothing, most of all signed nothing."

Hatton leaned forward. "Lady, she signed to your death."

I looked around the Law Lords and my close councillors. In the circle of stone faces was written one clear sentence: *And for that she must die.*

"No news yet of the six?"

"Madam, not yet." Walsingham's face as he approached across the park was livid with strain. Behind him Davison, his trusty secretary, looked spent and stark-eyed too—when had they last slept? Yet Walsingham's bow was as brisk as ever. "We have his next letter, but he has not named them." *Yet to take my life as he had pledged they would, they must be all around me, close at hand . . .*

Who were they?

Beyond us ran the river, wide and lazy here at Richmond and tonight slow-rolling like molten lead in the dull purple August evening light. All around, courtiers and their ladies, townsfolk and strollers, clusters of servants, dotted the green as far as eye could see. Away to the right, a lone figure lingered to see me pass. As I stared at him, he slunk away.

I gripped Hatton's arm. "Say, any of you—*who is that man?*"

All gazed after him, but only young Cecil spoke. "A newcomer to court, an Irish gentleman, if it please Your Grace—they call him Barnwell, I do believe."

Irish—Catholic too?

Davison was slipping away even before the jerk of Walsingham's head had ordered *Look into him!* In an agony of sudden fear, I cast round the little group—Burghley and Hatton, staid in their long gowns; the poor half-sized youth Cecil; Walsingham, armed with nothing more lethal than his bundles of documents; and behind us only my women Parry and Radcliffe, Anne Warwick and Helena of Northampton. "I see I am well defended here among you," I protested tremulously, "when not a man about me wears a sword!"

Where was Raleigh?

Where was Robin?

But we all knew that the assassin's bullet, poison or dagger point, come when it may, will pierce a wall of swords. And this was what I had to live with all the dreary while Walsingham unravelled all the threads that led us back to Mary.

"She must go to the Tower!" pronounced Burghley.

"She may not!" I wept afresh. How could I forget my own imprisonment there, the sight of the scaffold, the stink of fresh blood reeking from it no matter how much fresh straw they put down?

"Where then, Majesty?"

"Some vacant estate—away from London!"

Burghley pondered. "What of the house of the young Earl of Essex, serving with my Lord of Leicester in the Netherlands?"

"So be it."

My young lord objected, of course, pouring forth letters from Zutphen, where the English forces lay at siege—but I could rule him then, in those far days . . .

And while she was there, Walsingham pounced on Babington, on Father Ballard, yes, on the Irish squire Barnwell too, for he was one of them, and the rest of the "six"—now swollen to twelve, nay, twenty and more. They all died for their treasons, but not before their words and writings had convicted Mary too.

She came to trial in Fotheringay, and I saw she had none but the best. One crisp October morning Burghley loaded his gouty frame onto a plodding palfrey and, with Walsingham beside him, took the Great North Road. Thirty-four nobles sat on the commission, even old Papists like the Earl of Shrewsbury. Walsingham left his trusty Davison to bear me up, and the first task I gave him was to write to tell them how badly I lacked my Spirit and my Moor—and then to write to Robin to say I missed him even more.

But his reply brought a sorrow deeper than the pain of his absence, painful though that was:

Weep with me, Majesty, when I report to you my sister's loss, the sole hope of her house . . .

Sidney was dead, young Philip Sidney, poor ill-fated youth! And his poor little wife, Walsingham's plain daughter—childless she was, not even a son of his body to console her widowhood.

He died most bravely . . .

The paper slipped from my hand to the floor, my eyes darkened, but the words wept on in my brain:

. . . at the siege of Zutphen. Fighting against the forces of the King of Spain, he took a mortal wound high in the thigh. As he lay burning in a high fever, when they brought him water to ease his agony he commanded it to be given to the common soldier who lay next to him: "For I see," said he, "that your need is greater than mine . . ."

"Your Majesty, word from Fotheringay—oh, madam, forgive my intrusion—shall I call your women—?"

"No, no, Davison, I shall be myself in just a moment. Speak, give me the news, I will collect myself."

Blinking with indignation, Davison composed his honest features as he proffered the despatch. "The Queen of Scots will not plead to the charge, Lord Burghley writes us. She says she is neither guilty nor not guilty but a sovereign queen, a stranger in your land, and subject to no subject, only to God."

"Aach!" I screamed, and tore the paper from his hand. "Still she plays games with us! Give me a pen here!"

Trembling with fury, I sat down at the table and pulled the candle nearer. The hot wax seared my hand, the quill spat ink like venom as I carved my rage into the parchment:

You have in various ways attempted to take my life and bring my kingdom to destruction by bloodshed. These treasons will be proved on you, and now made manifest. It is my will you answer the nobles and peers of my kingdom as if I myself were present. Act plainly without reserve and you will the sooner be able to obtain favour of me, Elizabeth the Queen.

"Hah! There!"

Almost panting, I threw the parchment at Davison's hapless head. "Order them to bring her to the bar of that court!" I screeched. "Even if they have to drag her there with camels! See to it!"

He bowed and hastened out. "Majesty, it is done!"

Of course, we faced a stream of protest from all over the world—one by one the ambassadors of France, of Spain, of the Holy Roman Empire blasted us with rage and reproach. Coolest of all came the word from Scotland, where the twenty-year-old King James now saw his chance to be King indeed, and more, my heir. His pleas for Mary's life were barely dutiful, certainly not filial! Which all thought disgusting, but to me showed that whatever his faults, my godson was no hypocrite. And to all of them I gave the same reply: *"It must be done . . ."*

And done it was, in solemn, proper form, the charge put to her face in open court: ". . . to answer in the matter of Sir Anthony Babington— and moreover, as you have been the head and fount and most pernicious source of all plots against our lawful sovereign Queen Elizabeth, you now stand accused as a most toad-spotted traitor, being by birth of Scotland, by breeding of France, and by religion a true child of Spain—and thus a daughter of debate and sister of that Whore of Babylon, the Pope of Rome . . ."

"Good words, and well phrased!" I exulted to Davison. "Let her answer that!" For now we had all six of her "gentlemen," including the Irish traitor Barnwell, and we knew it all.

But she was never short of a ready answer—or a bare-faced lie.

"I know no Babington!" she ringingly declared.

Her own letter to him was put before the court.

"I did not write that!" was her next resounding perjury.

Her two secretaries, without the rack or any other torture, swore on the Book she did.

"They are all lying!" came echoing back now. "On the word of a queen!"

Her word?

My arse!

No—that at least has a fundamental ring of truth—her word, none!

By the time that Babington, the Jesuit Father Ballard and the other "gentlemen" of the plot came to their trial, I was in a frenzy. "Let them all feel the full rigour of their punishment!" I screamed. At his execution, Babington's lips were still murmuring *"Parce, parce, Domine"* . . . "Spare me, spare me, O Lord!" when the hangman cut his heart out and held it up in his hand. And had I, who remembered the burnings under Mary, ordered such diabolical torments? Weeping, vomiting, I sent a fresh command: "Let all the rest of them hang till they are dead before the butcher-surgeons begin the castrating and quartering."

And Mary caused all this.

Even then, she fought on, like a dying gladiator. Her last cast was at Burghley. "You are no fair judge—you are my enemy!"

And what did my Spirit, my best servant, the very right hand of my soul, reply in his dry lawyer's voice? "You mistake me, madam. I am merely the enemy of the enemies of my Queen!"

She had no defence but lies and bluster, tears and protestations—all piss and wind! What could the verdict be but *Guilty as charged?*

Now we saw how she was hated and how I was loved! Church bells tolled the tidings from every steeple in the land, bonfires blazed from Cornwall to Carlisle, psalms and prayers rang out on every corner, as all England cried to dance upon her grave. Two decades of detestation for "the She-monster," "the Mermaid," and "the Whore" boiled over, and they hungered for her death, thirsted for her blood, clamoured for retribution.

Yet still I fought to save her, like a mother tiger for her cub. When Walsingham came south covered in pride and satisfaction, I would not sign the warrant for her death.

He stood like one struck by a lightning bolt, then began to shake from head to foot. "Give me one reason, madam," he shouted, yellow and trembling, "why you would spare this bosom serpent who in twenty years has never ceased to try to sting you dead!"

"Sirrah, I'll give you three, five, six!" I howled in anguish. "She is a queen and one of God's Anointed, she is a woman and my kinswoman, she is a Tudor, and she is my heir! And when subjects come to take the lives of kings, who knows what chaos follows? If I do this, why, in years to come, any could use her death to plead the death of another King of England—or even argue, God defend us, that nations need not kings! Away, leave me!"

And leave me he did, to take to his bed and nurse his liver, bursting now with bile. So ill was he that not one of our doctors could help him, except for a Portuguese newly come to London fleeing the Inquisition, a Jew called Lopez. I sent Walsingham medicines of herbs and simples and broth from my own table, but otherwise he could not move me. Him I could handle—he was only one. But my Parliament made five hundred angry men, and they would not be denied.

They outflanked me then, I do confess—Walsingham, Burghley, Hatton and the rest. When they said it had to be put to Parliament, I readily agreed: I wanted her guilt blazed forth to the whole kingdom, to the whole world! What I did not see was that once my Parliament-men had hold of it, I could not save her.

They bearded me in Richmond as the year ran out, walking in the garden, drearily counting the last yellow leaves, a hot deputation. The Speaker's bow was polite enough, but his grim-looking jaw and ugly eye told another story. "Lady, we call for justice, justice, justice! The Queen of Scots is condemned, her life already forfeit! We see no reason under law why a just condemnation should not be followed by a just execution, as with any criminal in the land."

"Were it for my own life," I told them tearfully, "I would not touch her! But I do not think of myself alone. Pray you, then, good men all, accept my thankfulness, excuse my doubtfulness and take in good part this answer answerless!"

But they would not take it.

They had been baying for her blood since Norfolk's death, ten now, no, fourteen years before. And with the success of Philip's strike against William the Silent, with the knowledge that I, too, walked in daily danger of death from an assassin, they could not now be stopped. I thought to hold them with my power of veto—La Reyne ne veult! . . . The Queen will not permit it! But I was over-ridden, trampled down.

My father would not have stood for it: he would have had his way! But my task was harder—not to take life but to save it—and so they overbore me. And for that I never will forgive myself.

With Zutphen taken, back came Robin from the wars. He rode through the night to be with me as soon as his ship landed and came to me as he so often had before, as the dawn was breaking. Yet in this winter world no birds were singing. And with the first light, even with the love in his eyes, I could not help seeing a head not thinning now but almost bald, a face reddened and puffed up from the hard ride, and a body stiff with old muscles too long forced into armour, too long kept in the saddle.

"Robin—oh, my heart!"

Yet there was joy in his return, and triumph too.

"Madam, may I commend my stepson the young Essex?" demanded Robin, glowing with pride that night in the Presence, when all the Court turned out to welcome the heroes home. At his signal a tall figure loomed up from behind the sconces into the light round the throne.

Was this the boy who had left with him? For sure, he had brought me back a man, and a fine one indeed . . .

Tall, taller than Robin or Raleigh, he had an ardent grace that taught the candles to burn bright, glancing from the tortoiseshell depths of his bright black eyes. His tumbling curls, midway between brown and gold, had little gleaming glow-worms in their depths, and his smile, too, brought light and colour to the darkest day. Yet his glance was without malice, his boyish grin open as sunlight, and his bow unaffected, unfinished even, in a way that touched my deepest part . . .

"Honor him, lady, for he triumphed at Zutphen, leading the charge like the young Alexander when he first blooded spurs and sword on the field of Chaeronea—"

The young man started, and half turned away. "Pray, sir, spare your praises!" he said fiercely. "I am not worthy!"

He was blushing!

How long was it since any man had blushed in my presence?

How old was he? Twenty? Oh, God, only nineteen?

Oh, Jesus, Cupid, spare me . . .

Robin waved him aside. "Now to the Queen of Scots, beloved lady—you must sign the warrant for her death . . ."

They all protested love, said they adored me.

Why, then, did no one help me?

I dreamed then of the man who would do it for me, for her—the pillow on her face, the slow-wasting drops slipped into her food. I scattered hints like loom weights; I even wrote urging her keepers to "do their duty," and speedily too. But Christ, these tender consciences! No man would do it. And though I wished her dead, I could not sign the warrant for her death.

Why not? Why did I delay? Hear me, and I'll tell you.

Even that Mary who had hated me, my hated sister, had held her hand from striking off my head when her own Lord Chancellor, my enemy Gardiner, and the Ambassador Renard, that stinking Spanish fox, were pressing for my death.

I saw myself in Mary, in both the Marys. And I saw another. *How could I of all women send a woman to the block?*

Oh, now she came back to me, in my sleep or my white nights—in grotesque mockery, her head tucked underneath her arm, walking the Bloody

Tower, her hand at her throat, saying with a wild laugh, "Fear me not, Master Executioner, for I have but a little neck . . ."
My mother.

Never would I have thought my little body had so many tears in it. A black Christmas came and went at Richmond, Candlemas looming found us at Greenwich, and still they hounded me by night and day: *Madam, you must sign! Sign the death warrant!*

Candlemas came in with the break of February, and we gave thanks for the Feast of the Purification of the Virgin. I always loved the dazzle of the candles that the feast was named for, the golden bloom they cast, sweet as God's grace, no matter how much the Puritans railed against them as idolatry. Was it that that weakened me when my cousin Harry Hunsdon came to my chamber attended only by the Secretary Davison very late that night? Or was it the sense of his blood, our blood, Boleyn blood, blood of my mother and her sister, son as he was of Mary as I was child of Anne?

His grim look sank my heart.

"Majesty—may we enter and disturb your peace?"
Peace?

Behind him came my other cousin Howard, his face dark too with concern and meaning. *His father had protected me from sister Mary—could Charles, now coming into his father's place as Lord High Admiral, save me from this Mary in his turn?*

"Madam, we come to say only one word. It is written, *Strike or be stricken, strike or be stricken.*"

I saw the dark shape of terror lying in wait, felt the assassin's blade as it flashed from behind the arras, and screamed as the hare does when the hounds sink their teeth into her haunches. *"By God's blood, let me sign!"*

Madly I traced my way through the serpentine forms of my ELIZABETH R, sometimes keening in pain, sometimes laughing the disordered laugh of a Bedlam woman. "See there, I have signed! Bear the news to Walsingham! it will go near to kill him outright!" I threw the heavy parchment to the floor. Davison hasted to gather it up, scrolls, seals and all, and lap it tenderly in blood-red velvet. "Madam, I will."

God, they were hounds, snuffling the trail of blood! At least that would silence them for a while, get them off my back. For I knew they would not proceed to the execution without my agreement to the time, the place and all the details, as with the Earl of Norfolk. Now at last, could I hope to sleep a little?

"Leave me now, damn you!" I howled. *"Leave me in peace!"*

Dear Jesus, God have mercy, how was I to know?

Yes, I must bear it. But when I face my Maker at the last account, I can do no better than the child's defence: "She started it! She tried to kill me first!"

And I was happier once the warrant was signed, I confess. The next day and the next and the next, a pale sun finely gilding all the fields round Greenwich, we were on horseback not long after dawn, Robin and Essex and I. Now I raced the young Rob, not the old, for we soon had him outdistanced as my young lord clapped his spurs on and challenged me for victory. On the third day we were heading back to the palace when across the water meadows came a sound that I dared not credit . . .

"What's that?"

Essex cocked his bright head. "Church bells, Your Majesty. But why do they ring out now?"

"Ask me not! *Follow!*"

I spurred the screaming mare every inch of the way back. At the gate-house a little crowd was gathered, in front of them a smaller group of men not talking, standing apart. As I threw the reins of my horse to a groom and leaped down into Essex's strong young arms, they were there to greet me, Burghley and Hatton, Hunsdon and Howard, Knollys and the invalid Walsingham, and behind them Davison. All were clothed in black, though even their sable silks were not as ominous as their faces.

"Tell me not it is done!" I cried in terror.

Burghley bowed like an angel of death. "My lady, it is done."

"*How*, done?"

Burghley inclined his head. "By due process of law. Your Council met as soon as the warrant was in our hands. It was sealed by the Lord Chancellor and despatched to Fotheringay. And there it was executed upon the Scottish Queen."

"How—died she?"

"Very bravely, Majesty, firm in her faith."

Hatton stepped forward. "You deny the lady! It was her finest hour! She died in a crimson petticoat, flaunting the blood of martyrs—"

A groan, a sigh, a sob, seemed to issue from my depths and split my being: "*Away, all of you! Away!*"

I never heard the rest until years after—the great red wig that bounced off with her head, revealing the sparse grey hairs underneath, just as mine would have done; the lips that went on moving in prayer for an hour and more after her head was severed; the little dog that crept nuzzling to her skirts as she lay on the ground, then afterwards ran to the head and licked her face, and would not be led away . . .

Already now it was too much to bear. Shaking and speechless, I looked round the group. Only the boy Essex wore the badge of innocence in the scarlet flush searing his cheeks. By Robin's face he knew already—they all knew.

They had taken her life. They had taken from me my right as their Queen, my royal prerogative to decree *how, where* and *when,* taken out of my hands the decision I had shrunk from—God Almighty!—for twenty years now.

They had put us in the hands of France, of Spain, of the Pope, of Scotland even, as pure regicides whose sin could not go unpunished . . .

They had without my choice made the urchin James of Scotland now my heir—after my death, now my only heir.

Stammering, reeling, I grasped for Essex's hand, found his strong arm at the ready and leaned into him.

"Who sent the warrant?"

"I did, Your Majesty." It was Davison, the trusty servant—trusty Judas!

"Guard! Ho there!" Speechless, I pointed at him, and the guard led him away. I gasped for breath. "I will have him hanged! And you—you—" I turned on Burghley and Hatton. "You will pay for your presumption—I ban you from Court—you are anathema to me, now and henceforth—"

"Majesty, no!"

Hatton was on his knees, weeping and plucking the hem of my gown. But Burghley straightened his old shoulders and drew himself up. "As Your Majesty wills." Proudly he bowed his head. "But a word in our defence. What the Queen did, she did foully and treacherously, and she was rightly called to account and punished. What we did, we did openly, under English law, and the end was just. Without her death, these plots against you, lady, would still have flourished like the Hydra, sprouting fresh heads until the heart of the beast was cut out. While she lived, you never breathed secure in your own kingdom, and our whole nation lay in mortal dread."

In all the crowd, not a breath stirred. He paused, and began again in the same voice.

"Now have we shown the Pope, the kings of France and Spain, the Jesuit Fathers, the devils of Douai, the whole world, the value that we place on our religion, on our country, on our Queen. We have scotched the 'Enterprise of England,' the great Roman revival on these shores! Now they know that England is Protestant, will be Protestant, for so long as the waters of the sea beat round this isle! Madam, remember Latimer, burned at the stake in your sister's time, when he heartened his companion in the flames? *Be of good cheer, Master Ridley,* said he then, *and play the man, for we shall this day light such a candle by God's grace in England as I trust shall never be put out.* Your Grace has kept alight this precious candle, and we, too—yea, every man of us—would give our lives to see it not snuffed out."

Quietly he gathered up his long velvet gown. "For me now, I take my dismissal—nay, my disgrace is my honour at your hands, I take it with joy. And I dare swear that when Your Grace comes to bethink herself, you will see then, and know for all of God's good time to come, that what we did we had to do, what we did was set down by God's own hand on high from time before time, and if I die for saying so, I cannot think we did wrong!"

He bowed, and never turning his old back on me, slowly withdrew, as they all did in a dreadful silence, and I was left weeping.

L X I

Now the evil was upon us. Now the hunt was on—and England, poor quivering England, stalked by the mighty hunter, was at last brought to bay.

It was Mary's work again—that deadly hand that even from the grave never ceased to move against me. For her last writing was to will the throne of England to her dear cousin of Spain. To all Catholics, then, England was Philip's now. And the Most Holy Catholic King of Spain and of the Low Countries, and now *Rex Anglorum,* was coming to claim his own.

What of James in Scotland, you demand, what of her own son, should he not inherit her claim to the crown?

A wife may be divorced, even a husband. But who has power to divorce their own child? Who but Mary would even try? Making her last will, Mary set aside the son of her own body in favour of a half-mad Spaniard she had never seen. And Philip, crazed with age and rage, loss and defeat, took up the challenge. He would assume his right-presumptive against me—he would make a Holy Crusade against the Queen of Heretics, the heretical Queen.

Yet still it seemed that we might fight them off by other means. That springtime I still suffered like an invalid, and slowly, only slowly, did I pull round from Mary's death. It was long before I forgave Burghley and the rest and had them back to Court, but forgive them I did. And early summer brought me a wondrous tonic. Once again the little man of Plymouth stood before me to report how he had kept my last commandment. Around his balding pate the light frizz of hair stood like a mischievous halo. "Well, Sir Francis," I challenged him, "I told you *harry them, harry them.* Have you played ducks and drakes with the King of Spain?"

His wide blue eyes dancing, he made his reply. "We have Draked them at least, madam, you may be sure. In Cadiz harbor we burned above thirty-seven of their ships!"

I gave a shout of laughter. "Then you have singed the King of Spain's beard!"

"No question—with a vengeance! Afterwards, plying the sea-lanes of the Spanish Main, we took and burned no less than a hundred. And then happening to be at Cape St. Vincent, making for the Azores"—his eyes rolled innocently—"we came upon the carrack *San Felipe—*"

I leaned forward, my blood racing, "What, the *Saint Philip?* The King's own treasure ship?"

"Majesty, *yes!*" He cackled with delight. "And so loaded with silks and spices and silver bullion that she could scarce draw water!" Like a conjuror, from between his fingers he twirled a shining coin. "And besides her emeralds, rubies, sapphires, opals, pearls, I have a hundred and fifty thousand of the brothers and sisters of this fellow to lay at your royal feet —I bring a carpet of gold for you to tread upon!"

Oh, how I loved it! Burghley brought a moneylender, Palavicino, fresh from the Bourse. "Tell Her Majesty what you have told me."

The Italian bowed, and fingered his moustache. "With the loss of the *Felipe,* Most Excellent Majesty, the cost of the King of Spain's credit throughout Europe has now soared to eighteen, twenty per cent—he can borrow nowhere for a centime less."

I adored it! I leaned forward greedily. "And mine?"

"Eight per cent, Serenissima, and falling. You have inflicted a mortal wound on his main arteries, his lines of cash."

I wept with satisfaction. That one action bought us a summer of peace— of peace and joy—

I have to tell you—joy as I never knew in all my life. That first summer with Robin, you will say, what of that? That was long gone in memory, he was gone. And now? Another "he" was now, the boy called Essex, he was here, he was mine.

I can see him still, that tall frame leaning down to me, his strong striding gait as he hastened to my side, his clear gaze, his open heart, open to me in all the ardour of his nineteen summers—who could resist it?

So, he was nineteen, while I was—the age I was—what did it matter? There was nothing to it: he pleased me, passed the time for me, that's all.

All that summer there were sweet walks amid the tumbling roses and honeysuckle bowers, long talks deep into the night when we two alone were awake amid the slumbering guards and the last of the courtiers. He would not seek his bed, he never came to his chamber except with birdsong and dawning, and then only to shrug off his doublet for fresh apparel to attend me again . . .

Oh, it was sweet, he was sweet, he was so sweet . . .

And there came, too, a little sourness with the joy, which was its own relish to my jaded palate. Raleigh was jealous! So he fought all the harder for my favour. He sent out ships to find the New World he had promised me, there to found the "Virginia" he had dreamed of, ordering his men to bring back monsters, Indians, whatever they could find in tribute for me. And one day at Court, his blue eyes snapping and his bow at its most ceremonious, he had a surprise indeed.

"I trust Your Majesty will enjoy this, for it has cost me a good wetting!"

"This? This weed?" I turned the shrivelled brown leaves in my hands. "Why, how so?"

"When I was taking this 'weed,' as you name it, madam, I called my man to bring me a yard of ale. Coming upon me, the booby cried 'Fire! Our master's on fire!' and threw the ale all over me to put me out—to the ruin of a good doublet!"

My curiosity was now running riot. I fingered the limp leaf, silky between my thumbs. "Explain, sir! How, on fire?"

"Madam, this weed you smoke!"

And whipping out a small white clay pipe with a bulb on the end of it, he stuffed the leaf into the bowl and set fire to it, puffing energetically all the while upon the stem. "This is the way of the Indians of the New World, who derive great benefit from it. Aaah!" He closed his eyes and drew the scented flume into his lungs. A look of bliss passed across his face. "Now, Majesty, you must try!"

I looked around. Beside me stood Mary Radcliffe, pale as a lily, as she always was. Would the weed bring color to her cheeks? "Radcliffe . . ."

"Madam?"

Oh, the sweet purity of her! One puff and she was primrose-green, all sick and fainty, coughing and puking, not fit to be seen. Walsingham's daughter Frances, Sidney's widow, only just returned to Court after long mourning for her husband, led her away.

"Here, mistress!"

Raleigh had pounced on another of my ladies, the young Elizabeth Throckmorton, orphan daughter of my old servant Sir Nicholas, and though cousin to the traitor Throckmorton, still one of my favourites. "Try this for your lady!"

"Indeed, sir!" she replied, laughing up at him, her bonny brown face alight with youth and mischief. "I'll venture for Her Majesty—at your bidding!"

"Why, there's a wench!" He stopped, and looked at her for the first time. "What do they call you, Bess, or Bessy, is it?"

We went on to try the weed all round the Court, turning the strange word "tobacco" in our mouths as well as the tongue-stinging spume, and in the head-spinning, gut-wrenching stink and taste and feel of it, I never thought to say, *Call her not Bess, she is no man's plaything, nor are you, sir, a free man when I am your mistress and you are in my service.*

Raleigh had much to do with his new worlds; Essex was still learning the ways of the old. Yet two stallions can never keep together in one field. They quarrelled, violently and often. Boy as he was, Essex went hard at my Walter till I could take no more.

"Beware, sir," I burst out one night in the Presence, "of attacking those nearest to me, or I may speak words of your mother you would not wish to hear!"

He turned as pale as death. "My mother, madam?"

"Yes, that witch Lettice! And you should look to your sister Penelope, loose-sided as her mother, rumoured now to be a bed swerver to her husband the Lord Rich!"

He quivered like a stag when the bolt finds his heart. "Even at your hand, I will not stand for this! Nor will I stand by to see my affection cast down in favour of a wretch like Raleigh, who means so much to you!"

And storming and cursing, he flung out into the night. Yet I soon had my hawk back on my wrist, contrite and humbled, feeding from my hand —*I could tame him then* . . .

But the chill winds of autumn blew our sweet summer idyll away, and my enemies nearer our shores.

"We must make peace!" I moaned to all who would listen. But my lords' iron faces round the table said, *It must be war.*

Now I needed my new gallant's innocent devotion and all the diversions he could put me to. He brought a friend of his, Kit Blount, to Court, and together they adored me and tilted for my favours. And in reward I made him my Master of the Horse—just as I had done Robin.

But still the warmongers nipped and picked, nibbling away at the fabric of my peace.

"Consider this, madam!" urged my cousin Howard, the Lord Admiral, his shrewd eyes on my face. "The King of Spain now has ten, twenty, forty thousand men not twenty miles away in the Netherlands under the Duke of Parma! In the Azores his fleet has defeated Portugal, captured her galleons and secured her to his side. At Terceira there he beat the French, and his Admiral then boasted he could throw six hundred ships and eighty-five thousand soldiers down the English throat at a week's notice. We flout his religion, harry his ships, support his rebellious subjects, usurp 'his' throne. What now will hold him back from our destruction?"

"Oh, Charles—"

Under the strong lineaments of his manly English face, I could still see the boy I had known as old uncle Howard's son. How fast the sons were replacing their fathers!

And yet it was true that Spain now feared nothing from a defeated France . . . and that with Mary dead, I had lost my insurance there . . .

"But we do not know that Philip bears such rooted hate against us," I protested.

"Give me the money, madam, and we will know!"

Yellower than ever since his illness, Walsingham had lost none of his inner fire. "With the cash to pay for it, we shall have intelligence second to none! We shall know if he plans to attack from the Low Countries, or send a force by sea; if he sets sail, how many and with whom, where to, on which day; and what he thinks comes after. Lady, I swear the King of Spain will not so much as pick his ears but you will know of it, yes, even to the weight of the earwax!"

"God's body, Walsingham, money again? *How much?*"

Que voulez-vous?

What could I do?

By the spring of '88, then—Walsingham was a genius!—we knew all that we needed, and more, far more, than we ever wished to know. Each day brought news of another thing to fear.

"One hundred and thirty ships stand in Lisbon harbor, with a frontline strength of twenty great galleons, ten galleasses and five newly rigged mighty merchantmen, all armed for war and fitted now for sail," a grim-faced Walsingham informed a tight war cabinet. "With them come sixty-odd second-line galleons, each one twice as big as the biggest of our ships, and with them seventy troopships, scouts and hulks."

An armada, then.

In a white silence each of us pictured the forest of masts, the floating fortresses standing proud of the water, every one higher than the Tower of London. Walsingham went on. "King Philip has given command to the first of his nobles, the Duke of Medina Sidonia. And he commands nine thousand sailors, two thousand galley slaves, nigh on three thousand cannon and above twenty thousand soldiers."

We few . . . we hapless few . . .

Walsingham's dry voice was droning on. "The Duke of Parma in the Netherlands is ordered to stand by to rendezvous with the great fleet, to add his forces to their ranks—for the invasion of England. He has written his lord and master"—Walsingham threw down a copy of the despatch—"that he will prepare his own barges to make landing—"

One thing at least was clear as day to me. *"They must not make landing."*

Hunsdon raised his eyebrows. "Your Majesty fears the Catholics will rise in support?"

"Never! They will not rise!" I swore. "Not for the King of Spain! No one in England has forgotten Bloody Mary and the fires of Smithfield—they will fight!"

But no one dared to say "Amen!"

Oh, we would fight. No man made doubt of that. The City of London, asked how many men they could supply to defend her, asked what we would need. When told five thousand men and fifteen ships, they swore to double the number, and if need be, double that.

But if the enemy made landing . . .

"Rob, you will defend me?"

Oh, how tired he looked . . . and he rubbed his side as Kat had done before she died—was he in pain?

He smiled his old Robin smile. "Defend you? Lady, say *die* for you—rejoicing and singing psalms like a weaver, if your sweet life were saved!"

Painfully we struggled out of our sleep of peace to put all England on a war footing. Howard was Lord Admiral; Burghley, in charge of affairs at home, and Walsingham abroad; Hatton, Lord Chancellor to rule and sweeten my unruly Parliament. They would save England, if any could. But Robin was my champion, my defender: he must save me. "You shall be my Lieutenant-General, to command the land forces and defences," I told him. "In which capacity I look to you to save both of us—and all of our good people!"

For we would fight—we would all fight, we would go down fighting. And that fighting spirit of little England won me some strange admirers. How God loves to jest! My new admirer was none other than the Pope.

"What a valiant woman this Englishwoman is!" he told the French Ambassador. "Not even Queen of half an island, she braves the world's two greatest nations, France and Spain, by both land and sea, and taunts their kings by her excellence in all things. What a crime of God that she and I could never marry—our children would have been the wonder of the world!"

I laughed along with all my Court when we heard this. But that night at Greenwich, as the night deepened and hope burned down with the candles, came a storm of fear and recrimination—if I had married Philip when he offered, when first I came to the throne, could I have spared my beloved land what was to follow?

Certainly, yes.

But at a price no English heart would pay.

No, we would fight!

Within my chamber a small group of my women murmured drowsily in a far corner, as doves coo softly, roosting in midnight elms. By the great fireplace, filled with green not glowing branches now in June, fragrant with ferns and bracken, one of the pages slept the blameless sleep of his seven summers, curled up with the dogs.

Outside I knew my yeoman, gentlemen and guard kept double watch now, while I watched for England.

England—my England—this England of ours . . .

This England . . .

This England never did nor never shall lie at the proud foot of a conqueror. Come the three corners of the world in arms, and we shall shock them!

Beyond the casement rolled on silent and unseen England's green hills and pastures, our noble forests, mighty rivers and small sparkling streams, great cities and thatched market towns, broad highways and fair harbours—a paradise of God. I thought of all my people, honest men and sturdy toiling women, children and babes in arms whom we had fought to bring up in the light of truth, not fear; freedom, not tyranny. Across the meadowland the sighing waters sucked and sang, and a lone nightjar purled through the damp sweet air.

This earth—this realm—this England . . .

In my heart now I saw our little land beating back to the first dawn of life among these hidden isles, this secret place lost in the mists at the edge of the universe, and beating onward, too, ceaselessly on, to worlds and races yet unknown to man. Closing my eyes, I swore a silent, secret oath to God and to my soul: *We shall keep the faith.*

Let the world come against us! We shall fight them to the death.

We shall fight while there is English earth to bear us up, English soil to

soak up our blood, we shall fight while one good English arm can wield a
sword against our enemies.
   We shall fight while England lives.
   We shall never surrender!

L X I I

They shall not pass . . .

"Who's there? What, have they landed—? No, come in, I was not sleeping, only dreaming, in a doze—oh, Robin, what news?"

   My chamber was a pool of glimmering silence. In the light before
dawn, I could not read his face.

   "Lady, a new Bull from the Pope."

   The Pope? Still shitting Bull? Did it matter now?

   "From my admirer? Why, what's he saying now?"

   "He calls upon all Catholics to rise up against you and to fight with
Spain when their army makes our shores."

   "He still believes his word will put me off my throne?" I was indifferent. "On the usual grounds, bastard, usurper, heretic, and so forth?"

   "And one more, Majesty." His eyes were glinting like the boy Rob I
had known. Narrowing his eyes, he peered down at the paper in his hand:
" '. . . for that she has used an infamous variety of lust to keep men in
subjection to her foul fleshly needs, using black arts to entangle in sin
and entrap the greatest of her nobles in her damnable and detestable
vices, her filthy turpitude . . .' "

   I looked at him, keeping my face straight. "Does His Holiness name
any of my poor male victims, these men I have enslaved with my lust?
Anyone we know . . . ?"

   He made a great play of consulting the parchment once again, and our
eyes met in a sweet, sad smile. "There is one Robert Dudley, Earl of
Leicester, here . . ."

Yet darker news was even now winging towards us. Walsingham's gold—
my gold!—or the King of Spain's—had bought us eyes even in his most

secret places; we could look into his close-stool. So we knew all his preparations moment by moment as he knew them himself. We were there at the musters, we oversaw every knot of every ship's rigging, we knew even as the armourers rolled them on board how many cannonballs were coming to pulverise poor England—one hundred and twenty-three thousand, seven hundred and ninety-two! So we knew then the day, the very hour when the King of Spain's great army of the sea wheeled west out of Corunna, set its course east across the Biscay and made for open water.

The Armada was coming.

They had near on three hundred galleons, while my fleet mustered under thirty. With the ships of Drake and Hawkins, Raleigh and others of my privateers, and then the craft that every shipyard now was sweating night and day to throw together, we might make a hundred.

Three against one, at best.

They had two thousand galley slaves, three thousand cannon, ten thousand sailors, twenty thousand handpicked fighting men.

We had the boys and men of Sussex, Essex, Kent.

And then the Duke of Parma with his fifty thousand men sat waiting on our doorstep, his fleet of barges uncounted and uncountable, for his shipwrights were building them faster than our spies could keep record.

Yet David beat Goliath.

We had our English hearts, the best hearts in the world.

"No, Robin, I will not fall back to Windsor. We can defend St. James's here as well as any, if we have to . . ." *For if we fail to hold them in the Channel and they make London water, then all is lost, and I am lost with it.*

I took his hand. It felt dry and hot, but his face as I brushed it with my fingers was sticky and cold. *He must have some oil of vervain, and that potion of all-heal and heart's-ease Dame Katherine Parr used to have mixed for my father—I will send it. Oh, how I love him.* I stroked his pale face, almost forgetting my own fear-tortured gut. "Get yourself off to the coast now, rally the muster, for I shall come by and by to inspect my troops!"

Lord of Hosts, God of battles, Thou that givest not always the battle to the mighty but may stir up Thy strength for the few, bless and keep my poor soldiers, hearten them against their most fearsome foe . . .

Robin gone, Essex gone with him, Raleigh gone, only the little half-man Robert Cecil left to help me, none to defend or save me . . .

Save what had always saved me, God and my good courage—

That night I spent a long time at my toilet, rubbing wolfsbane into my temples—*God, grant me a wolf's strength for what I have to face.*

Alone in my chamber, I tried to pray: *Lord God, Father God, Father of love I never had, Thou hast set me on high, but my flesh is frail and weak. And now the terror is upon us, there is nowhere to hide, and now I must be strong for others, not myself. If therefore I at any time this day of battle chance to forget Thee, do not Thou forget Thy child and daughter—touch my heart, O God, that I again remember Thee and Thy great purpose for myself, my country and for all my people.*

Yet if I could have had another prayer, it would have been: *Oh, God, let me be there, let me not die alone!*

"The ships of Spain are sighted, madam—the runner is even now fallen from his horse."

"Robert, I thank you."

All that July storms raged over Europe, clouds and tempests blackened the sky, nature was so offended by the belligerence of man. Then at last, on the fifth day of the third week of the month, it came, darkening the sun.

At three o'clock the watchers on the Lizard *saw the great nightmare creep over the horizon till the sea and sky turned black. Across the wide rim of the bowl of the world, the line of ships stretched farther than eye could see— ships built like towers, keeps and castles, breasting the waves in a perfect crescent, in such numbers that the horns of this devil moon were seven miles apart . . .*

Under full sail they came, in a high wind, yet so leisurely that it seemed as if they mocked our terror with their slow, stately dance. So heavy were they that the winds laboured to drive them, and the very sea was heard to groan under the burden.

Then came the first of our losses, when the poor simple soul on lookout, after giving the word, cried "Jesu have mercy!" and lay down and died. Yet my little Drake, playing bowls on Plymouth Hoe with his friend and kinsman the old Devon seadog John Hawkins, calmly paused and looked up at the sky. "Play on!" he commanded carelessly. "Finish the game. The King of Spain will stay for our convenience."

Yet for all these brave words, we all knew the great unspoken truth. Everything turned on England's little ships.

"God smiles upon us, madam!" said Robert stoutly when the news made London. "For our fleet is ready, here at our defence and not somewhere off England chasing its tail while the ships of Spain slip past!"

As some had counselled for our strategy, *he was too smooth to say—not least my fiery young lord Essex, who would have had us rush out looking for battle instead of waiting till we could take them in our own time and in our own waters.*

That night the cruel crescent, too proud for evasion or concealment, weighed anchor outside Plymouth. And when they awoke at dawn the next day, they found that all our little ships had slipped out of port and lay in wait behind them. How I laughed when I heard this! "That will teach them, Robert!" I exulted. "They laugh at our cockleshells at their peril!"

Robert smiled. But he was very pale. "Please God it may be so, Your Majesty."

Now every hour or half hour a rider from the sea brought the next despatch. I had them in my hands within minutes of their arrival, still wet with seawater, rain and mud, or sweat, or blood.

"They must make for Calais, madam, we know that," my cousin Howard the Lord Admiral sent furiously from his flagship in the fleet, "to rendezvous with Parma and provide safe cover for his barges. Until then we may only harry them at a distance, to avoid loss of any of our fleet."

"Yes!" I sent back. "And God speed! Robert, order them to stand off!" For the loss of even one of our ships did not bear contemplation.

Yet how hard it is to fight a sea battle on land! Standing off, we felt the poverty of our firepower—blast after blast of shot was loosed off with all the sound and fury in the world, only to fall harmlessly into the sea. I wept with rage to think of the prodigious cost, the vast waste of money, the sheer pointlessness of it all!

"Bid them *engage!*" I wept. "For some of them at least we must destroy before they make Calais water! Is that beyond our people?"

"Madam, your Vice-Admiral Sir Francis Drake sends to say that this is what they must and will do now."

"So be it! God give us victory then!"

How swift God is to punish our over-reaching, humble our pride with strong indignity! The word reached me in the privy, my woman Warwick, Robin's brother Ambrose's wife, hammering on the door. "Madam, evil news!"

"God help us! What?"

"Your Majesty's cousin the Lord Admiral, sailing too near the wind, is taken by the enemy!"

In Warwick's eyes I saw what stumbled out of the garderobe, an old woman still fumbling with her petticoats, struggling to adjust her skirt, tears in her eyes, her face cracked with shock. "So, fool!" I grated. "Is this all? What more?"

"All the ships stand on the turn of the tide, madam, the galloper says, both the Lord Admiral's and the galleons that surround him. And when it turns, from the lie of the Spanish ships, the shore watchers say, they will ram the flagship, sink it and send all our men to their deaths!"

"What?" My screeching would have shattered glass. "No mercy for a great lord, our greatest lord of the sea? No ransom even?" But as I spoke I heard the evil whisper, *Victory or death . . . death or victory . . .*

LXIII

They laughed at our little ships, the Spaniards—did you know that?—just because their huge hulks could not turn, nor wheel, nor fly about with every light breeze, as ours could do. Their galleons being so mighty and high-built, they thought our cockleshells nothing but bum-boats, tubs and clinkers. "Poison comes in small bottles!" they jeered at my seamen from their lofty floating battlements.

They thought they had my Charles, my Lord Admiral, our commander in chief, in their hand, and with him the victory firmly in their grasp. They even gave orders for a victory Mass! But God is just. And our English hearts of oak would not give up without a fight! At the first turning of the tide, while the Spanish dullards were still rubbing the sleep from their eyes, three of our little boats like whippets slipped in between their great galleons' legs, ran under their huge shoulders and threw a line to the Admiral's trapped ship. Then they towed her head around in a trice with a display of seamanship the Spanish still talk of to this day, and while the great galleons were still struggling to weigh anchor, they had her out to safety and the open sea!

"Now God be thanked!" I cried. And to cousin Charles I sent a flurry of despatches, laughing, weeping, railing, exulting, reproaching, ordering "Attack without fear or favour!" "Take care, proceed with greatest caution!" "Forward!" "Retreat!" "Onward!" "Fall back!" till my clerks were in a frenzy.

And still victory stood like the turning of the tide, going neither this way nor that. We trailed them up the Channel, my sailors and commanders performing prodigies of courage.

And still the foul weather raged, with storms and tempests defying the calms of July and showing nature ready to turn back the seasons as punishment for our offence against peace and against God.

"What news, Robert?"

"First blood, Your Majesty—one of their warships holed above the waterline and limping, the *Rosario,* and the treasure ship *San Salvador* damaged beyond sail—both signalling surrender."

"A warship and the treasure ship! Good, by God! Oh, our God is good!" I cried with joy, and Robert rejoiced with me in his quiet way. But our anxious glances said, *Two? Is that all? And what are two out of three hundred?*

I neither seemed to eat nor sleep now—but, then, who in England did? And day and night were not what they were before, but became one endless pacing round broken only by a fitful half-crazed trance when the body cried, *No more!* And out there, out in the wild grey storm-lashed sea, day in, day out, through driving rain and winds that wheeled and veered like the hosts of hell, the hellish hosts of Spain lumbered on up the Channel while all around them the little English nipped like terriers in and out, savaging the great clumsy hulks like blind bears.

"What news, Robert?"

"You shall be first to hear, Majesty, when anything arrives."

"What day is it? I think I have lost count."

"This is the sixth full day of battle, lady."

"And tomorrow—"

Robert nodded. God, he grew paler every day!

"Speak, man!" I almost cried. But he did not need to speak for me to hear him. And in any case, what was there to say?

For tomorrow they made Calais.

Of course we had thought of fire ships, we had planned them long before! Why, no less a man than Walsingham himself was in Dover at this moment, presiding over the tons of pitch, the tar-soaked clinkers, a veritable force of fire to gladden the heart of any salamander. Perhaps Philip's prayers or the caterwauling of his three thousand tame monks chanting round the clock in his great cathedral palace deafened God's ears to our good Protestant prayers. At any rate, He turned the wind against us, and Walsingham's floating tinderboxes were trapped in Dover, unable to poke their noses out of harbour.

So when the great fleet of Spain rode tamely at anchor outside Calais, our lookouts looked in vain for the help they needed now. But they were not men to lose time and tide weeping for what could not be. Howard called the commanders and all the captains onto his ship for a council of war. And there they took the fateful decision that was to decide our fate, when they clasped hands, swore a great oath and vowed to stake all England's future on one frantic, desperate throw.

Praise God I was not there. The Almighty blinded my eyes to this, deafened my ears, in His great wisdom, of that I was sure! For how could

I ever have taken that decision, countenanced that sacrifice—*even I, I who have made so many of my own, sacrificed so much that I held dear, and for the same cause too, for England, always England, this England of ours . . .*

Drake sighed, they say, as he closed his sky-blue eyes, then opened them to declare, "I'll give the *Thomas.*" Hawkins wept openly as he muttered thick with tears, "From me, let it be the *Hawk.*" Then Frobisher came in, and others too, until all ten were committed. Ten of the best and fastest ships in the fleet, freely given by those who owned and loved them, to serve as fire-ships to drive out the devil of Spain's mighty Armada.

And so, instead of the old wallowing tubs, the wrecks, the skeletons of ships that could sail no more, could not hold a straight line, but drifted at random if they fired at all, we sent a fire-ship fleet from hell straight to the Spanish heart. Left in all their glory, not stripped of canvas, masts and all, as fire-ships always were, not tiny tar-boats but the finest four-masted schooners under full sail, trimmed and tight-rigged they bore down on the Armada where it rode at anchor like every sailor's dream of his own death.

Indeed they seemed, all said, like the death fleet of a great Norse chieftain from the ancient days of heroes and sagas, bearing to Valhalla in a cloud of flame a mighty warlord and all his warriors. For they sailed in perfect formation, holding their course so true that no one who saw them from the Spanish ships could believe they were unmanned. And they sailed straight and true into the middle of the Spanish fleet and brought with them fire and brimstone, terror and death.

"Now sir—what news?"

A shore watcher stood before me in St. James's, his own face bloodied from a great fall he took as he raced me the word.

"Your Majesty, God fights for us at last, and grinds your enemies under His heel!" He was weeping with a blend of wild emotion, a kind of grief mixed with a savage pride. "For God Himself now scales down their pride with tempests, roasts them with shot and shell—now they cut their cables and ram each other in the frenzy to escape—oh, God, to hear the cries, the screams of pain and panic, as we blast them and blister them with red-hot fusillades, rain down molten lead, cut them to pieces—one galleon as she turned over under our bombardment was seen pouring blood from the lee scuppers, so many men were pumping their life's blood away in her, making the sea as dark as wine for half a mile around—"

Victory or death . . .

 Or death, or victory . . .

Even Robert's face had a little colour now.

"From the Lord Admiral, Majesty—all good, so far as the battle goes."

I tore the parchment from his hand and squinted like a gorgon to squeeze out the words:

Majesty, Queen of battles, your servant salutes you! This night your commanders, led by Vice-Admiral Drake, truly a firedrake now, breathing flame and fury, lit by a sacred rage, sent in fire-ships among the foe as they lay at anchor in Calais water, and in piteous panic they are now all broken up and fled. Albeit at such cost, for your commanders wept for their beloved ships even as they laughed to see their triumph, so went the day to us.

Now God be praised, we have scattered your foes and they run before the wind. Those that cannot run, using their dead to plug the holes below their bilges, now limp on up the Channel, and we pick them off at our leisure, one by one. Now outside Calais, where they were to rendezvous with the Duke of Parma, the Dutch men-o'-war turned out for us to keep them apart.

By threes and fives, now all at sixes and sevens, the enemy make what speed they can out of the Channel and away up our eastern coast. Our English harriers hot in pursuit found the whole Channel choking-black from coast to coast with barrels and baggages, drowned horses and pack mules, even ships' cats thrown off by the crews to lighten them for flight. Amidst the chaos we have hunted down the Admiral of the galleasses, and have run him aground off Dover, and without this Don and his ships the evil crescent cannot re-form.

When last sighted, the stragglers were off Yarmouth Road under full sail, making what haste they could for the North Sea. We shall chase them from the face of our waters, pursue them without mercy if we have to drive them all around Scotland and back out to sea again . . .

Your Majesty's most devoted and triumphant kinsman and servant, the Lord Admiral the Lord Charles Howard of Effingham.

They were gone.

The tall ships were defeated, the Armada blown apart and scattered to fly before the face of God.

We faced each other in a trembling dawn, my lords and I, none daring to rejoice even at this precious moment of victory. Raleigh had raced from Dover to report, his blue eyes sea-washed with exhaustion, his mouth set with grim foreboding. "The battle is not won! It merely shifts to Yarmouth, where they may regroup and ply back to make landing on the south coast."

Burghley nodded. "Even now they may still brave it to attack back up the river from the sea, to make London by way of the Thames, following their King's orders to do or die. And there is still the Duke of Parma with his legions standing by in Calais, ready to embark."

"My lord of Leicester!"

We had not heard the usher's hasty knock before he threw open the door and Robin came striding in, tearing off his hat. My heart pulled like a bruised muscle at the sight of him, then dropped to something worse. He looked sick with haste, grey with exhaustion, his smile sideways with some dread unspoken thing.

"The land defences are our trouble now." He took a breath, and his sad eyes found mine. "Ill news, Your Majesty, which I determined to bring you myself. With or without the aid of his colleagues, the Duke of Parma is launching his troops from Calais. With our ships all fled after the Armada, the Channel stands open to them. They may land unopposed—we lie undefended before them."

LXIV

Undefended before them . . .

I gathered the dregs of my strength. "We must look to the land defences now for the last throw!"

For what else did we have?

"Robin, return as my Lieutenant-General to our armed forces, cheer them in my name. Tell them I will come to Tilbury to inspect the land defences and put heart into my troops."

Was it to hearten the men? Or to hearten one woman—namely, myself? Or merely because I missed one man so badly that I had to see him?

I knew this much, I was dying of inaction, dying of something—and after the torment of the days and weeks of the Armada battle, I must break free of this war of attrition or lose the will to win.

"Send for the Mistress of the Robes! And my women, call for all my women, now, this instant!"

"Majesty, it shall be!"

Now, after all the hours of forced inaction, I was on fire to be let out of this prison of a palace. I was sick to my bones of playing the Princess in the Tower, and longing to be free. And if God smiled on Parma and the troops of Spain made land, I was not safe even in the Tower of London! No, the only place for me now was down at Tilbury surrounded by my men.

Yet to defend me, they had to know what they were fighting for. As I paced the floor in a nerve storm of excitement, I resolved to give every man jack of them something to die for if need be. "All my jewels! Let me have all my jewels here at once!"

Never did a bride of Christ passing to her life out of our world, or an impatient virgin coming at last to the altar, prepare herself for her great moment more carefully than I did that day. "No, not that gown, fool! Nor this one, it hangs like a sack! Oh, hurry, will you? Make haste, make haste!"

"Even for your Coronation, madam, you never gave more love and thought to every detail!" warbled Parry, shaking her grey head. "And that daffodil yellow always became you—yellow silk with, let's see, with amber, lady? Agates, perhaps, or your favourite pearls?"

I caught the eye of Radcliffe as she fastened on the sleeve of my gown, and we shared a silent moment of sad pain. For Parry's world was darkening now: fumbling in the jewel cases and treasure boxes, she could no longer tell an agate from an aigrette, and the gown I wore was not yellow but purest white.

It had to be white, as in the past Parry would have known—white for our innocence, white for the purity of our cause, above all white for virginity, for my maiden grace. Then I must add silver to vaunt my royalty, gold for divinity, and some symbol of a warrior queen to show the men that I shared in their battle, that I was ready and willing to withstand each blow as they would have to do.

The robe I chose was velvet, soft as swansdown, white as a rabbit's scut. The overgown and bodice were silvered with filigree scrolls, and silver Tudor roses spangled the wide kirtle and huge padded sleeves like stars in springtime. Then pearls—*always pearls now, nature's unshed tears, pearls for tears*—great pearls of the Orient and far India, three and four deep edging the neck and waist, swinging in ropes from my girdle, bedecking my wig, clustering my ears and fingers, swathing my throat. Around my neck came a gauzy ruff of silver tissue, around my shoulders a long floating scarf of cloth of gold.

"Magnificent!" breathed Radcliffe, and I knew she spoke the truth. Yet I had to look like a warrior now as well as a queen.

"Your Majesty, let me send to the Armoury," advised the young Cecil.

"Lord God—and the Tower Armourer—only knows what they have there."

"Robert, there is no time!"

"Madam, I'll have my man there and back before you know he's gone!"

How useful he was grown! Back with all haste came a slender breastplate made of solid silver, perfectly fitting for the occasion, and a perfect fit.

"Who wore this?" I demanded as they buckled it on. But no one knew. Was it my father as a boy, playing at tilting? Or did my mother disport herself in it at some ceremonial masque? It could even have belonged to Edward when he made that last progress in armour through the streets of London just before he died. *All gone now, all gone—but not in vain: we shall defend this land of yours to our own deaths, we shall never surrender . . .*

With it came a matching helmet just as finely made. I had it carried before me on a cushion of white satin by a tiny page clad like a prince of elfland, all in white satin and silver too. I went bareheaded, like a heroine of old riding to battle, and I knew I looked a perfect Amazon, a warrior queen. And in my hand I bore my weapon of war, a silver truncheon, chased in solid gold.

Burghley's command to the counties had been plain enough: *Muster the greatest number of armed defenders ever seen on English soil.* Now the ranks of men covered Tilbury's hillsides and the valley in between, a black tide as far as the eye could see, lapping back to the horizon and down to the water's edge. On a rough dais hastily thrown up, the little knot of commanders and their captains stood forward to greet me. And all the hours of preparation—*God, how long it all took now, the gown, the ruff, the wig, the complexion, the glaze!*—were worth it for the second of admiration that flared in my young lord of Essex's eyes as I rode up on that great white gelding and saw him standing beside Robin at the head of all his men. *My lord—oh, my sweet lord—how is it with you . . . ?*

But Robin it was who spoke. Holding my bridle, he began levelly enough, but I could hear what lay behind his voice. And as he moved up, a full troop of men closed around us in a tight, protective ring. "Majesty, still no firm word yet of the Duke of Parma. With the winds still against us in the Channel, we can get no more intelligence beyond that first report from Calais that he has launched his troops. If he has done so, they will be here tonight. And with our ships still away harrying the Armada, they will slip through our defences."

"What of the Dutch? Will their ships aid us, block Parma's barges?"

"No word."

I looked down at his fierce and anxious face. The pits of his eyes were bruised with sleeplessness, and his hand was pressing again, pressing at his side. *Oh, Robin . . .* I looked at the massed thousands, standing mute and motionless, sweating in the sun. My ships had done their best. We could not fight two sea battles with one fleet. On these landsmen and countrymen—men? By the foremost ranks, most of them hardly more than boys—and on these arms, these shoulders, now did all depend. "I must go among the men."

Robin shook his head. "Madam, dear lady, take my word against it. The whole object of this invasion is to put you off your throne. Now that they are landing, one or more of our own men, a Catholic or malcontent, could easily have been suborned to turn against you. If you go down among the ranks, expose yourself to danger, it would take only one pistol, and their work is done!"

Behind him was Essex, treading on his heels. *How could his eyes be so bright and yet so black . . .*

"What do you think, my lord?"

He threw back his head. "You must retire, Majesty. I shall myself conduct you back to London and command your defence."

Oh yes . . .

No . . .

I smiled down into their troubled eyes. God, I felt weary! And old, so old, seeing and knowing more than both of them. "My lords, consider this. None of you can defend me. For I have no defence but the love of England, and my people's wish that I should be their ruler and not the King of Spain. If they must face the brutal soldiery of Parma, his Switzers and swinish Hessians, the sweepings of seven countries, then I face it with them. I have no more than one life to lay down, and I do not fear to lose it in England's service."

Essex's face tightened, but from Robin's I could see he had expected this. His smile came sweetly now and full of love. "Then, lady, let us lead you to your men—"

"And through my men," I corrected, "for I would not have any man here miss the rare spectacle I have made myself for his benefit!"

Up and down we went, then down and up, till every rank and file had been inspected. In all the battle lines of tight-packed men, not a soul moved nor breathed, all the little world of Tilbury held its breath. At last we came back to the dais, where we had begun. I turned my gelding, and began to speak. "People of England—"

A light wind off the river stole my words and whipped them away unheard. *Oh, God, strengthen me now, I beseech you, for now or never I must be strong indeed.* I raised my voice.

"My loving people—"

As I spoke the line at the front broke rank, and wave by wave all followed, all the troops falling as one man to their knees. Before me a young lad was weeping openly, whispering to himself, "God bless Your Majesty! Bless your sweet face!"

I found my voice again through a mist of tears. "My loving people, we have been told we should take heed how we commit ourself to armed multitudes, for fear of treachery." I threw a glance at Robin, who grinned back with a rueful, loving nod. "But I assure you, I do not desire to live in distrust of my faithful and loving people. Let tyrants fear! I have always so behaved myself that under God I have placed my strength and safeguard in the loyal hearts and goodwill of my subjects. Now I have come among you resolved in the heat of battle to live and die among you, to lay down for God, for my kingdom and my people my honour and my blood, even in the dust!"

I was weeping now along with all the men. *"I know I have the body of a weak and feeble woman, but I have the heart and stomach of a king, and a king of England too!"* Now the blood surged to my heart like wine, and I soared to my defiance. "And I think foul scorn that Parma or Spain or any prince of Europe should dare to invade the borders of our realm! So now I will myself take up arms, I myself will be your general, judge and rewarder of every one of your virtues in the field. I know already that you all deserve rewards and crowns, and we do assure you, on the word of a queen, that they shall all be paid. In the meantime my Lieutenant-General shall be in my stead—and I promise you, no prince ever had a more noble or worthy subject—not doubting but by your obedience to my general and your valour in the field, we shall shortly have a famous victory over the enemies of God, my kingdom and my people!"

The cheers were deafening. But sweetest of all was the whispered word of my young lord as his strong young arms swept me from my horse: "Majesty, you are Queen of the world, Queen of all hearts! This day you have put courage into the meanest man here, and fired with love the boldest!"

These words were my consolation, nay my food, in the long nerve-torturing hours that followed. Would Parma come? Or was he playing cat and mouse with us? I paced about that hillside till night was fading, talking easily with my captains as if I had not a care in the world. But all the time I never took my eyes off the far horizon where the road led in from the sea.

Yet was it the silver dusk as it slowly fell late that midsummer night? Or simply my old eyes? For when he came I did not see him. Only the shouts of the camp followers at the outer edge of the ranks told of his arrival. And there he was, no mere galloper but an intelligencer from

Calais, gasping and blurting: "Parma will not sail! He has given up the cause, dispersed his men, and himself sails back to Spain!"

"Praise the Lord! Now God be praised!"

"And bless Her Majesty! God bless the Queen!"

"The Queen!"

"The Queen!"

"*The Queen!*"

Above the roars and cries of men in triumph, one small voice whispered in my ear: *I have done this—I, Elizabeth—Elizabeth the Queen.* And oh, it was good!

That night we dined in Robin's tent, feasting on sucking pig and good roast beef, and as they raised the ruby-red wine again and again to my health in the circle of kind candlelight, I was never happier, I was Queen indeed.

We told ourselves that the threat to England was not quite over. We could still hear at any moment, so we said, the long-dreaded cry "To horse! To horse! The Spaniards are coming!" But we did not believe it. In our hearts we felt the victory, seized it and savoured it till our souls were so packed with gladness we could feel no more. And then, if we could have stilled our world for just one second, stayed the mighty turning of the globe, stopped the earth on its axis at that moment, I would have done it—for that night I touched, we touched, the still centre at the heart of things—

"No more, my lord?"

With a gentle negative, Robin waved the man away. I stared at his plate, where his good viands lay almost untouched. "You are not eating?"

"My dearest lady, I leave that to you and to the young blood!" He smiled fondly at Essex. "I am not hungry."

A thought came to me. "You are still unwell? Did you get the medicines I sent you?"

"I did indeed, dear madam, and have found them greatly helpful for my pains." Again he rubbed absently at his side. "And once our enemy is certainly despatched, I thought to call upon the Jew who cured Walsingham of his jaundice, the Portuguese Dr. Lopez, to take his opinion. And then I shall crave your dearest permission to go north to take the waters of the spring at Buxton—that was known to be sovereign in the time of the Romans, and will for sure cure me now."

"And you will not have long to wait, sir, I dare swear!" chimed in Essex, flushed with youth and wine. "For we have the Dons on the run, I will wager to that! Parma will not show his sheep-biting face upon our shores. We have the victory! We have won the day!"

Robin and I exchanged a glance at this: *The young—God bless them!*

But my young lord was right. By dribs and drabs, by over-hasty posts and over-long despatches, by words and letters, scribbled notes and last words and oaths and sighs and tears and prayers and dying screams and curses, the true tale emerged.

We had won the day.

We had thrown down the hosts of Belial, put down the mighty from their seat. The broken fleet of Spain sailed on, not daring to rendezvous, not even to pause to share their shot or victuals; in their terror now it was each for himself, catch as catch can. Some were lost at sea as they plied round Scotland, others washed up on the coasts of Ireland, where the treacherous kerns had their heads for footballs and their eyes and ears for dinner. Of those who sailed safely round England and struck out again into open sea, many, weakened by warfare and starvation, fell into the hands of corsairs and were sold into the galleys, where the poor souls labour still. Of the great host that had so proudly left Spain, less than a thousand men ever limped back.

Such was God's verdict, such His vengeance, for them death and dishonour and the scourge of His wrath.

For us, there was relief and then rejoicing. When the word came in that all our foes were gone, I commanded a service of thanksgiving and myself chose the text. At my command then did my Archbishop, my Whitgift, whom I called my little black husband, begin on the Collect:

"Now is our great and mighty Queen Elizabeth like Deborah of old, who rose up triumphing among the tribes of Israel to sing this song of joy:

" 'Praise ye the Lord for the avenging of Israel. Hear, O ye kings, give ear, O ye princes, for I will sing unto the Lord, I will sing praises to the Lord our God.

" 'Awake, awake Deborah, utter thy song, for the Lord hath made thee to have dominion over the mighty: O my soul, thou hast broken the horse hoofs and thrown down the prancings of the mighty ones.

" 'So may all thine enemies perish, O Lord: but let them that love Thee be as the sun when he goes forth in all his might.' "

"And after Deborah," observed Burghley smugly as he and I and young Robert his son and Robin and Walsingham shared a companionable glass as the dawn rose, for none of us wanted to go to bed that night, "after the great war leader Deborah, you recall, my best lady, that the land of Israel had peace for forty years?"

I laughed. "Nay, for England, let me prophesy—peace in our land, peace and good joy for four hundred and forty years!"

And we toasted to that, and called for more wine and grew merry and even riotous.

Yet as I spoke the still small voice breathed again in my heart: *Let the rule of God last a thousand years in this land, this hour of ours will never be forgotten. Till the end of time, all souls that call this precious island home will thrill to the memory of how little England fought this mighty Spanish Armada and beat them from our shores.*

THE ENVOY TO MY FOURTH BOOK

Non nobis, Domine . . .

Not unto us, O Lord, be the power and the glory, the victory and the might.

Not unto us foreknowledge of the future, to see the dark hand moving to shear life's precious thread even at the height of love and joy and thanksgiving.

How was I to know?

I never said, Good-bye, love, *never bid him farewell.*

He came to kiss hands on his leave-taking, and his eyes were as ever now, loving, warm and sad.

"When will you return?" I demanded fretfully. "For I shall have need of you before the next Parliament session—those troublesome men from the shires are sure to object to the subsidies that we must still raise for defence—and there is still the matter of Ireland—"

He held my hand for longer than courtesy dictated. "Madam, there will always be the matter of Ireland. For that Godforsaken country now stands in such a case that only God—or some young god on earth—has power to cure it."

He half turned to the door where his man stood nursing a thick travelling cloak, for though it was September now and still golden warm, he seemed to feel the cold.

"Take care of Her Majesty, boy!" he rallied Essex, standing at my side, playfully punching the bright padded scarlet-and-cinnamon shoulder roll of my lord's fashionable rig. "If I dare entrust an unfledged youth with such a sacred charge!" Of course, my lord's fine auburn-brown brows darkened and burned fiercely at "youth" and "boy," and as we laughed at his high protests, Robin's leaving passed off.

Did he know then?

I am sure he knew.

For as he parted from me, he raised my hand to his lips and said, "I leave you now to my young lord's love—and England's. Farewell, my Queen, my dearest—"

Did he also murmur under his breath as he turned, or did I only dream it afterwards, "Farewell, my love"?

I should have gone with him to his horse, held his stirrup as he mounted, had a last kiss from the saddle as I always used to do.

But "Majesty, dance!" commanded my young flame-clad lordling, and burning with him I sprang into a galliard and did not even watch Robin to the door.

Then came a letter, at the end of August—oh, how he lied to me!—for he wrote words of comfort: "I continue with the medicines you sent me, and find they do much better than any other thing I have. But I write now only to know how my gracious lady does, whose health and happiness are to me the most precious things in the world . . ."

I smiled to receive this, and then set it aside. I would answer it next day . . . or the next day . . . or the next . . .

But the next thing was a trembling youth standing before me, mumbling and white with dread at the news he had to give.

Robin was . . .

No, no, even now I cannot say it without grief and fury—yes, fury, for if he had told me truly how he was, I could have sent my physicians.

At the very least I could have sent to the first man of my kingdom all the servants and nurses, knights and squires—yes, even the ladies—fitting to attend the dying of a man like him.

As it was, he died almost abandoned, alone and untended save for one or two simpletons who did not flee from his fever in fear of the plague. He had there the Irish scribbler Spenser, who was acting as his secretary, and that Edmund was one of the few to lament his passing in verse. "All his greatness vapoured to naught," he wrote.

Fine words, fine words! But when my lord was vapouring to naught, burning of an ague, clutching his side and screaming, who was with him? Just as when he fell ill before at Wanstead after I learned of his marriage with the she-wolf, he was untended by any save for chumbling old witches and country clowns. Now no one was there to soothe his sufferings, kiss him tenderly one last time, close his eyes with love.

And there was none to mourn him.

Least of all Lettice—for she, his wife, the she-wolf, vampire, harpy, witch as she was of all the wicked world, no sooner had she hearsed and coffined him than she married again.

Yes, the funeral baked meats did coldly furnish forth the wedding feast!

The lustful whore wed herself to a man young enough to be her son—indeed, he was the dearest friend of my lord her son. He was young Blount, Christopher Blount, who tilted for me with my lord of Essex and then fell under her spell.

Well, she would not live to grow fat on her treachery to Robin! I took back from her all his estates, wrenched from her every tithe barn, every tenement; I drove her out of Kenilworth and repossessed it myself; I bled her of every farthing he ever owed me; I hunted her down like the bitch-wolf she was, and I had no mercy.

He left me everything—as so he should, for everything he had was mine, everything he had I had given him. But one thing he left me that he bought and chose for me to be his legacy, his last gift.

Pearls.

Pearls for virginity, for the moon, for Diana, goddess of virgins, the tears of nature, for the grief of the world.

A triple rope of six hundred pearls, the world's finest, with a pendant of diamonds for majesty and emeralds for jealous love.

But all this came later.

Then, I could do nothing.

Nothing at all.

He died on my birthday.

What was God trying to tell me?

Did he die murmuring of me, calling for me, crying for me? The mumbling mongrel, the idiot from his village who brought the news, could not tell. "He died, my lady. That's all I know. He died."

"Leave me."

I did not rave, nor shout. I sat quite quietly until all had left me, from Parry down to the pageboys, then I crossed the chamber and shot home the bolt. I was very calm.

Farewell love.

On the table lay the note he had sent me about his medicines and his state of health. Carefully I inscribed it "His Last Letter," and sealed it with a ribbon. Then I sat down and waited.

Waited for it to pass.

Waited and waited.

And I did not wait alone. I heard his voice, he was with me all the time. We talked of many things. But above all I scolded him for his neglect of himself, his neglect of me!

How can you leave me so? *I wept to him.* How can you leave me?

Lady, lady, he replied in that dear voice of his, *lady, my love, I shall never leave you.*

The sun went up, and the sun went down, and I did not stir. Night came and went, and I wandered a little, in my mind and in my chamber, but always I came back to my chair and our conversation.

Sometimes I thought I heard my voice crooning the songs we used to sing together. Oftentimes people came and spoke and knocked on the chamber door and called from outside, "Majesty, are you there? Are you within?"

Fools—where else would I be?

Except in the grave, in company with my lord. Now, there we would be private—there we would embrace as we did on that one day when we came together, that day of miracles, that day at Kew.

Oh, my lord, my lord . . .

My new lord came too, the young one, but his voice was harsh and empty through the oak door, his loud bluster rang hollow in my ear, and I did not hear him. And he, too, went away.

At last came the voice of Burghley, quiet as always: "Madam, I trust you're well. Pray you stand back from the door, for we are coming in."

Boom! Boom! Boom!

It thundered like the ending of the world

Boom, boom, boom.

Boom, boom . . .

How long they strove I do not know. But at last the black oak, harder than iron, splintered and gave as they stove in the door. In through the void tumbled four huge Court porters, sweating and gasping and pulling their forelocks, their faces looking as if I would say, Off with their heads! To the Tower with them!

And there was Burghley, gathering his robe primly as he ducked through the door, for all the world as if he strolled in his own garden.

"Good day to you, dearest madam," he said conversationally. "I trust you have taken no harm these past four days."

Behind him his son Robert, Walsingham, Hatton and my cousins Knollys and Hunsdon shouldered through the pillars of split oak, carefully dodging the dagger-like splinters, and all bowed before me. Burghley waved his hand. In darted Radcliffe and Bess Throckmorton, Carey and Warwick, with all their maids.

"See, madam, here are your women to ready you for your people," continued Burghley, calmly as before. "For they clamour to see you, to rejoice with you. And we have triumphs and celebrations, services in the Abbey and St. Paul's, and the Ambassadors of France and Italy, Savoy and Venice, Austria and Poland, all queue for you these four days to lay their letters at your feet."

Stepping forward lightly on his tiny feet, little Robert took up the tune. "For now you are Queen of the world, madam, and all the world craves your advice and support. See here, Your Royal Grace—" He flashed open a heavy leather wallet and produced a parchment. Under it lay warrants, sealed and unsealed, decrees and patents, screeds of vellum ready for my hand. "We need your signature on this . . . your word on that . . ."

Of course, they had me then.

After thirty years, Burghley knew how to handle me.

And life went on.

I went on, there and then. I was unrobed and toiletted and re-robed and new-wigged and bedecked in shimmering satin, diamonds and pearls, until like our victory itself I shone forth like the sun in splendour and my people gloried with fireworks and cheers, ballads and bells, till they rang the town hollow. There were three days of tilting and cockfighting and bear-baiting and carousing and wenching, and on every one of them the Armada was defeated twenty times over, to the joy of all.

And I never mentioned his name to a soul again.

But in my own way, in my own time, I had said what I wanted.

Farewell, my love.

Here Ends
the Fourth Book
–*LIBER QUARTUS*–
of My History

GLORIANA

Book the Fifth, and Last,

-LIBER QUINTUS-

of My History

We had defeated the Armada, the mightiest force the world had ever seen. We, England, and I, Elizabeth, Elizabeth the Queen.

I was a living legend, the wonder of the world, the paragon of women, the paradigm of queens. For a woman still fallible—and yes, God help me, even more imprisoned in the flesh than ever, besides being mired in politics and frantic for ready cash—a living goddess was no easy thing to be.

We had singed the King of Spain's beard, plucked him by the nose, slapped him across both cheeks, taken down his breeches, bared his backside to all the world and birched it so soundly that he would not sit in comfort for the rest of his life.

It was a great, a mighty, a world-famous triumph. Yet we still had to go on. I had to, England had to, now and forever, now at once.

Now?

Can't go on, must go on.

And so my lord came in.

As long as we had Spain to beat back from our shores, and the Douai missionaries, the enemy within to conquer and hold down, as we did all through the eighties, I could keep Cupid at bay.

But now . . .

For him, for my young lord—

To have the entree money could not buy, the free access to my presence, yes, to my Privy Chamber, the chance to whisper in my ear, the nearness to the throne that all my life men fought for—and now, at our height of triumph, would have pledged a mine in India to share—would not the man who could command all that have felt himself blest indeed?

Would you not think my lord would count himself a god among men in the favour of my eyes—and be grateful?

When first I loved him, I was a thing of fable, a legend from a former age and yet the pivot—no, the architect—of the world's present, the once and *future Queen. Hardly a soul alive in England now could remember a time when I was not on the throne.*

And I was also a woman like no other, rich and royal, breathing desire and delight, tempests and torments, whether I danced, or rode, laughed at life's follies, wept at grief and loss, or smiled into love's eyes.

So what if I were a little past fifty—and he—a little younger! What would another man, countless young men, have given to enjoy that unrivalled closeness—that sweet intimacy of walks and talks—which we enjoyed in the springtime of our love?

O my love, my love—now I can say it, sweet love, sweet lord of love . . .

When I loved you first, my lord, my love, then was I singular, talented, splendid, and above all lovely, in your eyes and my own . . .

And you? Slowly you grew rougher, coarser, bolder—no longer the boy blushing, but the man of reckless strength just breaking out of control, the violence lying underneath the lace and velvet only just in check—

And I? Jesus, why codge and cog?

You were the tall and wayward man with the red beard who would explode in anger if he did not get his way.

And it frightened me, made me flare, made me squirm—after a life of silken smoothness and satin flattery, it excited me, why should I not confess?

You were so like my father—were my father—

And so was I. For I, too, could not help loving and desiring—above all, desiring to give where I loved.

For I knew now that I loved my lord of Essex as my father had loved my mother. And as a man who measured his own worth in the weight of his coffers, so Henry parcelled out his love for her in the value of his gifts.

What is love without power, or power without love—love to give, power to give—to give, to give . . . ?

I could not honour my new lord with titles, for his own earldom from his father was one of the greatest. More, as a Devereux, the blood of all our finest families ran in his veins. Yet I could gild the lily with ceremonial honours. And I could give him money, grant him monopolies like the sweet wines that were for him the foundation of a tidy fortune, and what he prized still more, the chance to blaze forth at the very head of the State, when he would shine out like a star, a king among men, a baby god.

But what I craved to give him was not the shining but the substance, not the gloss of honour but the garment itself, to wear and grow into till he truly was what he appeared—star, king and god in one. I meant to teach him mastery, mastery of himself and others—as he had mastered me.

Beyond redemption. For I loved him in a way I never knew before. Oh, I loved Robin—how well I loved him, you alone know. And I loved dear faithful trusty Hatton, who was so tall, and danced like a dream of joy; and I

loved Raleigh for his eyes of lapis lazuli and his wicked wit—yet never
desired them as I now desired my lord.

It was a love I knew fed its own destruction. I knew from the first I loved
him in a way he never could love me. I loved him as a man, and he loved
me as his Queen, as his patron and the source of all his wealth, as an old
love-forgotten spinster, never as a woman.

Yet Christ knows, a winter face and withered breasts, a belly creased with
purple and thighs crumpled like dewlaps, do not make the fire in the loins
burn any lower! Two fires indeed now—for as I writhed in the agony of love
for him, I was consumed, too, by the flames of self-disgust from the rich,
endless torment of these lustful thoughts.

"Wager on me, Your Grace!"

To see him playing tennis, sleeves rolled up to show his golden forearms,
his shirt lying open to the waist, flashing a torso as perfect as any hero of
Roman marble, to glimpse the outline of the muscles of his breast, the strong
brown nipple, the hairs sprouting at his waist . . .

"What says Your Majesty?"

To have him on the dais in the Presence incline his noble height to me,
hang down his head to my imperious whisper till his brown-burning curls
teasingly brushed my cheek and set me burning too . . .

To have him kneel to me, lips and eyes smiling, that long strong face level
with mine, to inhale the green strength of his fragrance, the hot spice of his
pomander, to have his hand by mine on the arm of my throne, his cheek not
a foot from my caress—to have all that, and then not to crane into that
warmth, that scented manliness, not with one finger trace the back of that
tense brown hand, stroke that cheek, take that face between my hands, cover
it with kisses and then drink my fill from that full man's mouth, sucking
forth his soul till mine died too . . .

Not to do that—or any of it—though by day and night my love and my
groaning flesh were goading me to do it—can you wonder that I was crabbed
and snappish, tearful at times and vengeful at others, hating to be crossed
and even more hating being humoured, pandered to as if I were a child or
lunatic . . . ?

What a jester is God! Now, when I could at last have taken a lover—when
I knew, my monthly courses being over for this last year and more, that I was
safe from childbearing, safe from disgrace and shame—now when all the
world, the King of Spain excepted, admired and adored me so much they
would have forgiven me anything—now I could have had any man, any king
in the whole world, now I found myself mad with love for a boy who never
saw it, not even when it reared itself beneath his nose and said, Love me, I
beg you! Love me, and take me! Swive me as lustily as a swineherd swives
a milkmaid, till my head reels, my eyes bubble, and my lungs choke for
breath even as I cry for mercy—reeling, bubbling, choking, dying—

But he never saw it.

Never saw it—because he only saw what he had seen all along, from the first time he met me, when at nine years old he had turned his face away in harsh recoil and would not be kissed by me, not even by a queen, because of what he saw—

Because he saw a wrinkled old woman, face like a lizard, painted and varnished till her glaze cracked like old earthenware every time she smiled.

I would not beg his love—nor could I command it. I could not make him love me as a woman when I did not stir him or his senses as a man. So I took what I could get, enjoyed what I had. And never ceased to pine for what I had not and could not get, never would get.

I freeze, I burn . . .

If he had once kissed me, even once laid his hand upon my breast, taken my nipple in his lips, laid me before him, unclothed me and admired my naked length—only once . . .

But he never did it—worse, it was all too plain he never even thought it. And I could not stop thinking of it.

When I should have been thinking of so many, many things.

L X V

GOD BLEW WITH HIS WINDS, AND THEY WERE SCATTERED.

It has a ring, no?

What do you mean, no? I chose it myself for the Armada medal the Royal Mint struck to commemorate the victory! It pleased the people well. It pleased me well. And there was no thought of pleasing you when it was chosen.

Enfin.

Alors.

So, then!

The war was over: now the war could begin.

Now at once, as we had sowed dragon's teeth, we had to look to reap the whirlwind, the tempest of Spain's hate. Should we sit tight and wait for it to waft its way once more to our shores, or carry war into the enemy camp as we did before, strike at the Spanish ships in their own harbors, attack their armies entrenched within their own walls?

And I had to think of the succession—think of handing on a country strong in its boundaries, strong overseas. Young James of Scotland, as I heard, was a great bookworm, not much of a warrior . . . half Tudor, then, at least. Should I supply the other, fighting half to keep England at peace?

My young lord, flushed with our triumph and even more with the Order of the Garter I now gave him, to Raleigh's fury, fought for more fighting—he was all for aggression, more anger against Spain.

"For now is the time to drive home the lesson, Majesty!" he urged, his black-gold eyes afire. "Now we have them on the hip, now we may take them any way we want!"

Even his dearest rival agreed with him. "Believe your men of war, madam, your swordsmen, your defenders, not your penmen who sit all day in Council, your lily-livered scribes!" Raleigh begged me. "Now is the time to dash all that great Spanish empire to pieces, make the kings of Spain no more than kings of gypsies, figs and oranges, as they were in days of old! Strike, madam! Only strike!"

Strike or be stricken, strike or be stricken . . .

But Burghley, wracked with his gout again now that he no longer had a greater terror to keep it at bay, closed his pain-wearied eyes and with drawn breath still counselled "caution—pacific caution!"

"Caution? God's truth, *caution?*"

The very word was poison to my lord, he could not stomach it. He burst out in furious reproach and castigated Burghley till I had to terminate the meeting. Hours later when I sent for him to my chamber, he was still seething. "Madam, forgive me—but these tedious old fools!" he swore and cursed as he came through the door.

I laughed at his angry face and impetuous tossing gait as he strode up and down. "What, have you learned nothing from your wardship with the cleverest man in England?"

I saw his eyes startle, and he spluttered with contempt. "Who, lady? My Lord Burghley? Cleverer than your spymaster Secretary Walsingham, or even than Raleigh, much as I hate him? Surely not! Cleverer than his nephews, the Bacon brothers, sons of your old Lord Keeper? Your Grace knows them not as yet—they are still at the university in Cambridge—but I promise you from my days in Lord Burghley's house as his ward, these are two of the sharpest brains that ever England bred!"

I was intrigued. "Why, then, does Lord Burghley not bring them forward for a place in my government?"

To that, as I thought, he had no answer, for there was none. If these two Bacons were not preferred to my attention by my dear old friend Burghley, that could only be because they were not worthy of my service! Meanwhile his own boy, the pygmy Robert, every day grew more and more to my hand, like the one cherished utensil that makes every task easier. He was a jewel, bright and patient and hard as a rock in his clever little heart—and if I could not love him, then at least I could trust him as I trusted his father.

As my lord did not. "The Bacon brothers are misjudged, unjustly handled by their uncle, your Lord Treasurer Burghley! As God's my witness, madam, you shall see they are fit for your royal service—above all, Francis. I must have a good position for him! For as I am a knight in your life's service and, moreover, the best of them that serve you, I shall show you, I shall prove it to you, you shall see!"

I loved it then, his arrogance to tell me what to do, his assumption of the right to choose my people and to command employment for those he called his own. After so many years of smooth and submissive devotion, hailed as Diana this, Belphoebe that, in maundering poetry and moaning verse, O sweet Empress of the Night, and all the rest of it, after all this his rough magic enchanted me—the angry flick of his eye, the quick lash of his contempt however swiftly cloaked, his lordly domination, made me freeze and burn, made me burn, made me freeze . . .

Yes, yes, hold your tongue, God damn you! Do not dare to tell me that I must have known that I would pay for it, as every woman does who makes that fool's choice of a man with her quim, not with her Queen's part, with her weak body, not her royal mind—

I knew already.

And all too soon he showed what he thought of me.

"Compromise, compromise!" I schooled him. Always seek the middle way, that is what we mean by diplomacy!"

I would not make war on Spain, for wars cost money, money I did not have. Yet no more would I sit upon my throne, my finger in my eye, thumb up my bum, waiting for Spain to return at her leisure to make war on me! Night after night that summer and autumn, I pored over endless lists, reports, despatches, numbers of Spanish ships known to be wrecked, ships believed lost, ships now thought to have got back safe to Spain and in what state. And bit by bit a strategy emerged.

They wanted an expedition, Raleigh and Drake and my lord and all my young hawks and that fool they called Norris, though he was not all fool neither, for he had done well under Robin in the Netherlands—*no, tell the truth now, for the sands are running down*—"Sir-Jean" Norris, as the Dutch called him, had been the mainstay of the army there, Robin's right hand as an experienced warrior, no, a leading player in that theatre of war. And he knew of warfare by sea as well, or I would not have set him with Raleigh among that handful of men who gave me secret warning of the only places on our little island where the deep-drawn ships of the Armada could have made landing—Norris knew all that.

Why, then, did he—did they—band together to urge a new expedition, give me such bad advice?

Or—truth now—did I just listen to my lord, who was in love with the enterprise from the outset? Did I want to be in love with anything he loved as a way of getting close to him, if I could not have him?

If I did, I paid for it! To equip the fleet, I put my hand into my pocket, fished around to the depths of both my plackets, found the pounds and

pence that the war party demanded, but with much difficulty. I had to
borrow on the Bourse, raise credit from foreign moneylenders, things
were so bad. God's legs, how it pained me! "Tell me again," I ordered
Drake as he stood before me, "what is this venture for? And what rewards will you and your fellows bring home this time?"

"Majesty, I can say no more than I and Sir John Norris and your own
Earl of Essex have told you twenty times!" he said with more sea captain's choler than courtly compliment. "We sail to Lisbon, where any of
the rats that swam from the wreck of the Armada will be assembling, and
fire them out. That will put paid to the war fleet of the King of Spain
once and for all, and then you and all England may rest secure from
Spain and Rome, the Pope and all priestly plotters evermore! Then once
in Lisbon, to harry the King of Spain on a new front, we shall stir up the
Portuguese against the Spaniards and remind them of their true King,
the dispossessed Don Antonio—"

*Don Antonio—Jesus, yes—victim of Philip's lust for dominion and even
now, so Walsingham had told me, hot-footing it to England to enlist our
help against the usurper Spain.*

"Yes, yes, continue, I am listening!"

"Then, Majesty, we make sail for the Azores, where we may hope for
rich pickings on the Spanish Main—"

"Yes, yes, rich pickings!"

I turned the words greedily in my mouth. Money, treasure, funds, cash,
I had to have them! My gold hunger now was hurting me as much as my
love hunger for my lord, and almost as much as my sad and rotten
teeth . . .

*My coffers were so empty! All the war chest gone in the struggle against
Spain, drained and depleted. Gold! Gold! I had to have it, we needed it,
England had to—*

*I, we, England? I and we were the same, I was England and she was I, the
mother country, the country I had mothered, the only child I had—*

What was Drake saying? ". . . for this is the time of year when the
annual shipment of gold and silver from the deep mines of Peru is sent
back to Spain. We may have it, lady, if you so wish, shiploads of bullion
bars, ingots and nuggets and pieces of eight—and more jewels and treasures than you have seen before—"

*Oh, I had seen, I had possessed the great crosses of emeralds, crowns of
diamonds, reliquaries of rubies, sapphires, agates, amethysts—gross, vulgar
things, of course; it was an act of true Protestant faith to the Reformed
Religion to break them up, sell the inferior gemstones and have the better
ones reset for the greater glory of Elizabeth, of England, of our God. More of
these to come?*

Yes! Gold, jewels and rich pickings, yessss!

A large diamond in its circle of sapphires winked its agreement as I extended a beringed hand for his embrace. "Go then, Sir Francis! And as you have done before, Drake them thoroughly for me, yes? But I warn you, I look for more than a singed beard this time, more, much more. I want them grilled and carbonadoed, toasted and roasted, both fore and aft!"

The little man bobbed on his stumpy legs, and his thinning halo of hair quivered with merriment. "Gracious lady, I can only make you the old gamester's answer—let the huntsmen see the quarry, let the dogs see the stags, and you shall have blood, you shall have all the guts you crave spitting and spilling for your assay, you shall have Spaniard-killing till England itself cry out, *Enough, we are sated, we can take no more!*"

And so said all of them, save Burghley and his son—above all, so said my lord.

And so I was persuaded.

Why did I listen to these men, listen to any save Burghley and little Robert, listen to anything they said?

Make no reply, do not tell me, I do not want to know.

And while they were making preparations for this great enterprise—*great indeed, as far as money went! At first I was asked for no more than five thousand pounds, and that was more than enough! But then by ifs and buts, and lies and flourishes, and false sums and evasions, it soared to eight, then twelve*—while all this turmoil was in train, my blue-eyed Raleigh, still blue-eyed but a boy no more now against my fine young lord, took a fit of jealous pique to find himself no longer the hero of the hour, hero of my heart.

"I must crave your leave of absence," he demanded stiffly one dank day of spring when the dullness outside seemed to have seized the Presence too, so grey were we all, "for Sherborne, Majesty, for my lands in Dorset, and thereafter for Ireland, where my estates are sore in need of my attention."

So Raleigh went from the Court. I soon forgot him, for the flurry at the door told me that news was at hand.

"Madam, a post from Scotland: from the Court of King James."

There he stood, the Scots envoy, a short, freckled, sandy, rawboned thing, and as soon as he opened his mouth, I was back with cousin Mary of Scots in the days when she and her emissaries had badgered and bothered me with their rough demands. *God, what an accent! How I hate the Scots! Is it true that they grow hair even between their toes, as Kat used to say? And how did she know?*

What was he saying? "My King and master seeks your good advice, my bonny lady—"

Bonny lady? Truth, I was these days more of a bony lady—hush, take a compliment as it comes—

"My lord King James desires to take a wife, after the commandment of Our Lord. His eye has lighted upon a princess of Denmark, the young Anne of Skandenborg, daughter of King Frederick—and he most humbly desires to take Your Grace's view before he makes a venture."

Does he now? I snorted to myself with satisfaction. And so he should! He should take my advice, he should give me grateful thanks! For in beating off the Armada, we have also reasserted his own claim to my throne, over his fool mother's efforts to will it to Philip of Spain. And how it goes from now on will depend on how he treats me, his godmother, cousin and—albeit distant—aunt!

I frowned at the envoy and pretended to confer with Burghley and Walsingham standing by the throne. "Marry the daughter of the house of Denmark? We shall have to think about this."

But in truth this marriage pleased me, pleased me well. It meant that James, for all Mary's machinations, for all the Romish guile of his Guise uncles, meant to be Protestant firm and sure, for along with England, the Danes were among the tiny handful of Protestant royalty in the whole world. The Danes! I laughed aloud. Indeed, they had offered for me even before I was Queen, at the time when my old admirer Erik of Sweden was also hot on my trail—so I might have been Denmark's Queen, the greatest of the Danes.

I nodded at the Scot and smiled his dismissal. "I shall bethink me. Come to us tomorrow and you shall take our word back to your King. Indeed, I have much to tell him, much advice to give him. Is he still plagued by your ranting Covenanters, like that fellow Knox? He and I both must guard against the evil of Puritans, Presbyterians, whatever they call themselves, for they are caterpillars of the commonwealth every bit as much as the maggots of Rome! But for his marriage—well, until tomorrow."

I turned to go. As I did so, I saw Throckmorton snivelling into her sleeve. Whatever was ailing her? "For God's sake, girl, does the very mention of marriage bring tears into your eyes?"

In a flash it came to me—she had fooled herself with hopes of Raleigh, and finding him so faithful to me that he would sooner leave Court than see another man in the ascendant, thought herself slighted! And now perhaps with weddings in the air, in default of Walter she feared she would be paired off willy-nilly with some undesirable, some hateful creature that I knew nothing of.

She was her brother's ward now that her father was dead, and hence at his mercy. I knew that. Well, no man would force her while I was her mistress! I took her by the hand and patted it sharply. "Take my word, wench, you shall not marry against your will, I can promise you that. You shall remain a virgin with me here till the North Seas run dry, never you fear!"

She dropped her eyes. "God bless you, ma'am!" she mumbled.

Lying besom! No wonder, then, she could not meet my eye! And I was innocence itself—or, rather, roundly deceived. Fool that I was, I suspected nothing.

No more than I did when my sweet lord was hanging round my throne, hanging on my every word as if his one thought was of me, to be there, to be with me, when all the time he was far away, a thousand leagues away from me and mine . . .

I could not grant his wish to join the Drake expedition against Spain, that went without saying. But he forced me to say it. And with constant badgering, forced me to shout it, scream it, ram it down his throat: *"You shall not go!"*

"By God's body, madam, by God's body, blood and bones!" he swore. *How could he know that was my father's favourite oath.* "On my knees I beg, do not wrong me so! You take my manhood when you refuse to let me go and fight! Why do you hold me back from adding to your glory and to England's?"

"You are so sure of victory, my lord!" I snapped back. "May I not hold you back from girding me with your defeats and losses?"

But the loss I feared was not money but his life—or even one single second of his company.

Then came the day I awoke, and after throwing the bread she had brought at the maid's head, for God knows it was harder than her numb-skull, I demanded, "What news of my lord today?"

"My lord? Of Essex?"

The rain was coursing down the windows—I can still see her face stark in the watery light.

"Who else, looby? Send for him at once!"

But I got nothing back but blank-eyed stares and green gawpings and dangling hands and idiot evasions. When I cried for my women, none dared speak to me. Christ, I could trust none of them since Kat died! Now I was weeping, crying, howling, *"Where is he?"*

Once again it was Burghley who had to break the news, and the sight of him brought on another paroxysm: *Jesus, God, tell me, how will I manage without this man, as soon now I must.*

Fat now he was, half-crippled and breathless, but still rising from his carrying chair with all due ceremony to bow before me as he sadly said, "Your Majesty—he is gone."

LXVI

"How—when—*gone?*"

Burghley's old eyes were as sad as a weeping spring. *Was he thinking of all the other times he had had to do this for me, break such news to me?* He stifled a sigh. "My lord of Essex is gone, madam, to join the fleet—the expedition against Spain—to win glory for you and for England—"

"*Glory for himself!*" I wept. "He cares nothing for me, still less for England!"

Oh, it was plain enough what he thought of me. What could he care for me, to leave me so? I must give him over, leave this cruel and unprofitable love, I must, for the health of my soul! But who can talk down a disordered heart, master an unruly love by reasoning it out of existence? I loved him more, if that were possible, the less he loved me, a story every woman knows . . .

"Get me pen and ink, command a messenger on the fastest horse!"

Burghley bowed. "Instantly, Majesty."

I wrote breathing fury, in letters of fire, to command his return. But his ship was halfway down the Channel, he could not be brought back.

The weeks dragged by: I lived like a widow. They tried to cheer me, my women, all save the widow herself, Frances Sidney. Now her face was yellower than her father's, her Puritan piety fiercer, and in church she prayed longer and harder for the fleet than even the silliest of the maids. Why should she do that? Too pious by half! *I must get her a husband.*

Those who never sleep the simple sleep of innocent exhaustion, who are condemned to woo the God of Oblivion all night long and still to be spurned, never welcome the morning. As I tossed and turned in the last moments of a fretful doze, I could hear a warbling, no, a tuneless chirping outside the bed hangings.

> "Some say he's black,
> But I say he's bonny,
> The fairest of them all,
> Oh, my handsome, winsome, Johnny . . ."

"Who's there?" I called querulously. The chamber was thick with the smell of the night soil, for the Grooms of the Stool were not yet about their duties. I shifted unhappily. Oh, my teeth ached so in the morning these days, before Radcliffe had applied her oil of cloves to them and Anne Warwick washed round my mouth with aqua vitae. Bess Throckmorton's chubby-cheeked face came beaming through the curtains. "I, madam—with good news! Sir Walter Raleigh is returned to Court, with tidings of Ireland, America, his plantations and people there—"

"Oh, hold your tongue, girl!" I grumbled fiercely. "And don't be a fool! He loves you not, or he would not leave you!"

Her eyebrows lifted, and she stared at me with her round open eyes. I felt a rush of rage—*was she thinking the same of me?*—and anger made me harsh. "Command my breakfast here at once, bread and strong ale, not the small beer. And put Sir Walter out of your silly head! He will never marry while he needs to buy my love to stay ahead of all his creditors—least of all to a penniless, dowerless, fatherless girl of no family such as you! Now close the curtains and let me rest!"

I heard her small sad snivellings round the chamber as I lay on my pillows vainly trying to doze off again. And hers were not the only tears shed there that day.

Then the next morning Burghley came again, God bless him, as the night candles burned out and the sun came up, and a sweet damp English dawn awoke to the sound of wren and robin, dove and blackbird, while a late nightingale still called her liquid lamentation from the woods.

Burghley bowed. "Your Majesty, despatches from the fleet. They have taken Corunna, with no loss of life. And my lord of Essex was the hero of the hour."

Tears, idle tears . . .

"Command him back. Promise him war service if he must be a hero, but say he can serve me nearer the throne's interests than the Azores, or the Canaries, or wherever he is—"

And nearer England—nearer to me . . .

Another chasm of time, another desert of the heart, another long, lean Lent.

And less time now, so little time to waste . . .

At last he came, returned to face my fury. As he strode through the door, through the ranks of the Queen's Guard, I saw the men snapping to, eyes wide, faces aglow as if at the return of some great Caesar or all-conquering Alexander. Suddenly a worm of jealousy—*no, fear*—stirred at the bottom of my heart. So they loved him now, the people, for his prowess against their great enemy Spain, their blackest bogeyman! Was he courting popularity for himself, at the expense of mine? A fatal memory of our history stirred. Just so had the usurping son of Gaunt, Henry of Bolingbroke in King Richard's time, won the love of the crowds and put that Richard off his throne!

And this on top of his gross disobedience and defiance in leaving me against my strict command—God in heaven! I could not wait for him to approach the dais, but skipped from the throne to fall on him, to make him pay!

Or so I meant. But then, seeing his face, his eyes, all the hard knot of rage melted into tears, then into whispers—he was kissing my hands as I leaned into him, and then the warm strength of his arm, the comfort and feel of him, the smell of his pomade, his sweet head bending down, his lips murmuring, "Majesty, it was for you, I went for you, all for you, only for you . . ."

How could I believe this, fall for all this?

How could I command music and feasting, plays and interludes, dance as I never had since Robin died, even graciously ordering him to take out Bess Throckmorton, and Raleigh to dance with Frances Sidney when I tired, to give those two poor drabs a little pleasure, so generous was I in love?

How could I?

You may well ask! All the more so as the great naval expedition, the war on Spain to end war, the raid of all treasure raids, was a gross failure, a complete and costly debacle, in every regard!

My cousin Howard's normally bold eyes would not meet mine as he made his report: as Lord Admiral he felt the shame, the waste of it, in his heart's core, though God knows he had had no more command over the commanders than I did. His level voice ran on till I could no longer contain myself.

"What? The fools came upon *half of Spain's fleet* holed up in Corunna, and through quarrelling among themselves, succeeded in letting it go?"

Howard's mouth tightened as he tugged his neat fair beard. "They burned one galleon."

"Then at Lisbon, the Portuguese declined to rise and aid them in the name of Don Antonio? And as for treasure—hah! All they brought home was a shipload or two of the pox!"

Howard tapped an angry foot. "Your Majesty forgets the grain ships they seized off the Cape Verde Islands."

"I forget nothing! The whole spoils of that haul will make less than a tenth of what I shelled out to equip the fleet!"

I would not see Drake. He had undone all the good work he had done against the Armada, and he was a hero no longer. He would never sail for me again, that I swore to, and I kept my oath. But my lord? Did I upbraid him? Yes—but without conviction. And why did I believe him when he threw all the blame on the others and swore that he had fought, lived and breathed all that time only for me?

Why?

He said he loved me.

Ask any woman who has listened to this, loved it, drunk it in, sucked it up, swallowed it down, drained the last drop of submission to a worthless man—

No, never say that! Words ran away with me, I ran away with myself, he was not worthless, never, no—

I loved him! He could not, then, be worthless, I would not have it, I, Elizabeth, Elizabeth the Queen!

Yet God in heaven, while he fooled and farted round the world, playing his war games and dedicating them to me, laying them at my feet as a tomcat on a farm kills a great grey and greasy rat rotten with plague and shotten with burst bowels, and proudly lays the stinking useless thing at your feet, as he did then . . . while he did this, the whole of France was bursting apart, splitting from neck to navel, unseaming itself from the nuts to the chops, in the last spasm of its civil war. Here on the fringe of Europe, here in England or else in Denmark and the Low Countries, even in Portugal until it fell under Spain, in all these countries we had escaped the worst of the Romish hatred, the vile power of the Popes to counter the Reformation, fight back against our Protestantism, and as they did so to maim, garrote and burn, torture and kill. But in France and Spain they took the brunt of Popish power, and their sufferings were terrible.

What am I saying?

Simply that the last child of the Regent Catherine, that poor witch of the Medici, mother of so many sons, all of whom lived to eat lead, drink poison, swallow steel, suffer vile and violent deaths—her last son, Henry III—

I sighed a heavy sigh to the rider from France. "Monsieur, how many of your black-clad brethren now have stood before me with news like this?"

"*Majesté?*"

Poor frog, he had no idea what I was talking about.

He was talking of another French king dead—another assassination, for Henry III was murdered—and yet another Henry, Henry IV, King of Navarre, now on the throne of Valois. But no Valois he: this French King was, God be thanked, a Protestant!

"Ink there, and parchment—nothing but the best!" I cried in delight. "And have the scriveners standing ready with the monarch's royal seal!"

"Most dearest King and cousin, brother in God—" I wrote to him in my own hand four or six times that summer with advice and cheer, sending prayers and exhortations for his success, and was not too piqued when he did not reply. He was of course fighting a civil war, fighting for life and throne, even for his capital, held against him by the Papish hordes. Robert Cecil, blending his father's foresight with Walsingham's groundwork, brought me the word: "All Protestants, all over Europe, are rallying to his cause!"

He looked into my eyes with his clear, clever gaze, and I read his meaning.

As my lord would surely rally to him too—he would run away to play soldier in France if I did not stop him. But if I did, he would defy me again, steal away again, and I would not know where he was . . .

That night it was high summer, and we danced beside the Thames. The lanterns made a hundred weeping moons upon the shining water as I let him go.

"If you must fight, my lord," I told him, trembling with the effort to look calm, "by God's bowels of belief, get you to France!"

His fair skin, ever his best barometer, flushed like fire with wonderment and joy. "To France, gracious Queen?"

"Do not repeat my words like a great natural, a chattering nuthatch!" I savaged him.

He reddened now, an angry sunset presaging a storm. "I am no natural! Not even for your good Grace—!"

"Oh, get to France—go and help the King of Navarre win Paris from the Papists, for till then he is a king without a throne!"

"At your command, madam!"

As he stormed off, Walsingham appeared with his scrivener, bearing his heavy load of papers, as he always did.

"Despatches, madam, for your signature."

"What, at this hour? No ill news from France?"

"No, Majesty, all is well." But he looked yellower, greyer and more livid than ever I had seen him, and for the first time his dull daughter Frances, the widow Sidney, was attending him; he was leaning on her arm. *Was he, too, getting old?* Roughly I rallied him. "God's love, my lord, this news of the French affair, and Henry of Navarre now King, should go near to warm your liver, cure it of what ails you. Now with the Armada smashed and France turned to our faith, you may truly boast that God has shown himself a Protestant!" I clapped my hands for a servant. "Will you raise a glass and drink with me to that?"

Walsingham's thin lips pursed. "By your leave, madam, no, my papers call me—" And he hurried off. Smiling, I waved the wine-bearer away.

Truly old Walsingham never heated his liver with anything save anti-Popish passion, and in all my life I never saw him down a drop of anything useful. I would send my physician to him, the Jew Lopez.

Let us see, too, what an herbal draught might do. Back in my chamber I called for service. "Parry!"

"Here, lady, where?"

"Here, Parry, you fool, over here by the hearth—"

She was as blind as a bat now, but still loyal as ever, and still as useful. "For my lord Walsingham—have them send that tonic of verbena and heart's-ease that Dame Katherine Parr used to make up for my father."

Parry pondered. "All-heal and heart's-ease, lady, as I remember, not verbena, as we had made for my lord of Leicester in his last illness, was it not—?"

"Parry, see to it, talk to me not of the past!"

God is a humorist. He likes to sport with us. Yet if God's a jester, a greater one is Death. While I was keeping him at bay with my simples for Walsingham, the King of Terrors fetched me a blow from behind I never looked for. As she went to the stillroom to command Walsingham's remedy, Parry herself was taken with a catalepsy and fell down without speech or motion. I visited her daily, fed her broth with my own hands and ordered her to get well—on pain of death! On the third day she opened her mouth and spoke. "I nursed you in your cradle, did you know that?" she whispered fondly. Then she closed her milky eyes and fell asleep.

I never knew that. And now there was so much I wished to ask her, and it was too late.

Now Death had whetted his scythe, he seemed determined to cut a swathe through all those around me. Next to fall was Ambrose, Robin's elder brother.

"Warwick, be comforted!" I told his widow Anne.

Frances Sidney took her hand and smoothed her weeping face. "God has a special place for widows in His heart," she tried to soothe her. "It is His will—we must be patient." But there was little cheer to offer there, for like young Frances, Anne was childless too: Ambrose was the last of their ill-fated house.

Super flumina Babylonis . . . By the waters of Babylon we sat down and wept . . .

His funeral was sumptuous, with five hundred black-clad paupers following him to his grave. As I prayed I thought of old Northumberland their father as he was when I first knew him, the envy of all men with his five fine sons on his heels, John, Ambrose, Robin, Guildford and Henry. Who would have thought that his whole line would perish, that not one of them would leave a son, save only Robin's by-blow by the Douglas, the boy who could never inherit?

Come away, Death . . .

Walsingham went the next April just as the daffodils began to peep. The grieving Frances as a dutiful daughter now had another cause of grief, and another set of mourning weeds. Bess Throckmorton wept too, God knows why, till with so much water she became dropsical, her breasts and belly, hands and feet puffed up, and I had to send her away from the Court to the clean air of the country. Burghley and I wept and prayed together for our old comrade-in-arms, and I did not recover any joy of life till Burghley had me to Theobalds for a long retreat on that summer progress.

Yet even our progresses, once our summer high days and holidays when we travelled merrily from place to place, were not as they once were. Now to dismantle the entire Court and Council, to pack our whole lives into boxes and carts, to transport above a thousand or two thousand people, for a Court was as big as any market town, and then to be on the road for weeks and months—these days it was an ordeal to me, and no pleasure anymore. Oh yes, I saved good money when I enjoyed my subjects' lavish hospitality in place of my own! And I still loved to meet the people, see their joy in me and hear their rough-hewn tributes of loving cheer. But it was not enough now for the effort it cost.

Then Hatton sickened. Like a fool he kept it from me till it could not be concealed. Then I sent out another messenger for Dr. Lopez, my Portuguese physician who had fled the Inquisition, sat by another bedside, administered more broth and fresh threats of mortal fury should he dare to die, and his smile was as sweet as ever as he promised to obey.

But like all of us, Hatton was subject to a greater law than mine.

"He has voided no urine for a week or more," said Lopez, his shoulders moving in the shadow of a shrug. "All within him from the breastbone down is dissolved into pus, and his feet are turning black."

I started violently. "Never say so! For God's love, man, you can save him! Why, the lady of the Strachey was recovered after a lying a month in a swoon—"

He brought his slender fingers to his lips and looked at me out of his sorrowful, ancient eyes, eyes full of death. "Majesty, if you hang me for it, as the great Alexander hanged the doctor who could not cure his best beloved Hephaestion, I cannot save him."

"God bless you ever, dearest, sweetest Queen!"

He died smiling, and pressing my hand. Jesus, could not such a fine long dancing body, bellied out graciously now with years and honours, keep in a little life?

Kit—my only faithful lover, the only man who never married but stayed

*true only to me, my servant ever and no other woman's to his dying day. You
were the last man I ever kissed, kissed with the kiss that thickens the blood,
shortens the breath, makes the heart clap its wings against the ribs like a
dove in a cage. Wait for me in heaven, I look to see you there, I shall have
need of you . . .*

My Hatton died the third week of November, and I wept all winter
long for him. I could weep now as I recall him—his high step in a galliard, his dark beard, his touch, his love, his kiss—

Weep not, sweet Queen, for tricking tears are vain.

*Was it the rogue from Stratford who said that, the little bald player and
playwright who looked like a woman's tailor? I seem to think his bombast
was in a livelier vein. But I forget.*

What, all my old lords dying? Who could I talk to, who could I turn to?
God, spare me from this never-ending line of men in black telling of
death, smelling of death—*making me think of my own.* And who could
replace them?

"Robert? Where is Master Cecil?"

"Here, madam—at your service!"

I looked at his narrow pale face so like his father's, his smiling eyes, his
old head on young shoulders, his neat little hands, and said to myself, *Sir,
your time has come.*

At Theobalds I knighted him, and back in London had him sworn in as
a lord of my Privy Council. That night I supped my wine with satisfaction,
rolling it round my tongue. Robert. Yes. He would make a good penman,
clever and faithful in the sober silks and the long dark gowns he favored
to hide his crooked shoulder and pygmy frame. He would balance the
war men like my lord in every debate. He would serve England well, he
would serve the State.

Then a pang took me, took me hard. *My teeth, with these sweet comfits?
Or my heart?* So much for England—what of Elizabeth? Raleigh was
gone back to Ireland once again, Oxford now taking more interest in the
common players than in me, and the young newcomers like the Earl of
Southampton and the two Pembroke brothers, sons of my old Earl, still
wet behind the ears, too green and unschooled for my taste. I wanted
men, young men, about me, not boys! Where was the man to flame in
fire-bright, red-tongued velvet, where the strong lord verdant in green,
gambolling in cerulean, sprouting in crocus yellow like the hope of spring
—the man who would serve not the State but me?

Where was my lord?

My lord of May was in Normandy, where he went to fight for me and
King Henry and the light of truth in France. He wrote to me in the
sweetest vein a woman could hope to hear.

Most fair, most dear, most excellent sovereign,

While Your Majesty gives me leave to say I love you, my joy is like my affection, unmatchable. If you ever deny me that, you may end my life but never shake my constancy. For were the sweetness of your nature turned to the greatest bitterness that could be, it is still not in your power, great Queen as you are, to make me love you less . . .

Ever Your Sweet Grace's

Robt. Devereux, Earl of Essex

Jesus, God, I could not endure it.

"Order my lord home . . . now!"

What did I care what the chattering magpies made of it, of him, of me, of a young man rising through an old woman's dotage? I wanted him back and had the power to command it—and why should I not?

And I had a thing to celebrate that required his presence. A new toy, but a great one.

Nonsuch!

None Such—the finest palace in our land.

When my father built it and named it, he meant it to be just that—Sans Égal, None Such, without equal. And even more than his treasured "White Hall," None Such palace was to be a wonder of the world. And who but sister Mary, ever in dread of anything splendid, lavish, sensual, sensational, would have *given it away?*

Rot her, she gave it to the Earl of Arundel when she came to the throne, to buy his loyalty and keep that slippery old Papist sweet. She hated it, Burghley told me, because its thrusting towers and cloud-capped pinnacles, its teeming turrets and huge proud facade, seemed the essence of my father to her tormented soul. The Henry of her dark days lived on for her in every brick and stone, every bulging boss, every fear-some gargoyle, every huge splendid statue, above all in the kingly scale of it—why, the very gatehouse was five stories high! And she gave it away! But now the old Earl being dead—for death's clouds now and then shake out a little silver—his last survivor found it politic to offer it back to me.

It was the best palace in England, and built to last forever.

Soul, heart and hands, I grabbed for it. "Yes! *Mine!*"

Now all I wanted was my lord to enjoy it with.

And back he came, burning in flame and ochre slashed with gold, crested with gold, and I? I could have eaten his gold buttons. Yet there was to be *nonsuch* hope and pleasure as I had dreamed of—as it should have been . . .

It was a shining May, winter long gone, Bess back at Court, happily now recovered from both her dropsy and her weakness for my Raleigh.

And as I knew for sure, he never cared a toss for her: on my instructions Robert had taxed him with it, and he laughed the idea to scorn, swore on his soul he loved me too much ever to marry—so neither now paid each other the slightest attention.

Even the wretched Sidney girl had at last picked up, laid aside her widow's weeds and shown a readiness to smile in the Presence, to laugh with my lords, and with them quiz Sir Walter about his America, his "New Found Land."

Yet that night my lord was troubled, and child that he was, could not rest till he had troubled me. Leaning on the arm of my throne as we watched the dancers, telling of France and the carnage there, the times he had seen death, almost touched it, looked it in the face, suddenly he announced, "Death and Desire are bedfellows, lady. I have seen twenty-four summers, and who knows when Death will call? If I die in your service, like your lords of Leicester and Warwick, who died without issue, I leave not a wrack behind. A man should marry, should desire to marry."

"Marry? Never speak of it!"

Never think of it! howled my heart.

And I silenced him. But still with sore unease I watched as later on he took out the bouncing Bess Throckmorton to dance. Then it was Radcliffe and a few others, but later still, Bess again. And I thought she hung on him, earnestly seemed to interrogate him, with not a few anxious glances thrown at me.

Perhaps, after all, he was safest in France . . .

But I could not part with him again so soon! And while I dithered, she was brought to me. It was near the dinner hour, the sky had at last cleared after a morning of rain, my lord had sent from the stables to say that the horses were ready, we could at last ride out, and I was not minded for interruptions. "Jesus, who's this?"

A great sow of a woman the guards were bundling into the chamber, huge head solid on a neck like a tree trunk, mammoth breasts fighting their greasy bindings, dark wet patches at the nipples—*God, was this thing a mother?*—filthy, stinking.

She was as rank as rotting offal, she reeked of the sty. My gorge rose and I looked wildly round at my ladies. "Smelling salts, one of you! And send for a chamberer to bring fresh fragrance. *Who is this woman?*"

Robert stepped forward from the little group of men around the creature. "She is a wet nurse, madam, arrested drunk and brawling in Deptford—I had her brought to you for what she said in her cups." He turned to the woman. "Speak now. Tell Her Majesty what you told me."

One eye gleamed wild and cunning as a sow in farrow through a solid mat of hair as she whined, "And I'll not be hanged for speaking, you swear, Your Honour?"

"I swear you will be hanged," said Robert pleasantly, "this very moment, if you will not speak!"

And out it came, amid snuffles, tears and curses, and endless pleas for mercy. *A lady of the Court who found herself great with child—lying in secretly in a house in the East End—delivered of a baby boy, and this sow hired as the wet nurse—and a great lord who came to the house and stood godfather to the babe when it was baptised straight afterwards—a tall lord with curling brown hair and bright black eyes, who stooped a little in his bounding walk—*

"Enough." Robert nodded to the guards. "Take her away."

I stilled my wringing hands. "Do not—hang her for this!"

Robert smiled. "No, a good whipping will suffice. If the beadles lay on heartily, you may lose a little skin from your nether regions, madam," he informed the woman amiably, "but from the size of you, you have plenty to spare. And your life is safe—as long as you hold your tongue."

They dragged her screaming away as I sat screaming inside.

I lifted a hand to Robert, patiently awaiting my will. "Order Mistress Throckmorton to be confined to her chamber."

And a great lord who came there, a tall lord . . .

"And have my lord of Essex brought here to me at once—under armed guard."

He was white and trembling, and the soldiers who guarded him in a worse state yet, to see their hero brought so low.

"Madam, what is this?"

"Traitor!" I screamed at him. "You are married to her, no, Bess Throckmorton, and the father of her child?"

"Traitor? I?" He was like a man sinking in a quagmire who cannot save himself. "Majesty, no!" he forced out through pale lips. "I am not married to her, I never fathered any child. I am as innocent of her flesh as she is of mine!"

"And why, sir, why," I wildly howled, "should I believe you?"

He threw back his head, drew a deep breath and closed his eyes. "Because, my dearest lady, the traitor you seek is not here, it is not I . . . for I . . . I am already married."

L X V I I

He stood before me in my chamber, grinning like a dog, and thought I would as ever be pleased to see him. With him he had brought back from Ireland the scribbler Spenser, a little man with graceless hair short-cropped like a damned Puritan, poorly clad in black, with bands at his neck like a jobbing clerk, which indeed he seemed to be now. He was a man who at another time would have had a warm welcome, and even now I tried to show civility.

"You served my lord of Leicester, am I right, Master Edmund, before you went to Ireland as the Governor's secretary?"

He gave a jerky bow. "He was my first, best patron, may it please Your Majesty." A nervous laugh. "He liked my little sonnets, the love pieces I called the *Amoretti,* and he would commission pastorals from me." *Yes, and he also used your pen to attack me over my French marriage with your fool satire "Mother Hubberds Tale," when the Duke of Anjou courted me, as I recall. Well, let be—they are all dead now.* "Pastorals, hah, master secretary? Was the world better, think you, in that golden age, when men were true, when vows were kept, and honour was more than just an empty word?"

Raleigh was staring intently at me, feeling for my mood. Now he sprang in gaily. "If we talk pastorals, madam, command this man reveal his heart to you. He has a poem in progress that must have the distinction of being the longest piece ever written in your honour! It is an epic to rival the *Aeneid*—even Homer's *Odyssey*—and will establish, madam, for all time your peerless place as the Muse of Poetry in these islands, the Goddess whom we all love, serve and obey."

"All about me? All to honour me? Well, sir, you have my blessing!"

"May I then, Majesty"—he broke off, fumbled, dared—"may I beg the favour of your name—your goodwill for the title—may I call it after you —*The Faerie Queen*?"

"You may!"

"Oh, madam!" And off he skipped there and then, flushed with success, to enter it for publication.

We were alone.

Now I could play with Raleigh as he had played with me. "A little wine, sir?" I smiled at him pleasantly. "My lord of Essex thinks to be married, he tells me. I told him I should take it for the act of a traitor, and I have banned him from the Court, packed him off to his estates while I ponder the penalty. What is your view of this? What think you of marriage?"

Did I detect a shadow of alarm fleeting across the back of those still-wonderful blue eyes? "I think of it, dearest lady," he said cautiously, feeling for his ground, "as of an honourable estate, which Our Lord Himself called holy—"

Holy, he says! A sharp nip was called for. "But Our Lord never married!"

He laughed uneasily. "Yet we of His lesser generation—weak in the flesh—may find it hard to follow His example—"

Oh yes, sir, wriggle and squirm with your weak flesh as you like, you have no way off this hook! "And for the procreation of children too, was it not so ordained?" I said easily.

Now he was sweating—a light film covered his upper lip with the faint sheen of dread, even beneath the crisp black curls of his moustache. Yet his years of soldiering had given him a hard nerve. He did not flinch. "Yes indeed, lady."

"Indeed, when a man and woman lie down together, a babe or two may hardly be avoided, would you not say?"

He knew then. And he took it like man. "True, Majesty—it will out."

"Well, sir, get you gone."

I took no pleasure in pulling the legs off spiders to watch them writhe in agony and try to wriggle hopelessly away. So I dismissed him. But as he bowed and withdrew from the door with a last level glance, I called one of my gentlemen. "Have the Captain of the Guard wait upon me at once—with an armed band."

To make an arrest.

And carry the traitor straight to the Tower!

> *As you came from the Holy Land*
> *Of Walsinghame, of Walsinghame,*
> *Met you not with my true love*
> *by the way as you came?*

> *Such a one did I meet, good sir,*
> *such an angel face*
> *Who like a queen, like a nymph did appear,*
> *by her gait, by her grace.*

She hath left me here all alone,
all alone as unknown,
Who sometimes did lead me with herself,
and me took for her own.

Yet true love is a durable fire
in the mind ever burning,
Never sick, never dead, never old,
from itself never turning.

He sent me this and other love pleas from his imprisonment, but I was not to be placated. No, for I was sick with fury, sick and shaking, my gut plaguing me as ever, my bowels turning to water. Helena, Warwick and the maids were all standing around with their eyes on the ground as I came limping in from the garderobe, stinking of the closestool.

Only Helena rose to the occasion, her tall figure stepping forward calmly to take my arm. "Shall I send for Dr. Lopez, madam, or one of your other physicians?"

"No, girl, no!" I wept. "They could not cure me of my lord Leicester's betrayal, and they will not now!"

Radcliffe came forward with a silver salver bearing a thimble glass of ratafia and some cherry wafers. "Your Grace has eaten nothing all day long—pray you, take a mouthful of some sustenance?"

I waved it away. But with her look of love and sweet concern, my self-control broke again. "Oh, God," I lamented. "Is it the same again as it was with Robin? Is this God's punishment for living too long? To see events coming round again for a second torment?"

Between them Warwick and Radcliffe were getting me to my bed. Helena took my hand as they tucked me in, and in her flat, still-accented Swedish tones, dropped this quietly into my ear: "Except that Your Majesty never loved, nor"—she hesitated delicately—"enjoyed the love—of Sir Walter as with Lord Leicester. And now Your Grace still has, still enjoys the love of my lord of Essex—"

Warwick was on my other side. "Lady, take a drop of Radcliffe's cordial—it is very soothing, it will help you sleep . . ."

Essex's love. I was beginning to drowse. *Yes! That at least I have, that is true. He writes me daily sweet and manly missives of his devotion: "My marriage was never for myself, but all for her—an act of piety—I was forced to take pity on her—"*

I clutched Warwick's hand. "That wretch Raleigh could not make that excuse! He bedded her for lust! And right under my nose!"

And for years—two years at least . . .

"Is he taken to the Tower?"

"As you commanded, Majesty, they both are. They await your pleasure."

Robert it was who unravelled it for me—not that it took much unravelling. His little eyes were bright with genuine sympathy as he bowed before me and proffered a parchment. "Sir Walter Raleigh sends you letters of apology and atonement, Your Majesty, with a poem or two—"

I screamed aloud and struck it from his hand. "I want no apologias, nor no poems neither! Only the truth!"

"Truth, then, my lady," he chirped equably. "Sir Walter and the lady looked and liked, and by degrees he parted her from her virtue. So then she was with child—"

I knew it! That was the "dropsy" that had puffed her up—and I took pity on her, sent her from the Court to recover in the pure country air!

"—and Sir Walter married her. And when you sent her into the country, she hid instead in her brother's house by Mile End and gave birth to a son. At which Sir Walter engaged the aid of the Earl of Essex to stand godfather to the child. Though they are rivals, yet Sir Walter thought the Earl would sympathize with him in his plight, being as he was himself under the shadow of a secret marriage, a union contracted without Your Majesty's good leave—"

I sprang to my feet and paced about the chamber. "It is not the same! Their marriages are not the same!"

Beside my bed lay the letters from my lord explaining all:

Hear me, Majesty, on your sweet soul, hear me!

In Zutphen I first knew her, when she flew to her lord's side and nursed him till his death—and he himself on his deathbed made me promise to care for her. I saw him as a hero tragically slain before his time, and his last wish as a sacred trust. Your late lord of Leicester, who loved Your Majesty as much as myself, if that were possible, would confirm this, had God spared him. To marry the lady was a debt of honour that no knight could refuse. But while I am bound to her by honour, I am riven to you by love, by dearest love . . .

Yes! He still loved me. I caught up the latest of his letters and pressed it to my lips. As who would not love me, against *her,* his wife, against the poor wretched widow Sidney . . .

For to say truth, I had nothing against Frances his bride. Thinking of her lean and boyish body, her cow's eyes always piously fixed on the floor, her pallid skin, her hair and eyes unfashionably black in a world where my red-gold curls and porcelain colouring were the only thing, I could even feel sorry for her. He could not love her. I was his love, though in respect for my position and the distance between us, he could not show it. And he of all men should found a noble house and line, procreate children, lest his title—and his beauty!—die with him.

Yes, it was a marriage more like a duty, indeed more like a penance imposed on him by God than an indulgence of the lustful flesh.

I could overlook it, if not forgive. And I missed him so horribly, I must have him back!

But not for myself alone. Now it came to me. With all the old men dying, for England's sake I must bring on new men, young men. My lord was strong and brave, a tireless fighter, and a loyal Englishman to his heart's core. He could be made useful—I would put him on the Privy Council as one of my leading lords and advisers.

Still, I hesitated. Could I combine England's interests with my own? Yes! said my pride. Why not? I always had! I would school him, tame him to my hand. He could be rehabilitated, forgiven.

Not so Raleigh. He was dispensable. And all the more so as swordsmen were suddenly out of use.

The change was simple, sudden and violent, as peace always is. It came on the wettest day of that dismal summer when it seemed God had opened heaven's sluice gates, so tirelessly did it rain. Pent up indoors at Nonsuch, we all grew fretful and turned inward, so the word was all the stranger when it came.

There would be no more war in France.

Our troops were no longer needed to support the Protestant King Henry against his Catholic subjects.

In a fever I strode up and down the terrace where I was trying to take the air during a break in the rain.

At least we will save money, with—what?—two, three hundred thousand crowns so far spent with no hope of recovery . . . Frantically my mind sought some grain of comfort in the news Burghley now gave me, struggling to rise from his carrying chair as his men helped him up. *"What? He said what?* Oh, seat yourself my lord, do not stand on ceremony!"

With a sigh, Burghley eased himself back on his cushions, Robert standing grave-faced at his side. "Madam, the King said, *'Paris is worth a Mass.'*"

"And for this he turns from the true faith, from the light of our religion, gives up the cause of Protestantism in his land and *converts to Rome?* God, that I were a man!" I was weeping with rage. "I would eat his heart in the marketplace! Get me ink and parchment." *And let me have some comfort.* "Send for my lord!"

The words spilled from my pen:

To my cousin King and seigneur of France, le Roi Henry IV:

It is told me that to make peace in your land, you have yielded up our faith to embrace Rome. Ah, what grief this gives me, what regret, what groaning I feel in my soul! Can you expect any good outcome of an act so iniquitous? I can only hope that sounder inspiration will come to you. I have set you in the front rank of my devotions, and pray for you day and night.

Your loving sister as ever, if you are as ever too—if not, I have nothing to do with you!

ER

Burghley smiled when he read it. "I see Your Grace has lost nothing of your powers of reproof. But lady, fear you not. We have not lost an ally, for in the weakened state of his poor country, King Henry will never dare to make war on us. And you shall see that with France now united, the King of Spain will turn his attentions to her as his oldest enemy, and we shall be small beer—this move indeed will help us."

Soothed a little, I returned his smile. "Let us hope so—for I fear we may have our hands full here at home!"

For by now I knew that peace would bring no peace to the wicked such as I, a woman hard at war with love and with herself. And as my lord loved war, so he was not minded now to let me have peace. Would you not have thought that with his great rival Raleigh disgraced through his foolish marriage, himself known to be king of my heart and a great deal else besides, all given freely at my hand—*sweet wines, rolling woods and champains, great estates and their rents, which rolled along, too, punctually every quarter*—my sweet lord would have been sweet indeed, would have been well contented. But—my endless cry from this point on—*I should have known . . .*

I sent for him with my new resolution to use his gifts for England firm in my heart. I tried to keep my distance, treat him more coolly when he returned from the country, where he kept his wife. But the play, our late-autumn tragedy, was not played out yet. Now in adversity must the wise man call his philosophy to his aid . . .

I schooled my soul to acceptance of the King of France's dereliction by turning again to schoolgirl exercises, translating Boethius's great work *De Consolatione Philosophiae* from its noble Latin into less than noble English, my rage against the King, against Raleigh, against all faithless men, simmered so. But the exercise did its work. I renewed relations with the errant King and released the traitor Raleigh and his drab Bess Throckmorton from their confinement. I even found a use for him when my privateers took the best prize of all, the *Madre de Dios*.

Madre de Dios! Mother of God indeed! She was the King of Spain's own merchantman, the greatest of his fleet, a floating castle that took six hundred to man her seven decks, and towering like a castle above the water, she was laden with treasure from the East Indies, a fabulous hoard! Jewels and ivory, silver and gold, sandalwood, silks and spices, tiger's teeth and Chinese bedsteads, musk and ambergris and peppers and peacocks' tails. I sent Raleigh down to Plymouth to take charge of it for me, then banished him back down to Sherborne, where his "Bessy" lived, to try how he liked the *holy matrimony* he praised so much!

The spoils of the *Madre de Dios* brought me a hundred thousand pounds from the sale of her cargo of peppers alone. We had peace with France, and as Burghley foresaw, nothing to fear from a distracted Spain. Now I could think of restoring the Treasury and feeding our lean coffers, now we could read and ride and sport and play, have the players every night if we so chose, and lutes and laughter and dancing till dawn. And now, too, I had new life and new blood at Court, the youngsters borne to London on the wave of joy and hope that followed the Armada: new names, new men, Carey and Pembroke, Coke and Cumberland, Southampton, Howard and Harington, yes, even the Bacon brothers my lord loved so. What though they were the sons and daughters of my first courtiers, that I had worn out a whole generation and descended to the next? Was I ever a woman to complain of youth and beauty, whatever its source?

We had it all to play for, my lord and I—but still there was the tinder-box of his youth, his love and pride, ever ready to take spark . . .

And still it rained. July and August wept into a sodden September and a lost harvest, then on into November, when even my Accession Day jousts were drowned out in mud and water, valiantly though my knights and heroes struggled. I dispensed praise and rewards as ever, yet my heart was like the red clay the hooves churned up in the lists. But one white night saw me awake to a dawn as clear and sweet as the birth of a new world.

"Quick, girl!" I prodded the maid asleep on her pallet with an urgent toe. "Rouse up my women, call my gentlemen, I will ride at once. Have them send to my lord of Essex to attend me at the stables!"

Now I was happily hastening down to meet him, forging through Non-such's chain of courtyards, my people at my heels. *He will be there at the stables as he always is, to choose my horse for the day, assist me to mount, cup his sweet hand for my instep and fly me into the saddle, take my ankle in his strong brown fingers as he adjusts my stirrup, touch my hand to the reins . . .*

Then he will turn his sweet face up to mine—"It pleases you, Majesty?"—then he will vault onto his own mount, throw his marvellous leg over the crupper and be mind for a fierce canter, a wild gallop, whatsoever I wish . . .

Already now the deep familiar heat, the burning spreading from my centre till I shudder, freeze, live and die . . .

"Nay, man, she must be told! How can we hope to keep it from her?"

Suddenly through the low stone archway close ahead burst a huddle of men locked deep in angry talk. My cousins Harry Hunsdon and Lord Howard, the lady-faced newcomer the Earl of Southampton and his friend the young Earl of Pembroke, attended by their men—what were they all doing up at dawn like this. "My lords?"

They looked aghast to see me. Even cousin Hunsdon, eleven years my senior, fat and bald and staring seventy summers in the face, had the air of a boy thief caught red-handed and seeing the noose swinging before his nose. "We did not think to see Your Majesty at this hour!"

I smiled fiercely. "Tell me, cousin—why not!"

"Madam . . . I . . ."

He stammered to a silence. All around stared, at the milk-washed sky, at their feet, everywhere but at me. It was left to one of the young hotheads, Pembroke it was, raw and untutored, his handsome face aflame, to blurt it out. "My lord Essex and Sir Christopher Blount, coming to words about Your Majesty, agreed to make it blows. They met even now at dawn, for a duel in the water meadow."

"Jesus, *no!*"

Southampton smiled a shallow, catlike smile. "Both live, Majesty. But—"

He held an agonizing pause.

I fought down an instant hate. *"But,* sir? Speak out!"

"My lord of Essex took a wound—"

"God, is he hurt?" In panic I struck Hundson's arm. "Send for my physicians, now, at once, send for Dr. Lopez!"

"No need, no need!" Hunsdon soothed me. "It is but a flesh wound and the barber-surgeons were in attendance; they are with him now."

"A flesh wound?"

His flesh—my wound—

Southampton seemed to snicker again—or was it just the composition of his features as he stroked his leg high in the fleshy part, inward up to the thigh? "Here, in the groin"—he smirked—"which I think may hurt him less than his pride, having lost to Sir Kit—he is pinked only."

Relief burst out as anger in me. "God's wounds, he knows that brawling and duelling are expressly forbidden at our Court! In my father's time, men lost their hands for this! How dare he challenge Blount? Now surely it was time someone took down his pride to teach him better manners!" I turned to Hundson. "What possessed him? Why did he pick this quarrel?"

Hunsdon sighed. "Because Your Majesty favoured Kit Blount after the jousting: because you sent him a piece of your gold and red-enamelled chess set, my lord swore no *knave* should have *his* queen . . ."

What can I say?

When I should have taken down that pride, I saw it as love. And I loved it in him.

Yet well I know that when two men fight over a woman, it is the fight they want, and not the woman. And a man who would fight his nearest, dearest friend, as Blount was to my lord, would fight with anyone.

God, that I had him there—I could have slapped his face for risking death in such childish foolishness! Yet he was like an unbacked colt, he would have his way.

And his way was the way of war. Cheated of France, he wanted war on Spain. Spain now became his war chant: recovering from his wound, he never ceased to press it. And to his side flocked all the young hawks who thought like him to find death or glory in the cannon's mouth. And as he was a leader to all of them, so he himself looked around until he fastened on a fair cause for his sword, as he saw it.

"Give countenance to Don Antonio, favour him, madam," he urged. "For with His Excellency here at court, we have the perfect claimant in him, to advance his rights against Spain!"

Don Antonio. Yes. I should have known that he would find an ally there, that two such adventurers would be soul brothers. For myself, I had no time for the Pretender—the truth was I had been avoiding the half-pint Portu-guese, who lurked about the Court, refusing to receive him. Philip had in-vaded his borders, stolen his country and put him off his throne—all this was true. But I would no more interfere in others' wars and others' quarrels than I would fly to the moon. It was true, too, that Philip had imposed the hideous Inquisition on his new captive country, causing many good souls to flee, Christians and Jews, among them my own physician Dr. Lopez. But I had my hands full with the fight against Rome here on our shores! I would not carry the battle a thousand miles away!

No, the Pretender would get no help from me. I told young Cumberland, who could be trusted as the ward of my old Earl of Bedford, that the Don's great moustachios pleased me not. And truly they were both fearsome and foolish—but I feared more the imbroglio with Spain that he would drag us into. I would not risk dear English lives, much less good English cash, to embroil myself in affairs so far away and challenge Philip on his own home ground. But to my lord, Don Antonio was a hero of old romance, a man wronged, whom we should restore.

But as hotly as my lord pressed for war, Burghley and Robert, my old cousin Knollys, and Howard, my Lord Admiral, all pressed for peace.

"I shall show you, sirs, the evil that is Spain!" he vowed and swore.

Now our scenes at Council seemed like the Armada again as the battle raged to and fro. So much for my hopes of making him a valued lord of advisement—he would heed no advice but his own! Often now my lord would storm from the table, a thing I never knew before, and could only be blandished forth by grovelling gifts . . .

. . . which I gave—and gave—not only money but my very self.

After one of his high storms I had to be bled for a rush of humours to the head. As the thick glistening carmine oozed into the cupping glass, I saw my life running out for him, my heart's blood let for him, this pelican lover who would eat up my love, my life and all and drink me dry.

"Your Majesty faints?"

"No, Doctor, no—on, press on!"

And on it went, our love song, our tragicomedy.

"Majesty, grant me—"

"Madam, I must have—"

"Your Grace cannot but say yes—"

Now he grew stronger, flourishing in my love and thickening the air with his demands.

"Yet he carries his heart on his forehead, madam," observed Robert drily. "Where my lord favours, the world can be in no doubt."

"I favour those who will serve Her Majesty as men and not as eunuchs!" my lord responded angrily. "Men who will show her that we must have war on Spain!"

"As your lordship pleases."

If ever a man turned the other cheek, it was my "Pygmy," as I nick-named Robert. Equable, cheerful, even merry among the endless trials of the Court, supporting now much of his father's role as well as his own, he never failed to return a fair answer to my lord's demands. To no avail.

"He hates me, madam, Sir Robert, as his father does!" my lord pro-tested. "But they shall see I can carry war outside the Council Chamber! And I must have my own men in your government, men I can trust. I must have the Attorney-Generalship for Francis Bacon, and a post for Anthony his brother, my chief adviser, my king of intelligence in the war against our enemies—"

"God's pettitoes, sir, must me no musts, and Bacon me no Bacons! That Francis of yours is no man of mine! And the danger you dream of does not exist. I am safe in my kingdom now, safe in my people's love!"

His eyes had lost all their little agate love-lights as he stared blackly at me and said quietly, "Madam—you shall see."

That summer progress had not taken us far—not like our journeys of the early days when I thought nothing of going as far as Northamptonshire. These days I kept a tighter circle around London, yet still would have no man think I could not sit a horse or last the day out in a shaking litter as I always did. But bad news travels anywhere, everywhere, and always faster than it ought. So we were found at Theobalds, Burghley's great house in Hertfordshire, which I always loved.

For he knew how to please me! Every stone of the place had been built for my delight, every wing added to accommodate my desires. For me his masons built the Green Gallery in the Middle Court, where I could pace beside a map of the whole of England painted on the walls, while the Fountain Court had my portrait done in marble, in the line of descent from all the kings and queens of England, and a vast Great Gallery too, spacious enough to walk with my entire Court and any visiting ambassadors and their trains to boot. I loved the lofty archways and high turreted towers, I loved the loving welcome I had there.

After dinner Burghley retired, pleading age and fatigue. But as Robert squired me through the gardens among the purling fountains, white marble statues and avenues of limes, out popped Burghley from a summer house clad as a hermit, with bell, book and candle, to announce his retirement from the world and beg my favour on his son to replace him.

"Not so, not so, my Lord!" I laughed with delight at his prank. "I cannot retire you, I need you too much! And why should I give you up when I can have two Cecils for the price of one!"

Despite his rueful smile, I thought that pleased him. And I was heart-warmed to see him on his feet again, his carrying chair used only for moving between the buildings.

That night in the Great Hall I was served with the height of ceremony, so I was well contented.

I was in such peace, such happiness, all I wanted was my lord. He had promised to return by nightfall from the city, where he had pleaded urgent business to wring from me a day's leave of absence.

"Majesty, greetings!"

He came upon us as ever like a fresh breeze of spring blowing our clouds away. But to my eye, which read his skies like the best weatherman, there was a fearful hint of storm.

"Truth, your lordship has missed good sport!" exulted my *bête noire*, the young Southampton, leaping to his side. "We had a bearbaiting today to honour the Queen. To see the bear chained to the stake, his little red

eyes darting about for the next mastiff, to hear his roaring as they tore
his flesh and flanks—"

My lord cut him off with a brief bow. "Forgive my rudeness, sir, but my
errand will not stand on courtesy. Nor will my duty to my Queen."

He sank on one knee by my chair and warmly grasped my hand. Even
so are beggars made blissful by meagre crumbs—*his hand on mine—he
was raising it to his lips, covering the crabby back of it with kisses—*

"Hear me, all of you! Guard, ho! Stand close to the Queen!"

A pregnant terror settled on us all. My blood rose to his as he hotly
announced, "Now have I guarded her sweet presence while all of you
sported or slept! I alone have loved her enough to keep watch and ward!
And I have uncovered a vile plot that touches her most nearly. Her
Majesty stands in hourly danger of her life! And I myself have conveyed
the assassin to the Tower!"

LXVIII

It is the royal prerogative alone to commit to the Tower—but let that pass.
Trust makes for treachery—that saying is as old as time itself. And when
the wolf prowls, look to the shepherd as well as the sheep.

"Hac urget lupus, hac canis angit," *said the old poet Horace: "Oh, I am
caught between the wolf and the dog."*

"He is well named 'wolf,' Your Majesty!" my lord went on in that same
strange exalted vein. "For if ever a vile creature sought to devour unseen,
strike underneath the cloak of Your Majesty's good kindness—"

Howard and Knollys, Warwick and Radcliffe, Burghley and Robert,
the Pembroke brothers, Southampton, and Cumberland and all my people were standing like country mummers gawping for their cue. I could
not breathe. *Who will take command, who will help me here?*

"My lord?"

He grasped my beseeching hand, brought it to his lips and covered it
again with a hundred fervent kisses. "He wrought against your life when
your Majesty most trusted him—"

Who had I trusted? I cast an anguished glance around my lords, my cousins, all my young men—*God, is there never to be rest and peace?* "My lord—what are you speaking of?"

"Why, dearest lady, of the wolf and his master in this plot to take your life, the King of Spain!"

Now it was farewell Theobalds as the carters and carriers fumed and swore, as the mules stumbled under loads ill-packed in haste, as the beds so recently assembled now had to be struck to their timbers again, and every fork and platter, every bow and brooch and boot and shoe, had to be packed up for our return to London to meet the crisis there. As the men cursed up and down outside and the maids ran to and fro within the house, I held a council of war to establish what we knew.

My lord was in his element, his fine face strongly working with emotion, his eyes bright with excitement, laughing and striding up and down, unable even to keep his seat.

"While you all dozed like dormice in the sun," he exulted, "I waked and kept watch, for Her Majesty and for England. And my Anthony"— he bowed importantly in my direction, he could not resist it—"the older Bacon, whom Your Majesty so dispraised, has woven for me a web of intelligence so fine that a summer mayfly could not slip through it. And we have caught a stinging thing indeed!"

I could not bear it. "Who? What? *Speak!*"

"As your Secretary knows"—my lord nodded at Robert, sitting pale and composed but suffering inside, I could tell, as we all were—"it was agreed to keep a watch on the house of Don Antonio and his Portuguese retinue for fear the Spaniards might try to take his life, have him murdered right here in London, as they did in Holland with William the Silent—and as they have tried so often, through the northern Earls, the Italian Ridolfi and our own traitors Throckmorton and Babington, to attack you too."

"Jesus, why torture me? Why rake up the past?"—*reminding me of all those fears, all those sick, silver-white nights that once you helped me through—oh my lord, my lord, what are we coming to, what are you doing to me?*—"Get to the point!"

The hot colour surged into his cheeks. "The point, then, madam!" he said angrily. "Two of the Don's servants being suspected of plotting against him, suborned by Spain to turn against their master, they were taken—Sir Robert knows this!" Again Robert bowed his calm acquiescence. "And they were put to the manacles, where they made a full and free confession."

I was beside myself. "And they said *what,* my lord?"

He triumphed like a schoolboy when he knows he has delivered his best enemy for a birching. "They testified not that they were plotting against the Don, but that you, madam, were the target! And that the agents of King Philip have suborned your own physician the Jew Lopez to poison you!"

Lopez—lupus.

Lupus *the wolf.*

Now I saw the point of all his punning.

But my Lopez—the man who ministered to Robin, kept Walsingham alive for longer than Dame Nature ever intended, tenderly eased my poor Hatton's final agony as he died by inches from his centre—Lopez? If I knew anything of men, he was no traitor, nor no poisoner!

The tears flowed from me, I could not contain them. "You put these rogue servants to the manacles? Under torture like that, men will say anything, implicate anyone! You are a rash and temerarious youth to move against the doctor in this matter! You cannot prove it! I know his innocence well enough!"

I should have known then that to challenge him would be spur enough. I tried to rein him: I appointed Robert and Burghley as his fellows on the three-man commission to examine Lopez.

"Majesty, he is innocent, and there is no plot," Burghley assured me after hours of probing interrogation.

"Madam, you are deceived!" my lord insisted, and set himself to prove it.

Now our old fear of Spain awoke again, and in such an atmosphere one plot, one fear, begets another faster than scorpions spawn. When Walsingham was alive, the lines of his spy network were kept neat and taut, and if a fly was caught, if a wasp struggled and a limb or a wing or two were torn off, even if a worker left the hive on a flight that never brought him home, I never saw it, never felt it. Now dirty things and clammy mysteries bobbed their black heads above the waters, broke the still surface of the oily slime and released their noxious stinking fumes into the air.

"What word of Dr. Lopez?"

"Majesty, nothing yet. But my lord swears he will confess a terrible conspiracy in time."

"I will not have him put to the question—no rack, no manacles, they know that?"

"Madam, they know—and they obey."

Can't go on, must go on.

Death goes on, life goes on.

Now as my poor Lopez sweated his life's fear into the stones of the

Tower, so were other clouds gathering. Those sunlit days at Theobalds with old Burghley sporting in the park now seemed in retrospect a miniature moment stolen from eternity, frozen in time, preserved between grey skies and the endless, thankless rain. Now as my birthday drew on this September, I refused all celebration, there could be no rejoicing.

No, of course it was not because this year brought me to my threescore years, damn you for thinking that! Sixty summers is nothing to a woman such as I!

But who could rejoice when once again we saw the failure of the harvest in our suffering land? The corn lay flattened in the sodden fields, the barley black and blasted with wet rot, crows dined upon the murrain-ravaged flocks, and the countryfolk saw starvation staring them in the face. Now from every church on every Sunday the low murmuring grew: *Domine ut quis, ut quis, Domine . . .* Why, Lord, why, wherefore art Thou absent from us, why is Thy wrath so hot against the sheep of Thy pasture?

Sleeplessly Robert toiled to amass the facts: "Grain now ten shillings a bushel in London, Majesty, up from seven—"

"Ten shillings? What are we coming to?"

"Fifteen in Bristowe, eighteen in Shrewsbury—"

"Now God have mercy!"

Early in autumn, the poor started dying. But for every wasted babe, every old man hastened to his end, a savage heart rejoiced. In truth the malcontents, the trouble-stirrers, the makers of mischief who live only to gnaw at the fabric of happiness and contentment, were never happier. Now would they seek advantage, now would they look for their chance to bolt and run away with us, and I grew fearful as I felt the reins of government twitch in my hand.

For our moths of state were not merely those who flew in from Rome, or fed on the fat of Rome, or looked to the hot breath of Rome for the wind beneath their wings. No, we had homegrown gnashers and gnawers, wilful and ignorant and as determined to win their way as any Popish Prelate, even the Anti-Christ himself.

It started with my Parliament-men, always a self-regarding, power-seeking bunch of meddling windbags! Now they were well in session, and my Lord Keeper, the faithful Sir John Puckering, had his hands full with them. He came from the House of Commons with a handful of my lords to wait on me at Whitehall. They found me mouldering in my chamber, without the will to distract myself on the virginals or join my ladies in a hand of cards, for my lord was absent on the Lopez business and I had no heart for joy that day. But Puckering's report would have raised the fire in any belly.

"He calls for *what?*" I could not believe my ears.

"Liberty of speech, he says, Majesty, according to the old freedoms of the House—"

"Wentworth, you say? Is he the Barnstable man who bothers me with the pamphlets?"

"Member for Liskeard now, madam—yes, Peter Wentworth," self-styled libertarian and pamphleteer. And he has others with him."

"Liskeard? So the foot of England—nay the big toe!—dares to lecture the head! I will not have these ranting fools instruct me what to do! Free speech, he says? You see what follows when a subject thinks to question the royal prerogative, to lecture a queen—what comes of letting lowborn men get hold of the idea that they are fit to govern, fit to rule! When once such blasphemous treason takes root, who needs a monarchy? Who needs a king?"

"But he is no traitor in what he says, Majesty," urged Puckering. "It is an ancient right—"

"Under the crown! And only under me!"

"But such freedoms—"

I stamped my foot hard enough to grind all these dissenters into the ground. "I'll freedom him! Convey Master Wentworth the Queen's compliments and consign him to the liberty of the Tower! And let any of his fellow praters and pamphleteers accompany him, if they will! I will not hear a single word more from any of them!"

There was a silence louder than all my shouting. At last my old cousin raised his head to speak.

"Yet though they have given your Majesty many annoyances, your Parliament-men," Knollys began, his dark face as always bright with Puritan fire. Trust him to defend this caterpillar of the nonconformist conscience, this worthless Wentworth! "Still, madam—"

"Annoyances? This villain Wentworth is not half of it. All my reign long they have badgered me, always badgered me! First over the succession, then my marriage, later the Scots Queen, not to mention their never-ending interference over matters of money and religion—"

"Still, madam, they have never failed to vote Your Grace the subsidies you needed—"

"I needed? That I needed for *them!* To make war for them, to hold peace for them, for them and for their comfortable wives and little children—"

"And you need not fear their loyalty now! Nor should you punish their honest speaking out against the abuses they see both in Church and State!" He wagged a gnarled finger of warning and fixed me with a glare. With a shock I saw every one of the twenty-odd years he had over me carved on his face, he looked as old as time itself. "I grieve Your Grace will turn aside from flushing out Popish treasons to turn on your own good people—"

"These Puritans and preachers are not good people! They are sedi-tious weevils, wilful, ignorant! Cousin, you know that bigots are as dan-gerous to the State from the one side as the other!" I struck my hands together in frustration and paced up and down. "Remember sister Mary, all for Rome? Then in comes brother Edward and the world turns arsy-versy for another zealot, another dogma? No, no zealotry! Always the golden mean! Let us have a gentle veil across the soul's windows so that no one can peer within."

Another silence, this time of agreement. The loyal Puckering sighed. "And Wentworth, madam? May I suggest—"

Oh, I was weary of the whole pack of them! "Wentworth? Save your breath, do not beg for him! No, let him rot there in the Tower—till he makes a frank and full submission on his knees before me!"

Which he would not, of course, stiff-necked and self-righteous as any Pharisee, as all the Puritans were! I ordered him all prisoner's comforts, even threw in the little Mistress Wentworth; she moved in with her hus-band into the Tower, and there they lived—at my expense!—as snug as bugs in a rug. But I would not soften and let him out. And his fate had a wondrous salutary effect upon his Parliamentary peers, all of whom sud-denly found their appetite for free speech dwindled to a widow's mite—I had no more from them.

But every age, every time, finds a race of those who the more they are thrown down, the more they will flourish. Next came a fish of very differ-ent flesh—called himself Marprelate, Martin Marprelate.

Why hide it? If I could meet the fellow now, I would laugh and slap his shoulder, shake his hand and say, Sir, I have hunted many a fine quarry, coursed hare and hog, chased and shot down the greatest stags of the forest, but you gave me the best run of all for my money!

At the time, though, I was not amused. In truth, I was frantic—for still I could hear the endless marching tread of my cousin's warning from Scots Mary's time: Strike or be stricken! Strike or be stricken!

"Did Your Majesty call?"

"No, no, go back to sleep, girl. If I need you I will wake you."

A sweet girl, that new maid, Burghley's granddaughter Elizabeth—named after me, of course, and—God!—a Cecil of the third generation of my service, by his favorite daughter Anne, sister of Robert, who was unhappily married to Lord Oxford, and now lately dead. I had taken the girl in among my ladies to cheer her up after the death of her mother, along with another little Bess, Elizabeth Vernon—there were battalions of Bessies now!—yet still she remained dull and dutiful. *I must get her married. One of the sons of Pembroke? No, the young Southampton, that vain boy who hangs around my lord—marriage would improve him, he could do with a good wife! And I could do with parting my lord from his boon companions like Southampton, and from his newfound hobby of this endless plot-detecting, politicking with the Bacon brothers, to allow me more of my lord's time and attention . . . more love, more joy . . .*

But before that, we must catch this rogue Puritan, this Martin Marprelate, who had us all by the ears. Some unknown hand was writing scurrilous attacks on my Church, condemning my bishops, even myself, in savage satire. The people—starving, murmuring, restless—were being inflamed against their lawful government, and we might have riots if he could not be caught.

But we could not catch him! None knew who he was, where the tracts came from, how they found their way onto every street corner, into every tavern, every breeches pocket. All I could do was put the best brains of the kingdom to work against him and await their success. Still pent up in my chamber by the rain, I was engaged in a desultory game of chess with my dear lord when Burghley came with Robert to make his report. In a corner my lord's shadow the egregious Southampton was prattling with my new maid Vernon, but even he fell silent as they approached. My heart sank to see that my old Burghley had resumed his carrying chair again, but his manner was as sharp as ever.

"The tracts come from a press in London, lady, that we know," Burghley told me, "for we have seized them in Cheapside and High Holborn with the ink still wet. And we have the printer—he was taken last night at dead of night as he and his men tried to move the press to a new lodging."

"Wonderful!" I exulted. "Then it can only be a matter of time before we have the author—this Martin Marprelate as he calls himself. And then—"

I paused vindictively and let the baleful threat hang in the air.

My lord sprang from my side and took a turn about the chamber. "And then, Majesty?" he said with an awkward laugh.

I stared at him. *Oh, he was lovely—oh, how love shatters all thought, all concentration—but no more of that!* "Why, to the Tower with him, if not to the gallows! We'll mar his pen and his prospects, too, if he threatens to mar our priests and prelates, the very princes of our Church. And the same for any who have truck with this sedition, who read or harbor these tracts, or pass them on."

He laughed again, more wildly than before. "What, then, of me, my lady—what will become of me?"

His hand was in his breeches pocket, and I knew at once what he would draw out. I could not read the little stark black lettering as he thrust the thing at me, but I knew what it would say.

The Epistle of Martin Marprelate for the reproof and overthrow of all horned masters called Bishops, all proud prelates, petty Anti-Christs, enemies of the gospel and the swinish rabble of covetous wretches calling themselves vicars of the church . . .

And he talked to me of the enemy within? "Oh, you fool, you fool!" I cried passionately. I could have boxed his ears! "Have you no sense of your own safety, your own survival? Do you see so little, care so little, that you do not see that ours is a house of cards, that under God we all stand or fall together? Take away the bishops and you take away the idea of true and God-vested authority. Take away that and farewell lords, farewell King!"

I burst into tears and clutched for Robert, standing silently by. "Find the Marprelate! For if he lives to mar our prelates, he will mar all. No priest, no King!"

They never caught him. The printer was put to the torture but never breathed a word; they have a fierce gall, these Puritans. But with random raids on Puritan houses and the haunts of those who called themselves "the Godly," we uncovered their secret cells and at last put out their fire. After seven fine flourishes, seven separate tracts, each one more vicious than the last, we drove the Marprelate to earth, and he never wrote again. But I gave orders that the watch was not to be relaxed. Oh, I had Hydra's heads and Hydra's eyes then for the threats to me and to my kingdom. And still they came, they came from all around.

For the Douai treason mill had not stopped turning, and a martyr's death was still the highest crown the apprentice priests of Rome could entertain. Time and again we would have saved them—why, Raleigh stayed the hanging of one priest in the West Country when he heard the fellow praying fervently for me, until he realized that the wretch was using his last moments on this earth to beg God to bring the Queen of England to the Church of Rome!

"At which I kicked him off the ladder myself, Majesty!" he reported grimly to me by letter. "But having more mercy on him than the foul Papists would have on us in the same circumstances, I allowed him to hang till he was dead. Thus he saw and felt not his privities hacked off, his bowels drawn out and his quarters cleft, as others have to do."

Some mercy, then—which most of them were too stubborn to take. Yet there was one—stubborn was not the word. Still, he had a soul of beauty.

As I in hoary winter's night stood shivering in the snow,
Surprised I was with sudden heat that made my heart to glow.
And lifting up a fearful eye to view what fire was near,
A pretty babe all burning bright did in the air appear.
Who scorched with excessive heat, such floods of tears did
   shed,
As though his flood should quench his flames which with his tears
   were fed,
"Alas," quoth he, "but newly born, in fiery heat I fry.
"Yet none approach to warm their hearts or feel my fire but I.
"For which as I am now on fire I work to do men good.
"So will I melt into a bath to wash them in my blood."
With this he vanished out of sight and swiftly shrank away,
And straight I called unto mind that it was Christmas Day.

Who would have thought a Jesuit to have had this in him? But he was no ordinary Papist, no ordinary priest or father confessor, Robert Southwell. He called it "The Burning Babe"; his mind was running on the fire all the time he was in the Tower. But he was not burned, of course—he was no heretic, but a traitor.

A very brave one. Worse than Campion they tortured him, thirteen times in all. And his soul flowered in this garden of blood till all who saw him marvelled. And like Campion he went to his death as to his wedding, serene in joy.

But let no one tell you these men were martyrs. He died justly! There was room for only one religion in my land. There was no saving them.

And my lords, my people, above all my Londoners after Southwell was arrested, were in no saving humour, not for any Papist, much less for a Jew. For months my Lopez held out against the questioners, saving his life daily, inch by inch. Then one day of April the sun shone, and I had a sudden longing for the river. The threat of rain notwithstanding, I commanded my lord's attendance. We could take the air in the Royal Barge with the Queen's Music, the whole consort in a barge behind us singing madrigals for spring . . .

"Madam, here comes my lord."

"Where? Oh, I see him!"

Just the sight of that lofty frame bounding towards me on the landing stage, that well-set body in its white and gold towering above his companions, the mincing Southampton and his good friend Blount, set my heart dancing. But not for long.

His bow was of the skimpiest—*did I imagine it, or was his courtesy diminishing to me now?* But his eye was on fire. "I have proved it, as I said I would! I have uncovered a most dangerous and desperate treason against you, dearest lady!" His voice was ringing out across the water—*was he enjoying this? Yes!* "As I told you, the point of the conspiracy was to be Your Majesty's death, the manner poison, the instrument Lopez—and now at last he has confessed it!"

My heart set like stone. "You had him put to the torture."

His ready anger raced up his cheeks. "No, madam, I did not—you did forbid it!"

"What then?"

He gave a careless laugh. "On my orders they—showed him the instruments."

Showed him the instruments. Parce, parce, Domine . . . *Spare me, O Lord. For the man of imagination, of feeling, of quick apprehension, that sight does all the work of the men in leather aprons.*

My lord flaunted himself before me like a summer swan. "And I was proved right all along—for he confessed!"

So the heavens darkened now for my poor wolf. With his own confession out of his own mouth, I could not save him. For three months I delayed signing the warrant while the crowds were baying for his blood. And for three months my lord kept after him like a dog at a rat.

What I could do at the end, I did—ordered him to be left hanging till he was dead, like Raleigh's priest—though not like Southwell, where they must have their pint of blood, and guts, and privates. And I refused to call in Lopez's property to the crown, but left it to his widow. But for long enough, his dark shape stalked my dreams.

As it still does.

He talks to me in the words of a play they made upon him for the public stage, which still rings in my ears. He stands before me making that other Jew's demand, the one who sought his pound of flesh from the merchant, after the Christians in Venice baited him so: "Your lord heated my enemies, and cooled my friends. What was his reason? I am a Jew. Hath not a Jew eyes? Hath not a Jew hands, organs, dimensions, senses, affections, passions? Are we not fed with the same food, hurt with the same weapons? If you prick us, do we not bleed? If you tickle us, do we not laugh? If you poison us, do we not die . . . ?"

And as he asks me this, I have no answer.

My lord called Lopez a wolf and rejoiced at his destruction. But as I looked at his strong white teeth and glad grinning countenance, a line of Terence I read with my master Grindal came fearfully to mind: "Auribus teneo lupum, nam neque quo amittam a me, invenio, neque uti retineam scio" . . . "For now I find I hold a wolf by the ears, and I do not know how I can get rid of him, nor how I may keep him."

LXIX

He had bested the Jew, the King of Spain, the Portuguese traitor-servants and the Cecils to boot—now was my lord riding high. And though my wild horse wrung my heart with every new high-stepping pace he took, God knows it suited him. Now in joy was he generous, loving, kind —that May he brought me tokens like any shepherd to his sweetheart, sweetening my heart indeed. And how I loved the caprice of his attentions!

"Your Grace should wear white more, it becomes you," he ordered carelessly and commanded for me a glimmering gown of samite of Jerusalem, pale as a pearl in an oyster.

"I have a mare for you, a dapple-grey, lady, with an eye almost as gentle as Your Majesty's own, and a lion heart like yours too. She will take you many a merry mile—when will it please you ride?" Did he know this was what Robin used to do?

Best of all was a gift one night that midsummer when the stragglers slumbered in corners, the guards drowsed at the doors of the Presence, and we two alone of all the world were wakeful, as in the very springtime of our love. He lay beside me couched on a vast cushion of red velvet, bright in his silks of saffron gold, those wondrous legs disposed at their ease. I looked at him and sighed my silent heart out, as I had done so many times before.

Oh, my sweet lord . . .

You smell of lavender and pomegranate . . .

What it would be now, to slip down from my chair and lie beside you on the cushions?

To stroke your face, tangle your brown curls till all the ochre and flame lights flash out of them—to touch your jaw, your cheek, trace and explore every inch of your neck, to feel the soft rounding at the top of your spine . . .

To draw your face to mine, to kiss you as I want to, know your wide man's mouth, feel your darting, probing tongue. Then your hard hand on my breast, your fingers reaching to strip off my bodice, remove my kirtle and leave me in my shift . . .

To fumble with the forty crested buttons of your doublet, to assist with trembling hands as you shrug off your breeches and hose, to have you draw my shift in one bold movement over my head, laughing, "Come, madam, come! What need you have more covering than a man?"

And then to have your hand, your seal upon my breast, your touch upon my body, your possession, your mastery, your long length, your flesh, your manhood, your love in mine, yours, all yours . . .

Oh, how sweet it was!

I was too old to blush now for such thoughts. But I closed my eyes to hide them from his view. And as I lay, half dreaming, half in heaven, I felt him take my hand.

"Majesty, look!"

On the third finger of my right hand he was slipping a ring. In a heavy frame of gold, a black-and-white intaglio portrait in miniature winked up at me: a fine white profile on a black ground, the raised ruff and hair shining brown. I knew that face as well as I knew my own—no, better, now I looked less in mirrors and more at him. It was my lord.

"Ohhh—"

I could say nothing. Marvelling, I drew it off my finger to admire the workmanship. Inside the ring, all the back of the jewel was enamelled with tiny forget-me-nots on a white ground, glowing blue as true as if they nestled round our feet beside white daisies and gold kingcups in a bright water meadow.

His eyes were blue-black in the gloaming as he whispered, "Madam— forget me not."

Forget? I pledged him then to wear it always—and upon the hand holding this quill, scratching this parchment, in spite of all, there it sits still.

I had a ring made for him in return, pressing it on his hand one night in the Presence when the dancing was hot and we were hotter, both on fire with the love, the feeling, what you will, that grew between us. "If ever you need me, dear my lord," I whispered him, "send me this ring and it shall command you whatever you most wish in all the world."

He raised it to his lips and slipped it on his finger, a plain band of gold enamelled round in black, as fitting for a man—but inside, unseen, it bore an engraved "posy," as the girls called it then, a little pledge of love returning his own love-words back to him: *forget me not . . .*

That summer we lost Raleigh to his lust for adventure and his lands overseas—and even more, to his greed for gold, for like me he was suffering from a well-nigh fatal consumption of the purse. Money! We rubbed our hands like usurers as we mourned our empty coffers.

"It is there, somewhere, Majesty, I know it, it is no mere sailor's dream," he murmured sombrely, staring through the casement with the same far regard I used to see in the eyes of my seaman Drake. "El Dorado! The Land of Gold!" But he sailed and returned with no more than a little metal ore and some bright black stones the London jewelers called marcasite, worth nothing, and both of us no richer than before.

Yet rich in love, I cared less than I should, and much less than I would have done before. And that Christmas we had a season of joy and feasting such I could not recall. It began with a wedding of my little maid Elizabeth, Burghley's granddaughter.

She came to me in her bridal gown to have my blessing before we processed to the church. Pale as a lily beneath her garland of red and white carnations, her modest gown as plain as any nun, she was the perfect bride.

"Now, Bess," I teased her, "did I not pledge my royal word to find you a good husband? And now must you, my old friend"—I turned to Burghley, being borne along behind the bride—"throw aside that chair of yours and dance at this wedding!"

His watery old eyes brightened as he returned, "Lady, one word from you and all cripples must walk! I shall dance with my heart for your kindness to this maid."

But I rallied the girl to cover my embarrassment, for in truth, my machinations had brought her a royal jilting. My first choice for her, the wretch Southampton, my lord's companion, to my fury flatly refused to marry—not merely little Bessie but any maid. "Madam, I copy you," he sneered—*what was wrong with the man?*—"I choose single blessedness over the joys of holy wedlock!"

"Say you so, sir!" I hissed in rage, peering at his long silken tresses cascading in one golden lock down over his left shoulder, his wary eyes with their veiled regard, his thin, sensual lips. *What, was the man another of the race of Sodom? For sure I knew that he consorted with the players, and the man Shakespeare had made a poem to him luxuriating in Venus's adoration for the fair youth Adonis, my cousin Hunsdon the Lord Chamberlain told me. Was Sodom his persuasion, or merely Onan?* Whichever it was, try as I might to make this marriage, I could not force him to it!

Any more than I could rein in my lord of Essex, whose extravagance now was a daily heartache. I felt for sure my lord was fooling with his money—with my money!

For he did not have a penny except what I gave him. And how he squandered it! Look at this business of needing his own intelligence service, politicking against the Cecils, forming his own party of followers for the love of God! Little by little, then, I was withdrawing some of his rents and his perquisites. With all England starving, even my sweet lord must learn to cut his coat according to his cloth!

Yet no thought of penny-pinching would I allow to spoil the fun that Christmas.

And we had good sport, I and my lords, that Christmas at Court. What though the odious Rich creature, the Lady Penelope my lord's bold sister, chose to come up from the country and inflict herself upon us?

"Your Majesty's most humble servant."

I looked at her with disfavour as she made her curtsey, now grown in minxhood as she was grown in body. She was as huge and high in the belly as a man-o'-war—faith, she was always a-breeding! How many children by her husband—the last of which, rumour whispered, Lord Rich had not put there himself? And now despite her condition, she was flaunting herself harder than ever, setting her cap at all and sundry. But what of it? If her own lord could look on and smile, then so could I.

And I smiled still through another vexation when, puke-pale and weeping, my new maid of honour Elizabeth Vernon was dragged to me by a furious Mistress of the Maids and forced to confess that she was with child. Oh, I slapped the silly strumpet's head as she stood there snivelling and confessed the father was Southampton! For I had that great lady-thing down as an arse-man all the way, and I hated to be wrong. Worse, he had not only ruined her but married her, defying my right to choose her husband! That merited more than a few more slaps, together with a generous handful of sharp tugs of her hair, and brought them both a salutary spell in the Tower. But in my own contentment, I could afford to be kind. Even when I found that the hussy Penelope Rich had wickedly given Southampton and the Vernon house-room for their ruinous amours and even egged the girl on, I would not let her spoil the joy I was taking in my lord's company.

For he was so good to me! Yes, you may sneer at an old woman who must pay for a young man's favours, but his favours, I swear, when he shone like this, were beyond money, beyond price! Of course, I never saw his own wife—she was no trouble to me. And in any case, I did not mind poor Frances, who, like a true wife, showed her duty by breeding; though he kept it from me and never spoke of her, I knew from Robert when she gave my lord a son, and I rejoiced for him at that. He kept her at his mother's house, where the still-hated Lettice still lived, God blast her, in retirement, for I never forgave her for marrying Robin. Thus with Bess Throckmorton, Lady Raleigh as she now was, tucked away at Sherborne Abbey on Raleigh's lands down there, I had all the she-wolves off my hands, and could enjoy my lord indeed.

L X X

Mary swore when they opened her, they would find "Calais" carved upon her heart. When they anatomise me, the curse will be "Cadiz."

It will be lying next to "Ireland" in that stone ruin, that graveyard of my heart. But Cadiz came first.

Cadiz.

It was to be my lord's greatest triumph, his hour of glory. The truth is, while I sought him as a courtier, he always courted fame in arms. I saw him best in silks and satin, when he dreamed of leather and cold steel. Me, I was content to let Spain slumber: he would always rouse a sleeping dog simply to hear it bark. I liked a war that was no war—where the King of Spain would not risk hostilities and I need not run the cost of keeping a war party in arms. But for my lord there was no party like a war party, and to the party he must go.

This one began at Greenwich in the midst of our dear delights, where I awoke one morning from an uneasy doze to the sound of a dull rumbling like thunder. But it was too early in the year for thundery storms, and besides, the sound I was hearing now did not roll and break as thunder did. I did not need to call in fear for my lord: he was already in attendance in the outer chamber, to greet me hotly as I emerged with the one word I dreaded: "War!"

"God's truth, what do you mean?"

"Cannon, madam, besieging Calais! You hear war!"

Behind him stood cousin Howard my Lord Admiral, Robert and Burghley, Raleigh, my old cousin Knollys, and the Lord Warden of the Cinque Ports, Lord Cobham. Cobham came forward, grey with sleeplessness, his stiff bow showing the long hours on a horse that had brought him to this dawn meeting.

"Your Majesty, the Spaniards have invaded France and have reached the northern coast. They lie at the gates of Calais!"

I reached out for my lord. "What of the French?"

He gave me his arm, his voice thick with excitement. "The French and the Netherlanders both have fought like Trojans to throw them back. But they have failed."

Raleigh shook his head. "And if Spain gets so much as a foot into Calais, yes, even a toehold there—"

Cobham's urgency could not be held in check. "—then we are back where we were when we faced the Armada in the knowledge that the Duke of Parma's troops stood by in their tens of thousands to pour into our land!"

Robert stepped forward. "Yet they did not invade!"

"And the affairs of another sovereign State do not concern us," Burghley said heavily. "We must preserve our peace!"

"Peace?" snarled my lord. "It must be war!"

Yet to keep peace, often means making war. That night I dreamed of Mars the god of war as a youth full-armed in black-enamelled armour, like my lord's, in a black helmet with the visor down. He stood on a dark hill and called aloud to a great throng of people, all dark, all in darkness, in a terrible voice, Now once again we must carry war out of the kingdom like burning coals, not wait for them to come hissing down upon us.

Then he turned slowly towards me, lifting off his helmet with its nodding sable plumes. And his face was my lord's face.

I was Bellona again then, goddess of war: his mother, lover, above all his Queen.

"Let it be war, then—but far enough away to keep the peace back home."

"To Cadiz, then, madam," my lord pressed, his fine face alight with zeal. "Let us set fire to King Philip's beard, burn his warships and raid his treasure fleet. Enriching you, we will succeed in crippling him, and keep him out of Europe, out of Calais, for all time to come!"

Briskly he laid his plans before me—fool that I was! While I thought him the perfect courtier, he had been plotting these schemes of war. He planned to make for Cadiz, then sail to Trinidad in the Indies, then on to the Spanish Main.

"And you return—when?"

"Majesty, how can I say?"

God, did I have to let him go?

And God, did it have to cost me fifty thousand pounds?

What if it cost me his precious breathing life?

I knew from Robin when they were at Zutphen that my lord was fearless in any battle. To check his rashness, I placed my cousin Howard the Lord Admiral in charge of the fleet. Himself he would be the General-in-Chief

of the Land Forces, Howard the Lord Commander. Raleigh should go
too; he was good by land or sea, he knew what he was doing. Like an old
hand, he also knew how to serve, and with grace accepted others' authority. Not so my lord, who always had to lead, who knew no more authority
than his own will. He was quarrelling, Howard wrote, before the ships
left the Channel.

Despatches from Howard reached me twice and thrice a day, raging at
my lord's high temper, his ill-grace, his refusal to concede, let alone obey,
his desire to win all the glory and keep it for himself. And in every clash
my Howard, who had kept the peace between seven commanders during
the Armada, now found himself defeated by one.

"By God!" I wept as I struggled over the letters. "I must take down his
high heart and break his will!"

But a still small voice inside me cried, Too late!

They took Cadiz. "They claim a famous victory, madam," little Robert
came bustling in one drizzling autumn morning to inform me. "Galleons
burned and others seized, the city sacked, and fine plunder too, so my
Lord Howard writes."

My lord wrote too, in a vein of high martial fury:

*Now, Majesty, picture the battle, with your great cannon shaking the
earth and making the heavens thunder, myself fighting your enemies with
your honour on my sword, your name on my heart, and your soldiers
fighting like tigers till the breach was made through holes too small to
admit a rat!*

I brought the parchment to my lips, and the fool tears flowed. Robert
stood by in sympathetic silence, then with a twinkle added, "And my lord
of Essex your Land Commander, I hear, showed his true mettle in his
treatment of the women!"

I laughed through my tears. "How so, the women?"

Robert opened his eyes wide. "Why, he forbade all rapine by his men,
a thing unheard of! And made them stand a guard of honour while the
women left the city, with all gallantry!"

This and other stories winged their way home faster than love itself.
When he came then, he sailed into London on a wave of the people's
hunger, for victory, for a hero, for anything to take their minds off their
empty bellies. Well then, let Gloriana welcome him as her hero! As I
rode to the docks to greet him—*yes, I had grown impatient, I could no
longer wait for him to come to me*—I saw the crowds: from the gates of
Whitehall they lined the street shouting and cheering as far as eye could
see.

As so they should, for I had dressed with care: an overgown of cloth of

GLORIANA 513

gold crosshatched with agates, diamonds and pearls, a kirtle and train of gleaming white satin, huge padded silver sleeves and a gauzy veil of silver tissue round my shoulders. And the dress was the least of it.

"Jesus have mercy!"

When I awoke that morning, I hurled the glass screaming to the floor and fell into sobbing hysterics. "Christ's bones, I never looked worse! Call for Radcliffe! Where is Warwick? Call for . . . call for . . ."

Call for a new face, without these vile wrinkles, hag's pits as deep as hell: new teeth in place of the yellow and black survivors huddling like famine victims in the front of my mouth; new hair in place of these thin grey elflocks straggling across a patched and balding scalp; a new white throat, not this purple turkey's neck; a new bosom fit for a young lord's fingers—

"Majesty, you have never looked lovelier!"

They knew what to do, my women, and they did it: first the white, laid on as thick as lime paste over a hint of carnation, next the red on the cheeks, then a sharp carmine for the lips, and over it all the glaze of whites of egg, which I must be careful not to crack. Last of all came the wig, a triumph of rich red ringlets and curlicues, spangled like stars and towering like one of Philip's galleons—yes, that was better! And with my lord waiting, would his love not make me lovely, lovelier than ever?

The day was dull and overcast, all my people reluctant to risk their silks and velvets riding to London water, fearing rain. But I would go down to meet him. My heart was weeping, no, bleeding with joy: *he was home, he was here, no more sorrow, no more white nights alone.*

My guards threw open the great gates of Whitehall, and my train passed through. My heart soared. The sun now peering would surely put the rain to flight. And the sunbeams shining on my golden gown seemed to strike the crowd as always, judging by their cheers. Oh, my good people! My heart went out to them.

But as my horse paced nearer, I could hear what they were shouting.

"The Lord Essex! Bring us the Lord General!"

"God save the good Earl! Praise God for his safe return!"

"Where is the Earl? The Earl! The good Earl!"

And all the length of the Strand, all along the Fleet, up Ludgate Hill past old St. Paul's, Eastcheap and By Ward, it was all the same.

"The Earl! The Earl!"

"The hero of Cadiz, who saves us from our enemies, God save him!"

"Let us see the Earl!"

Oh, I had my cries too, of course.

"The heavens smile on Your Majesty!"

"Here's to our good Queen Bess!"

But the lips that murmured "I thank you, my good people!" were cold, and my heart was colder still. Now none cried "Remember good King

Harry," no one "blessed my sweet face." And not one cried "Long life!" but "The General! The Lord General! When shall we see the Earl?"

He stood on the prow of his ship where it lay in the Pool of London, craning to see me. As I approached he bounded from the deck and down the gangplank, his men flurrying after like so many moths, to tear my hand from the reins, to press it to his forehead, kiss my foot.

"Oh, my sweet Queen!"

He was weeping openly, bright tears of joy. And I? *Nothing.*

I had longed for his return, prayed and wept for it night after cruel night. Now he was here, it was dust and ashes, wormwood, gall.

How had I bred this viper, who could now turn at will and sting me, who could release against me the many-headed brute that all kings must fear, a fickle, hostile people, the angry multitude?

They were distracted now by his great victory against our ancient enemy, hated Spain. But with four wet summers, four failed harvests in a row, they were sick and starving, and like sulphur, could take spark at any flint . . .

I had thought to return with him the way I came, in a great ceremonial procession through the streets of London, myself on my dapple-grey mare, himself on a black charger I had brought behind. But what fool would give to the people any soul that they loved more than me? By water, then, it must be. Pleading fatigue, I commanded the royal barge.

His return thus gangrened, the news he brought made it rankle deeper still. For returned with him, my cousin Howard could not wait to bring him to account. How had he lost my good Charles's good will?

They had fired far fewer galleons than they had thought at first, Howard reported through clenched teeth, and the threat of Spain was only delayed, not destroyed. *Now I must unleash my privateers, the men Hawkins, Gilbert and Frobisher, to do the business, and pay for Spain's bloody nose all over again.*

They had lost the treasure fleet through arguing among themselves when my lord would not obey the commander-in-chief. As they stood by, the Don Commander coolly set fire to it all—*losing me—and his master!* *—some twenty million florins!*

I heard the furious Howard out in silence, thanked and dismissed him. Alone, I dropped my head into my hands. What a dismal tale of pride and folly! But one thing above all made the ice bite to my heart. I had to challenge him. "My lord—on this voyage, my cousin says that you dubbed sixty-odd knights?"

"It is the privilege of the commander to reward valour so!" he blustered. "His prerogative to make new knights of his own—"

Prerogative?

Kings have prerogatives. Not subjects.

I was very calm. "On such a voyage, two would have been in order, four aplenty, six too many. But *sixty?*"

He raised his voice in passion. "Do not question your loyal servant's action, madam, for my judgement tells me I must do as I see fit!"

In other words, *I may do what I like!*

Was it because one of his jumped-up threepenny knights was Robin's by-blow, that illegitimate son he had by the Douglas? Just to see the boy grown up and now come to Court as Sir Robert Dudley, just as Robin was in our youth, with Robin's eyes and hair and nose and mouth and walk and carriage, was torment enough—but to know that my lord set him there . . .

But worse was the fear—no, the knowledge now—that my lord had grown in his own mind into one capable of making or breaking, as a king might do. And I had grown a monster.

Other heads than mine took the point too. His creature Bacon, whom I had to admire though I could not like, gave him fair warning not to try me in this. "Make the Queen love you by loving service, as her lord of Leicester did," he urged him, "and not by war or courting popularity. When you are England's darling, not her own, I doubt there can be any image more dangerous to a monarch, much less a lady of the Queen's apprehension."

England's darling.

It was true, the people loved him, he could do no wrong. Their hero, as they thought, had saved me from conspiracy, and won them a war. His judgement had been shown in his unmasking of Lopez, his valour at the siege of Cadiz.

He was adored.

As I was adored once too.

And as I still adored him, come what may.

For fool as I was, like all fools—*all old fools, say it*—still I clung to him. Despite my fears, despite my rages, each time my fool heart turned against him, within days, hours, minutes even, it had swung back to him —as it always had with Robin . . . I needed him, needed his youth and life, as once again Death renewed his assault, picking off my inner guard, my old guardians, one by one. Now within weeks I lost my two old cousins, first of all Hunsdon, dear old Harry Carey, my Lord Chamberlain, son of my mother's sister; then my old counsellor, stern Puritan but loyal friend Francis Knollys, cousin to me through his wife, Harry's sister Kate.

And fool again, half mad with grief, old though they were, I raged at their departed ghosts, *How dare you, dare you die!* Knollys I had appointed to my Council the very day I came to the throne, and Hunsdon not long after. Both now had sons who stepped at once into their fathers' places and offices, good and loyal as their sires had been. And both were full of years and honours, both made a good death, nothing was there to strike me to the heart. But I mourned them hard nonetheless, and not just for myself: with their going, after Robin, Hatton, Walsingham, two more links of my once-golden chain were severed for all time.

Now who would tell me the truth?

And that year also snapped a third, and fourth—my Lord Keeper Puckering, and old Cobham, Lord Warden of the Cinque Ports, unnoticed till this recent crisis but invaluable still. I was alone now, more and more alone.

And the last was the worst. I had held Drake back from sailing again after he failed me at the first sack of Cadiz. But my old sea dragon begged for one last voyage, and there Dame Fortune left him, far out at sea.

He would choose no other resting place than the Spanish Main. Now in ever-golden waters his soul swims with God as the fishes cruise his bones.

And now I saw that for me, too, deep and deadly things were stirring in the depths of the world's darkest sea.

LXXI

Ireland.
   Worst of my woes, an endless sea of troubles, land of God's ire.
   Who is yet born who can heal this broken land?

Where is the woman who does not love a present, as a child does? Above all on Lady Day, when the rents come in and March goes out, when the primroses banish the snowdrops from the wayside, and in memory of Our Lady all women should be honoured? It was late morning and I was lazing in my chamber when the knock came. I raised my head from my hand. "Radcliffe, what's that?"

"Gifts, lady."

A book and a box, in the arms of a burly porter. "Open them!"

Her thin arms straining, Radcliffe struggled to lay the huge folio volume on the table by me, and opened the leather frame. " 'To our Gloriana, the most high and magnificent Empress renowned for her piety, virtue and all-gracious government, Elizabeth,' " she read, " 'by the grace of God Queen of England and France, Ireland and Virginia, Defender of the Faith, her most humble servant Edmund Spenser doth in all humility dedicate, present and consecrate these his labours to live with the eternity of her fame: *The Faerie Queene.*' "

I laughed for joy. "So the little scribbler has finished his epic of me?"

"Six books of it anyway," said Radcliffe, peering at the end—her eyes may have been thirty years younger than mine, but her sight was worse! "Please it Your Majesty to hear it?"

"Later, perhaps. Here, sirrah!" I beckoned up the porter. "What of this box?"

"From Ireland, Your Majesty," he said, tugging his forelock, "and a letter."

"Open it."

He opened his mouth in a wide, stump-toothed grin. "Nay, mum, I cannot read!"

"Warwick!"

With a curtsey to me, Warwick took the missive from him and began to read:

"To the celestial ruler of our earthly heavens, from her vassal soldier, Thomas Lee, knight, greetings.

"In Limerick, at the execution of an Irish chief who had been a great rebel, I saw an ancient dame take this between her hands and drink from it, as at a banquet of the gods. And I decided to make bold to send it on to Your Majesty in tribute to your greatness. Though lifeless, you will see it speaks for itself. I pledge your honour in it, with my duty to continue the same ever against your enemies in this God-shotten land.

"Yours in all duty,

Thos. Lee (Capt.)"

"An ancient lady drank from it?" pondered Radcliffe. "A fine goblet, madam, or a loving cup it must be, captured from those foul rebels." She turned to the porter. "Well, fellow, open up!"

The box was nailed down—he had to use a hand-iron to open it. Within lay a round shape swathed in rags to protect it. Fine glass, then—even Venetian?

The porter grasped the bundle and heaved it up.

"Careful, man!" cried Warwick.

Too late. From the bundle something fell and thudded to the earth. There to my horror it bounced, and then—oh, God—it *rolled,* rolled till it touched my foot and lay there grinning up at me: a head, a man's head, black and bloated, the lips moving as if in speech, alive with maggots, the eyes open and staring, each with black worms writhing through the pupils . . .

"Argh! Argh! Argh!"

I could not stop screaming—only to vomit, and then set to again till I was coughing up blood along with bile. Nothing could stop me, only a cordial from my physician, which brought on an instant swoon . . .

Ireland.

I had enquiries made about the sender of my "present," Thomas Lee. A ruffian knight, they said, who had served under my lord in the Netherlands and France. And it was true he had seen an old beldame take the head between her hands and thirstily drink the blood as it spurted from the rebel's severed head, for the chief had killed her son. As he had killed his own three sons and his brother before Lee had, without trial, hung, drawn, quartered and decapitated him—and then burned the old woman for a witch.

A cruel and brutal fellow, then, violent and desperate—but only such, they said, would serve in that Devil's arsehole, Ireland.

God's own forsaken country.

That was Ireland.

Yet England, too, was in no good array, with my lord now daily feeling for his own power, and set to be both horse and charioteer of England's destiny. He grew a beard in Cadiz, did I tell you that? It is a thing all men do once, then some will shave it, some keep it, some will tend to moustaches, others like Robin stick to imperial tufts. But it marks always the passage into manhood, a man reaching for power, for status, for self-sovereignty. Or for sovereignty pure and simple . . .

Red like a fox, his was, and club-cut. I hated it.

And I hated still more, oh, I dreaded now his ever-growing appetite for conflict. I had good reason to fear other things: his popularity with the people; his anger with my cousin the Lord Admiral Howard, whom he blamed loud and long for the failure of the Cadiz expedition, thereby sowing discord in Council; his long-standing enmity with Burghley and Robert, who were always "penmen" to him, no men even, mere eunuchs, scriveners, anathema to a man of war. But the root of my fear lay in his love of war, for which he hungered now more than ever to restore his hero's halo and his credit lost in Cadiz. For I knew that this urge of his spelled disaster: I could read the writing on the wall, though I could not see its date. And when it came, it came like so many of life's worst moments, quite unexpectedly.

We had met to greet good tidings, a small handful of my Privy Lords and I, for we had heard that day of the death of my old friend and enemy, Philip of Spain. The man who once had loved and desired me, proposed marriage to me, then hated and hunted me even in my own kingdom, had now gone to his last reward. Good news, I say, not from malice at his death but as a wished-for release, for he had suffered hideous torments in shuffling off his flesh. The maggots that had seized the Irish rebel's head in death had possessed him in life: for three months he had rotted away alive and conscious, devoured by worms that played in and out of his gangrened orifices, his weeping, stinking sores—which he forbade his attendants to clean, taking them as God's will and punishment for his fleshly sins.

We stared at each other, Burghley and Robert, my lord, my cousin Howard, and a newcomer to the table, young Knollys, newly made a councillor to take his father's place. He was still sweet and twenty-odd, young William, the age when men feel themselves immortal, and for sure my lord, and even the clever little Robert, felt that way too. But cousin Howard was a man of middle life and more, and those hard, shrewd eyes now playing warily on my lord had looked on death and known it would come for him. And Burghley—oh, the sadness of seeing him now! Crippled by gout and fighting for breath with every word he spoke—*how much longer would God spare him to help me as only he could do? For his brain was as good as ever, his instinct as sound, his grasp as sure.*

My cousin Howard broke the silence, and I knew he was thinking back to the Armada, when as England's commander he had waged his own war against the King of Spain. "God rest his soul!" said Howard sombrely. "And spare us all such an end!"

"Amen!" I seconded him. "Thank God he is at peace!"

"And so may we be, madam," wheezed Burghley softly, "for his son the young Philip lacks his father's spirit, he will not seek war."

"Ha!" My lord laughed loudly, in the old man's face as it seemed. "Why, then, sir, this is the very moment to offer it!"

Robert discreetly brought his fingers together, as I had seen his father do a thousand times, and murmured, "Blessed are the peacemakers . . ."

My lord fired up again. "Blast all you peacemongers, all you chicken-hearted penmen! he cried hotly. "Can you not see that only war will give us peace with honour, and the only honour men or nations ever have is won by war! Now we may pound them into pieces, make messes of their flesh, grind meal from their bones and leave nothing for the dogs of war to feed on but the palms of their hands! Oh, and for Her Majesty," he added, hastily recollecting himself but with scarcely a glance in my direction, "there would be galleons burned, cities and treasure taken, honour and renown—"

Just as at Cadiz and your other adventures! I thought balefully. He seemed to read my thought, throwing up his head and casting me an angry glare. "It is all for you, Majesty, all, all for you!"

Burghley shook his head heavily from side to side. Silently he pushed forward a little psalter that lay under his hand, and with a quavering finger traced Psalm 55: " 'The bloody and deceitful man shall not live out half his days.' "

My lord's face darkened violently. "God's wounds, sir, no man impugns me thus!" He was reaching for his sword. *What, against Burghley? Against a sick old man?* I reached out frantically. Only my hand on his arm beside me stopped him rising to his feet.

What was he thinking of? To my horror I could see his was not the only hand on a sword hilt, for my cousin Howard had half risen too. I shook my head, and he fell back to his chair; but his hard, shrewd eyes were fixed on my lord now like a poisonous serpent. My brain was reeling. "Well, my lords," I gabbled, "setting that aside, what about Ireland? The despatches now are darker every day. With the rebels there growing in strength, I fear an uprising—how shall we avoid it?"

"We may not avoid it, Majesty," said Howard grimly, "for Ireland is always in a ferment—we never have subdued them! Our only way is to send an army now, under a high commander to take charge of all these Irish captains and ruffians who are now in the field, but running riot without direction and failing to hold the country down."

Ireland always in arms—never pacified—send an army—if that fails, send another—always the story of Ireland—

My heart sank even as my stomach rose at the old dance of despair inside my skull and belly—

Men and money!

Never enough!

Never, never enough!

I gripped my stomacher and drove it fiercely in and down with both hands to still my roaming guts. Then I paused to steady my voice. "This high commander: who, then, shall it be?"

Knollys, the young Knollys, fair like his mother and nothing like my old cousin, coughed and ventured his first word in Council. "It must be a great lord, dearest lady, one who goes with Your Majesty's full authority, not just to crush the rebels but to draw good men to follow him."

"My Lord Treasurer?" I turned to Burghley.

"There is Lord Mountjoy, madam, a loyal servant and a fine commander."

"Or the young Lord Cobham," put in Robert. He eyed me shrewdly.

"Unless Your Majesty means him for the office of his late father as Warden of the Cinque Ports."

I glimmered at him: he had guessed aright.

"Warden of the Cinque Ports?" interrupted my lord roughly. He tossed his head. "No, no, Her Majesty means not Cobham for that!" He turned to me, his manner bare of a shred of respect. *Oh, he was changed! Sea-changed in Cadiz waters!* "I must have that post for the Earl of Southampton—he is low in pocket and he needs the revenues," he announced carelessly. "Nor shall I allow of Mountjoy for Ireland, when I am your Lord Commander of the Land Forces—"

He needs the revenues?

He will not allow—?

He is Lord Commander—?

Spain, Ireland weighing on me, the enemy in Calais, four harvests lost now and our people starving, and not a penny farthing in the Treasury, not a groat to help any of it, and my lord *would not allow—*

Something shattered inside my seething skull. *"He* needs the revenues?" I burst out in a frenzy. "And *you* must have war, you must command?" I turned to my lords. "By God, this man is King here, and not I!" Furiously I leaned across the table and grabbed him by the doublet. "Your man shall not prevail! Cobham shall have the Cinque Ports, and I —I, Elizabeth, Elizabeth the Queen—I shall decide who goes to Ireland!"

All around the board my lords sat frozen in horror, Burghley drawn up to me as if to put his poor old body forward in my defence, Howard next to my lord watching him as a man watches a scorpion.

My lord slammed his fist on the green baize. "God, you delight to thwart me!" he cried in a passion. "Yet Your Grace must see—"

"Little man, little man!" I was beside myself, I slammed the table too. "Is 'must' a word to use to princes? No, you must bow that stubborn neck, you must obey, you must obey my will, you must come and go at my bidding, as all your betters have been content to do!"

Across from me young Knollys's eyes were bursting with horror, while my cousin Howard, his face sharpened to stone, drew slowly to the edge of his chair.

"And go you must!" I screamed. "Get yourself gone from my Court, take your foul manners back to your estates in the country, and remain there until you have learned to serve me with better grace!"

I struggled panting to my feet. Now like a man in a dream my lord rose fumblingly to his. From a furious red of rage his face had now turned an envenomed white—he was glistening like a man in the throes of disease. In the whole chamber, not a hair stirred.

"Why," he said clearly in a strange low tone, "now I see what it is to serve"—he paused, and launched each word like an arrow carrying its own poison on its tip—*"a—bastard—and—a—woman!"*

A sound like a savage laugh escaped him. He pushed back his chair and half turned to go. As he did so, I flew forward, grabbed for that tall shoulder and pulled him round to face me. I could not hear all the words pouring from my open, screaming mouth. But these I knew came from the depths of my soul: *"No man calls me a bastard . . ."* Raising my hand, I swung back my arm and with all my strength struck him across the face.

"Now God save you!" His hand was at his hilt even as he spat these words in my face, his sword drawn, the madness of the assassin splitting his face like lightning. With a thunderous crash Howard's chair flew back as my cousin leaped to my aid, throwing himself between us as he turned to face my lord. "For Christ's sake, man!" he shouted. "Collect yourself! This is the Queen, Her Majesty, your sovereign lady! If you draw a sword on her, you commit high treason! Withdraw! Withdraw!" Roughly he manhandled him to the door, shouting as he went. "Ho, guard, there! Attend my lord to his chamber, he is not well. And send for Her Majesty's women with their smelling salts and what have you—she needs them at once!"

He is not well.

I am not well.

All is not well.

But as I fell back on my chair, gasping and swooning in young Knollys's arms, one thing at least I knew—who now must go to Ireland.

LXXII

Bastard.

I sat in my chamber, laughing and raging. To hear this again, after forty years as Queen!

Was it this one word that killed my love for him? For it was gone, and my heart was dead as a stone. Yet still there was England.

A baseborn bastard woman . . .

Should I have him thrown into the Tower? Locked up and done away with? For Christ Jesus, how I wished him dead! But as with Mary, I did not want to be his executioner . . . Like Mary, though, if given enough rope, would he tie his own true-love knot, and hang himself?

"You are awake, madam? I thought you slept a little."

"No, girl, no. Say, what is that horseman I heard in the base-court?"

"From Theobalds, lady—the Lord Treasurer sends to say he is safely arrived back home. He thanks Your Majesty for sparing him this summer's progress, and he looks to return to you in full health before the berries turn again for autumn."

But he left me as they all did, peaceably in his chamber, praying to Jesus for "the last sweet drop of death." And the darkness came down upon me as it did when Robin died, and I lay on my bed speechless and mourning three days and nights to make my farewell.

How could he leave me when I most needed him?

Yet when in fifty years had I not needed him?

Oh, my old, my best and dearest friend, have them make ready for me in heaven, I shall not be long now. And see they prepare me a royal welcome— you always sought my best interests, you always looked after me, I shall expect no less in that world-without-end kingdom where we shall rule together as we did below.

And the year wore away leaving one word behind.

Bastard.

He had said it to my face.

Was I a base woman?

Cynic I may be, Stoic I have had to be, but base?

Go kiss my basest part!

And so I said without words when I made my decision to send him to Ireland. For months he sulked on his estates, and I left him there. But to Ireland he must go.

Let him prove his loyalty and his service.

Let him at least pull something from this flaming ruin of my pride and our love, for our country if not for me!

Now without respite evil poured from that Devil's Dyke, Ireland. To Court, broken and trembling came my one-time laureate Spenser, now destitute, driven out of Ireland, his prospects as wintry as the weather.

"Those animals of Irish rose up against us to tear and ravage everything, everything fair and fine that we have built or brought into their bog of a land!" he reported, shaking in every joint. "A mongrel of a chieftain, leading his dogs of kerns—clowns, rather, but for their viciousness!—and his so-called 'gallowglasses,' every one of which would have better graced a gallows, laid siege to the English settlers within the Pale, village by village and town by town, slaughtering men like cattle and cattle like plague rats."

He had lost all, of course, as they all had. The young lord I had there as commander lost his sister to a raider who kidnapped and ravished her, and his life at a battle they called "the Slaughter of Yellow Ford," the worst disaster ever suffered on English soil. Spenser died too, of fright and grief, as many did. And among the casualties one almost as bad as Burghley's loss: my best maid Radcliffe, losing two brothers there, as she had lost two others in the Netherlands and France, now laid her pale head on her pillow and grieved herself to death.

I was dying by inches myself as my dear ones died. But one thing was as clear as a lighthouse beacon in all this sea of grief: *Someone must go to Ireland. Let it be him.*

Christmas came on as he prepared to leave. I would not have him part on bad terms, but determined to do all I could to ensure his success. I made him my Earl Marshal, the heraldic title of the premier commander of all England. And as the music played in the Presence, as resplendent in ivory slashed with ebony and all sweetness and fiery devotion he led me out to dance for what I knew must be our last volta, I gave him a last warning.

"My lord, I have swallowed much—"

He took spark at once. "Why, madam, so have I! Are subjects always in the wrong? May not princes err? I would not let your father, not King Harry, speak to me as you spoke! You broke all the laws of our affection—"

Who would believe this man called me a bastard?

I was calmness itself. "Enough. I have pocketed up your insult, it shall never be held against you. But take warning when you question my authority. What I may forgive touching my person, I can never forgive if you touch my sceptre or my State. To strike at me as a woman is one thing—to move against a monarch merits death."

"I move against you? Oh, Majesty!"

He threw back his gorgeous head and laughed his great laugh.

From that first meeting in his boyhood, I had watched my lord flourish for twenty-odd summers. Now, like a shooting star trailing downward fire, he blazed no longer than so many weeks. Yet he filled the skies with brightness to the last. No man left England with higher hopes and louder huzzas, women and boys running alongside his horse to kiss his stirrup and thread rosebuds through his reins.

As he took his farewell, kissing my hand, he begged my licence to return at will. He hesitated, then seemed to force out the words. "Because—I shall suffer in your absence—I shall wish not to be long from your side."

I trod down my weakness. "Destroy the rebels and you may return at once!"

Lingering over my hand, he seemed impervious to my harsh tone. "Guard your most precious person," he said quietly, almost wistfully. His fingers found the ring he had given me, and he gently turned it on my hand. "Oh, my sweet Queen!" he murmured as he played with it. "If I may beg you, care for my friends, cool my enemies, and—forget me not."

Christ Jesus—if only he had always been like this!

If only . . .

I was dancing on knives. Lightly I brushed the ring that I gave him. "Have no fear, my lord," I promised him from the dark well of my soul, "I shall not forget!"

Yes, I wept to see him go—would not you? And quarrelled with myself at his last words. Cool his enemies? God Almighty! Why did he always hate the Cecils so—who, dead or alive, never failed to do me service?

Not least in serving him! No general ever had a better army, upwards of sixteen thousand men and a thousand horse, for all the youth of England were afire—they sold the pasture now to buy the horse, to go to war with him. No expedition that we raised in all my reign cost me more money—above a quarter of a million pounds! It hurts me still to think it! And Robert it was who raised that money, begging, borrowing, bullying, to send forth my lord in the rank of my Vice-Regent and the style of a king.

For which I gave Robert the Mastership of the Wards as his reward, a place of power and money. I knew my lord would think it rightly his. But I meant it as a warning. *Take heed of your purse, my lord,* I was saying to him, *and what I have given already—for these lucrative posts are in my hand to give or not to give—mine is the power, mine must be the glory, I, Gloriana, I, Elizabeth the Queen . . .*

Yet the first despatches from his camp showed how far he was from heeding me, or mending his rash ways. And though I had expected it—*yes, you could say played God, designed it*—yet still it brought me to the brink of fury every time.

"Though your orders were to attack Tyrone the O'Neill at once," he wrote, "Your Majesty must allow your general in the field to judge the time most meet for this engagement."

The same refrain: *I will do what I like.*

He had taken that rogue his bosom friend Southampton with him, a man I misliked and mistrusted, the more so since he stole Bess Vernon from me. I had been sure then that the man was a cloak-clogger and a sodomite, and was furious to be proved wrong. "If he goes, he goes as your companion, not as my officer!" I warned him. Now came the arrogant word: "The Earl of Southampton I have appointed as Your Majesty's Master of Horse for the expedition—"

"By Jesus and His Passion!" I swore viciously to Robert. "Master of Horse? That man never so much as ventured in the lists to tilt with the weakest—never got his leg over more than a half-cocked gelding—no man knows less of horses!"

"There is more in the despatches," Robert said quietly. "And word from the captain here—"

God, my sight was so dim! I did not see the fellow with him till he popped up at Robert's elbow with a rough-and-ready bow, a hardy, warlike man with a cold, blank eye and an old scar on his jaw.

"My man in the field," explained Robert. "One of the Irish captains under your Lord Commander." *Yes, and sometime spy?*

The man squared his legs sturdily and began. "The army dwindles daily, our captains are drunk all night, the quartermasters rife with corruption, and we have no ammunition. My lord the General your Earl Marshal talks of a great attack, but the cavalry cannot be got into the field, the one arm of our warfare the Irish fear."

"God's bones! What of the Horse Master, the Lord Southampton?"

"Spends his time in his tent with one of the young captains, a handsome boy called Piers—"

"Enough!" *God, what cold comfort to be right!* "And the rebel chief?"

"Not yet engaged. But there are rumours that messengers come by night—dark talk of a treaty—"

A treaty.

I had forbidden it out of hand, on his allegiance—forbade him even to parlay when he should be dealing death. Attack! Attack! I had ordered him, no quarter, no debate, above all no treaty!

Whoever would make treaty with a rebel and a traitor was a traitor too.

By day and night it darkened now as his world rushed to eclipse.

"He has made twenty new knights? Forty now? Fifty? Why, send to say he might as well make them by the hundred!"

Why was he making knights? To create a band of men loyal to him, not me?

"He says the army is down by so many through disease and desertion?" *Truly Ireland is one vast boghole, and his own father died there of dysentery.* "But an army of sixteen thousand men now mustering no more than four?"

Unless he had diverted five or eight thousand to another place—to his own use, as his own private army—

So, what have we? He builds up his own party, his own army? Can I guess, then, the answer to the one last demand I had, which rose to a howl, then to a scream as I sent reproach after reproach: *Why does he not attack?*

I sent a new command revoking his permission to return when he so willed. "Never think of leaving Ireland till you obey my command!" I fulminated furiously. "March on the O'Neill at once! Attack, kill, extirpate all these filthy rebels, leave not a rat alive!"

Even now I do not know why he never did. It was the raison d'être *of the whole war—the one stroke by which he could have rescued his name and credit, redeemed himself as England's darling and, above all, done me the service that I craved.*

Was he afraid? After all his talk of war, when it came down to it, like a snail he shrank in his head. Weeks he spent skulking in Dublin, wasting time, losing men. And when at last he had to face the O'Neill, Tyrone the rebel, who in contempt brought all his forces down from the hills to brave him, he was left with a quarter of an army, no cavalry and no will to fight— for now he knew he simply could not win. Small wonder, then, that he parlayed with the shag-haired traitor for forty minutes, all unheard by any other, their horses beached out in the middle of a fast-flowing river with no one by for a mile.

When I heard this, I knew he was a traitor.

And I knew he would know I would know. He would know that even as they talked, a man or men like Robert's spying captain would be stealing from the ranks, taking the fastest horse and the fastest ship to bring me word of this breathtaking dereliction, this blatant defiance.

As they did, trailing me to Nonsuch. Once again we faced the wearisome upheaval of the summer progress, days on the road, life reduced to carts and boxes. And this departure when we left Greenwich for its sweetening removed my lord seven leagues further from my heart. I had ordered all his gear moved out of his apartments, for if ever he returned, he would lodge no more with me. Egerton it was, the Lord Keeper I appointed to replace old Puckering, who as my premier man of law brought it to me.

"Found in my lord of Essex's lodgings, madam, and submitted for my scrutiny."

I took the book from his hand and puzzled vainly at the gold spidering on the spine. God blast these weak eyes! I could not read it. Heartsick, I turned to the flyleaf: "To the most excellent Earl of Essex, Earl Marshal of England, Viscount of Hereford and Bourchier, Baron Ferrars, Lord Marchet of Bourges and Lyon, is dedicated this History of Henry they

called the Fourth, with an account of the overthrow of that vain tyrant
Richard II and his replacement on the throne—"

Sick? Oh, sick!

My traitorous gut rebelled at every word, but I ground it down. "My
Lord Keeper, have my lord's affairs returned to his apartments, he must
not know we have discovered this. And have the author—"

Egerton read my command. "Already in our hands, lady. He has been
put to the question, and he swears he dedicated his book and wrote of
the usurpation to the great Earl from no ill purpose whatsoever—"

I screamed with rage. "What else would he say? Rack him again!"

Three rackings later, the penman stuck to his story, and we had to
release him. But now the threads were weaving together in a pattern all
too plain. And on a mild pale night of that September, the mortal earth
all slumbering below but Virgo rising in a fair clear sky, I sat down in my
chamber to piece it all out.

It had not long been my birthday—do not ask me which one! But take
'33, the year of my birth, from '99, where we are now, and you are left
with two of the three letters that signify the presence of the Devil—who I
now feared was here.

The King of Spain's back door, Raleigh called Ireland. Whoever held that
sceptic isle held England at the barrel of a gun.

All the pieces of the game now came together like a child's toy. My
lord planned to hold Ireland as his fiefdom, as a power base from which
to strike against me. He was building up his army, his own war party, with
his new-made knights as officers, and the soldiers "lost" from the musters as his own men. He would not fight the O'Neill—still less root him
out, as I had ordered—for he wanted the rebel as his vassal King, to hold
and rule Ireland for him—for him and under him, not under me.

For this he had courted popularity, wooed the people, challenged my
power and tried to substitute his. For this he had studied the rise of
Henry Bolingbroke to the throne, and the fall of the second Richard. He
sought my overthrow! He planned to make himself King instead of me!

Thank God he was safe in Ireland! And with my command forbidding
him to leave, there he must stay till I could mobilise my loyal lords
against him, to drive him from cover and flush him out where I could
take him.

The pale and bony fingers of another lifeless dawn were now feeling
their wandering way across the sky. I lifted my heavy head. In the glass
ahead of me at my table, I could see huddled in an old faded linsey-
woolsey nightgown not Gloriana, not myself, but a ruin of a woman,
hollow-eyed, with a stark, shrivelled, naked morning face, grey hair like
witch locks all about my ears.

Oh, my lord, my lord . . .

If I had been a milkmaid with a pail on my arm, and you a young shepherd from the hills, would we have been happy?

If I wept now, would these tears be the last?

O my sweet lord . . .

My sweet betrayer . . .

In the still morning something stirred—a hubbub below shattering the dewy peace of dawn like a broken glass, shouts and oaths and clashing steel. And now running feet—*who runs at Court but one in terror, or God save us, one bent on death? Men's feet, pounding feet, they were coming, they were here—*

A scuffle at the door, my women screaming, Warwick leaping forward vainly to defend me, and in he bursts, the drawn sword in his hand pointed at my heart.

LXXIII

"None move an inch, if you value your life!"

Was it like this when my lord of Seymour burst in on my brother—and did Edward, too, know this moment of mortal, searing dread?

Domine, in manibus tuis . . . Lord, into Thy hands I commend my spirit . . .

I looked that moment on my last hour, and was glad to find it beautiful. Even beneath the streaks of mud disfiguring his features, he was fairer than ever, his fine skin blooming with the flush of his dawn ride, his hair tumbling freely in those vivid locks, his body lean and hard from soldiering, a new scar on his sword-hand glowing like the scar of the first hand that ever raised my blood and taught that fire in my belly how to glow, how to burn . . .

If ever any ask what men think of at their deaths and you hear wiseacres prate of high and holy things, do not believe them. Socrates died with his male member at full alert and standing to attention; all his companions saw it. "A miracle!" cried the wicked old sage. "An erection on my deathbed? Sacrifice a cock to the God of Love for me!"

And I, too, died that moment in the bliss of my lord's eyes, his body and his presence, and my only thought was of enjoying him.

Burning . . .

I was burning, burning—had I died and gone to hell? No—for my hands, my heart, my head, were as cold as ice.

And I forced myself to meet those dangerous eyes as coldly as I could. "Why, my lord, what is this?"

He laughed wildly, strangely. "Not treason, though it may look as if it wears treason's face! I mean no treachery—though I am returned to clear my name from treacherous tongues, and with it clear away my enemies from clogging round your ears, poisoning your mind against your most true and loyal servant—"

Who was with him? My gaze fixed on his strongly working face, I could still see out of the corner of my eye a wall of steel at the door, none of it mine—

Where were my guards? I dared not call them, for he might strike.

"My lord, spare the Queen, as you hope to see God's mercy!"

It was the faithful Warwick. My lord stared at her as if she were deranged, and not himself.

"Why, woman," he said wonderingly, "the threat to Her Majesty comes not from me!"

"No one doubts that, my lord," I purred. "Therefore why do you need this show of arms?" I waved towards the door. "There are none but women here, all of whom love and honor your great lordship." I gave them a desperate signal. And bless them, they all muttered through lips blue with fear, "And so we do, sir, so we do!"—like the chorus of a Greek tragedy.

He nodded, still in that strange, half-dazed way. "Yes, madam, as you say."

He seemed to breathe more easily now, and I saw my chance. "So pray you, my dear lord, withdraw to your chamber, shift your shirt and let me see you in your finest array. Now you are returned and I do not have to sit by like a widow mourning your loss, we shall have plays and music, we shall feast tonight, feast your homecoming."

And may God have mercy on my soul . . .

He threw himself at my feet and kissed my hands. "Majesty, it is done!"

And like a hurricane, he was gone even as he entered, his men of war with him.

He had seen me as no man ever had before, naked in my chamber. God, was it to punish me that you visited me with this final shame? Where now was Gloriana? Across the table the face in the glass stared out with the mute, brute look of degradation, of pain and shame beyond the humiliation that I had seen in the faces of town whores stripped for their lashing in the marketplace for all to come and laugh at.

Oh, I burned, I burned, I burned, and still I froze.

But I would not weep. I turned to Helena, standing like marble behind my chair. "Give me a headcloth, I beg of you, cover my head. And my furred chamber gown—and pray the boy build up the fire, for I am very cold—"

Now they all came alive in frantic activity. I raised my hand. "And at once—send for Sir Robert Cecil."

"By Your Grace's leave." The little maid could hardly find her voice from her still-lingering terror. "He is already in the ante-chamber—but he says he will await your gracious presence until you are dressed, to greet Your Majesty as you choose to appear."

My lord had brought no army, Robert said. There was no war party backing him up, no force come to put me off my throne, merely a bunch of his own creatures, desperate fellows who had chanced all with him to break from Ireland and make a run for home, trusting to my weak fondness and forgiveness to overlook the ruin of the expedition there. The great general had abandoned the war in Ireland and staked all on this last frantic throw, that much was clear. But what lay behind it, if he was in league with the Irish rebels or the King of Spain, the Pope or the Catholic King of France, to overthrow me and my government, that was a mystery still.

"Your Grace must sift him, probe him to the quick," said Robert gravely, "before he is taken and committed for examination and trial."

"Oh, God, must he be tried now? Must I—?"

Robert looked at me with his father's lawyer's eyes. "Your Majesty, consider. My lord as your Earl Marshal has refused every one of your orders in Ireland. He has parlayed with the traitor and your enemy, defied your express command not to return, and broken in on you with drawn and naked steel. For every one of these, his life is forfeit. My own father, if he had lived to do such things, could not escape the charge of treason and *lèse majesté*. There is no other way."

I howled with grief. "Your father, had he lived, would not have dared to speak to me thus!"

Robert diplomatically shifted his ground and pressed on. "But we must know if any more of Your Grace's enemies are still behind him—if the peril he placed you in was his own rash impulse or part of a plot. Then when we know our enemy, we who defend you may strike without mercy."

Strike or be stricken—strike or be stricken—

Oh, God, again?

His own rash impulse or part of a plot?

In my heart, even more in my gut, I knew the answer to that already. My fear, and not his malice, had spun that web of conspiracy I had dreamed up the night before, with Virgo rising, in the cold hollow hours before dawn. Yet, we must make sure. I must send for him. Yet, would he come?

A needless fear! He came to me unbidden just before the dinner hour, when the noon September sun played warmly through the casement and my chamber reeked goldenly of beeswax and marigolds and early Michaelmas daisies white as stars. Now I was Gloriana again, dressed as fine and fierce as for a state banquet to feast a dozen ambassadors. My gown was in the new fashion, heavy black velvet cut like a coat all in one piece, without a kirtle, but the waist nipped in as neat and trim as ever. From the neck to the hem all down the front ran a fantastic border of jewelled flowers, pearls shaped like marguerites with emerald leaves, rubies for roses on carved golden stems, and table-cut sapphires as deep as inkwells. My ruff was the highest, widest, whitest, stiffest, laciest ever seen on any neck, and my wig was adorned with a diadem like a pearl-and-sapphire halo encircling my head. Red bows for triumph ran around my waist and flourished at each shoulder. Now I was Gloriana, Venus, Juno, Iris, a rainbow in my hand, lightning in my tongue, and bolts of thunder at my command.

"Give my lord welcome—say he may come in."

Oh, and on my left sleeve I sported a ruby heart depending from a truelove knot of gold—would he notice, would he care?

He bounded in unconscious of wrongdoing, like a gazelle in an upland pasture or like Adam at the dawning of the world. He wore no sword now, and the dagger at his waist in its gilt and onyx sheath I knew was purely ornamental. In oyster silk frogged and crested with gold and beads of topaz, a gold chain at his neck, lace at his collar and one huge teardrop pearl—*my symbol*—in his ear, he still had power to dazzle my weak eyes.

"Your Majesty's forever—while you wish him yours!"

Oh, he was lovely!

Now the burning began again, spreading from my woman's heart, from the core of my womanhood, burning, burning . . .

He knelt before me, humble and sweet, chastened to my hand. "Favour me, Majesty, with one precious word!"

I kept my voice level and very low. "It must be a word of reproof for your defiance—"

He tossed his head with a flash of the old spirit, then knelt penitently at my side. "Punish me, lady, chastise me as I deserve!"

He hung his head down to me like a flower. I struggled for control. *"Why did you come?"*

His eyes were wide and startled like an afternoon fawn. He was very pale. "Why, madam, to see you!"

"What do you want?"

"Nothing but to serve you with a humble, thankful heart." He passed a wandering hand across his brow and ran his fingers through his hair.

"You are changed, my lord."

He answered low and puzzled, like a man lost in a mist. "Yes."

Was he well? This was not the man who had spurned me and scorned my orders. *On guard! On guard!* was thrumming through my brain. Yet in spite of all, my fatal heart was dancing.

Had he at last learned his lesson, was his proud spirit tamed, was my wild horse backed and broken to my hand, my rein, my spur?

All around me my people had been standing in pageant-like attitudes, stiff and unnatural. Now they relaxed. Helena came forward, her maids at her heels. "Will Your Grace dine with my lord? Take a little wine or a few comfits or dainties? We have an elder-flower custard just up from the kitchen . . ."

"Nothing, no, we want nothing, leave us."

At my sign they melted away and we were alone.

After so many pains and sorrows, he was here, he was now . . .

Kneeling among the cushions by my chair, he was very near, he was so close. The shaft of sunlight from the casement behind turned his hair to filaments of gold, gave him a halo like my own. Now I could see the ring of amber round the little love-moons in his eyes, see their black coral depths as never before. He had shaved the hated beard and now wore only an imperial just as Robin had, fine, clipped and manly, enticing to the touch . . .

He looked into my eyes, then dropped his gaze like a virgin at a bridal when they bear the bride to bed. His breath now was coming as short as mine, his fragrance of pungent spices invading my every sense, my being, like red fire. Now with unnatural clarity I could see each coriander curl clustering to his neck, the soft flush of his face, the red well of his marvellous wide mouth . . .

He lifted his head and looked into my eyes. His hand found mine; he was turning the ring he gave me on my finger, as my fingers found and caressed the warm hoop I gave him. "Oh, my lord, my lord!"

That ever I should call thee castaway . . .

His sigh came from the depths beyond his soul. "Oh, my sweet Queen!" He closed his eyes.

He was here, he was now, he was mine . . .

Oh, Robin, Robin, my love, my only love . . .

Closing my eyes like his, I slipped my hand up to his neck and caressed his face. Then as a woman who knew not what she did, I took his face between both my hands and drew his mouth down to mine for the long-dreamed-of, longed-for, long-forbidden kiss . . .

It was a kiss beyond imagination, almost beyond bliss—the kiss of soul made flesh in trembling wonderment, manna, ambrosia, a kiss long as my exile from the shores of love . . .

A kiss as long as life . . .

. . . as long as death—

He started like a foal under my hands, and his head snapped out of my grasp. He stared at me, a shadow-play of feelings chasing each other across his face. And suddenly I saw again the boy who had pulled away from my embrace twenty years before, the first time we had met, when he came to Burghley's house after his father died. Any young thing would have found me ancient then, painted and wrinkled then, and as far from his desiring as a Gorgon or the ancient Queen of Serpents, the Medusa herself.

What must he think now?

I did not care.

I had had my kiss. A Judas kiss, bitter and sweet, for the men of my guard stood now outside the door. But the kiss I wanted—the kiss I had earned.

Take what you want, and pay for it, says God.

That was for Elizabeth the woman. Now I must do what the Queen had to do.

"Guard?"

They brought him to the Privy Council, where all the lords who were with me and those who could be hastily summoned, Robert and Howard, Buckhurst and the Lord Keeper, young Knollys and the young Cobham, put him to the question.

"And though the interrogation lasted five hours, Majesty, they came to their decision in less than five minutes," Robert reported.

Robert never wore pomander nor pomade: there was no smell of man about him when he came into a room. Why should that be?

I closed my eyes. "And—?" I did not want to hear.

"They found no more than is already known. But my lord of Essex has no explanation for his actions, still less excuse. And for even the least of his offenses the penalty is death. Instant imprisonment, then, and a speedy trial may hardly be avoided."

I drew a breath. "Nothing more known?"

Robert paused, then placed a careful emphasis. "Nothing more discovered, madam, and nothing confessed. But his parley with the Irish rebel remains unaccounted for."

I laughed a dry laugh. "Yet not so great a mystery any longer, Sir Robert! If my lord did not plan to put me off my throne to seize it for himself, if he is not in league with our enemies outside the kingdom, then who is left?"

Robert pretended to consider. "It is true, lady, that his mind may be turning to another who may in years to come inherit your throne. But by your late father's will, to meddle with the succession is of itself treason."

Treason to contemplate who would succeed me?

Treason to give thought to the last of the Tudors, the King better known as Stuart, the young James?

They must all be thinking of him, parleying with him, in secret correspondence with him, I knew it! And with a queen approaching her Biblical threescore years and ten, I would have scant respect for a man who was not looking ahead, weighing the options, yes, and smoothing the way!

I met Robert's eye. It was as clear as a millpond, just as his father's used to be when most he pulled the wool over my eyes. "Well, Master Secretary," I said to him straight-faced, "any man engaged in such traitorous correspondence I hope would have the sense and skill to keep it to himself."

I stared at him hard, and he met my eye. "Absolutely, madam," he agreed. "For if he did not, he would not be fit to help a cat govern, let alone to live—still less to live and serve Gloriana, a monarch like yourself."

I nodded. "Quite so."

Robert hesitated. "What, then, of my lord?"

What indeed?

Imprisoned he must be—yet live he would, if I could help it! Through storms and scenes with Howard and Raleigh, even with letters against him from Francis Bacon, his sworn creature until, like Icarus, my lord flew too near the sun and the wisest of his followers found a new planet for their orbit, I would not take his life.

"Majesty, give me one reason why the great felon deserves not to die!" Raleigh implored.

And I could not—save only a lingering certainty that what he had done was not treason, he had not plotted against my throne. Wanton and childlike he was, yes, and infinitely hurtful—but not dangerous, except to my pride! He had offended my person, but there had been no threat to the State. I was sure, too, that the madness of his acts proved he was not himself. And now despite his guard of sergeants and men-at-arms, the sickness he had been nursing ever since he arrived in Ireland stole up on him and proved me right. Confined to York House on the river, he fell at once into a malady so severe the wonder was he had made England alive.

The Devil's Arsehole, they call Ireland—even the dysentery there is worse than anywhere else. *Now God save him from what had killed his father!* He lay between life and death, unconscious of the world, as the process of his punishment ground on. It seemed superfluous to issue a royal order confirming his indefinite arrest, debarring him from any public office and banning him to come to Court or within twenty miles of my presence, for he had not the strength of a day-old runt of the litter, and like that ill-fated thing could not even open his eyes.

Should he have died then?

God did not think so.

Yet something died. There was a death, without doubt. For when I kissed him, I kissed him good-bye, and the lord that I had loved was dead to me now.

Yet not quite to himself. As the year ran down to Christ's nativity and the New Year turned its wheel; as the world over, all men held their breath and prayed for the new epoch; as a new century was born with the year 1600 of our Gracious Lord, my lord, like Lazarus, was drawn back from death to life. Yet what is life without love, employment, company? Still more, without money, for now that my largesse and his cash had run out, all his creditors gathered like vultures round a dropping beast. Pent up in York House, he rotted in disuse while the world wagged on without him. I longed to release him—who but a brute would keep such a bird in a cage? And God had redeemed even the Prodigal Son . . . Yet already I was censured for my dangerous mildness, and not a lord of mine who would not now have rejoiced to see him coffined, and followed his hearse barefoot a dancing mile.

Even so, I tried! For like a doting mother, I still cherished fond hopes that her ne'er-do-well offspring would reform at last.

It was a mission fit to test out one of my younger lords, one who had never been his enemy and who might now stand his friend. "Convey this to my lord, in gentle terms. Tell him if he will but express his penitence, show true remorse, if he will undertake to serve me from now on in whatsoever I command—"

"Majesty, it shall be!"

Young William Knollys, pink-faced with his exertions, was back from York House before I knew he was gone. I gave him my hand to kiss. "Well, what did he say—?"

He paused, then turned his colour and took a pace or two of stiff embarrassment. "Surely I dare swear my lord is not himself—neither in mind nor in body! For when I came—"

"What says he?"

Knollys dropped to one knee. "Forgive me, madam!" he implored. "Do not hold me guilty of the violence of his language!"

"Say on!"

He muttered so low I could hardly hear the words. "Your Majesty, my lord of Essex said, 'By Christ, her conditions are as crooked as her carcass.' "

I smiled. *Almost as crooked, my sweet lord, as your poor wandering soul.* I looked at Knollys, mortifying before my eyes, and chuckled my reassurance. "Well, sir, let us see if the crooked old tortoise can see off the young hare! I thank you for your service."

Alas for my poor lord! Now with his lost discretion, the light of reason and clear judgement also burned down in his mind.

"Broken nights, Majesty, he suffers, and great screaming dreams," I heard from his keeper. "He fears for his life, and curses Sir Robert Cecil as the author of all his ills."

Oh, God, how could he? How could my lord, born nature's darling and a king among men, favoured in height, in face, in form, now so lose himself as to be jealous of a hunchback, a poor pygmy thrust into the world scarce half made up, a man whose very shadow the dogs barked at as he passed!

For his health of mind, then, as much as of his body, I ordered his release to his own house on the Strand.

"Still under supervision!" I warned Buckhurst. "By my Lords of the Privy Council. But he may now send and receive letters, admit visitors and begin his life again—so long as he gives offence to no man."

Nor no woman, I beg of you, my lord.

Would he accept this chance, this message, this reprieve? The next day, as I expected, his first letter was for me. I took it like a schoolgirl deep inside the bosom of my dress, down through the springtime water meadows below Richmond park, and as my people wandered at a distance, I opened the parchment with a trembling hand.

Most sweet Queen,
Your Majesty knows, who knows everything, that the lease on my monopoly for the sale of sweet wines in England runs out this day next se'nnight. Without it I may not support my life, content my creditors or hold my head up like the meanest man. If I may therefore conjure your beneficence to grant it me again . . .

The smell of the river was rank in my nostrils, and the greedy waterbirds, feeding and fighting, were harsh in my ears. *Oh, my lord, my pelican lord!* I hoped for love, humility and sweetness, and got a begging letter! Yet hardly even that, not so much begging, more a shouting, bullying letter with its loud demand: *Renew my income, take care of my debts, or I perish!*

I paced along the riverbank in bleak despair. *Oh, you are sick of self-love, dearest lord, and taste with a distempered appetite.* My mind was whirling, fears and desires for him besetting me, biting like a cloud of midges. Was there no hope?

Yet what is love but one long act of hope? And ruined love, when it is built anew, grows fairer than at first, more strong, far sweeter. *Out of the strong cometh forth sweetness,* God Himself taught us in the story of Samson. I pressed my hands together and brought them with his foolish letter to my lips.

I would not throw my Samson to the lions. I would do as I had done all my life, wait, wait on, and hope.

And all that year all the world waited for him, for me, for what we could not say. Behind every man about me, every act, stalked the great shadow of my unseen lord, and I could not forget him.

And a month later, as February opened with another Candlemas, another Festival of Light, another Feast of the Blessed Virgin and thus a day I never could ignore, I shined my light on him and ordered him set at full liberty to be himself again.

Yet to this day I do not believe he ever regained his true health and strength, his true self. And urging him on, nursing and feeding their own old grudge against me, were the two she-wolves his mother Lettice and his sister Penelope.

Lettice was always jealous of me from the time she was a girl. She had taken Robin from me, and paid for it with twenty years of disgrace. Now she was wife to Kit Blount, one of my lord's boon friends and followers, who had come with him from Ireland and shared in his fall. Her daughter the pert Penelope, meeting Blount in her mother's house, had found through him an illicit fondness for his kinsman, another Blount, Baron Mountjoy, and she was now his mistress. And Mountjoy himself was even now in Ireland as my commander in my lord's place, holding the key to England's ever-weak back door . . .

And this little knot, this nest of vipers—along with the foul Southampton and a rabble of Irish captains, among them the brute Lee, who had sent me the head of the dead rebel—met every day in Essex House, to feed his vanity and fan his madness.

Madness, yes. I use the word with care. Whom the gods wish to destroy, they first make mad. And only a madman would throw down his life like a gauntlet at the feet of a woman—above all, the woman who had fought for so long to save that precious life.

How would he use his freedom? How would he show me what he planned, what he thought?

I still hoped, as I held my breath and waited.

When it came, though, it came widdershins, black and deadly, sideways out of the sun. *But it was aimed straight at my throne.*

Someone paid the players, the Lord Chamberlain's Men, to stage the play of *Richard II,* showing the usurpation of the King. I screamed for Hunsdon my Lord Chamberlain, and pacing, raging, weeping, tearing my fan, I pitched into him. "These traitorous players of yours! And their hack Shakespeare—he took my shilling, I paid him from my own purse! But they are worse than whores, these scribblers, never a one born who will not sell his soul for money!"

Poor honest Hunsdon turned pale at my rage. "Majesty, throughout London the playhouses put on twenty plays a week, many of them histories of our country! I dare swear," he ventured tremulously, "that there is no danger in the play, no threat to your State, no offence in the world!"

My nerves were breaking. "God's lids, cousin, open your blind eyes!" I groaned in despair. *"I am Richard II, know you not that?"*

When would it come, the attempt on my throne?

For come it must now, the dogs in the street knew that.

Raleigh it was, my old sea dog and land-rover both, who could take soil of an enemy at any mile, who flushed him out. And he it was who fell upon me on that bitter peaking Sunday after Candlemas as I left the Chapel Royal with the word: "Majesty, arm yourself! For my lord of Essex is up in arms against you!"

LXXIV

I would have lain down both our lives to spare what was to follow. But it was written, by the left hand of God. And we His children had to bow to His scourging and then, weeping, kiss His rod.

"In the hour before dawn, I had warning, lady." Raleigh's words came tumbling forth. "An old soldier of mine, one of my captains when I fought in Ireland, came to tell me to keep clear of both the Court and City today, for he swore that all those here were likely to have a bloody day of it!"

Dies irae, dies sanguinis . . . Day of anger, day of blood—here at last? Oh, my lord, my lord!

We stood in the frozen churchyard, my lords quietly closing round me to a man.

Robert leaned forward urgently. "And could you get no more from him than this?"

"Where the attack will come?" demanded Howard.

"God's blood, I tried!" Raleigh exploded. "Though he came as a friend, I had my poiniard to his throat and through into his windpipe, and I swear he knew no more! But it is no secret where the rats who fled from Ireland have been gathering here in London!"

No—nor who would give a welcome to a useful swordsman, however big a blackguard—

"So at first light I took to the water and had the sculler row me down-river towards my lord of Essex's house," Raleigh hurried on, "where I heard a lookout shout the alarm, and the next second, gunshot was flying round our ears."

Armed insurrection, then—was he determined now to raise a treason even I could not pardon?

I looked into Raleigh's pale and vital face, and could have kissed his cornflower eyes. "Now God be thanked for your dear life, my Walter," I said fervently, "for His hand has preserved you!"

"Say, rather, the brawny hands of my good sculler!" said Raleigh grimly. "For at the first ball he backed water like a good 'un, and we shot off as fast as if we rode the the Devil's tail. But they are under arms there, lady, make no mistake! They offer war upon your peace, and a rising must follow!"

"Who are the ringleaders? Who now holds Essex House?"

Robert was as ever ready with the answer. "All those Your Majesty well knows: those we have had all this time under surveillance: my lord himself, his followers my lord of Southampton and Sir Christopher Blount, with a rabble of Irishmen, sergeants, captains and other lesser fry."

Oh, my lord, my lord, not one of them is worthy to unloose the latchet of your shoe! And will you put to sea in such a leaky sieve?

I wept then as Robert and Raleigh spoke: not, as they thought, from fear at your flight into revolt, but in grief at your descent, your fatal fall into such degradation, such sad foolishness.

It was all around me now, the smell of fear. And as we stood like children in a ring waiting for one to cry "Pax" to release us, there came a running, howling messenger, his face red with furious fire and the word we did not want to hear. "A plot against the Queen! They plot to take her throne, and afterwards her life!"

I had warned him, I had told him to his face—anything against myself I could pardon, but never an assault upon my throne. My throne? Our throne, this royal throne of kings, this Tudor heritage I had had from my sister, she from our brother, he from our father and he from his to the foundation of our line—how could I forgive an attack on that?

To get it nearly cost me my dear life. To hold it for England these last forty years has cost me my love, my hope of children, my health, my peace of mind, my life's liquor from my very veins.

"Have," "keep" and "hold" are three fine words. He should have known.

No mercy, then, for an Icarus whose mad folly led him to take on the sun. But even now, if he could do no more, if he could do nothing for himself and still less for me, he could still serve England. He could show our friends abroad and enemies at home that Englishmen still clung to the Tudors as they did that day at Bosworth when our line began. Let him raise his rebellion! Then the world would see that England knew only one sovereign, Gloriana, Elizabeth the Queen!

"Sir Robert?"

"Majesty?"

"We must do nothing rash—we must seek peace even at the point of the sword. Let us send a delegation of my Privy Councillors to wait upon my lord and his followers, asking him gently to come before the Council to account for himself."

"Madam, it is done."

I knew my lord's nature. And if my summons worked on that soft yet fiery clay as I was gambling that it would . . .

Well, we should see.

Did Robert guess my plan, sniff it out, feel it in his bones, as he did with so many of my schemes? For he implemented it sooner than thought itself. But his was not the hand that tipped the scales, no, nor mine neither. What was to be was written by a greater force than ours.

For now events took their predestined path, the course set in the heavens from time before time, before our earth took form and substance out of the liquid void, ordained for us even at the moment when the hand of God, shaping the race of men, gave us our dwelling place, fashioned the planets and lit up the stars.

My lords arrived to find Essex House seething with desperate riffraff, and a madness in the air as when the plague seizes a town and all cry "Sauve qui peut!" Standing in the courtyard with a Herald Royal, my Lord Keeper, the

*Lord Egerton, clapped his hat on his head and called upon my lord in a
great voice to disband his followers, lay down his arms and come at once to
Court, where he would be honourably treated. For which courtesy all four of
my Privy Councillors inside five minutes now found themselves the prisoners
of my lord, under lock and key in Essex House.*

So.

It began to work . . .

Now as we paced the entrance hall of Whitehall, another messenger
came panting from the road: "My lord has called a rising, and all London
follows him, all the City will take arms against the Queen!"

I laughed a little at the white faces circling mine. "Courage, my lords!
He may rise—they will not follow him! Not against me!"

And hanging in the air I could hear every man's sombre prayer: *Pray
God she may be right!*

*But like Cassandra, cursed with foresight by the god whom she had
spurned, I took no joy from my foreknowledge. For if I were right, my lord
would be plunged forever in a pit of wrong so deep that God Almighty could
not pluck him out.*

Now every minute brought a messenger.

"My lord has taken to the streets, with all his rabble army on his
heels!"

I had to know. "How does he look?"

"Wildly, madam, like a man in flight from Bedlam."

*Which now I think he was, for a heaving, sweating frenzy had seized his
soul. In years to come they will speak of my lord's "rebellion," his "uprising." In truth, it was more like a parade of zanies or lunatic beggars as he
ran madly through the City with his motley crew on his heels, crying, "For
the Queen! For the Queen! Rally to me, good people! They plan to take my
life! For God's love, rally—speak, hands, for me!"*

*Madness, madness: he was seized by seven devils, he was consumed by his
own evil spirits.*

"And in truth, the evil spirits of his world here on earth now do their
best to aid him!" Buckhurst observed grimly as the news poured in: Sir
Kit Blount urging his men to kill every soul in their way, and the fell
Penelope taking her coach to ride up and down London enlisting all she
met to stand up for her brother. "Yet here is a lord who no sooner had
she forced him into her coach than he hopped out through the door on
the other side. He has hastened here to offer you his loyalty—please it
Your Majesty to see him?"

"Later, later—there will come a time—"

Penelope. Doubtless she thought to queen it at my lord's side in his new

Queen-less kingdom. But now she was, like him, pissing her venom into the wind.

"News, madam, of my lord of Essex's force: less than ten score all told."

"They were making for St. Paul's, to raise the people after matins—"

"But they came too late to catch the congregation: not a man was there, they had all gone to their homes—"

"And in every lane and every street where he thought to find welcome, they all turn their backs—"

Oh, God, I could see the scene as if I had been there! Now he who always had found open hearts, open hands, open house, ran like a soul in hell to the Devil's drumbeat of slamming doors and clanging shutters, having to see the women who before threw kisses and rosebuds in his way now bundling children out of his sight as if he had horns and cloven hooves.

He came at last to the house of the Sheriff of London, demanding a force of the City militiamen and a clean shirt, for he ran with sweat although the day was bitter, biting, February cold.

"By all means, my lord," returned the officer with all civility, then ducked out of his back door to raise the watch and give the alarm.

They waited there an hour or more and then, giving up hope, fell back to Essex House.

And there I lost him: lost the sense of his sufferings, lost the man I loved.

When did my lord know that he had failed? That he had lost the game, and with it life and all? That he had thrown away the world and his place in it with this one desperate act?

Or did he know already that he had no future now without my love and favour, without my money, my continuance? When he lost me after the dash back from Ireland, when he invaded my Privy Chamber, raped my woman's privacy and pride, had he known then that he was a doomed man?

For doomed he was. Now like great Hector at the walls of Troy, his god abandoned him, he was alone. Back at Essex House, he shut himself up within his chamber, and what he suffered there no man could tell.

"My lord! My lord!" The hammering on the door, the urgent cries, never abated all the afternoon. "A boat stands at the water gate, the tide is on the turn, fly hence, fly now, you may take ship for France!"

But all their answer was a world-without-end silence.

The day wore on, London slumbering in its Sabbath peace and not a mouse stirring. Late in the afternoon the Mayor and all the aldermen, as bright as cherries in their chains and robes, waited upon me with the City's compliments. "In faith, Your Majesty, the troops we have deployed to ring the City complain of freezing in their idleness, they have nothing to do!"

And as the first candles woke to blooming life, as the light died on his last day of freedom, my lord released his hostages, broke his sword and tendered up his body to its fate.

They came to trial in Westminster Hall, he and Southampton, before twenty-five of their peers. Besides the rebellion, the armed rising to put me off my throne, he was found to be in treasonous correspondence with Spain, with Scotland, with any who would listen to his wild offers to place them on my throne, so long as they made him their Lord General. Young James of Scotland, I was grimly pleased to see, had been far too clever to agree to anything. Yet he had kept my lord on a string, as a politic ruler ought to do . . .

Now the trials began. Blount was tried the next day, pleaded guilty and lost his head the day after—as did the ruffian Lee, arrested making his way through Whitehall to my Privy Chamber in some wild scheme to save my lord by holding me to ransom. He went nimbly to the noose, denied the axe as a lowborn common man, and in truth he owed God more than the normal tally of deaths. And I like to think that the old witch he burned and the rebel chief he quartered and all the others who had cause to curse the hour of his nativity were waiting for him in the other place when he descended to begin an eternity of pleasant intercourse.

Yet still he fought, my lord, like the wild horse he was. Even at his trial, with his own guilt stacked against him, he tried to turn the tables on his accusers. "Hear me, my lords," he cried out, his voice ringing though Westminster's vaulted space, "if you value the Queen's life! For there is near the Queen a far fouler traitor than any can accuse me of being!"

"He says *what?*" I cried to Robert when he brought me the word. "That the lord I most trust, fondly trust, is guilty of high treason?"

Robert bowed his head. He was very pale. "And that he is in league with the Queen's enemies, that he corresponds with the King of Scots, the King of Spain."

I did not know whether to laugh or cry. "And this traitor is close to me, so my lord says?"

Robert drew up his puny inches with a strange dignity denied to bigger men. "As close as heart can think." His eyes were bright with tears, he was trembling violently. "Madam, he accuses me."

Oh, my poor Pygmy. Even now Robert could not escape my lord's deep-rooted malice.

"I do not credit it, not for an instant!" I cried with passion. "Nor will anyone else! Never think you need to defend yourself against this cruel slander!"

But he was stung to the quick. "Madam, I must!"

All night he laboured to compose his defence, and the next day at the trial he begged leave of the judges to clear himself of all that had been said against him. God! If I could have been there to hear him! For of all the lords and kings and great ones who have come to that ancient hall of Westminster, to that thousand-year-old seat of justice, to face their trial, Robert that day made one of the noblest speeches of all who ever fought for life or truth.

"My lord," he braved him out, "you charge me with high things, and I defy you to the uttermost. For wit, I give you pre-eminence: you have it abundantly. For nobility, I must also give you place: I am not noble, though I am proud to be a gentleman. I am no swordsman: Your Lordship has been favoured with such gifts, there again you have the odds.

"But I have innocence, conscience, truth and loyalty to defend me against the scandal and sting of slanderous tongues. I stand for loyalty, which I never lost. You stand for treason, which possesses your heart. I do confess that I have considered the future of our realm. I have said that the King of Scots has a claim to this throne, and the King of Spain did when the Queen of Scots made him her heir, and I deny this is treason—it is no less than truth. You, too, my lord, were a competitor with them, you wished to rule, you would depose the Queen!

"Ah, my good lord, if this were only your own tragedy! But you have drawn noble persons and gentlemen into your act of rebellion, and their very blood will cry vengeance upon you!"

Robert was applauded to the rafters, he was free and clear. Throughout all England the joy, the relief, echoed and re-echoed as the whole country gave thanks for my deliverance. Once more I was Gloriana, now I was again Elizabeth the Queen. For my lord, there was only one verdict, only one hollow cry of the black-clad judges through the sergeant-at-arms. I had told him that I could forgive any crime against me as a woman—*and as God is my witness, the man that I once loved, I loved still.*

But he had had my warning, and he had spurned it. The man who never would make love to me had in the end made love to his own death. His trial was fair, his judges honorable, the verdict inescapable.

Soon they brought me the warrant for his death.

And last night I signed it.

Here Ends
the Fifth Book
−LIBER QUINTUS−
of My History

EPILOGUE

More light there, for the last time, to keep all these ghosts at bay! And build up the fire, for the frost saves his fiercest nips for this graveyard hour, the hour before the dawn. A little wine now to sweeten my mouth, a little aqua vitae for my teeth, and let me light the last candle of my five-branched tale.

A bastard he called me.

Oh, how God loves to make circles as well as jests, how He loves to bring His mortal creation round and round! Now with the selfsame slur with which my life was born, so it draws to its end.

Was I a bastard?

My father toiled his guts out to prevent it! Had Clement the Pope proved clement to Henry the King when he needed a new wife, no question-mark would have touched me.

Why should I bother now to hide the truth? My mind is turning to that last account when the secrets of all hearts shall be laid bare. And why should I hesitate to share with you what I now see as God's last, best, royal joke?

When my father married my mother, he already had a wife. If he had even set aside Katherine formally, divorced her before *he wed my mother, I could have eased my conscience. But he was not the Sophy—and our God permits only one wife at a time.*

Yet he thought like a sophy. He believed he could shape his world to his thinking by act of will. And who can call him wrong? All his children succeeded him just as he willed it. And it was only right, by God's law and the order of their birth, that Henry's two legitimate descendants, Edward and Mary, should precede a younger child bearing the bar sinister—or at least the bar not quite true.

Yet if he had the power to work his will, why did he not will me legitimate? Oh, what use is it to bewail him now? Possession is ten-tenths of the law when it comes to power. Bastard or no, I have had it, held it, I have ruled, I will hand on.

And if I am a bastard, then all who knew my father will know where that comes from!

God, did I ever love him? For sure I hated him! Did I choose every man I ever loved as a shadow of him? Did I put down my last lord to exorcise forever the fear, the power of those big, rough, red-haired men reeking of manhood, action, sensuality, as they roistered through my life?

I do not think so . . .

No, his death serves a better, darker purpose. Though he broke my heart as a woman, he will do me tomorrow the last and greatest service to Elizabeth the Queen. The woman may have lost her love, her hope, her future. But the Queen in me has triumphed at last over the enemy within.

Who saw or knew of my deeper plan in this? They all saw a foolish old woman besotted with a beautiful youth who was all England's darling, and never thought to question further. I think Robert guessed—he was the only one about me now deep-versed enough in policy to see a hidden, purposeful design and trace it back to its source, to those deep wells that lie beneath the surface of our thought.

By permitting my lord to flourish in all pugnacity, all audacity, ever ready to challenge others and to put them down, I had controlled all my other warring and ambitious lords, confined them within the bounds I had laid down.

And by permitting—*no, I will not accept "encouraging"!*—his rebellion, I had killed it, and the spirit of rebellion with it. Through him I had shown City and Court, London and all the land, Europe and all the world, that my people never, ever, would rise against me! We had fought off wave after wave of those who believed that with the right leader, the right pretender, all the love my country had for me would be swept away, would be turned against me. But when they would not rise up even for England's darling, their great warrior-hero who had taken Cadiz and pissed in the eye of the mighty King of Spain, then my throne was safe indeed.

Now all around the world we could blow our English trumpet in every ear, show that my government was secure and chosen of my people, that I had won the last peace just as surely as I won every war. I had defeated the Pope and France—France, which all his reign had defeated even Great Harry!—I had seen Spain off with a bloody nose and a bloodier bum, and they would never go to war with us again.

I laughed. *Who knows? Before the world is out, this land of ours might well see another Spanish marriage—when the cry "The Spaniards are coming!" will be one not of terror but of joy?*

And now I could hand on my kingdom in a smooth and peaceable state to my successor.

My successor? You ask me who?

You know already! Ask yourself, with my views on due and right procedures, would I prefer to hand on to a junior or a senior line? Would I prefer an offspring of one of the silly women who came down through my father's younger sister, all those vain Grey girls, to a sober son of study and learning like myself, royal on both sides? Talk to me not of the sons of Catherine Grey! I will have no rascal's son come in my seat, the royal throne of England!

Oh, come now, stir your brains!

Who should it be but our cousin of Scotland?

James VI of that country will be the first of ours—descended from my father's oldest sister, whom Henry debarred, and happily skipping over his fool mother, the fat Catholic fraud Mary of Scots.

There are many consolations to a long life—above all, the joy of outliving others.

And above all, her!

Now the little Scots King will come into a kingdom in good order, and if I know my Master Secretary Robert, will have an easeful step up to this throne of English kings. But I am not minded to hand it over and slip off just yet! Now in this year of 1601, it is exactly one hundred years since the little Princess Katherine of Aragon, pretty, pink and pious, touched these shores as the wife-to-be of young Prince Arthur.

King Arthur and Queen Katherine—what of them if that frail life had held?

My father came to the throne in the ninth year of the fifteen hundreds—if I hold on another few years more, England will see a century of the rule of one father and his children. But I have done much for England—I have given my all! For her I never married, even my true love Robin, for her I courted half the world and fought the other half, for her I threw my last lord to his fate—all, all for her!—never ask me for more, still more, ever more!

And now, look there, beyond the casement, the sky lightens, and the night is done. This day is Ash Wednesday—day of ashes, day of his death, day to begin a mourning life for me.

Beside my bed drowse now two little maids, hardly more than children to my eyes—when I can see them with this fading sight! They snuffle lightly in their slumbers, curled up on the pallet with the chamber dogs in the light of the fire. Now I want company, now I feel myself alone.

EPILOGUE 549

Now is the very witching time of night. How is my lord as he awaits his hour? Does he pray, does he weep as I do, does he think of me?

"Majesty, ho, within!"

Christ, the knock frightened me! "Who's there?"

It was Warwick, bleary-eyed and, from her hasty toilet, newly awakened. "A strange message, madam, and a stranger messenger, come from the Tower. A boy—"

From the Tower.

"Let him come in."

Dwarfed by the burly guard, he was hardly a boy, more of a starveling, a changeling with odd eyes and cropped hair standing on end with cold. He seemed to bring the chill and damp of the Tower into the chamber with him, the stink of misery, the silent screams of pain. I shuddered as I spoke. "What are you, child?"

"Son to the Tower-Keeper, ma'am."

I closed my eyes under a flood of memories. *When I was in the Bell Tower and Robin in the Beauchamp—when he bribed the Tower boy then to bring me flowers with his message, and a robin's egg—*

I wept now from pure weakness. Warwick rushed smartly in. "Speak to the Queen, then, boy. Say what's your errand."

"From the lost lord who languishes in the Tower and must lose his head in the morning—he sends Her Ma'esty this."

He brought up a grubby fist and opened it. At my side Warwick gave a sharp gasp of recognition. Black and gleaming upon the boy's palm lay a silent circle of gold and enamel, a man's ring.

If ever you need me, dear my lord, I had told him when I gave it, *send me this ring, and it shall command you whatever you most wish in all the world.*

Oh, Jesus, Jesus . . .

Bitterness flooded me. He must know I could not reprieve him! How could he so cheapen his last hours with this weak, vain, grovelling appeal for mercy!

Yet my lord of Seymour died so, feebly and bitterly, spending his last night wretchedly scribbling letters of poison to me and sister Mary, stirring up hate against his brother—his brother the Lord Protector, himself doomed to kiss the selfsame block.

A great soul-weariness swept through me. *Tell my lord—*

Tell him what?

Oh, will these tears never cease?

"Come, boy, you tire the Queen." Taking the ring from his palm, Warwick stepped forward to hustle the child from the chamber. But he refused to budge.

"And the message!" he cried in alarm. "I am to give the ring *and* the message! My lord swore on his dying soul he'd come back and haunt me if I did not give the message."

"The message?" I did not recognize my own voice.

"I learned it! By heart he made me learn it! My lord says, lady"—the child's body froze in an attitude of concentration—"he says he yields this back to you along with his life, as freely as ever a man gave anything to the lady that he loved. His prays his love and his devotion will outlast his life, and that his death will purge his dishonour and disgrace. He trusts through God's mercy, not by his deserts, to see you in heaven. And until you join him, he hopes to shine down on Your Majesty all your livelong life and to be with you at the hour of your death—it is but passing through a gate, he says, where he who loves you gladly treads before."

Oh, my lord, my lord.

My love, my sweetest love.

The child's eyes glowed like lanterns. I paused. "Tell my lord—that the Queen accepts his ring."

His ring. It is on my hand now next to the one he gave to me. The Coronation ring they will have to cut off my finger, I know—it is too embedded now for me to draw off. But these two I will take with me to the grave.

What now?

The future now lies spinning away before me, stretching ahead in this quivering, silent world. Warwick has gone with the boy to give him his reward, and the maids are slowly stirring.

Both my lord and I now await the dawn.

In a little while he will leave his cell for that last walk on earth, and I shall walk with him each step of the way. I will be with him every second till he takes his last pace upon the scaffold, with him when he lays his head upon the block and throws his arms out in the final gesture to embrace his death. And I know as surely as if I sat inside his skull that his last thought, his last prayer, his last hope, will be of me, Elizabeth, Elizabeth his Queen.

And I shall wait then till God pleases for my call to follow after. And I shall see him there, not mortal now and tainted with his faults but as he was, and as he ought to be. There, where souls couch on flowers, we shall be granted an eternity of love and joy. With Dido and her Aeneas, Cleopatra and Antony, we shall not want for the best company.

Already I am half in love with death. And I am not afraid. I have no fear of going where my Kat and Robin, Burghley and Cranmer and Grindal, Parry and her brother, and all my lords of love have gone before. And there at last I shall look upon my mother, know the one who gave me life, at last feel a mother's kiss and the wonder of that all-embracing love.

They are all gone into the world of light, all calling me to follow. Now in my waking dreams I see them walking in an air of glory, and my soul strains to join them.

How will it be, I wonder?

What Scots Mary saw as she approached the block she did not tell. Sister Mary as she lay dying told her women, weeping with joy, that she saw little children all in white and gold playing and singing all about her—all the phantom babes the poor woman never had. But I hope and trust the angel choir of heavenly infants keep their distance from ancient virgins—my choice would be a quieter quietus, far removed from the young of the species, who in truth have never interested me.

And what now?

Life is for living. Lent is for mourning, and then spring, then Easter comes. For every thing, God teaches us, there is a season, a time to kill and a time to heal, a time to love and a time to hate, a time to weep and a time to laugh, a time to mourn and a time to dance.

I shall weep, yes, and then I shall dance. To my last day, as I think, I shall dance the dance of life itself, of eros and thanatos, of love and death. So, without dis-love or disloyalty to all my lords, to my love Robin, to my late last lord, I shall look for new partners. And as dancing goes, there is a fair youth newly come to Court fresh from the shires, the dew on his cheek, the fire in his eye, tall, with a horseman's body and fine legs and that hint of red in his hair, in his beard . . .

Yes, I shall try his skill. As God's my witness, I pray I shall never be too old to enjoy making a little winter love in a dark corner. I can still relish flirting, and I shall always need to be adored.

And in a few weeks now, as the daffodils gambol in yellow across our greening meadows, as the black-ash buds burst into their frail, five-fingered leaves and the beech puts on her misty robe of sweet viridian, I shall ride the face of England once again. I shall make summer progress as I always have through our pleasant pastures and our fertile meads, our well-stocked byres and little chubby farms. Before me shall unfold our noble woodlands and high upland plains, our rolling hills and fallows, our chalky downs, our mountain chains, the backbone of our land. Broad rivers and chuckling streams will play forth for me, smiling lakes and brooding forests wait for me, all the fierce, primeval strongholds of this land from the days when the things that dwell now deep inside the earth once were its kings.

England, my England—how I love this land! Her rivers pour their courses through my veins, her loam makes up my flesh, her soul my soul, her proud spirit my hope, my inspiration. And I have loved as I have lived, a woman of England to my heart's core, yes, to my heart of hearts! And when I die, what

bed, what last resting place so soft as the folds of this beloved land? What
mother's arms so gentle as the arms of Mother Country? I shall sleep sweetly
in this precious soil, borne round in her diurnal course, become part of this
precious sceptred isle—this blessed plot, this earth, this realm, this England
—my first, last, greatest love.

And I am now and forever the soul of England—I, Elizabeth, I, England,
Elizabeth the Queen!

FINIS

THE PERSONS OF MY HISTORY

ALFRED THE GREAT, King of Wessex 871–99

ALVA, Ferdinando Alvarez de Toledo, Duke of, commander of the Spanish forces in the Netherlands in the years before the Armada

ANJOU, Francis, Duke of, suitor to Elizabeth I, son of Catherine de' Medici

ANNE OF CLEVES, German princess, discarded fourth wife of Henry VIII; later decreed "the King's Sister"

ANTONIO, Don, pretender to the throne of Portugal

ARTHUR, Prince of Wales, son of Henry VII and older brother of Henry VIII; died aged fifteen

ARUNDEL, Henry Fitzallan, Earl of, suitor to Elizabeth I

ASCHAM, Roger, tutor to Elizabeth I as Princess and Queen

ASHLEY, John, husband of Kat, distant cousin of Anne Boleyn

ASHLEY, Katherine (Kat), governor to Princess Elizabeth in childhood, Mistress of the Robes and chief lady-in-waiting to Elizabeth as Queen

ASKEWE, Anne, Protestant martyr burned under Henry VIII

BABINGTON, Sir Anthony, Catholic conspirator against Elizabeth I

BACON, Anthony, son of Sir Nicholas Bacon, courtier and intelligencer, supporter of the Earl of Essex

BACON, Francis, son of Sir Nicholas Bacon, and younger brother of Anthony, courtier and scholar, supporter of the Earl of Essex

BACON, Sir Nicholas, Lord Keeper of the Great Seal, brother-in-law of William Cecil

BARNWELL, Robert, Irish Catholic conspirator; executed under Elizabeth I

BEAUFORT, Margaret, Lady, mother of Henry VII

BEDFORD, Francis Russell, Earl of, soldier and Privy Councillor to Elizabeth I

BEDINGFIELD, Sir Henry, custodian of Princess Elizabeth at Woodstock

BIRLEY, Hugh, traducer of Elizabeth I

BLOUNT, Bessie, mistress of Henry VIII and mother of the King's bastard, Henry Fitzroy

BLOUNT, Sir Christopher, friend and co-conspirator of the Earl of Essex and husband of his mother, Lettice

BOLEYN, Anne, second wife of Henry VIII and mother of Princess Elizabeth; beheaded on trumped-up charges of adultery

BOLEYN, Mary, sister of Anne Boleyn and mistress of Henry VIII, wife of William Carey, Gentleman of the Privy Chamber to Henry VIII

BONNER, Edmund, Bishop of London under Mary I

BOTHWELL, James Hepburn, Earl of, leader of the Scots lairds and third husband of Mary Queen of Scots

BREUNER, Baron Caspar von, Ambassador to the Hapsburg emperor Ferdinand I, uncle of Philip II

BROWNE, Lady, lady-in-waiting at the court of Edward VI and Mary I

BRYAN, Lady Margaret, royal governor to Mary I, Edward VI and Elizabeth I

BRYAN, Sir Thomas, courtier and husband of Lady Margaret

BUCKHURST, Thomas Sackville, Lord, diplomat and Privy Councillor

BURGHLEY. *See* Cecil, Sir William

CAMPION, Thomas, Jesuit priest and poet; executed under Elizabeth I

CAREY, Henry, Baron Hunsdon, son of Mary Boleyn, first cousin of Elizabeth I, Privy Councillor and Lord Chamberlain

CAREY, Katherine, daughter of Mary Boleyn and sister of Henry Carey and cousin of Elizabeth I, wife of Francis Knollys

CAREY, Katherine, daughter of Henry Carey, lady-in-waiting to Elizabeth I

CAREY, Philadelphia, sister of the young Katherine, daughter of Henry Carey, lady-in-waiting to Elizabeth I

CAREY, William, husband of Mary Boleyn

CARLOS, Don, Infante of Spain, son of Philip II

CATHERINE DE' MEDICI, Queen of France and mother-in-law of Mary Queen of Scots

CECIL, Robert, son of William Cecil, later first Earl of Salisbury, successor to his father as Elizabeth's chief councillor

CECIL, Sir William (later Lord Burghley), Secretary of State and Lord Treasurer, first minister of Elizabeth I

CHAPUYS, Eustace, Ambassador of the Holy Roman Empire

CHARLES OF AUSTRIA, Hapsburg Archduke, son of Ferdinand and brother of Maximilian, suitor to Elizabeth I

CHARLES V, King of Spain and Holy Roman Emperor, father of Philip II of Spain, nephew and defender of Katherine of Aragon

CHARLES IX, King of France, suitor to Elizabeth I, son of Catherine de' Medici

CHEKE, Sir John, Greek scholar and royal tutor

CHERTSEY, Sir John, gentleman-in-waiting to Princess Elizabeth

CLARENCIEUX, Lady Susan, Mistress of the Robes to Mary I

CLEMENT VII, Pope of Rome in the time of Henry VIII

CLINTON, Lady, lady-in-waiting, wife of Lord Clinton

CLINTON, Edward Fiennes de, Lord, Privy Councillor and First Lord of the Admiralty

COBHAM, Henry Brodie, Lord Warden of the Cinque Ports under Elizabeth I

COLIGNY, Admiral Gaspard de, leader of the Huguenots in the French civil war

CONDÉ, Prince of, Huguenot commander during the civil war in France

COOKE, Sir Anthony, Greek scholar and royal tutor

COOKE, Mildred, daughter of Sir Anthony, one of Katherine Parr's "academy of learned virgins," wife of William Cecil and mother of Robert

COURTENAY, Edward, descendant of Edward IV and pretender to the throne, prospective husband of Mary I and Elizabeth I

CRANMER, Thomas, Archbishop of Canterbury under Henry VIII and Protestant martyr

CROFTS, Sir James, courtier and Protestant conspirator against Mary I

DACRES, Leonard, Catholic rebel against Elizabeth I

DARNLEY, Lord Henry, descendant of Princess Margaret Tudor and second husband of Mary Queen of Scots; murdered by Scots lairds under Mary Queen of Scots

DAVISON, William, Secretary of State, disgraced for his part in the execution of Mary Queen of Scots

DENNY, Sir Anthony, Gentleman of the Privy Chamber to Henry VIII, host to Princess Elizabeth under Edward VI

DERBY, Edward Stanley, Earl of, Privy Councillor to Elizabeth I

DEVEREUX, Dorothy, daughter of the first Earl of Essex, sister of Penelope and Robert, later wife of the renegade knight Sir Thomas Perrott

DEVEREUX, Penelope, daughter of the first Earl of Essex and Lettice Knollys, sister of Robert, wife of Lord Rich

DEVEREUX, Robert. *See* Essex, Robert Devereux

DEVEREUX, Walter, first Earl of Essex, husband of Lettice Knollys and father of Robert, Penelope and Dorothy

DORMER, Jane, one of Katherine Parr's "academy of learned virgins," crypto-Catholic

DOWN, Mother Anne of Brentford, traducer of Elizabeth I

DRAKE, Sir Francis, seafarer and privateer, commander of the English fleet during the Armada

DUDLEY, Ambrose, Earl of Warwick, second son of the Duke of Northumberland and brother of Robert Dudley

DUDLEY, Guildford, fourth son of the Duke of Northumberland, brother of Robert Dudley and husband of Lady Jane Grey; executed under Mary I

DUDLEY, Lord Henry, youngest son of the Duke of Northumberland and brother of Robert Dudley

DUDLEY, John, Viscount Lisle and Earl of Warwick, later Duke of Northumberland and first minister to Edward VI; executed under Mary I

DUDLEY, John, Earl of Warwick, eldest son of the Duke of Northumberland and brother of Robert Dudley

DUDLEY, Mary. *See* Sidney, Mary

DUDLEY, Robert. *See* Leicester, Robert Dudley (Robin)

DUDLEY, Sir Robert, the Earl of Leicester's illegitimate son by Lady Douglas Sheffield

DYMOKE, Sir Edward, courtier and champion of the King at the Coronation of Edward VI

EDWARD, Prince of Wales, known as the Black Prince, eldest son of Edward III (reigned 1327–77)

EDWARD THE CONFESSOR, King of England 1042–66

EDWARD II, King of England 1307–27, lover of Piers Gaveston; deposed and murdered

EDWARD IV, King of England 1461–70, 1471–83

EDWARD VI, only son of Henry VIII and Jane Seymour, Prince of Wales; died aged sixteen

EGERTON, Sir Thomas, Lord Keeper under Elizabeth I, successor to Sir John Puckering

ELIZABETH, Princess of York, wife of Henry VII and mother of Arthur Prince of Wales and Henry VIII

ERIK, King of Sweden, suitor to Elizabeth I

ESSEX, Robert Devereux, second Earl of, son of Walter Devereux, first Earl, and Lettice Knollys, soldier and courtier, beloved of Elizabeth I; executed for conspiracy

FELTON, John, Catholic dissident; executed for posting Papal Bull against Elizabeth I

FÉNÉLON, Bertrand Salignac de la Mothe, French Ambassador to Elizabeth I

FERDINAND I, Holy Roman Emperor, father of Maximilian and Charles, suitor to Elizabeth I

FERIA, Don Gómez Suárez de Figueroa, Count of, Spanish Ambassador to Elizabeth I

FOIX, Paul de, French Ambassador to Elizabeth I

FORESTER, John, steward to the Earl of Leicester at Cumnor

FOWLER, John, Gentleman of the Privy Chamber to Edward VI, in the pay of Thomas Seymour, Baron Sudeley

FRANCIS II, King of France, husband of Mary Queen of Scots since childhood; died aged sixteen

FROBISHER, Sir Martin, seafarer and privateer

GARDINER, Stephen, Bishop of Winchester under Henry VIII; later, Catholic persecutor and first minister to Mary I

GAVESTON, Piers, murdered lover of Edward II

GAZE, Sir John, Lord Lieutenant of the Tower of London

GILBERT, Sir Humphrey, soldier and seafarer, kinsman of Sir Walter Raleigh

GRESHAM, Sir Thomas, financier, adviser to Elizabeth I and founder of the Royal Exchange

THE PERSONS OF MY HISTORY

GREY, Lady Catherine, descendant of Princess Mary Tudor, sister of Lady Jane Grey and cousin of Elizabeth I; illegally married to the Earl of Hertford

GREY, Lady Frances, Countess of Dorset and Duchess of Suffolk, daughter of Princess Mary Tudor, sister of Henry VIII, mother of Jane and Catherine

GREY, Lady Jane, descendant of Princess Mary Tudor, eldest of her line and cousin of Elizabeth I, Queen for nine days; executed under Mary I

GREY, Lord Henry, Earl of Dorset, later Duke of Suffolk, father of Jane and Catherine; executed for conspiracy against Mary I

GRINDAL, William, tutor to Princess Elizabeth

HASTINGS, Lord Edward, Privy Councillor to Mary I

HATTON, Sir Christopher, courtier, later Lord Chancellor, beloved of Elizabeth I

HAWKINS, Sir John, seafarer and naval commander during the Armada

HENEAGE, Sir Thomas, courtier, favoured by Elizabeth I

HENRY II, King of France and father-in-law of Mary Queen of Scots, lover of Mary Boleyn, killed while jousting

HENRY III, King of France, murdered by Huguenots

HENRY IV, King of France (also called Henry of Navarre)

HENRY V, King of England 1413–22

HENRY VII, King of England and father of Prince Arthur and Henry VIII

HENRY VIII, King of England and father of Edward VI, Mary I and Elizabeth I

HERBERT, Lady, sister and lady-in-waiting to Katherine Parr

HERTFORD, Earl of. *See* Seymour, Edward

HERTFORD, Lady, later Duchess of Somerset, wife of the Lord Protector to Edward VI

HOWARD, Lord Charles of Effingham, Lord Admiral and son of Lord William Howard, Lord Commander during the Armada

HOWARD, Katherine, cousin of Princess Elizabeth and fifth wife of Henry VIII, executed for adultery

HOWARD, Lord William of Effingham, Privy Councillor and great-uncle of Elizabeth I

HUNSDON, Baron. *See* Carey, Henry

HUNTINGDON, Henry, Earl of, courtier of Elizabeth I, distant descendant of Edward III

INNOCENT V, Pope of Rome

JAMES II, King of Scotland 1437–60

JAMES V, King of Scotland and father of Mary Queen of Scots; died when Mary was one week old

JAMES VI, King of Scotland, son of Mary Queen of Scots and Lord Darnley

JOHN OF AUSTRIA, Don, bastard half-brother of Don Carlos, Spanish Regent in the Netherlands

KATHERINE OF ARAGON, Infanta of Spain, first wife of Henry VIII and mother of Mary I

KNOLLYS, Cecilia, daughter of Sir Francis Knollys and Katherine Carey, cousin of Elizabeth

KNOLLYS, Sir Francis, Privy Councillor, husband of Katherine Carey, daughter of Mary Boleyn

KNOLLYS, Lettice, daughter of Sir Francis Knollys and Katherine Carey; wife of Viscount Hereford, later first Earl of Essex, and mother of Penelope and Dorothy Devereux and Robert Devereux, second Earl of Essex; later, wife of Robert Dudley, Earl of Leicester, and of Sir Christopher Blount

KNOLLYS, William, later Earl of Banbury, son of Francis Knollys

KNOX, John, Scots Protestant preacher and writer

LATIMER, Hugh, Bishop of Worcester and Protestant martyr

LEE, Thomas, captain in the Irish campaign and co-conspirator of the Earl of Essex

LEICESTER, Robert Dudley (Robin), Earl of, third son of the Duke of Northumberland, courtier and soldier, beloved of Elizabeth I

LENNOX, Margaret Douglas, Countess of, descendant of Princess Margaret Tudor and mother of Lord Darnley

LENNOX, Matthew, Earl of, Borders laird and father of Lord Darnley

LOPEZ, Dr. Roderigo, physician to Elizabeth I, Portuguese Jew executed for treason

MAITLAND, Lord William of Lethington, envoy of Mary Queen of Scots

MARGARET TUDOR, Princess of England, elder sister of Henry VIII, wife of James IV of Scotland and grandmother of Mary Queen of Scots and of Mary's second husband Lord Darnley

MARLOWE, Christopher, playwright and spy; murdered in tavern brawl

MARPRELATE, Martin, pen name of anonymous Puritan pamphleteer under Elizabeth I

MARY OF GUISE, wife of King James V of Scotland, mother of Mary Queen of Scots, and Regent of Scotland in her daughter's minority

MARY I, Queen of England, daughter of Henry VIII and Katherine of Aragon, wife of Philip II of Spain and persecutor of Protestants

MARY QUEEN OF SCOTS, daughter of James V, wife of Francis I of France, Lord Darnley and Earl Bothwell, Catholic pretender to the throne of England

MARY TUDOR, Princess of England, younger sister of Henry VIII; later married to Charles Brandon, Duke of Suffolk

MATILDA, daughter and heir of Henry I, Queen of England; never allowed to rule

MAXIMILIAN, Holy Roman Emperor, son of Ferdinand and brother of Charles, suitor to Elizabeth I

MEDINA SIDONIA, Duke of, Commander of the Spanish forces during the Armada

MELVILLE, Sir James, Ambassador of Mary Queen of Scots to Elizabeth I

MENDOZA, Bernardino de, last Spanish Ambassador to Elizabeth I

MONTAGUE, Anthony Browne, Lord Privy Councillor under Mary I

MORAY, Earl of, Scots laird, bastard half-brother of Mary Queen of Scots and Regent for James VI

MOUNTJOY, Charles Blount, Baron, Lord Lieutenant of Ireland

NORFOLK, Thomas Howard, third Duke of, father of Henry Howard, Earl of Surrey, Privy Councillor and Earl Marshal to Henry VIII
NORFOLK, Thomas Howard, fourth Duke of, son of the Earl of Surrey, Privy Councillor to Elizabeth I and Catholic conspirator
NORRIS, Henry, Gentleman of the Privy Chamber to Henry VIII; executed on false charges of adultery with Anne Boleyn
NORTHAMPTON, Edward, Marquis of, brother of Katherine Parr
NORTHAMPTON, Marchioness of. See Snakenborg, Helena of
NORTHUMBERLAND, 7th Earl of, Catholic conspirator; executed under Elizabeth I
NORTHUMBERLAND, Duke of. See Dudley, John, Viscount Lisle

O'NEILL, Hugh, 2nd Earl of Tyrone, Irish rebel and traitor to Elizabeth I
OXFORD, Edward de Vere, Earl of, courtier and theatre patron, husband of Anne Cecil, daughter of Lord Burghley

PAGET, Sir William, later Lord Paget, Secretary to the Privy Council under Henry VIII, Edward VI and Mary I
"YOUNG PAGET," nephew of Sir William Paget
PALAVICINO, Sir Horatio, international financier
PARKER, Matthew, Archbishop of Canterbury
PARMA, Alexander Farnese, Duke of, Spanish Commander in the Netherlands
PARR, Edward. See Northampton, Edward, Marquis of
PARR, Dame Katherine, sixth wife of Henry VIII; later, wife of Thomas Seymour, Baron Sudeley; died in childbirth
PARRY, Blanche, lady-in-waiting and lifelong companion to Elizabeth I
PARRY, Thomas, treasurer of Princess Elizabeth; later, Privy Councillor under Elizabeth I
PAULET, Sir William, later Marquis of Winchester, Privy Councillor to Henry VIII, Edward VI, Mary I and Elizabeth I, Lord Treasurer
PEMBROKE, William Herbert, Earl of, soldier and Privy Councillor
PHILIBERT, Emmanuel, Duke of Savoy, suitor to Elizabeth I
PHILIP II, King of Spain, husband of Mary I and suitor to Elizabeth I
PICKERING, Sir William, companion of the Earl of Surrey, conspirator against Mary I, Ambassador to France and suitor to Elizabeth I
POLE, Reginald, Cardinal, Papal Legate to Mary I, Archbishop of Canterbury and Catholic persecutor
PUCKERING, Sir John, Lord Keeper under Elizabeth I

QUADRA, Álvaro de la, Bishop Aquila, Spanish Ambassador to Elizabeth I, successor to Feria

RADCLIFFE, Mary, lady-in-waiting to Elizabeth I
RALEIGH, Sir Walter, courtier, soldier, explorer and poet, beloved of Elizabeth I
RANDOLPH, Sir Thomas, English envoy to Mary Queen of Scots

RENARD, Simon, Spanish Ambassador to Mary I

RICH, Sir Richard, later Lord Rich, lawyer and courtier under Henry VIII

RICH, Lord (Richard), grandson of Sir Richard, husband of Penelope Devereux, sister of the Earl of Essex

RICHARD, Duke of Gloucester, brother of Edward IV, later Richard III; killed at battle of Bosworth Field by Henry Tudor, later Henry VII

RICHARD II, King of England 1377–99; deposed and murdered

RIDLEY, Nicholas, Bishop of London, Protestant martyr

RIDOLFI, Roberto, Catholic conspirator against Elizabeth I

RIZZIO, David, private secretary to Mary Queen of Scots; murdered by Lord Darnley

ROBSART, Amy, wife of Robert Dudley

ROCHFORD, George, Viscount, brother of Anne Boleyn; executed on trumped-up charges of adultery with her

RUSSELL, Anne, lady-in-waiting to Elizabeth I, daughter of the Earl of Bedford and later married to Ambrose, Earl of Warwick, brother of Robert Dudley, Earl of Leicester

RUSSELL, Lady, lady-in-waiting at the court of Edward VI

ST. JOHAN, Earl of, Lord Treasurer to Henry VII

ST. JOHN, Lord, Lord Chamberlain to Henry VIII

SEYMOUR, Edward, brother of Jane and Thomas Seymour, Earl of Hertford, later Duke of Somerset, Lord Protector to Edward VI; executed under Edward VI

SEYMOUR, Jane, third wife of Henry VIII, mother of Edward VI, sister of Edward and Thomas Seymour

SEYMOUR, Thomas, Baron Sudeley, brother of Edward and Jane Seymour, fourth husband of Katherine Parr, courtier, soldier, suitor to Princess Elizabeth and conspirator against his brother the Lord Protector; executed under Edward VI

SHAKESPEARE, William, actor and playwright, principal member of the Lord Chamberlain's Men

SHARINGTON, Sir William, Master of the Royal Mint under Edward VI

SHEFFIELD, Lady Douglas, daughter of Lord William Howard; dubiously married to Robert Dudley, Earl of Leicester, and mother of his only surviving son

SHREWSBURY, Gilbert Talbot, Earl of, President of the Council of the North, Privy Councillor

SIDNEY, Mary, lady-in-waiting to Elizabeth I, sister of Robert Dudley, wife of Sir Henry Sidney and mother of Philip

SIDNEY, Sir Philip, son of Sir Henry Sidney and Mary Dudley, courtier, soldier and poet; killed at the battle of Zutphen

SIMIER, Jean de, French Ambassador

SMEATON, Mark, lutanist to Anne Boleyn; executed for alleged adultery with her

SNAKENBORG, Helena of, Swedish noblewoman, lady-in-waiting to Elizabeth I from girlhood and later Marchioness of Northampton

SOMERSET, Duke of. *See* Seymour, Edward

SOUTHAMPTON, Henry Wriothesley, 3rd Earl of, friend and co-conspirator of the Earl of Essex

SOUTHWELL, Robert, Jesuit priest and poet; executed under Elizabeth I

SPENSER, Edmund, secretary to the Lord Deputy of Ireland, poet

STORY, Dr. John, Catholic persecutor under Mary I and Member of Parliament

STUBBS, John, Puritan pamphleteer and dissident

SURREY, Henry Howard, Earl of, son of the third Duke of Norfolk, father of the fourth Duke; executed under Henry VIII

SUSSEX, Thomas Radcliffe, Earl of, soldier and Privy Councillor to Mary I and Elizabeth I

THOMAS, William, Clerk to the Privy Council of Edward VI, conspirator against Mary I

THROCKMORTON, Elizabeth, lady-in-waiting to Elizabeth I, daughter of Sir Nicholas and wife of Sir Walter Raleigh

THROCKMORTON, Francis, nephew of Sir Nicholas, Catholic conspirator; executed under Elizabeth I

THROCKMORTON, Sir Nicholas, Ambassador to France and Scotland under Elizabeth I

TOPCLIFFE, Richard, Master-Torturer to Elizabeth I

TYRRWHIT, Lady Elizabeth, stepdaughter of Katherine Parr and her chief lady-in-waiting

TYRRWHIT, Sir Robert, husband of Lady Elizabeth, interrogator of Princess Elizabeth under Edward VI

VERNON, James, brother of Richard, gentleman-in-waiting to Princess Elizabeth

VERNON, Richard, gentleman-in-waiting to Princess Elizabeth

VINE, Francis, gentleman-usher to Princess Elizabeth

WALSINGHAM, Frances, daughter of Sir Francis Walsingham, wife of Sir Philip Sidney and later of the Earl of Essex

WALSINGHAM, Sir Francis, envoy to France, Secretary of State and master of intelligence to Elizabeth I

WARNER, Sir Edward, Lord Lieutenant of the Tower of London

WARWICK, Anne. See Russell, Anne

WENDY, Dr. Thomas, physician to Henry VIII

WENTWORTH, Peter, radical Member of Parliament

WESTMORELAND, Charles Neville, Earl of, Catholic conspirator against Elizabeth I; fled abroad and died in exile

WHITGIFT, John, Archbishop of Canterbury 1583–1604

WILLIAM THE CONQUEROR, bastard son of Robert, Duke of Normandy, usurping King of England 1066–87

WILLIAM THE SILENT, ruler of the Netherlands, adversary of Philip II

WOLSEY, Thomas, Cardinal, first minister of Henry VIII, builder of Hampton Court

WRIOTHESLEY, Sir Thomas, Lord Chancellor to Henry VIII, later Earl of Southampton under Edward VI

WYATT, Sir Thomas, courtier and poet, suitor to Anne Boleyn

WYATT, Sir Thomas, son of Sir Thomas Wyatt, companion of the Earl of Surrey, courtier and conspirator against Mary I; executed